Land of the Sons

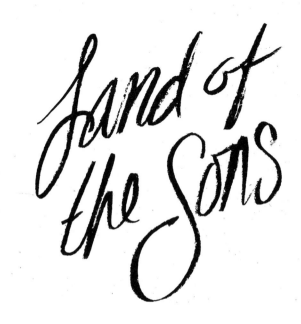

ON THE CAUSES
AND MOTIVES
THAT LED
TO THE END,
ENTIRE CHAPTERS
OF HISTORY BOOKS
COULD HAVE
BEEN WRITTEN.

BUT AFTER THE END,
NO MORE BOOKS
WERE EVER WRITTEN.

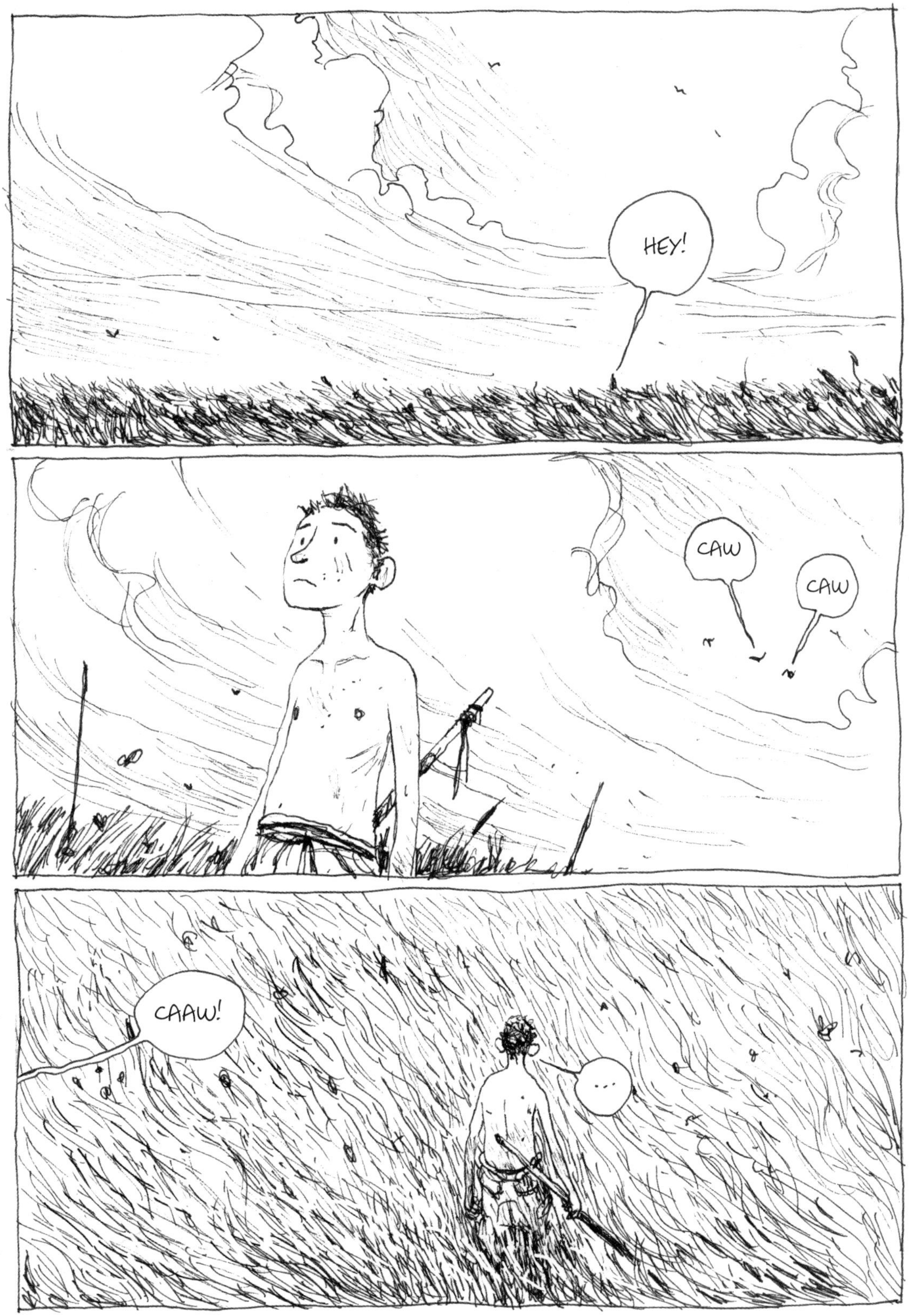
HEY!
CAW
CAW
CAAW!
...

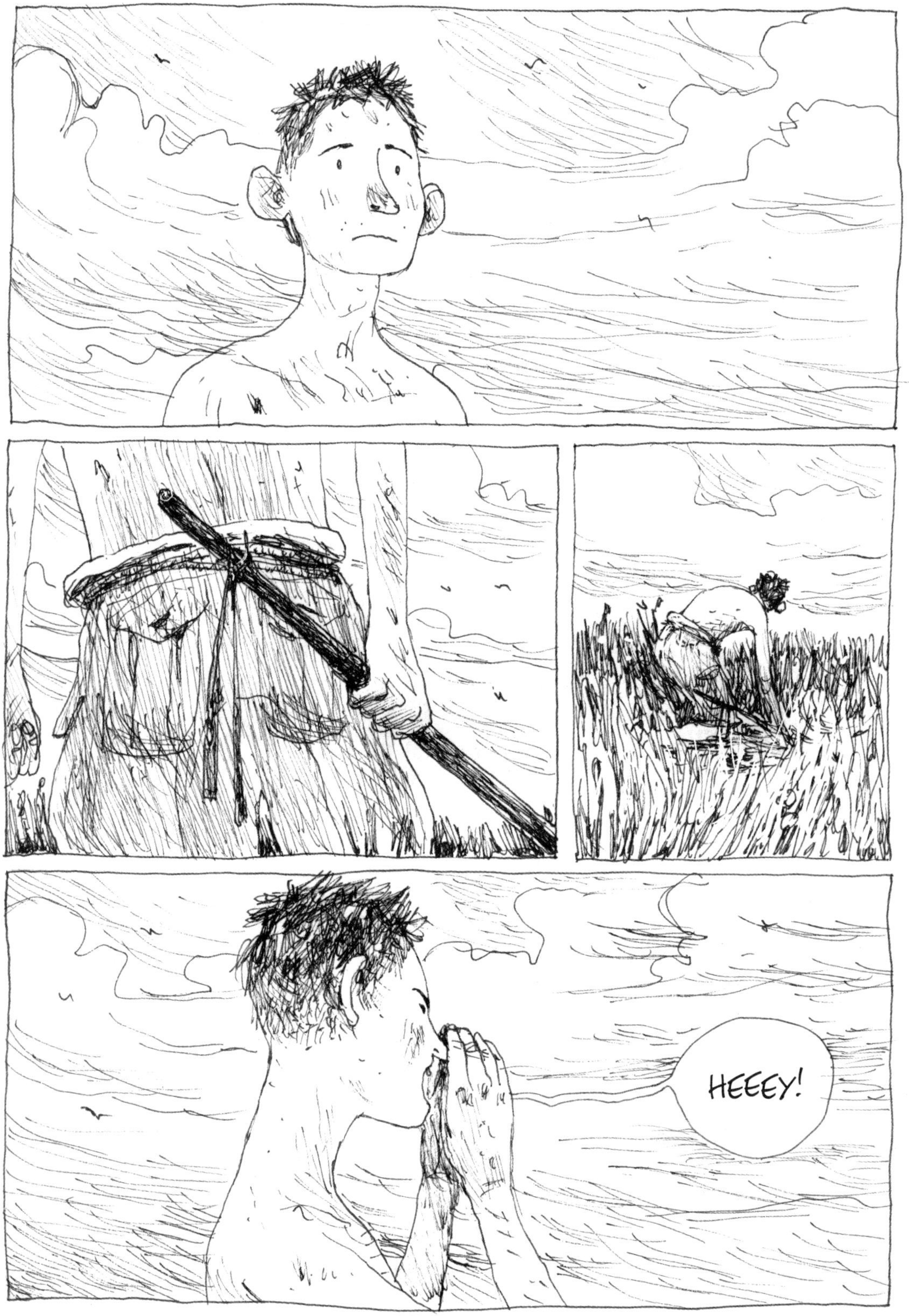
HEEEY!

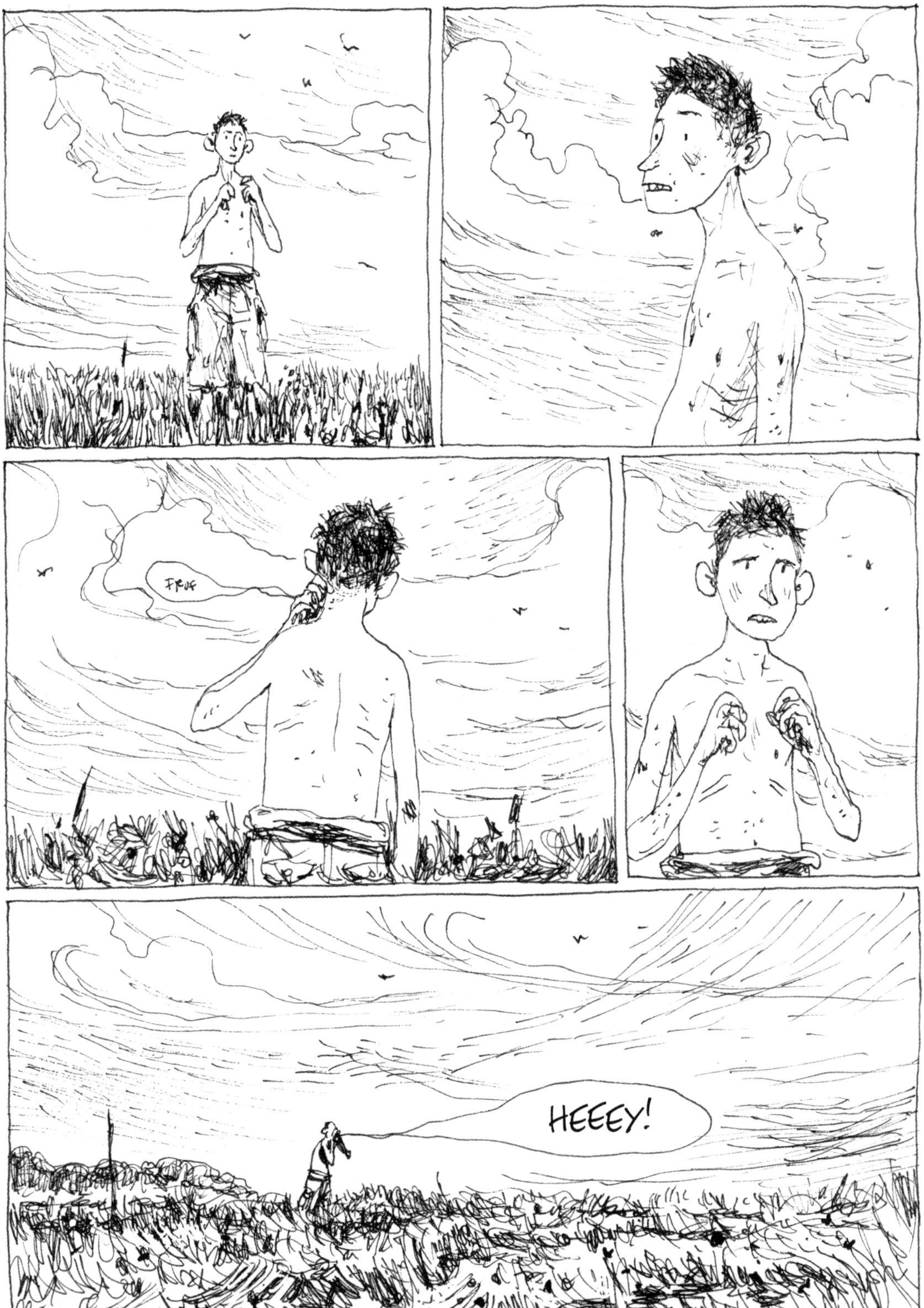
FRUF
HEEEY!

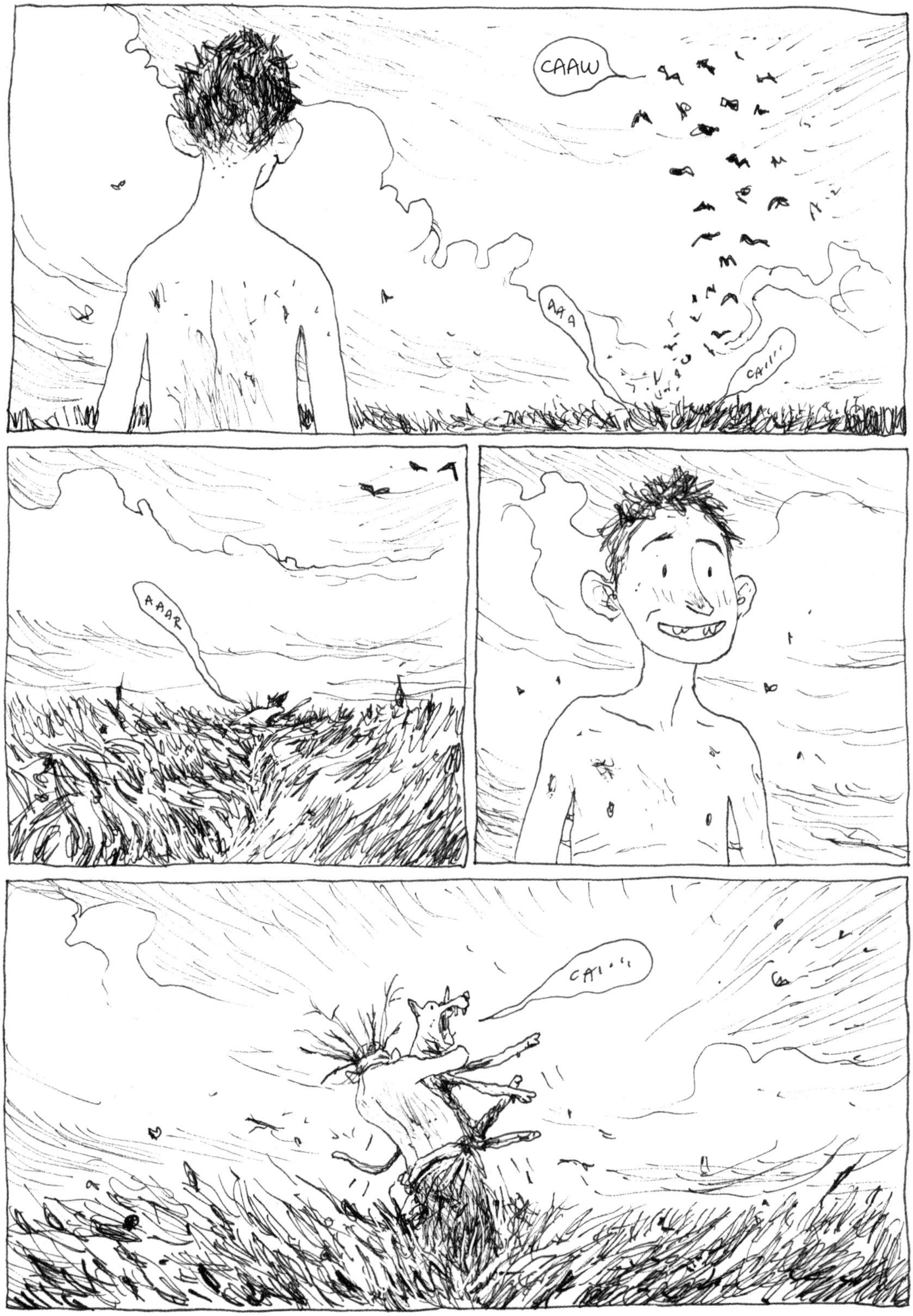
CAAW
AAA
CA
AAAR
CA

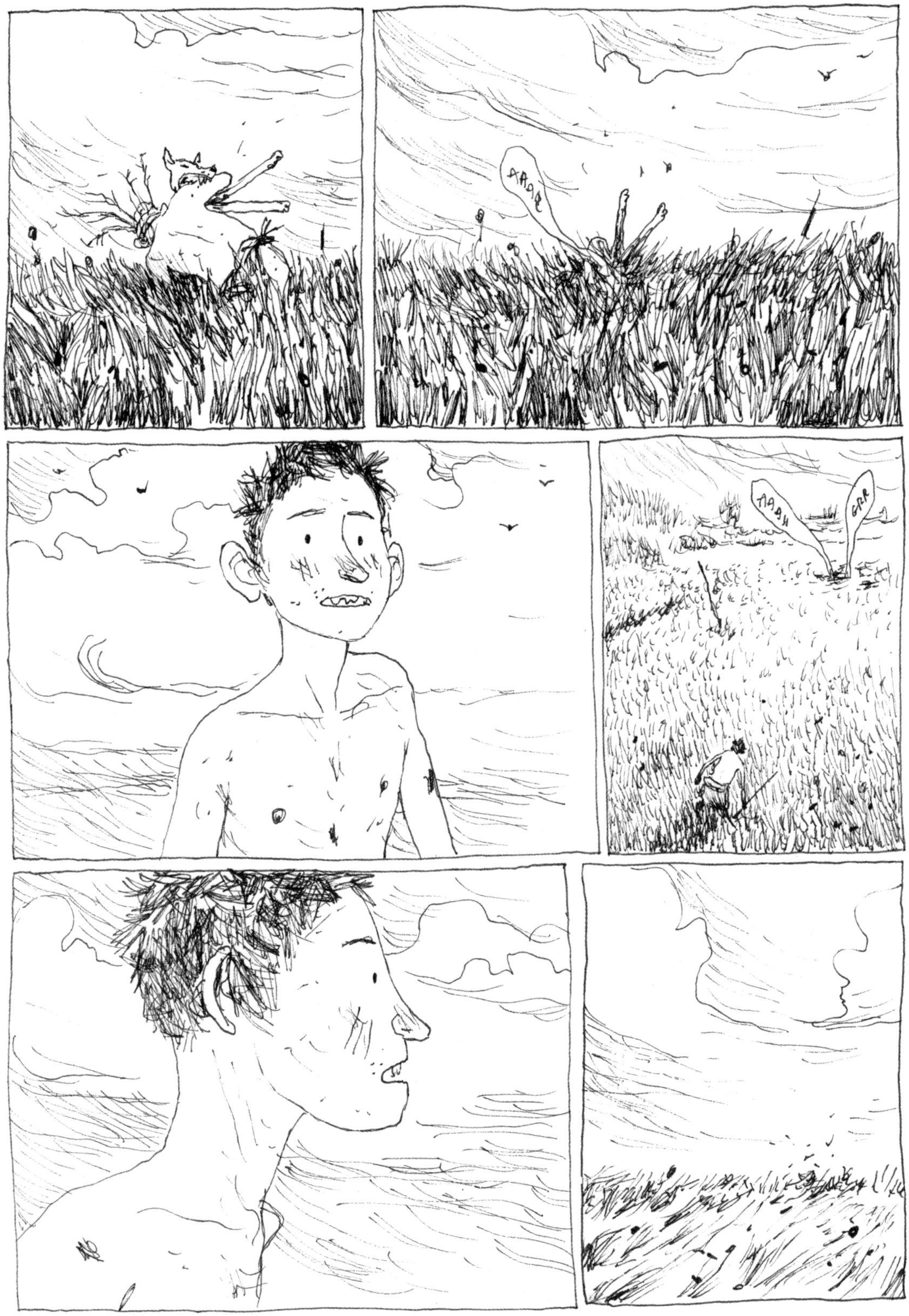
AAAE
AAAH
GRR

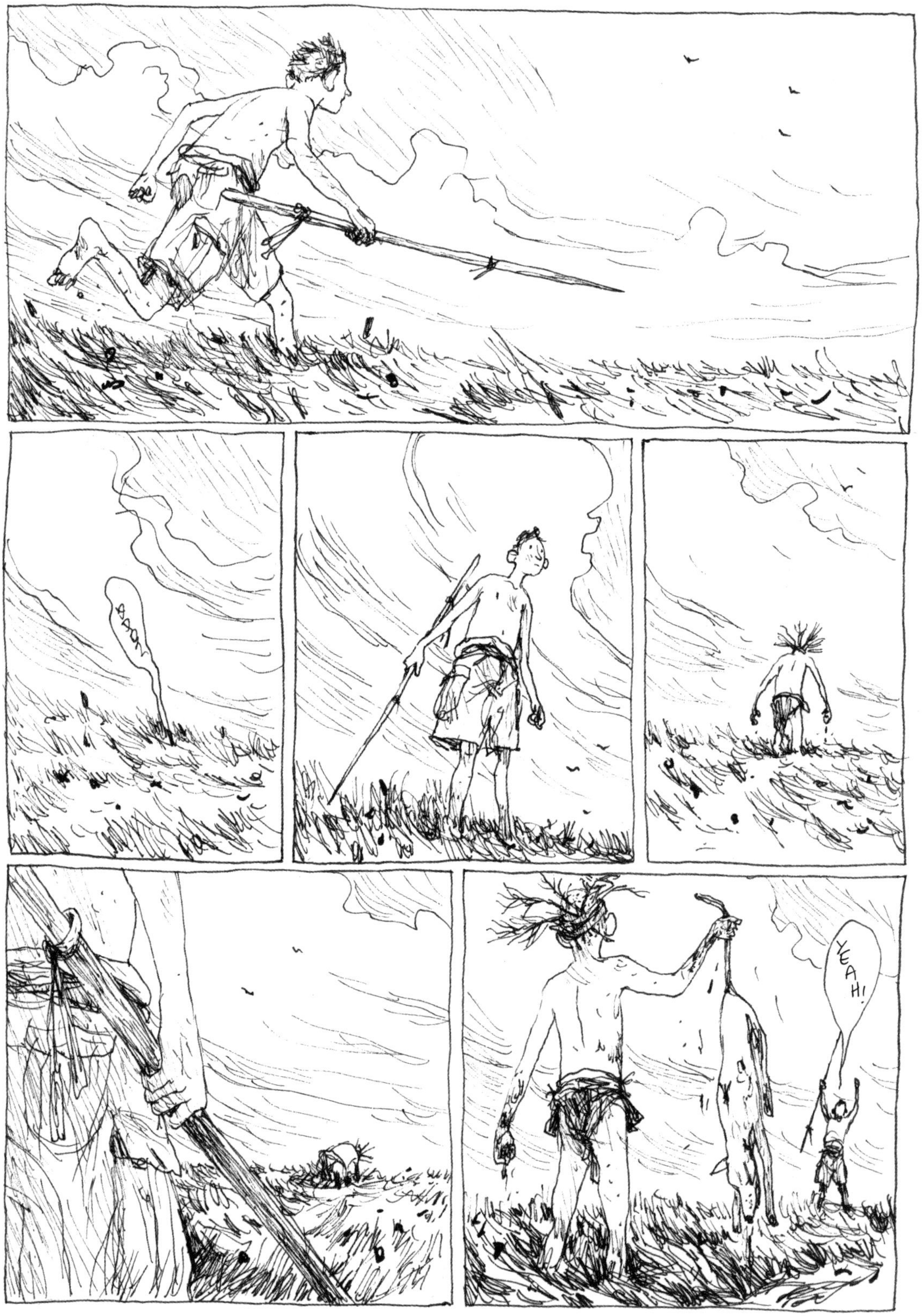
AAOW
YEAH!

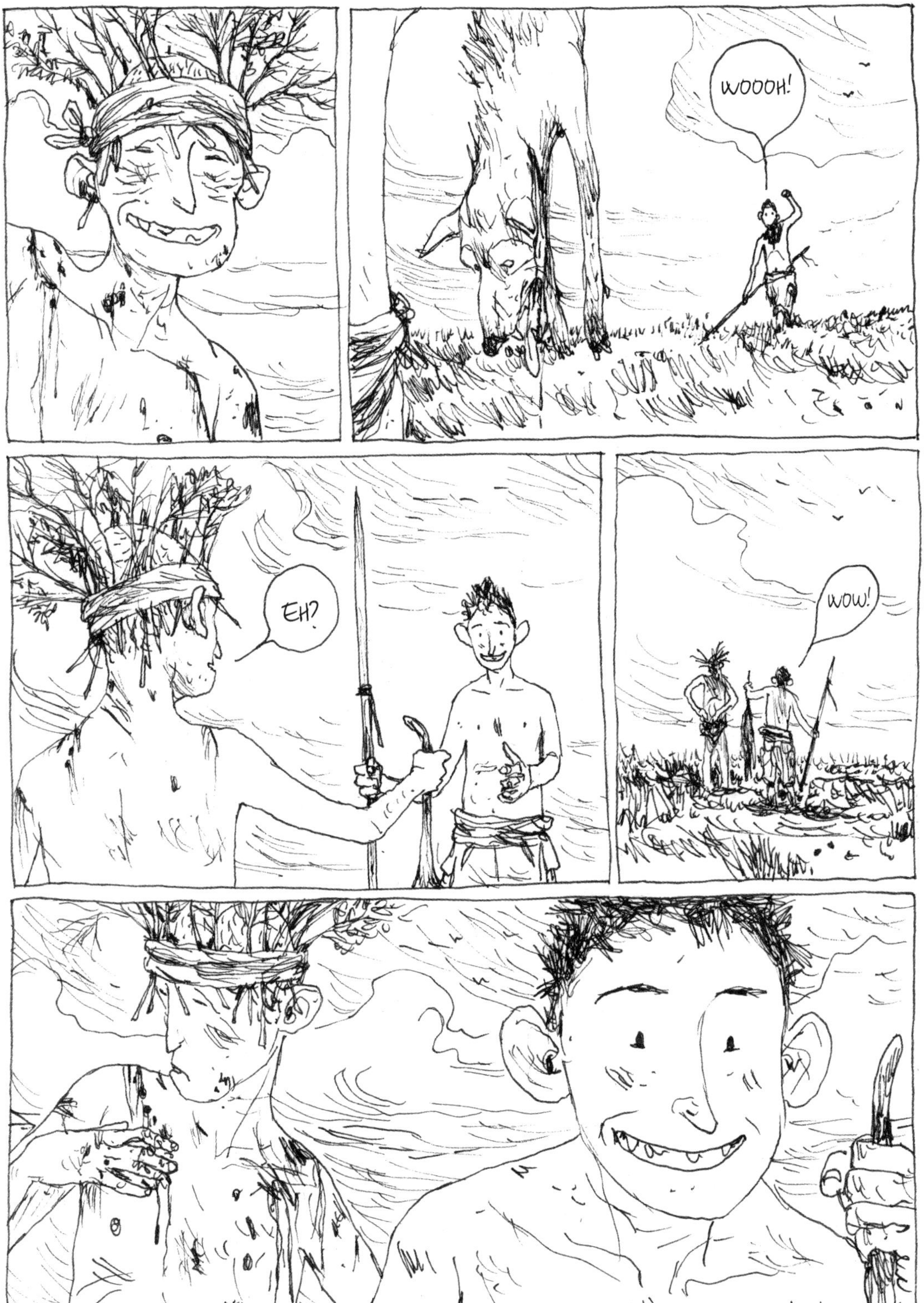
WOOOH!
EH?
WOW!

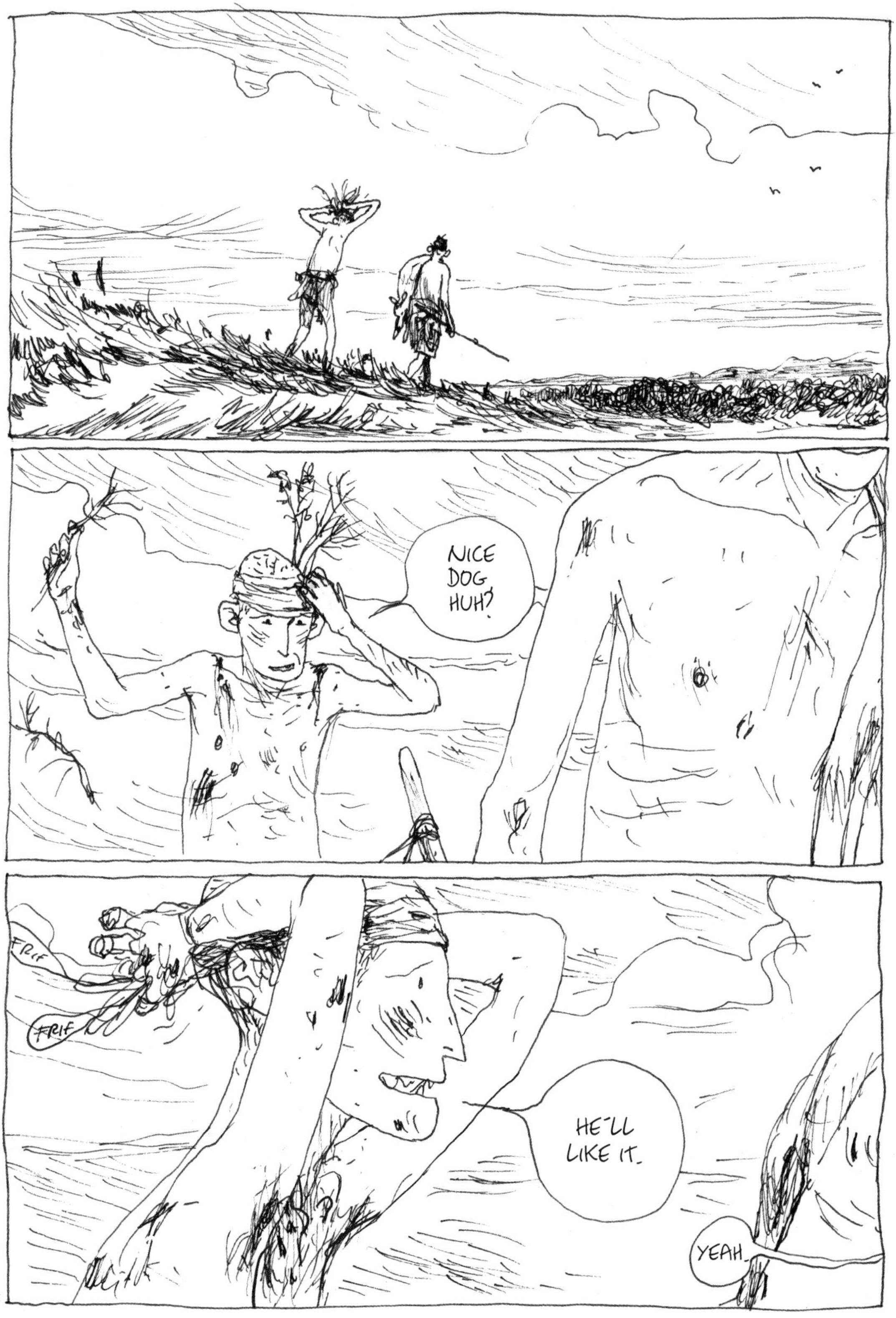
NICE DOG HUH?
FRIF
FRIF
HE'LL LIKE IT.
YEAH.

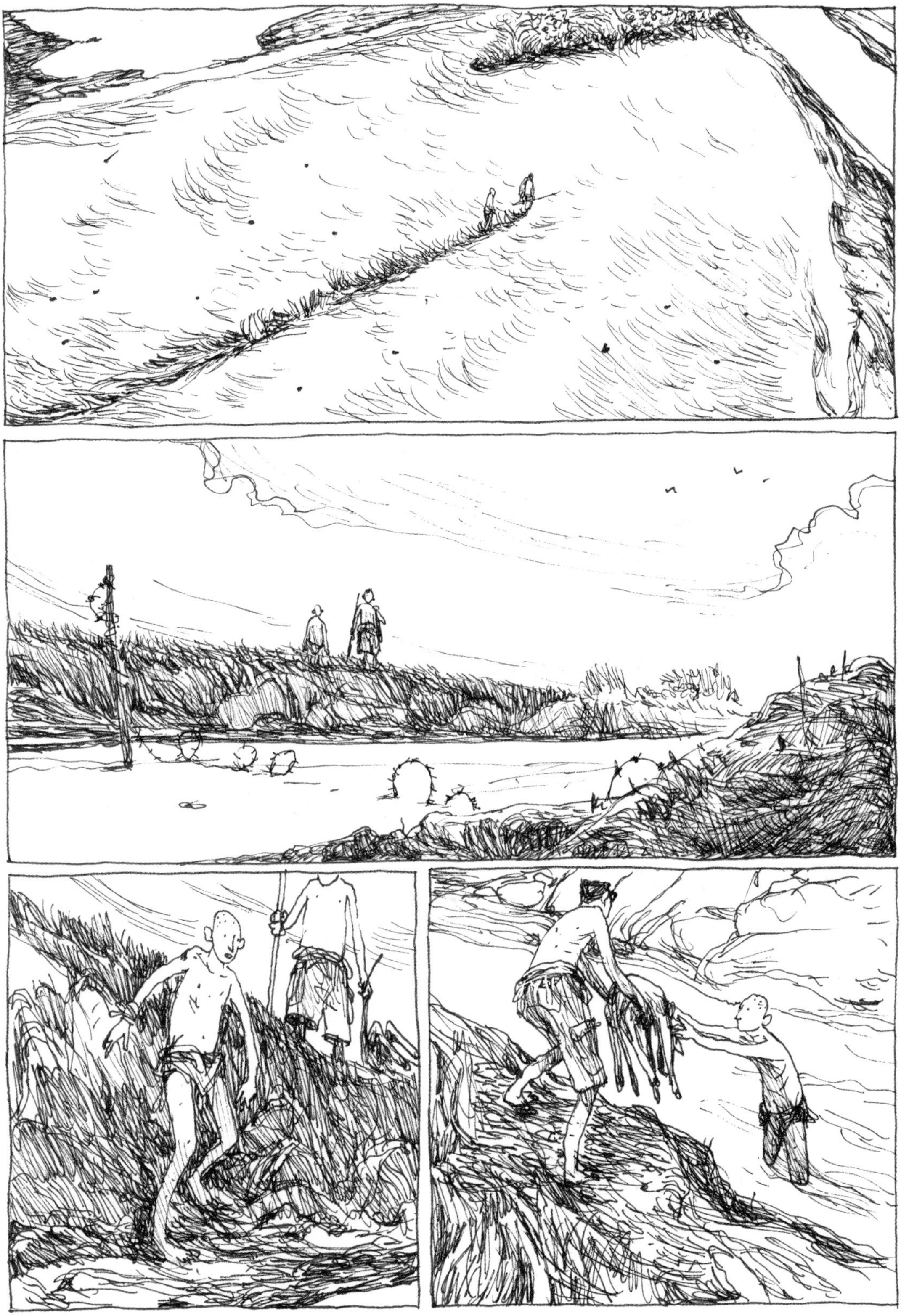

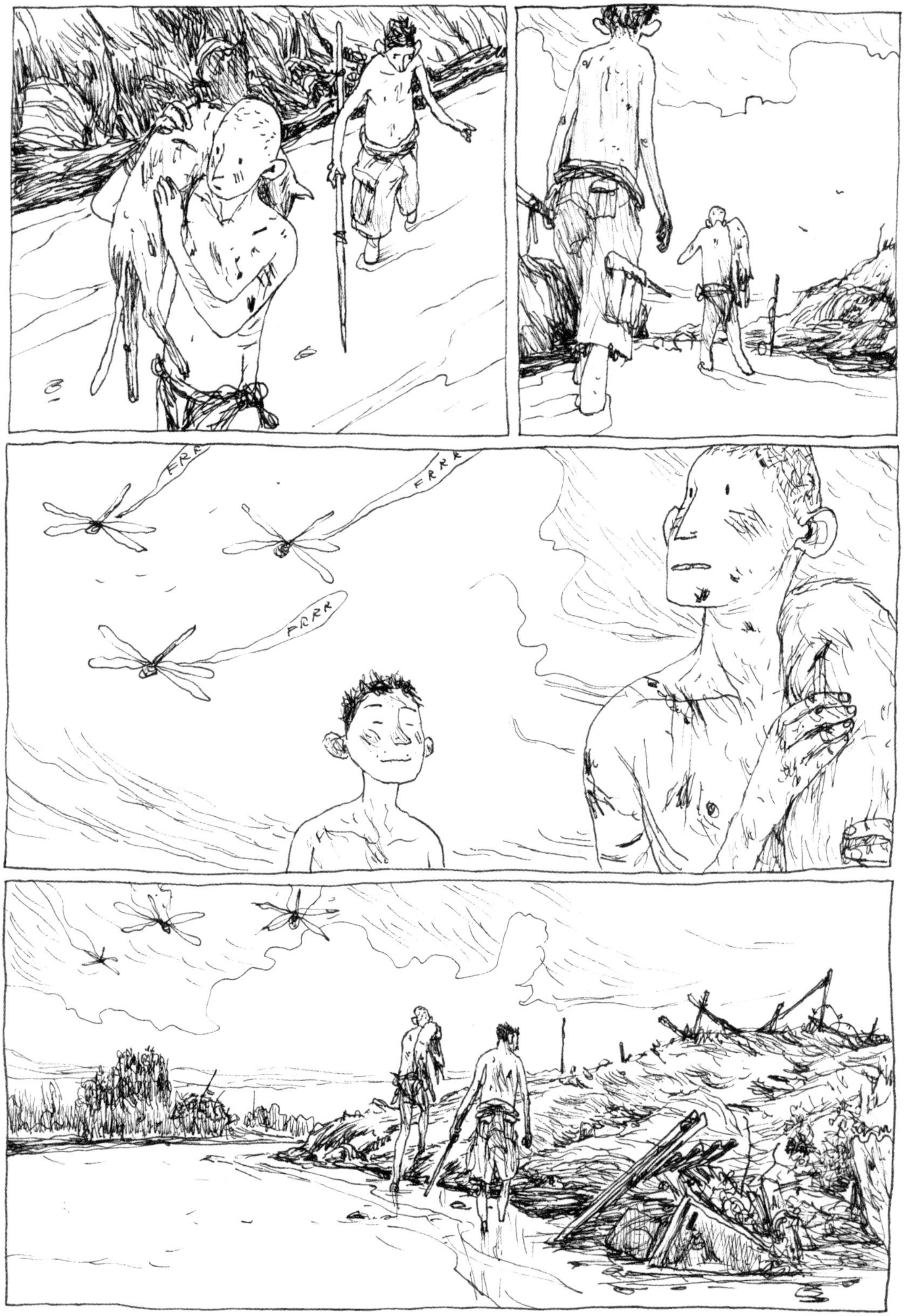
FRR
FRRR
FRRR

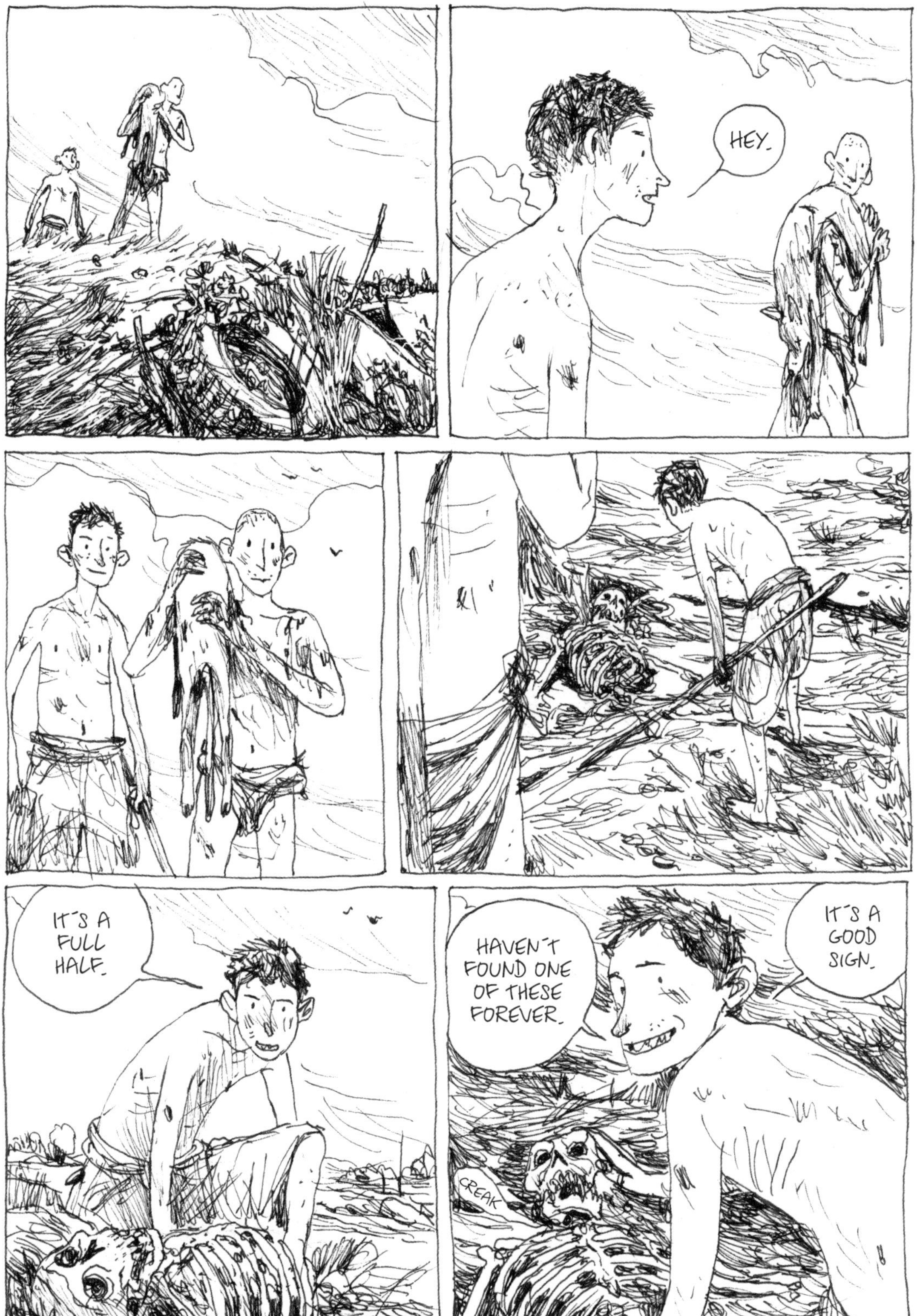
HEY.
IT'S A FULL HALF.
HAVEN'T FOUND ONE OF THESE FOREVER.
CREAK
IT'S A GOOD SIGN.

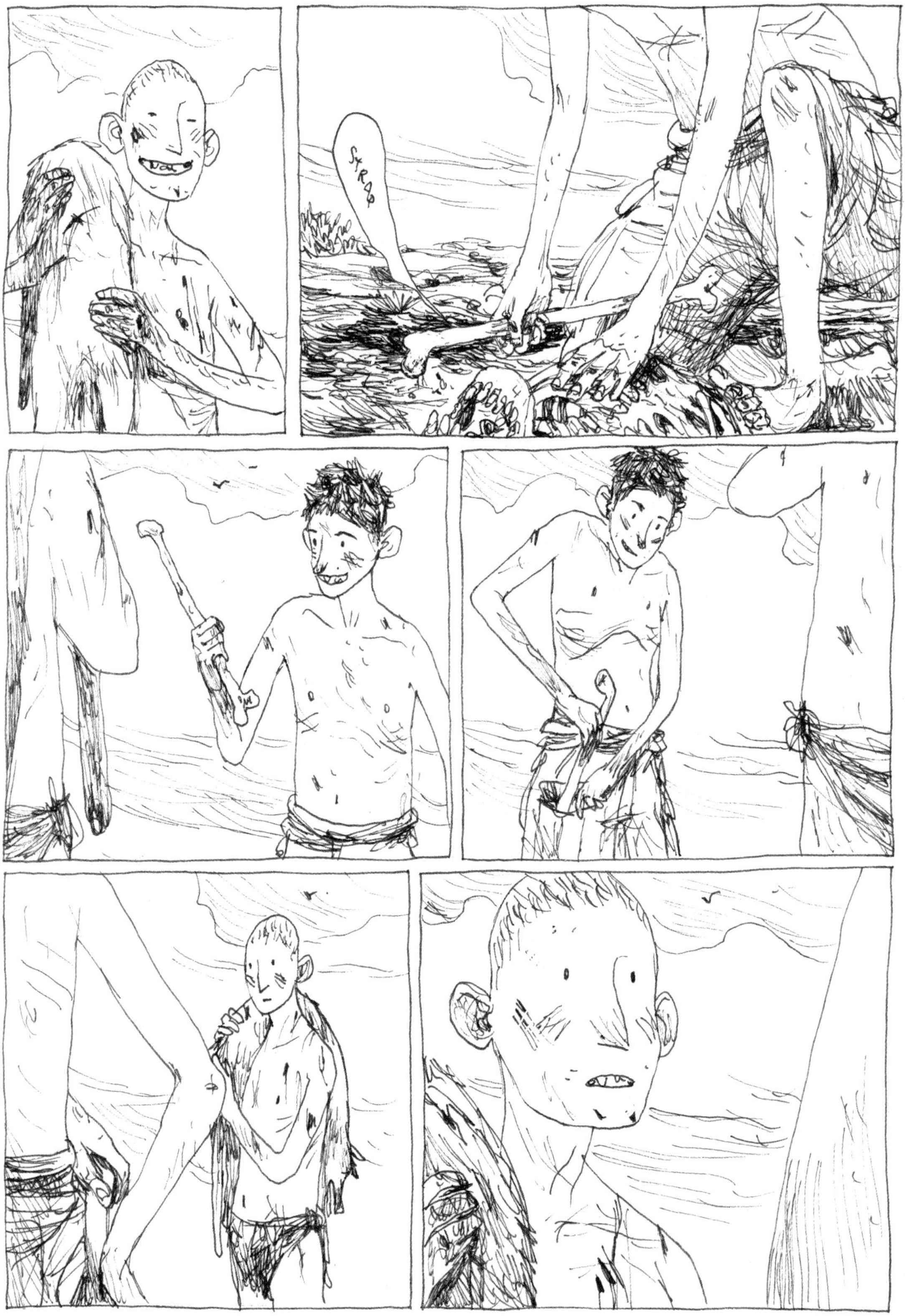

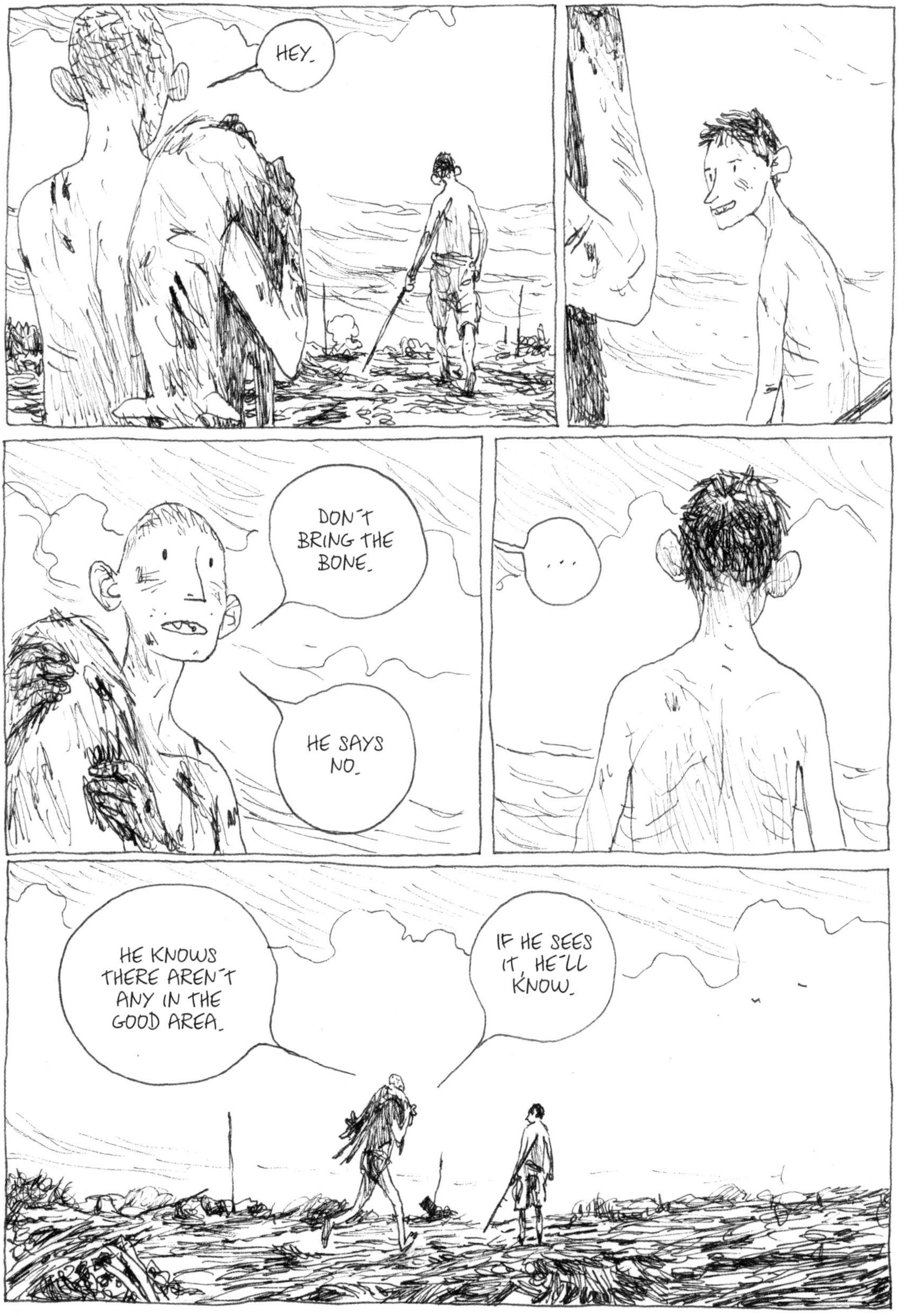
HEY.
DON'T BRING THE BONE.
HE SAYS NO.
...
HE KNOWS THERE AREN'T ANY IN THE GOOD AREA.
IF HE SEES IT, HE'LL KNOW.

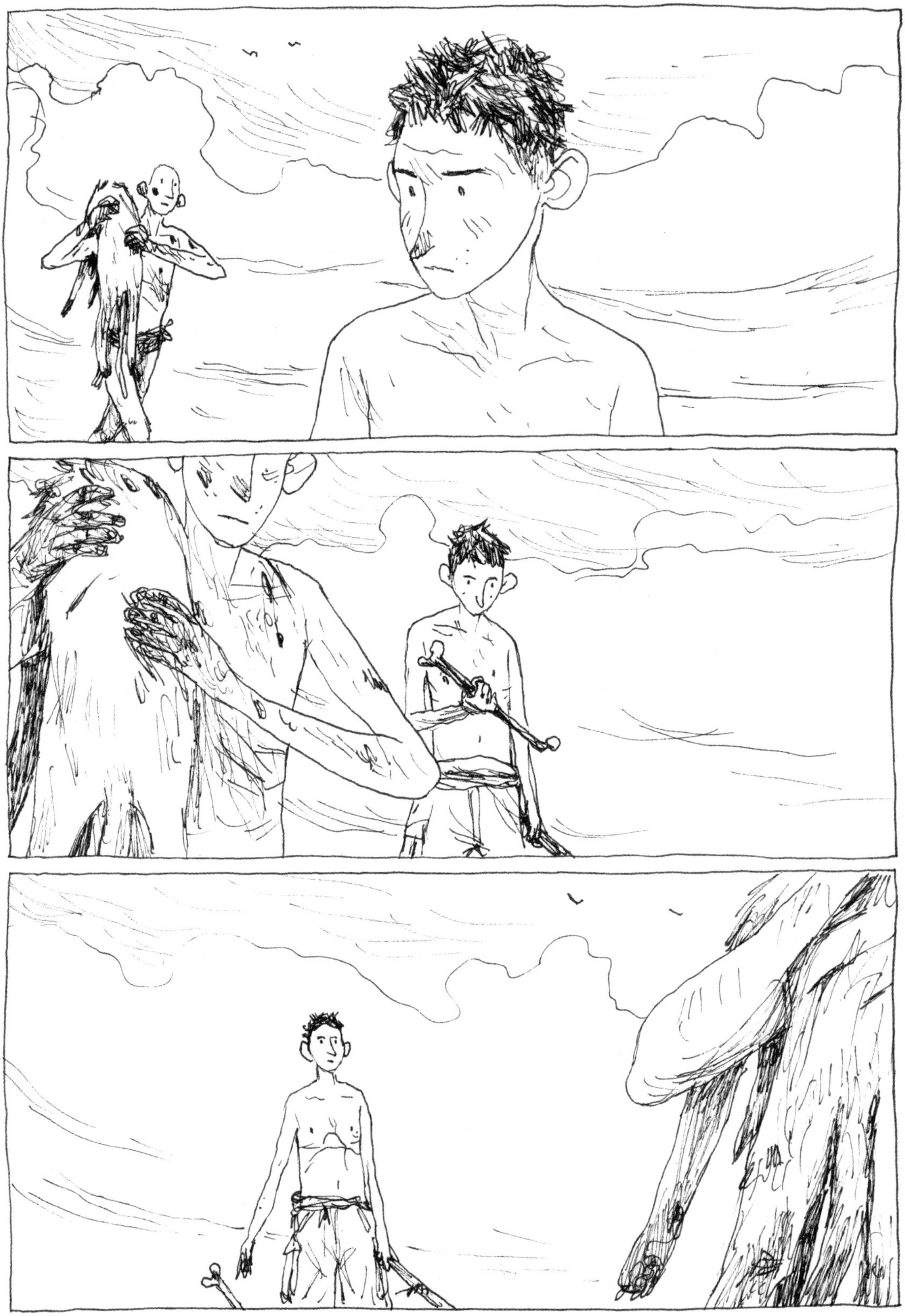

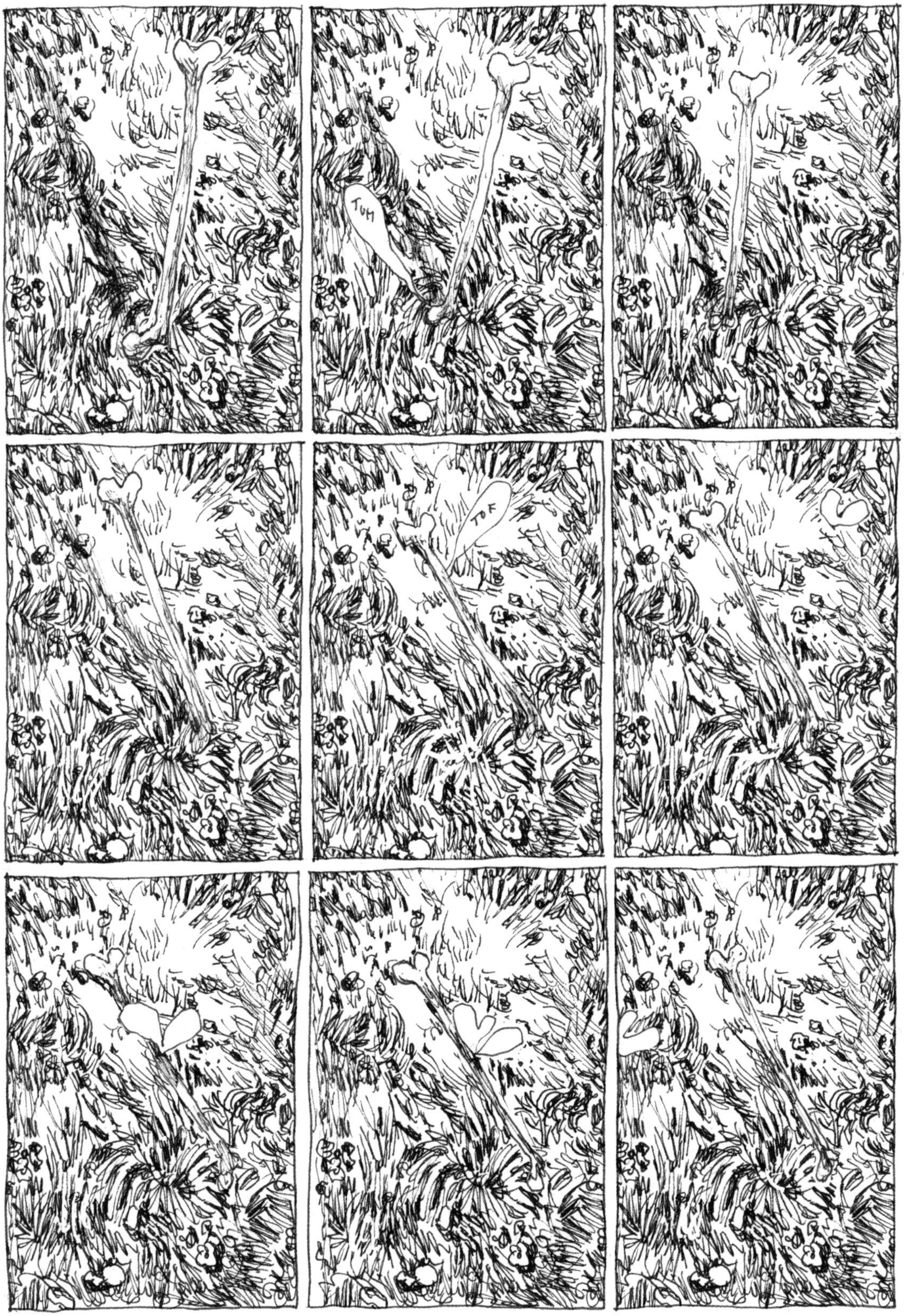
TUM
TOF

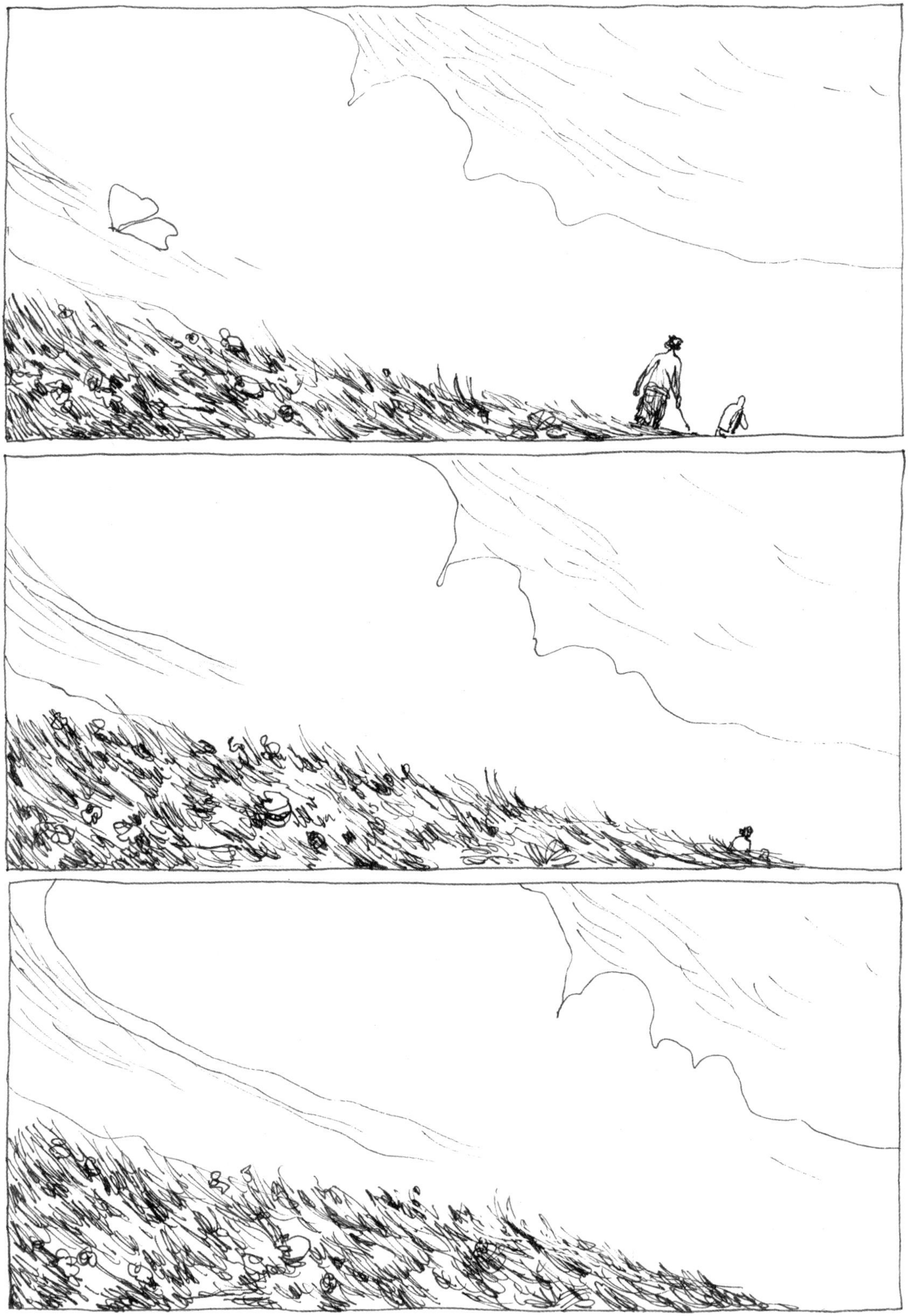

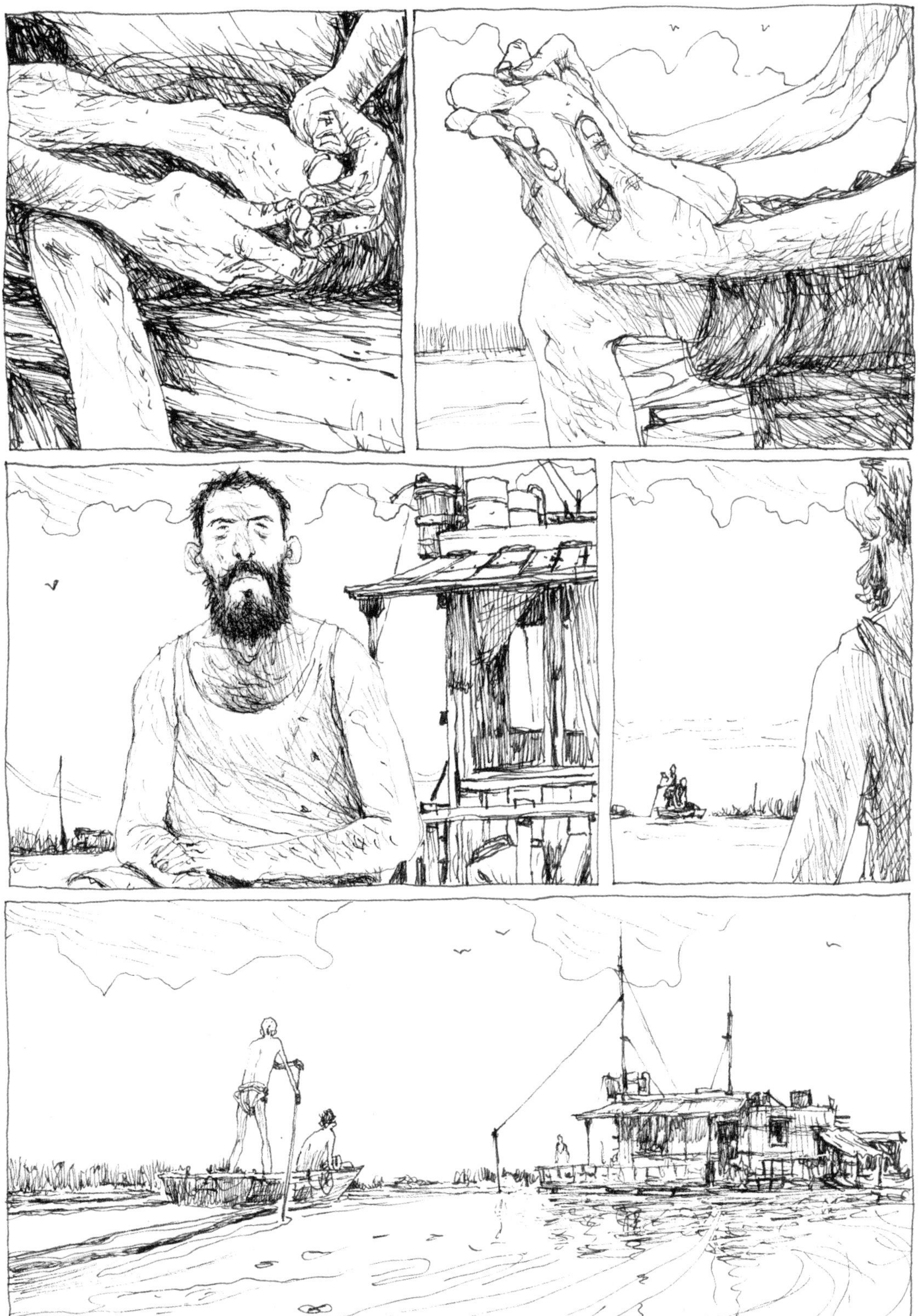

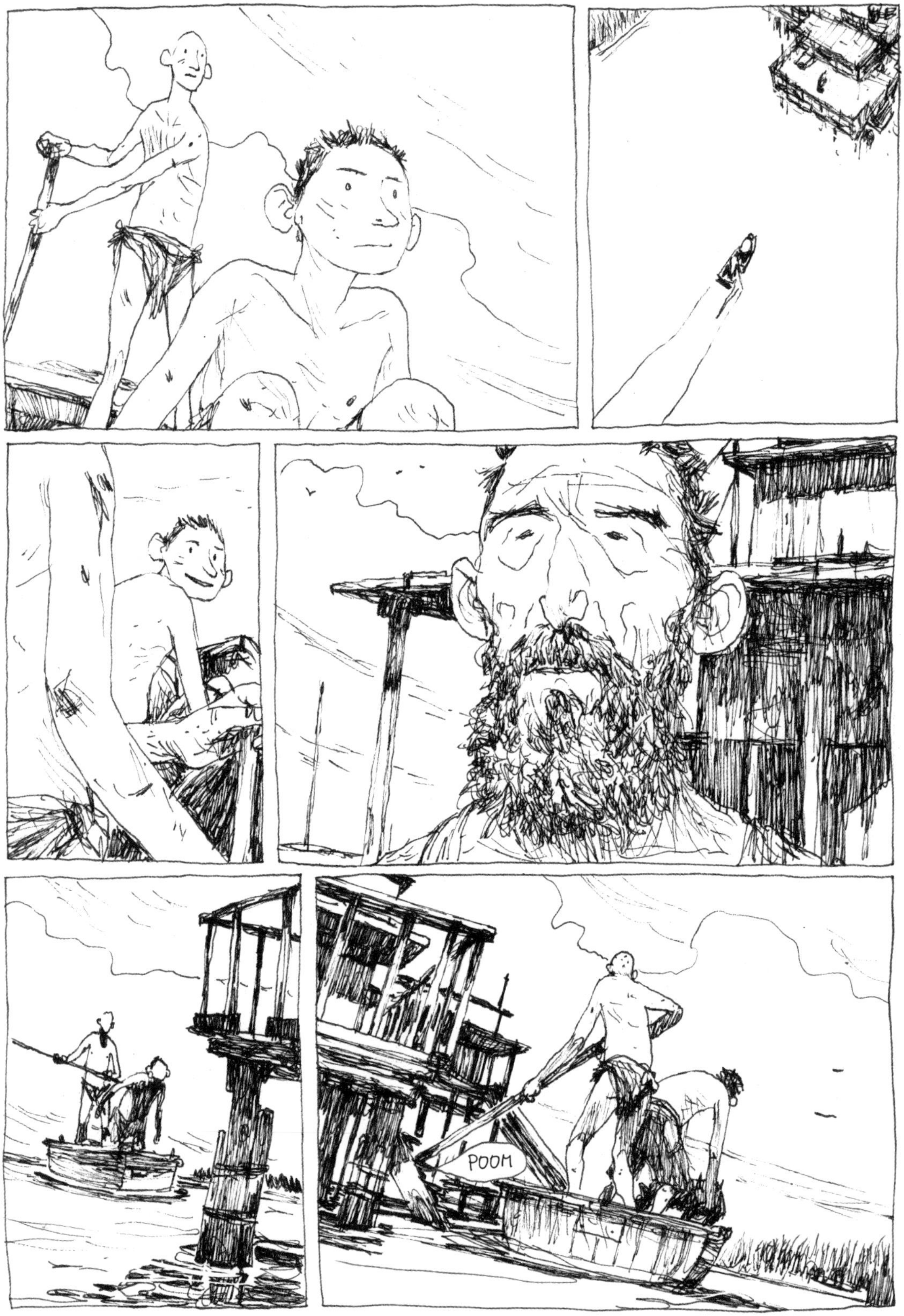
POOM

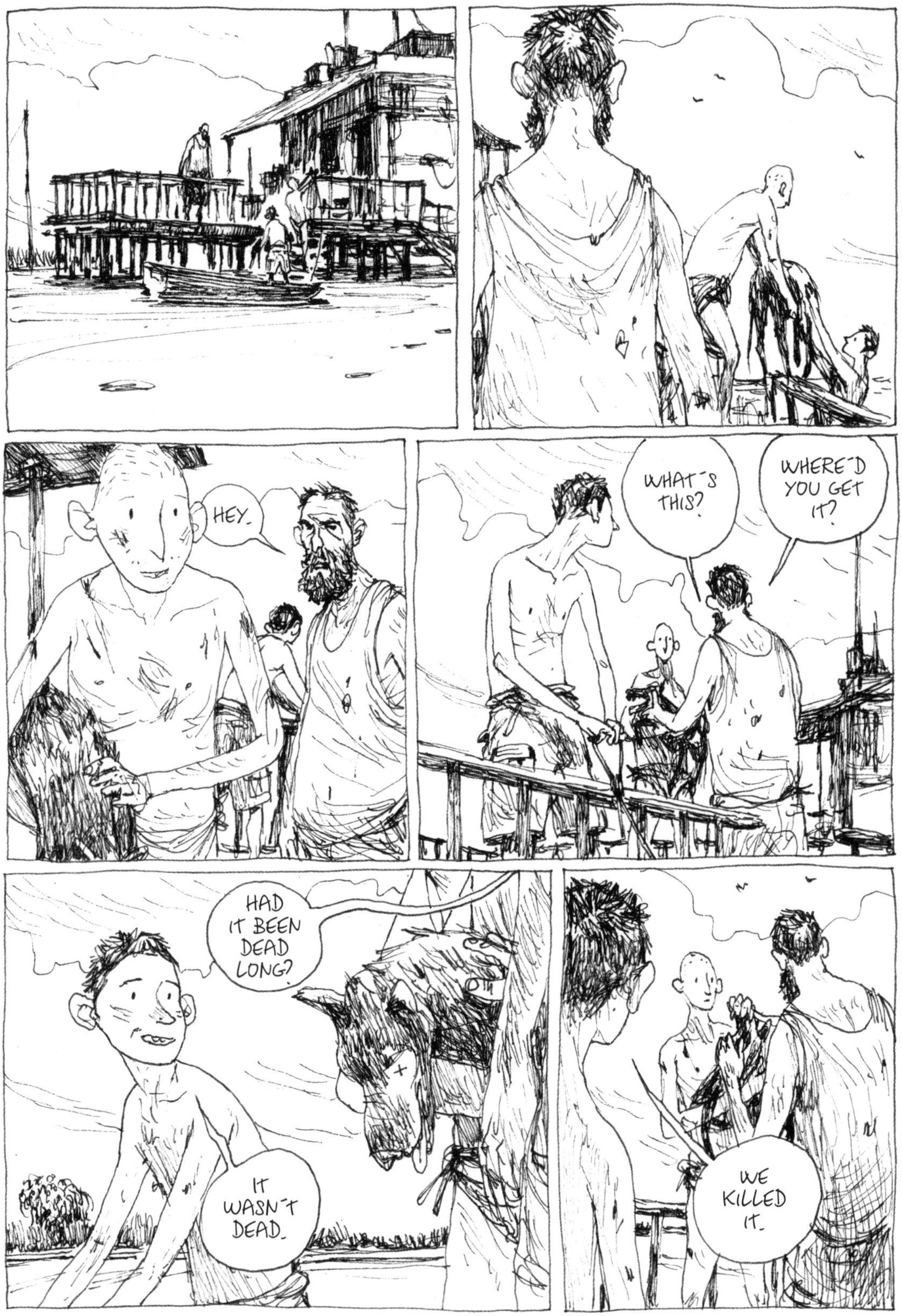
HEY.
WHAT'S THIS?
WHERE'D YOU GET IT?
HAD IT BEEN DEAD LONG?
IT WASN'T DEAD.
WE KILLED IT.

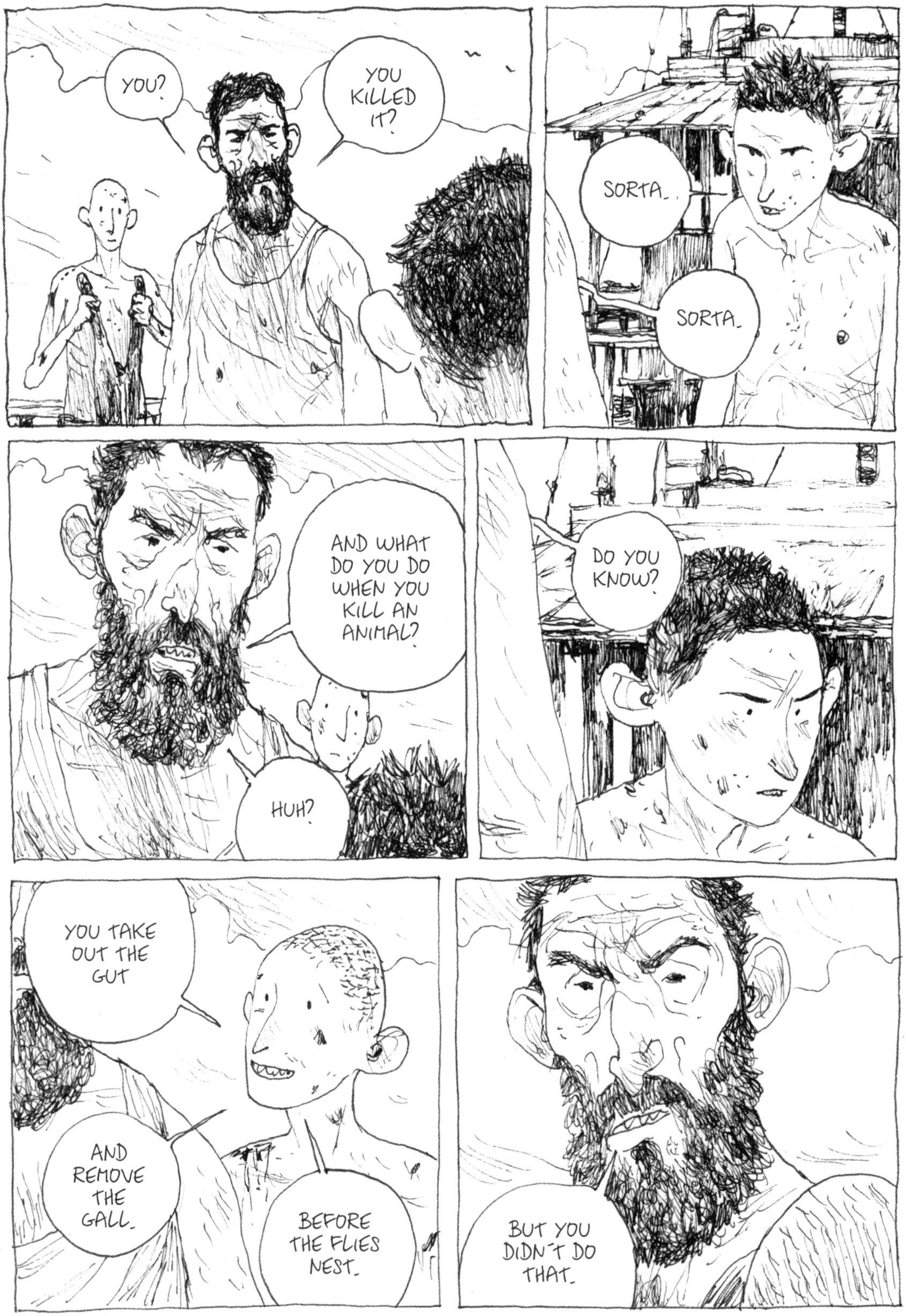
YOU?
YOU KILLED IT?
SORTA.
SORTA.
AND WHAT DO YOU DO WHEN YOU KILL AN ANIMAL?
HUH?
DO YOU KNOW?
YOU TAKE OUT THE GUT
AND REMOVE THE GALL.
BEFORE THE FLIES NEST.
BUT YOU DIDN'T DO THAT.

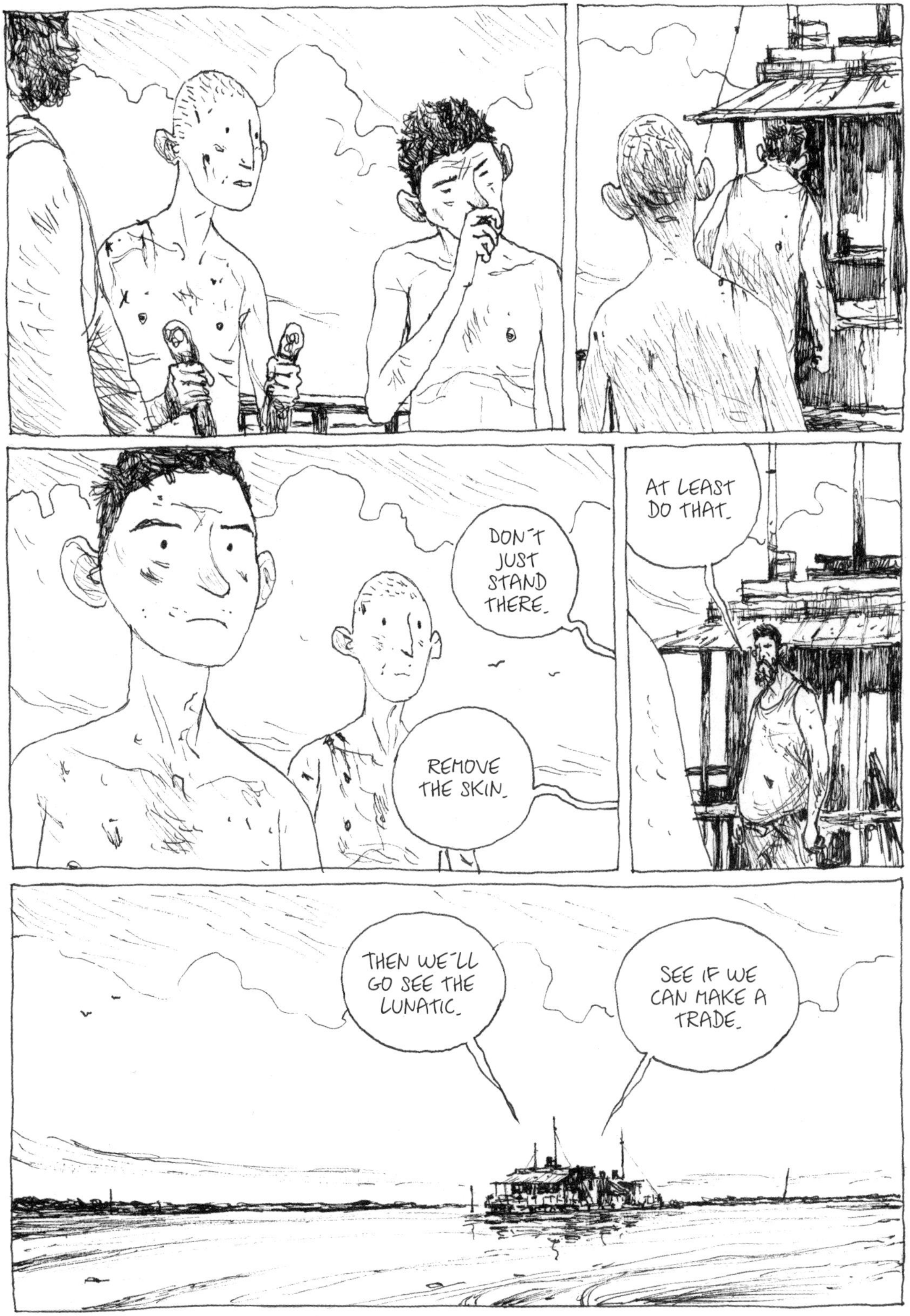

DON'T JUST STAND THERE.
REMOVE THE SKIN.
AT LEAST DO THAT.
THEN WE'LL GO SEE THE LUNATIC.
SEE IF WE CAN MAKE A TRADE.

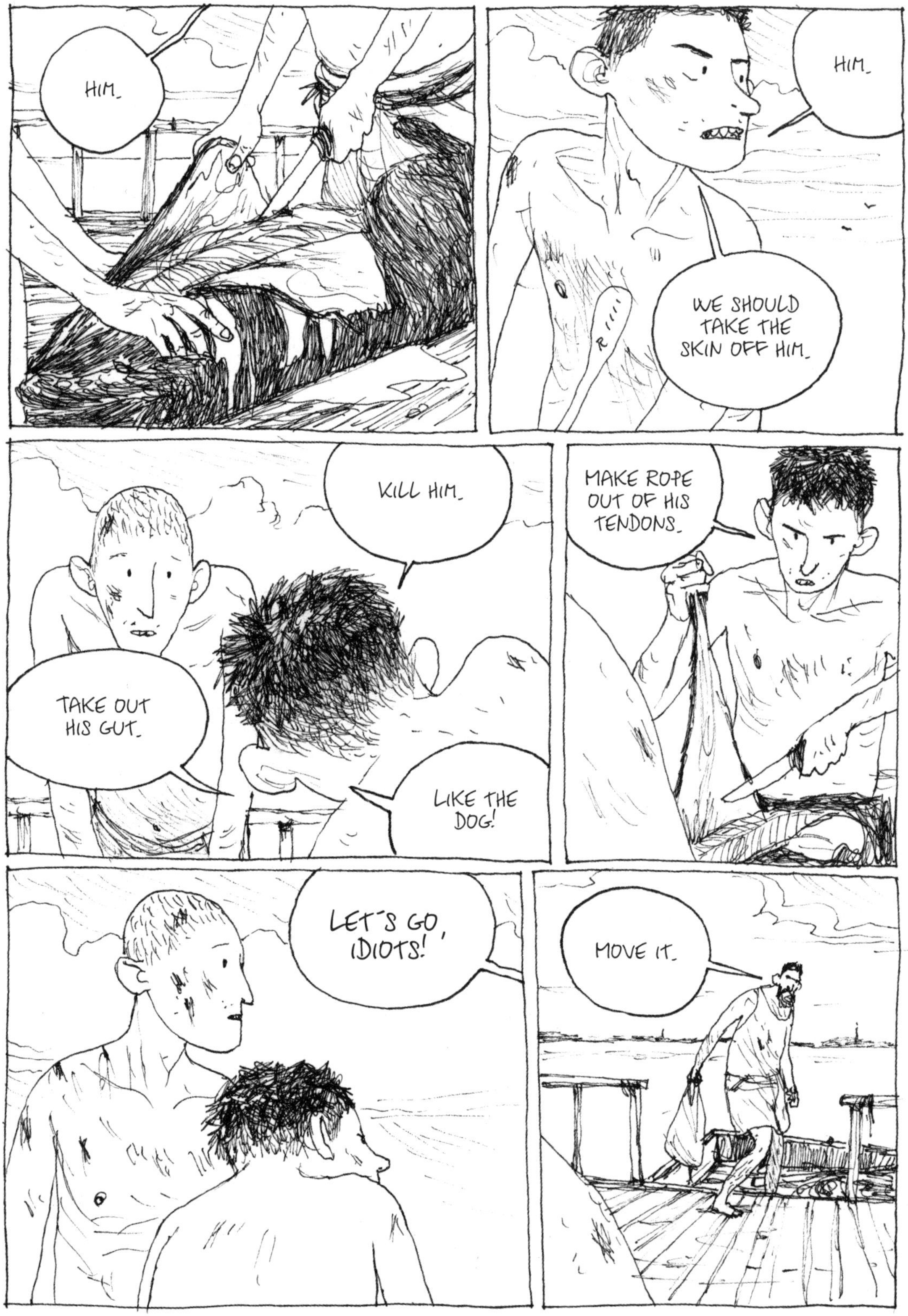
HIM_
HIM_
WE SHOULD TAKE THE SKIN OFF HIM_
KILL HIM_
TAKE OUT HIS GUT_
LIKE THE DOG!
MAKE ROPE OUT OF HIS TENDONS_
LET'S GO, IDIOTS!
MOVE IT_

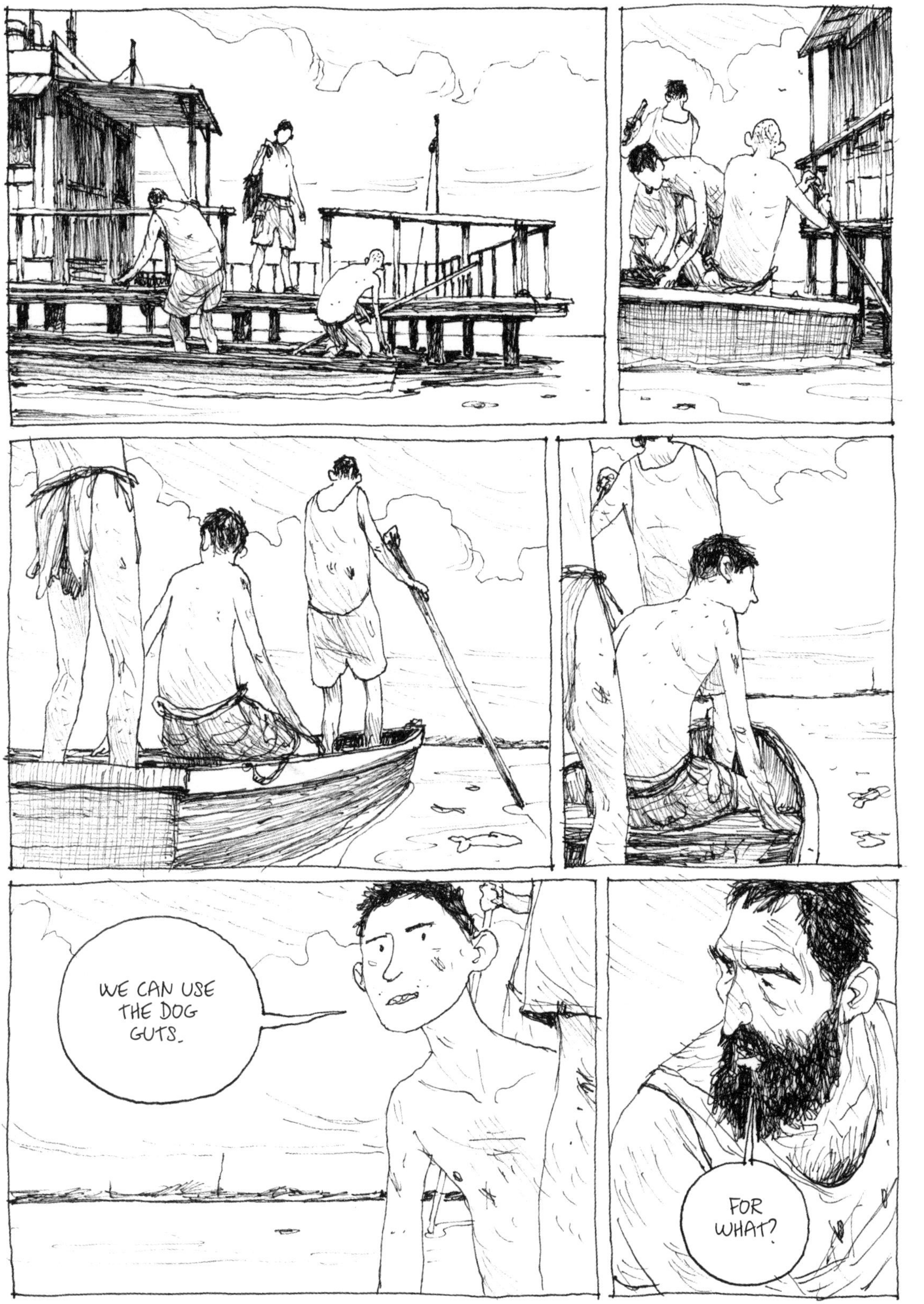
WE CAN USE THE DOG GUTS_
FOR WHAT?

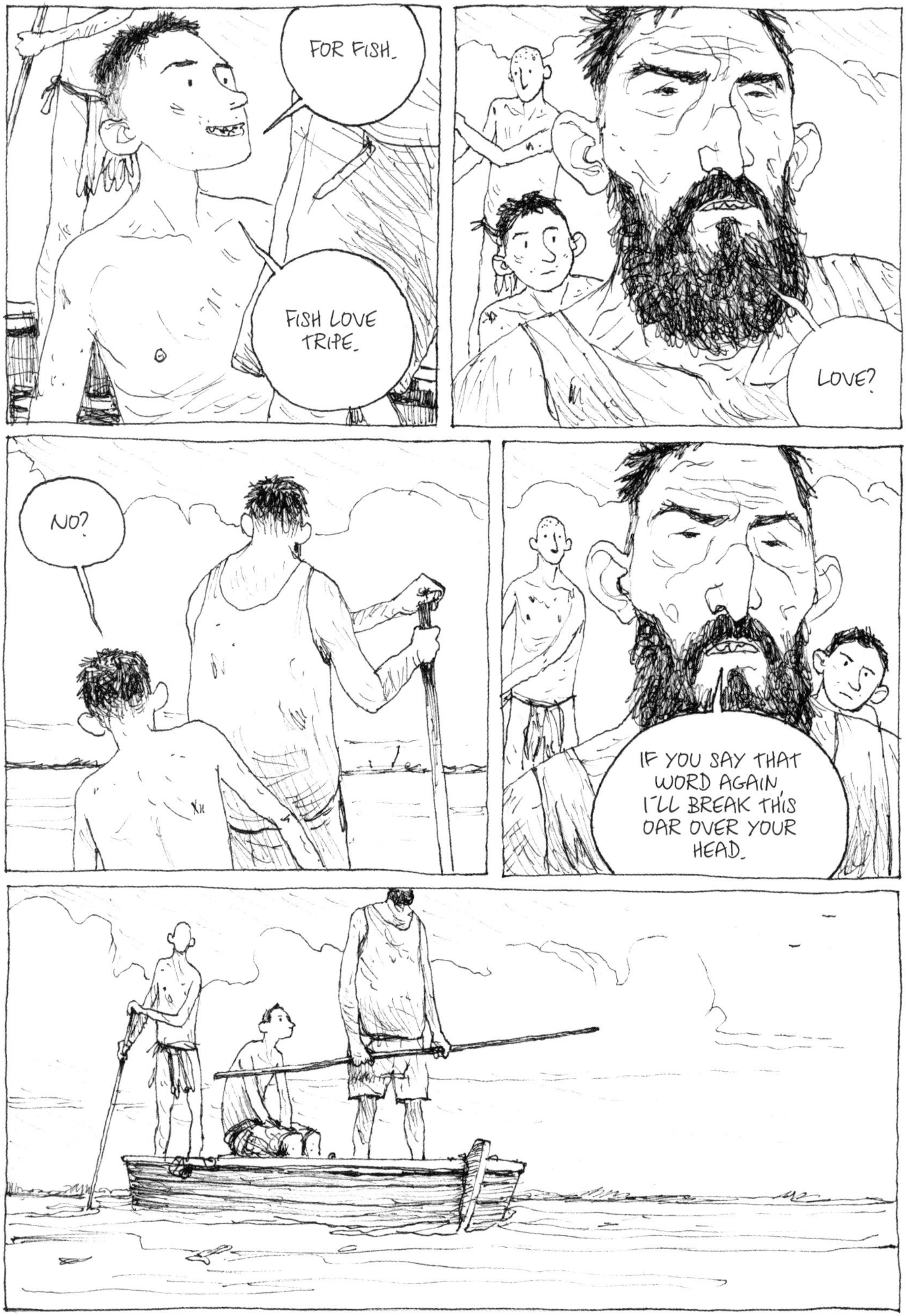
FOR FISH.
FISH LOVE TRIPE.
LOVE?
NO?
IF YOU SAY THAT WORD AGAIN, I'LL BREAK THIS OAR OVER YOUR HEAD.

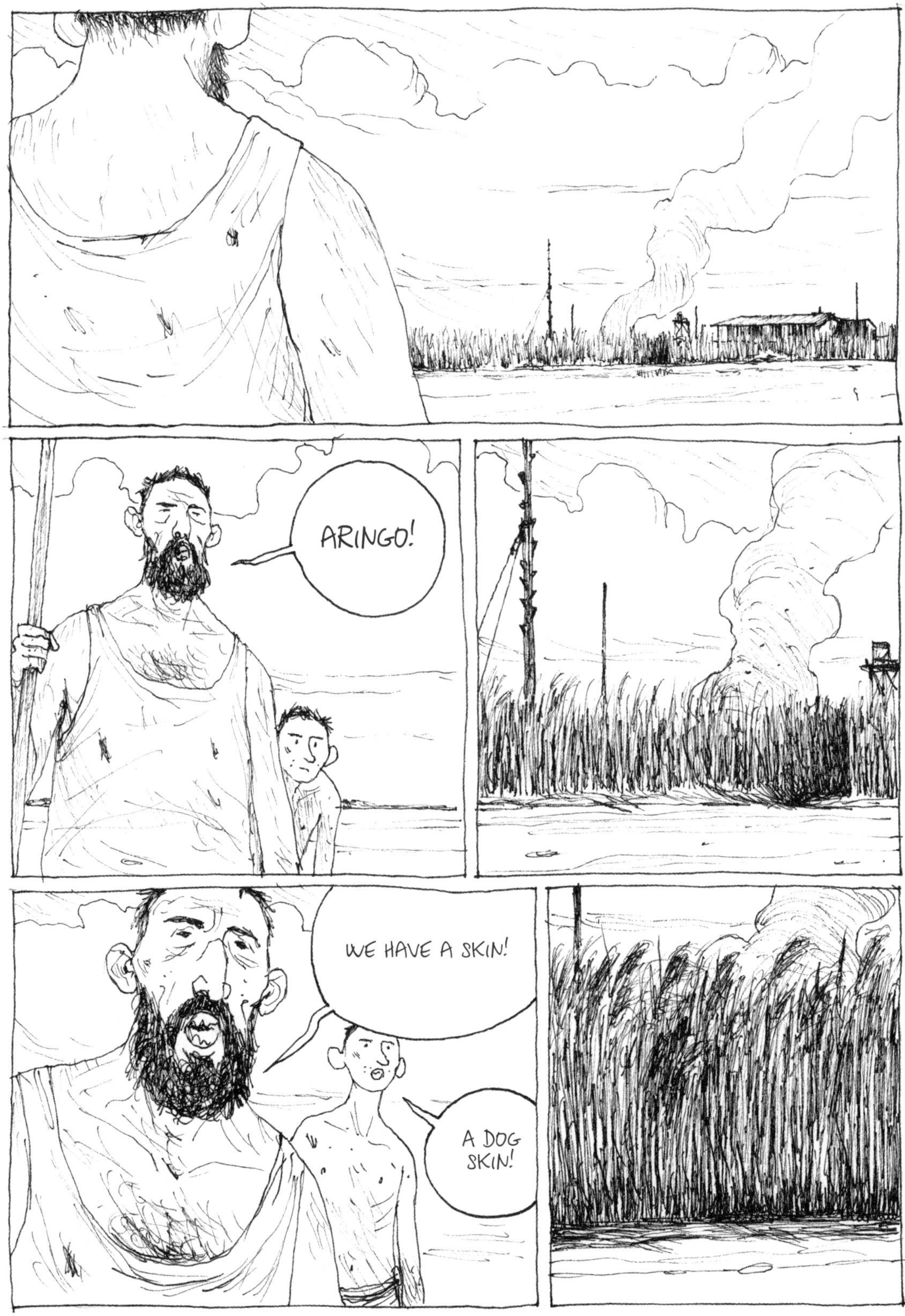
ARINGO!
WE HAVE A SKIN!
A DOG SKIN!

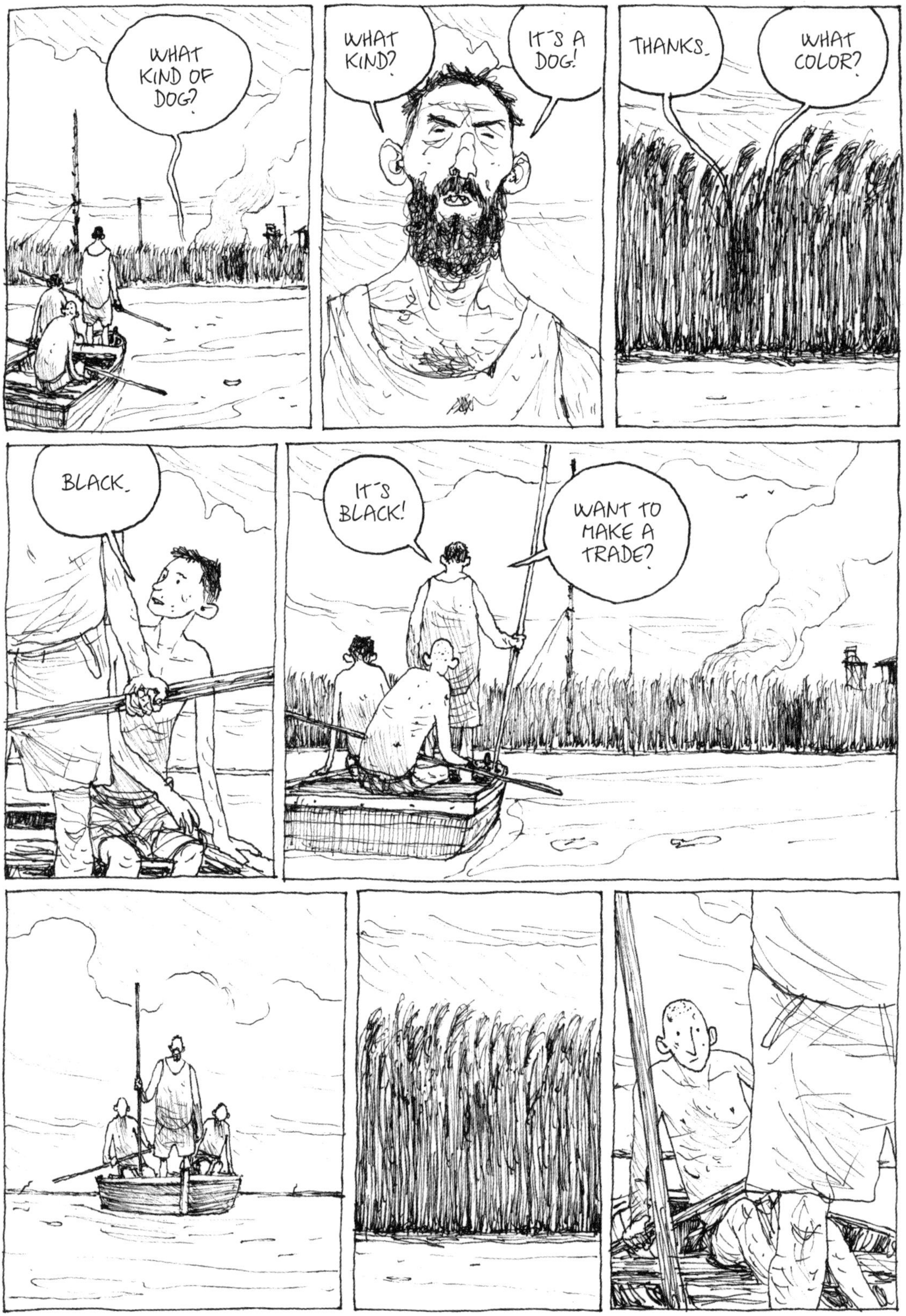
WHAT KIND OF DOG?
WHAT KIND?
IT'S A DOG!
THANKS.
WHAT COLOR?
BLACK.
IT'S BLACK!
WANT TO MAKE A TRADE?

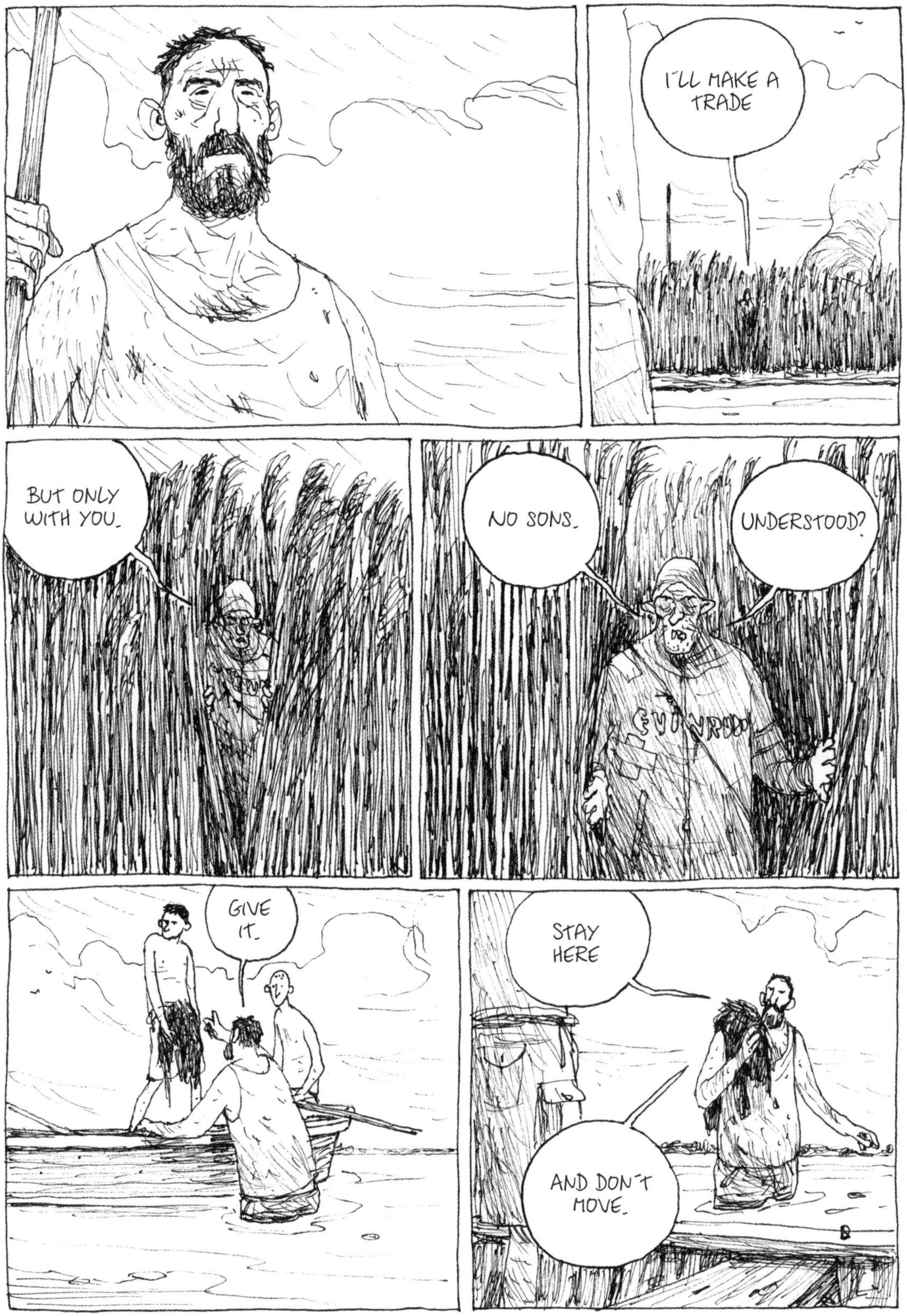
I'LL MAKE A TRADE
BUT ONLY WITH YOU.
NO SONS.
UNDERSTOOD?
GIVE IT.
STAY HERE
AND DON'T MOVE.

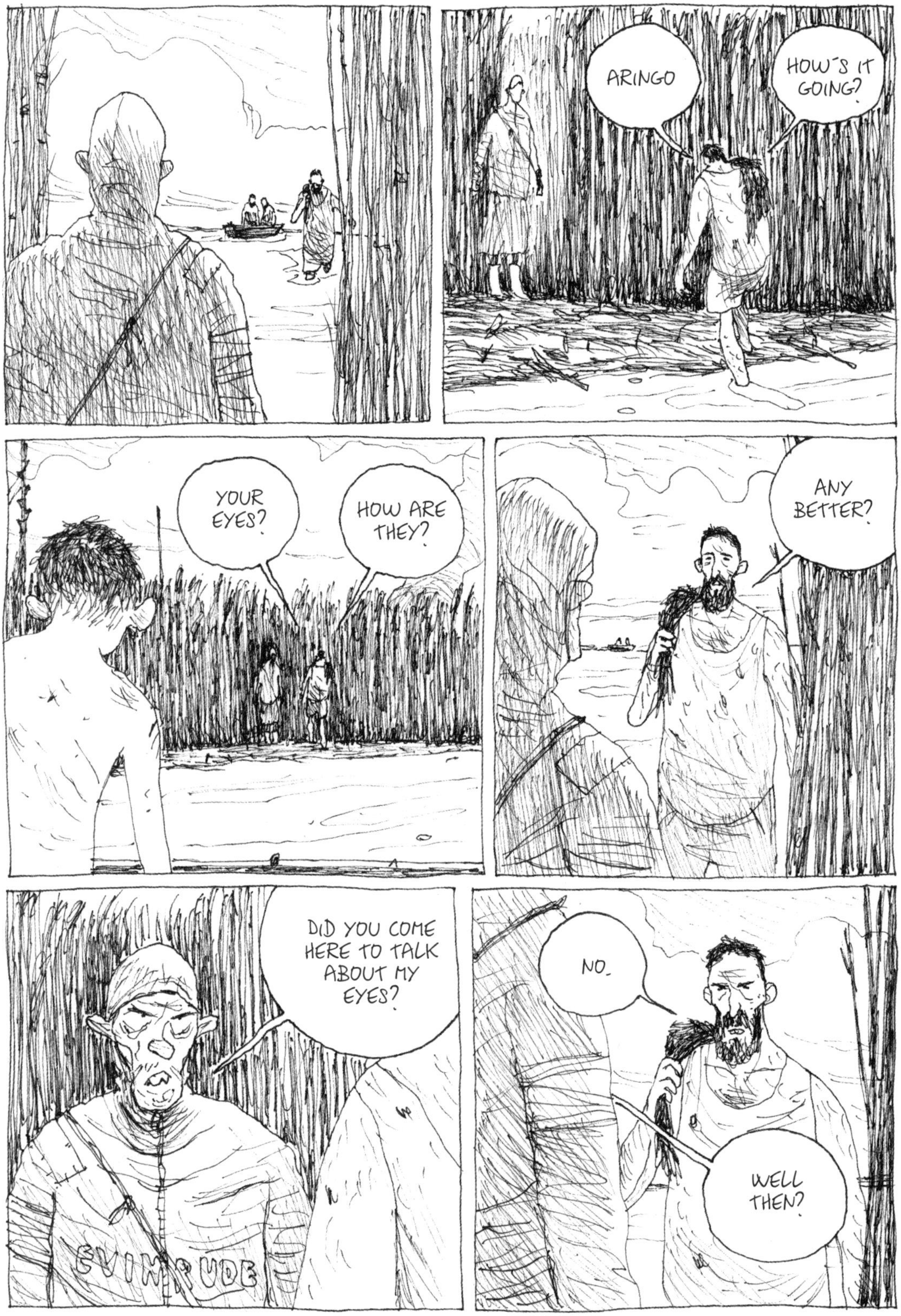
ARINGO
HOW´S IT GOING?
YOUR EYES?
HOW ARE THEY?
ANY BETTER?
DID YOU COME HERE TO TALK ABOUT MY EYES?
NO.
WELL THEN?

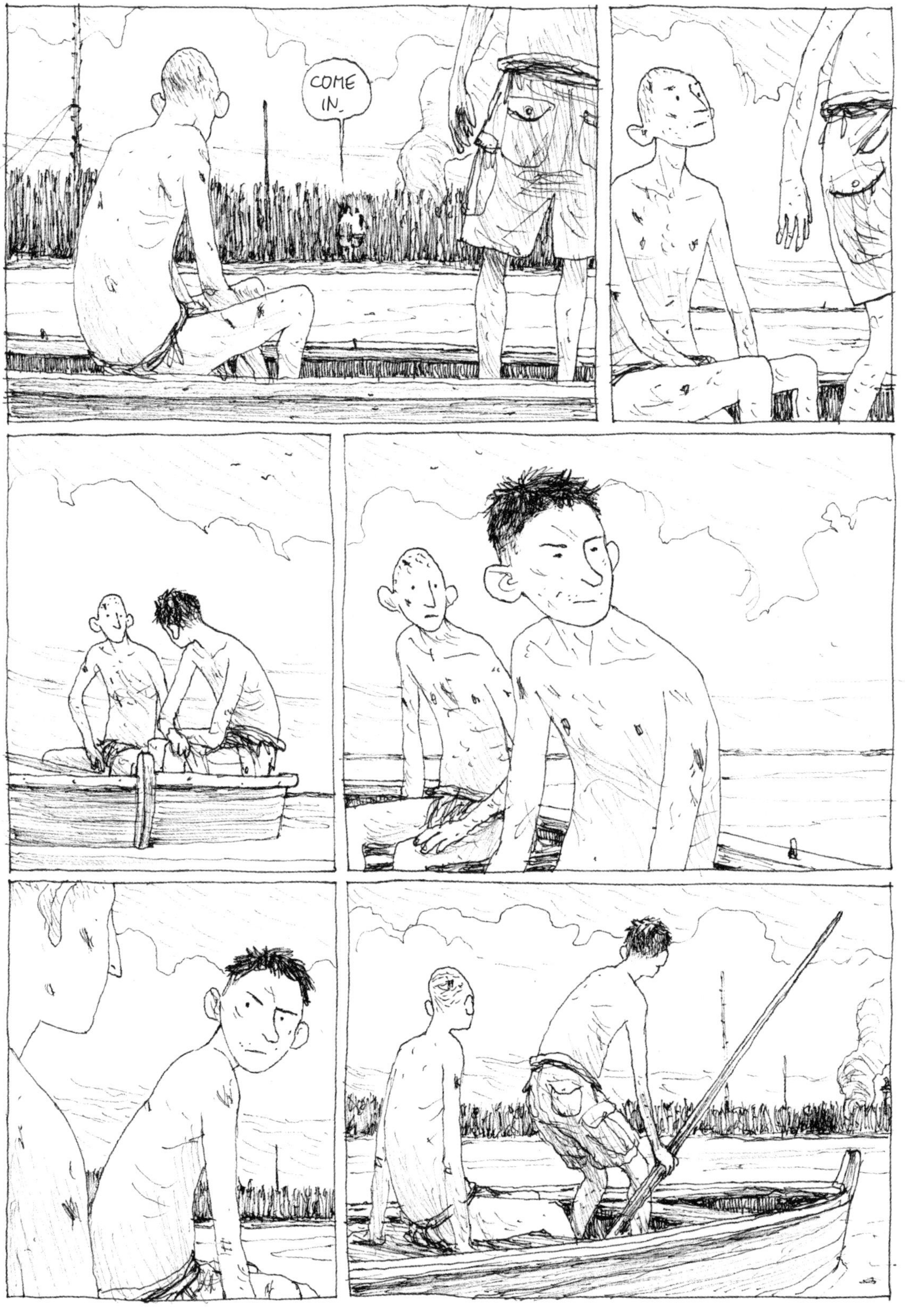
COME IN_

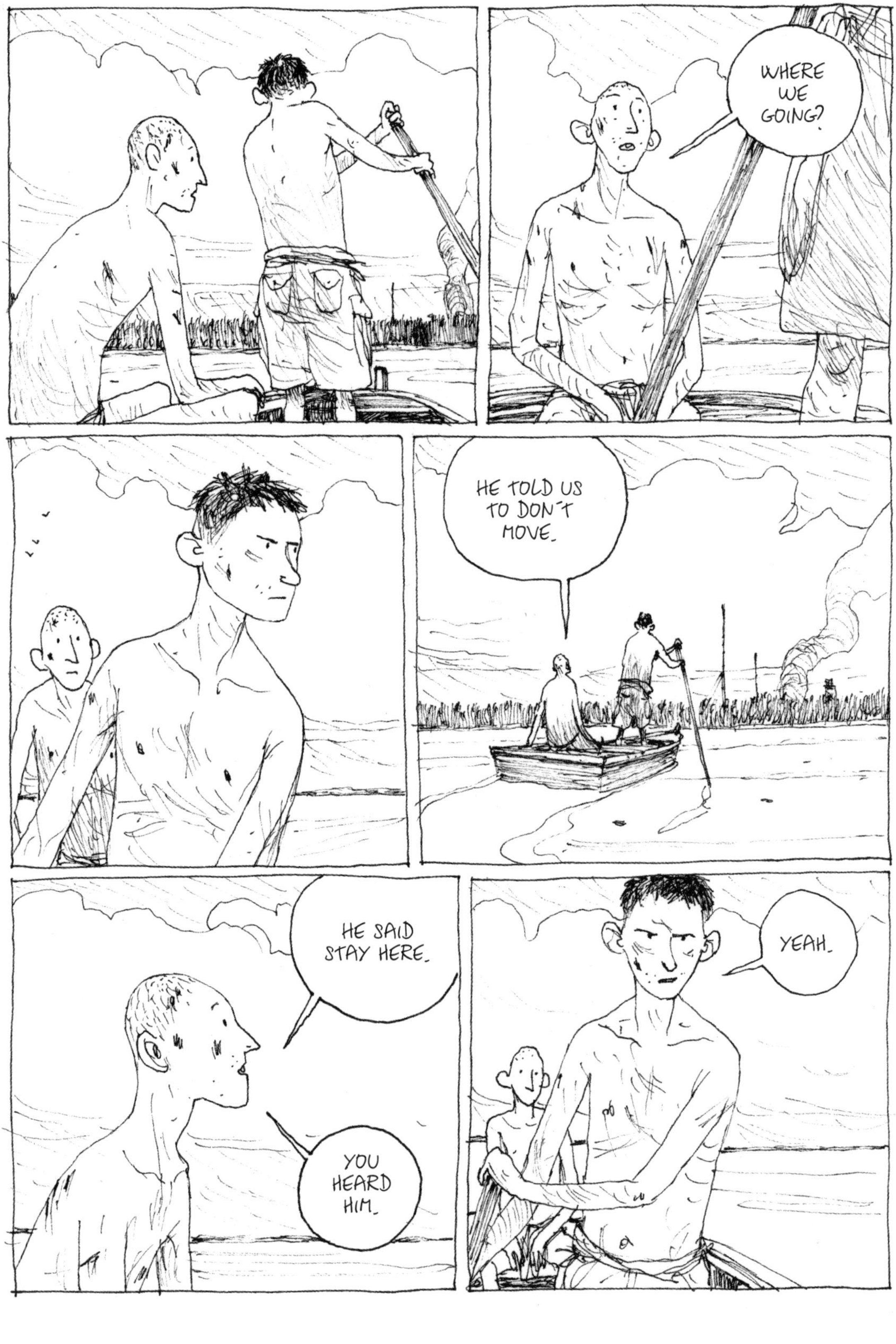
WHERE WE GOING?
HE TOLD US TO DON'T MOVE.
HE SAID STAY HERE.
YOU HEARD HIM.
YEAH.

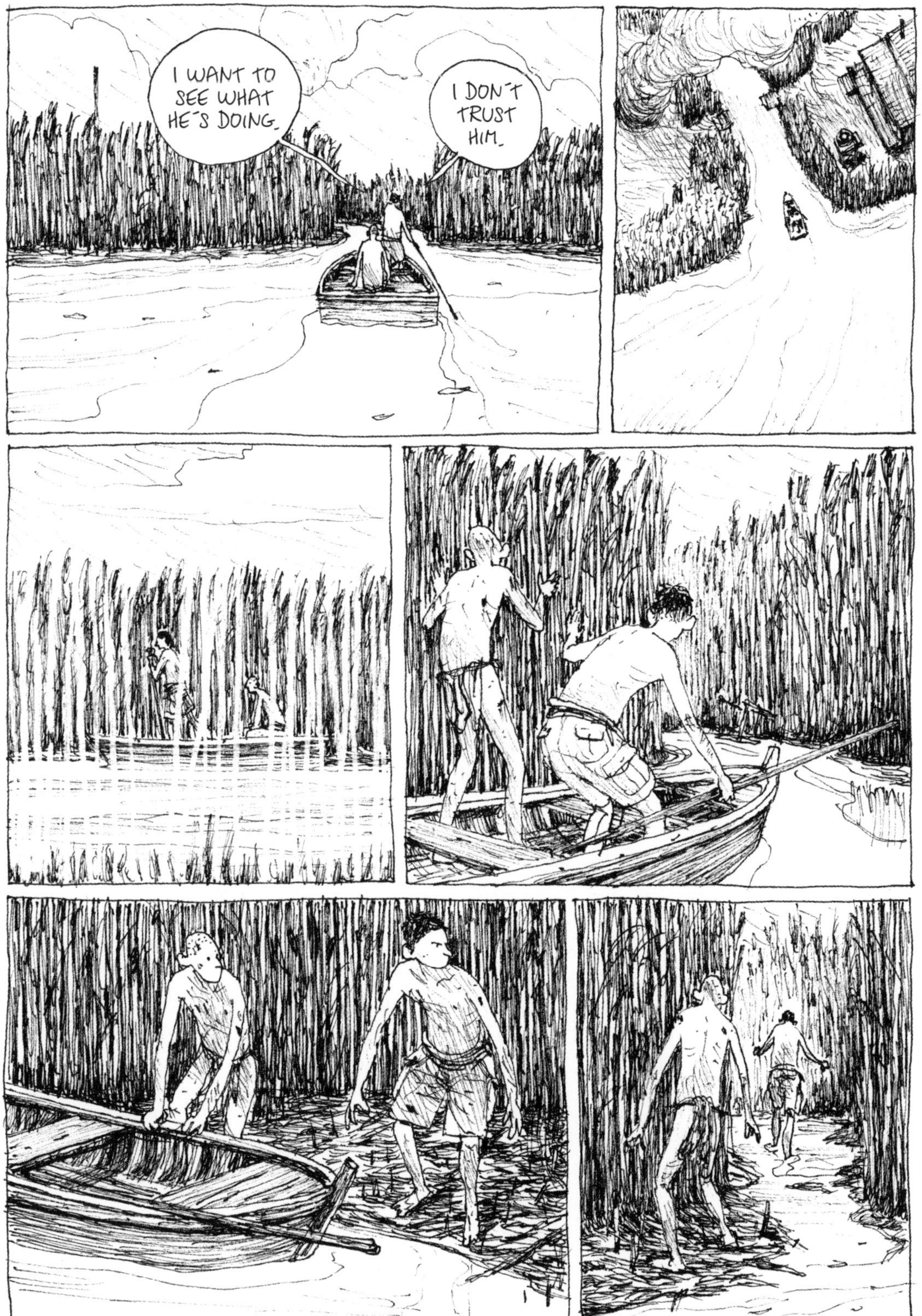
I WANT TO SEE WHAT HE'S DOING.
I DON'T TRUST HIM.

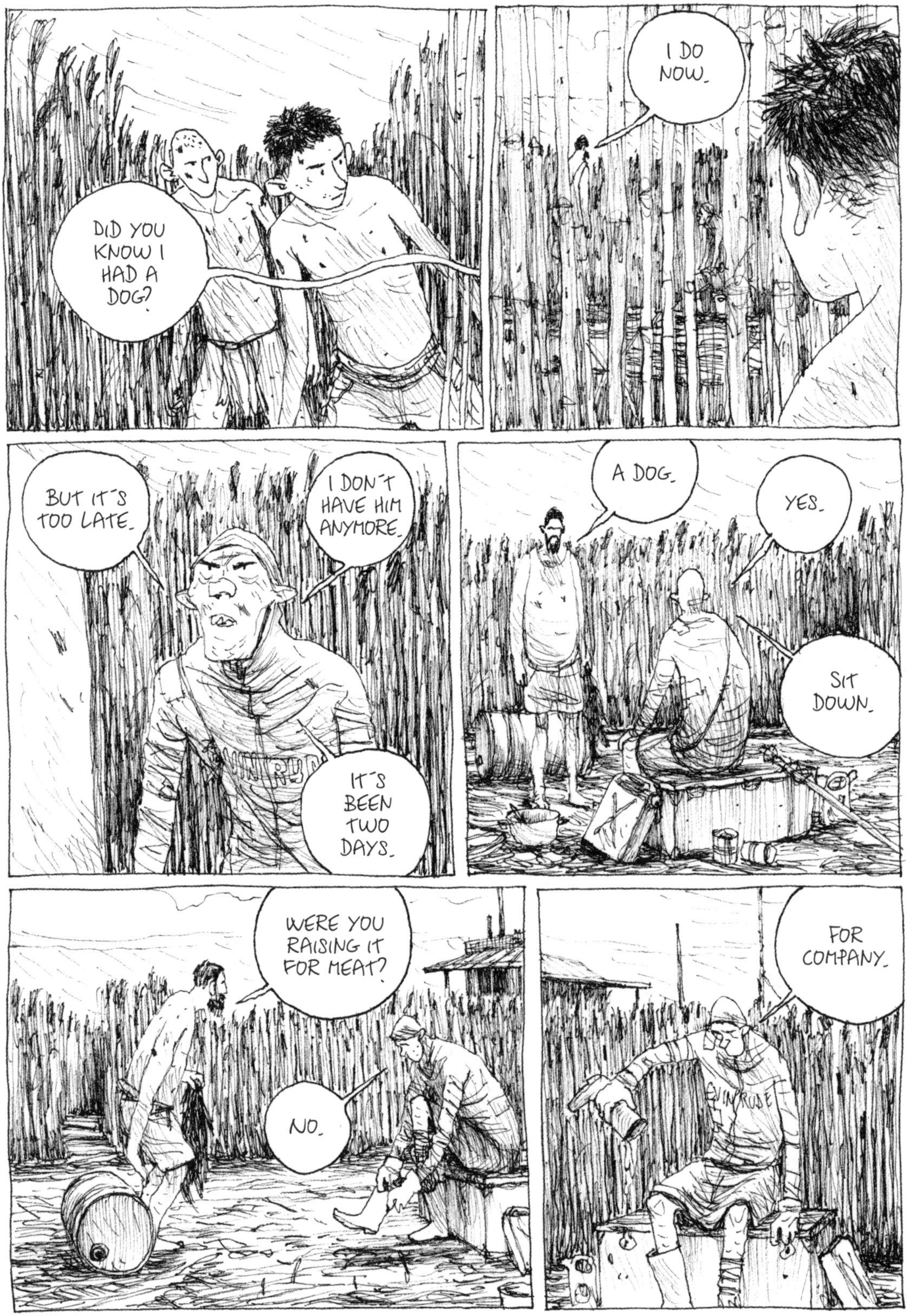
DID YOU KNOW I HAD A DOG?
I DO NOW.
I DON'T HAVE HIM ANYMORE.
BUT IT'S TOO LATE.
IT'S BEEN TWO DAYS.
A DOG.
YES.
SIT DOWN.
WERE YOU RAISING IT FOR MEAT?
NO.
FOR COMPANY.

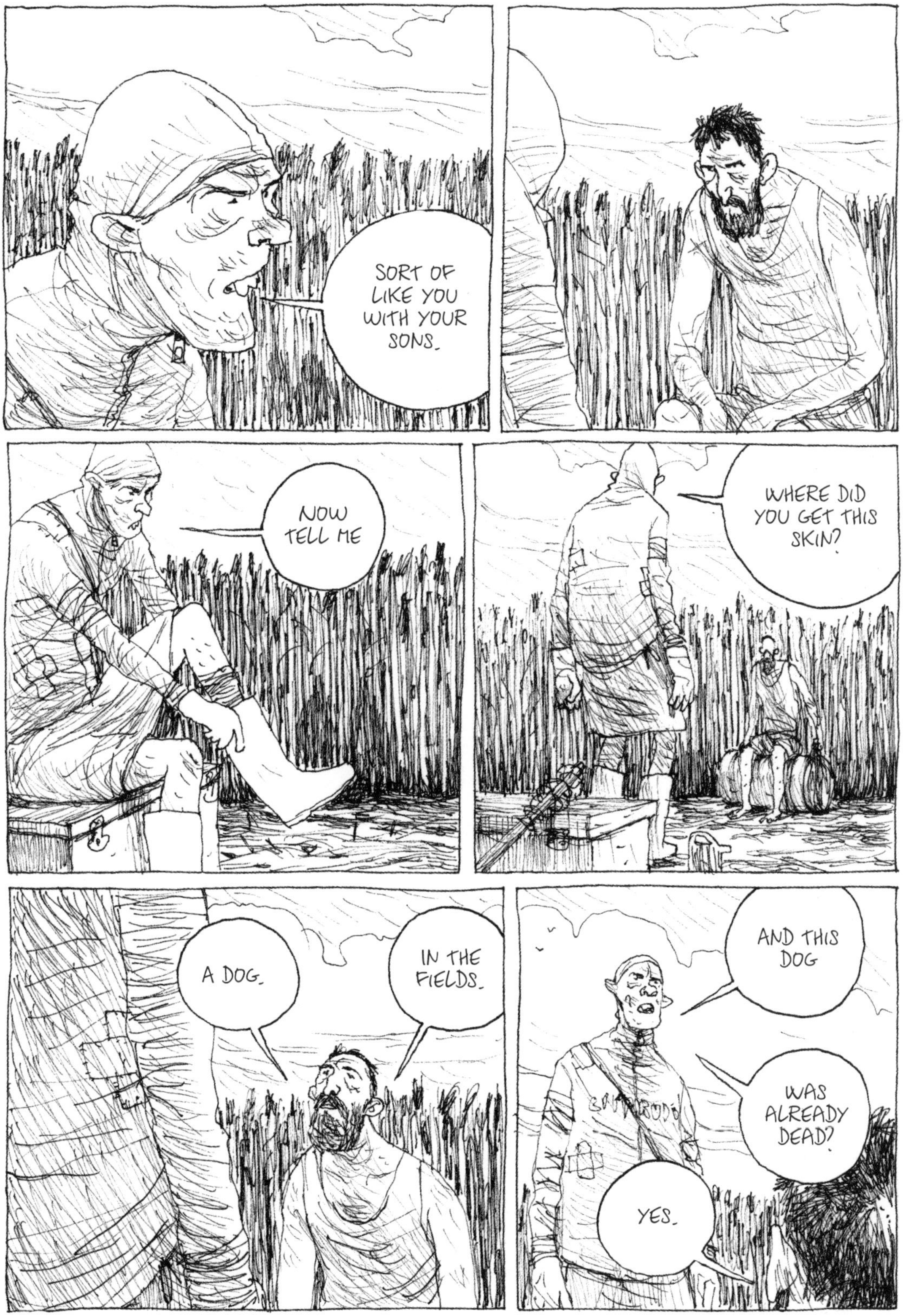
SORT OF LIKE YOU WITH YOUR SONS.
NOW TELL ME
WHERE DID YOU GET THIS SKIN?
A DOG.
IN THE FIELDS.
AND THIS DOG
WAS ALREADY DEAD?
YES.

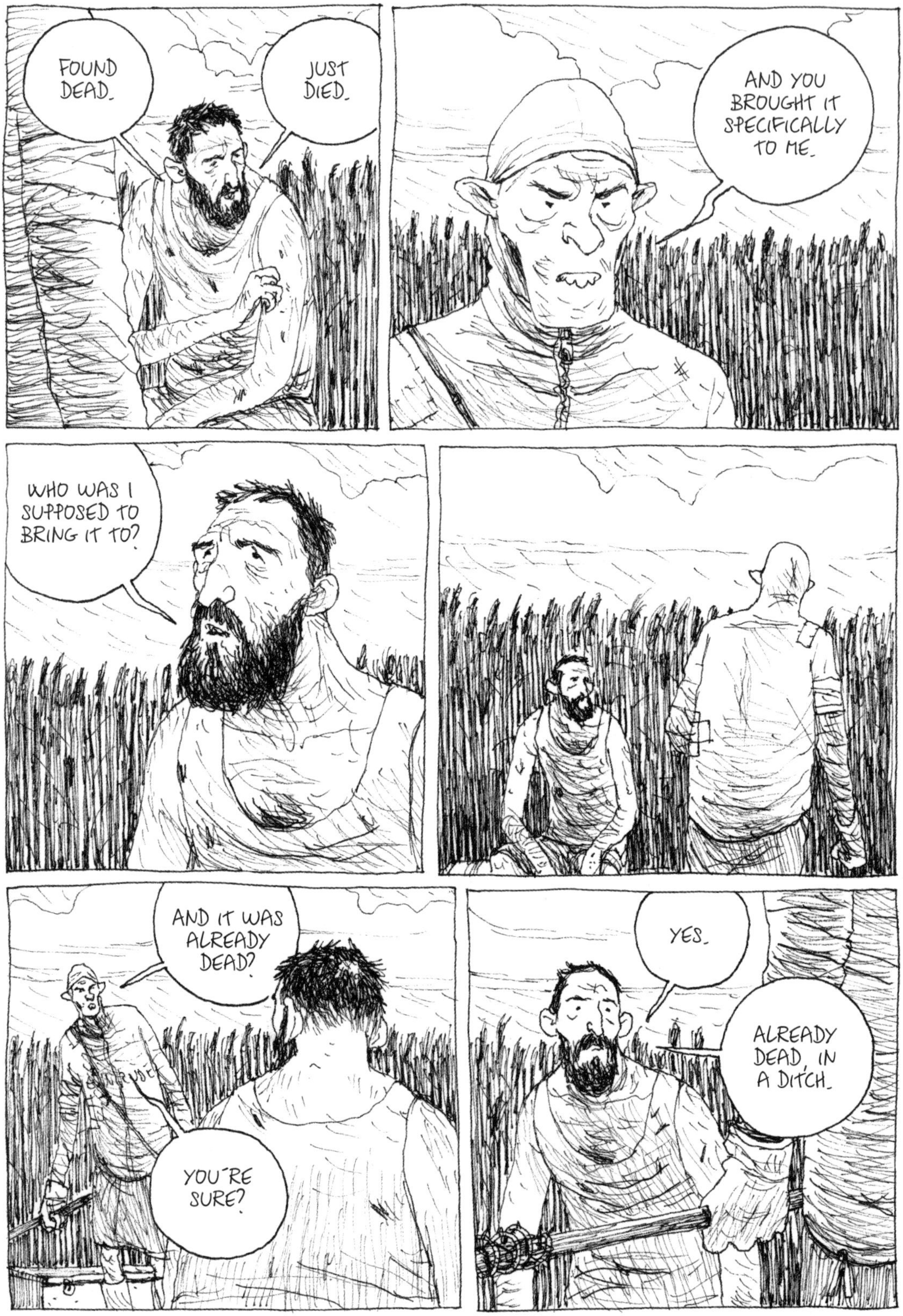
FOUND DEAD.
JUST DIED.
AND YOU BROUGHT IT SPECIFICALLY TO ME.
WHO WAS I SUPPOSED TO BRING IT TO?
AND IT WAS ALREADY DEAD?
YOU'RE SURE?
YES.
ALREADY DEAD, IN A DITCH.

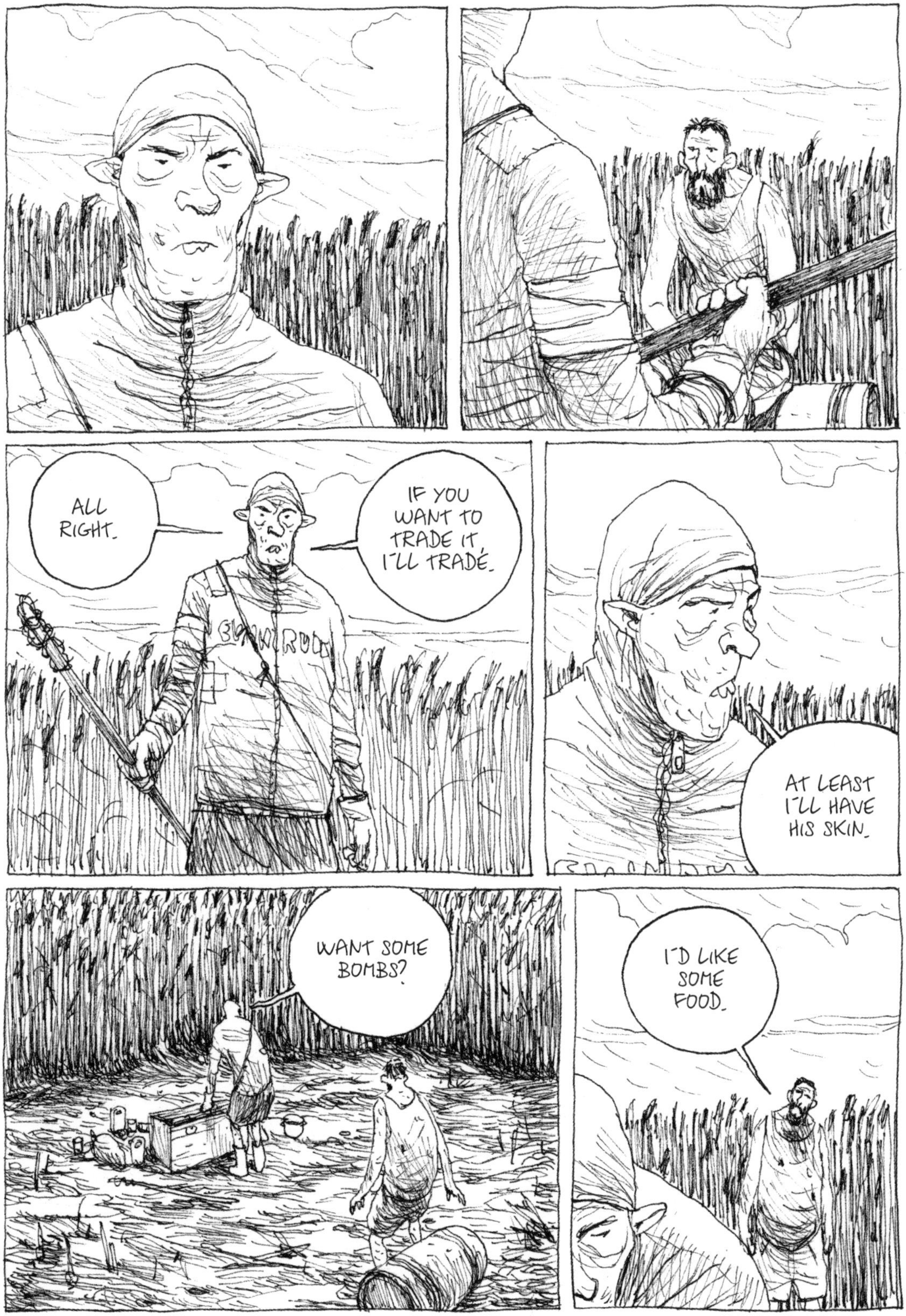
ALL RIGHT.
IF YOU WANT TO TRADE IT I'LL TRADE.
AT LEAST I'LL HAVE HIS SKIN.
WANT SOME BOMBS?
I'D LIKE SOME FOOD.

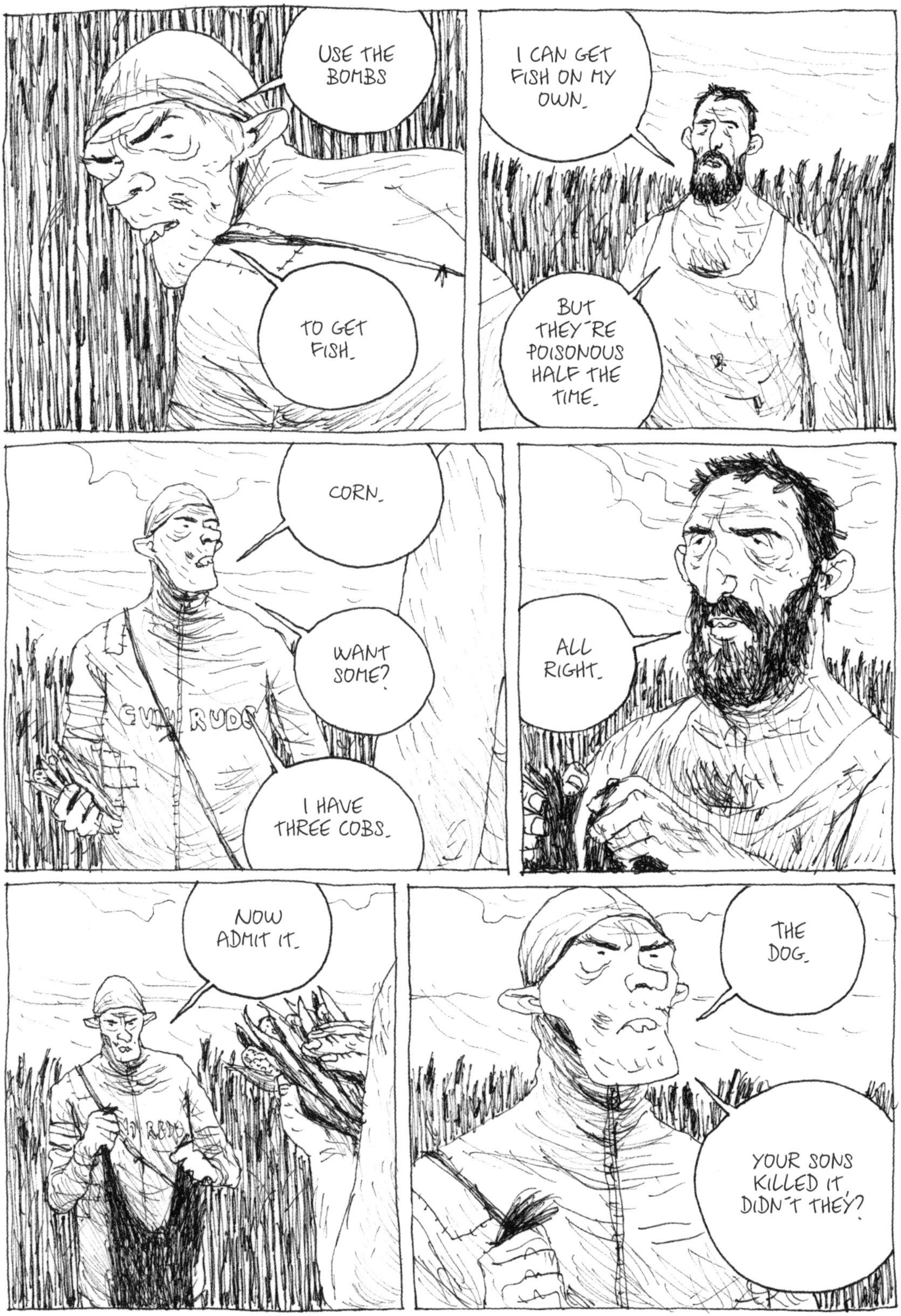
USE THE BOMBS
TO GET FISH.
I CAN GET FISH ON MY OWN.
BUT THEY'RE POISONOUS HALF THE TIME.
CORN.
WANT SOME?
I HAVE THREE COBS.
ALL RIGHT.
NOW ADMIT IT.
THE DOG.
YOUR SONS KILLED IT, DIDN'T THEY?

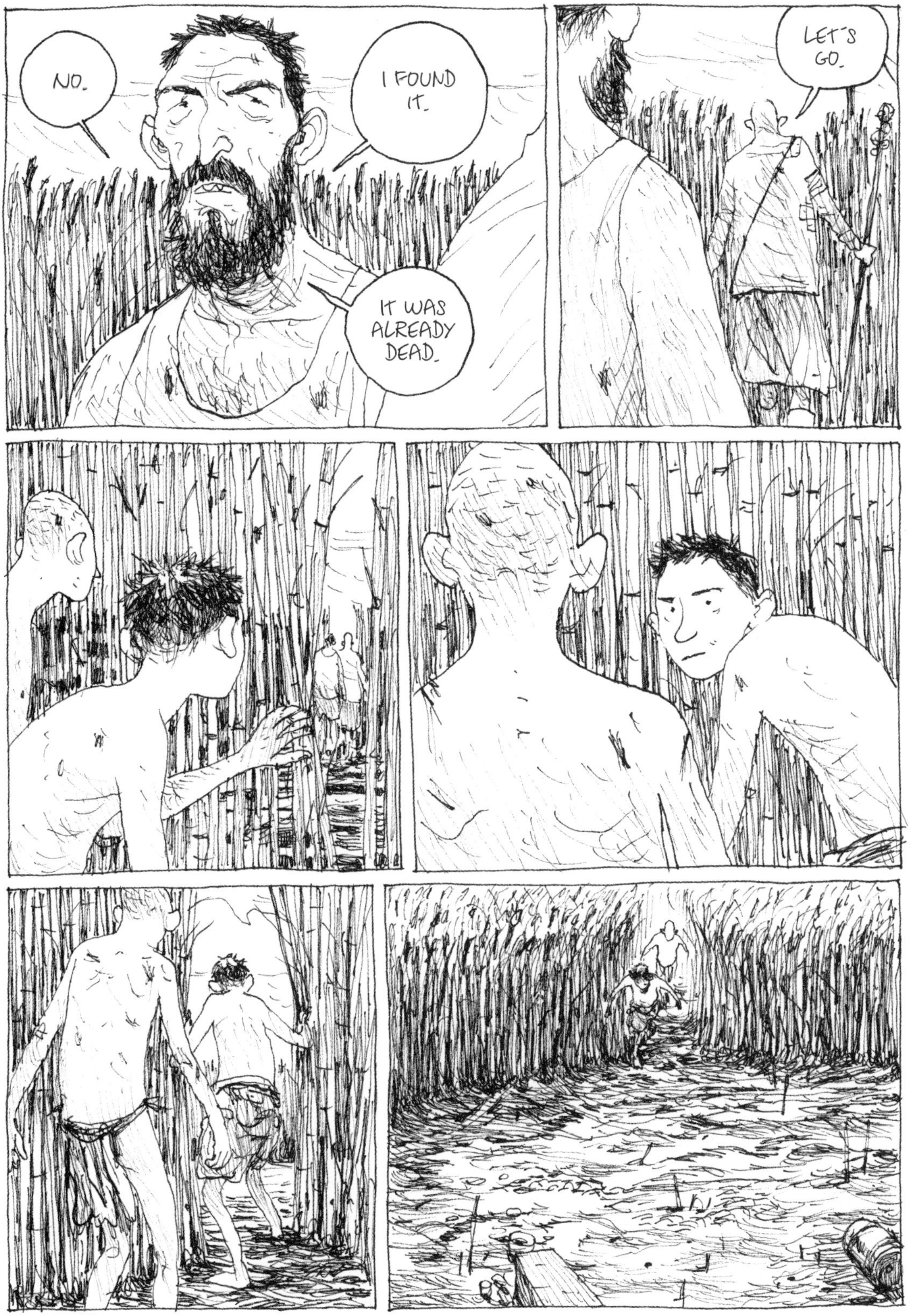
NO.
I FOUND IT.
IT WAS ALREADY DEAD.
LET'S GO.

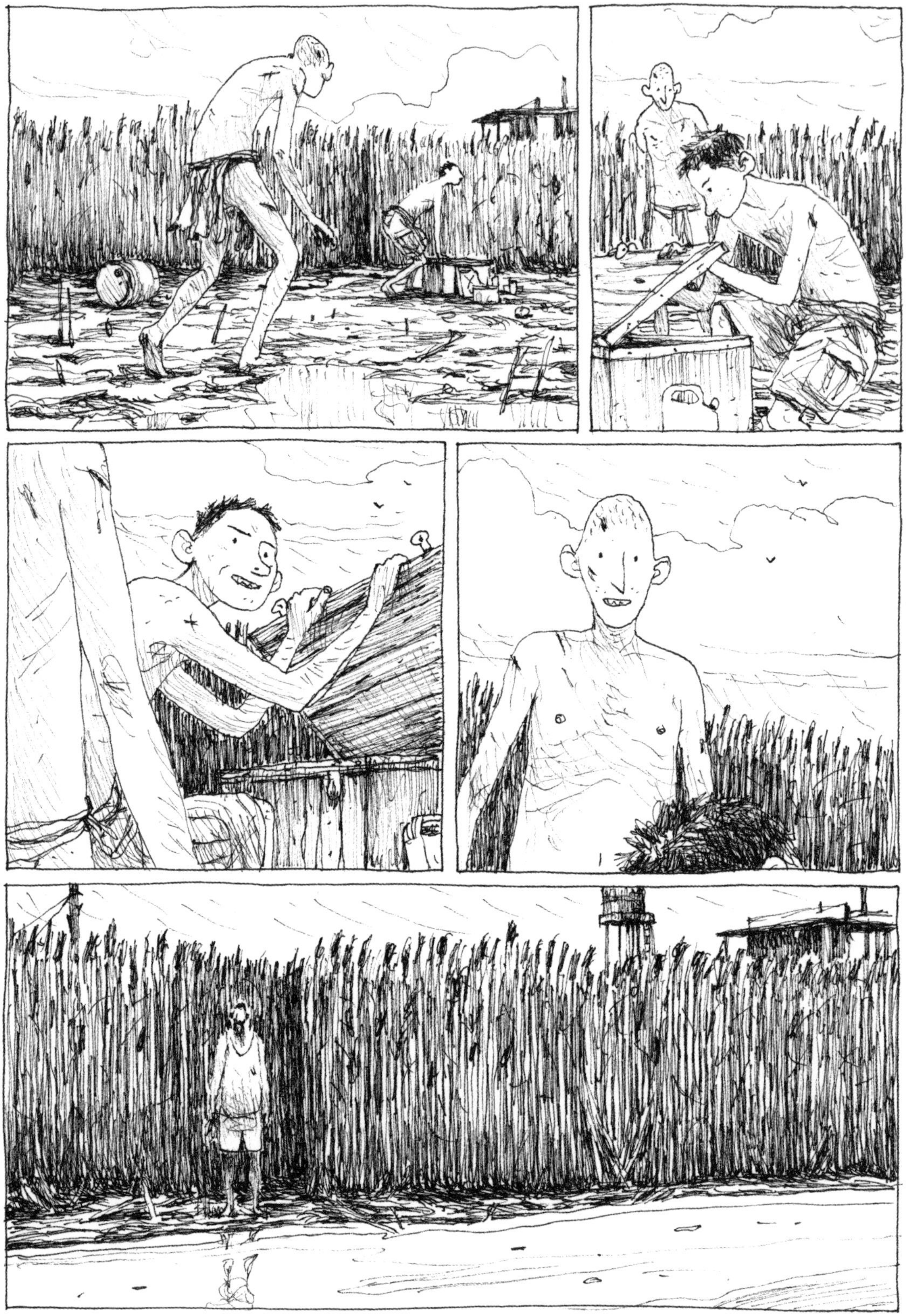

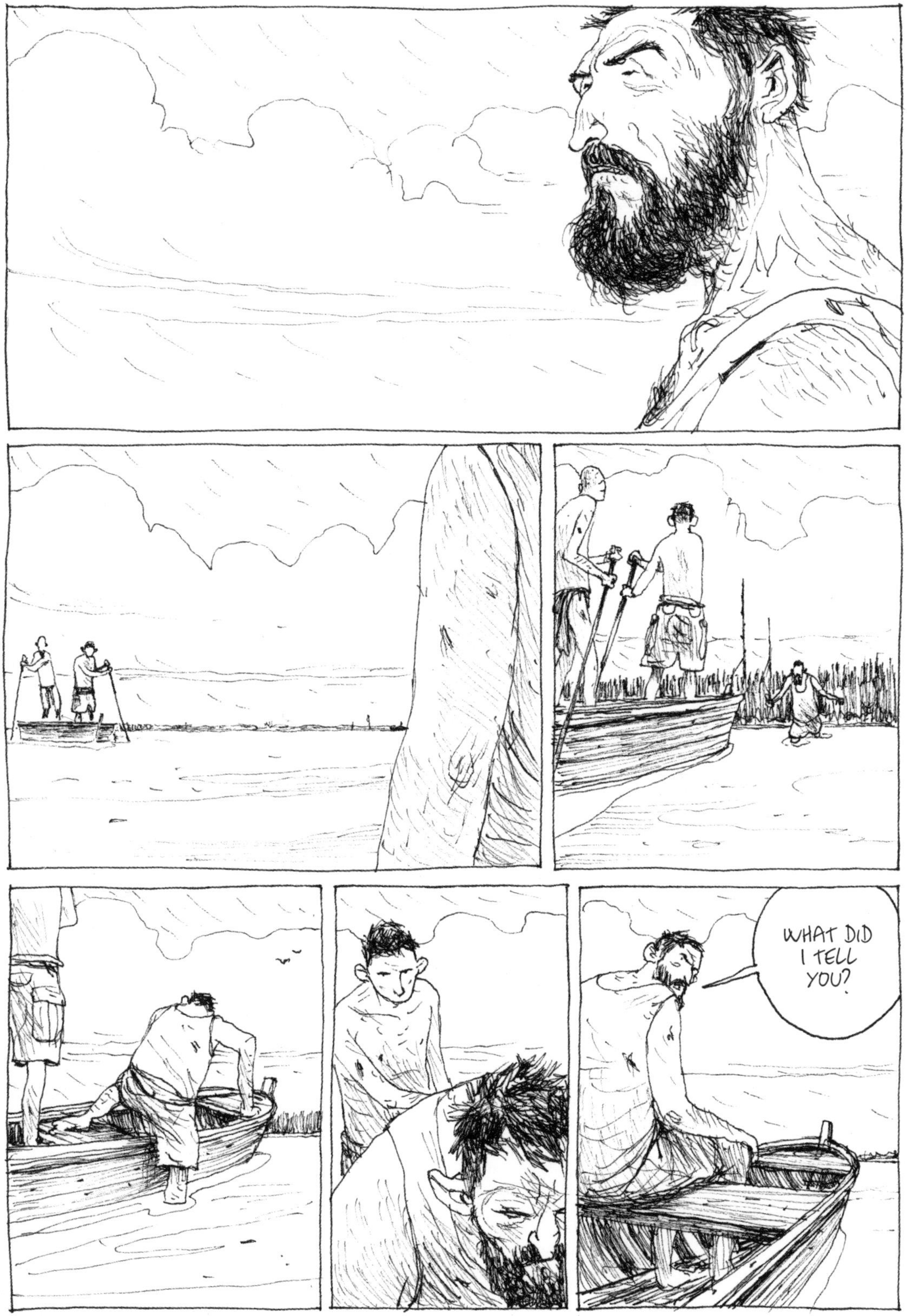
WHAT DID I TELL YOU?

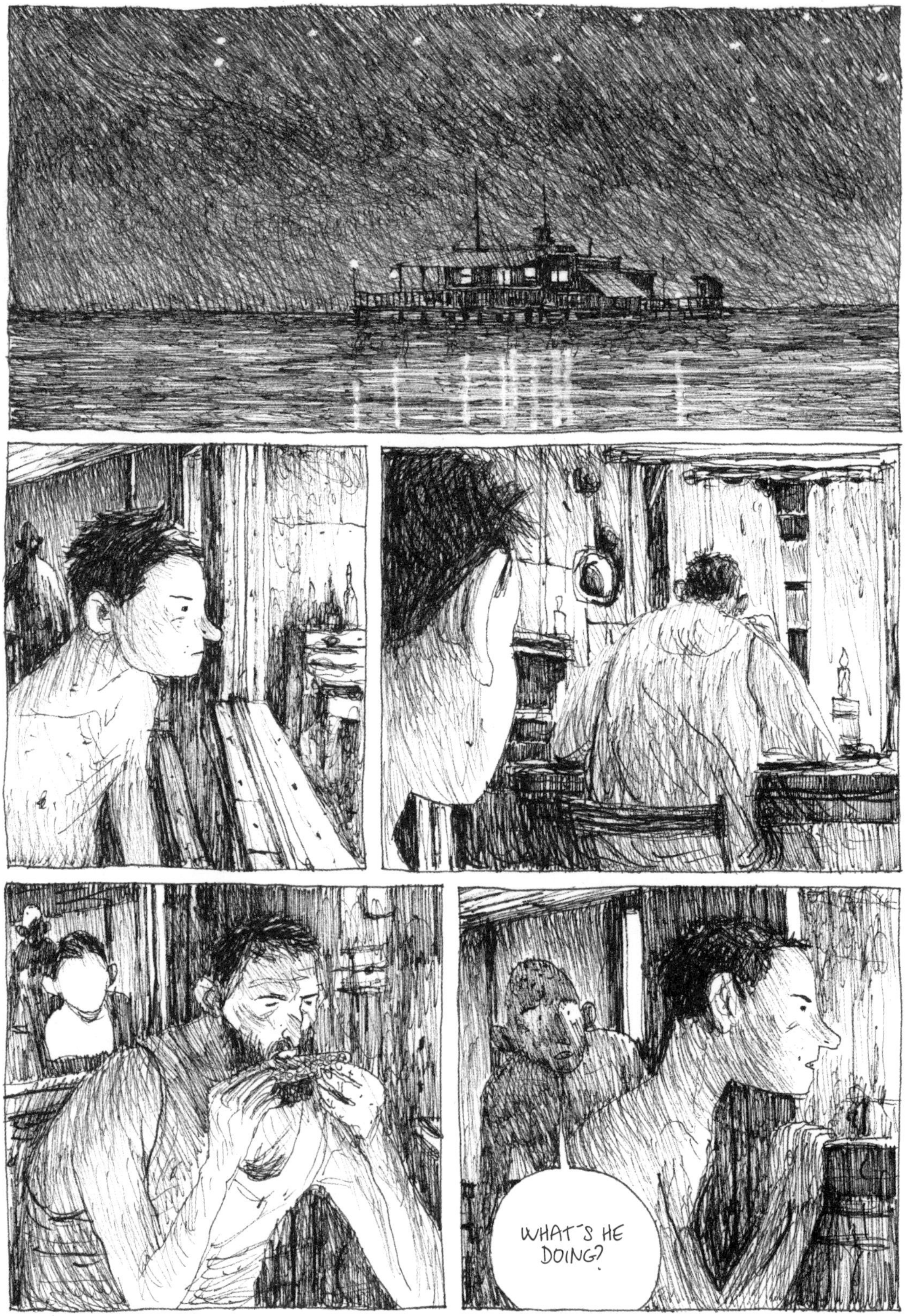
WHAT'S HE DOING?

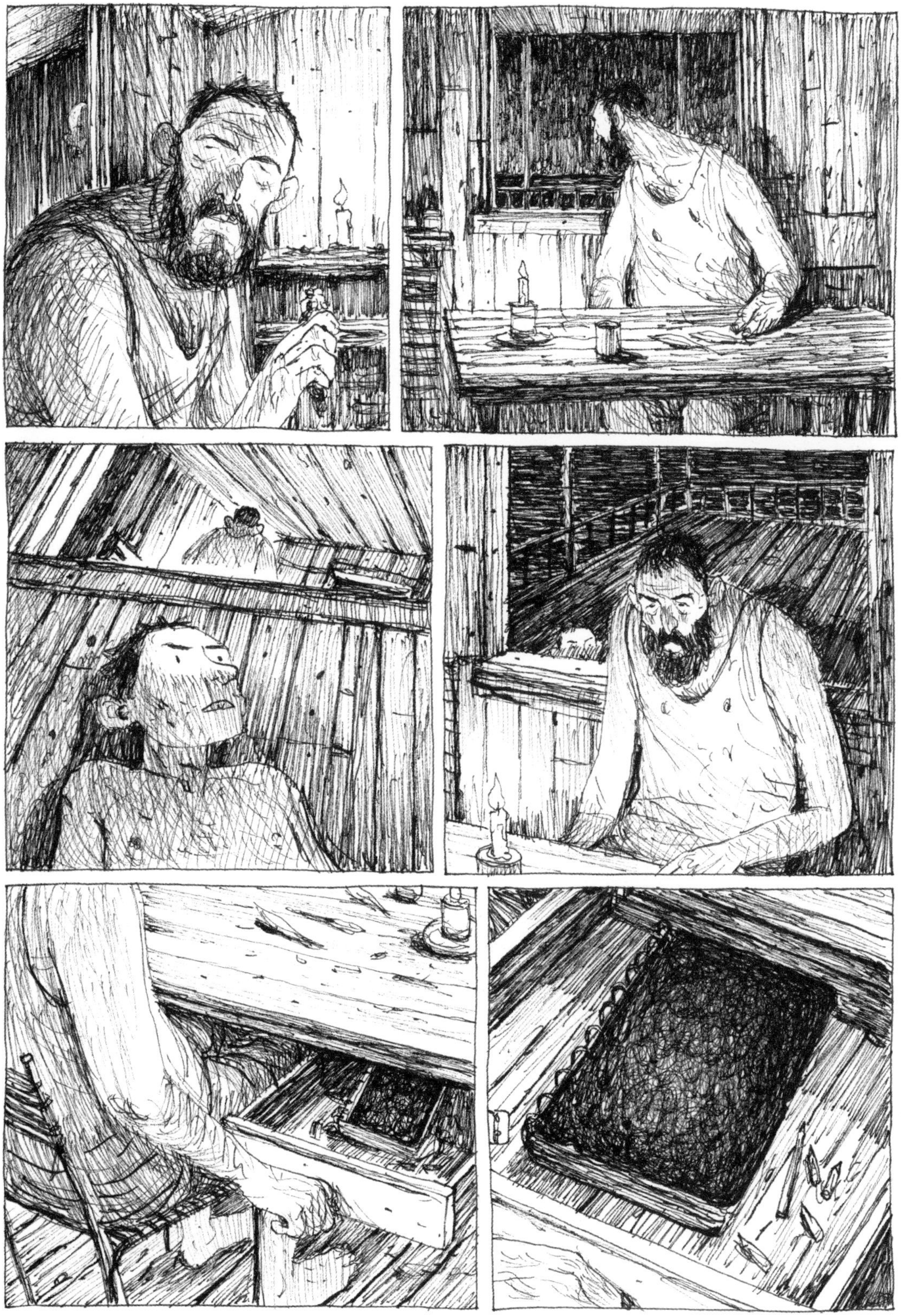

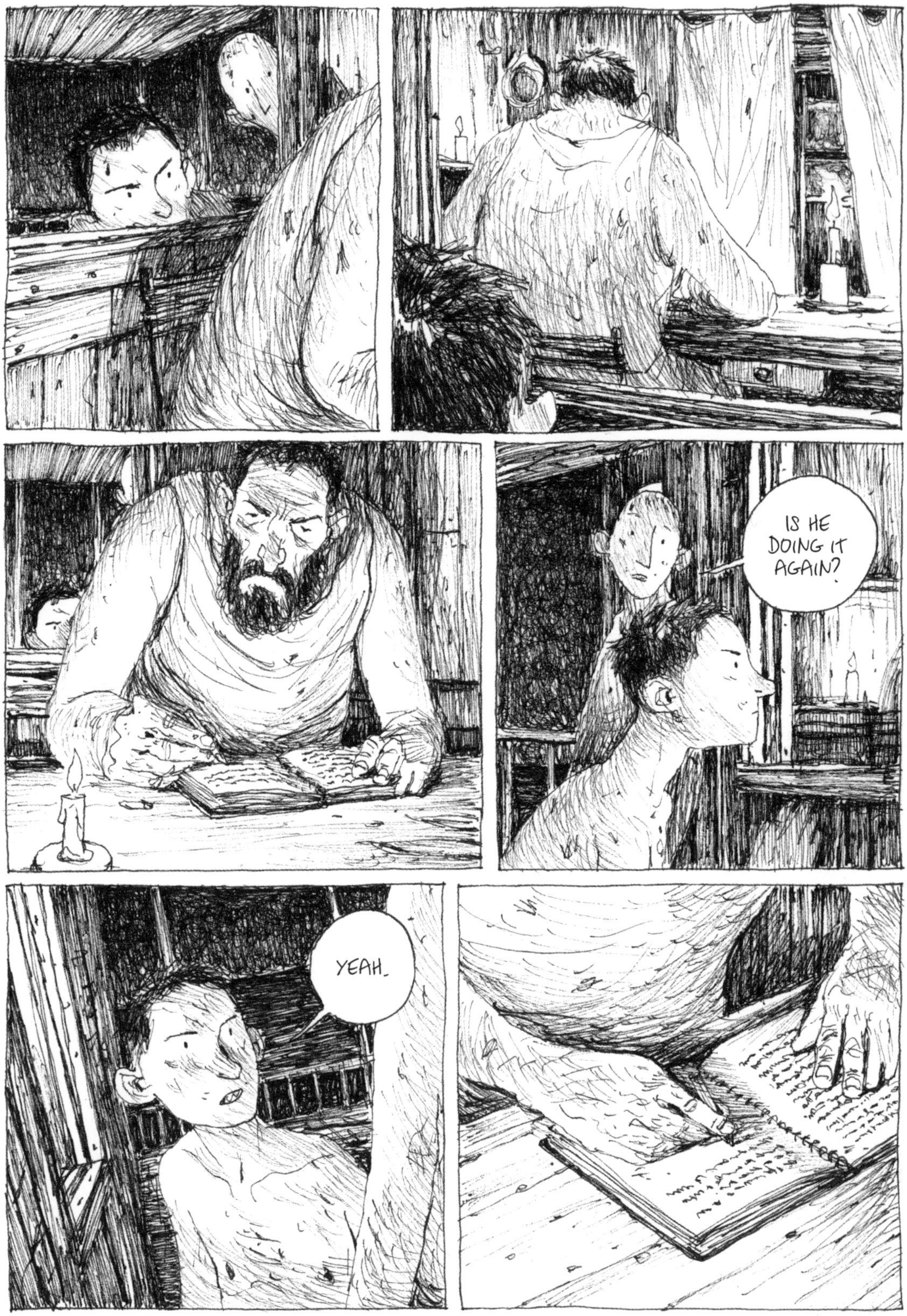
IS HE DOING IT AGAIN?
YEAH_

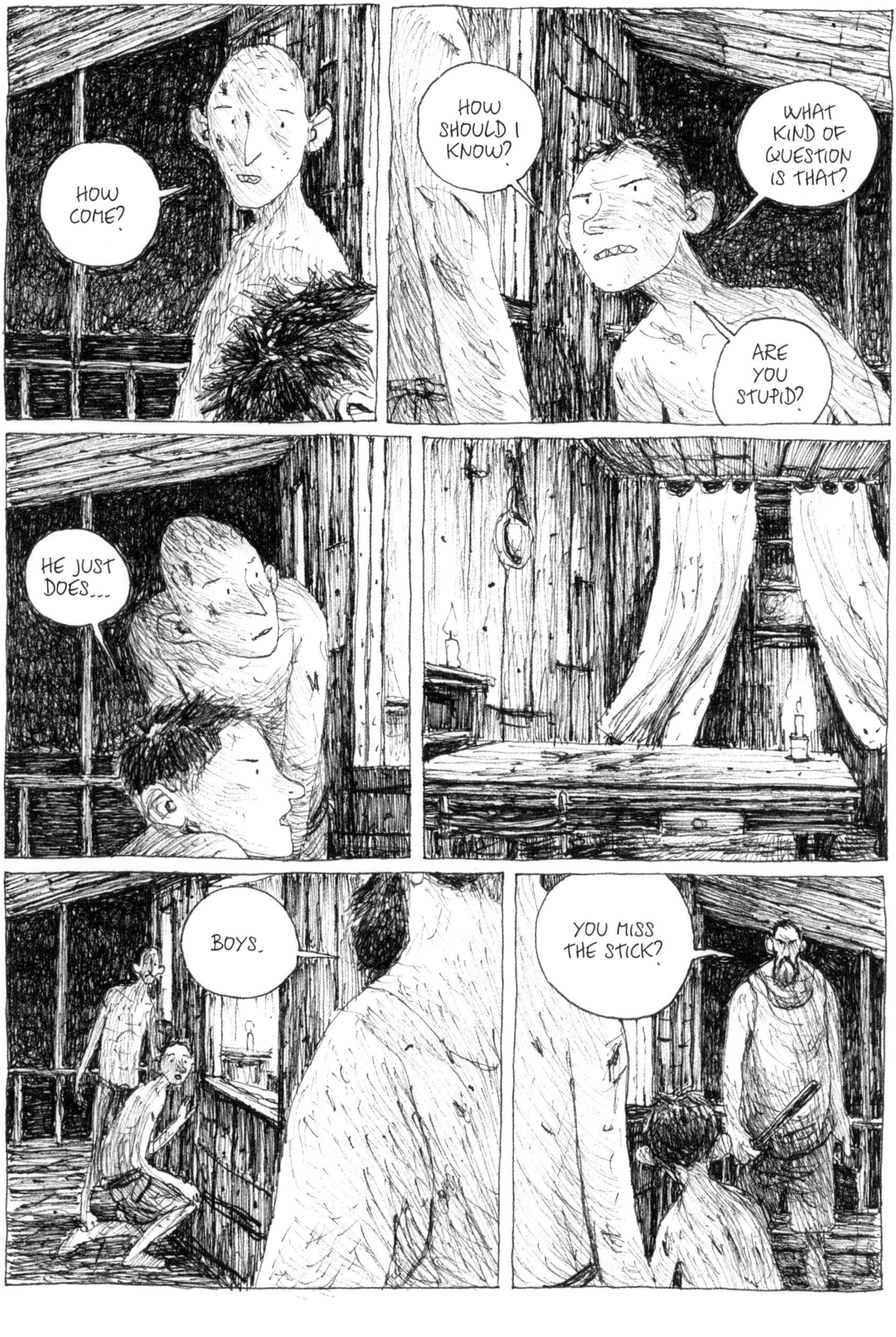
HOW COME?
HOW SHOULD I KNOW?
WHAT KIND OF QUESTION IS THAT?
ARE YOU STUPID?
HE JUST DOES...
BOYS.
YOU MISS THE STICK?

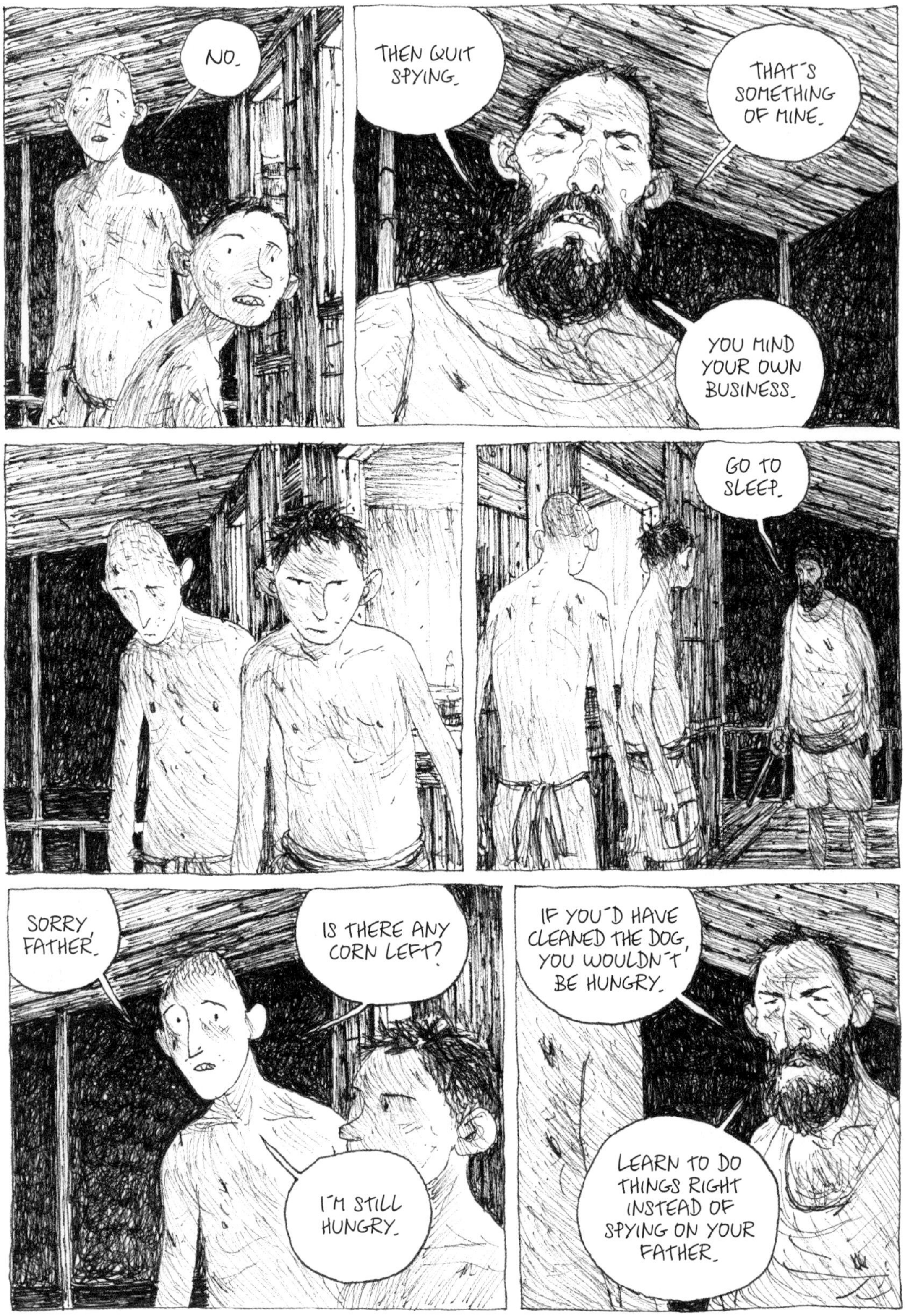
NO.
THEN QUIT SPYING.
THAT'S SOMETHING OF MINE.
YOU MIND YOUR OWN BUSINESS.
GO TO SLEEP.
SORRY FATHER.
IS THERE ANY CORN LEFT?
I'M STILL HUNGRY.
IF YOU'D HAVE CLEANED THE DOG, YOU WOULDN'T BE HUNGRY.
LEARN TO DO THINGS RIGHT INSTEAD OF SPYING ON YOUR FATHER.

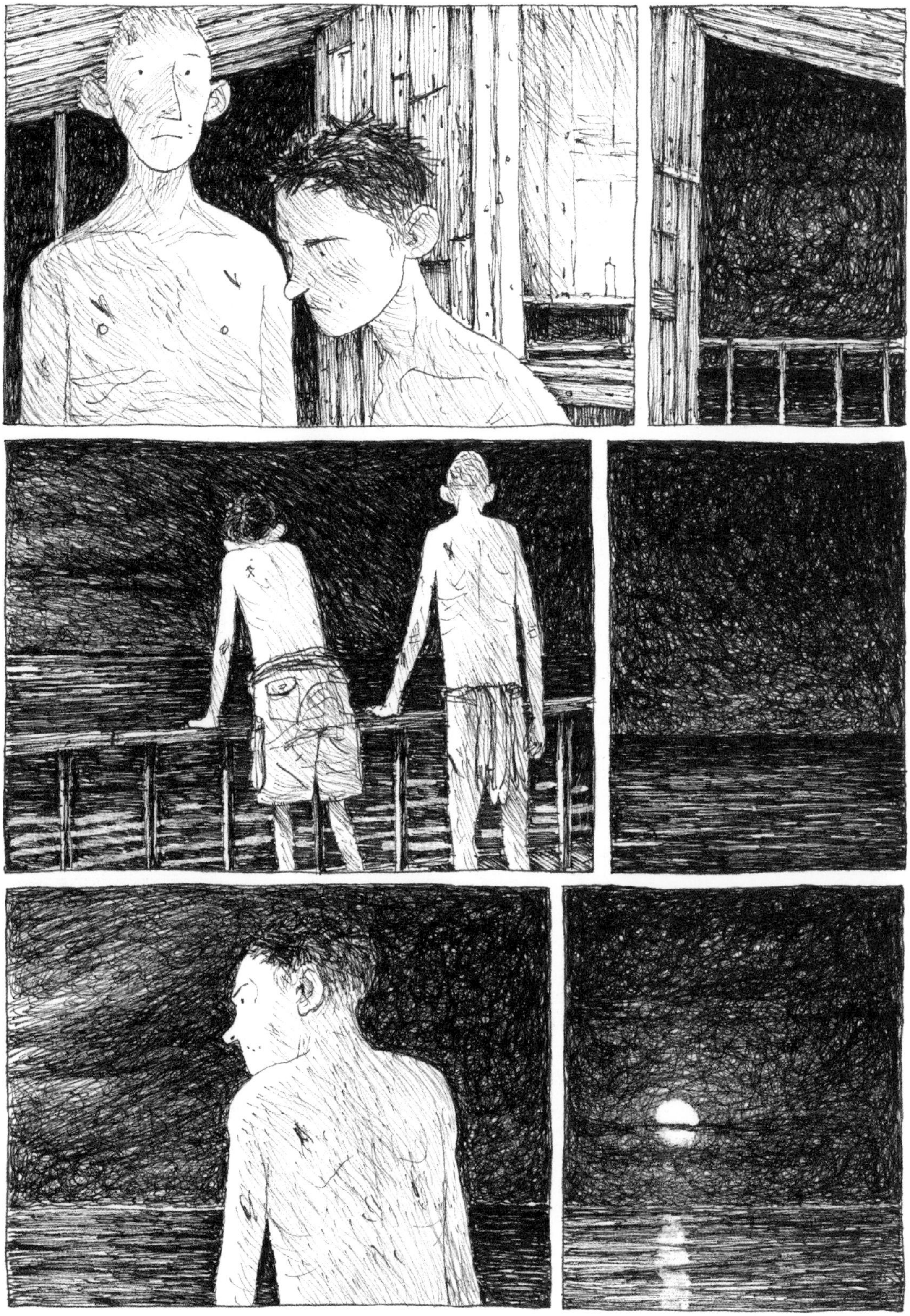

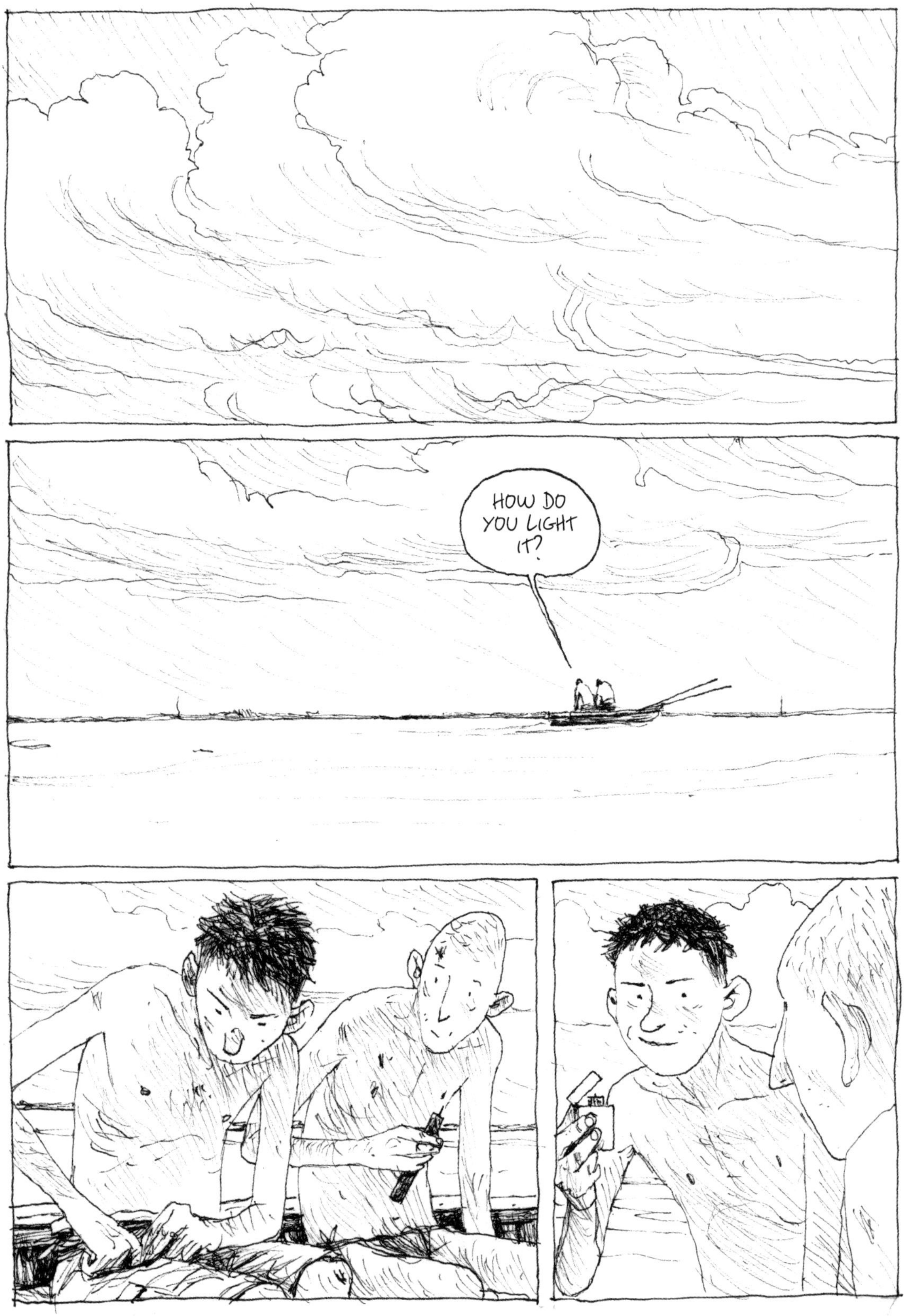
HOW DO YOU LIGHT IT?

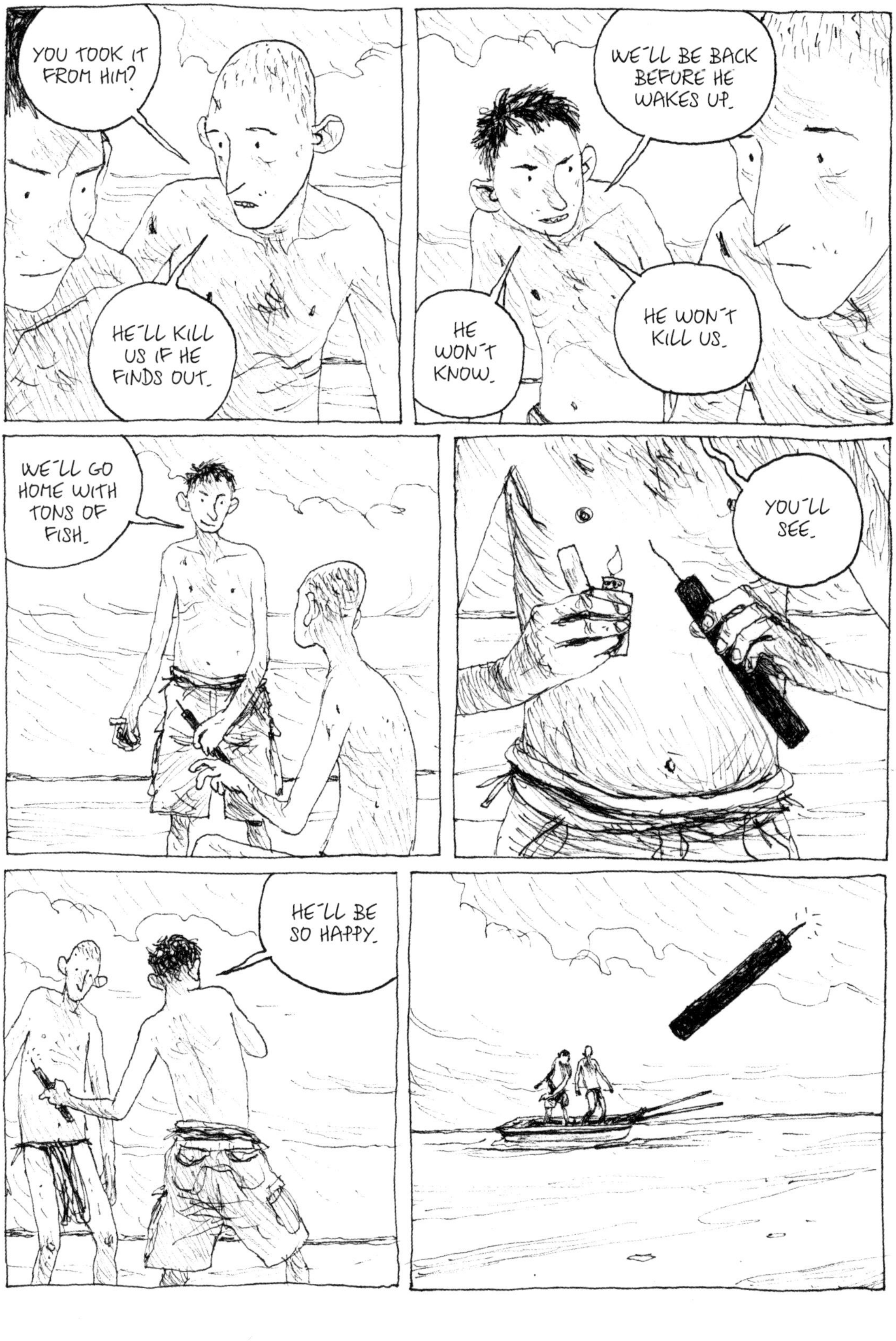
YOU TOOK IT FROM HIM?
HE'LL KILL US IF HE FINDS OUT.
WE'LL BE BACK BEFORE HE WAKES UP.
HE WON'T KNOW.
HE WON'T KILL US.
WE'LL GO HOME WITH TONS OF FISH.
YOU'LL SEE.
HE'LL BE SO HAPPY.

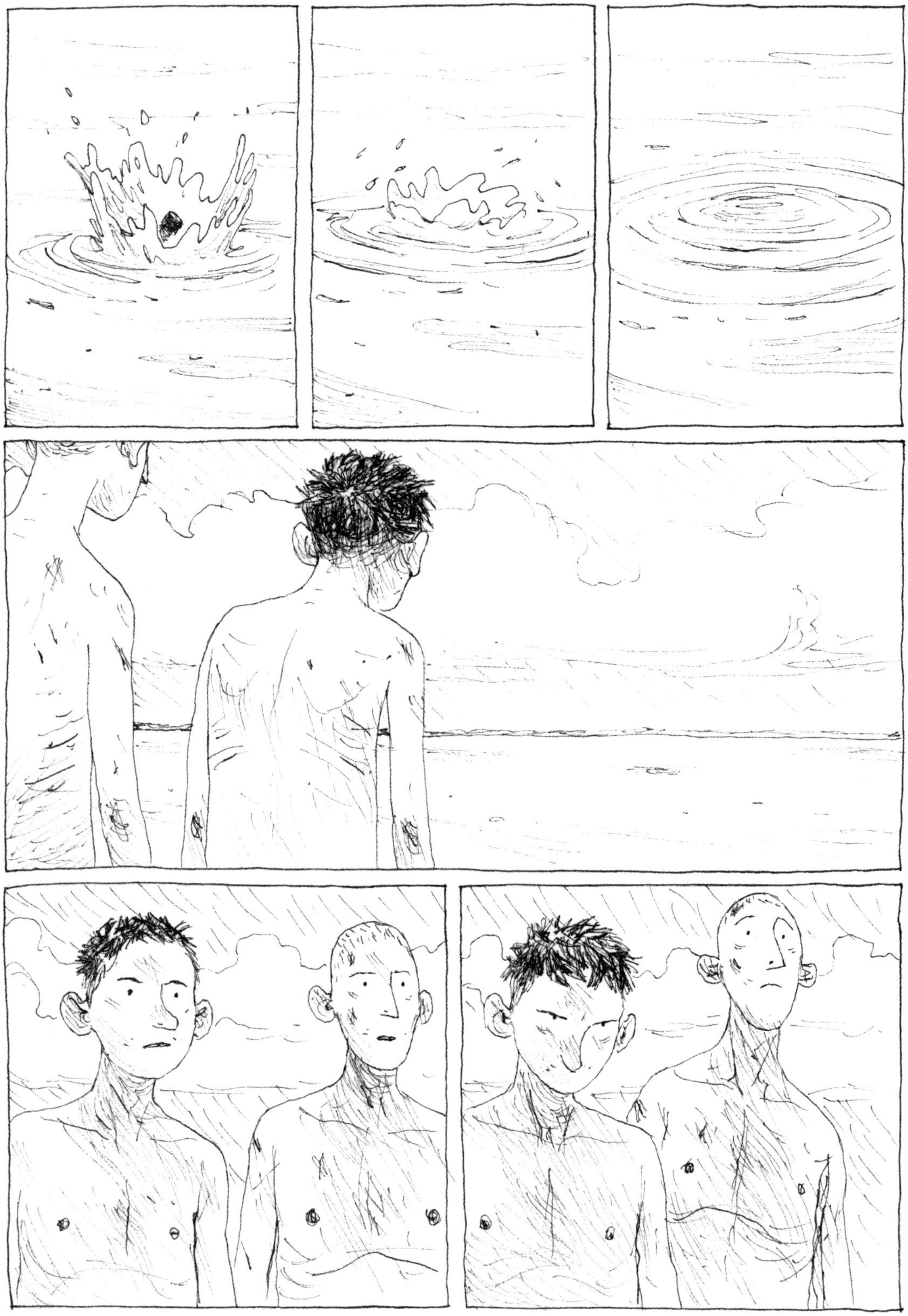

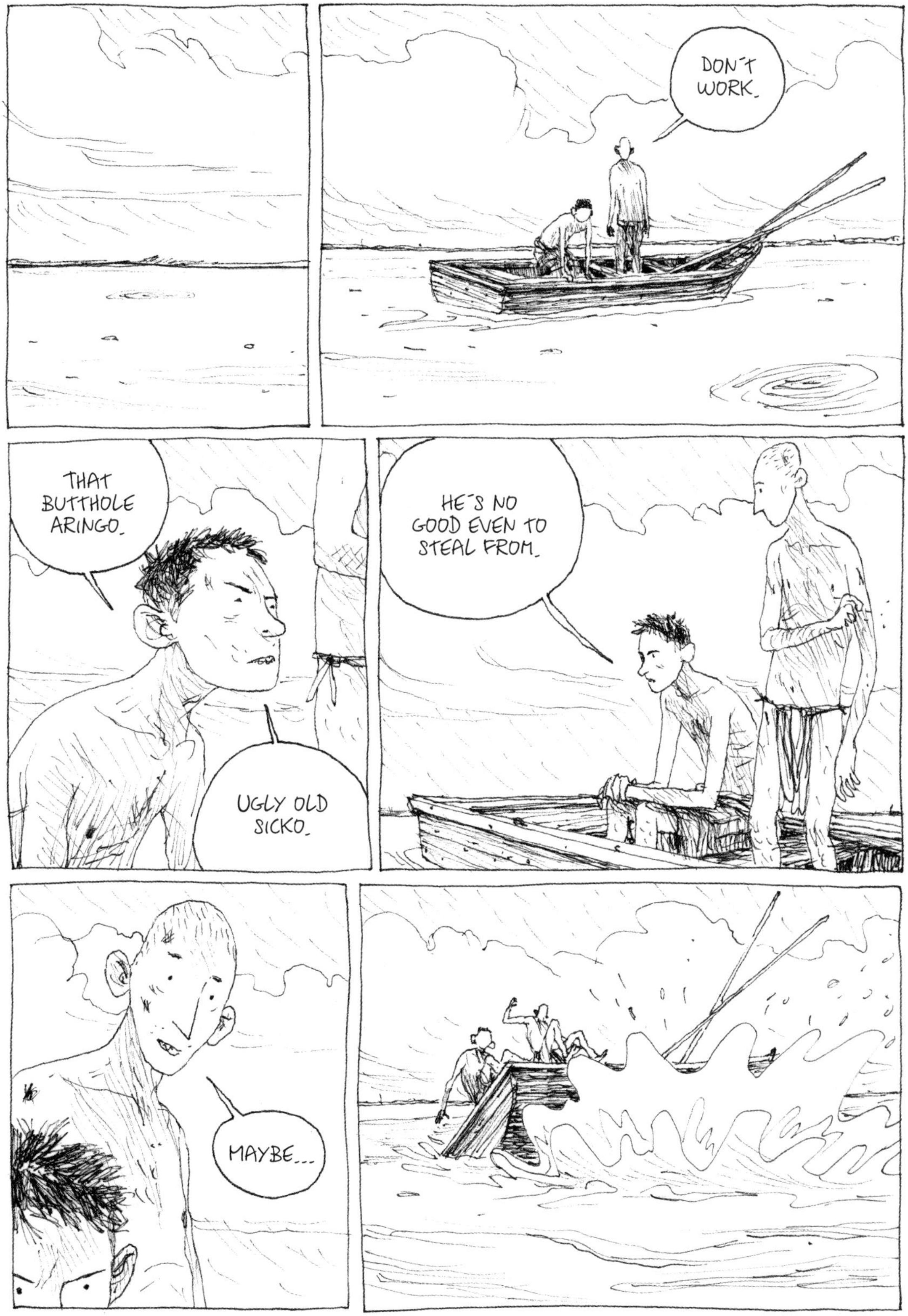
DON'T WORK.
THAT BUTTHOLE ARINGO.
UGLY OLD SICKO.
HE'S NO GOOD EVEN TO STEAL FROM.
MAYBE...

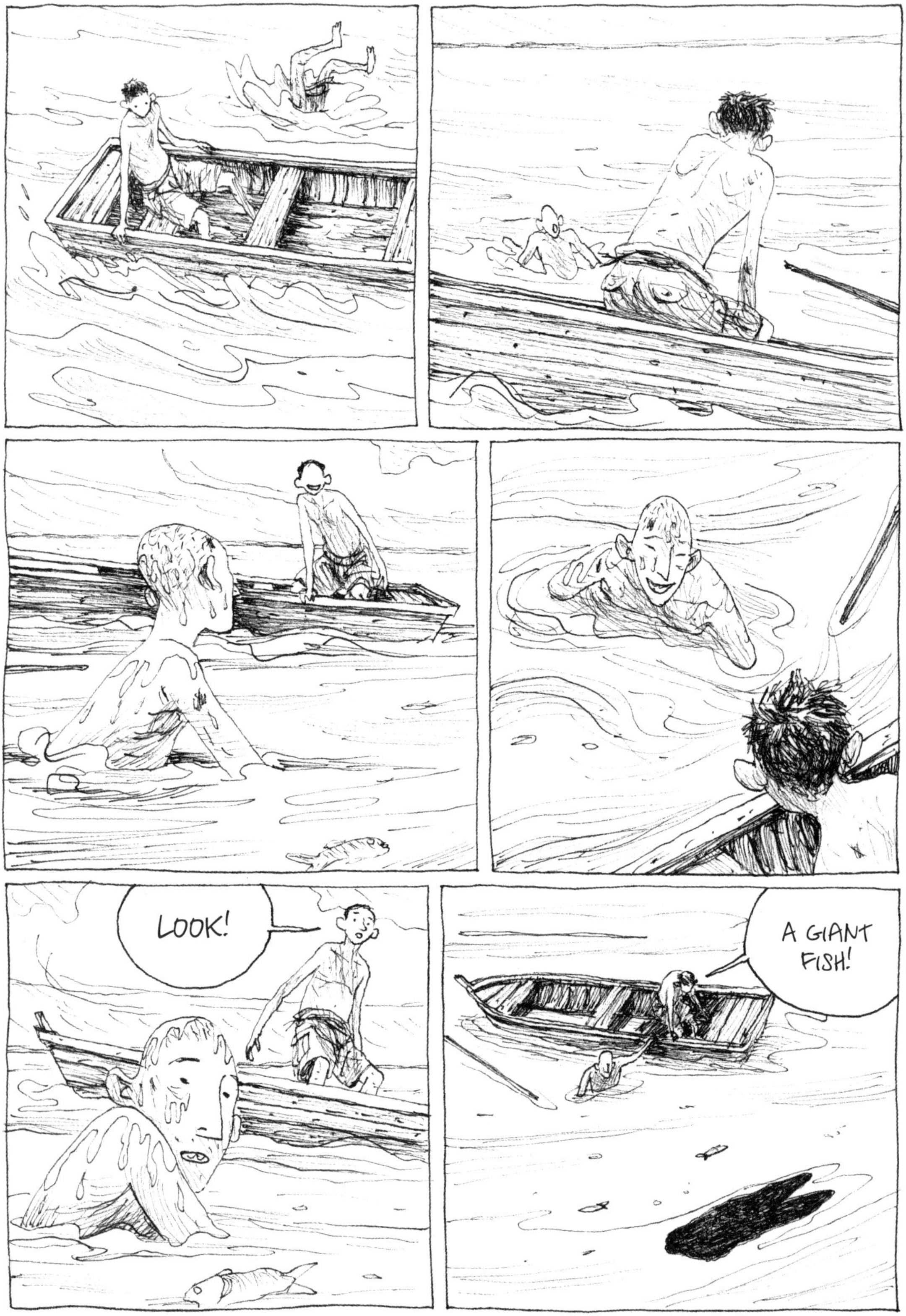
LOOK!
A GIANT FISH!

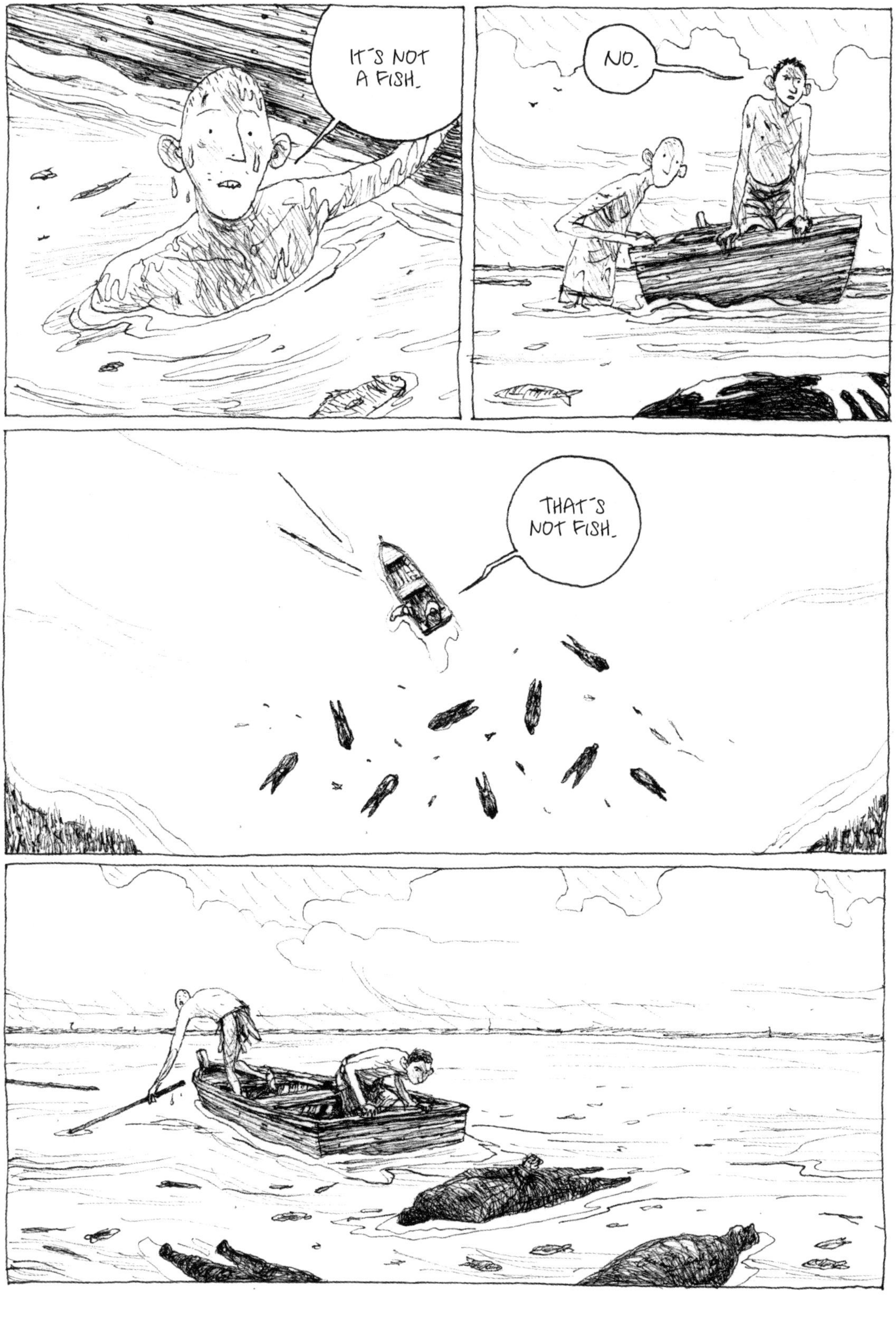
IT´S NOT A FISH.
NO.
THAT´S NOT FISH.

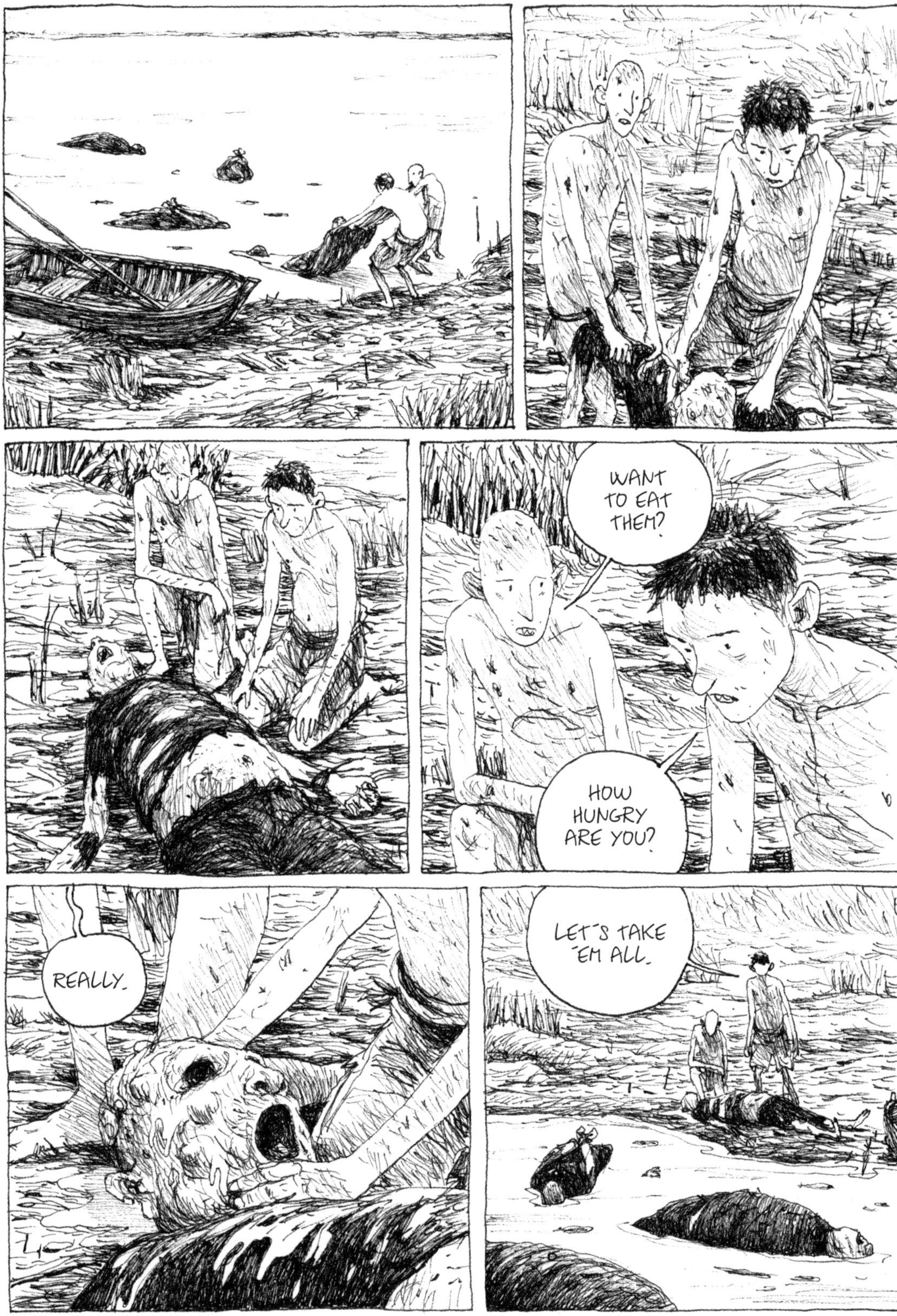
WANT TO EAT THEM?
HOW HUNGRY ARE YOU?
REALLY.
LET'S TAKE 'EM ALL.

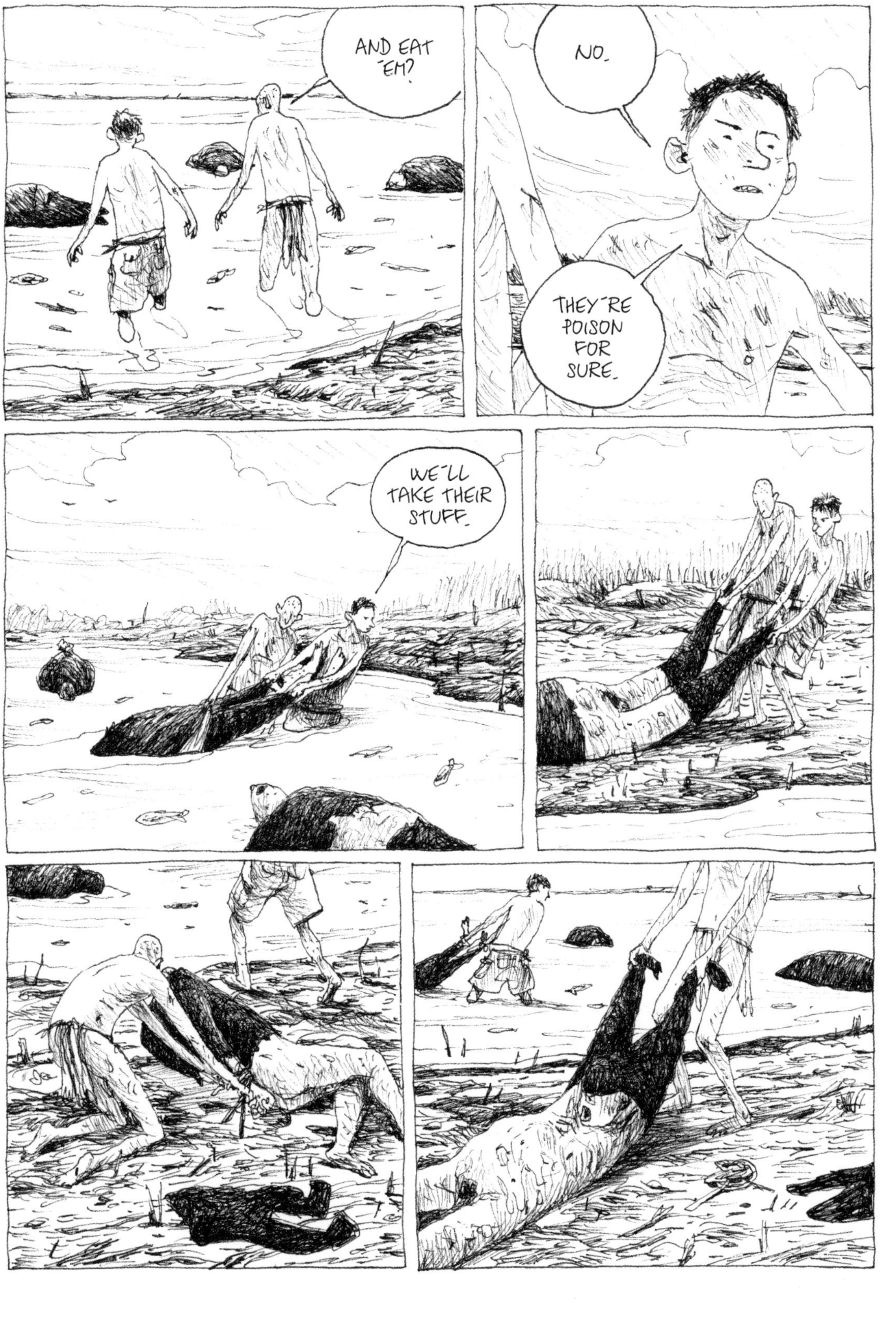
AND EAT 'EM?
NO.
THEY'RE POISON FOR SURE.
WE'LL TAKE THEIR STUFF.

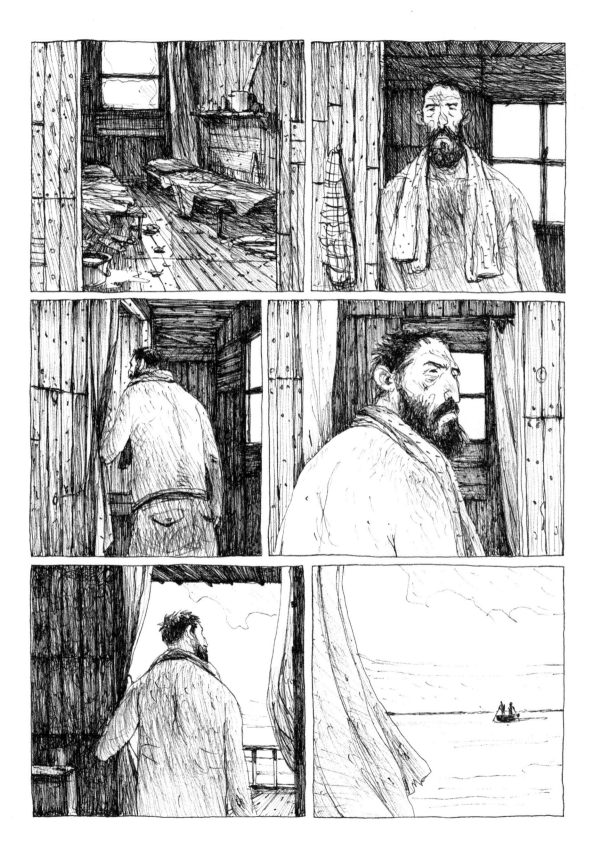

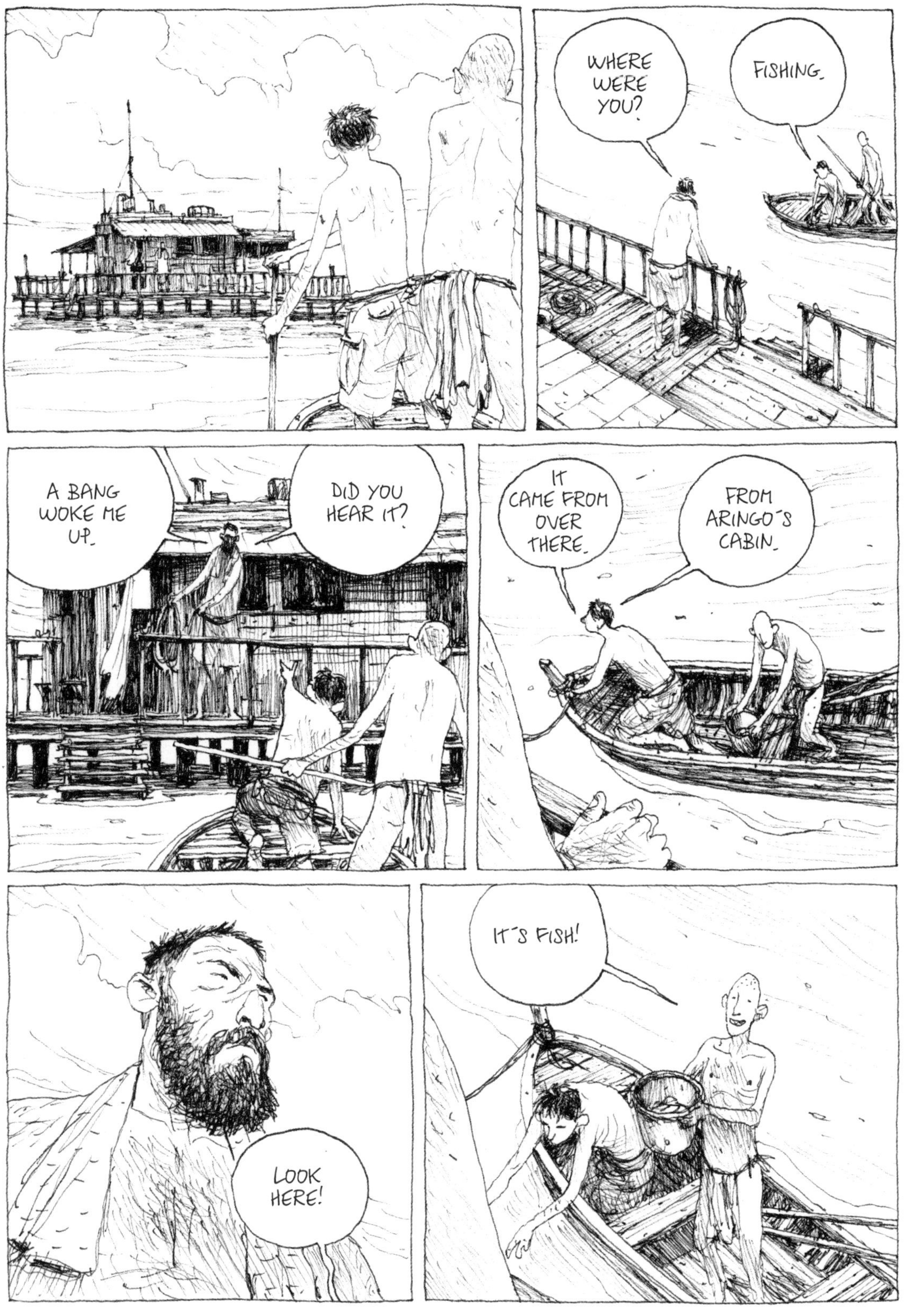
WHERE WERE YOU?
FISHING.
A BANG WOKE ME UP.
DID YOU HEAR IT?
IT CAME FROM OVER THERE.
FROM ARINGO'S CABIN.
LOOK HERE!
IT'S FISH!

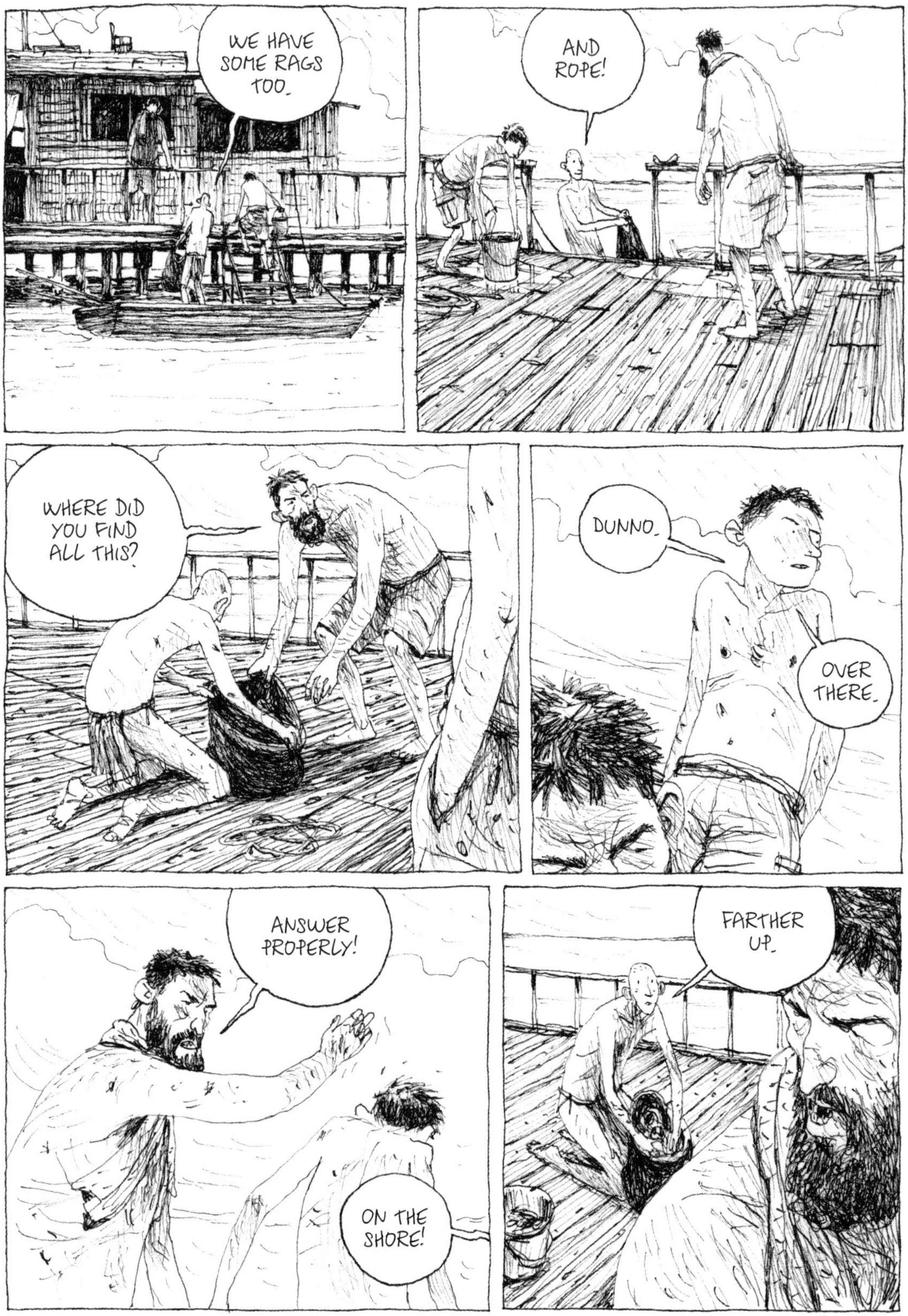
WE HAVE SOME RAGS TOO_
AND ROPE!
WHERE DID YOU FIND ALL THIS?
DUNNO_
OVER THERE_
ANSWER PROPERLY!
ON THE SHORE!
FARTHER UP_

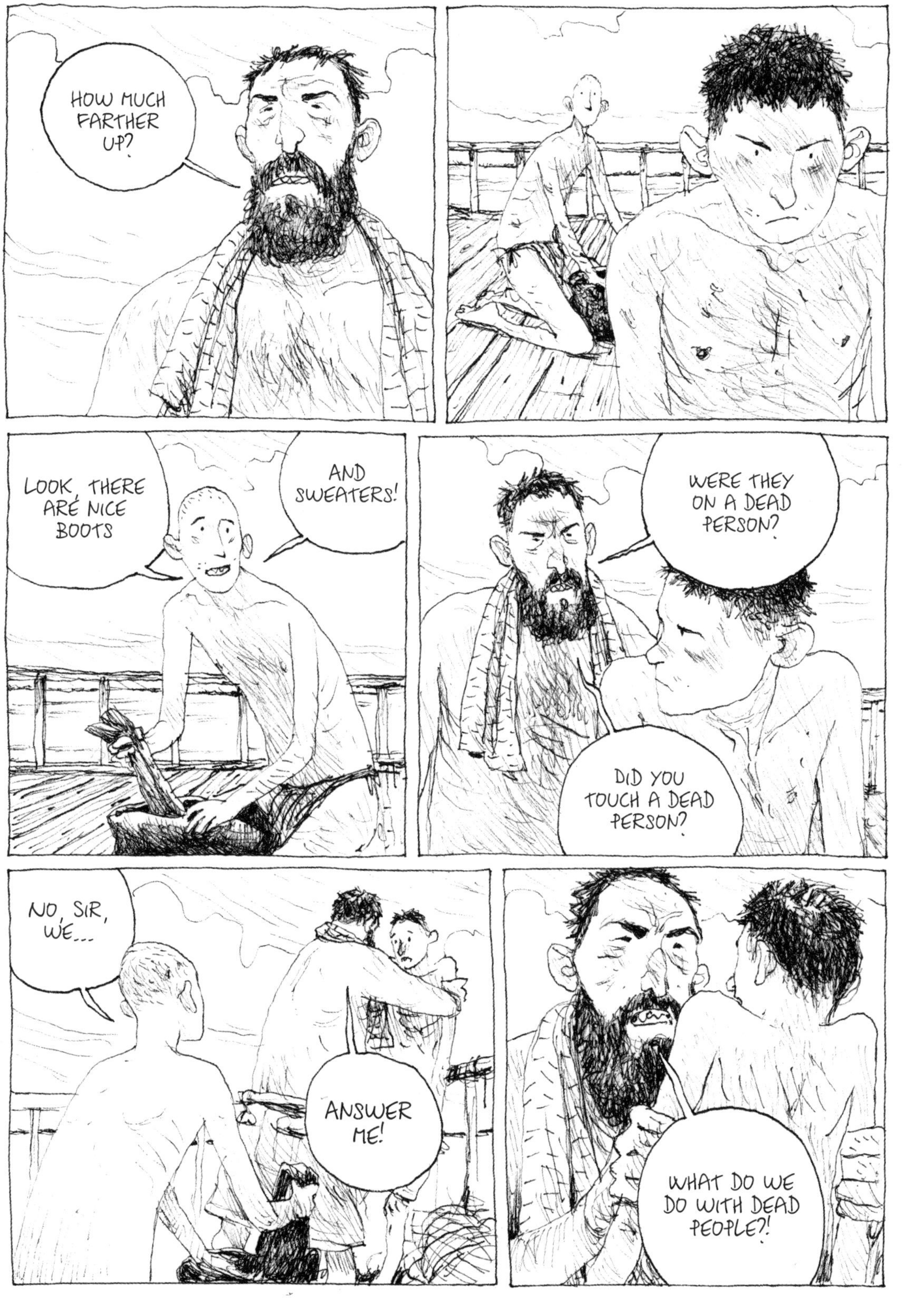
HOW MUCH FARTHER UP?
LOOK, THERE ARE NICE BOOTS
AND SWEATERS!
WERE THEY ON A DEAD PERSON?
DID YOU TOUCH A DEAD PERSON?
NO, SIR, WE...
ANSWER ME!
WHAT DO WE DO WITH DEAD PEOPLE?!

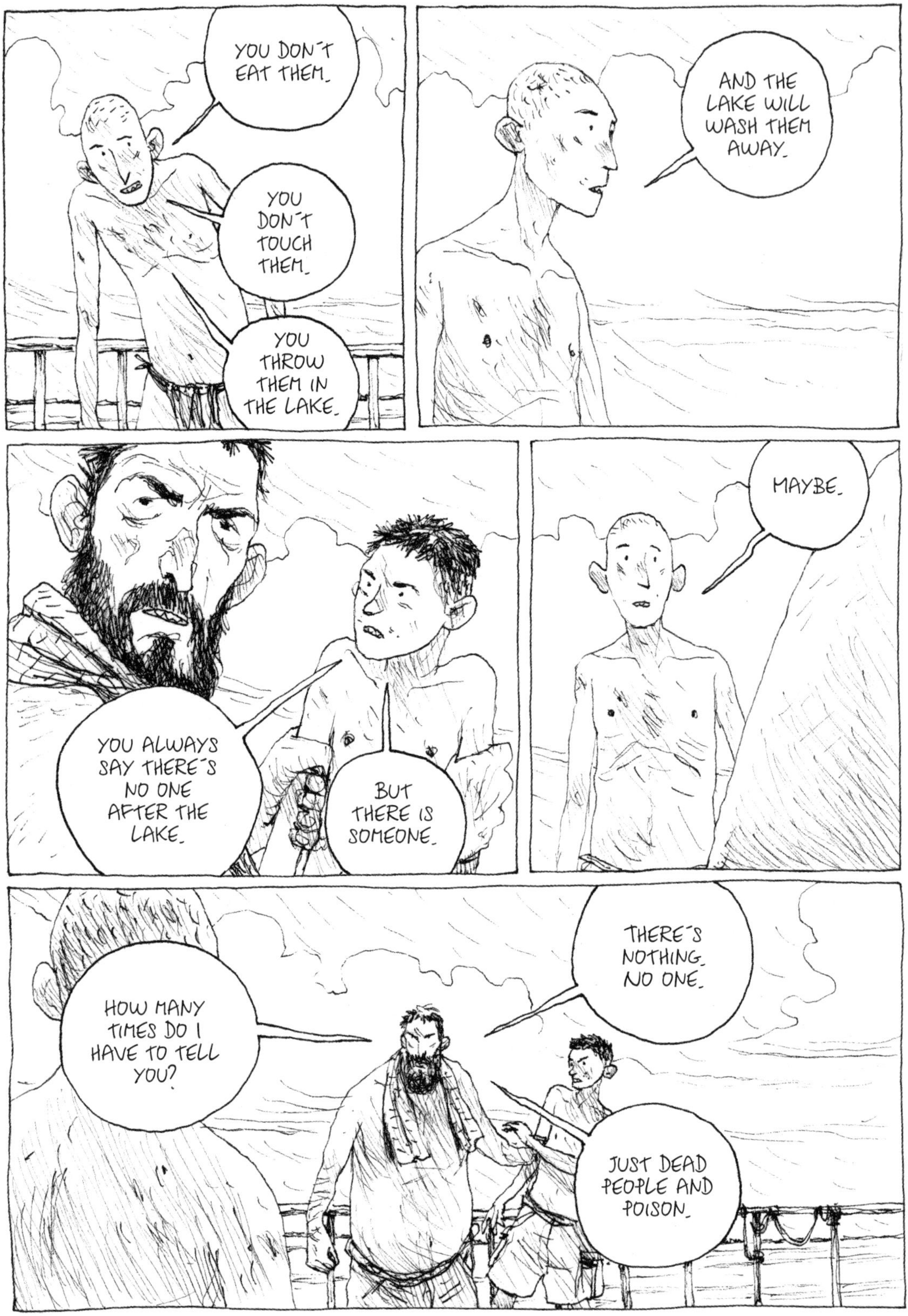

YOU DON'T EAT THEM.
YOU DON'T TOUCH THEM.
YOU THROW THEM IN THE LAKE.
AND THE LAKE WILL WASH THEM AWAY.
YOU ALWAYS SAY THERE'S NO ONE AFTER THE LAKE.
BUT THERE IS SOMEONE.
MAYBE.
HOW MANY TIMES DO I HAVE TO TELL YOU?
THERE'S NOTHING. NO ONE.
JUST DEAD PEOPLE AND POISON.

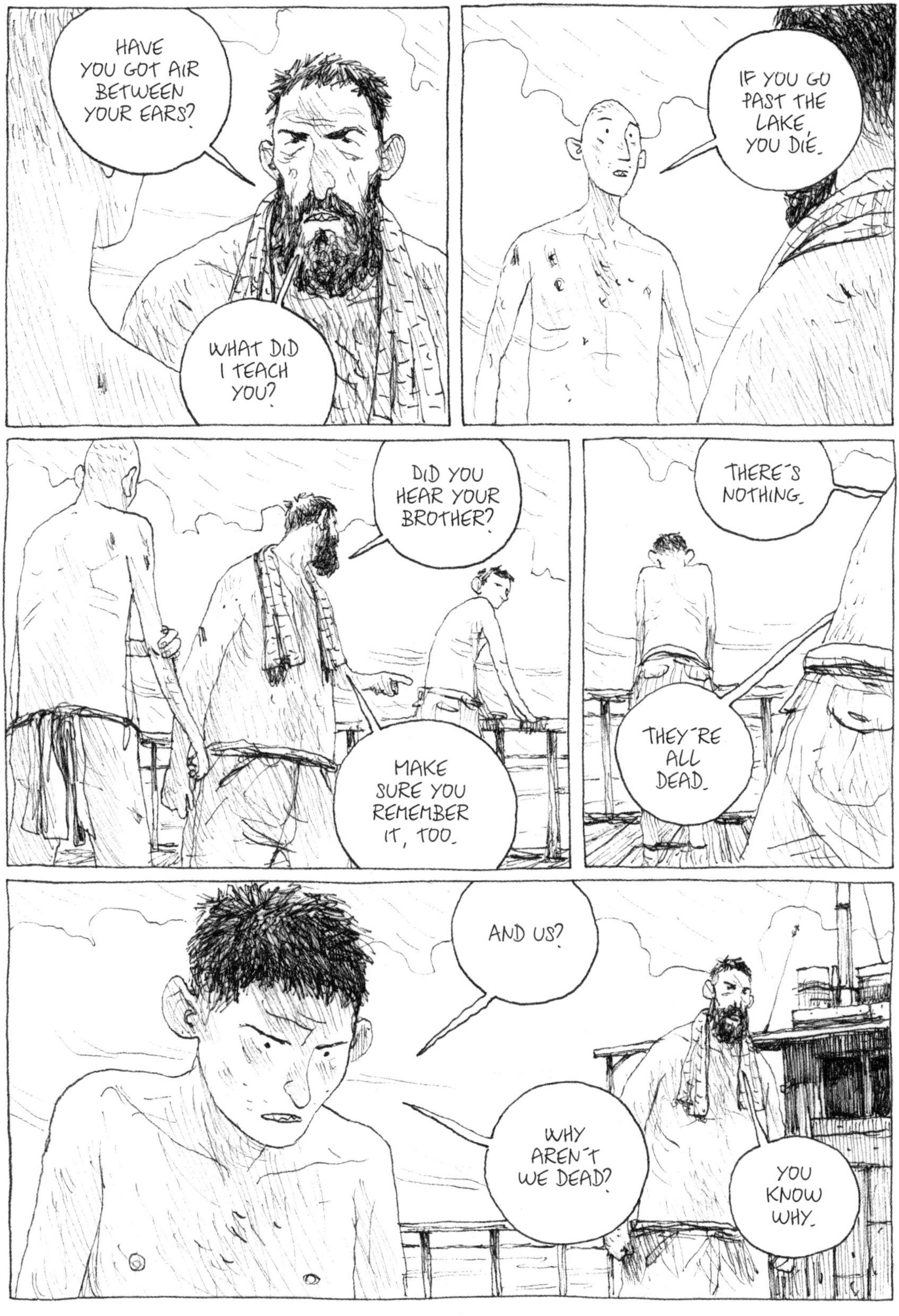
HAVE YOU GOT AIR BETWEEN YOUR EARS?
WHAT DID I TEACH YOU?
IF YOU GO PAST THE LAKE, YOU DIE.
DID YOU HEAR YOUR BROTHER?
MAKE SURE YOU REMEMBER IT, TOO.
THERE'S NOTHING.
THEY'RE ALL DEAD.
AND US?
WHY AREN'T WE DEAD?
YOU KNOW WHY.

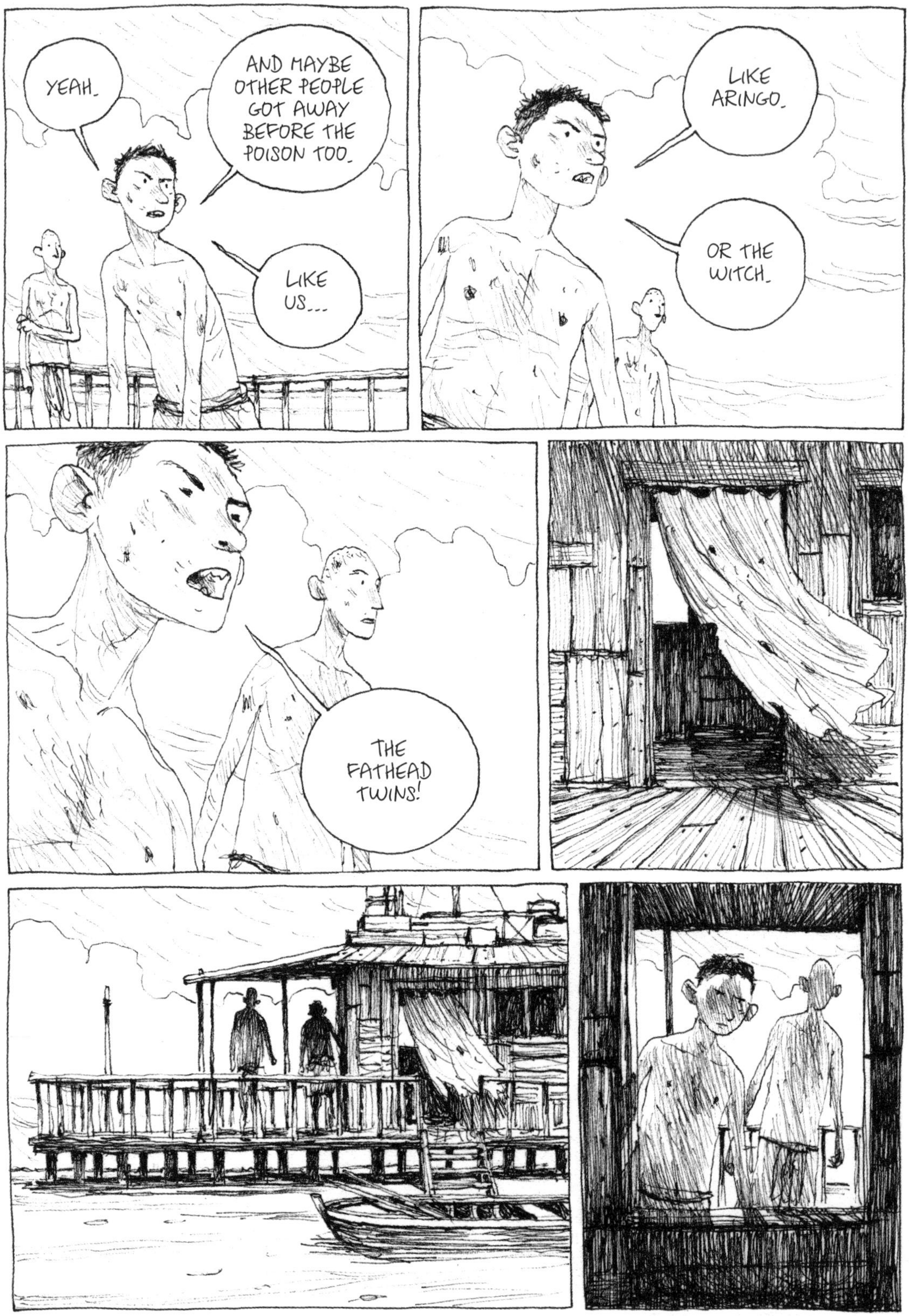
YEAH.
AND MAYBE OTHER PEOPLE GOT AWAY BEFORE THE POISON TOO.
LIKE US...
LIKE ARINGO.
OR THE WITCH.
THE FATHEAD TWINS!

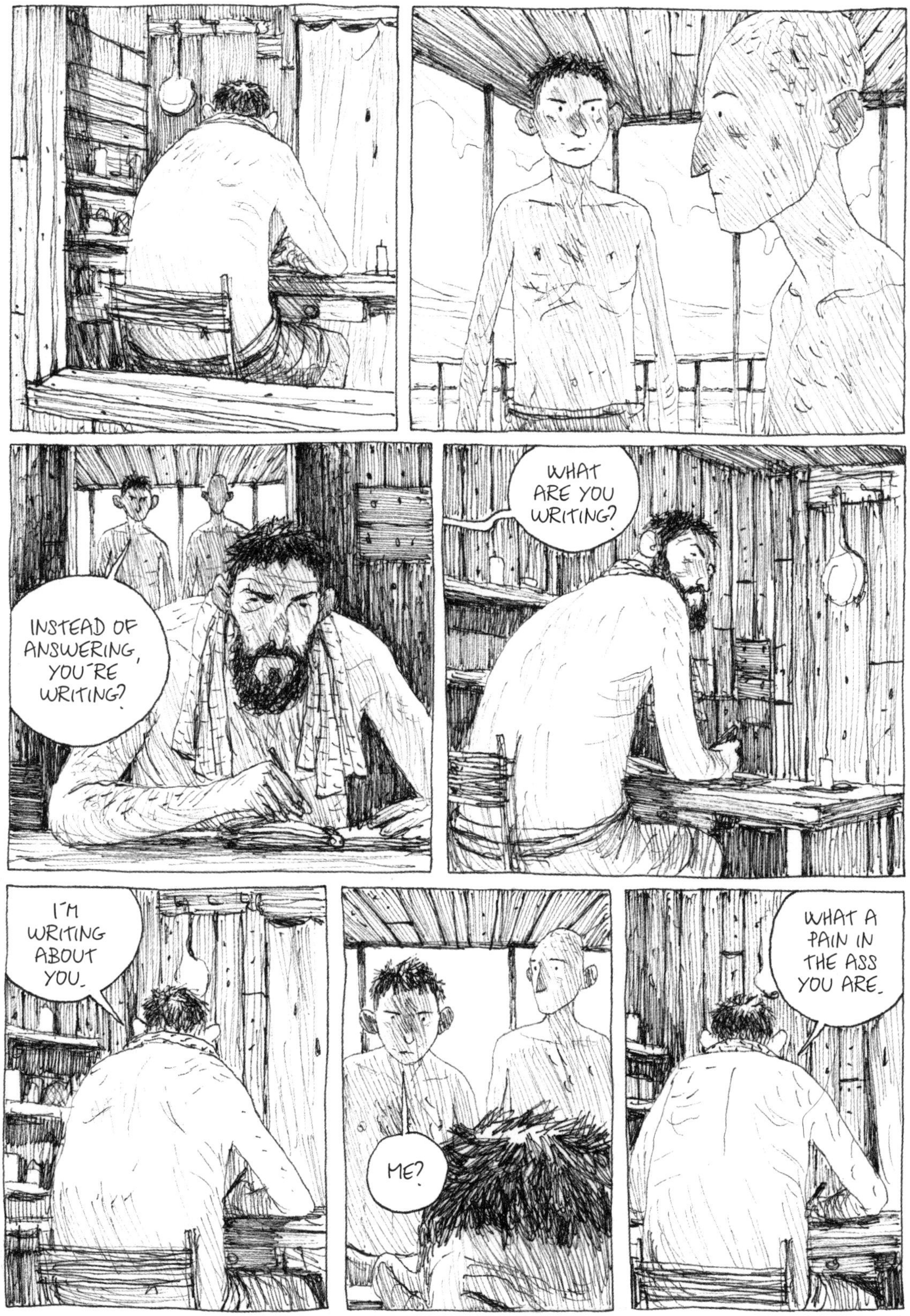
WHAT ARE YOU WRITING?
INSTEAD OF ANSWERING, YOU'RE WRITING?
I'M WRITING ABOUT YOU.
ME?
WHAT A PAIN IN THE ASS YOU ARE.

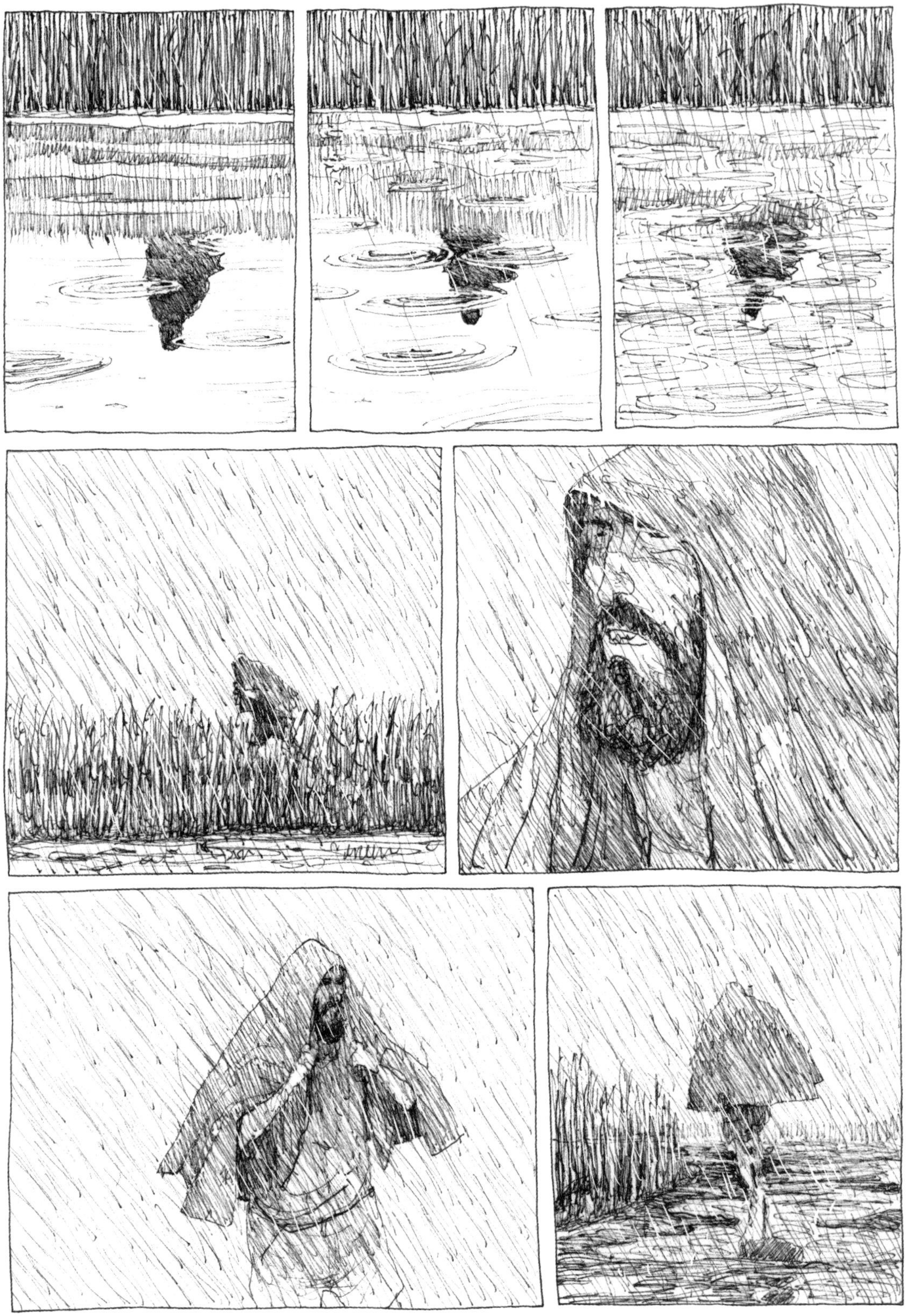

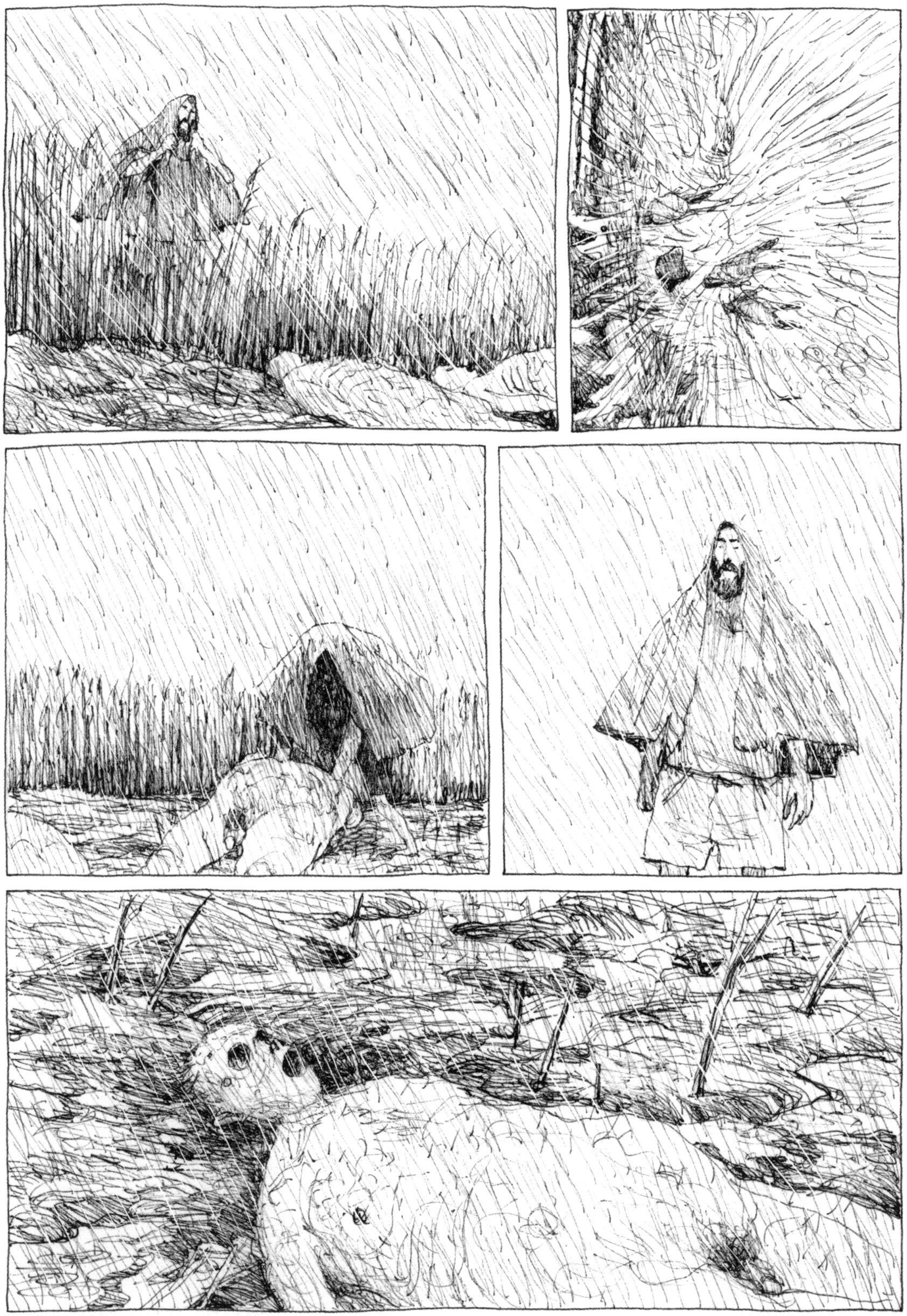

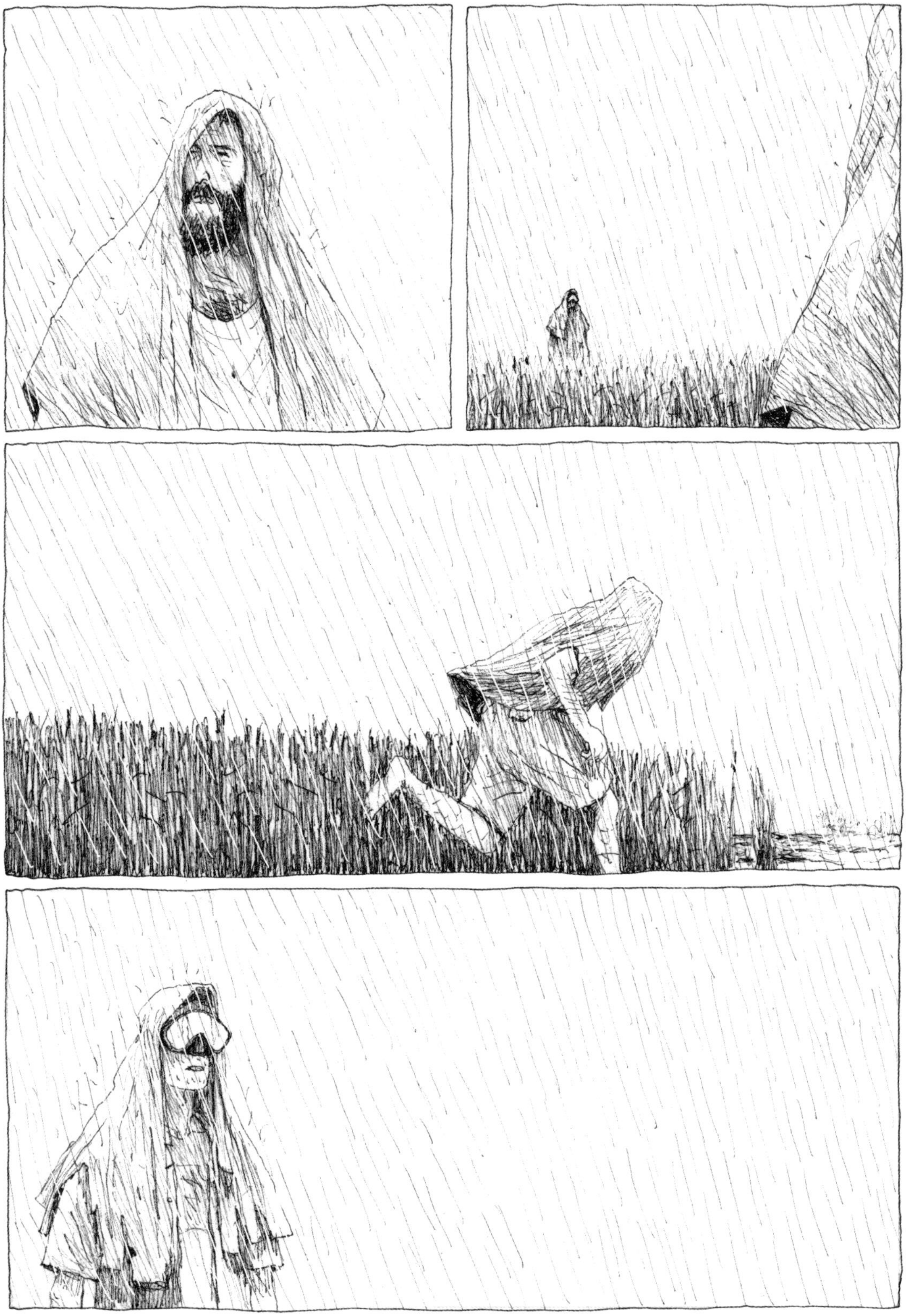

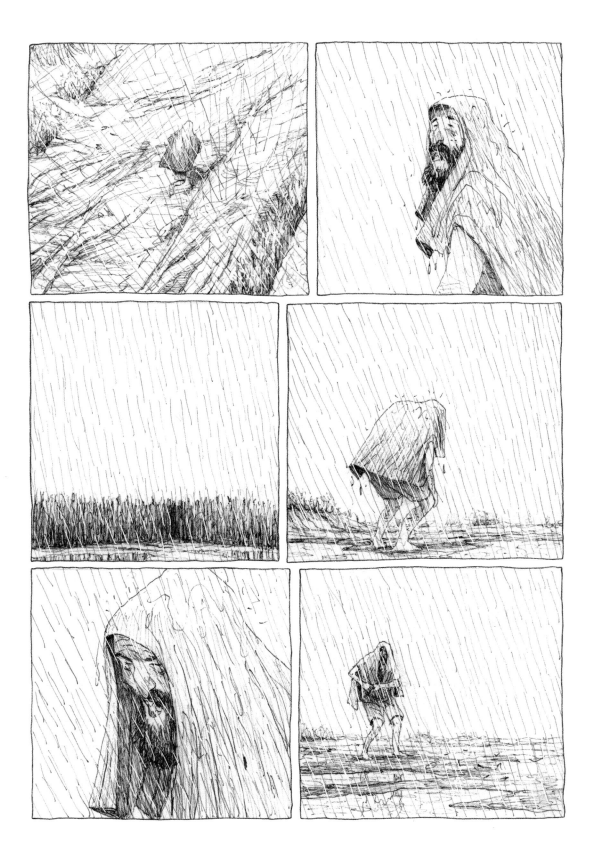

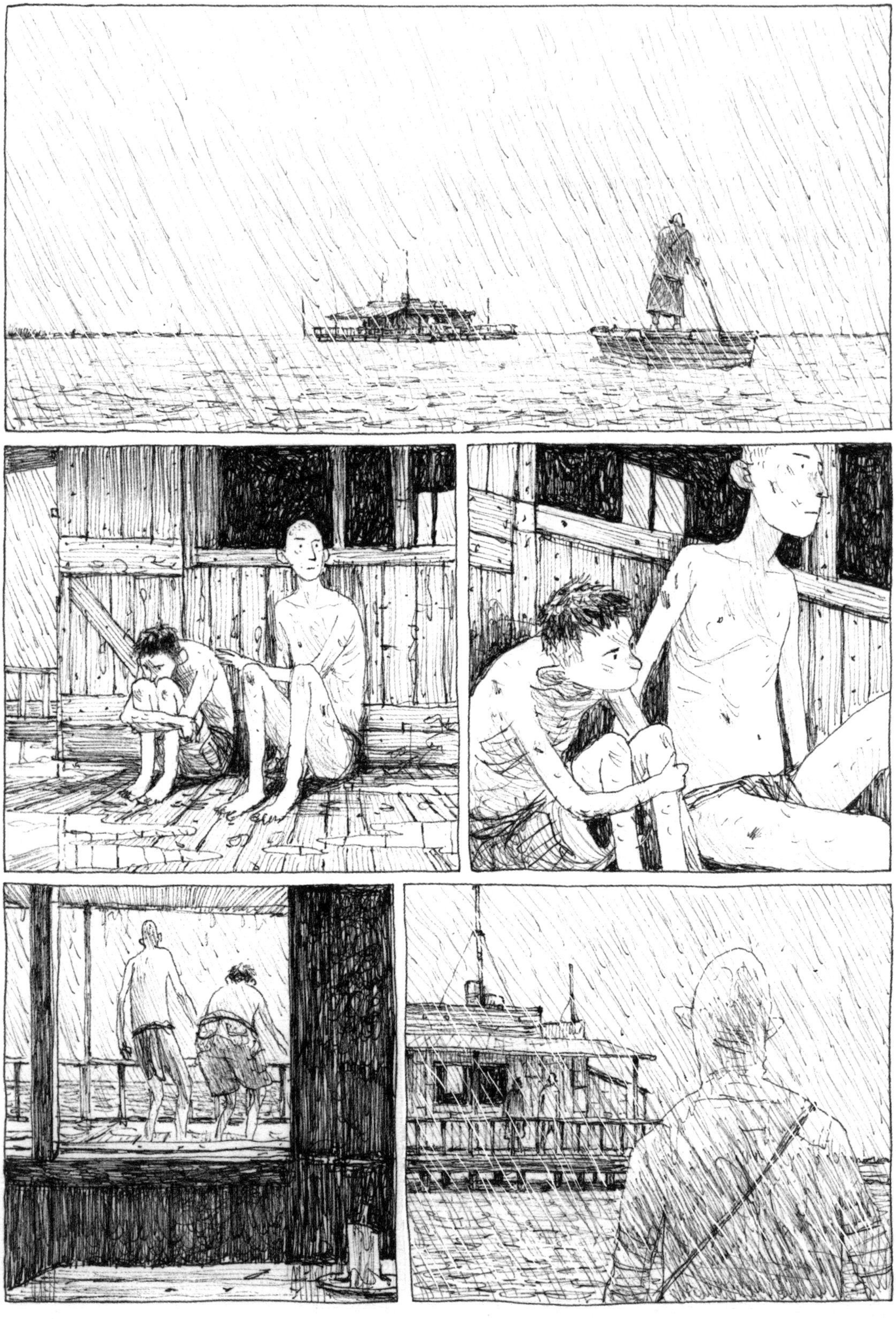

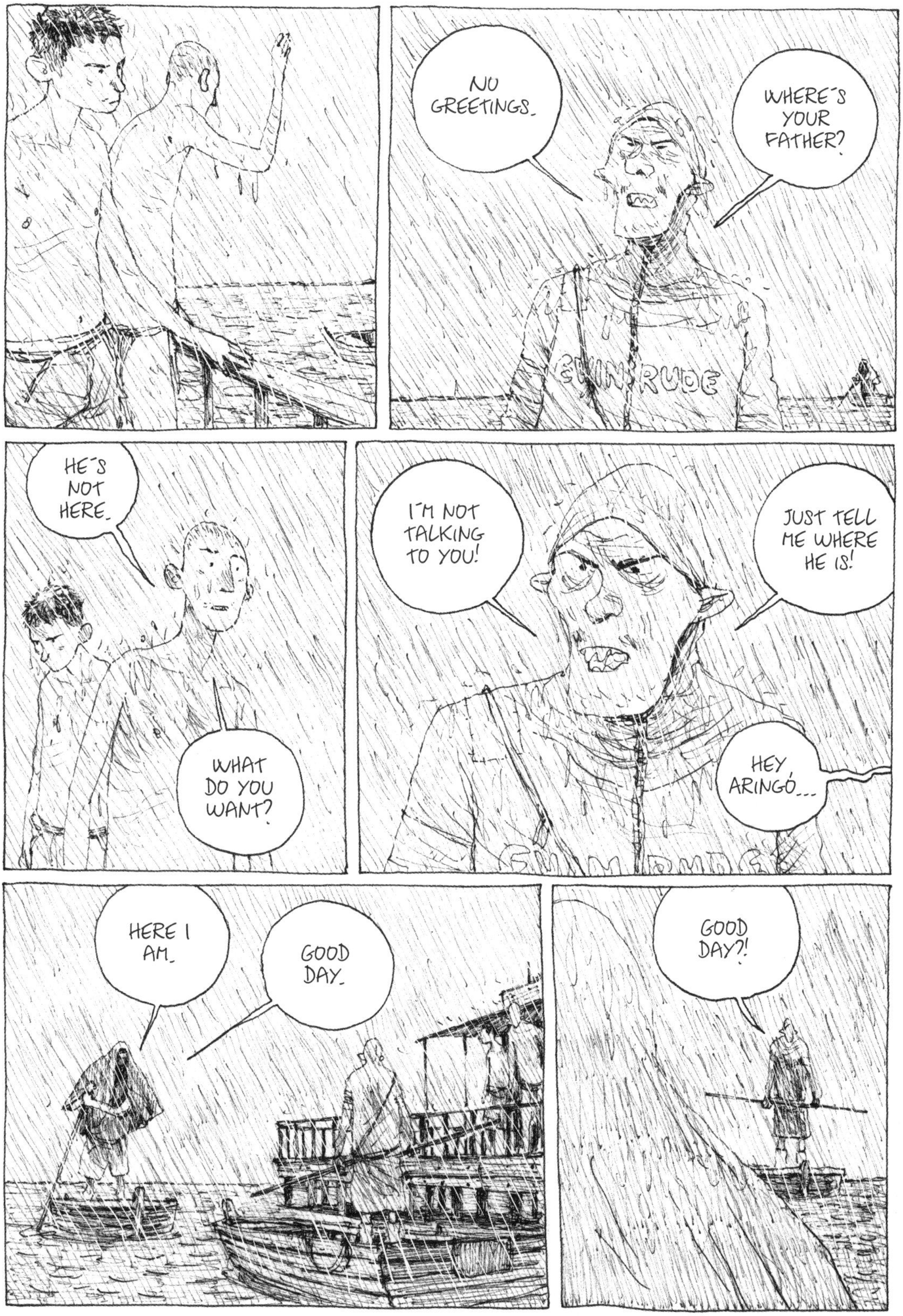
NO GREETINGS.
WHERE'S YOUR FATHER?
HE'S NOT HERE.
WHAT DO YOU WANT?
I'M NOT TALKING TO YOU!
JUST TELL ME WHERE HE IS!
HEY ARINGÓ...
HERE I AM.
GOOD DAY.
GOOD DAY?!

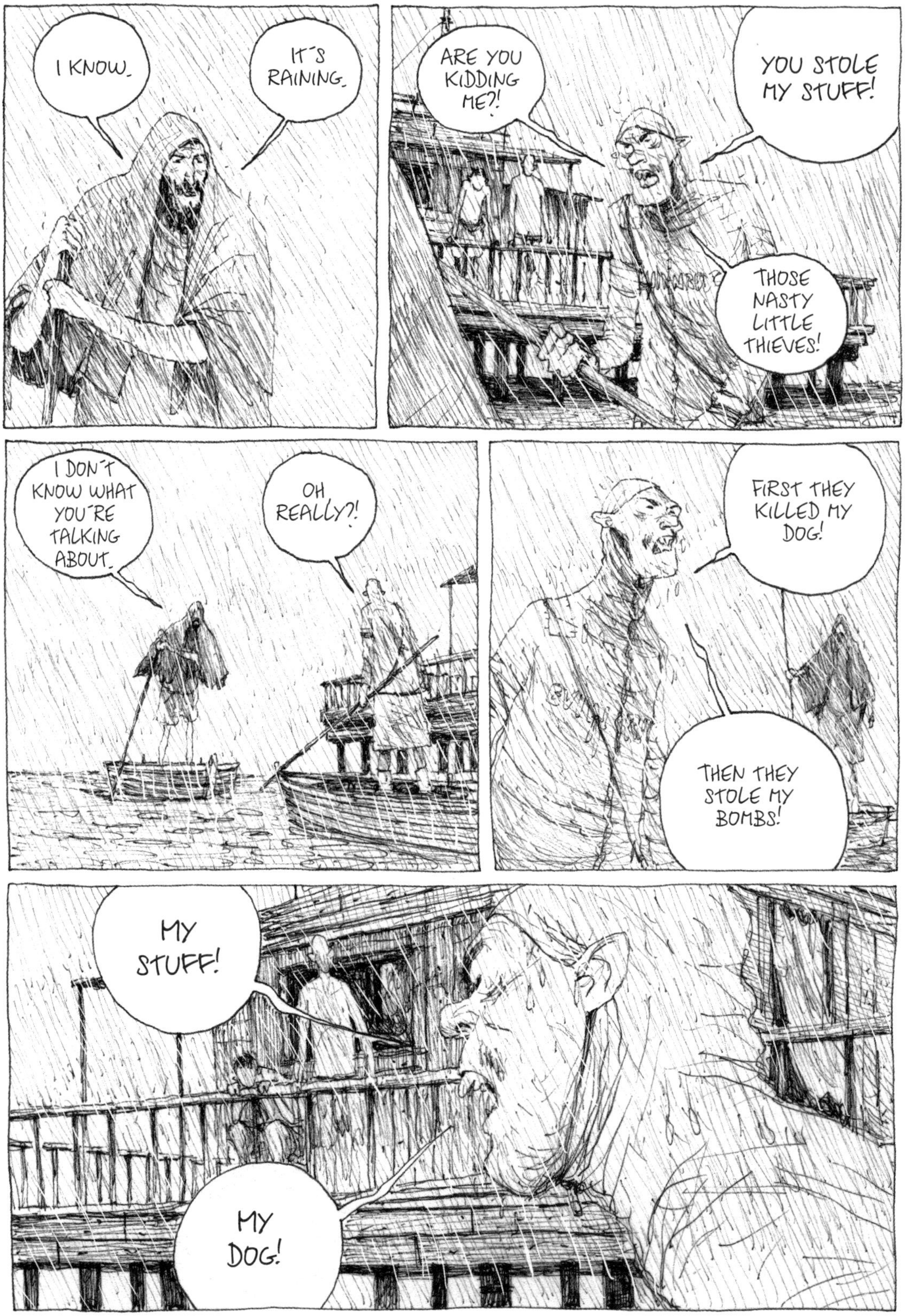

I KNOW.
IT'S RAINING.
ARE YOU KIDDING ME?!
YOU STOLE MY STUFF!
THOSE NASTY LITTLE THIEVES!
I DON'T KNOW WHAT YOU'RE TALKING ABOUT.
OH REALLY?!
FIRST THEY KILLED MY DOG!
THEN THEY STOLE MY BOMBS!
MY STUFF!
MY DOG!

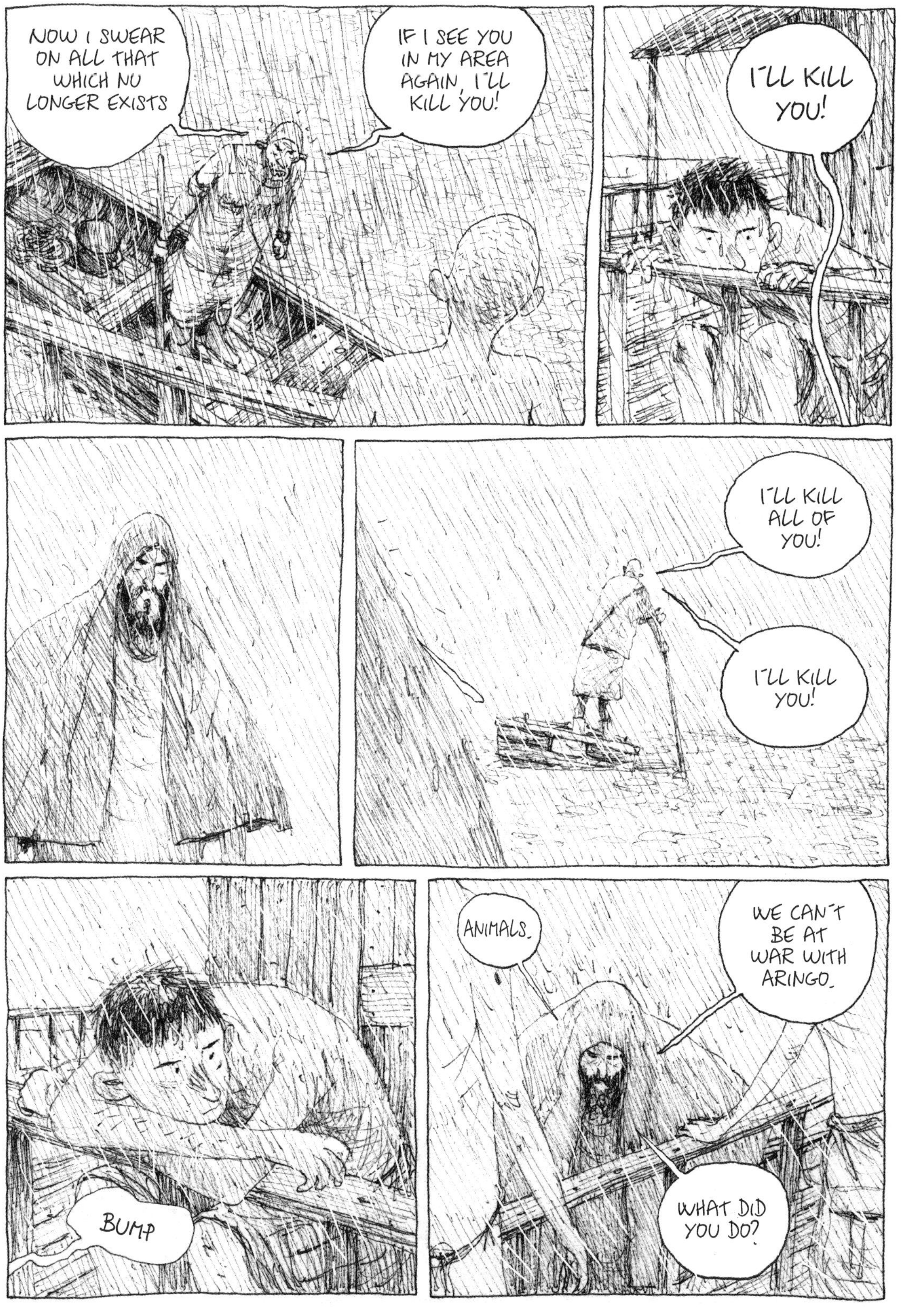
NOW I SWEAR ON ALL THAT WHICH NU LONGER EXISTS
IF I SEE YOU IN MY AREA AGAIN, I'LL KILL YOU!
I'LL KILL YOU!
I'LL KILL ALL OF YOU!
I'LL KILL YOU!
BUMP
ANIMALS...
WE CAN'T BE AT WAR WITH ARINGO...
WHAT DID YOU DO?

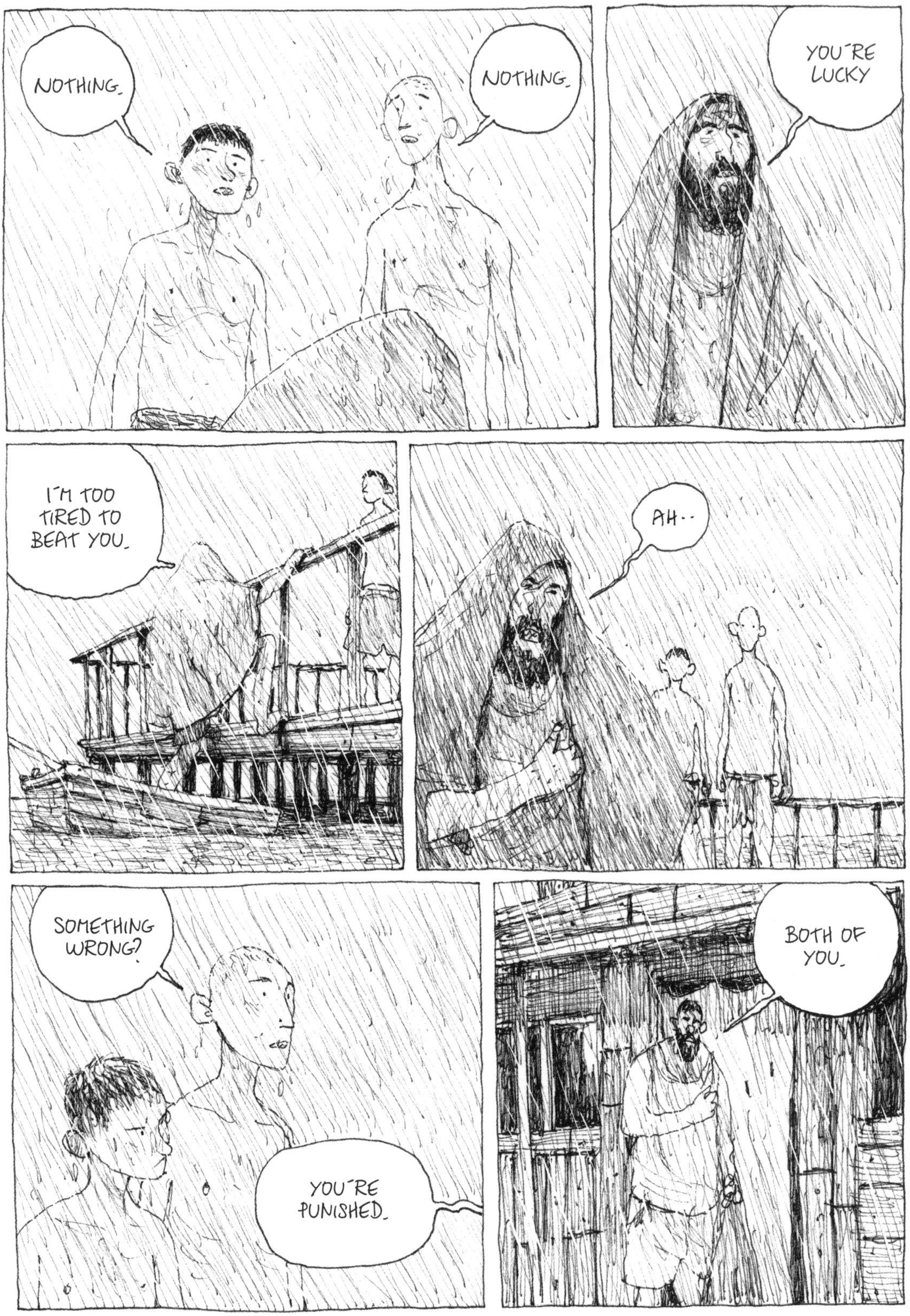
NOTHING.
NOTHING.
YOU'RE LUCKY
I'M TOO TIRED TO BEAT YOU.
AH..
SOMETHING WRONG?
YOU'RE PUNISHED.
BOTH OF YOU.

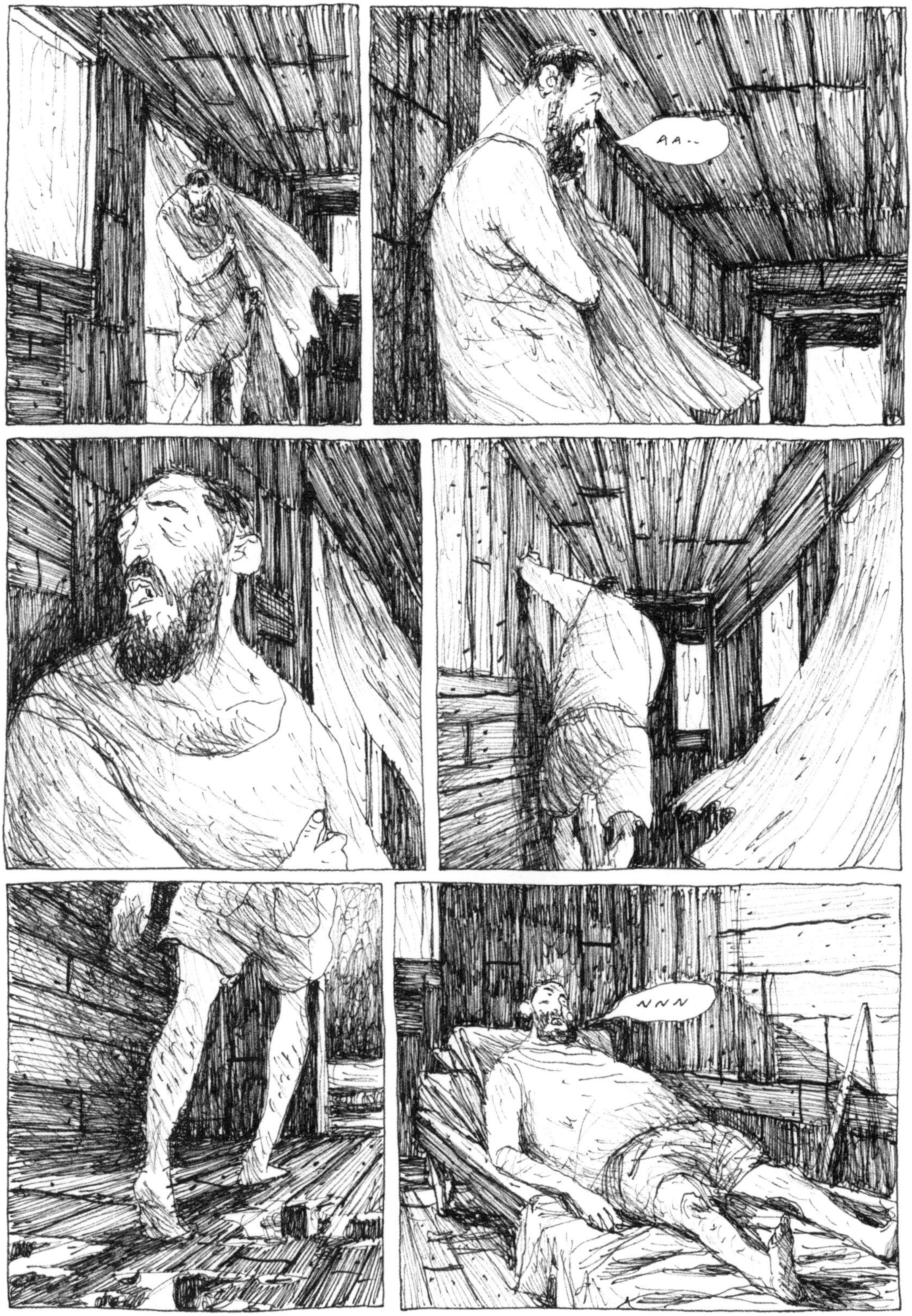
AA..
NNN

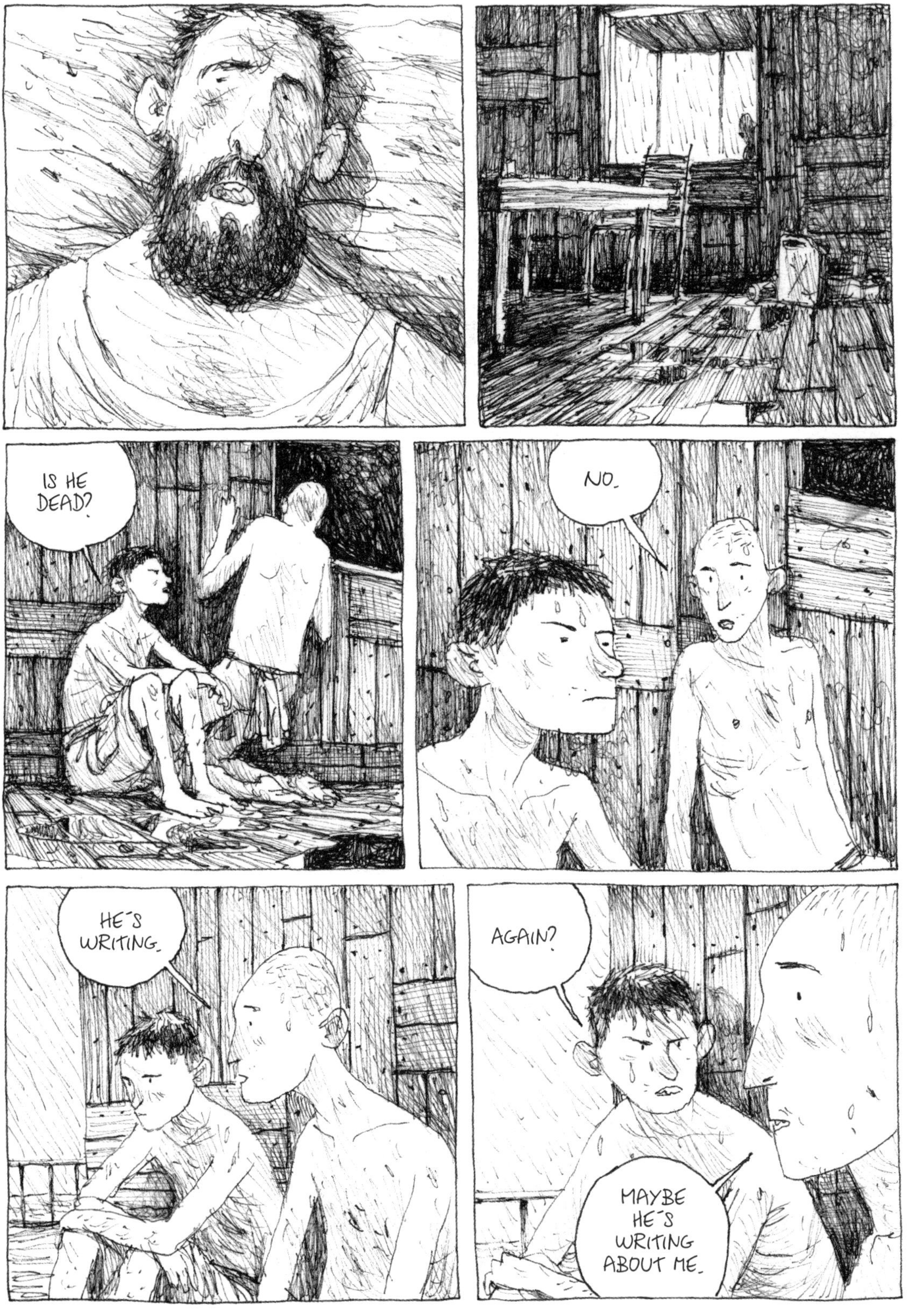
IS HE DEAD?
NO.
HE'S WRITING.
AGAIN?
MAYBE HE'S WRITING ABOUT ME.

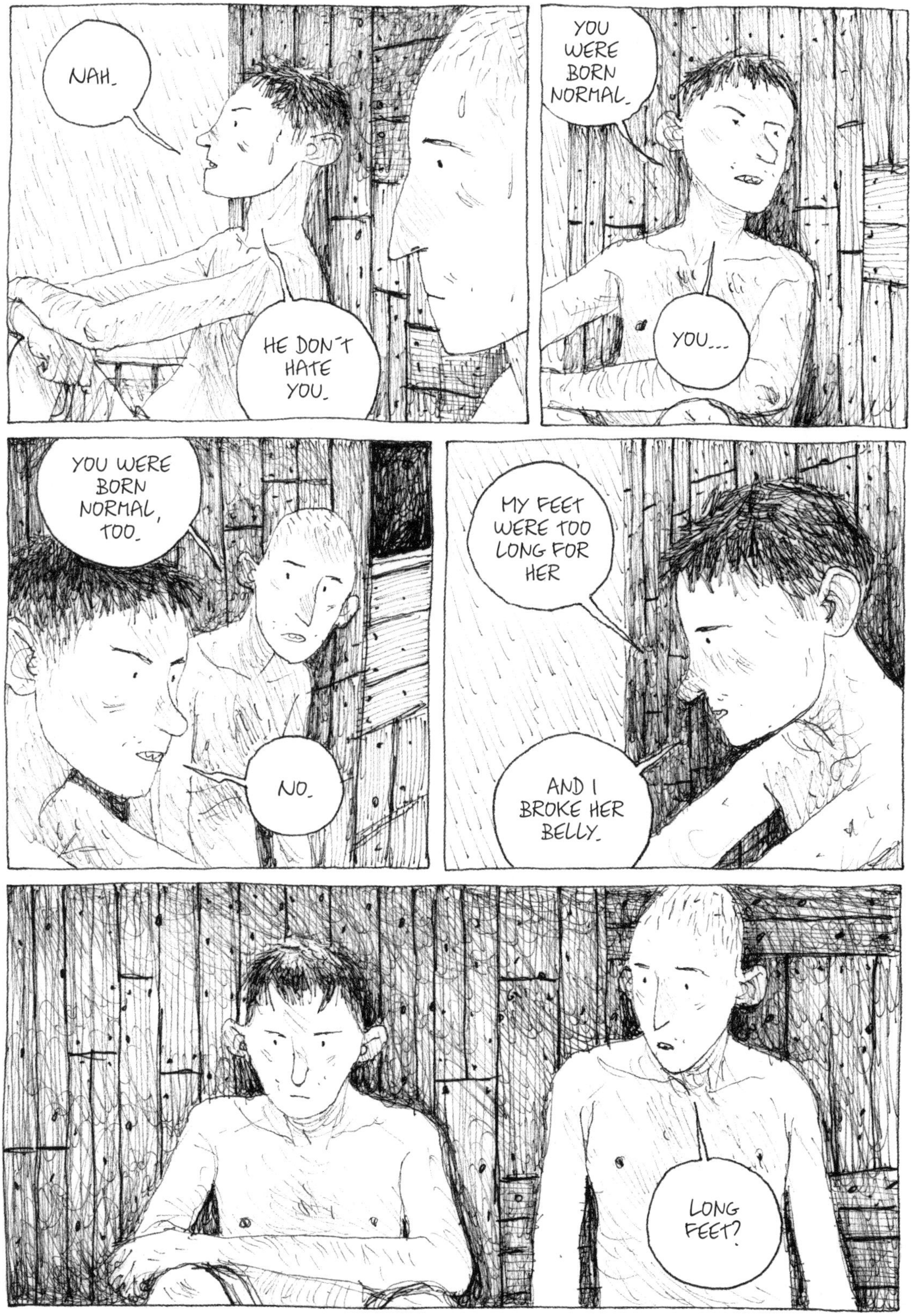
NAH.
HE DON'T HATE YOU.
YOU WERE BORN NORMAL.
YOU...
YOU WERE BORN NORMAL, TOO.
NO.
MY FEET WERE TOO LONG FOR HER
AND I BROKE HER BELLY.
LONG FEET?

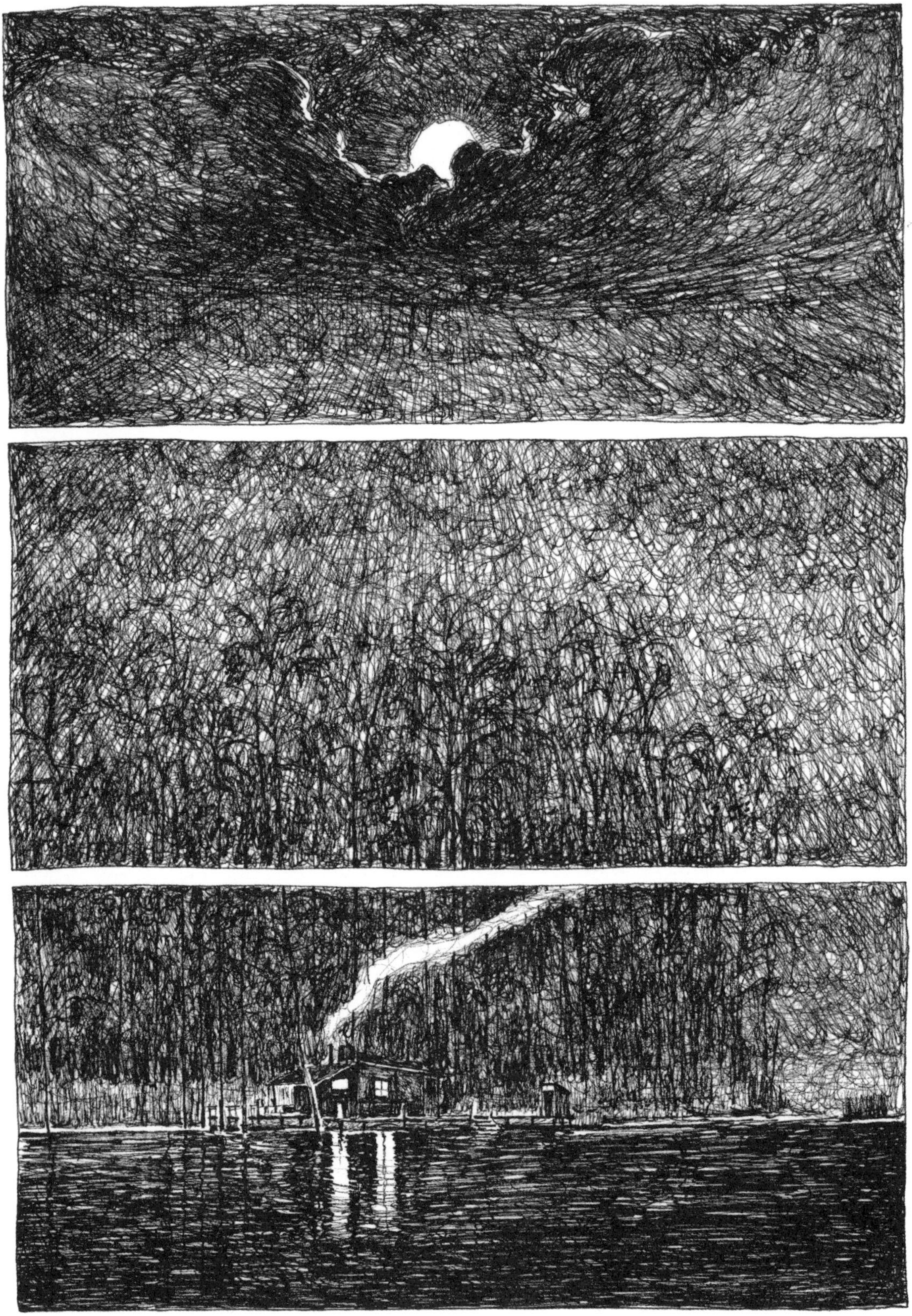

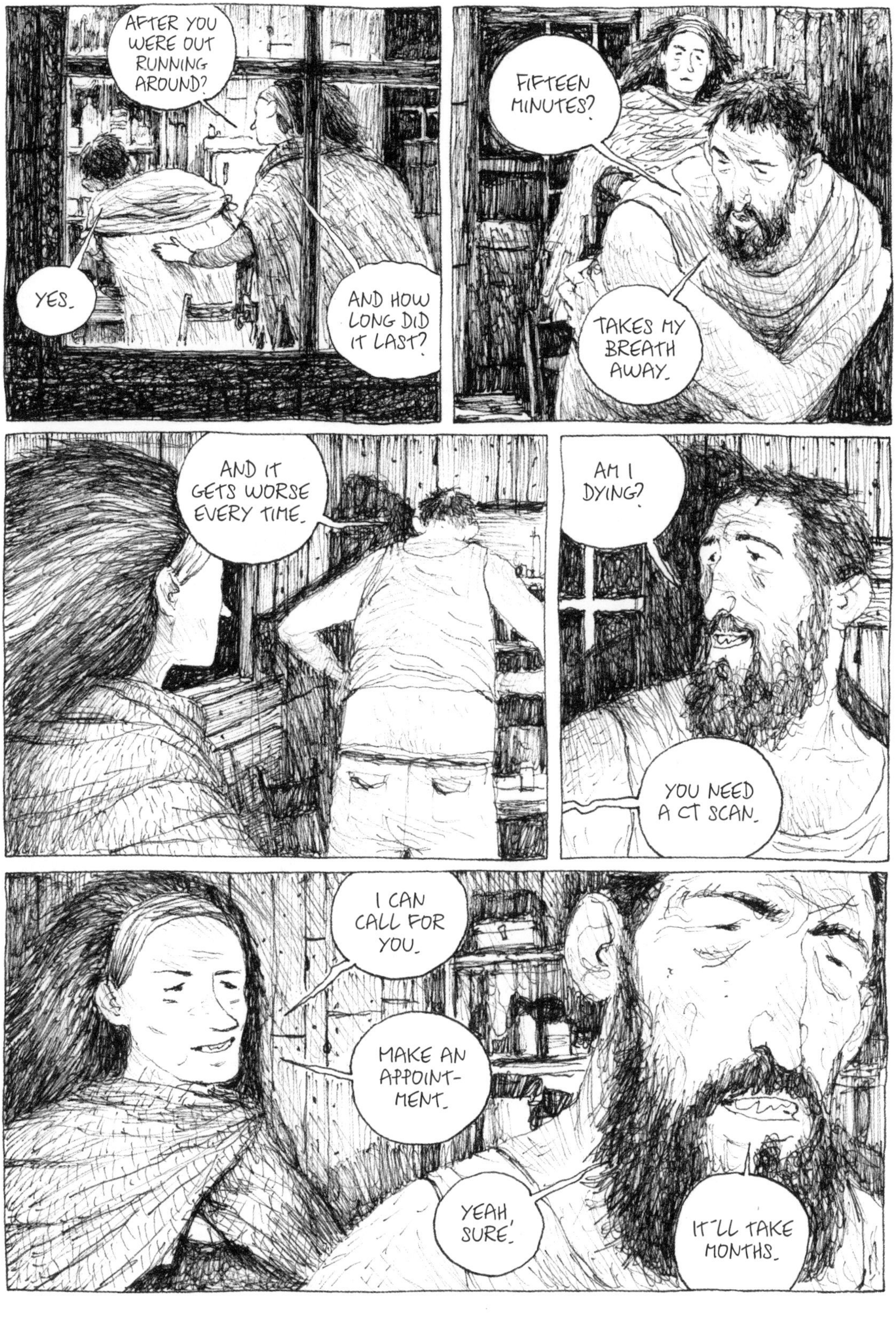
AFTER YOU WERE OUT RUNNING AROUND?
YES.
AND HOW LONG DID IT LAST?
FIFTEEN MINUTES?
TAKES MY BREATH AWAY.
AND IT GETS WORSE EVERY TIME.
AM I DYING?
YOU NEED A CT SCAN.
I CAN CALL FOR YOU.
MAKE AN APPOINT-MENT.
YEAH, SURE.
IT'LL TAKE MONTHS.

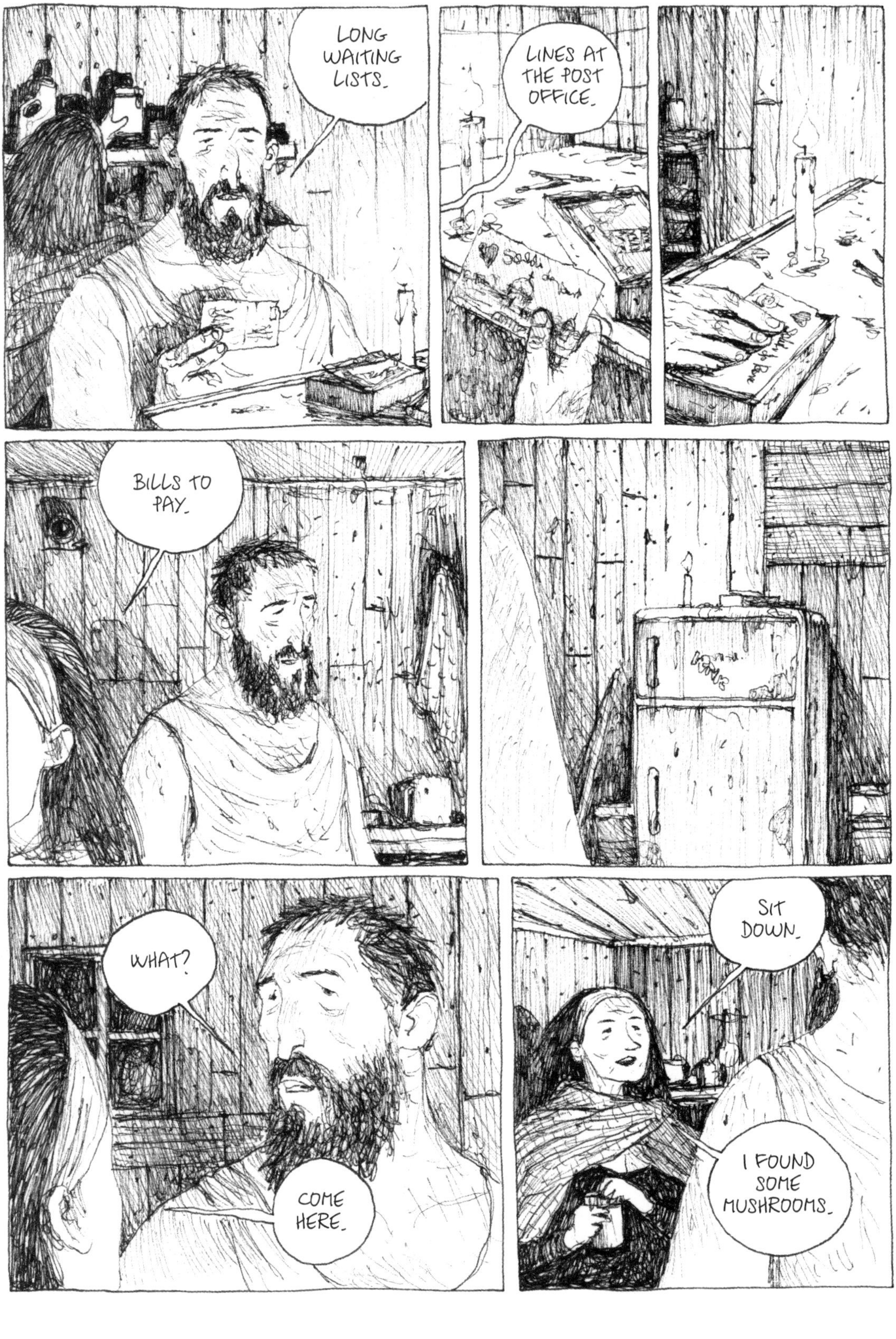
LONG WAITING LISTS_
LINES AT THE POST OFFICE_
BILLS TO PAY_
WHAT?
COME HERE_
SIT DOWN_
I FOUND SOME MUSHROOMS_

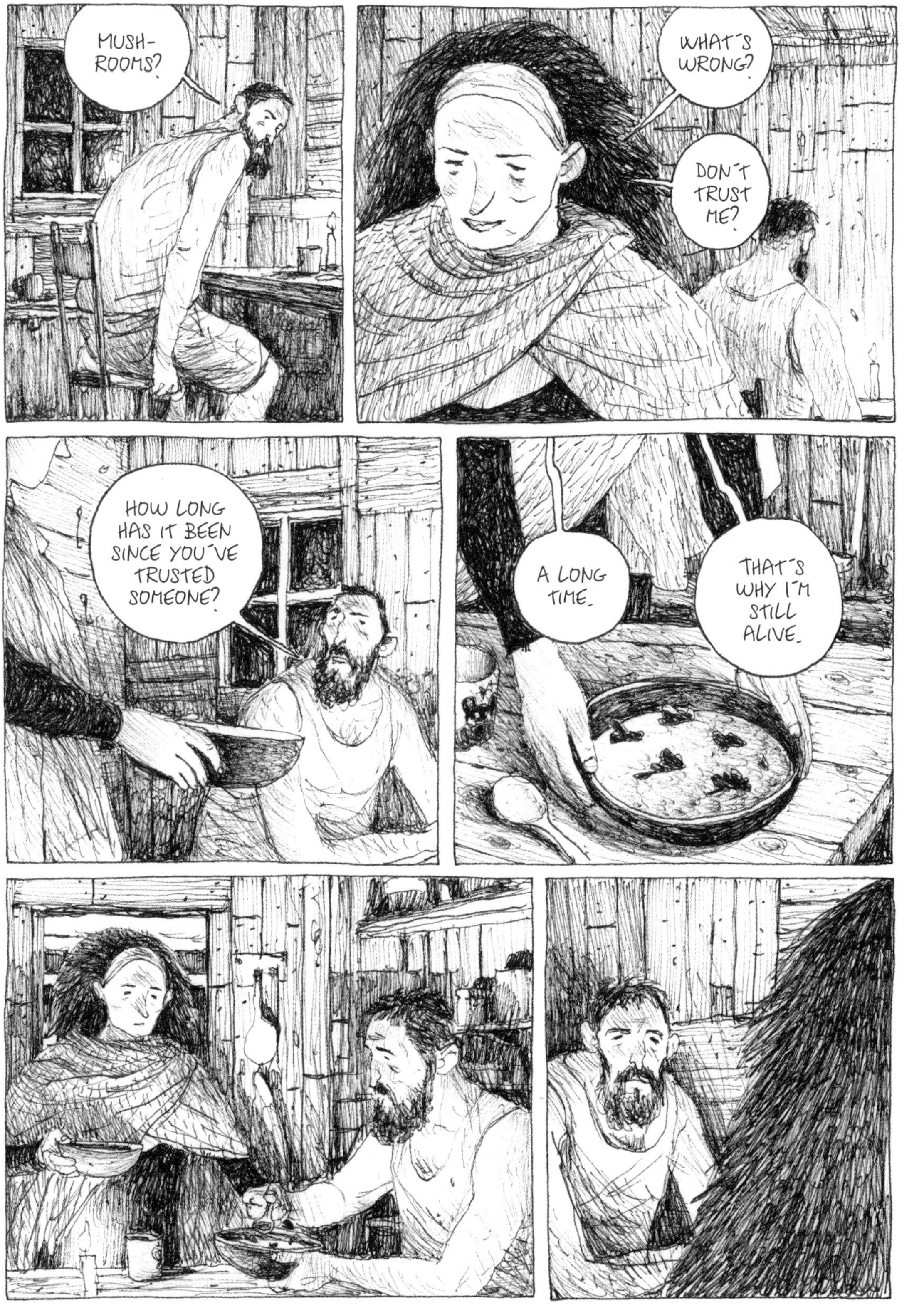
MUSH-ROOMS?
WHAT'S WRONG?
DON'T TRUST ME?
HOW LONG HAS IT BEEN SINCE YOU'VE TRUSTED SOMEONE?
A LONG TIME.
THAT'S WHY I'M STILL ALIVE.

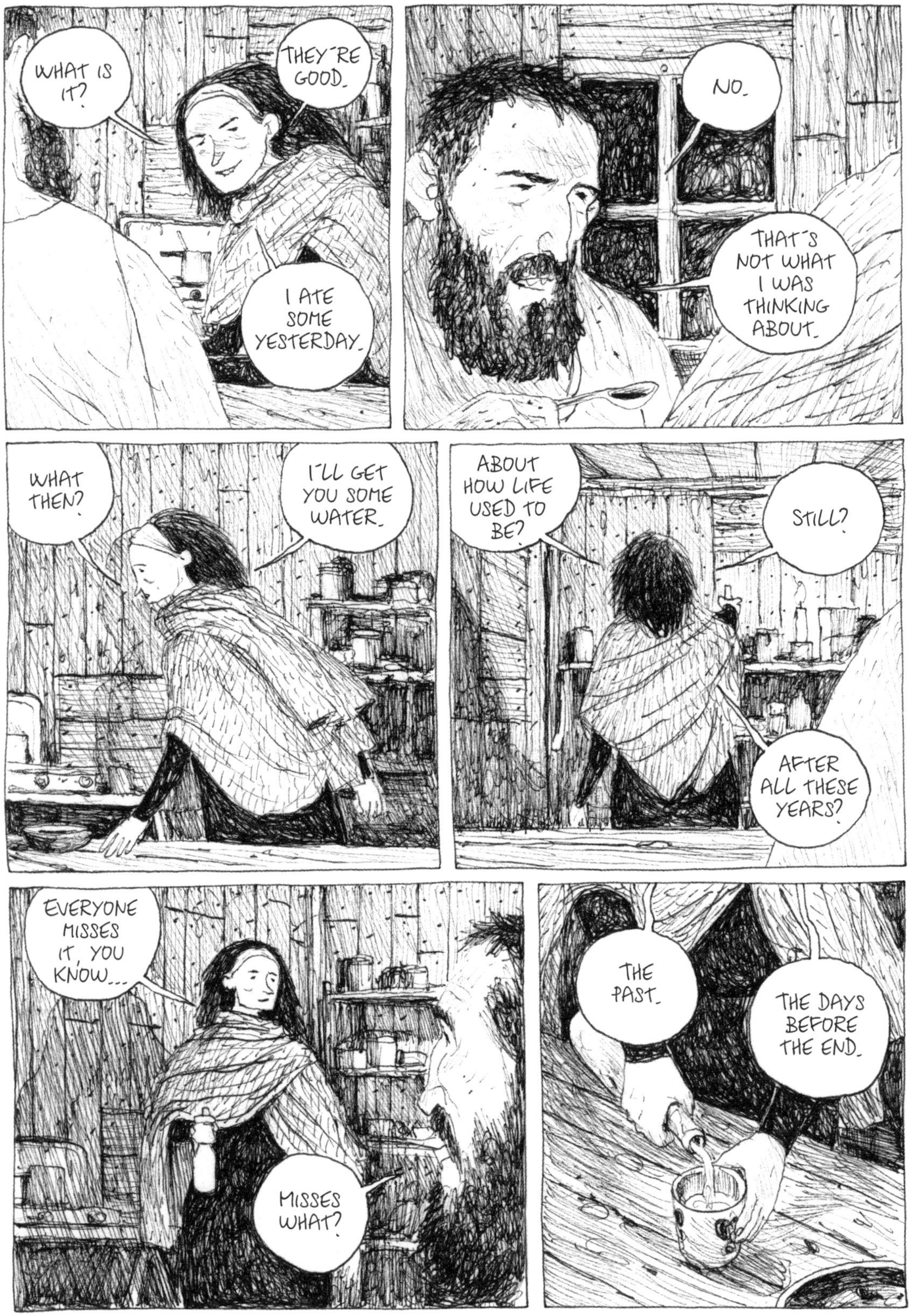
WHAT IS IT?
THEY'RE GOOD.
I ATE SOME YESTERDAY.
NO.
THAT'S NOT WHAT I WAS THINKING ABOUT.
WHAT THEN?
I'LL GET YOU SOME WATER.
ABOUT HOW LIFE USED TO BE?
STILL?
AFTER ALL THESE YEARS?
EVERYONE MISSES IT, YOU KNOW...
MISSES WHAT?
THE PAST.
THE DAYS BEFORE THE END.

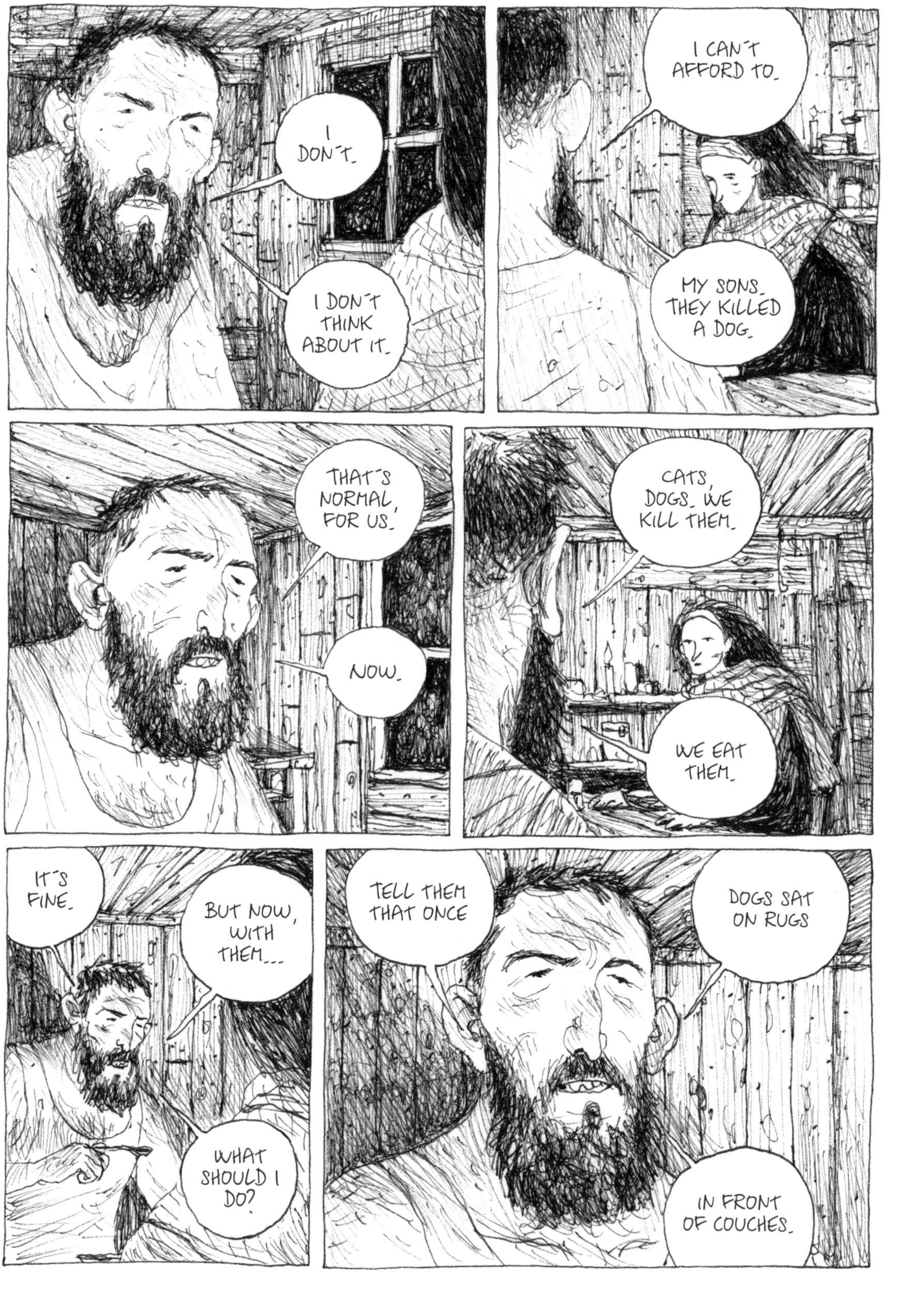
I DON'T.
I DON'T THINK ABOUT IT.
I CAN'T AFFORD TO.
MY SONS. THEY KILLED A DOG.
THAT'S NORMAL, FOR US.
NOW.
CATS, DOGS. WE KILL THEM.
WE EAT THEM.
IT'S FINE.
BUT NOW, WITH THEM...
WHAT SHOULD I DO?
TELL THEM THAT ONCE
DOGS SAT ON RUGS
IN FRONT OF COUCHES.

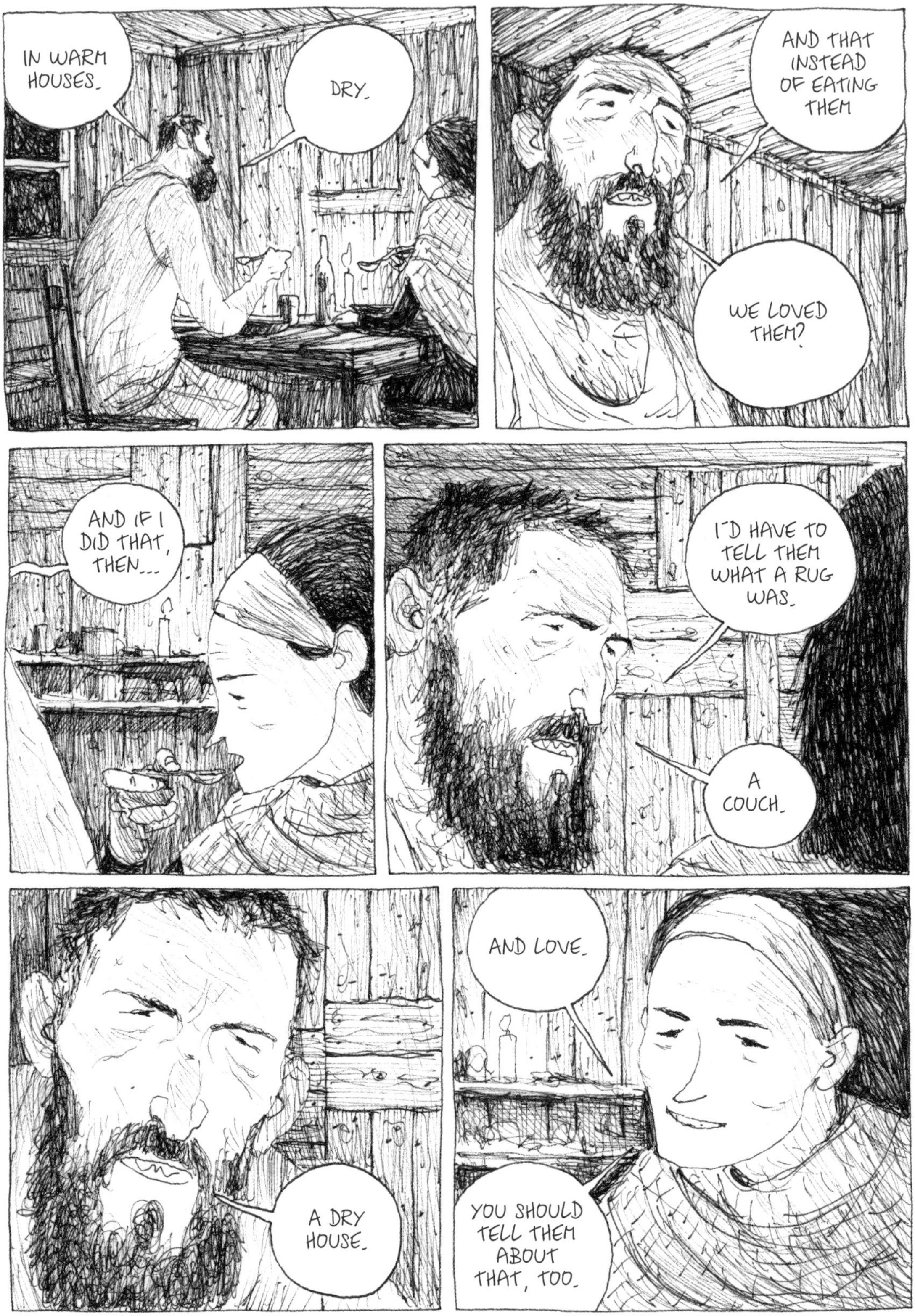
IN WARM HOUSES.
DRY.
AND THAT INSTEAD OF EATING THEM
WE LOVED THEM?
AND IF I DID THAT, THEN...
I'D HAVE TO TELL THEM WHAT A RUG WAS.
A COUCH.
A DRY HOUSE.
AND LOVE.
YOU SHOULD TELL THEM ABOUT THAT, TOO.

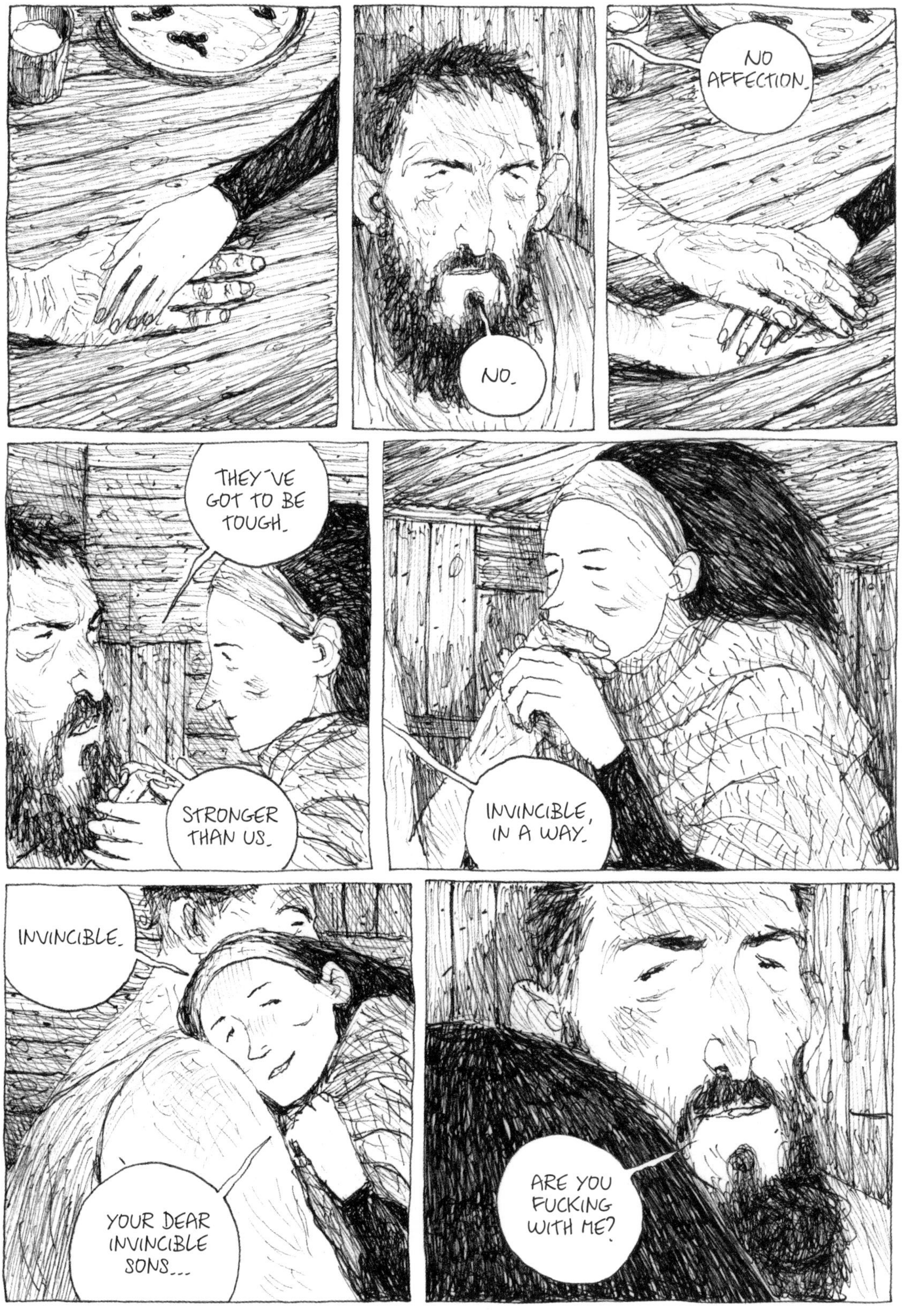
NO.
NO AFFECTION.
THEY'VE GOT TO BE TOUGH.
STRONGER THAN US.
INVINCIBLE, IN A WAY.
INVINCIBLE.
YOUR DEAR INVINCIBLE SONS...
ARE YOU FUCKING WITH ME?

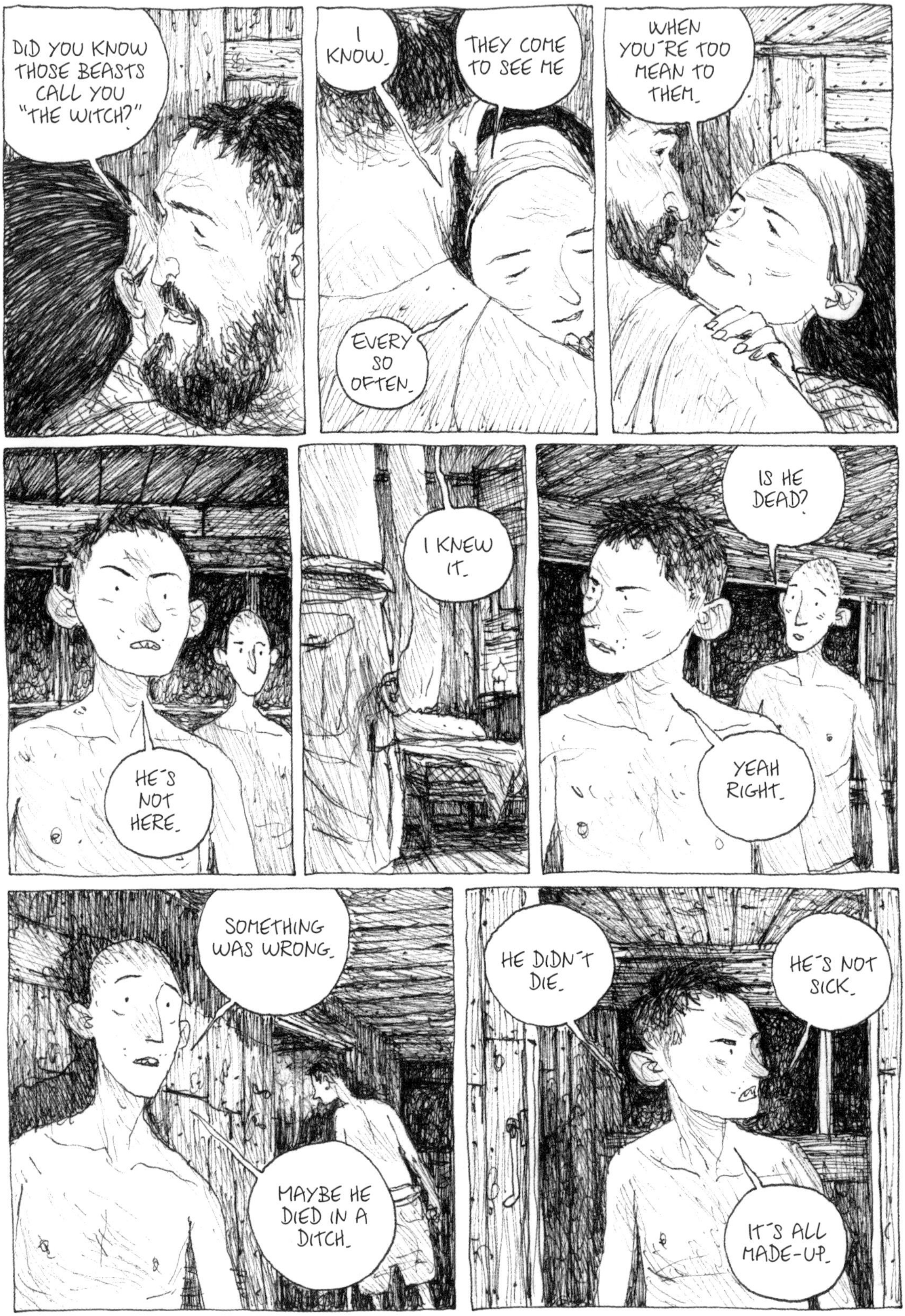
DID YOU KNOW THOSE BEASTS CALL YOU "THE WITCH?"
I KNOW.
THEY COME TO SEE ME
EVERY SO OFTEN.
WHEN YOU'RE TOO MEAN TO THEM.
HE'S NOT HERE.
I KNEW IT.
IS HE DEAD?
YEAH RIGHT.
SOMETHING WAS WRONG.
MAYBE HE DIED IN A DITCH.
HE DIDN'T DIE.
HE'S NOT SICK.
IT'S ALL MADE-UP.

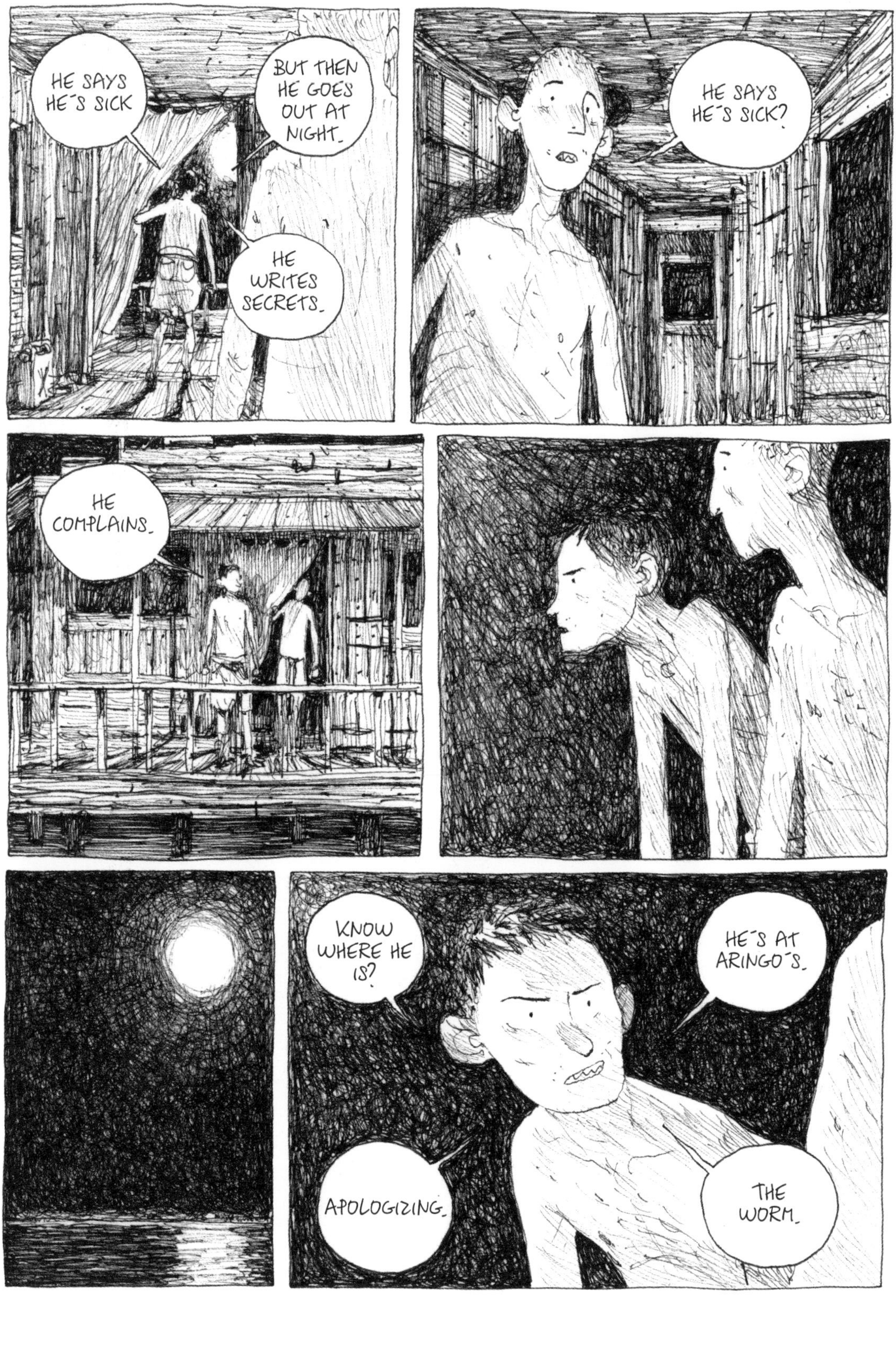
HE SAYS HE'S SICK
BUT THEN HE GOES OUT AT NIGHT.
HE WRITES SECRETS.
HE SAYS HE'S SICK?
HE COMPLAINS.
KNOW WHERE HE IS?
HE'S AT ARINGO'S.
APOLOGIZING.
THE WORM.

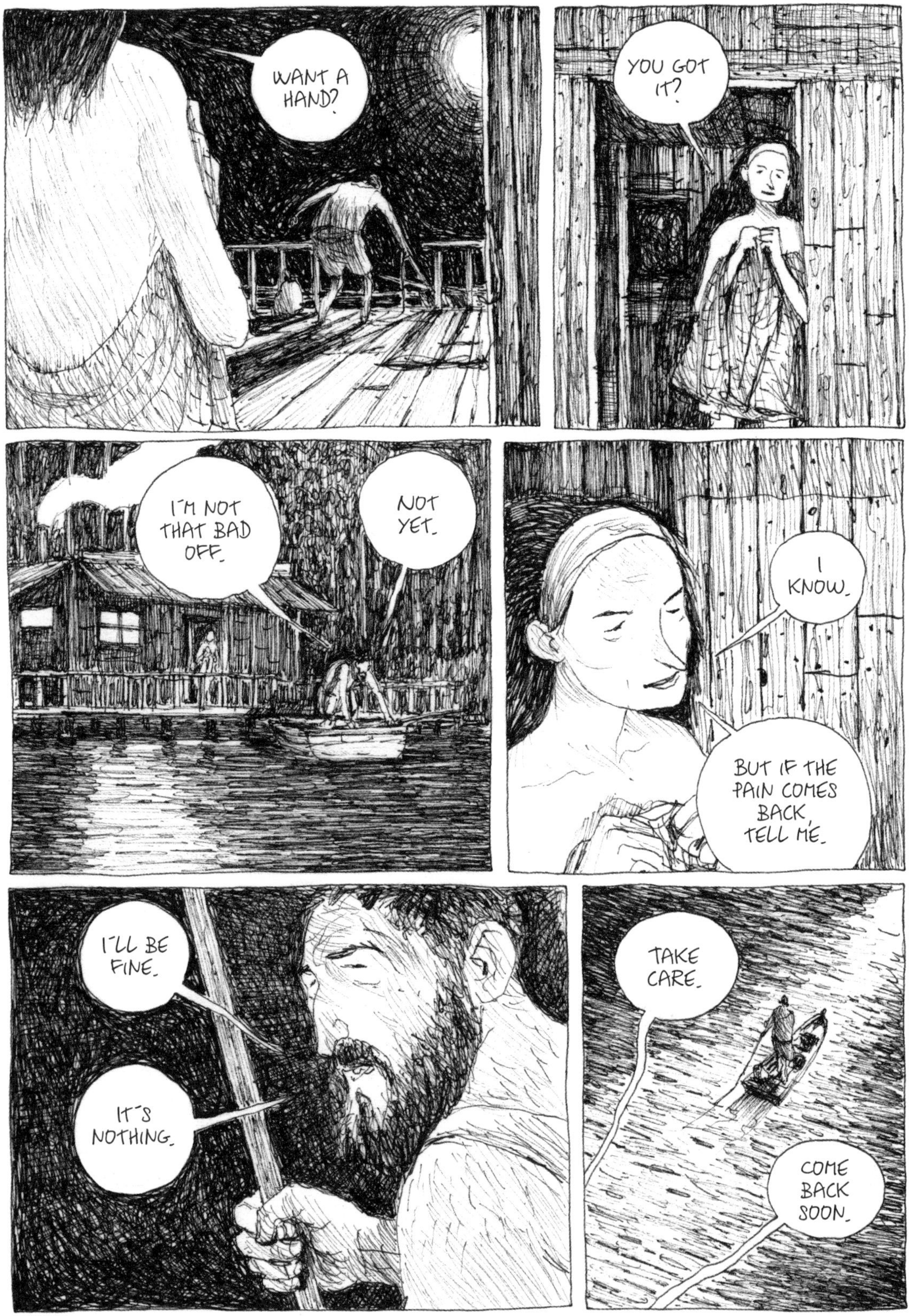
WANT A HAND?
YOU GOT IT?
I'M NOT THAT BAD OFF.
NOT YET.
I KNOW.
BUT IF THE PAIN COMES BACK, TELL ME.
I'LL BE FINE.
IT'S NOTHING.
TAKE CARE.
COME BACK SOON.

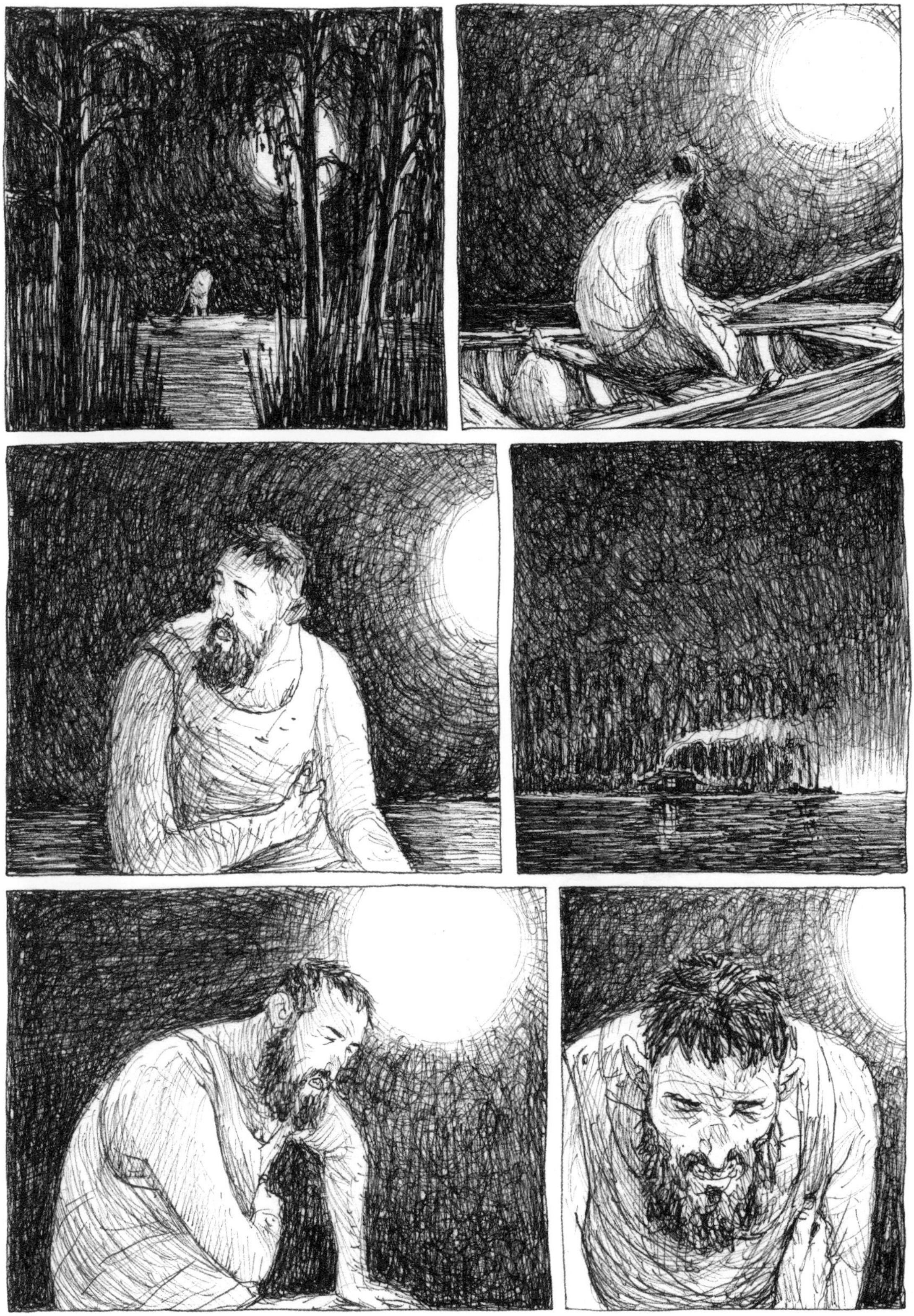

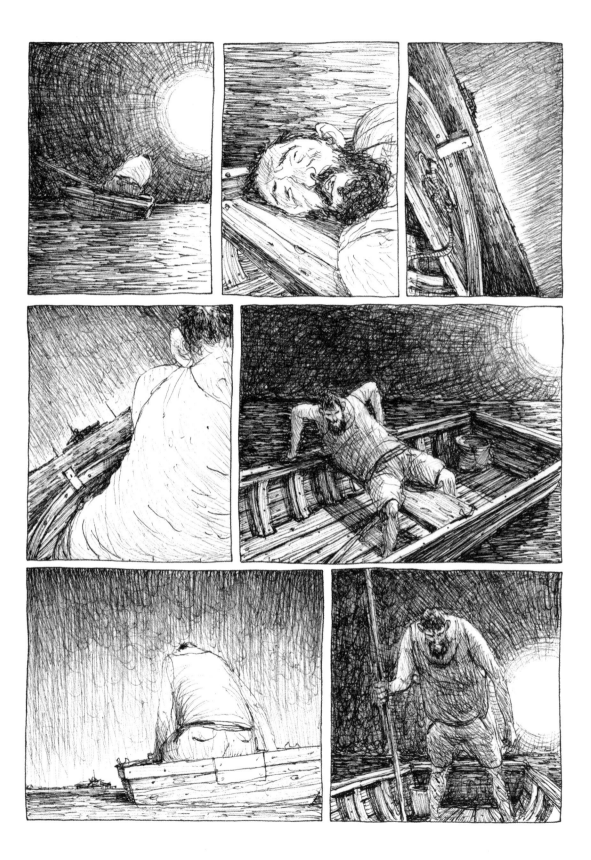

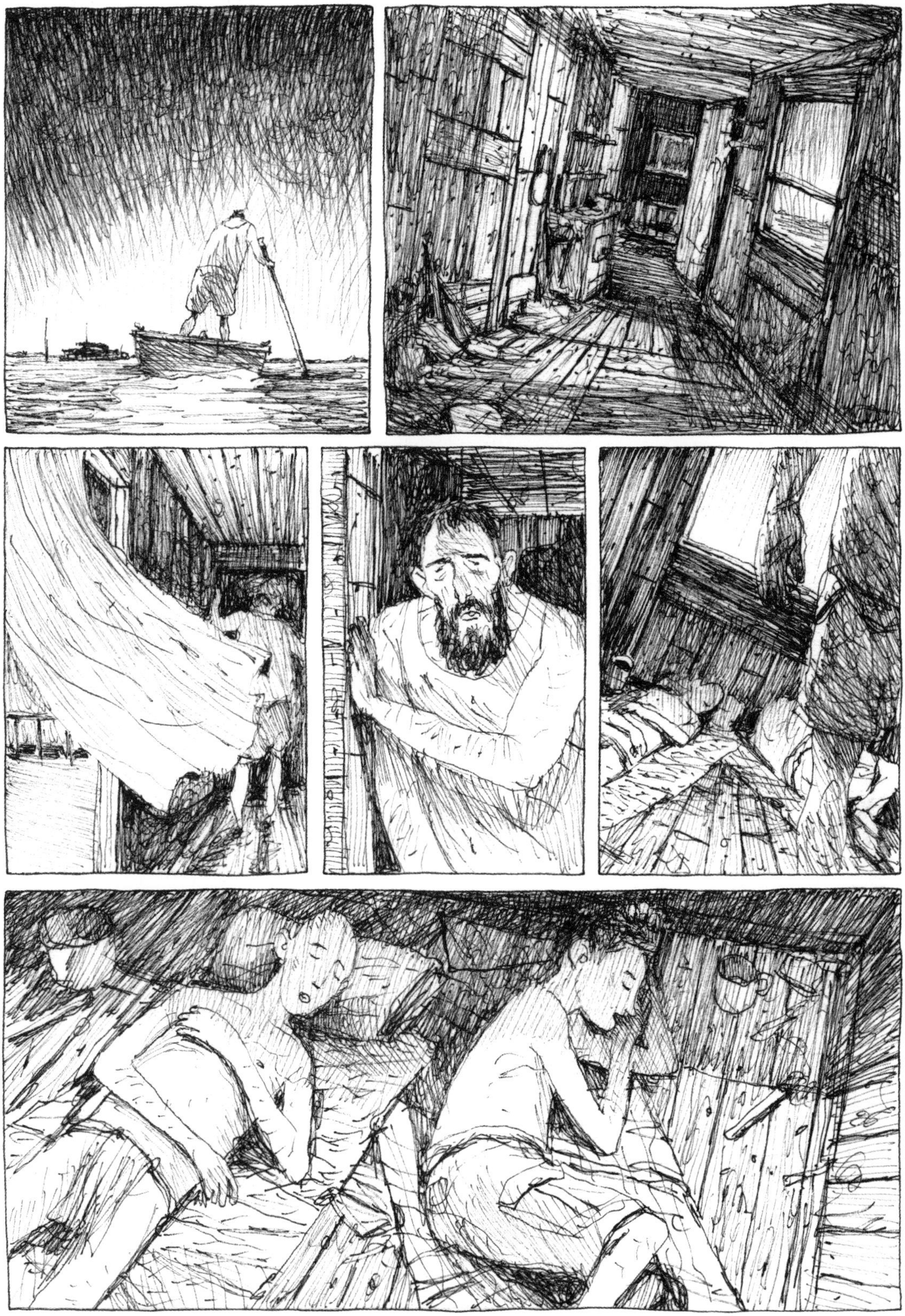

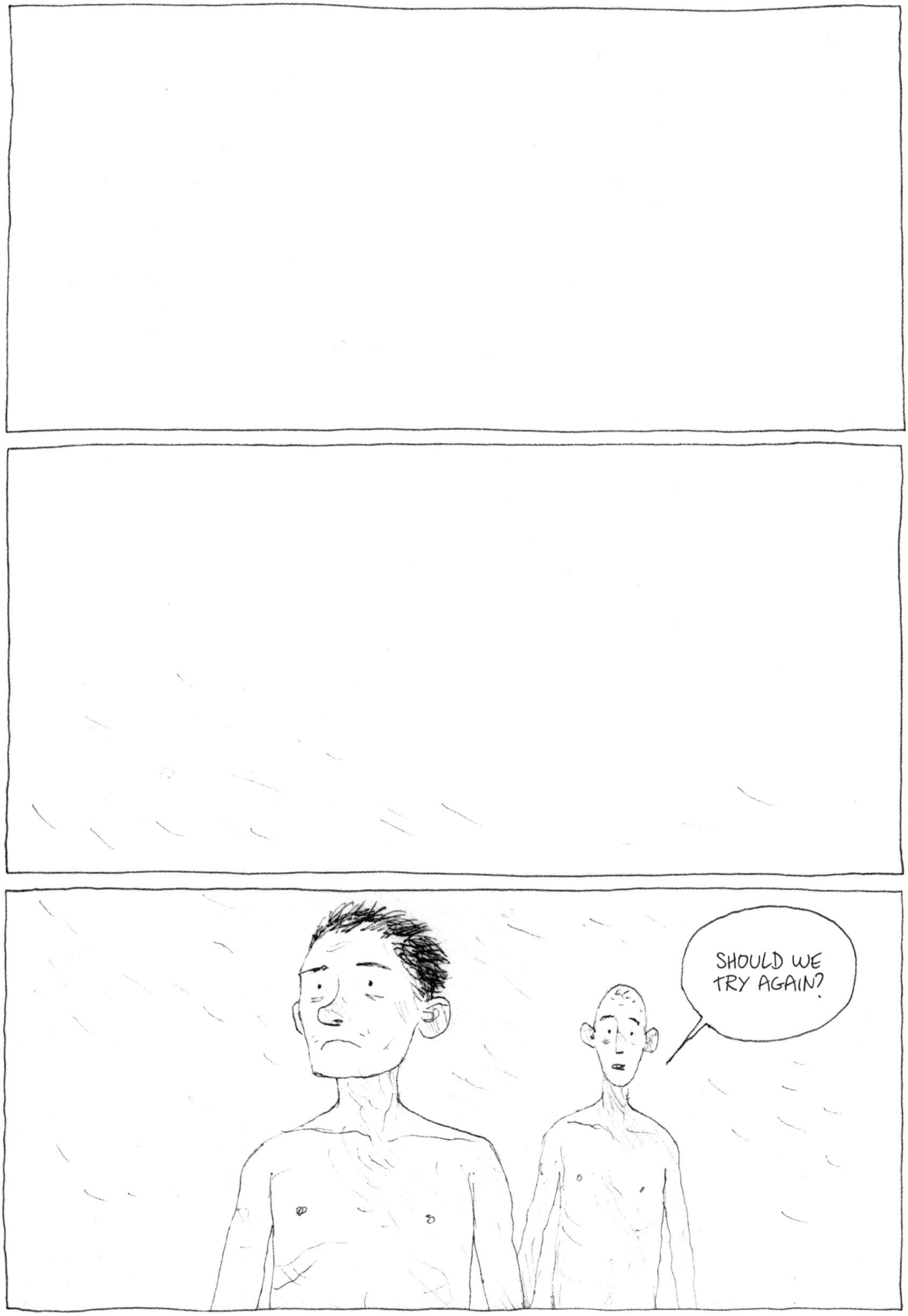
SHOULD WE TRY AGAIN?

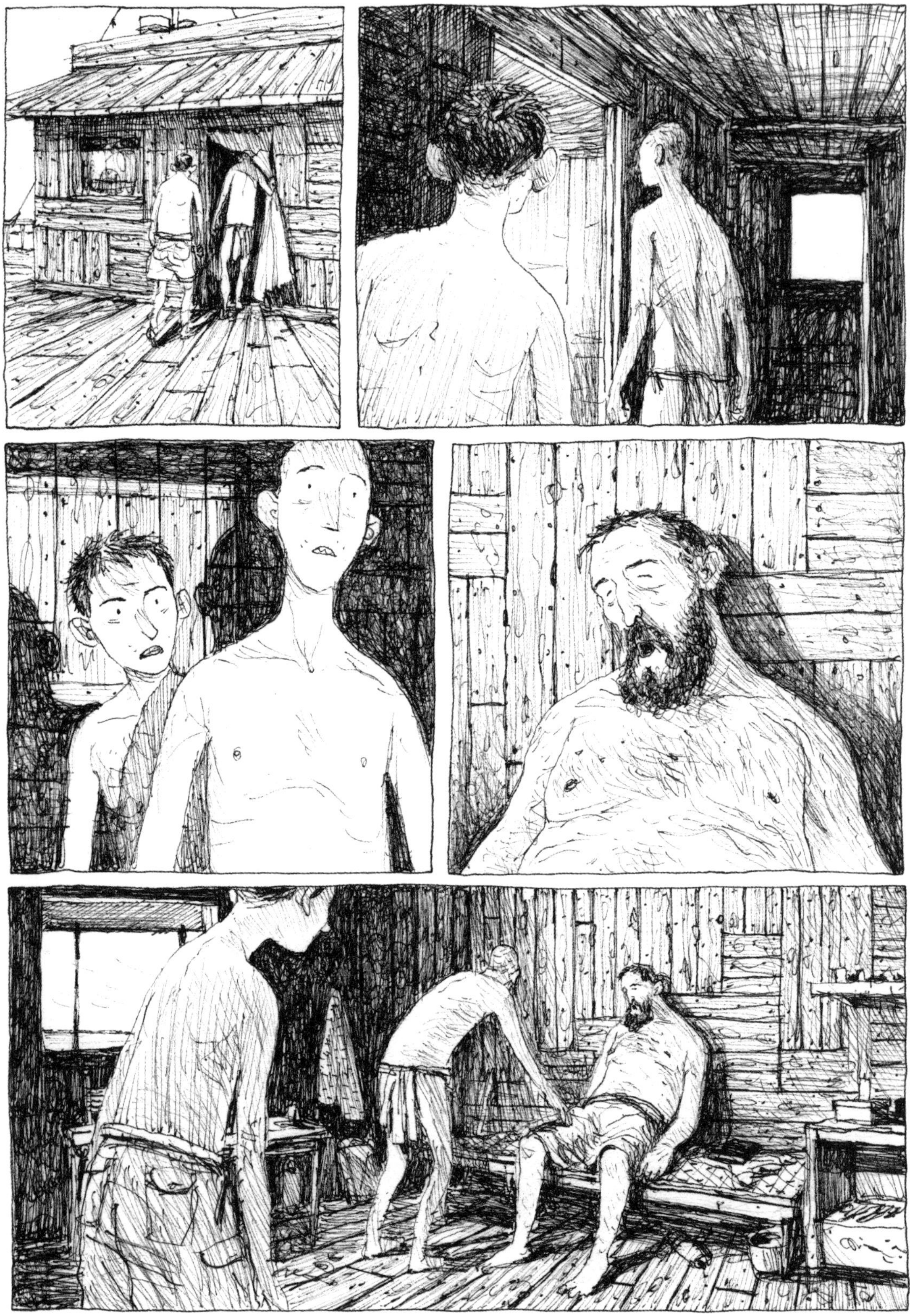

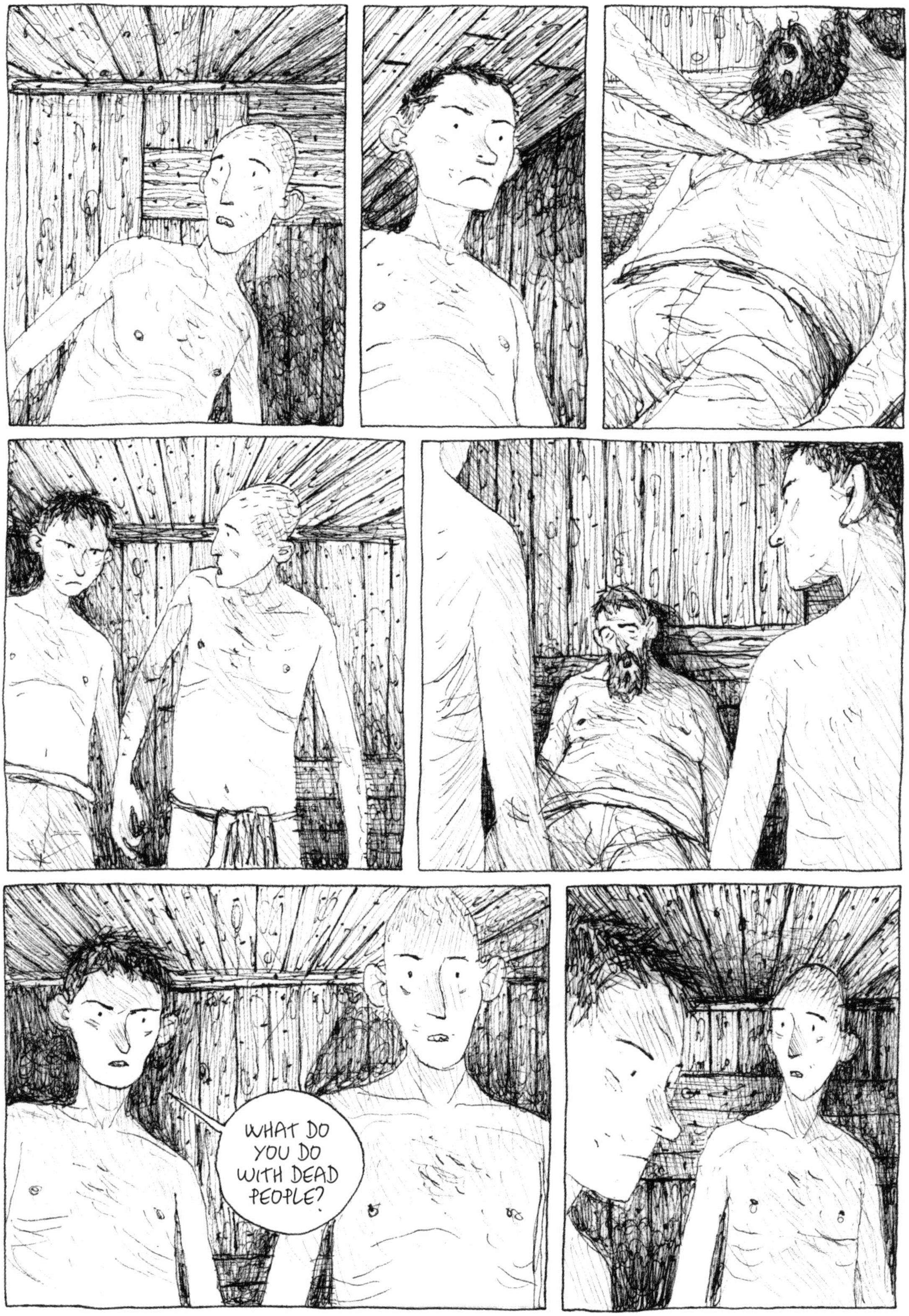
WHAT DO YOU DO WITH DEAD PEOPLE?

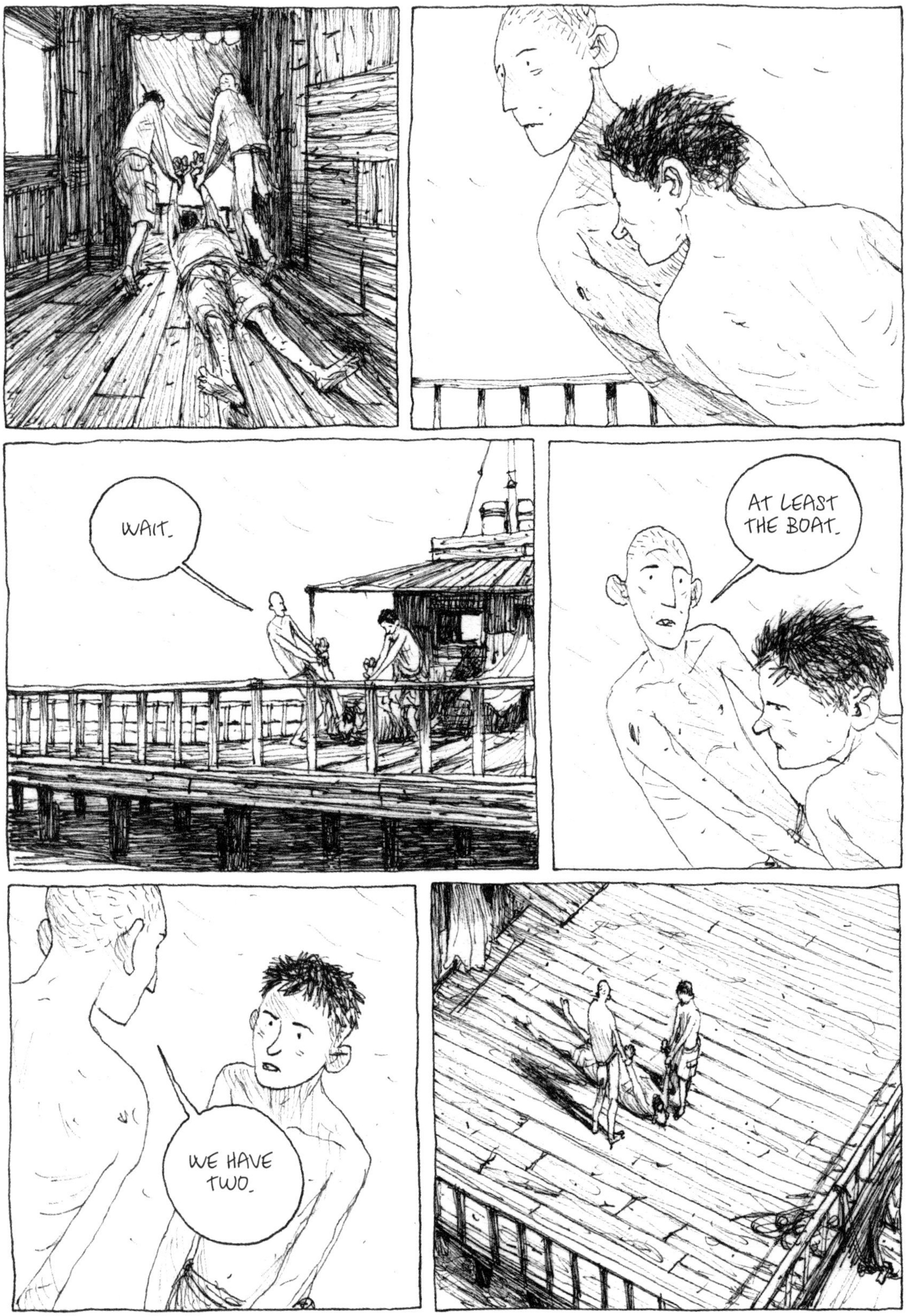
WAIT.
AT LEAST THE BOAT.
WE HAVE TWO.

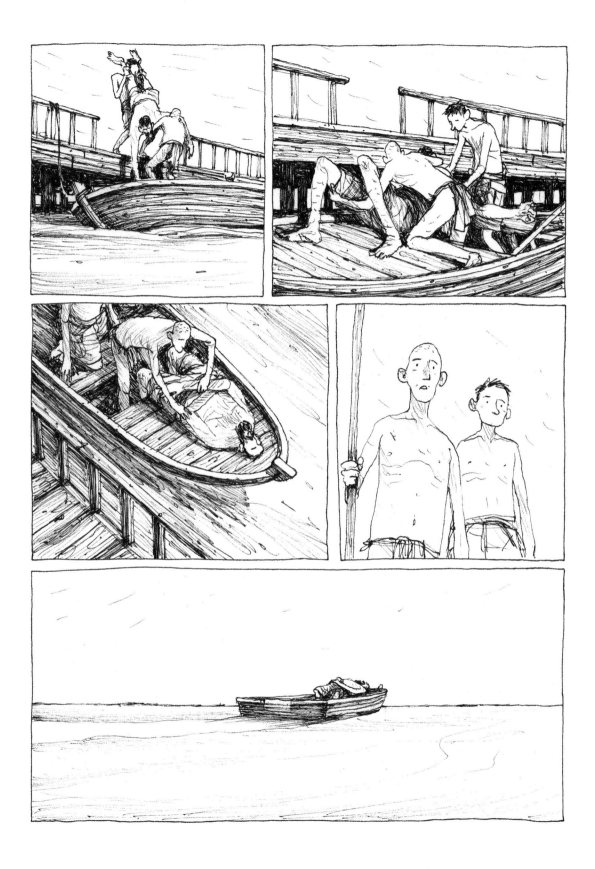

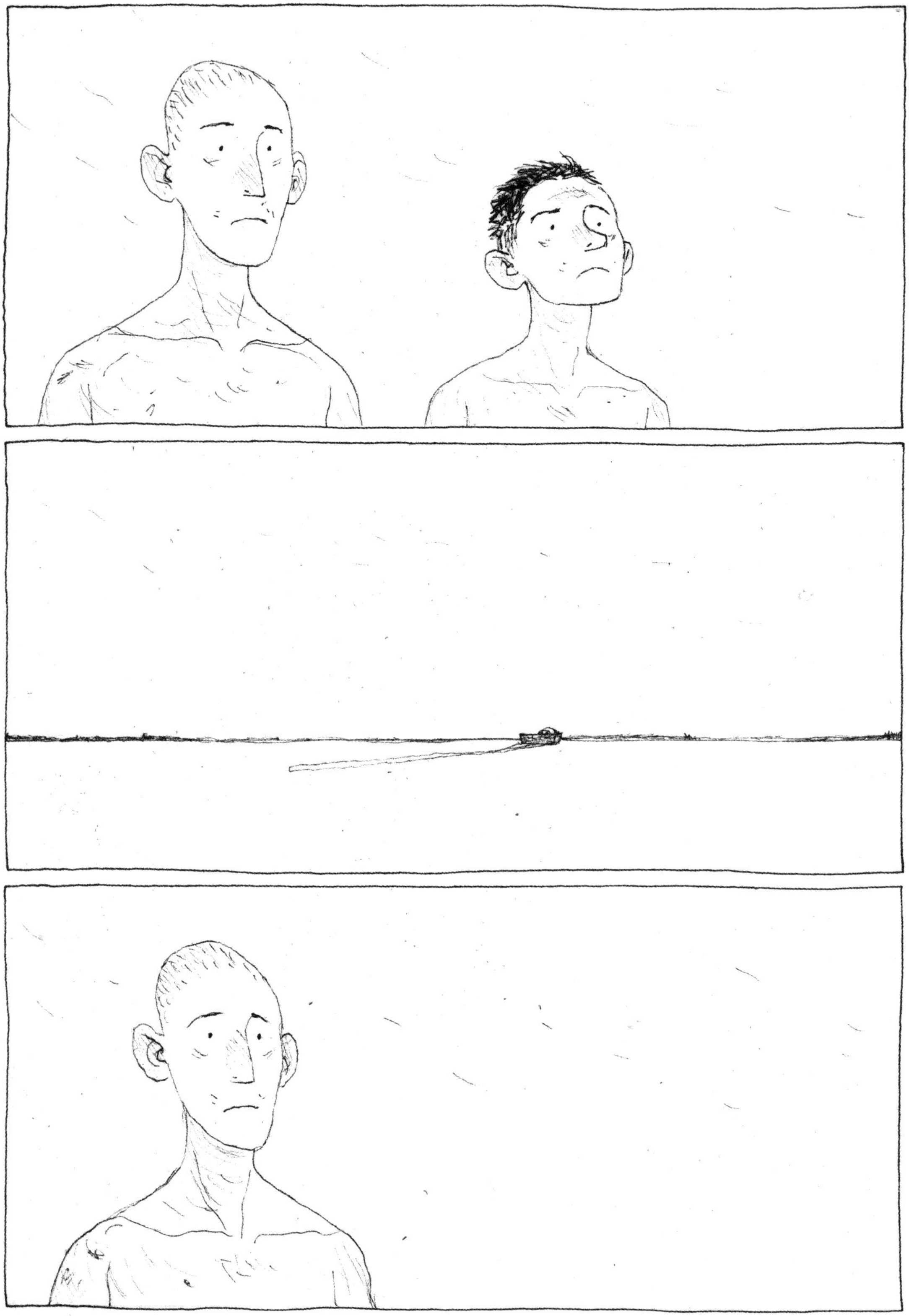

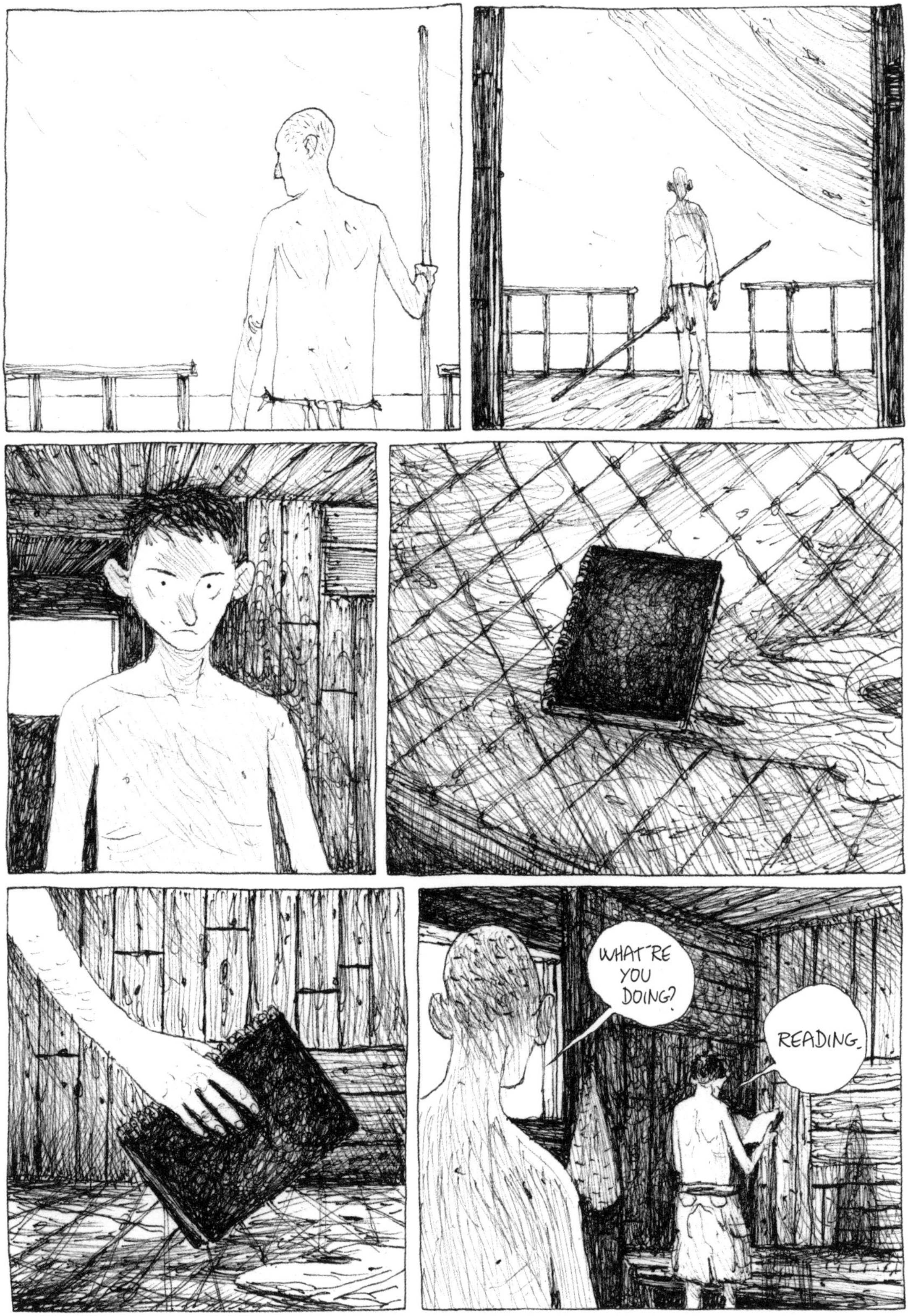
WHAT'RE YOU DOING?
READING.

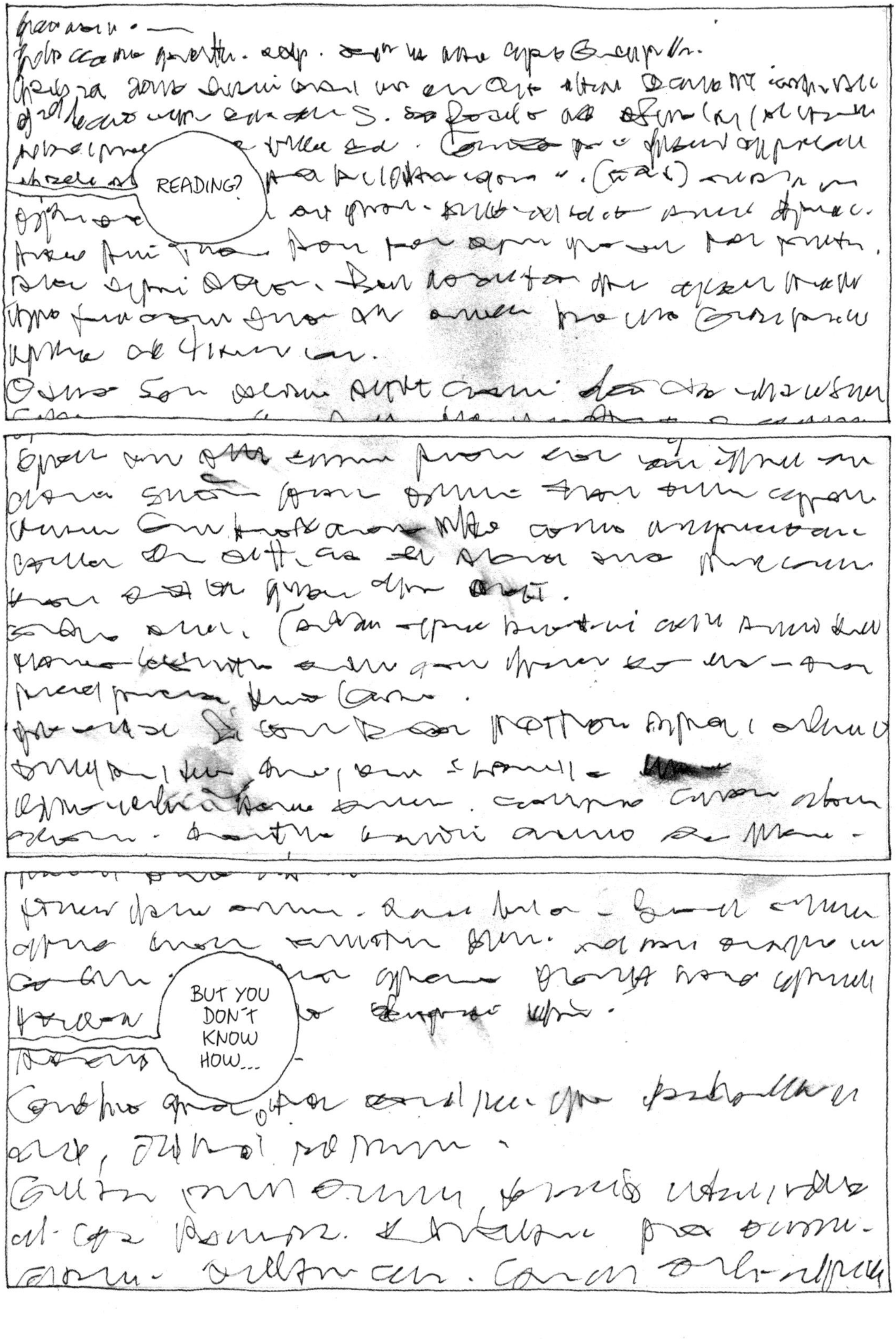
READING?
BUT YOU DON'T KNOW HOW...

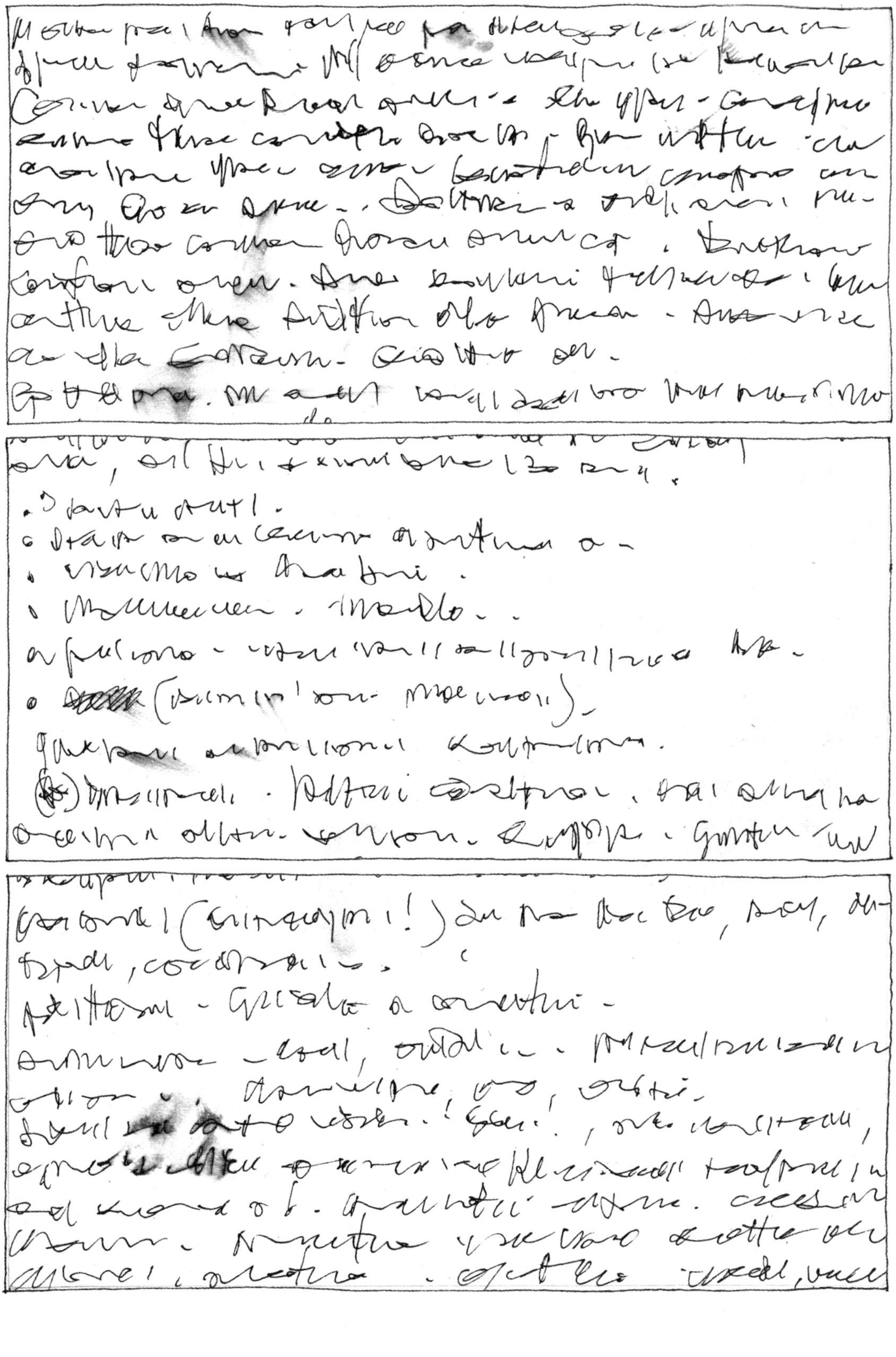

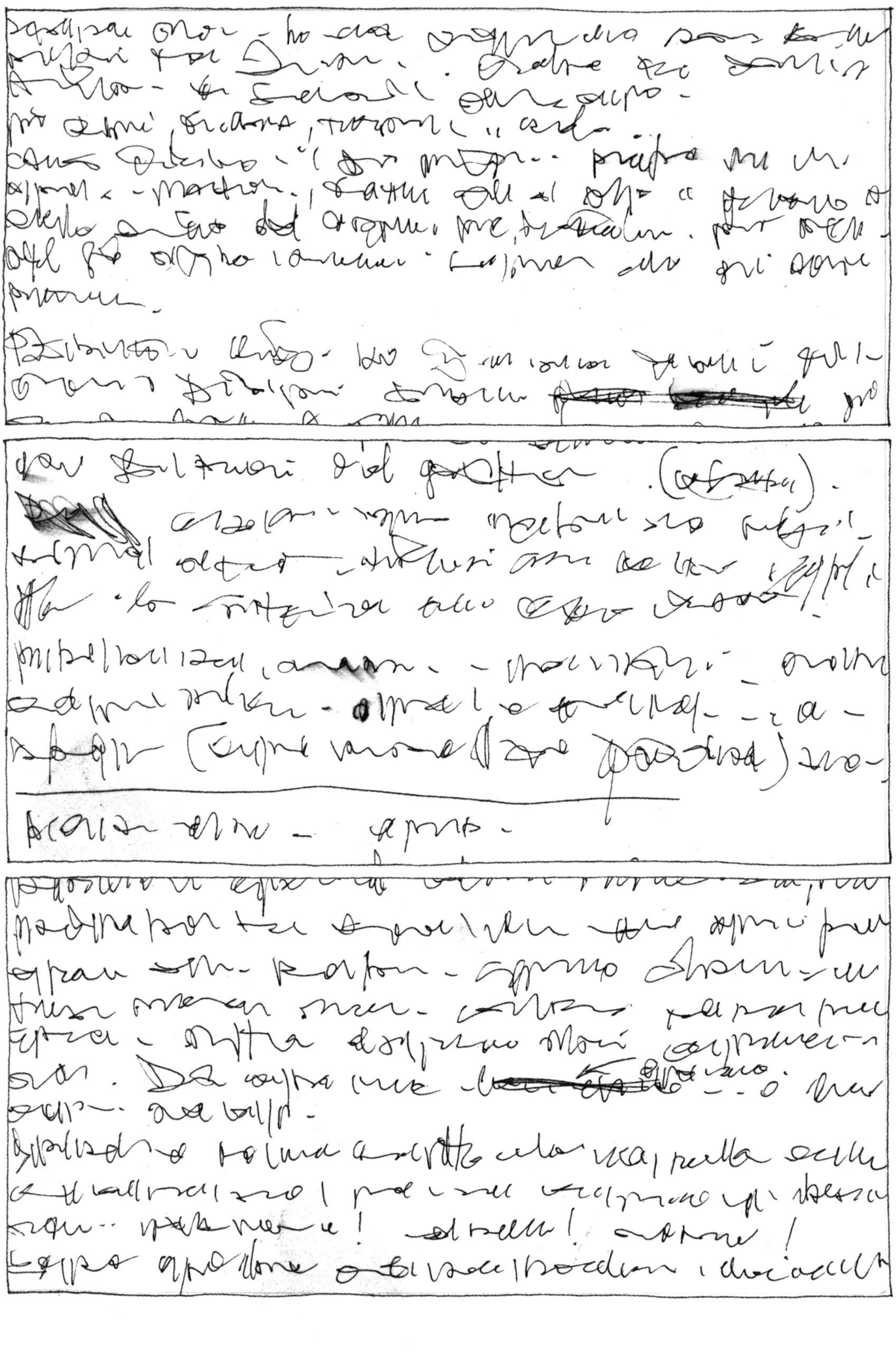

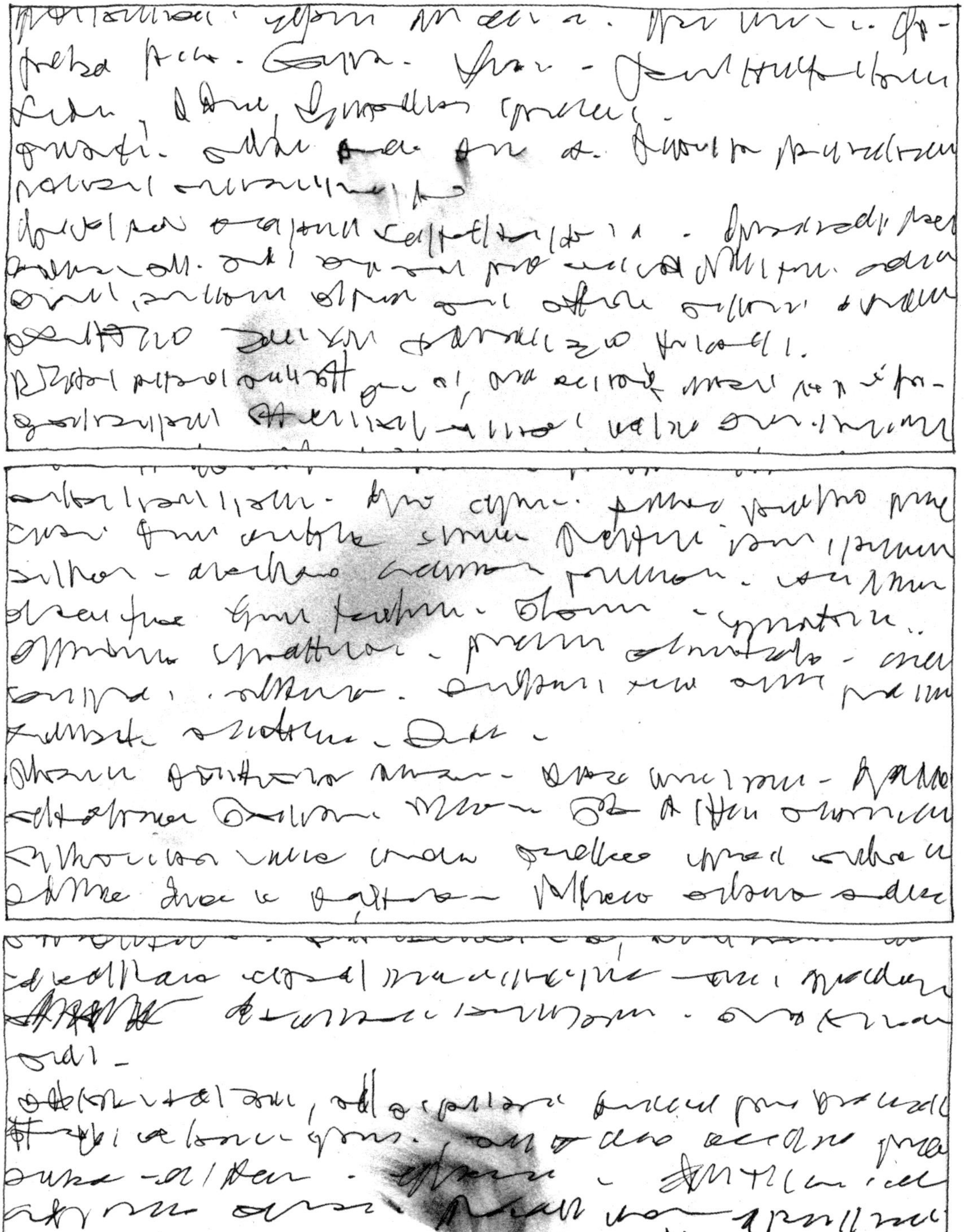

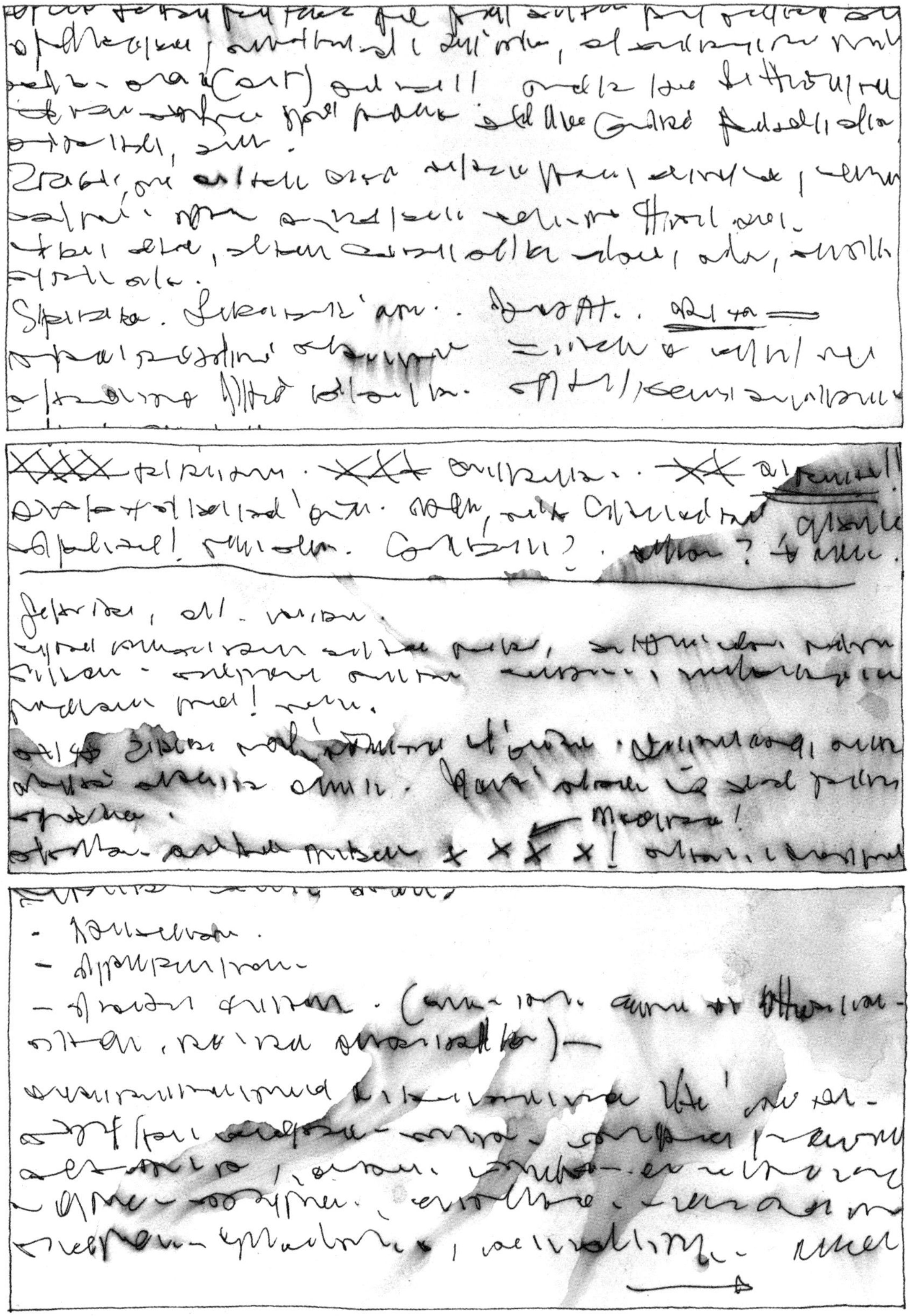

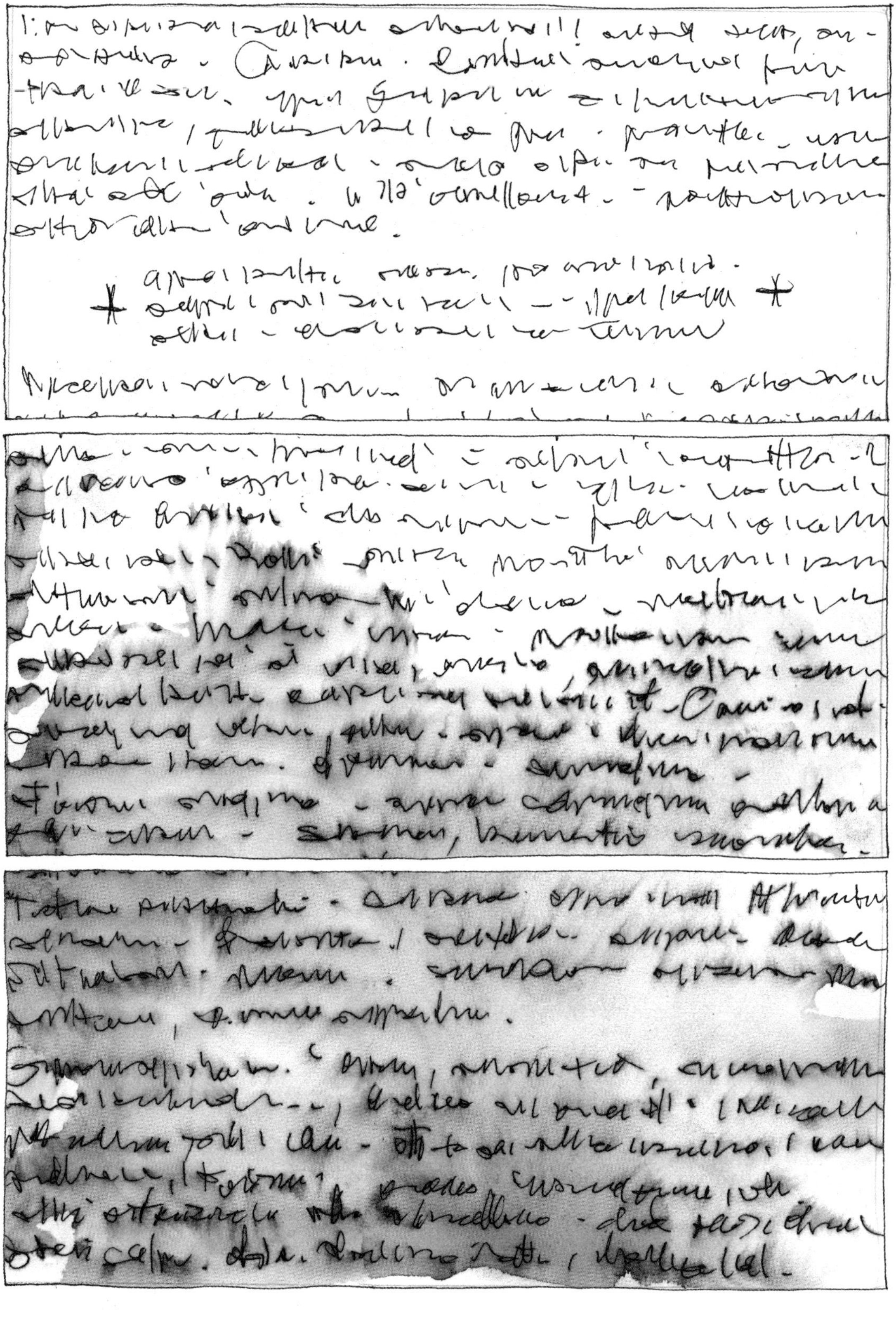

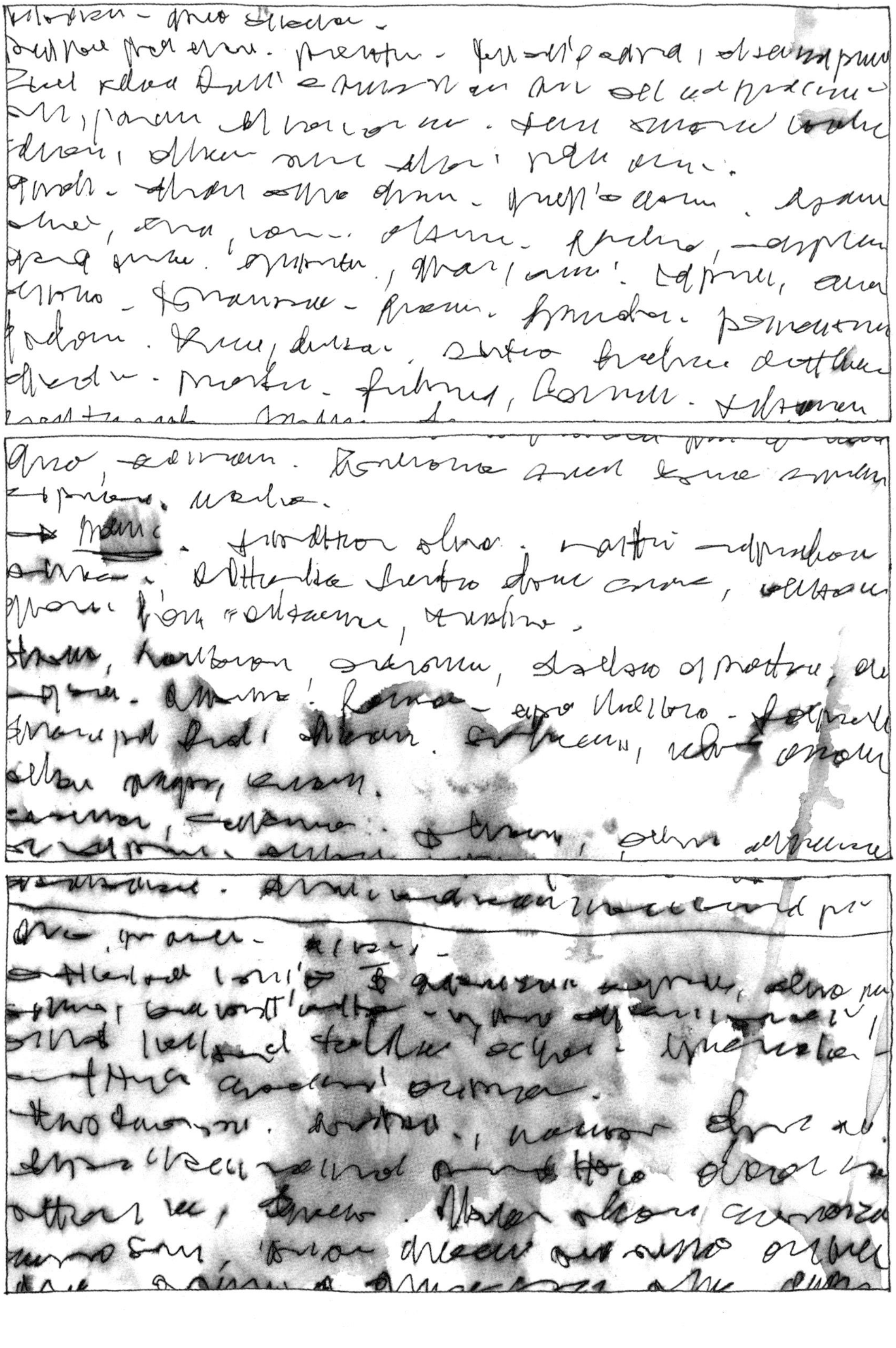

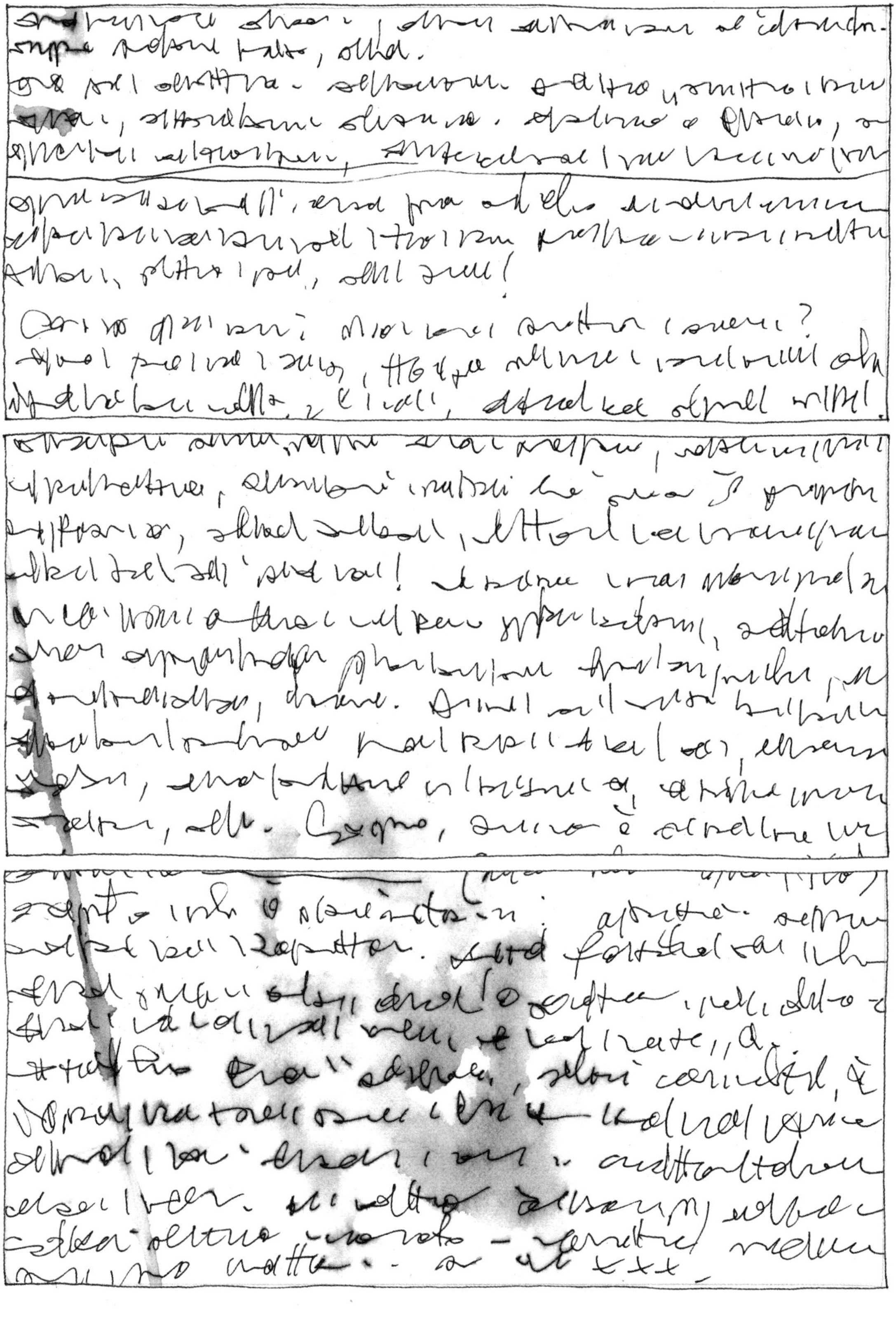

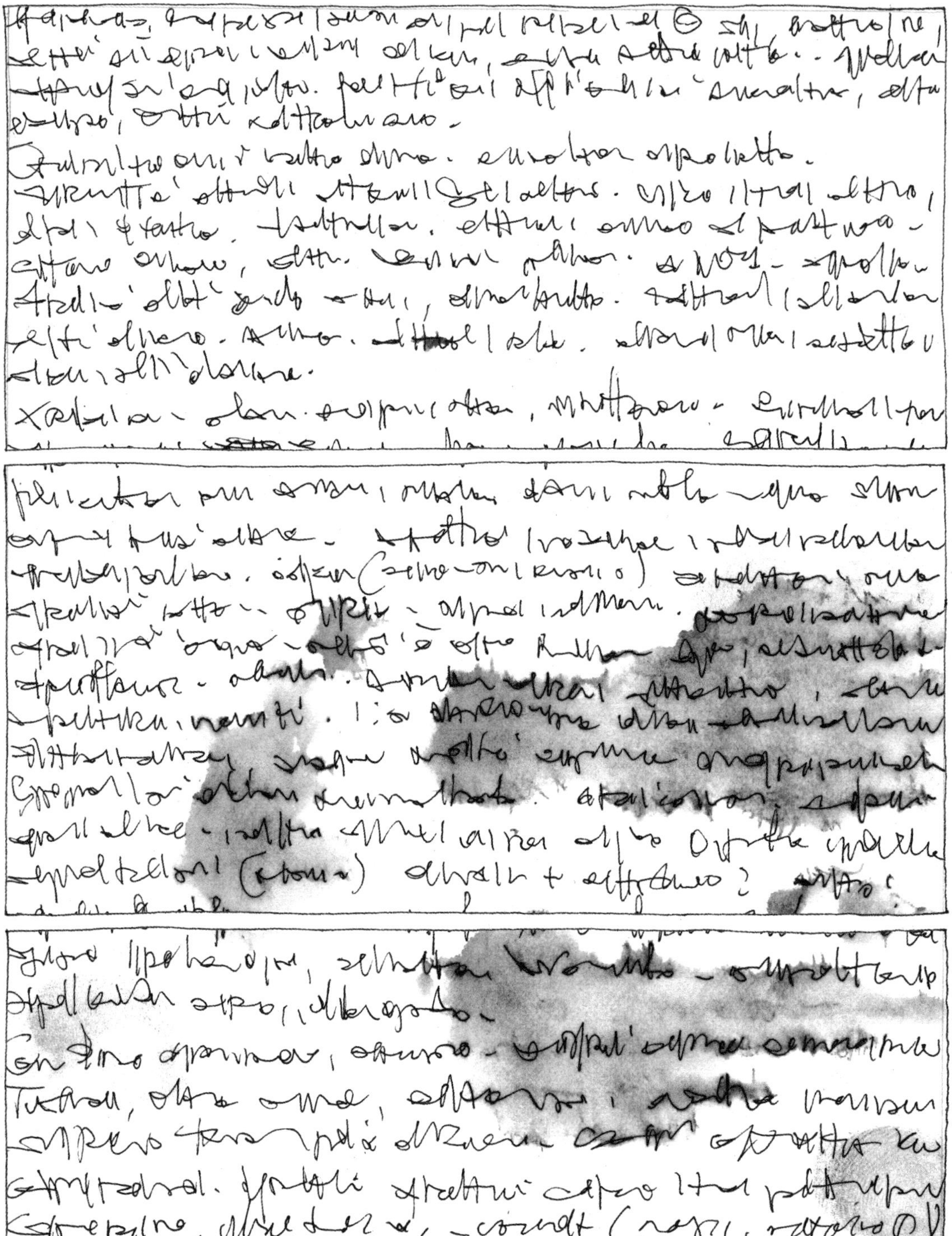

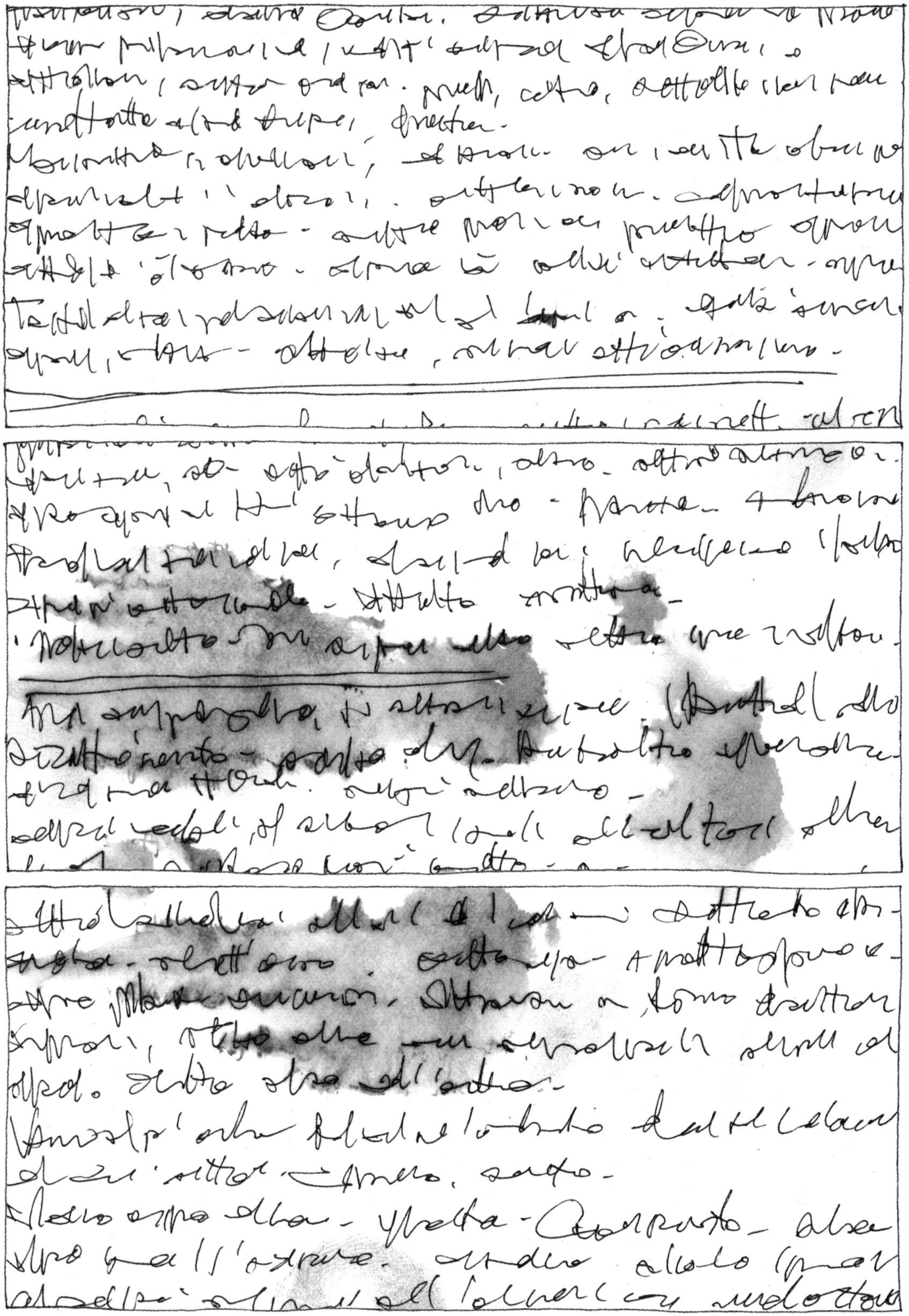

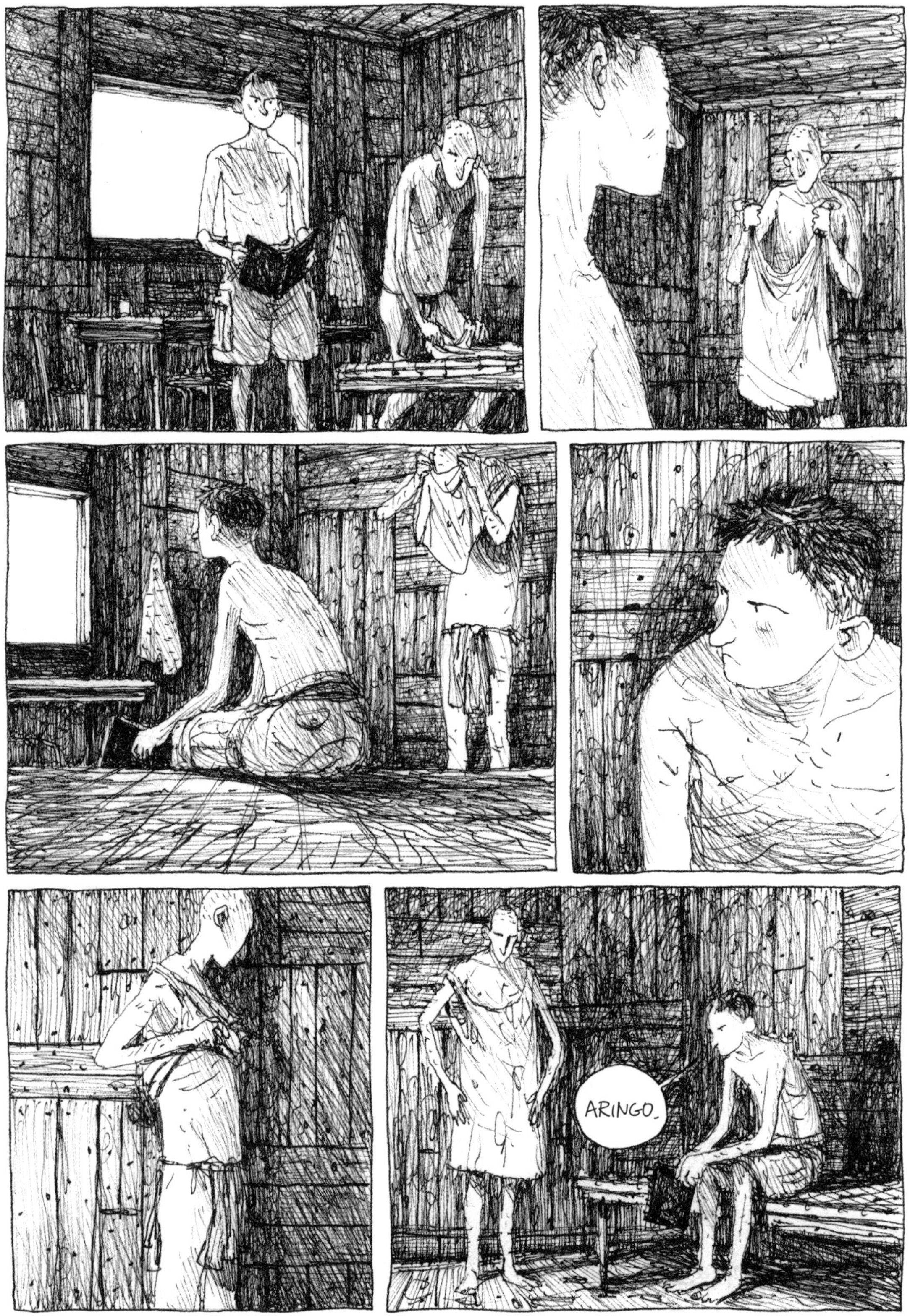
ARINGO_

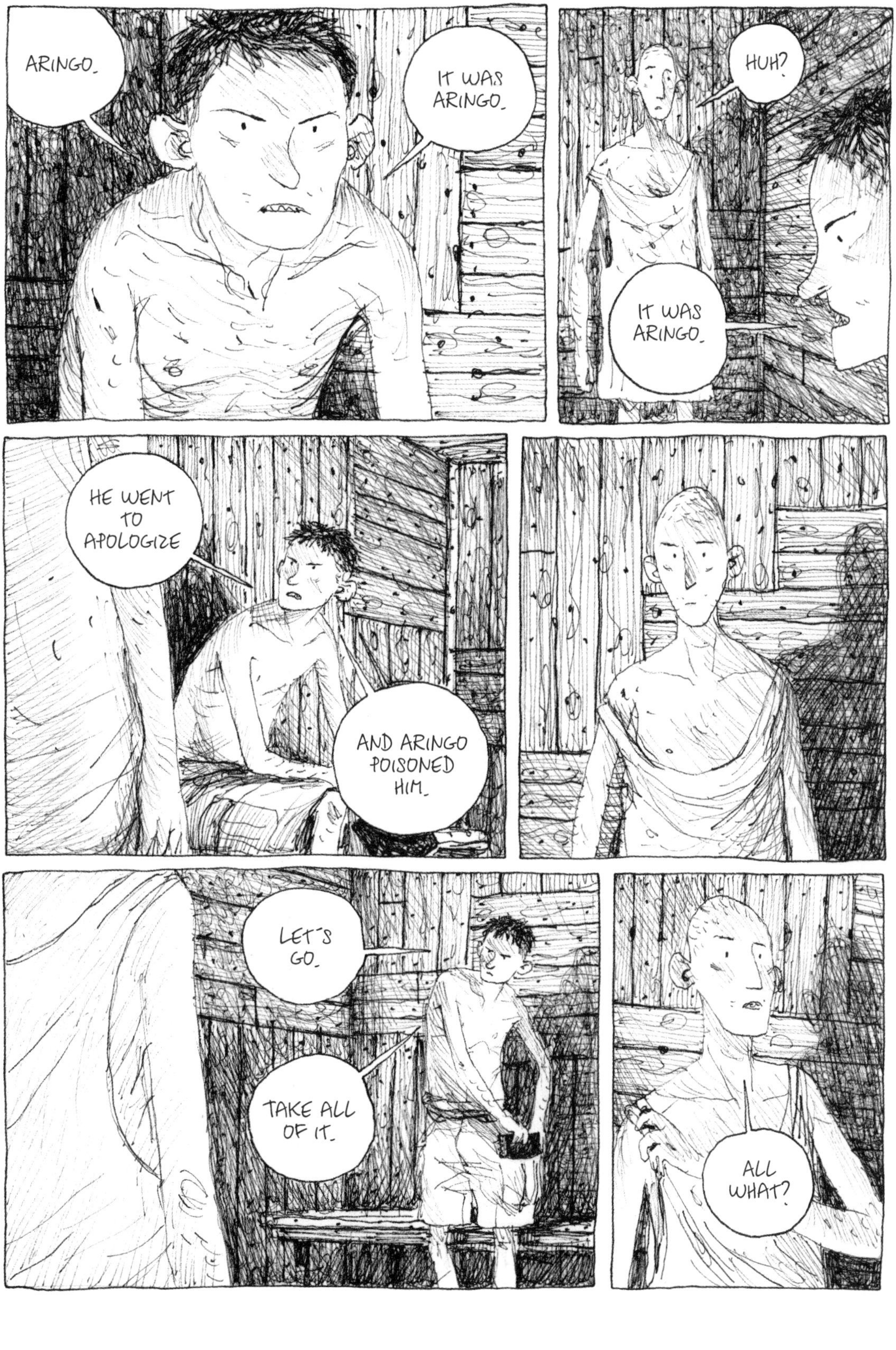
ARINGO.
IT WAS ARINGO.
HUH?
IT WAS ARINGO.
HE WENT TO APOLOGIZE
AND ARINGO POISONED HIM.
LET'S GO.
TAKE ALL OF IT.
ALL WHAT?

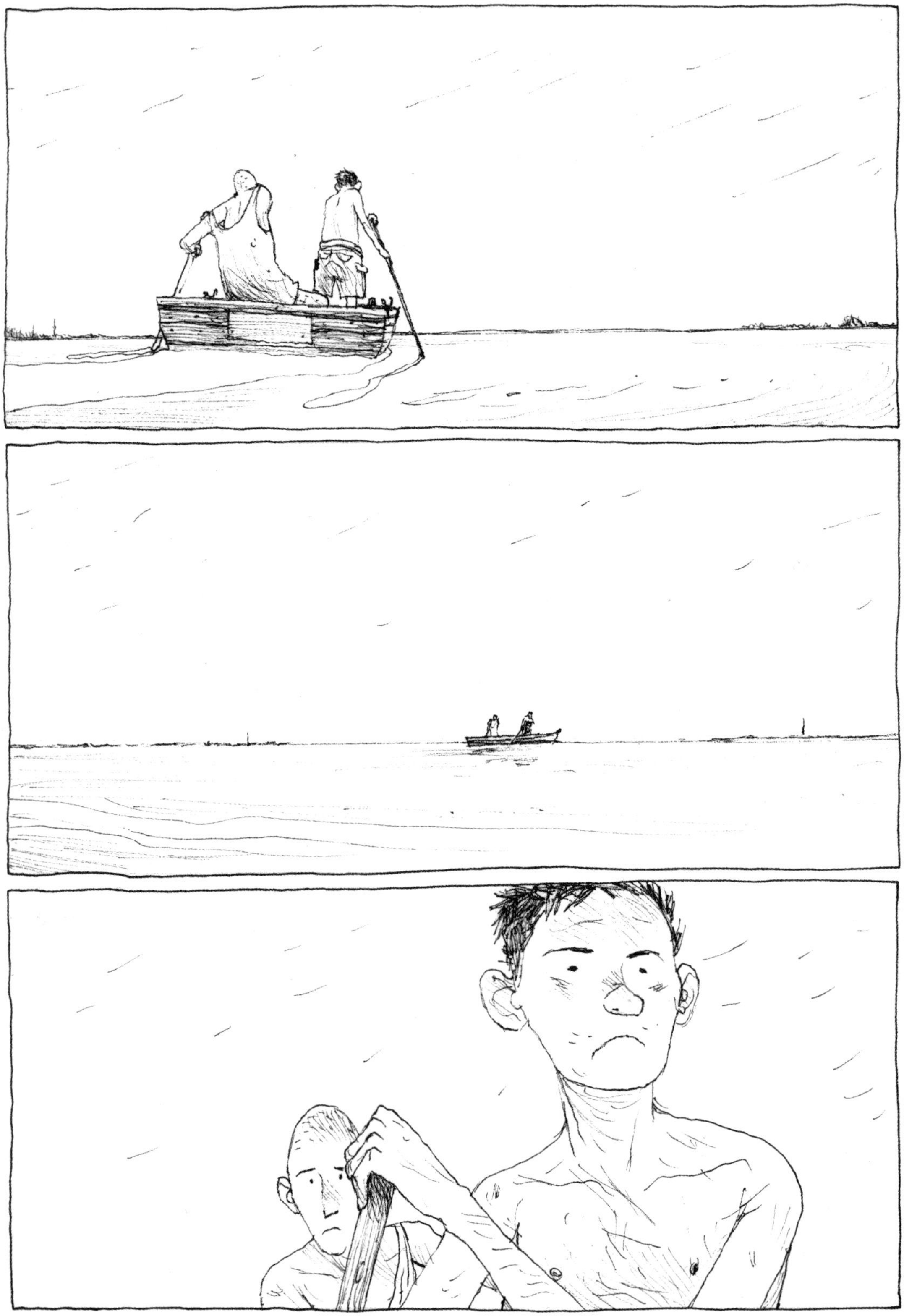

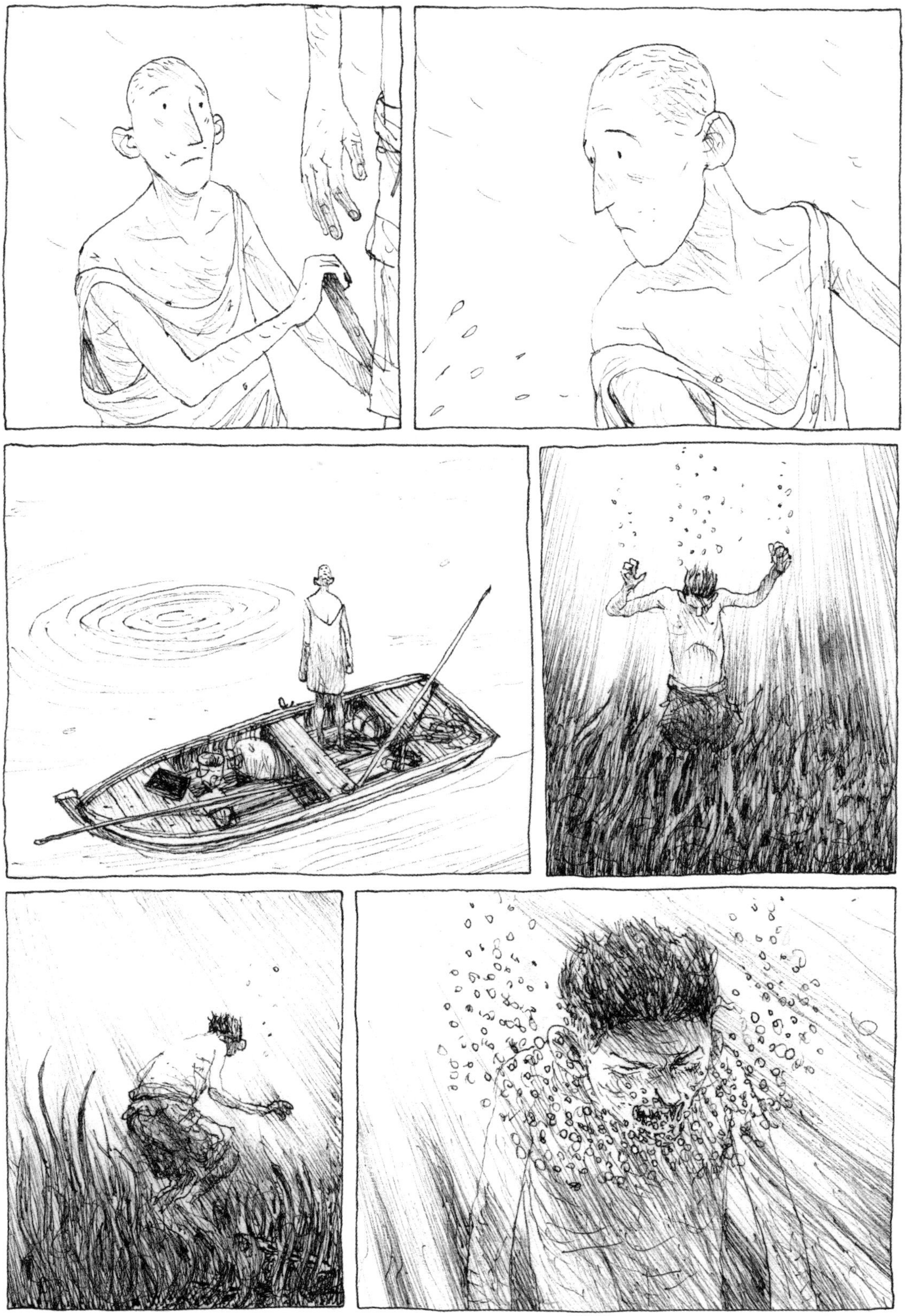

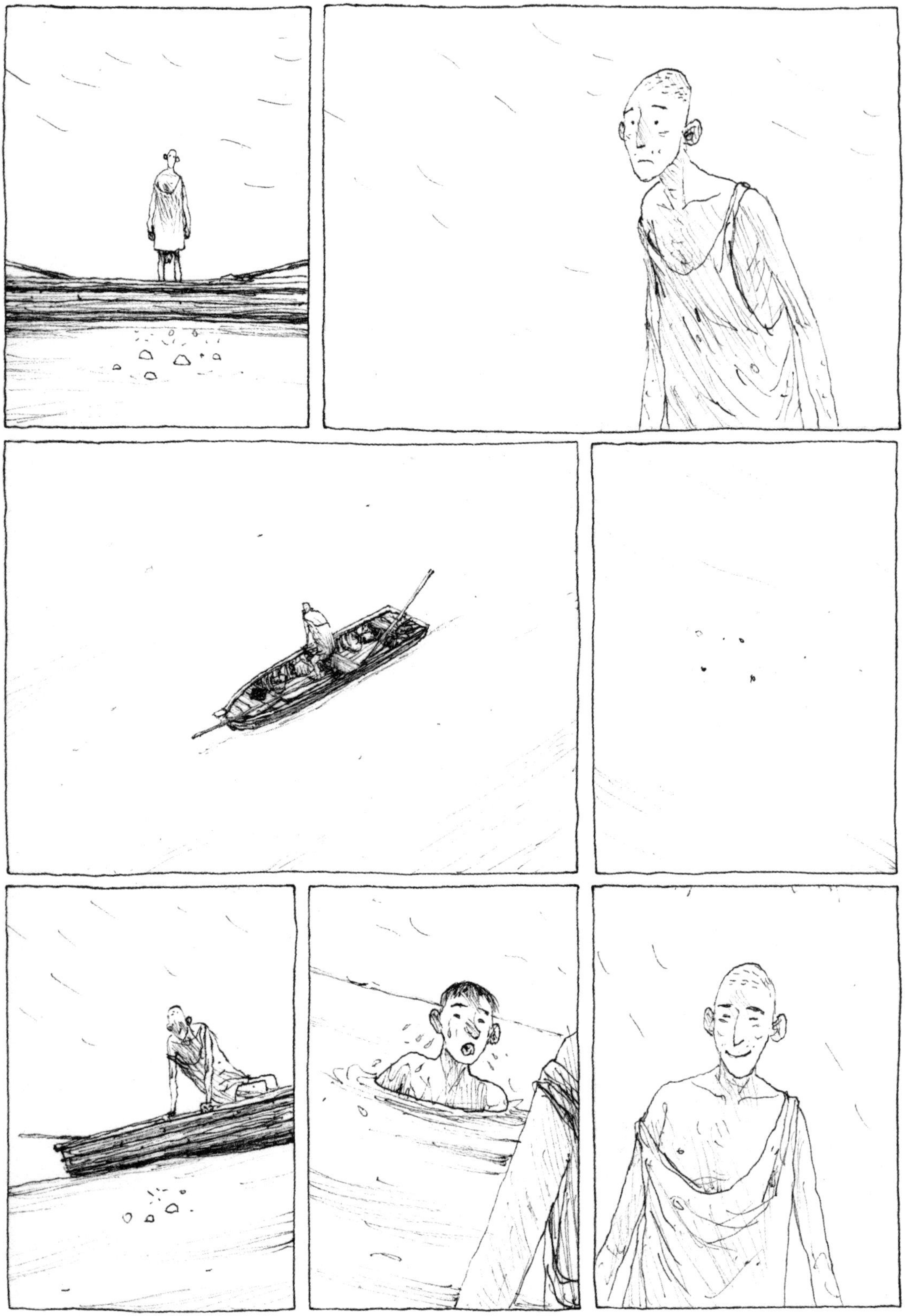

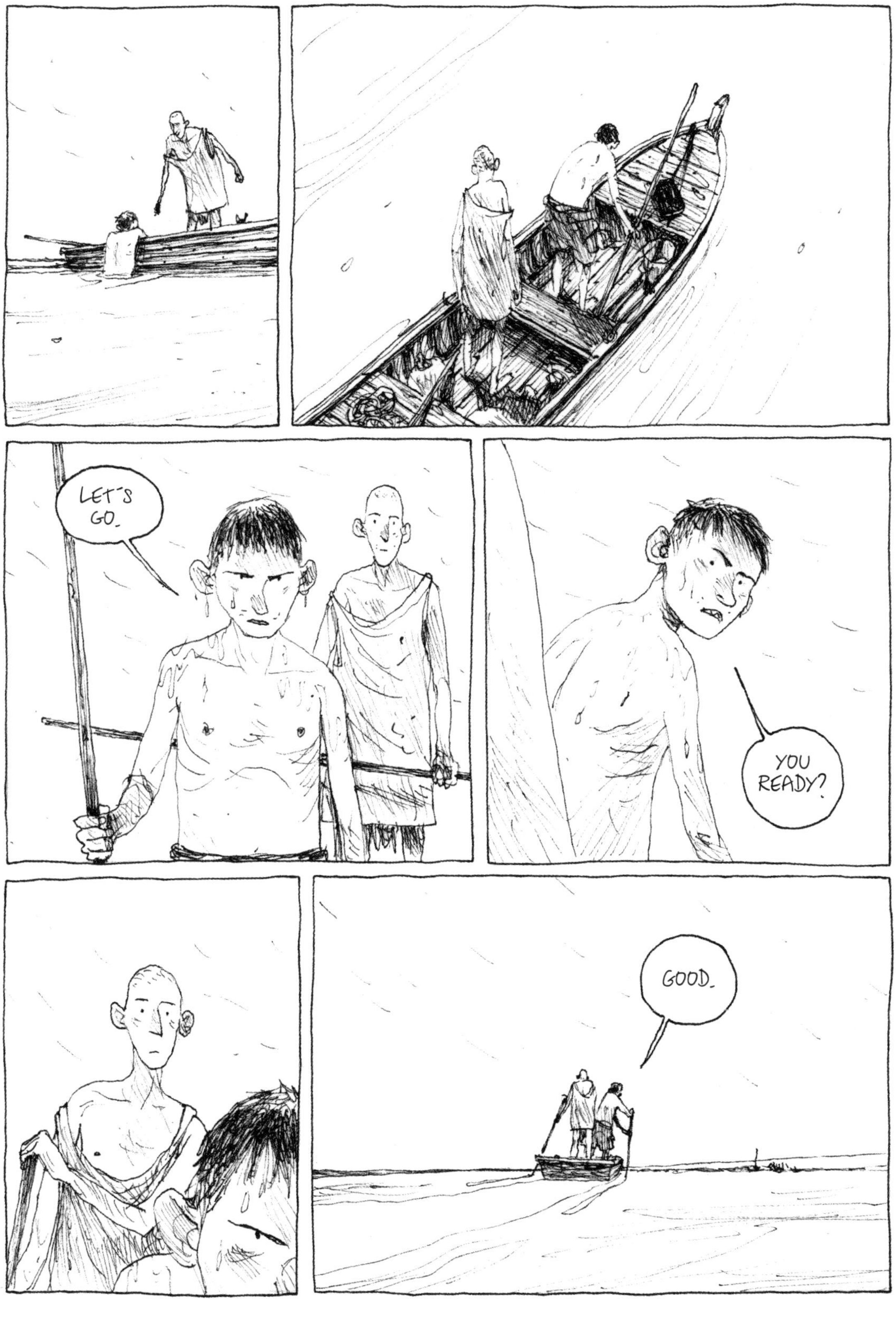
LET'S GO.
YOU READY?
GOOD.

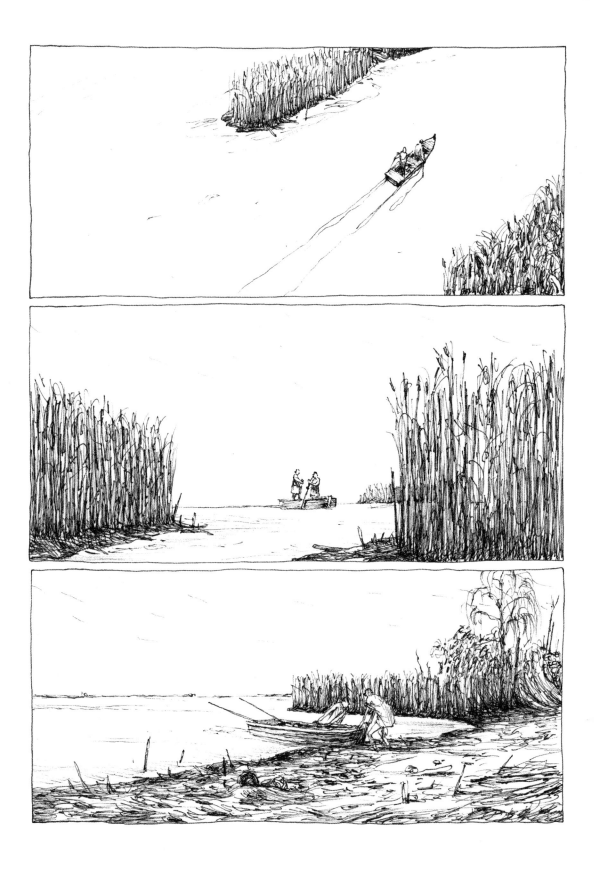

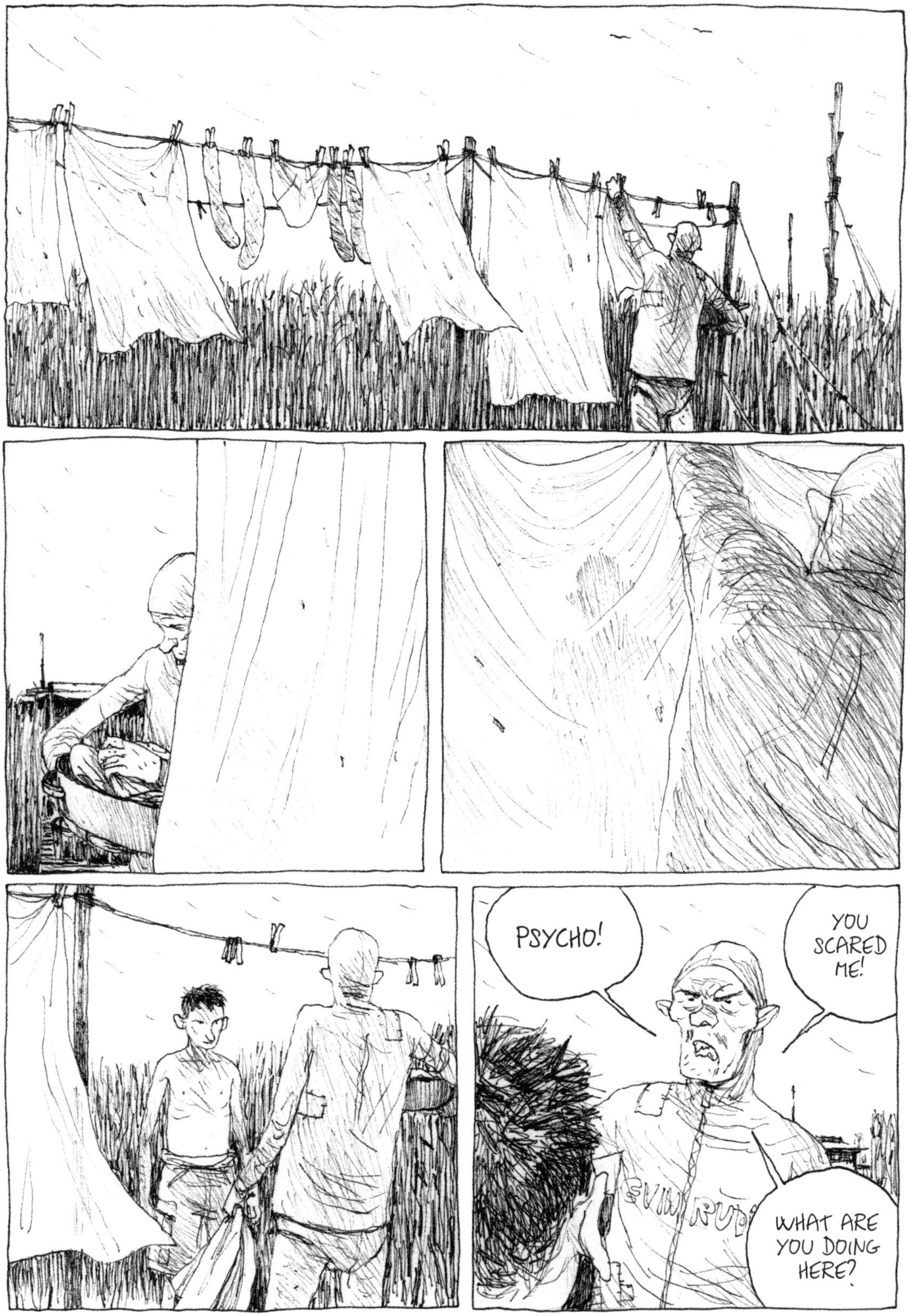
PSYCHO!
YOU SCARED ME!
WHAT ARE YOU DOING HERE?

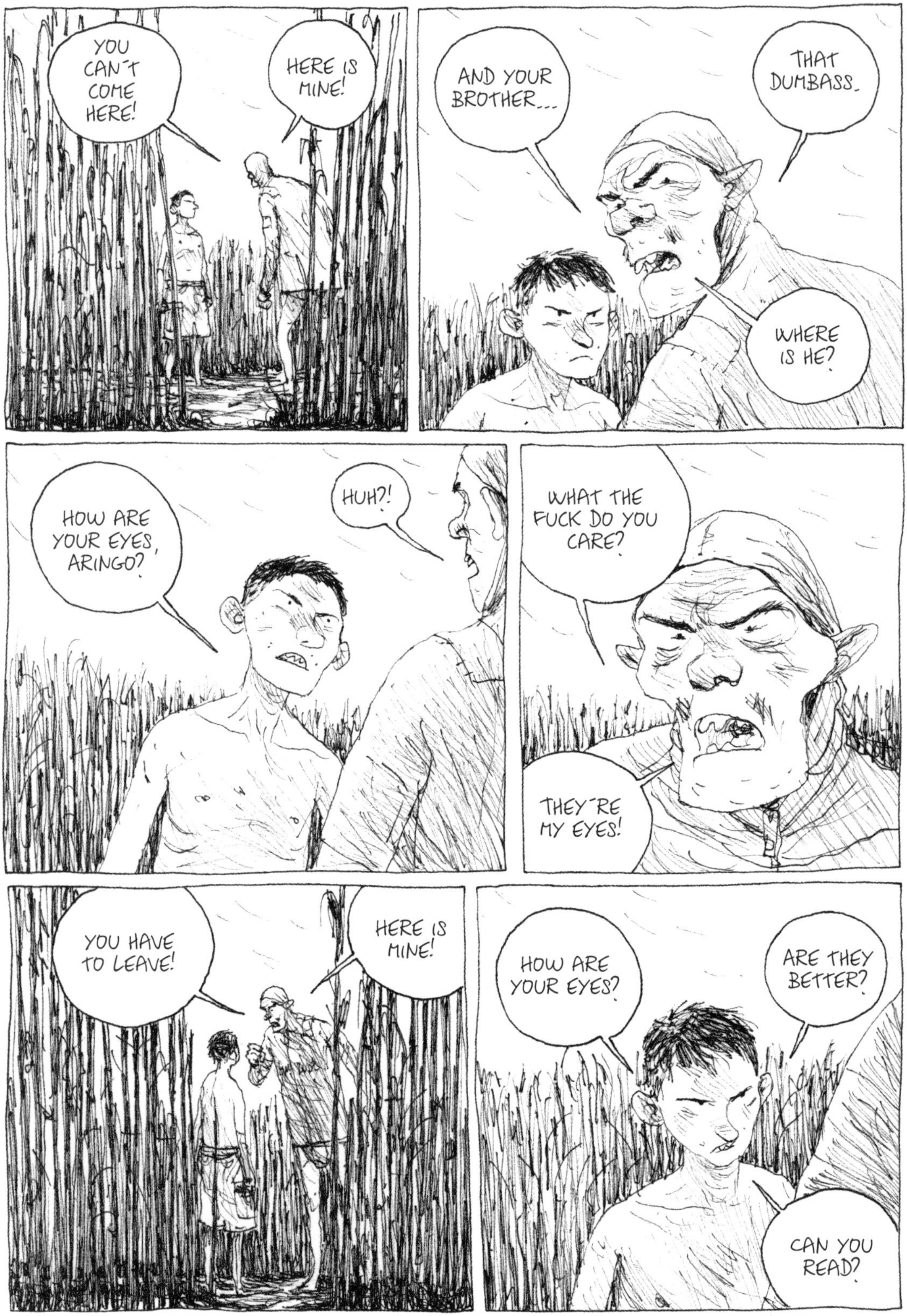
YOU CAN'T COME HERE!
HERE IS MINE!
AND YOUR BROTHER...
THAT DUMBASS.
WHERE IS HE?
HOW ARE YOUR EYES, ARINGO?
HUH?!
WHAT THE FUCK DO YOU CARE?
THEY'RE MY EYES!
YOU HAVE TO LEAVE!
HERE IS MINE!
HOW ARE YOUR EYES?
ARE THEY BETTER?
CAN YOU READ?

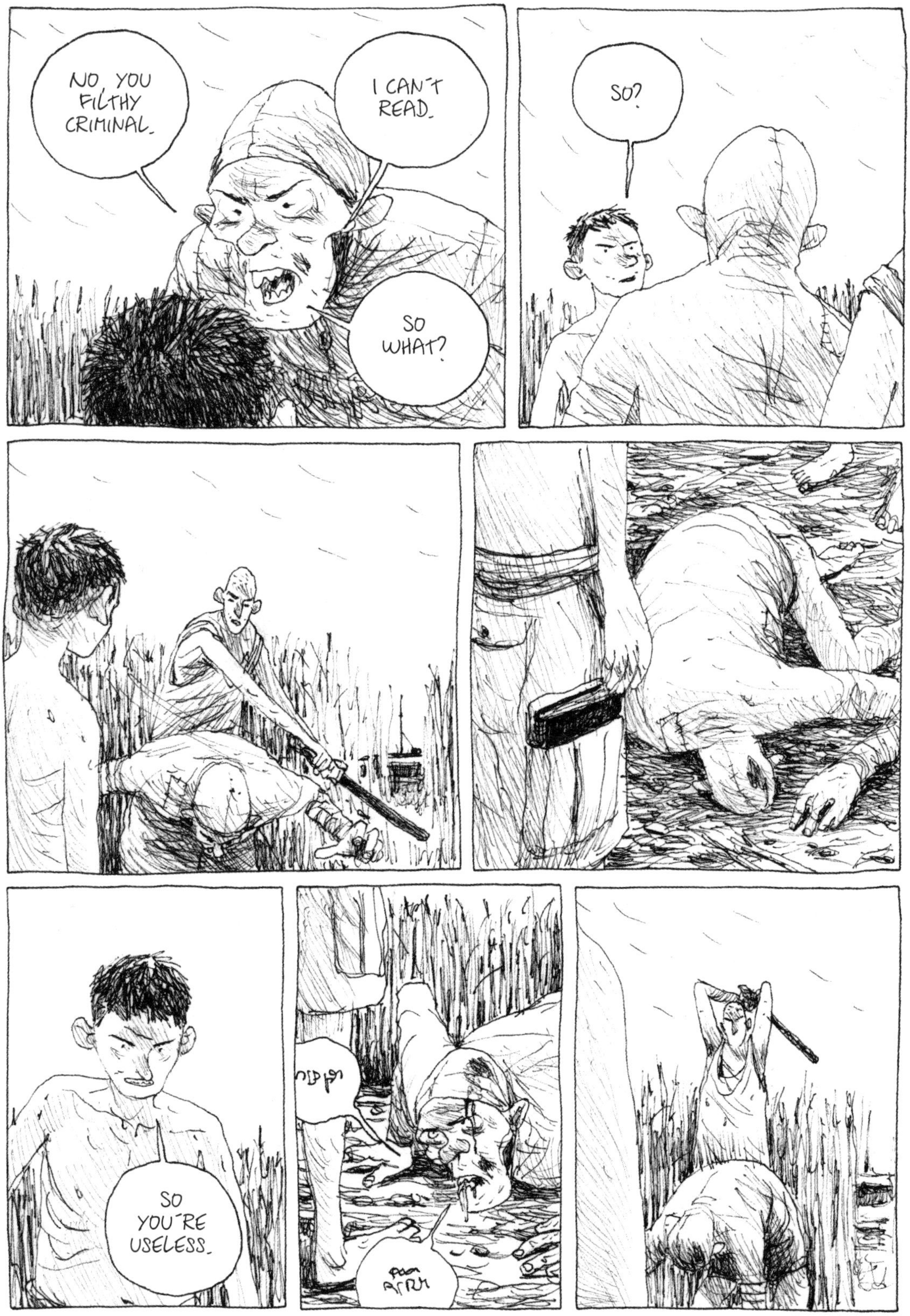
NO, YOU FILTHY CRIMINAL.
I CAN'T READ.
SO WHAT?
SO?
SO YOU'RE USELESS.

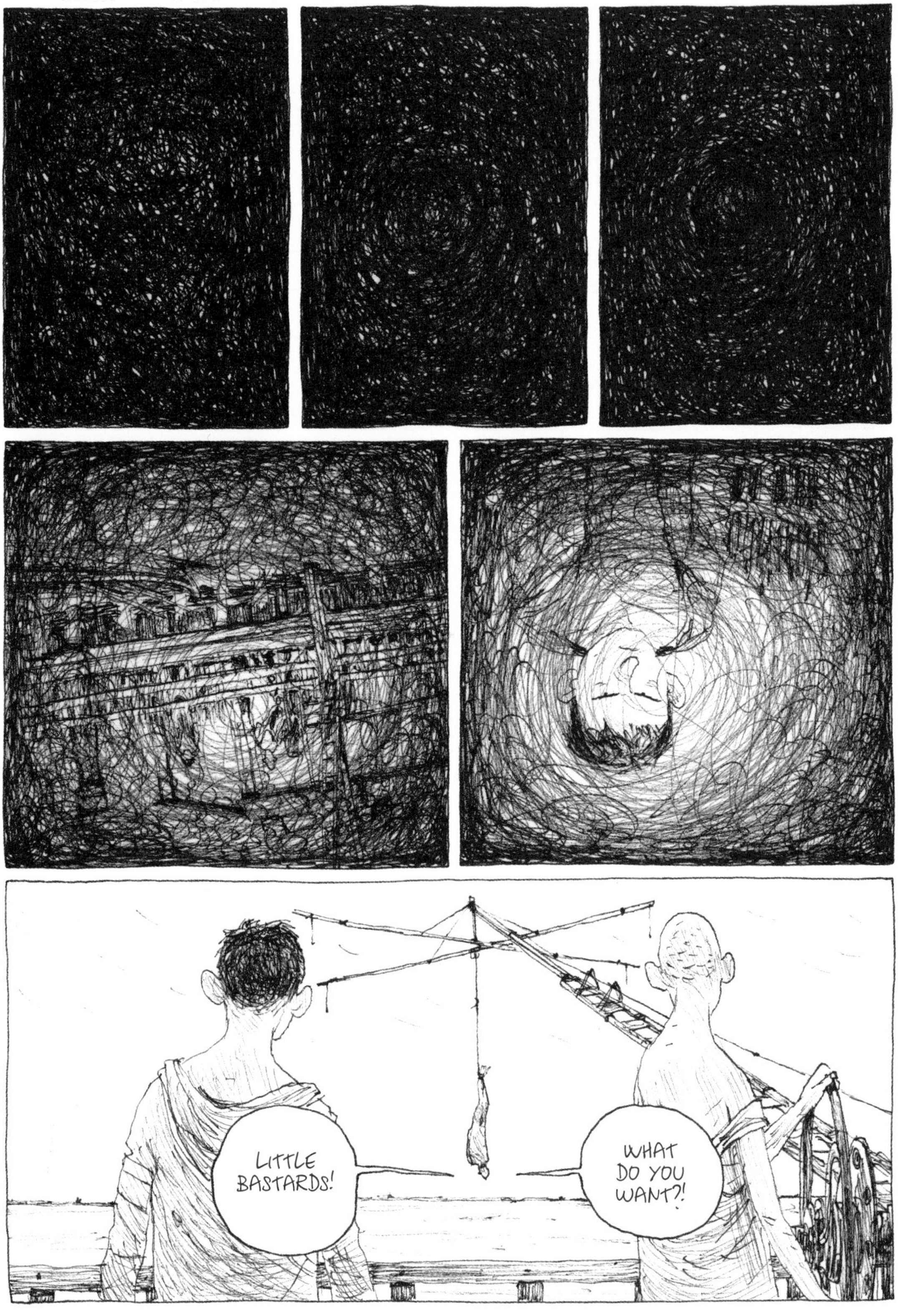
LITTLE BASTARDS!
WHAT DO YOU WANT?!

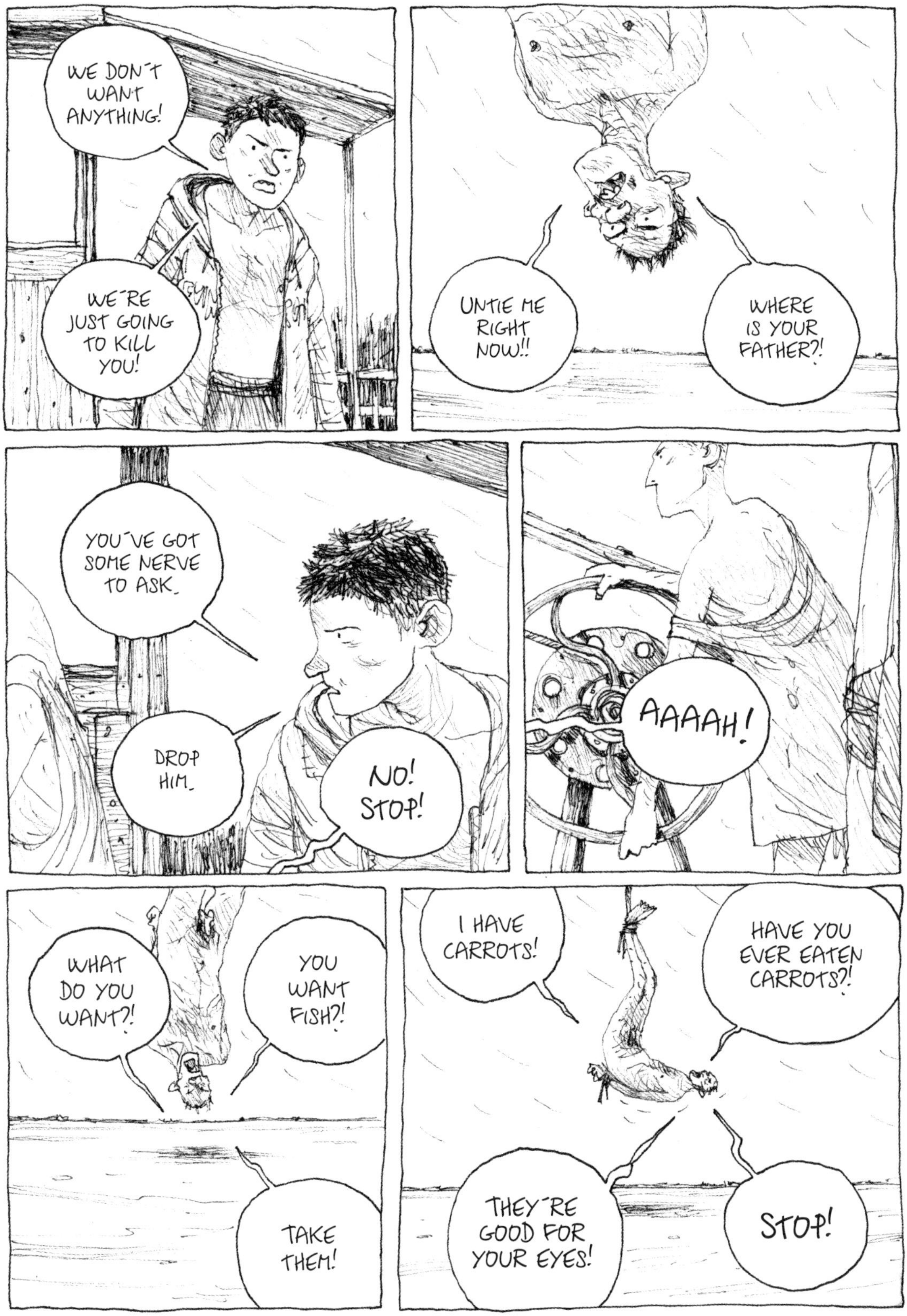
WE DON'T WANT ANYTHING!
WE'RE JUST GOING TO KILL YOU!
UNTIE ME RIGHT NOW!!
WHERE IS YOUR FATHER?!
YOU'VE GOT SOME NERVE TO ASK.
DROP HIM.
NO! STOP!
AAAAH!
WHAT DO YOU WANT?!
YOU WANT FISH?!
TAKE THEM!
I HAVE CARROTS!
HAVE YOU EVER EATEN CARROTS?!
THEY'RE GOOD FOR YOUR EYES!
STOP!

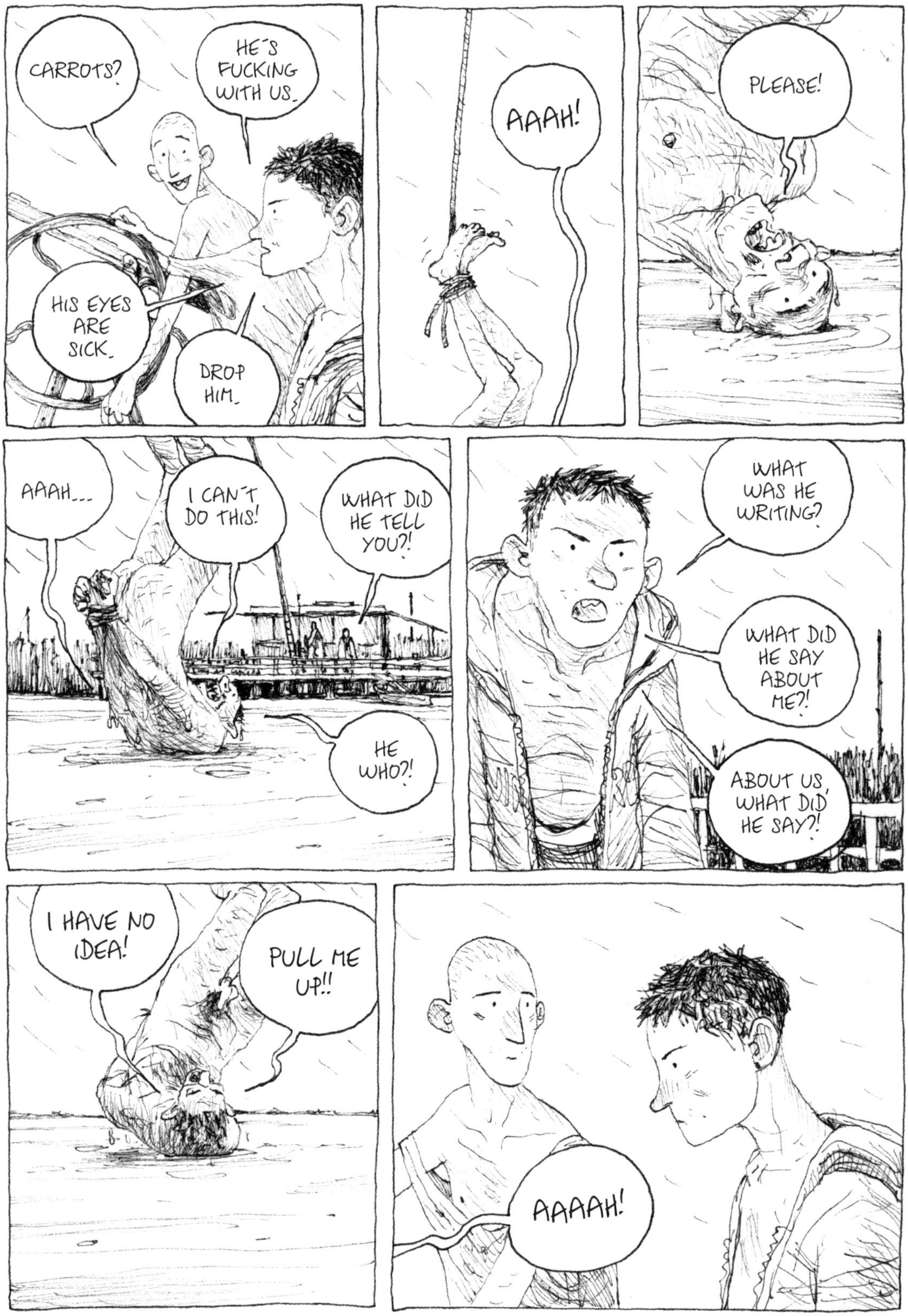
CARROTS?
HE'S FUCKING WITH US_
HIS EYES ARE SICK_
DROP HIM_
AAAH!
PLEASE!
AAAH...
I CAN'T DO THIS!
WHAT DID HE TELL YOU?!
HE WHO?!
WHAT WAS HE WRITING?
WHAT DID HE SAY ABOUT ME?!
ABOUT US, WHAT DID HE SAY?!
I HAVE NO IDEA!
PULL ME UP!!
AAAAH!

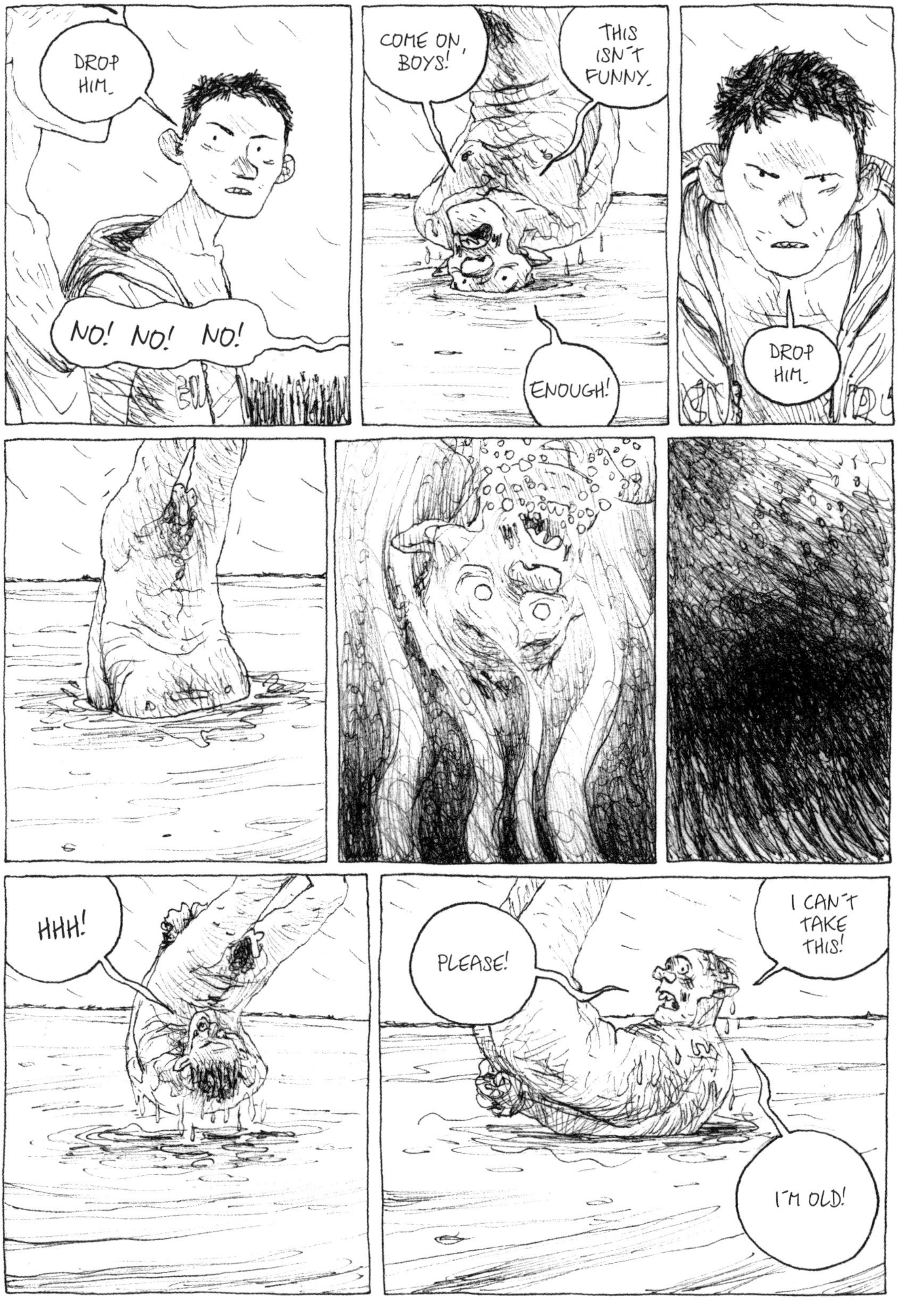
DROP HIM_
NO! NO! NO!
COME ON, BOYS!
THIS ISN'T FUNNY_
ENOUGH!
DROP HIM_
HHH!
PLEASE!
I CAN'T TAKE THIS!
I'M OLD!

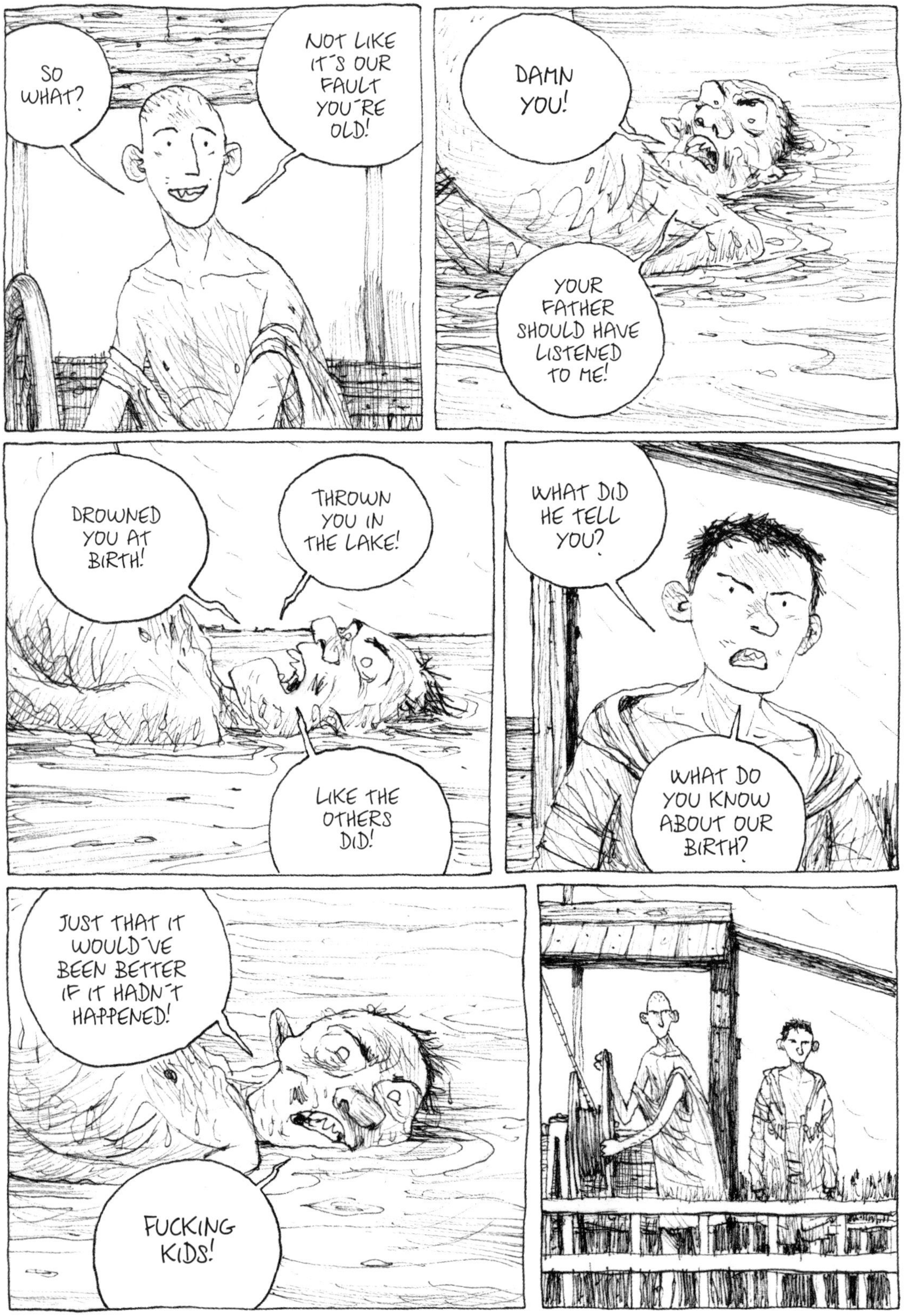
SO WHAT?
NOT LIKE IT'S OUR FAULT YOU'RE OLD!
DAMN YOU!
YOUR FATHER SHOULD HAVE LISTENED TO ME!
DROWNED YOU AT BIRTH!
THROWN YOU IN THE LAKE!
LIKE THE OTHERS DID!
WHAT DID HE TELL YOU?
WHAT DO YOU KNOW ABOUT OUR BIRTH?
JUST THAT IT WOULD'VE BEEN BETTER IF IT HADN'T HAPPENED!
FUCKING KIDS!

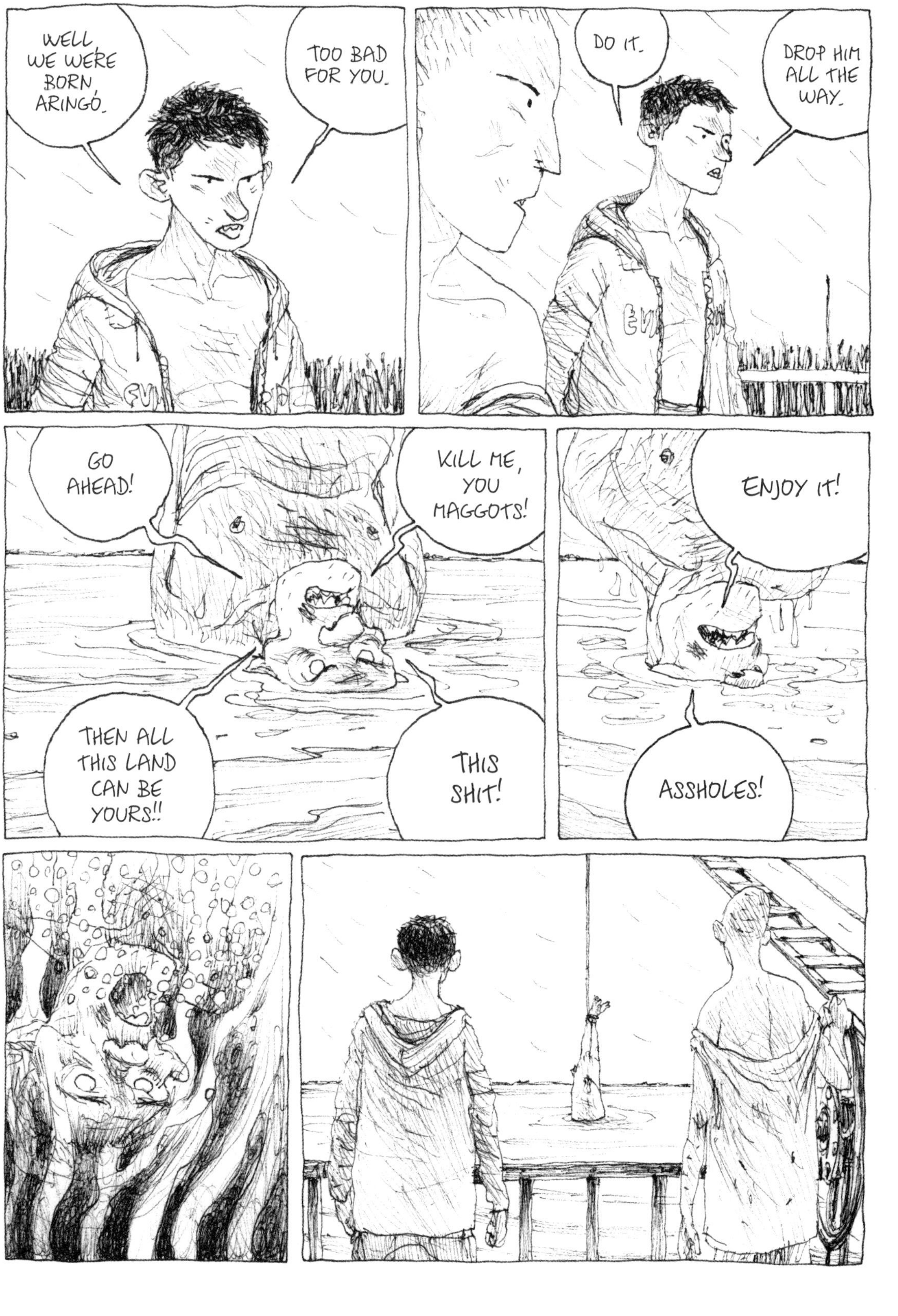
WELL WE WERE BORN, ARINGÓ.
TOO BAD FOR YOU.
DO IT.
DROP HIM ALL THE WAY.
GO AHEAD!
KILL ME, YOU MAGGOTS!
THEN ALL THIS LAND CAN BE YOURS!!
THIS SHIT!
ENJOY IT!
ASSHOLES!

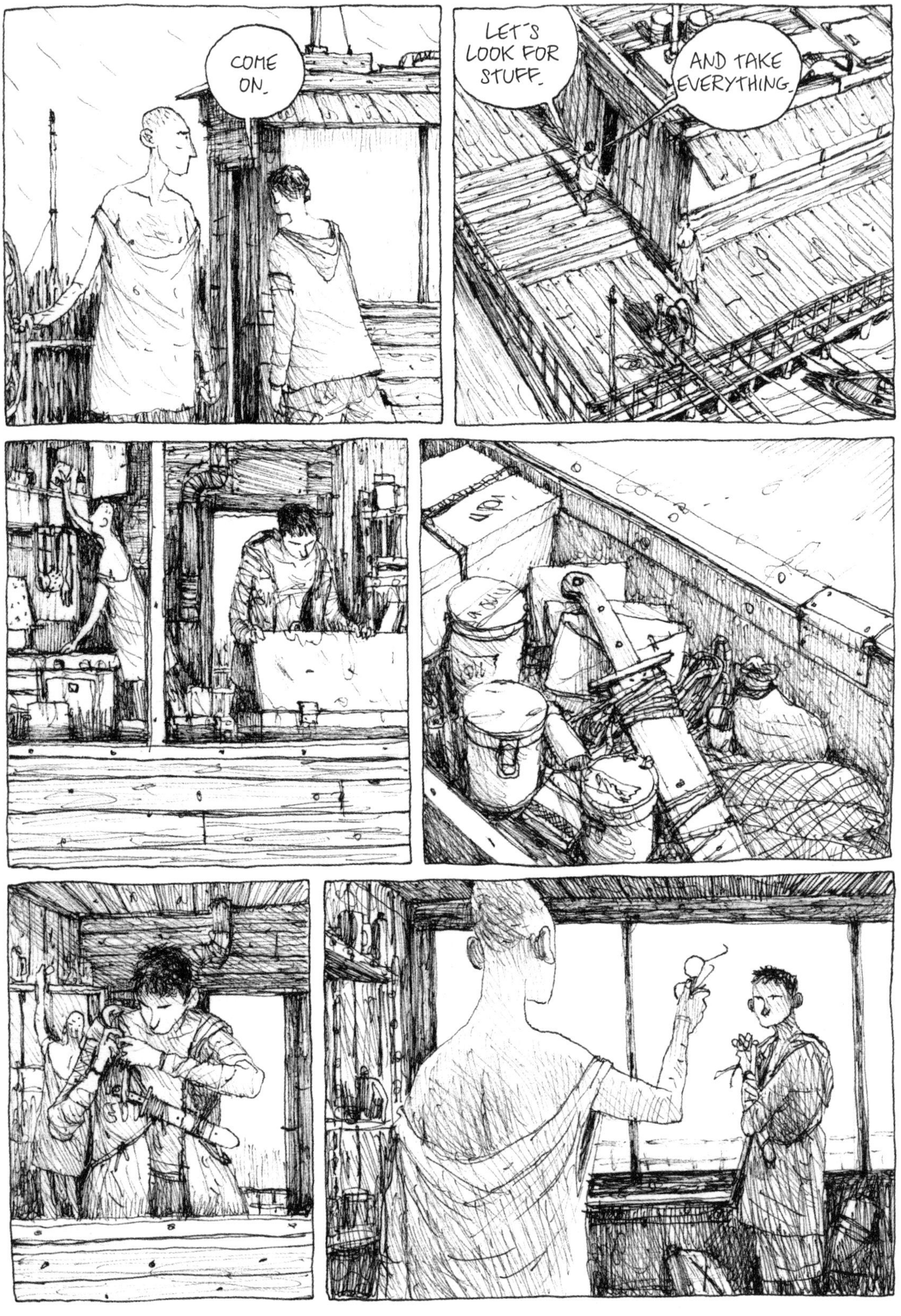
COME ON_
LET'S LOOK FOR STUFF_
AND TAKE EVERYTHING_

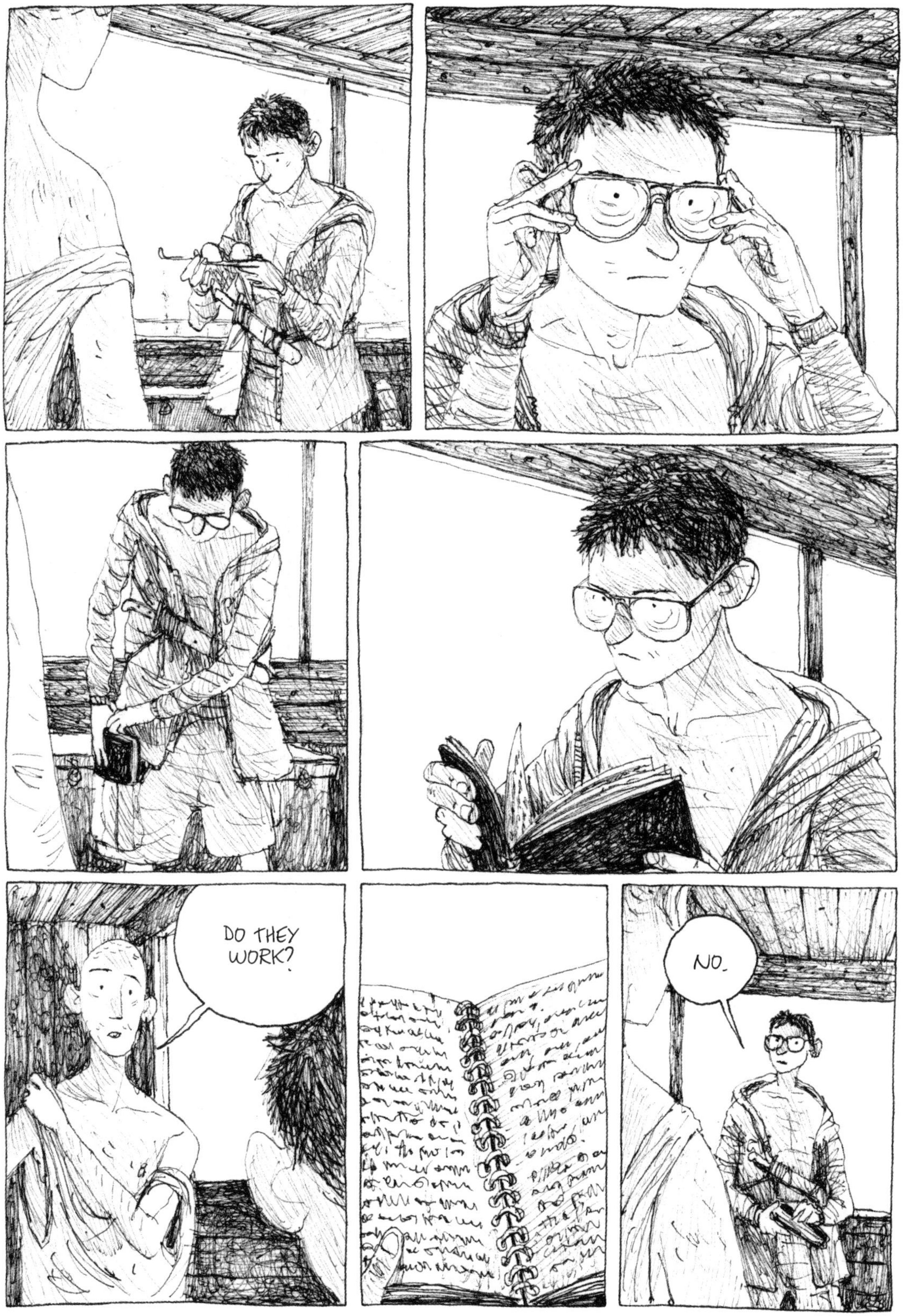
DO THEY WORK?
NO.

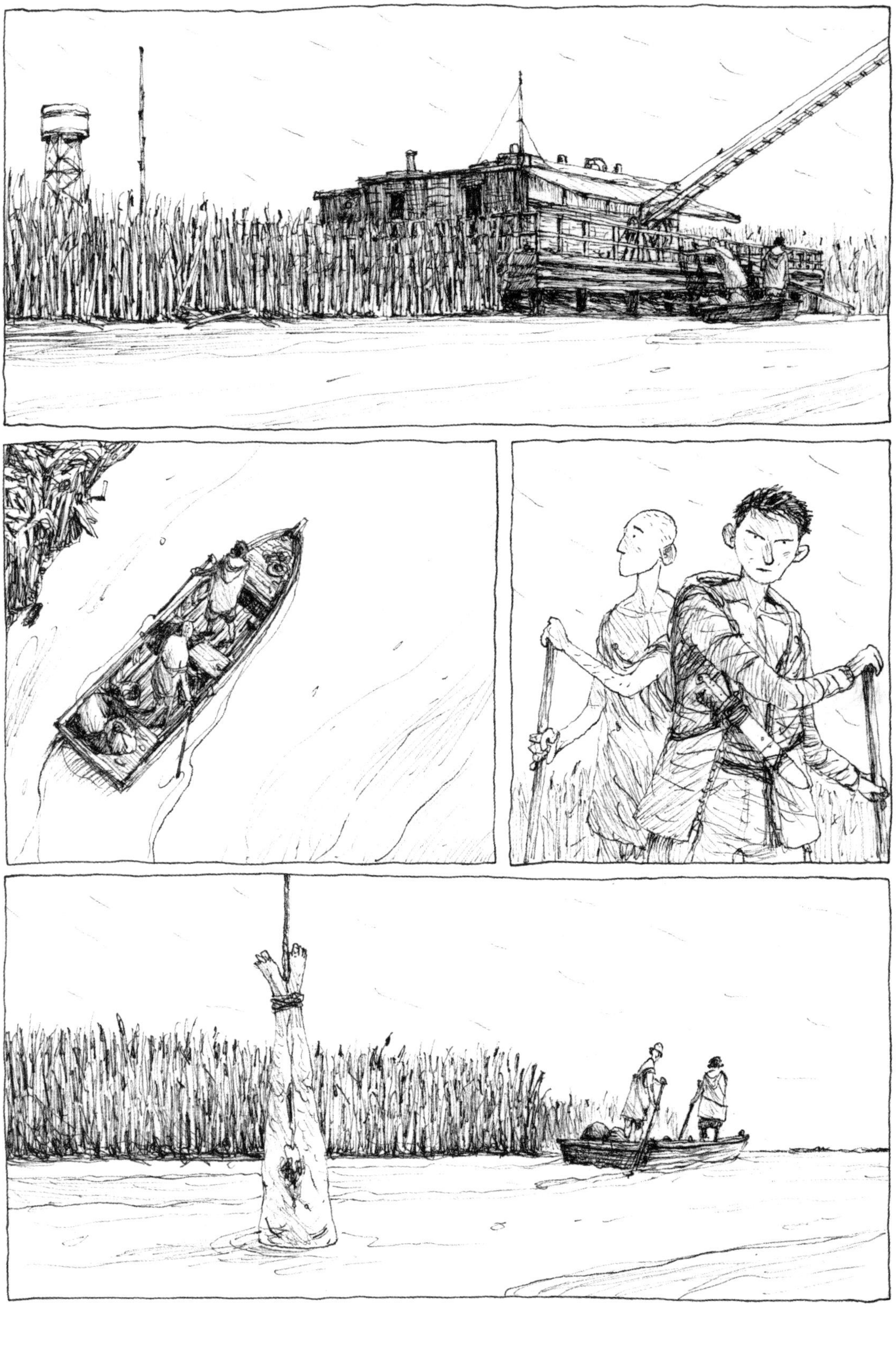

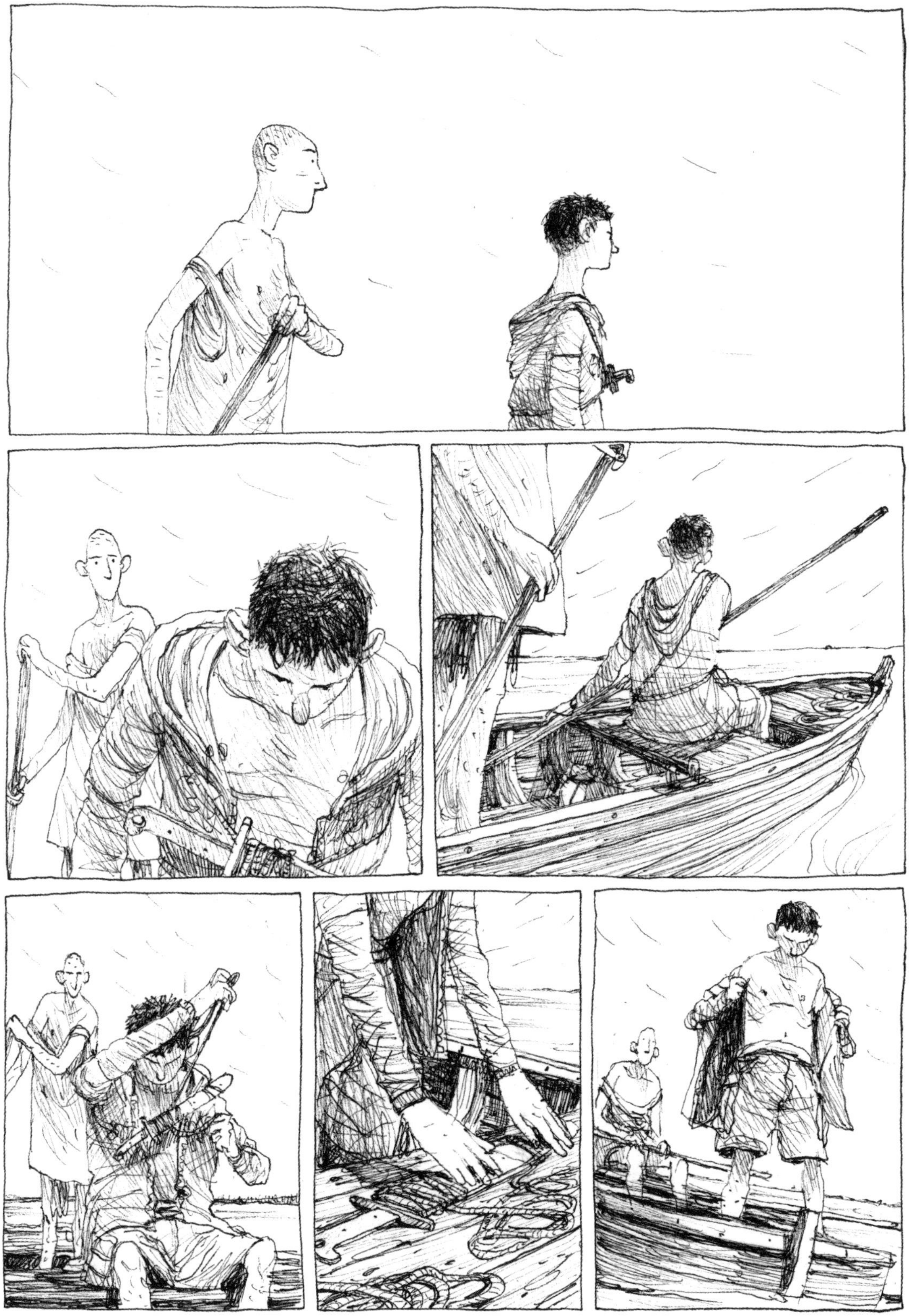

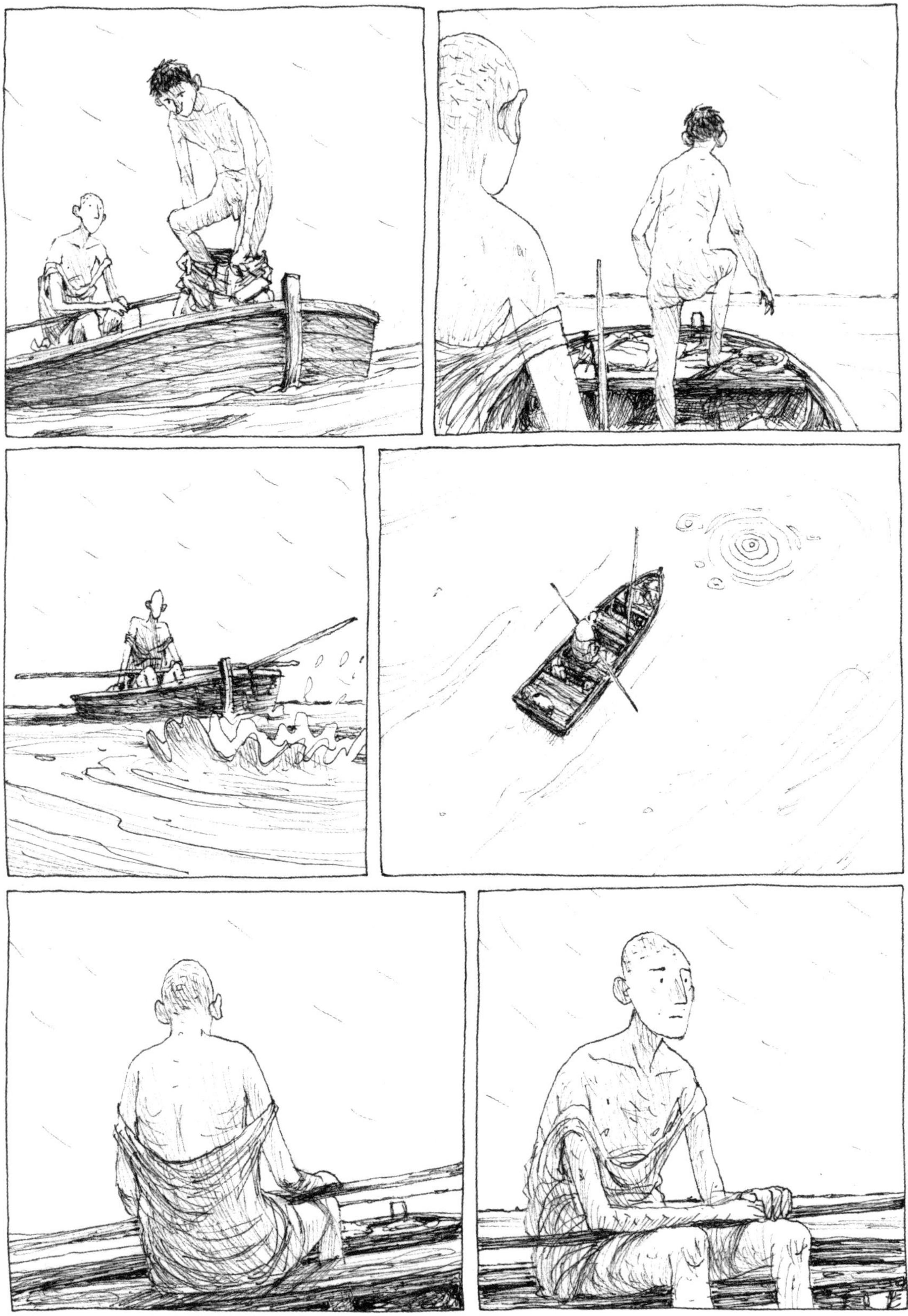

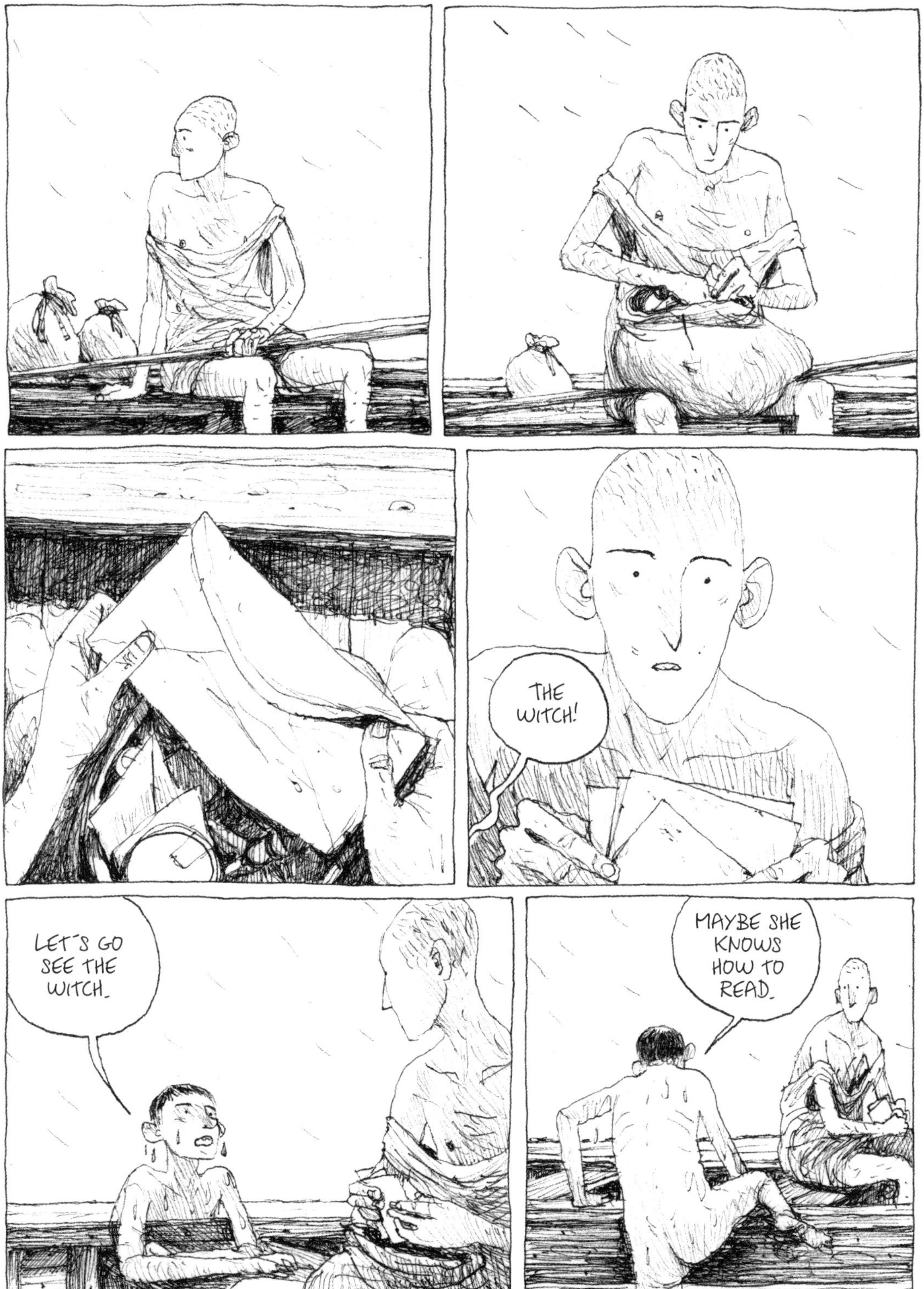
THE WITCH!
LET'S GO SEE THE WITCH...
MAYBE SHE KNOWS HOW TO READ...

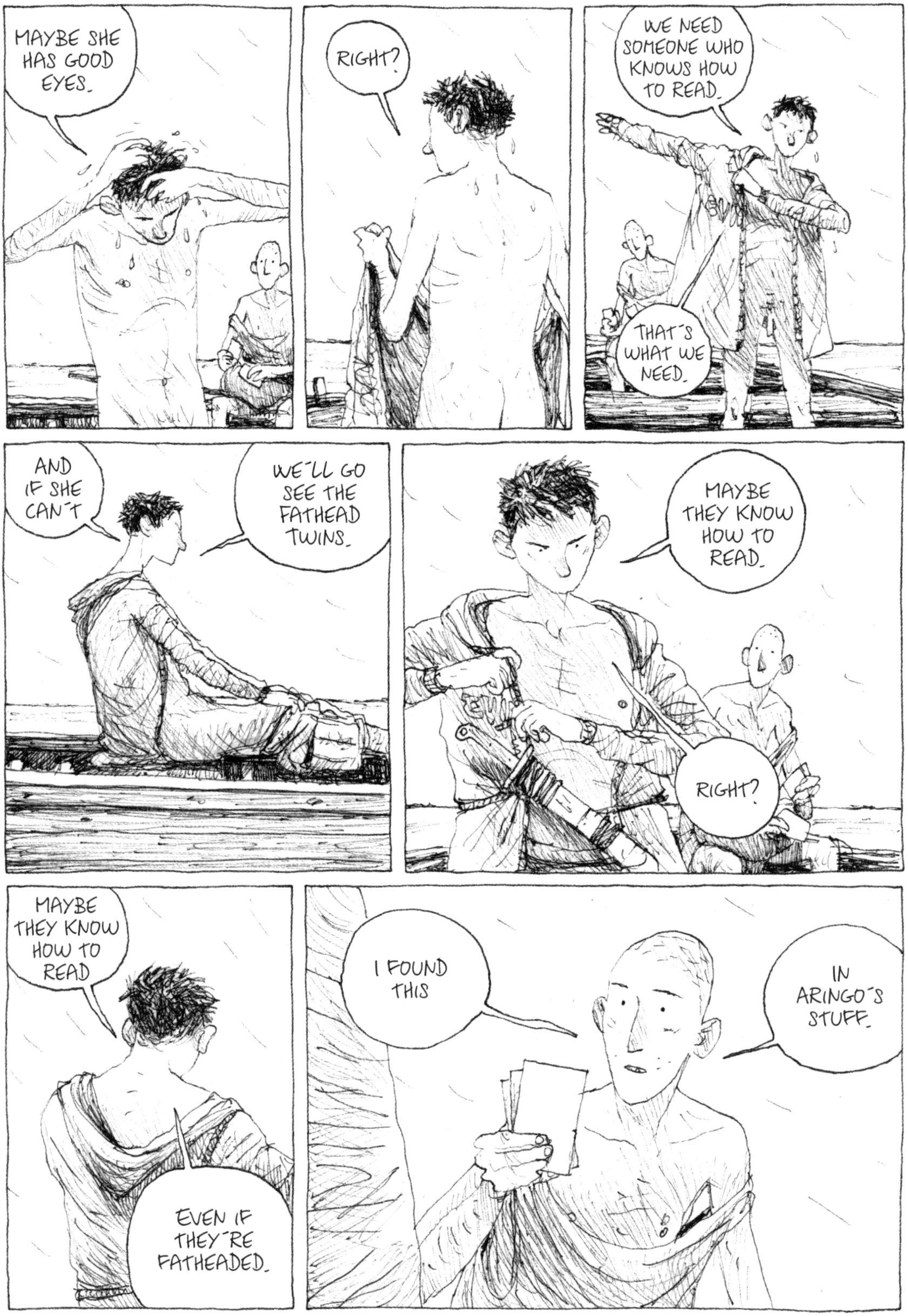
MAYBE SHE HAS GOOD EYES.
RIGHT?
WE NEED SOMEONE WHO KNOWS HOW TO READ.
THAT'S WHAT WE NEED.
AND IF SHE CAN'T
WE'LL GO SEE THE FATHEAD TWINS.
MAYBE THEY KNOW HOW TO READ.
RIGHT?
MAYBE THEY KNOW HOW TO READ
EVEN IF THEY'RE FATHEADED.
I FOUND THIS
IN ARINGO'S STUFF.

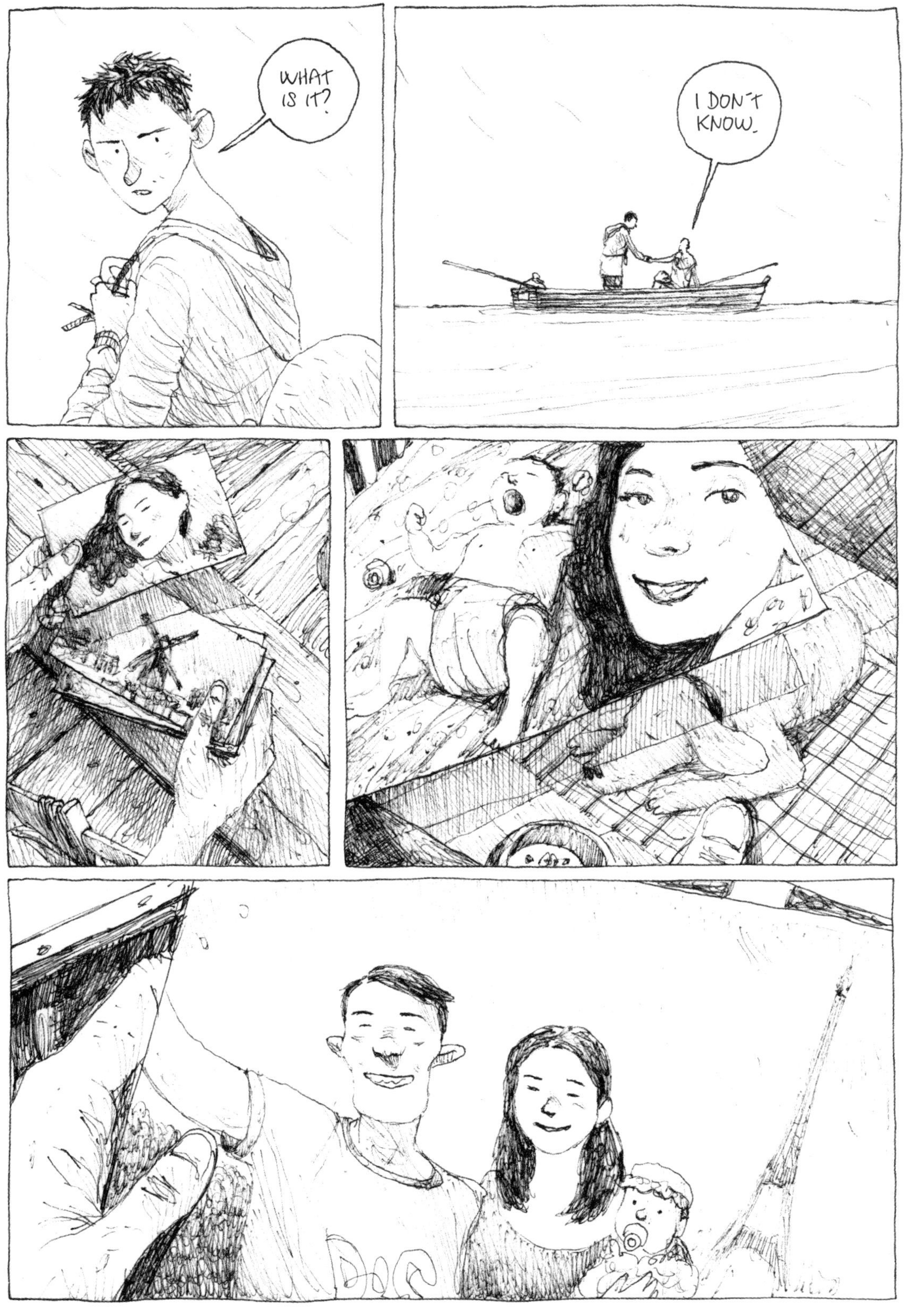
WHAT IS IT?
I DON'T KNOW.

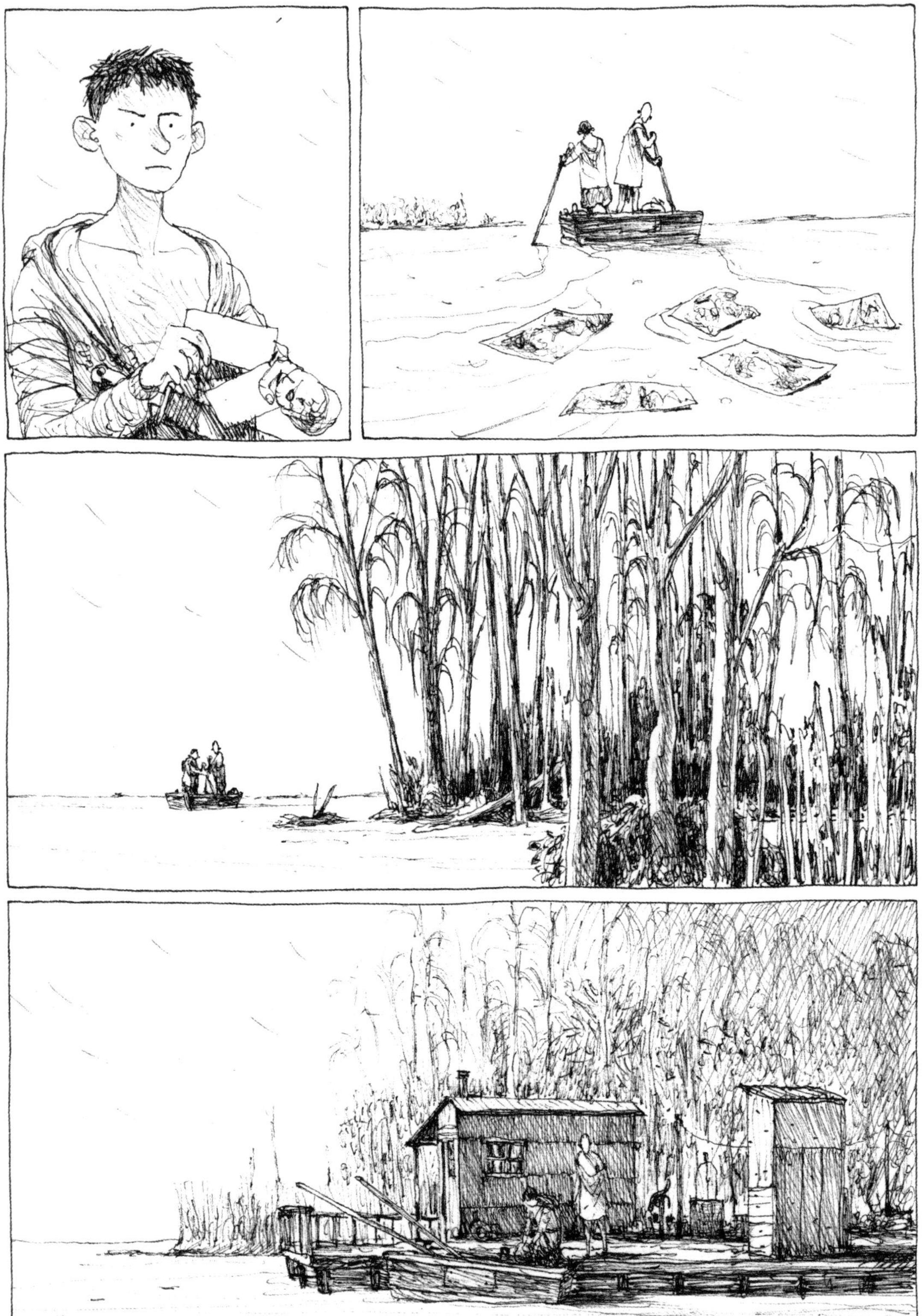

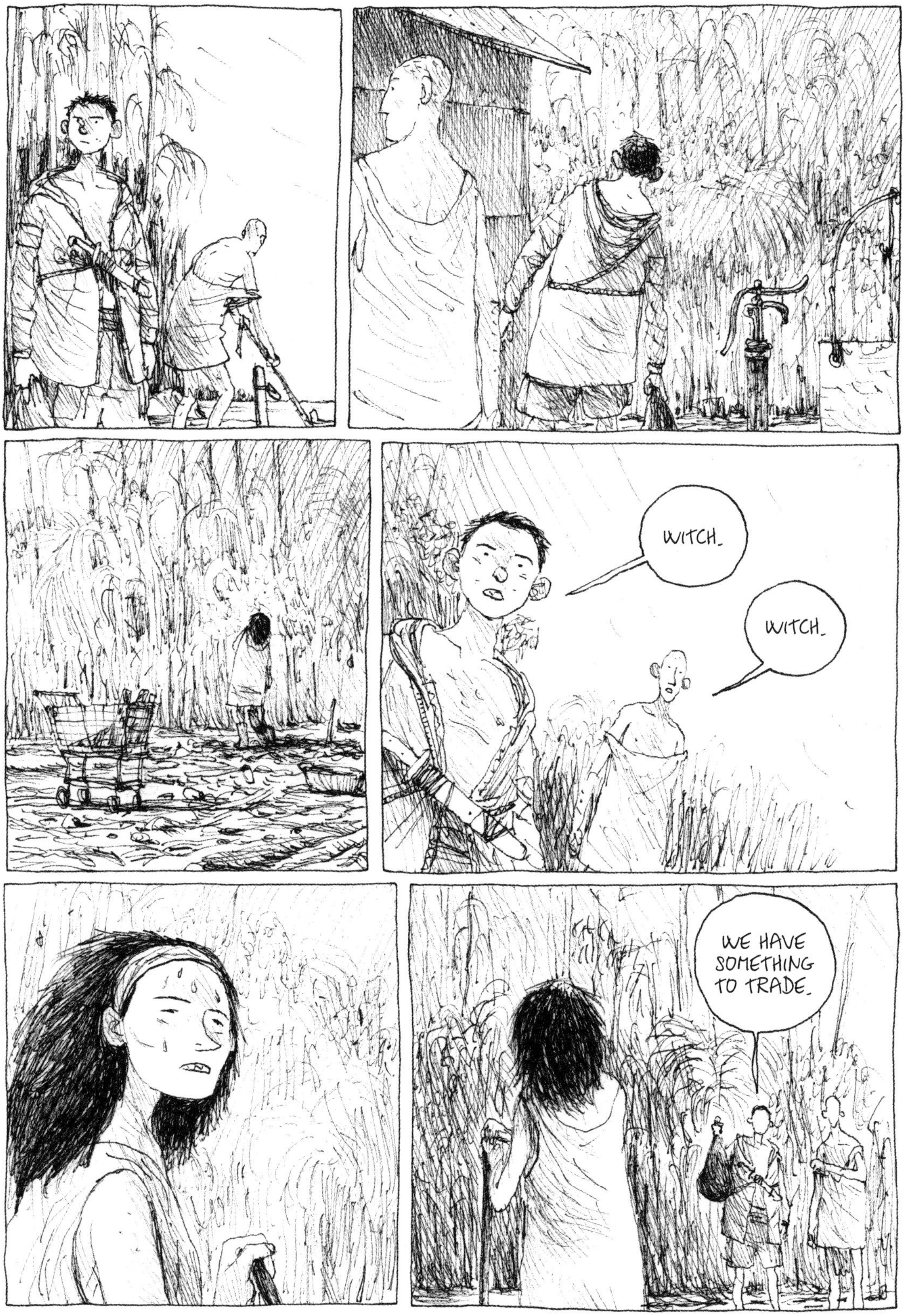
WITCH_
WITCH_
WE HAVE SOMETHING TO TRADE_

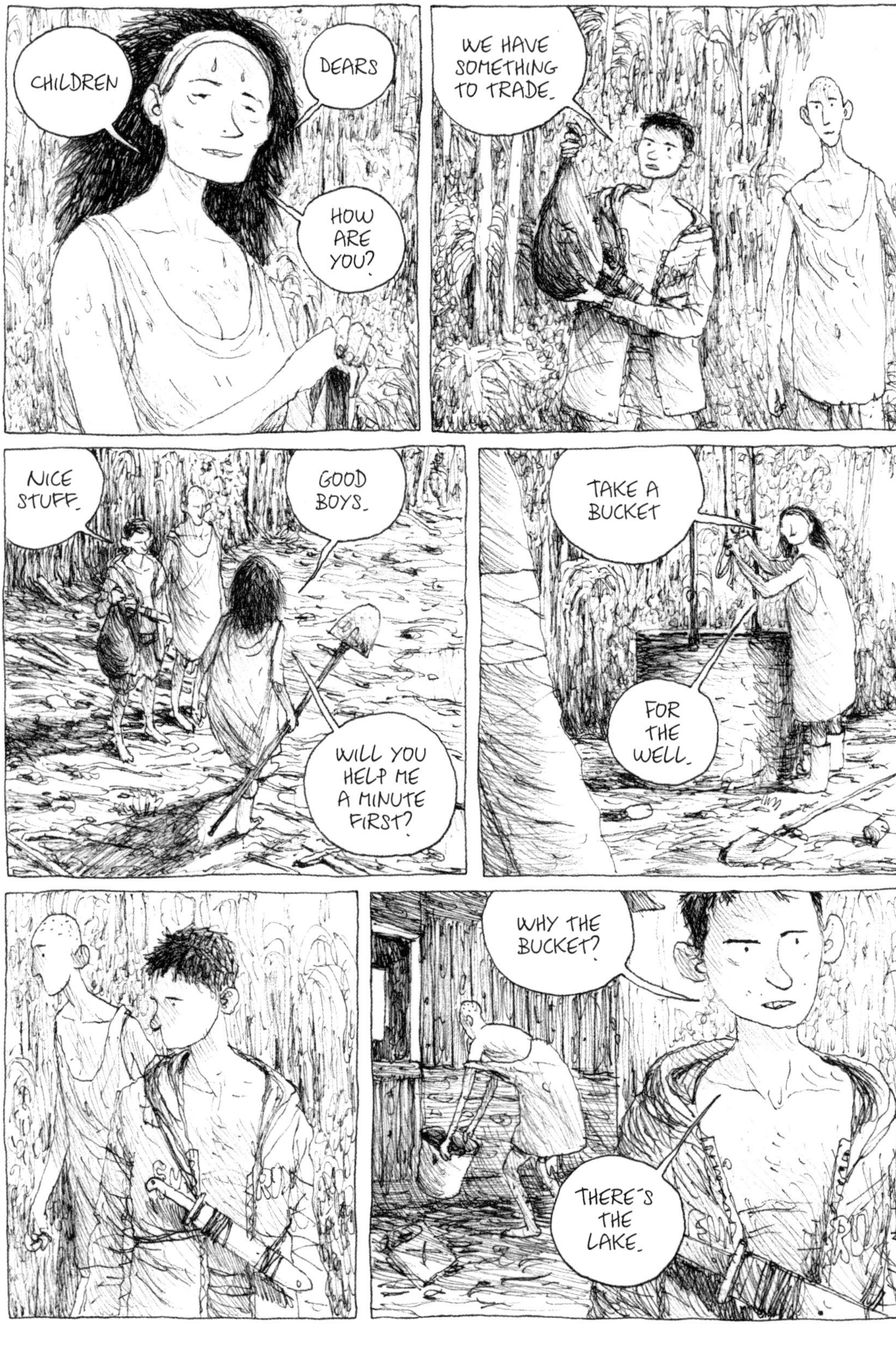
CHILDREN
DEARS
HOW ARE YOU?
WE HAVE SOMETHING TO TRADE.
NICE STUFF.
GOOD BOYS.
WILL YOU HELP ME A MINUTE FIRST?
TAKE A BUCKET
FOR THE WELL.
WHY THE BUCKET?
THERE'S THE LAKE.

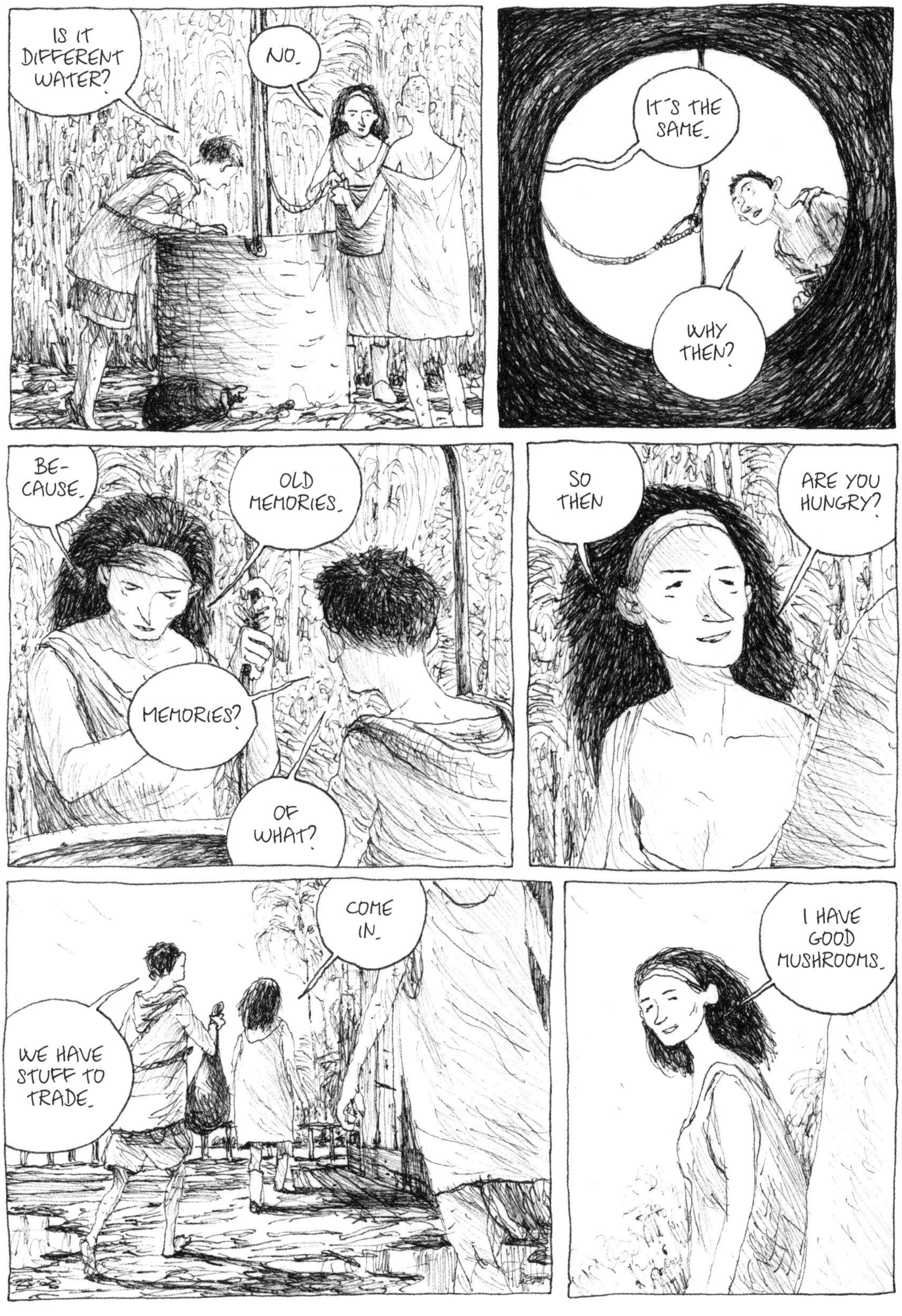
IS IT DIFFERENT WATER?
NO.
IT'S THE SAME.
WHY THEN?
BE-CAUSE.
OLD MEMORIES.
MEMORIES?
OF WHAT?
SO THEN
ARE YOU HUNGRY?
COME IN.
WE HAVE STUFF TO TRADE.
I HAVE GOOD MUSHROOMS.

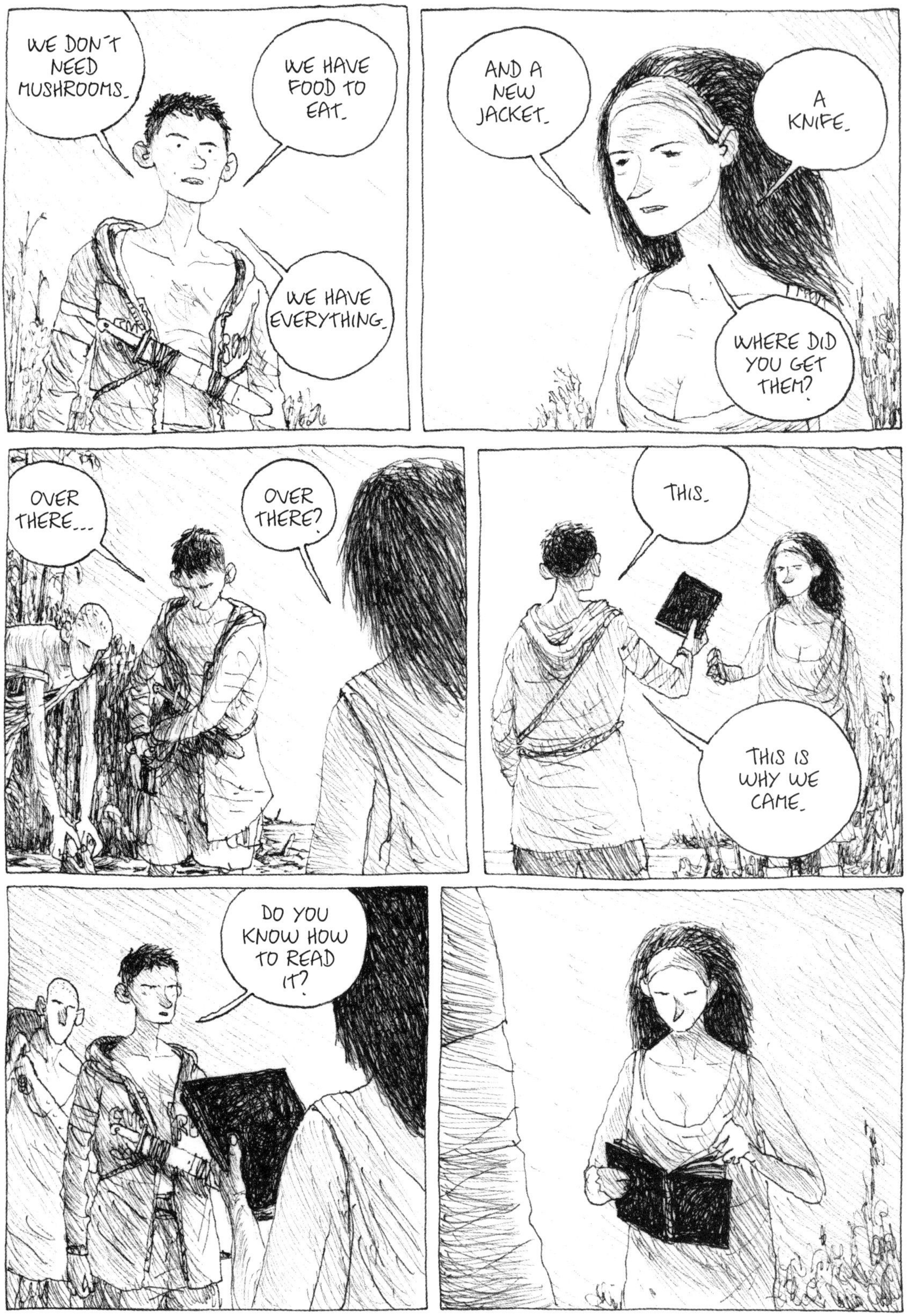
WE DON'T NEED MUSHROOMS.
WE HAVE FOOD TO EAT.
WE HAVE EVERYTHING.
AND A NEW JACKET.
A KNIFE.
WHERE DID YOU GET THEM?
OVER THERE...
OVER THERE?
THIS.
THIS IS WHY WE CAME.
DO YOU KNOW HOW TO READ IT?

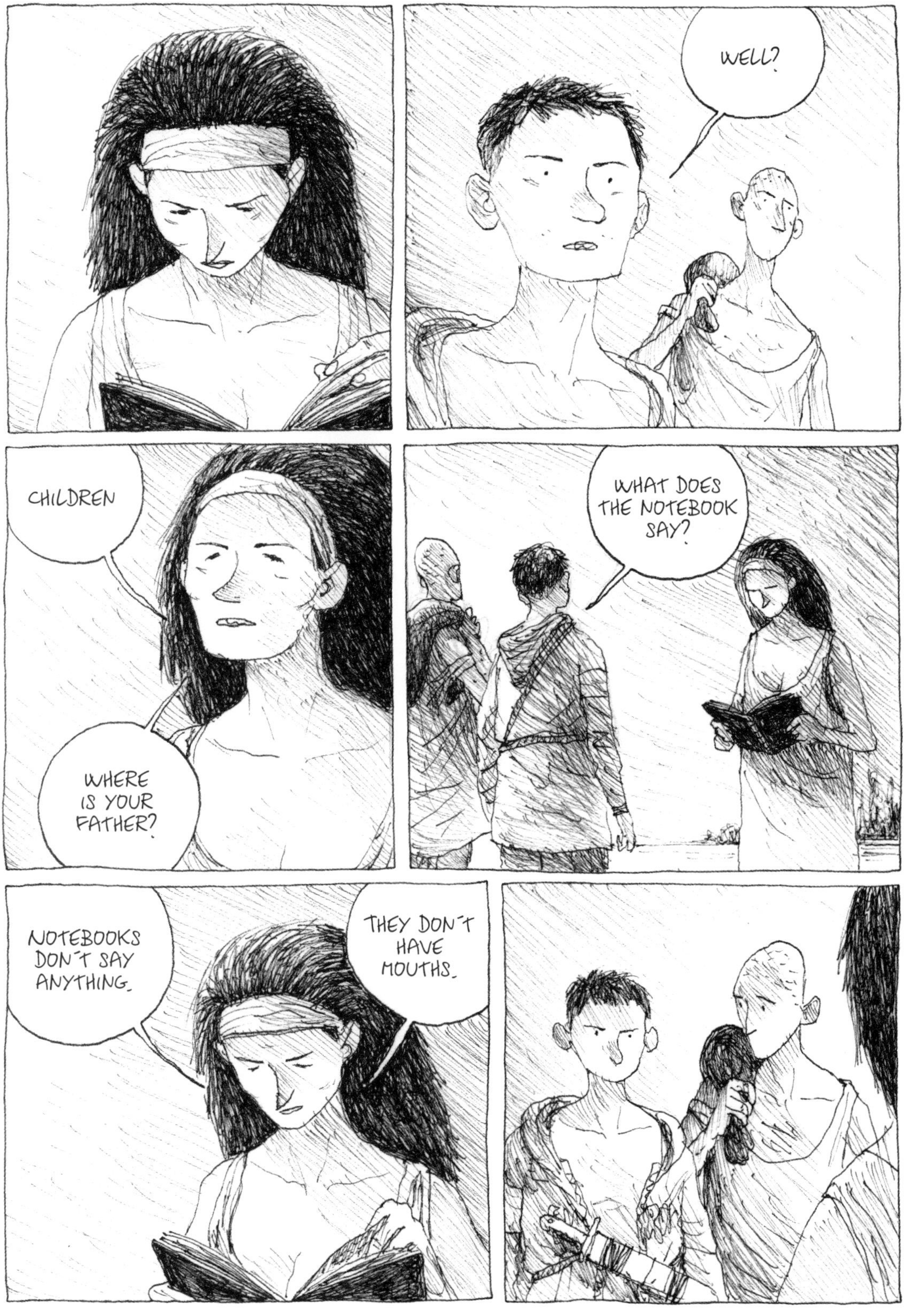
WELL?
CHILDREN
WHERE IS YOUR FATHER?
WHAT DOES THE NOTEBOOK SAY?
NOTEBOOKS DON'T SAY ANYTHING.
THEY DON'T HAVE MOUTHS.

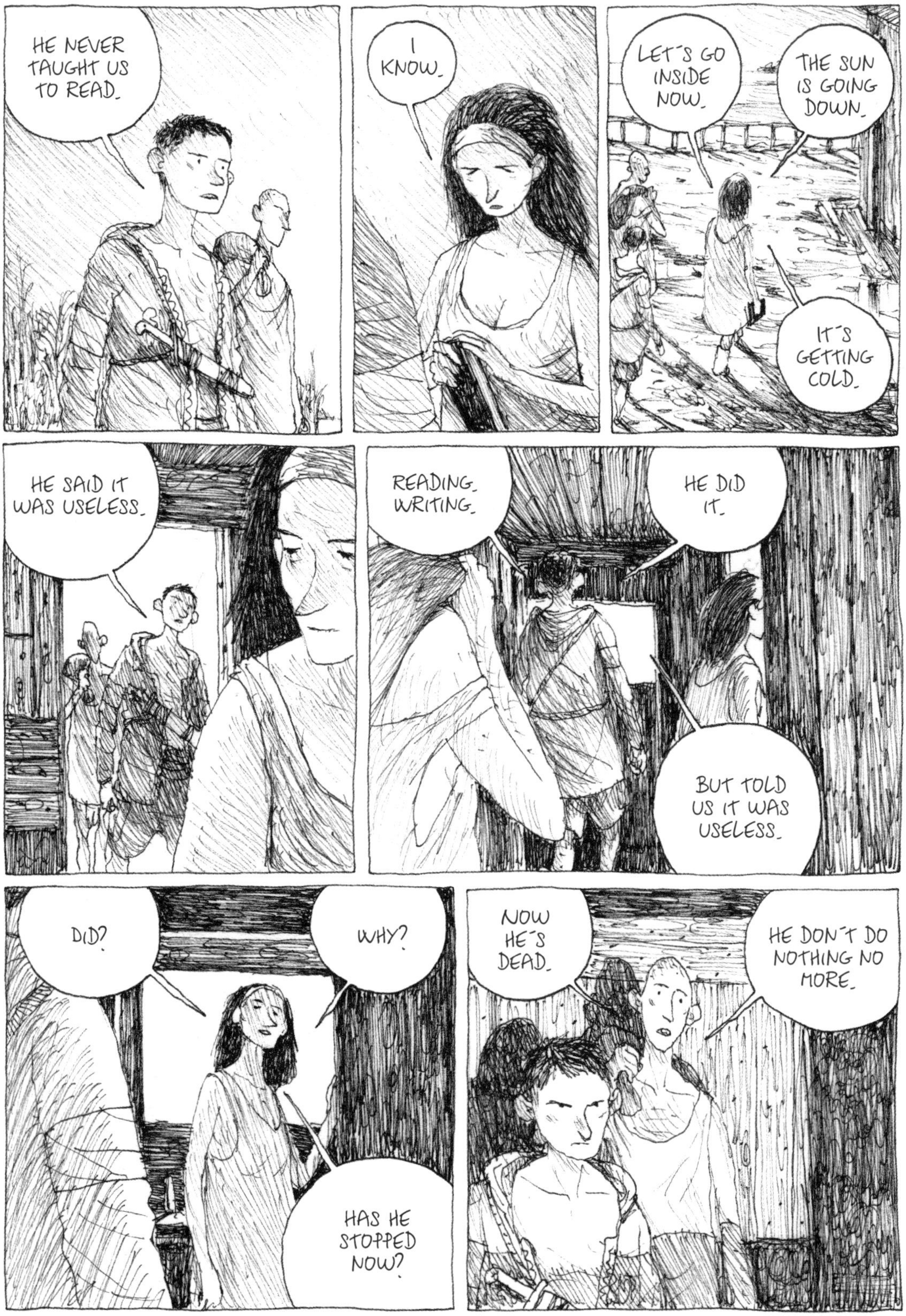
HE NEVER TAUGHT US TO READ.
I KNOW.
LET'S GO INSIDE NOW.
THE SUN IS GOING DOWN.
IT'S GETTING COLD.
HE SAID IT WAS USELESS.
READING. WRITING.
HE DID IT.
BUT TOLD US IT WAS USELESS.
DID?
WHY?
HAS HE STOPPED NOW?
NOW HE'S DEAD.
HE DON'T DO NOTHING NO MORE.

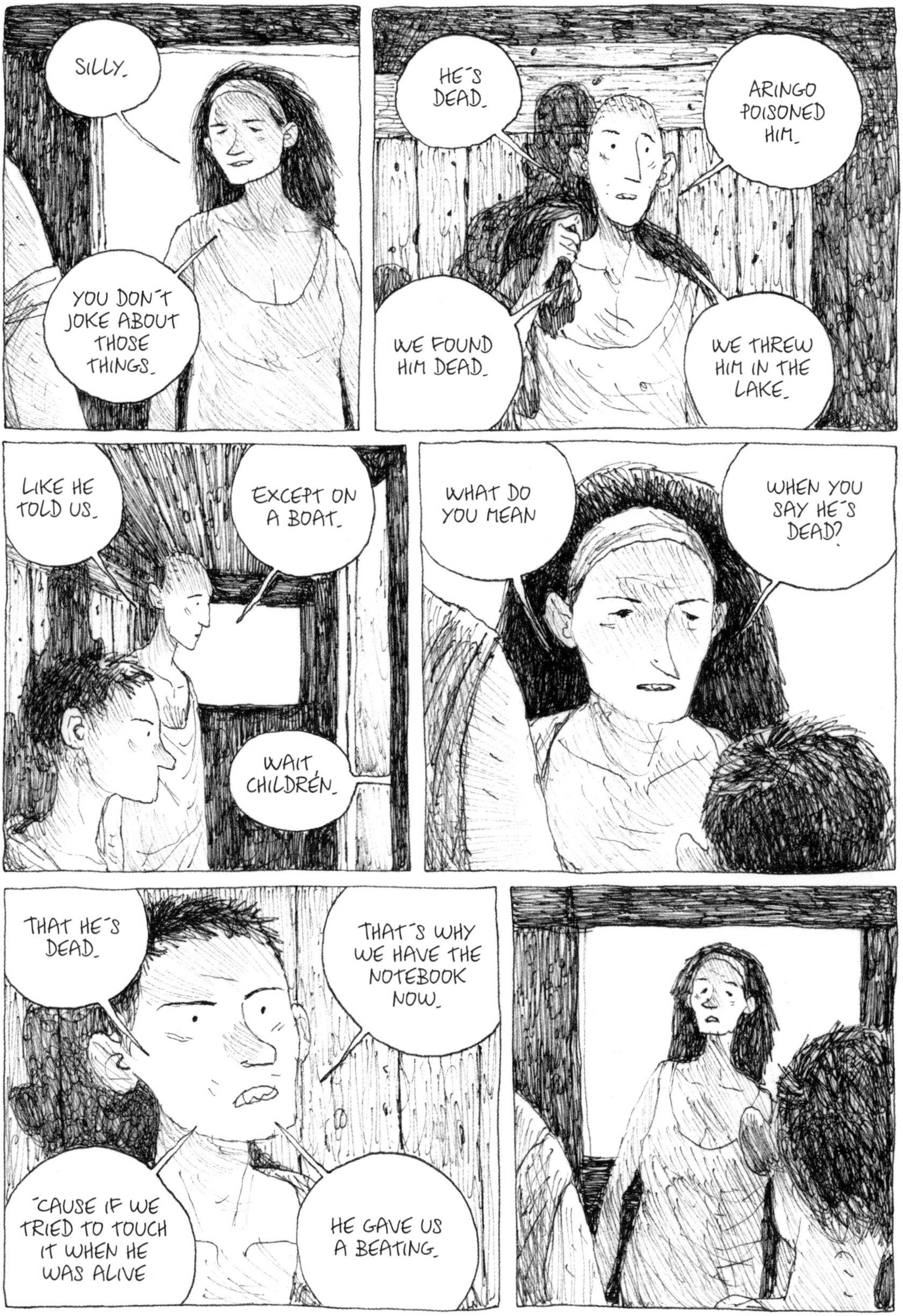
SILLY.
YOU DON'T JOKE ABOUT THOSE THINGS.
HE'S DEAD.
ARINGO POISONED HIM.
WE FOUND HIM DEAD.
WE THREW HIM IN THE LAKE.
LIKE HE TOLD US.
EXCEPT ON A BOAT.
WAIT, CHILDREN.
WHAT DO YOU MEAN
WHEN YOU SAY HE'S DEAD?
THAT HE'S DEAD.
THAT'S WHY WE HAVE THE NOTEBOOK NOW.
'CAUSE IF WE TRIED TO TOUCH IT WHEN HE WAS ALIVE
HE GAVE US A BEATING.

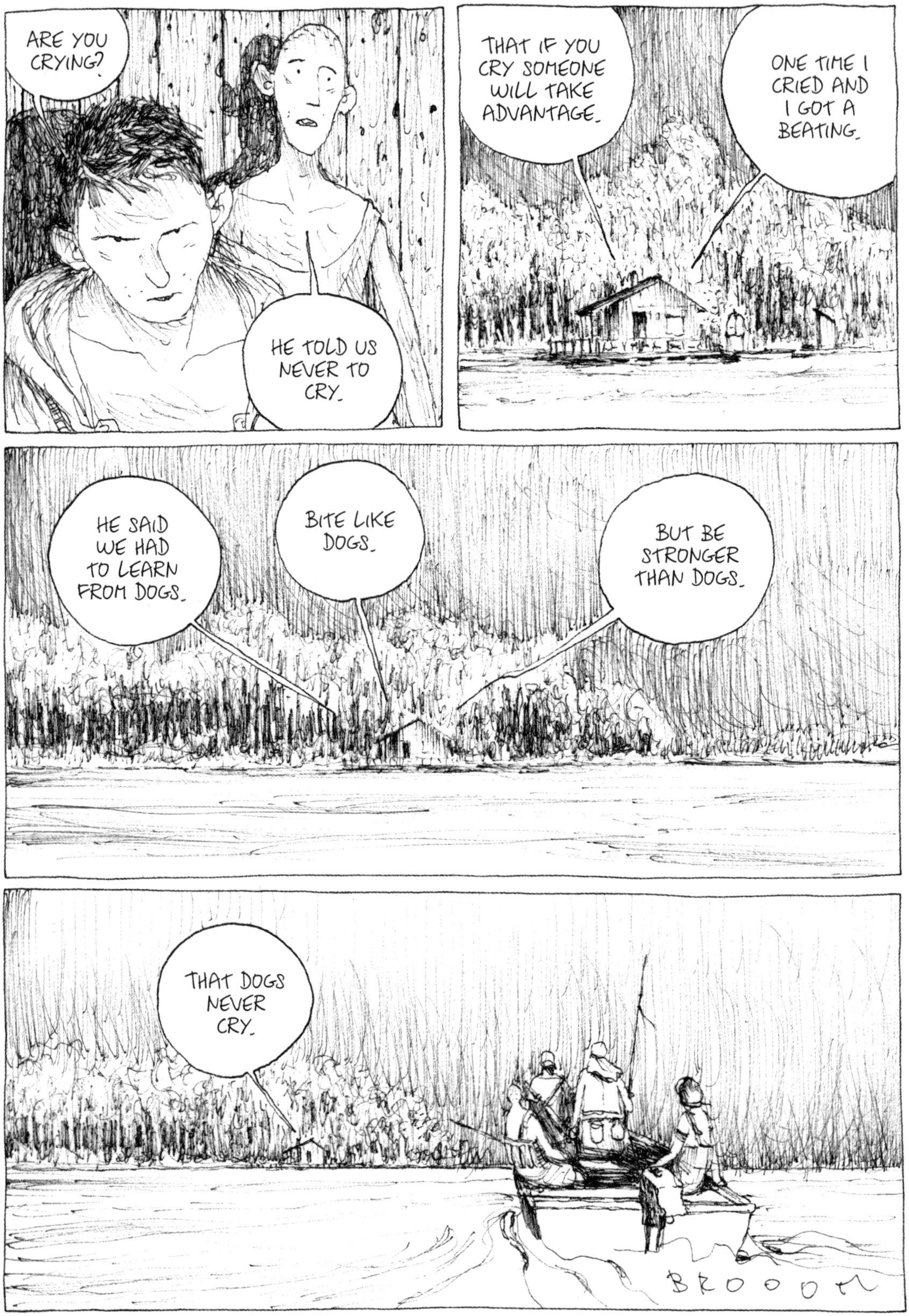
ARE YOU CRYING?
HE TOLD US NEVER TO CRY.
THAT IF YOU CRY SOMEONE WILL TAKE ADVANTAGE.
ONE TIME I CRIED AND I GOT A BEATING.
HE SAID WE HAD TO LEARN FROM DOGS.
BITE LIKE DOGS.
BUT BE STRONGER THAN DOGS.
THAT DOGS NEVER CRY.
BROOOM

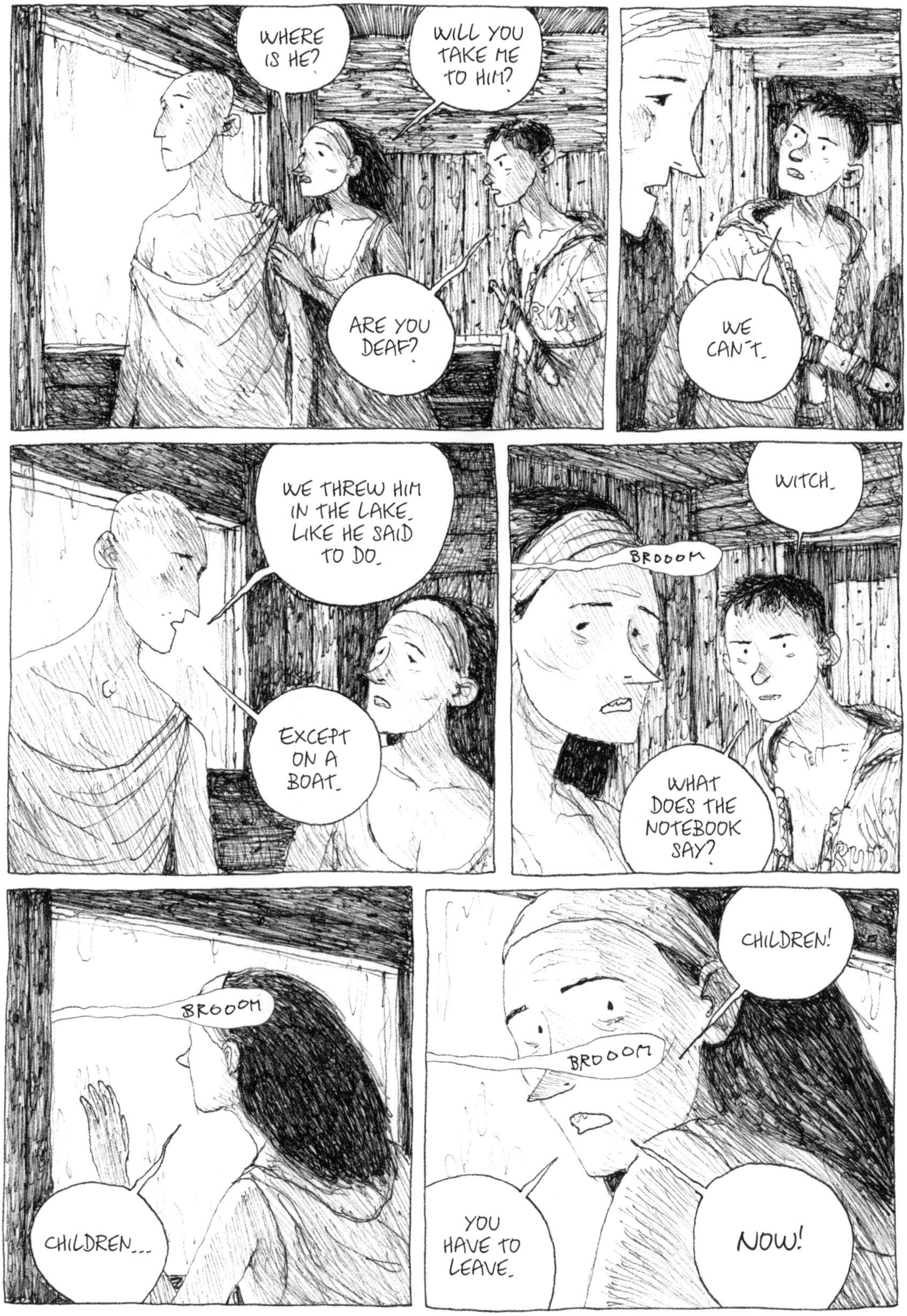
WHERE IS HE?
WILL YOU TAKE ME TO HIM?
ARE YOU DEAF?
WE CAN'T.
WE THREW HIM IN THE LAKE. LIKE HE SAID TO DO.
EXCEPT ON A BOAT.
BROOOM
WITCH.
WHAT DOES THE NOTEBOOK SAY?
BROOOM
CHILDREN...
CHILDREN!
BROOOM
YOU HAVE TO LEAVE.
NOW!

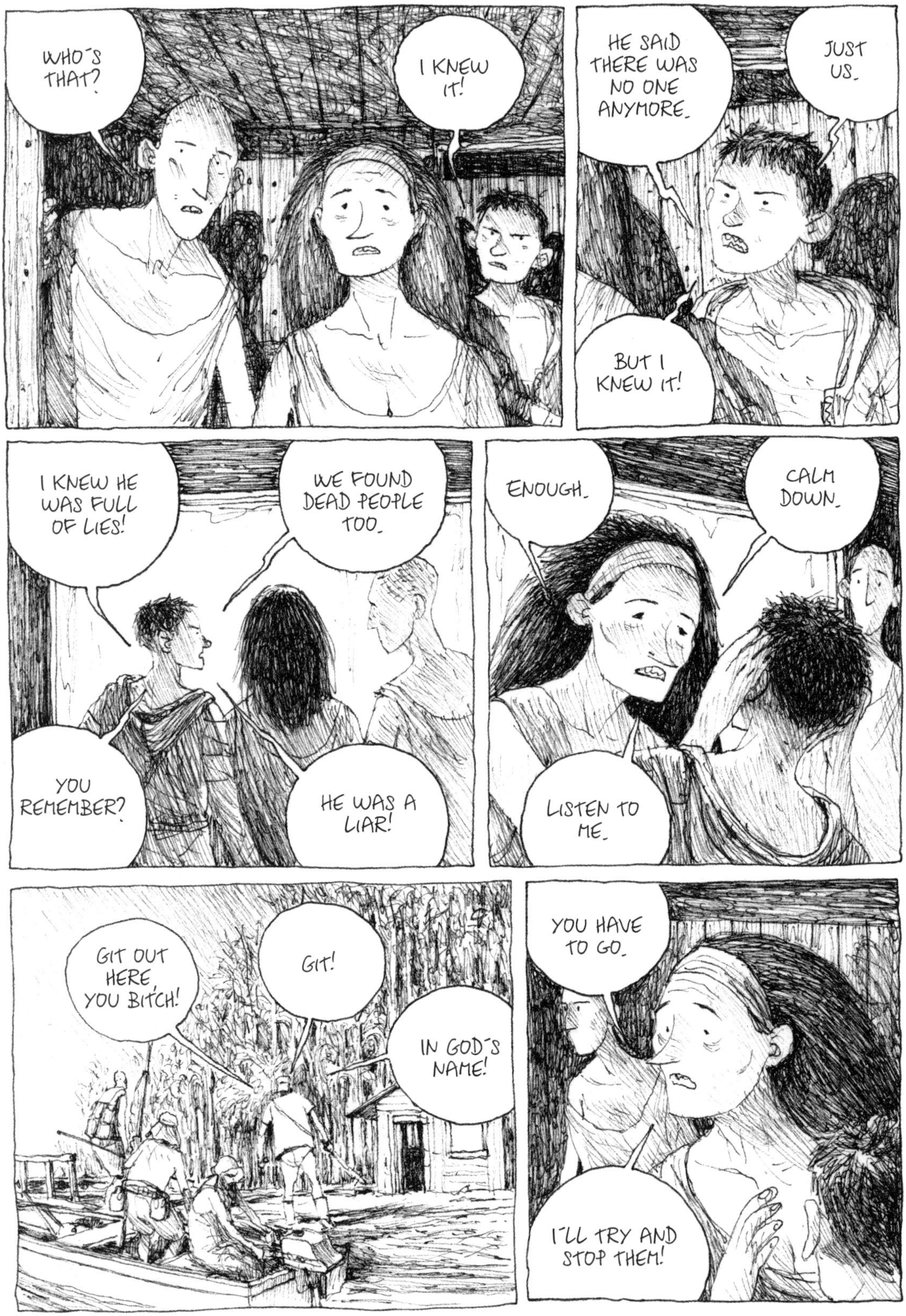
WHO'S THAT?
I KNEW IT!
HE SAID THERE WAS NO ONE ANYMORE.
JUST US.
BUT I KNEW IT!
I KNEW HE WAS FULL OF LIES!
WE FOUND DEAD PEOPLE TOO.
YOU REMEMBER?
HE WAS A LIAR!
ENOUGH.
CALM DOWN.
LISTEN TO ME.
GIT OUT HERE, YOU BITCH!
GIT!
IN GOD'S NAME!
YOU HAVE TO GO.
I'LL TRY AND STOP THEM!

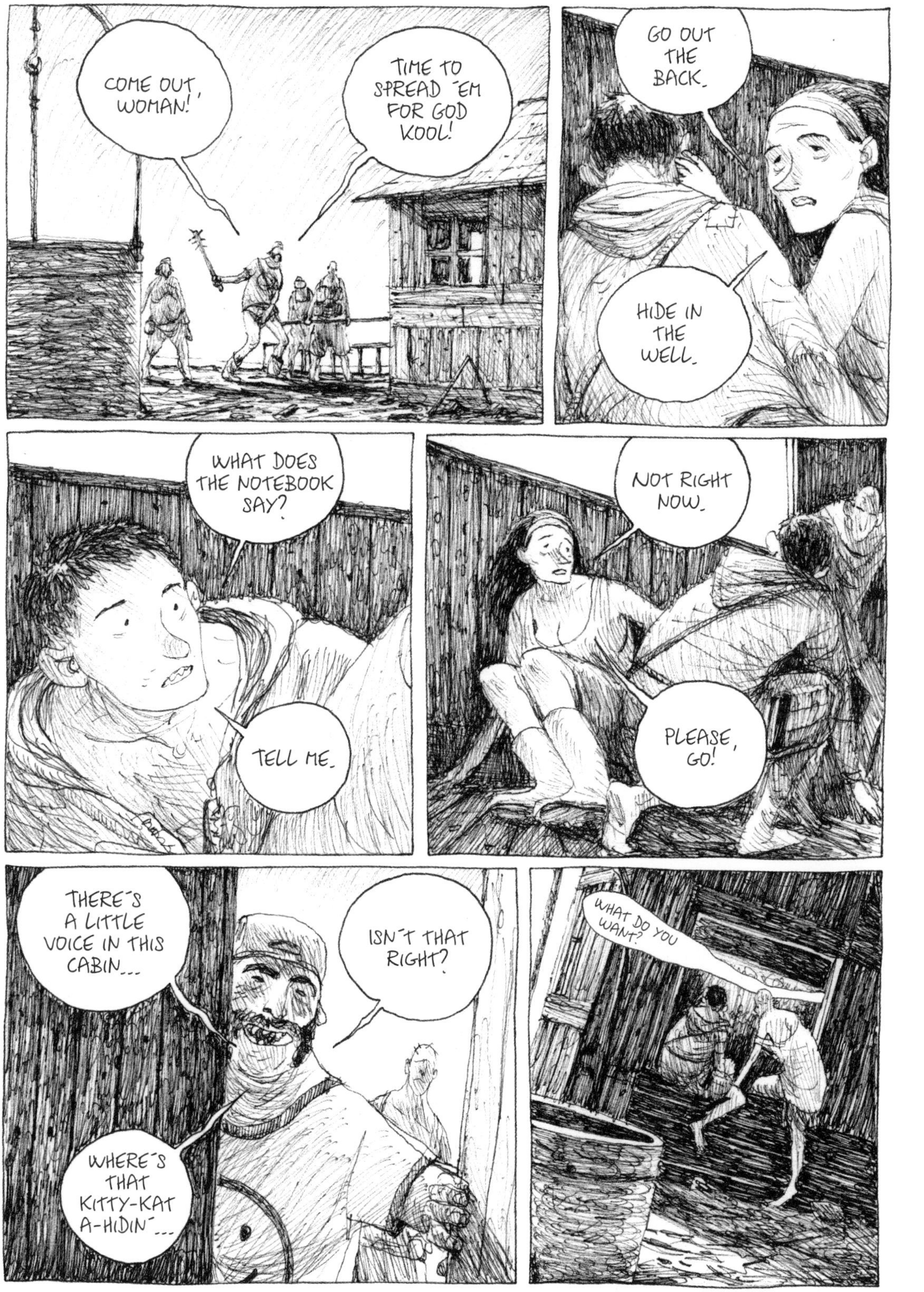
COME OUT, WOMAN!
TIME TO SPREAD 'EM FOR GOD KOOL!
GO OUT THE BACK.
HIDE IN THE WELL.
WHAT DOES THE NOTEBOOK SAY?
TELL ME.
NOT RIGHT NOW.
PLEASE, GO!
THERE'S A LITTLE VOICE IN THIS CABIN...
ISN'T THAT RIGHT?
WHERE'S THAT KITTY-KAT A-HIDIN'...
WHAT DO YOU WANT?

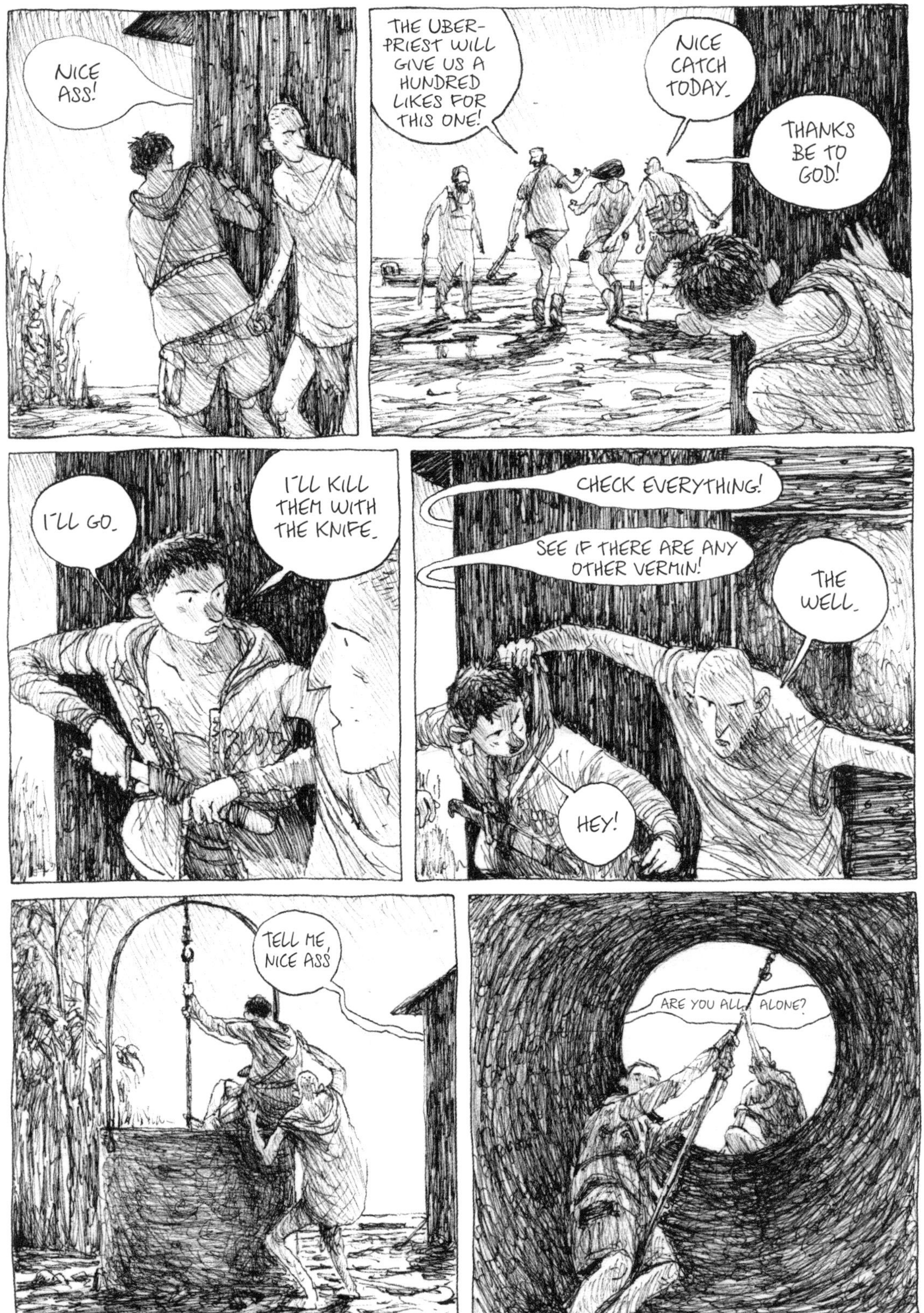
NICE ASS!
THE UBER-PRIEST WILL GIVE US A HUNDRED LIKES FOR THIS ONE!
NICE CATCH TODAY.
THANKS BE TO GOD!
I'LL GO.
I'LL KILL THEM WITH THE KNIFE.
CHECK EVERYTHING!
SEE IF THERE ARE ANY OTHER VERMIN!
THE WELL.
HEY!
TELL ME, NICE ASS'
ARE YOU ALL ALONE?

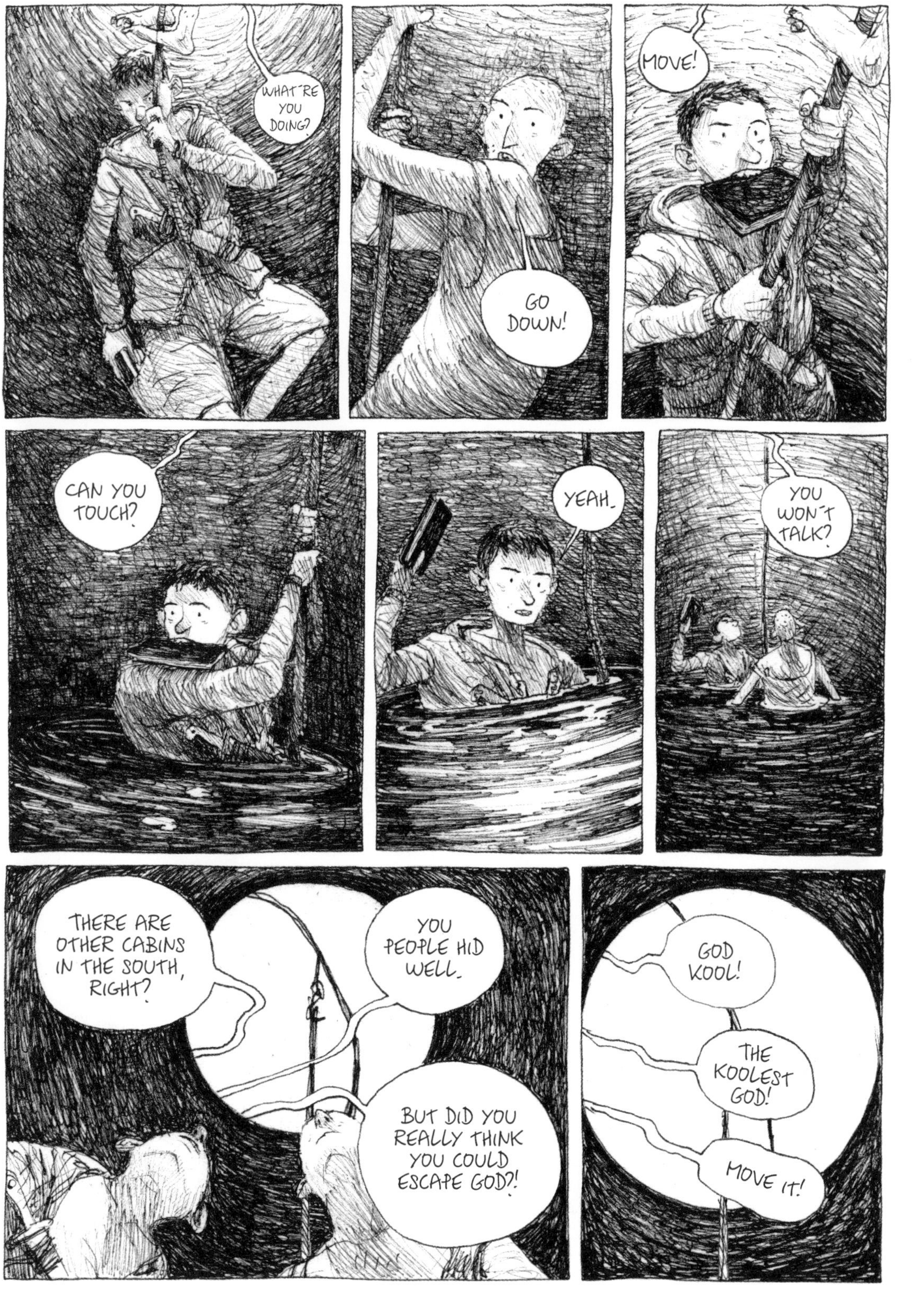
WHAT'RE YOU DOING?
GO DOWN!
MOVE!
CAN YOU TOUCH?
YEAH.
YOU WON'T TALK?
THERE ARE OTHER CABINS IN THE SOUTH, RIGHT?
YOU PEOPLE HID WELL.
BUT DID YOU REALLY THINK YOU COULD ESCAPE GOD?!
GOD KOOL!
THE KOOLEST GOD!
MOVE IT!

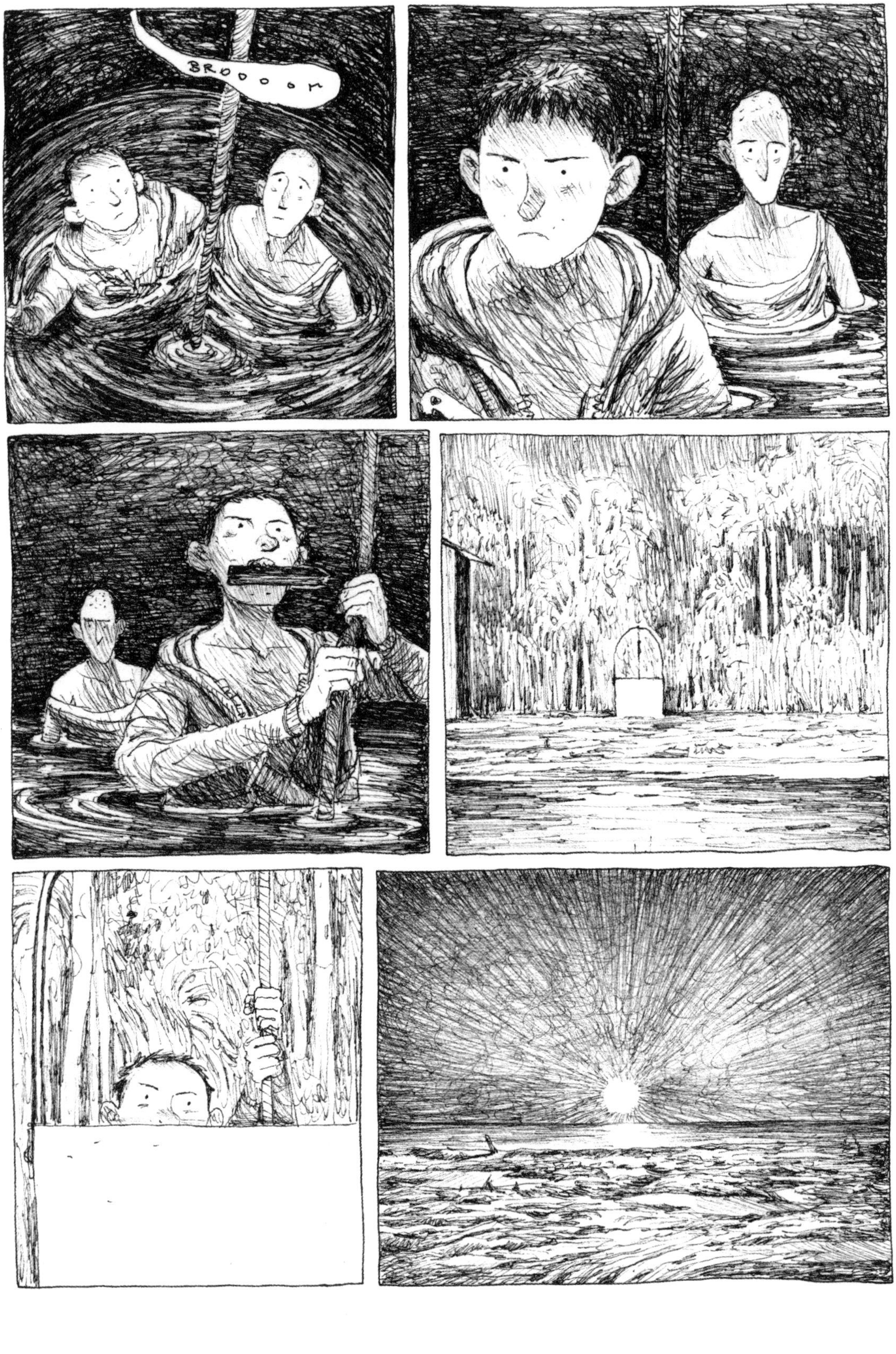
BROOOOM

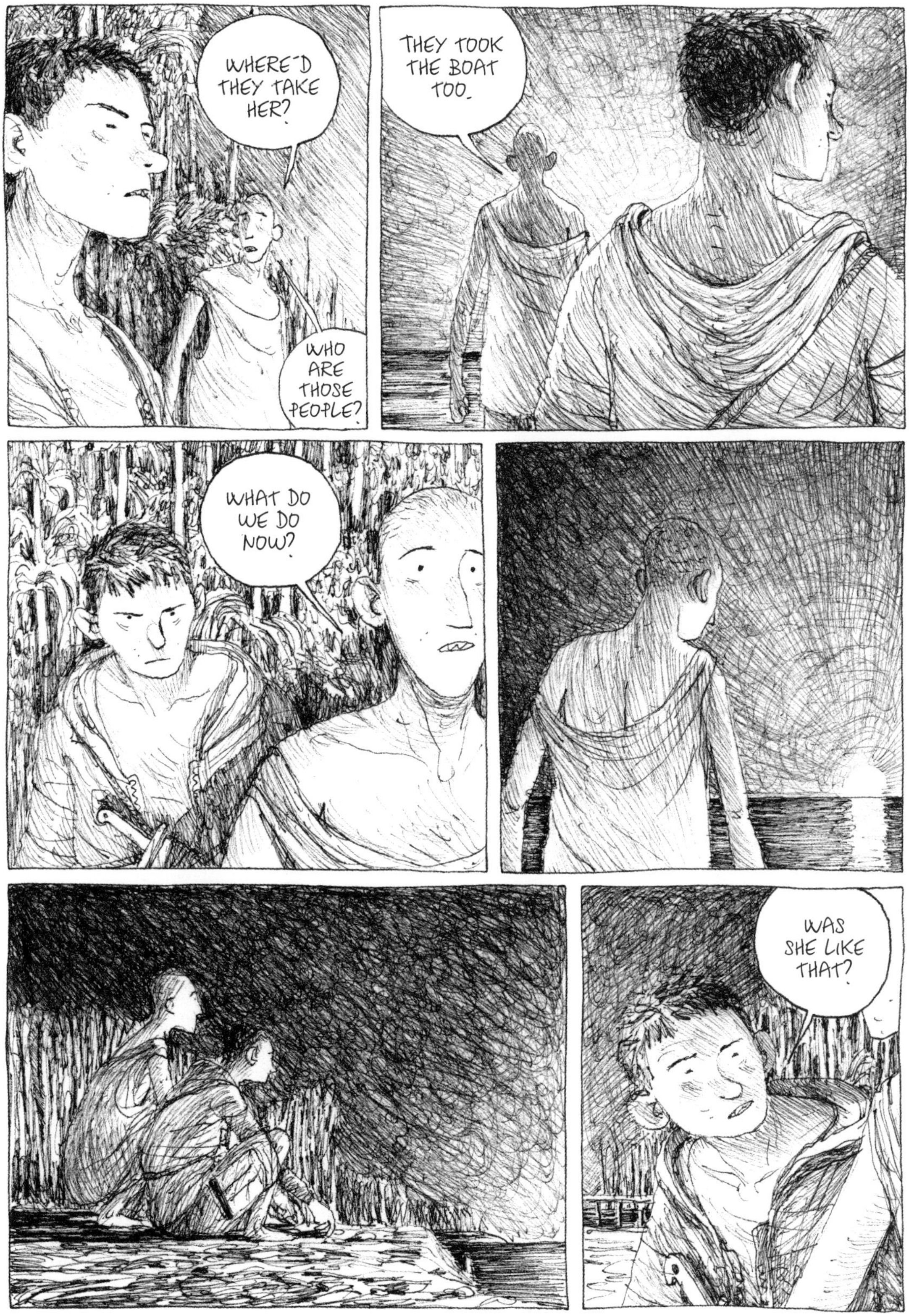
WHERE'D THEY TAKE HER?
WHO ARE THOSE PEOPLE?
THEY TOOK THE BOAT TOO.
WHAT DO WE DO NOW?
WAS SHE LIKE THAT?

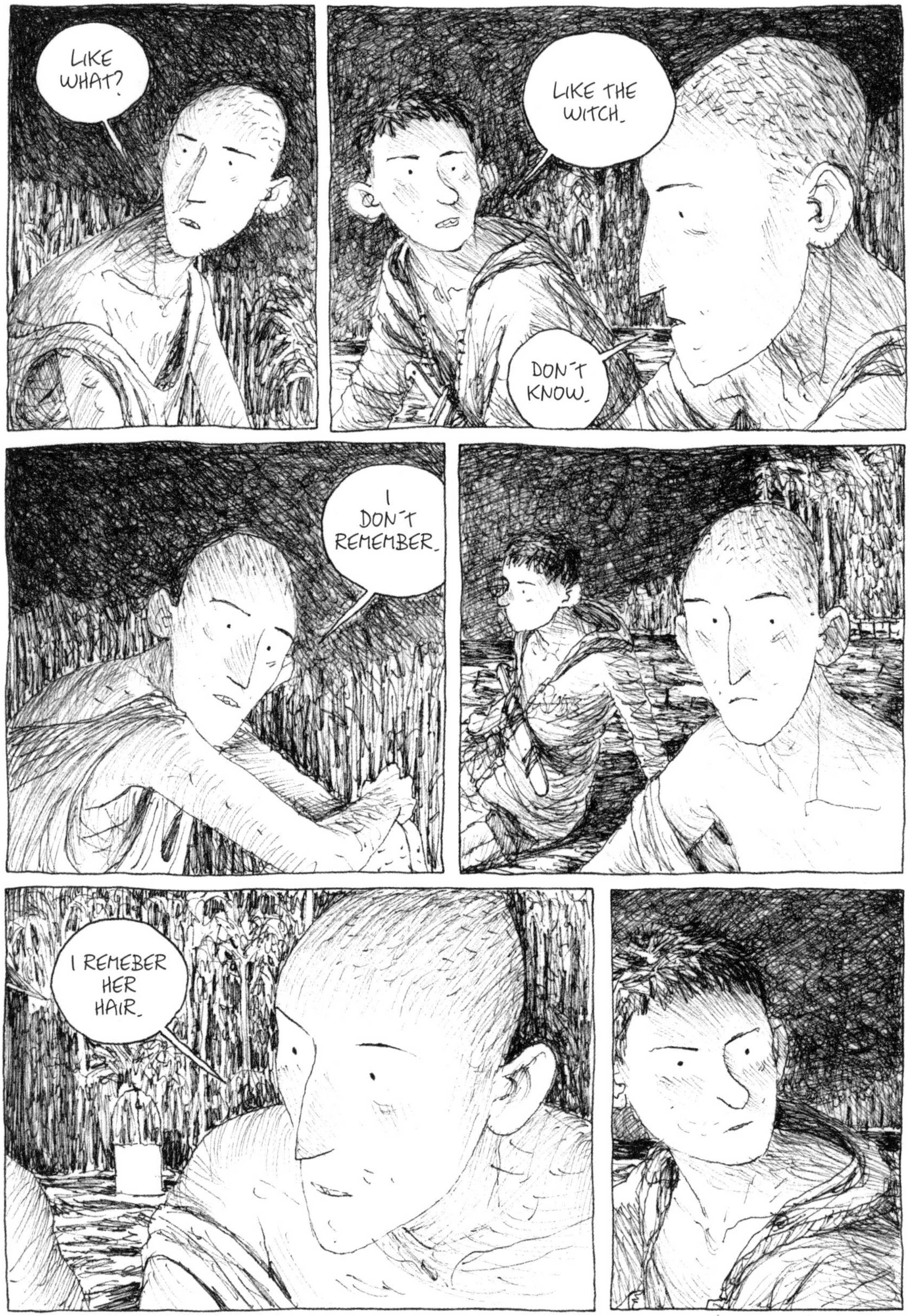
LIKE WHAT?
LIKE THE WITCH.
DON'T KNOW.
I DON'T REMEMBER.
I REMEBER HER HAIR.

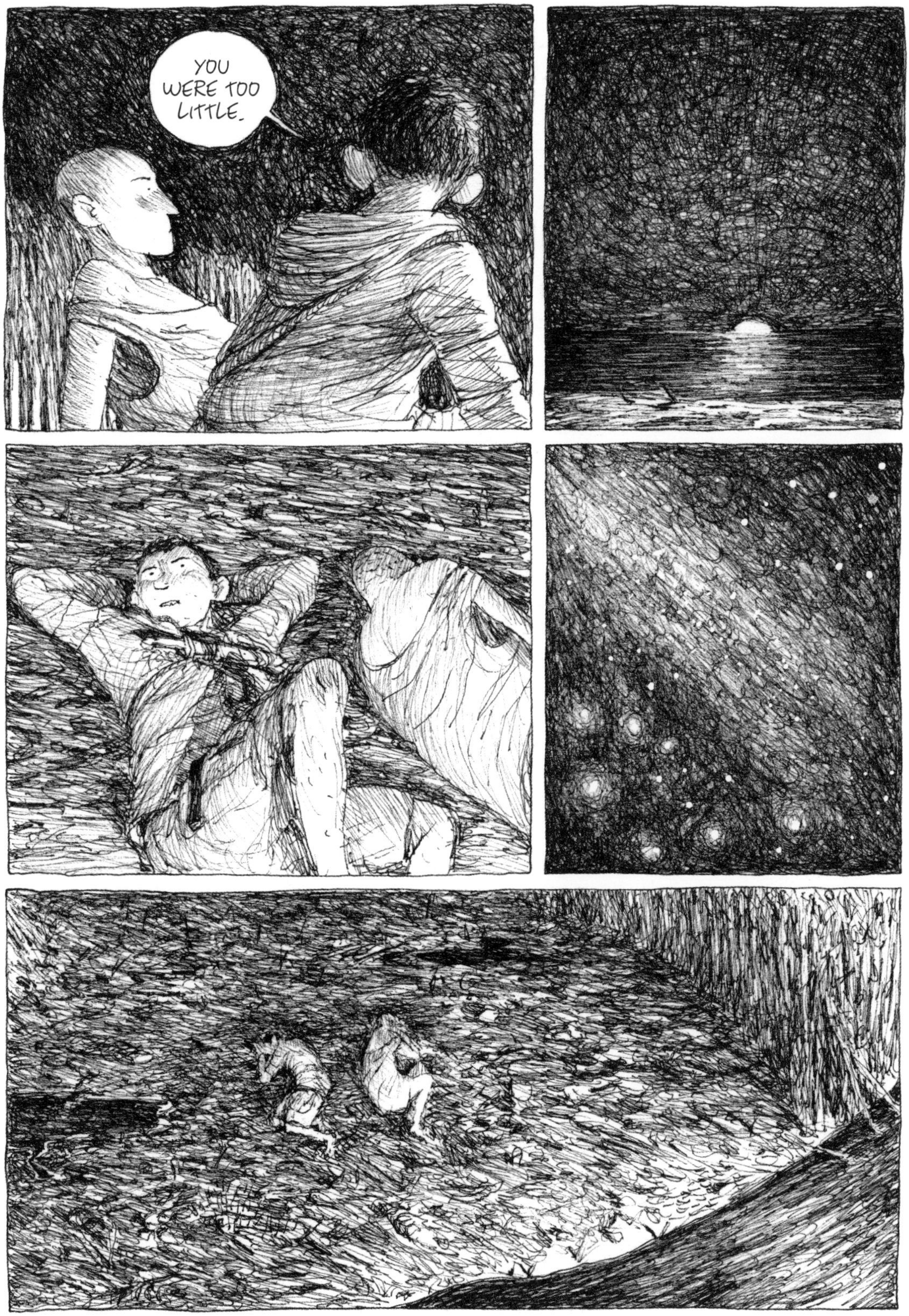
YOU WERE TOO LITTLE.

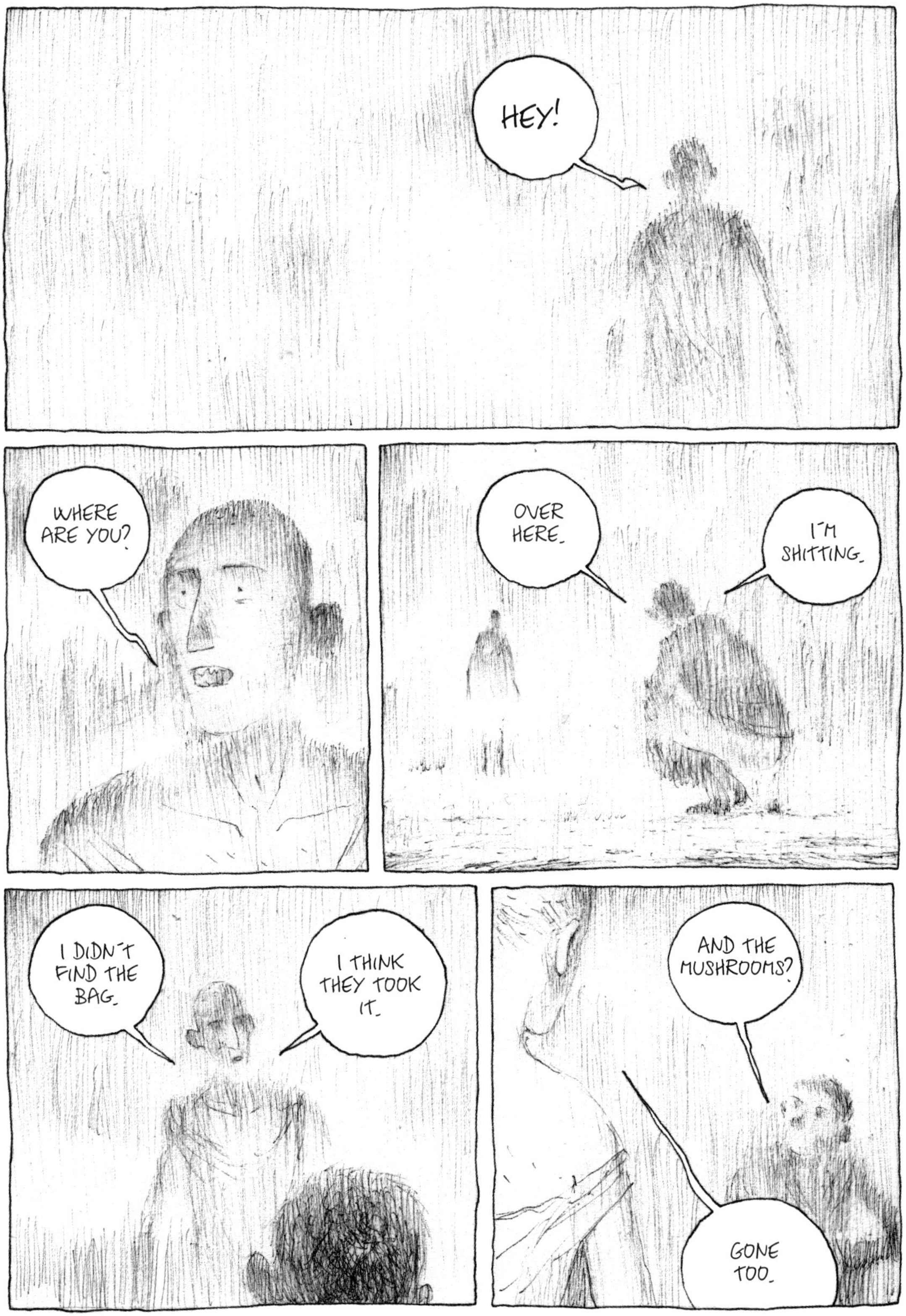
HEY!
WHERE ARE YOU?
OVER HERE.
I'M SHITTING.
I DIDN'T FIND THE BAG.
I THINK THEY TOOK IT.
AND THE MUSHROOMS?
GONE TOO.

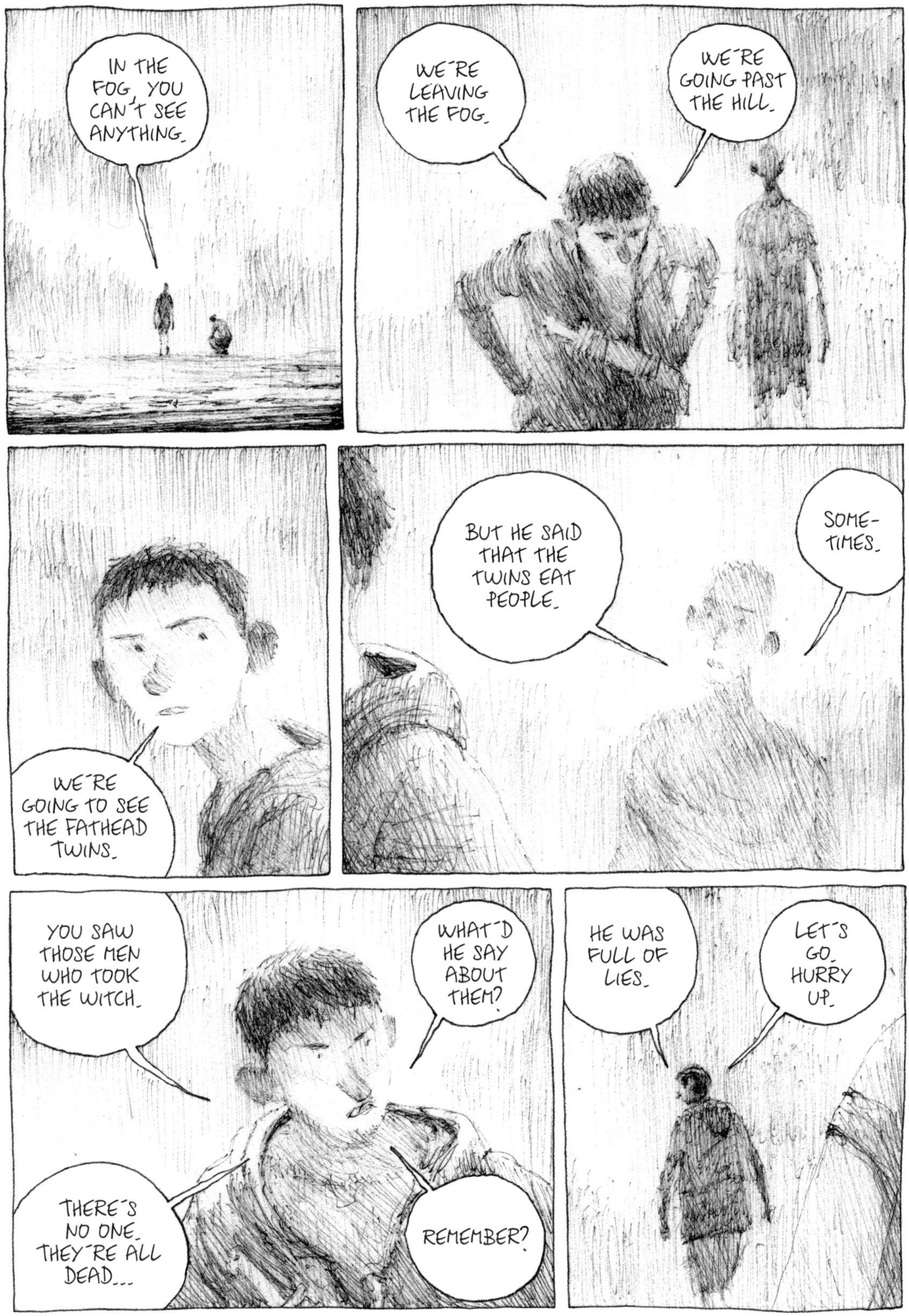
IN THE FOG, YOU CAN'T SEE ANYTHING.
WE'RE LEAVING THE FOG.
WE'RE GOING PAST THE HILL.
WE'RE GOING TO SEE THE FATHEAD TWINS.
BUT HE SAID THAT THE TWINS EAT PEOPLE.
SOME-TIMES.
YOU SAW THOSE MEN WHO TOOK THE WITCH.
WHAT'D HE SAY ABOUT THEM?
THERE'S NO ONE. THEY'RE ALL DEAD...
REMEMBER?
HE WAS FULL OF LIES.
LET'S GO. HURRY UP.

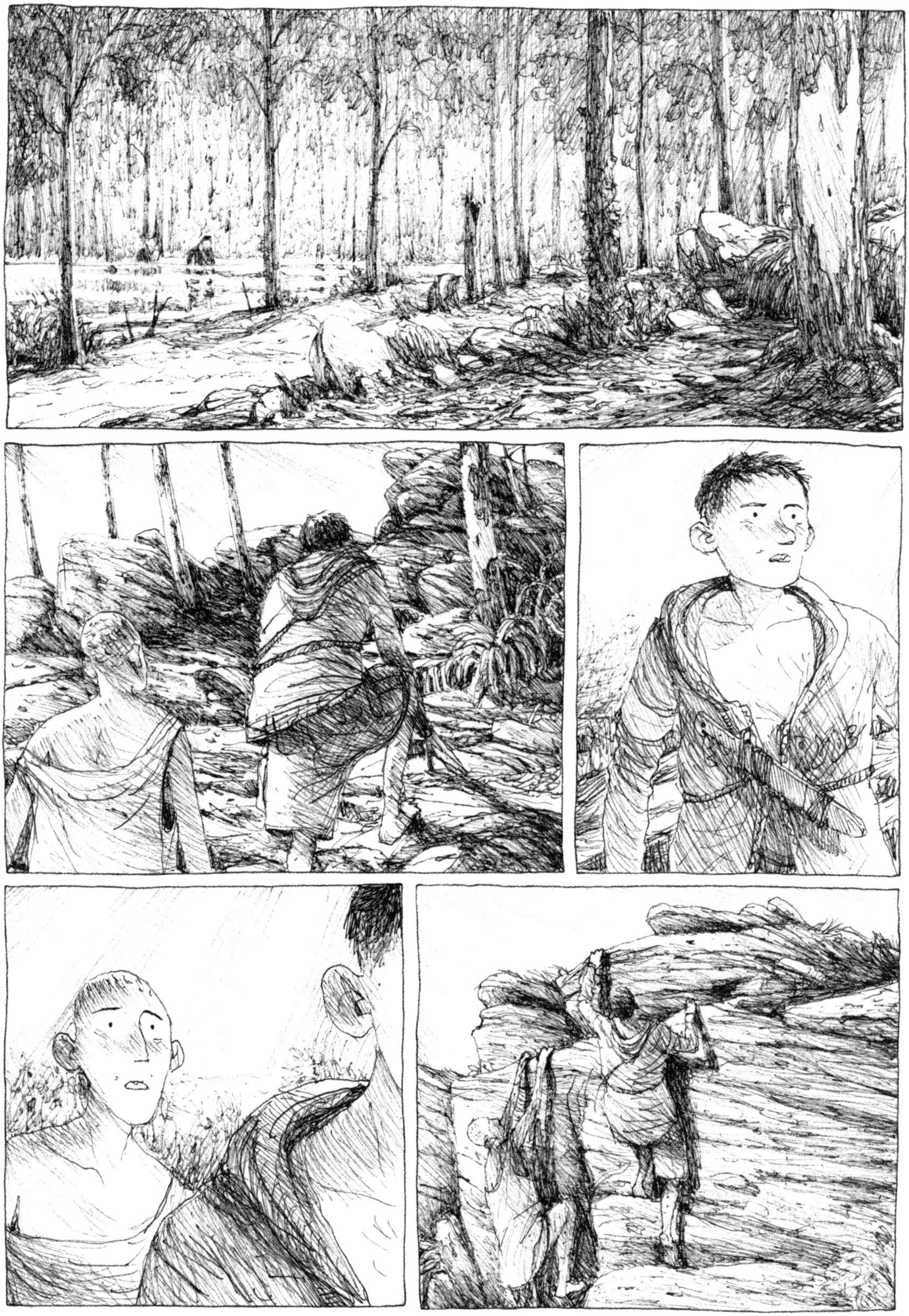

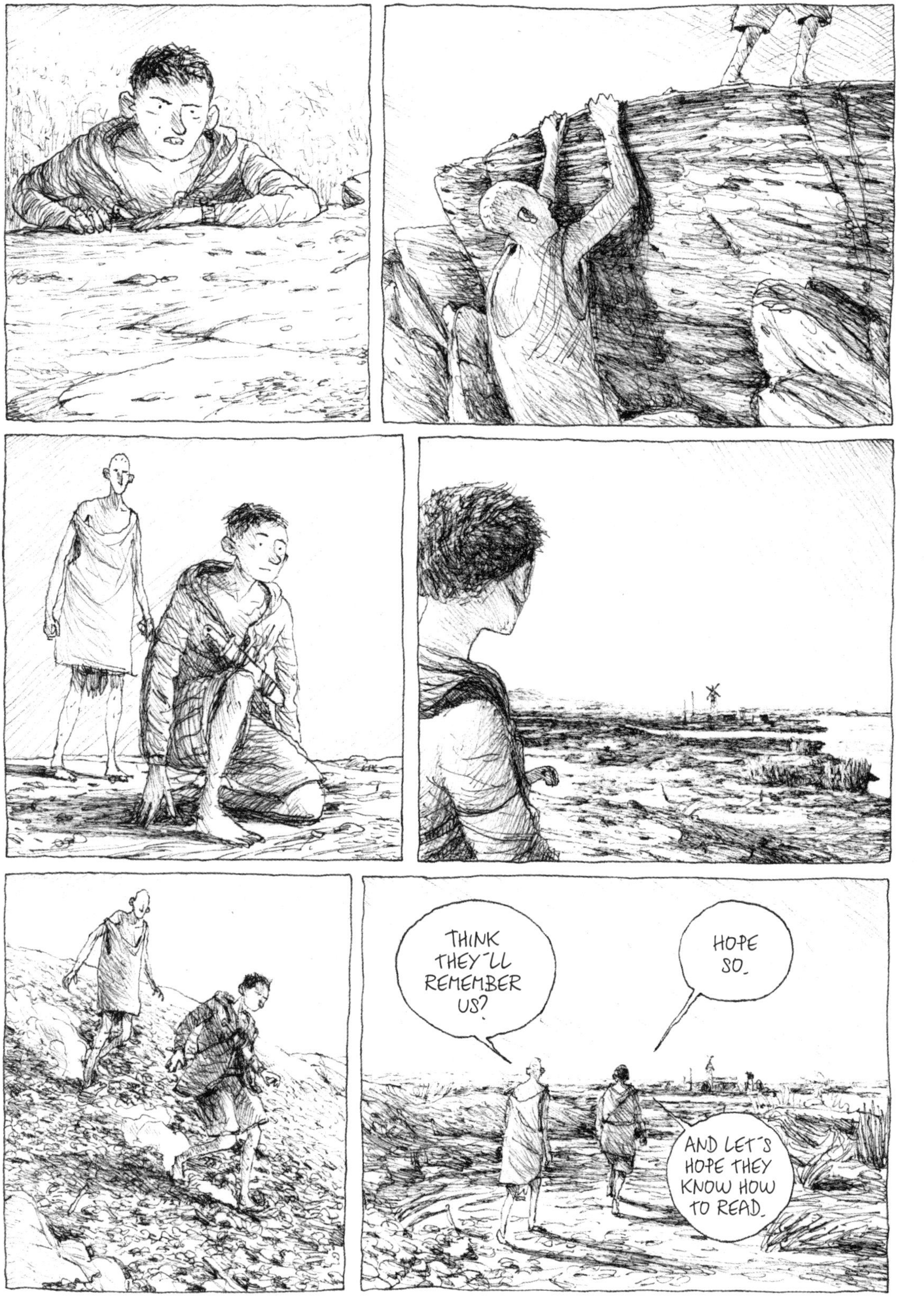
THINK THEY'LL REMEMBER US?
HOPE SO.
AND LET'S HOPE THEY KNOW HOW TO READ.

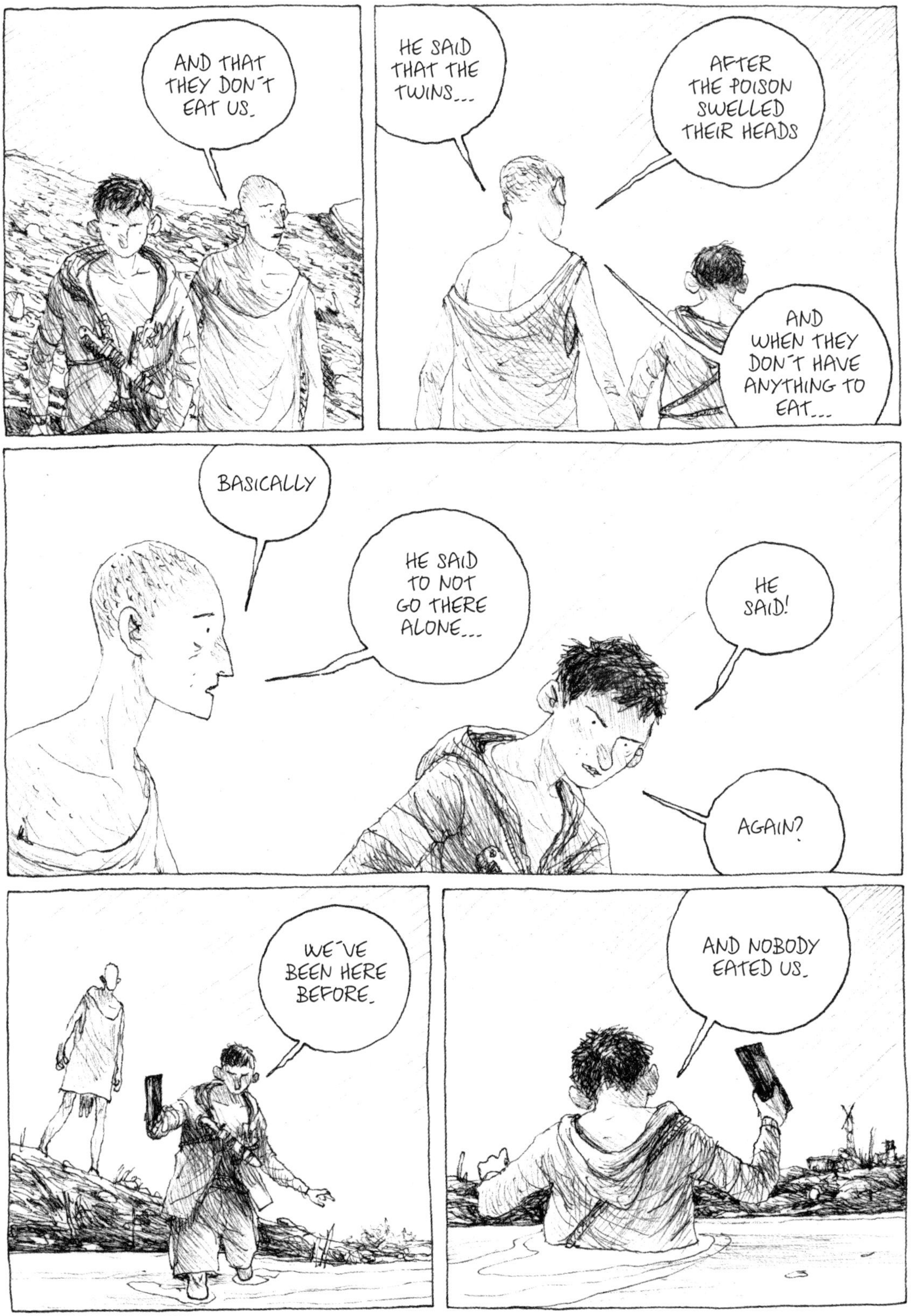
AND THAT THEY DON'T EAT US.
HE SAID THAT THE TWINS...
AFTER THE POISON SWELLED THEIR HEADS
AND WHEN THEY DON'T HAVE ANYTHING TO EAT...
BASICALLY
HE SAID TO NOT GO THERE ALONE...
HE SAID!
AGAIN?
WE'VE BEEN HERE BEFORE.
AND NOBODY EATED US.

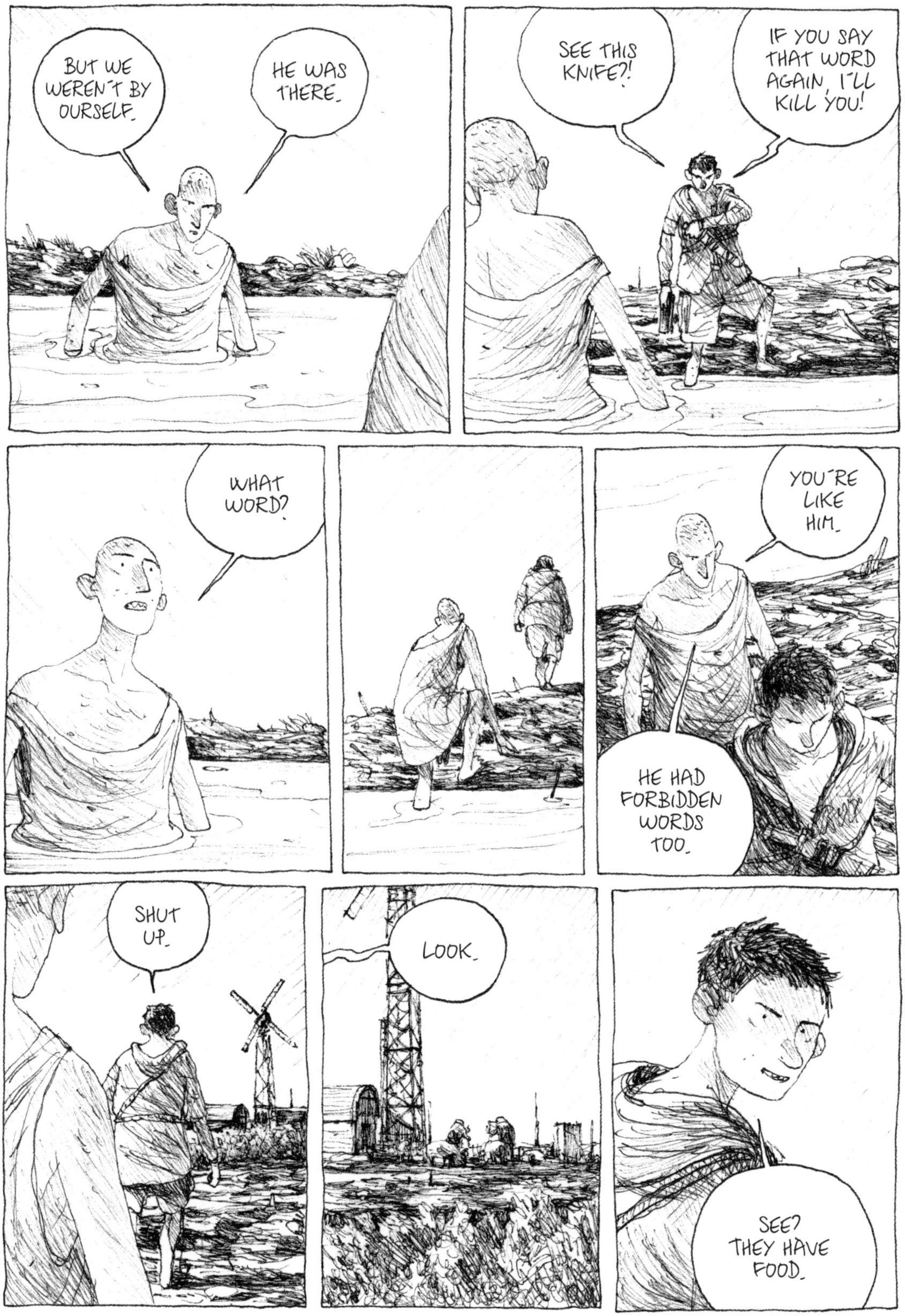
BUT WE WEREN'T BY OURSELF.
HE WAS THERE.
SEE THIS KNIFE?!
IF YOU SAY THAT WORD AGAIN, I'LL KILL YOU!
WHAT WORD?
YOU'RE LIKE HIM.
HE HAD FORBIDDEN WORDS TOO.
SHUT UP.
LOOK.
SEE? THEY HAVE FOOD.

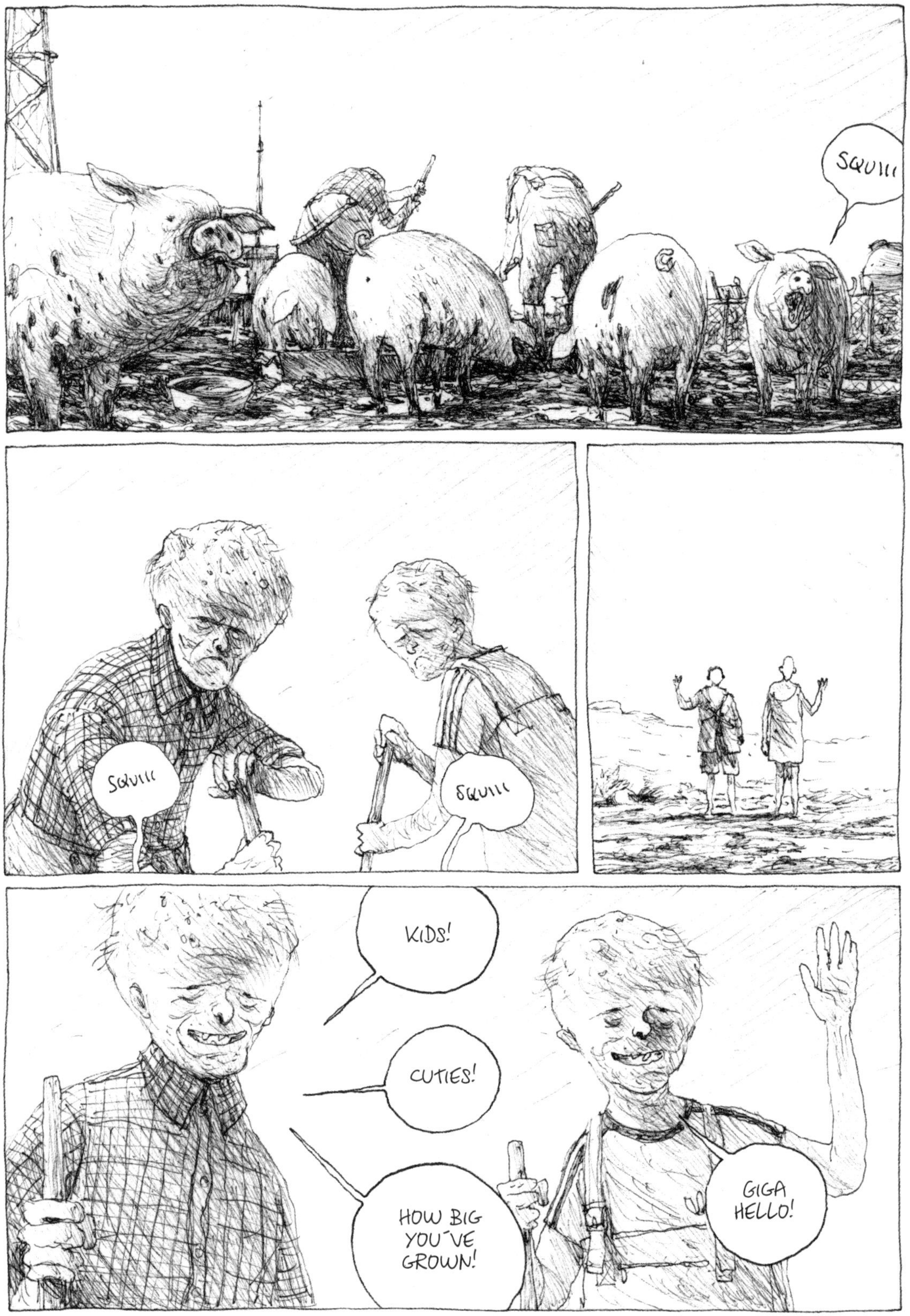
SQUIII
SQUIII
SQUIII
KIDS!
CUTIES!
HOW BIG YOU´VE GROWN!
GIGA HELLO!

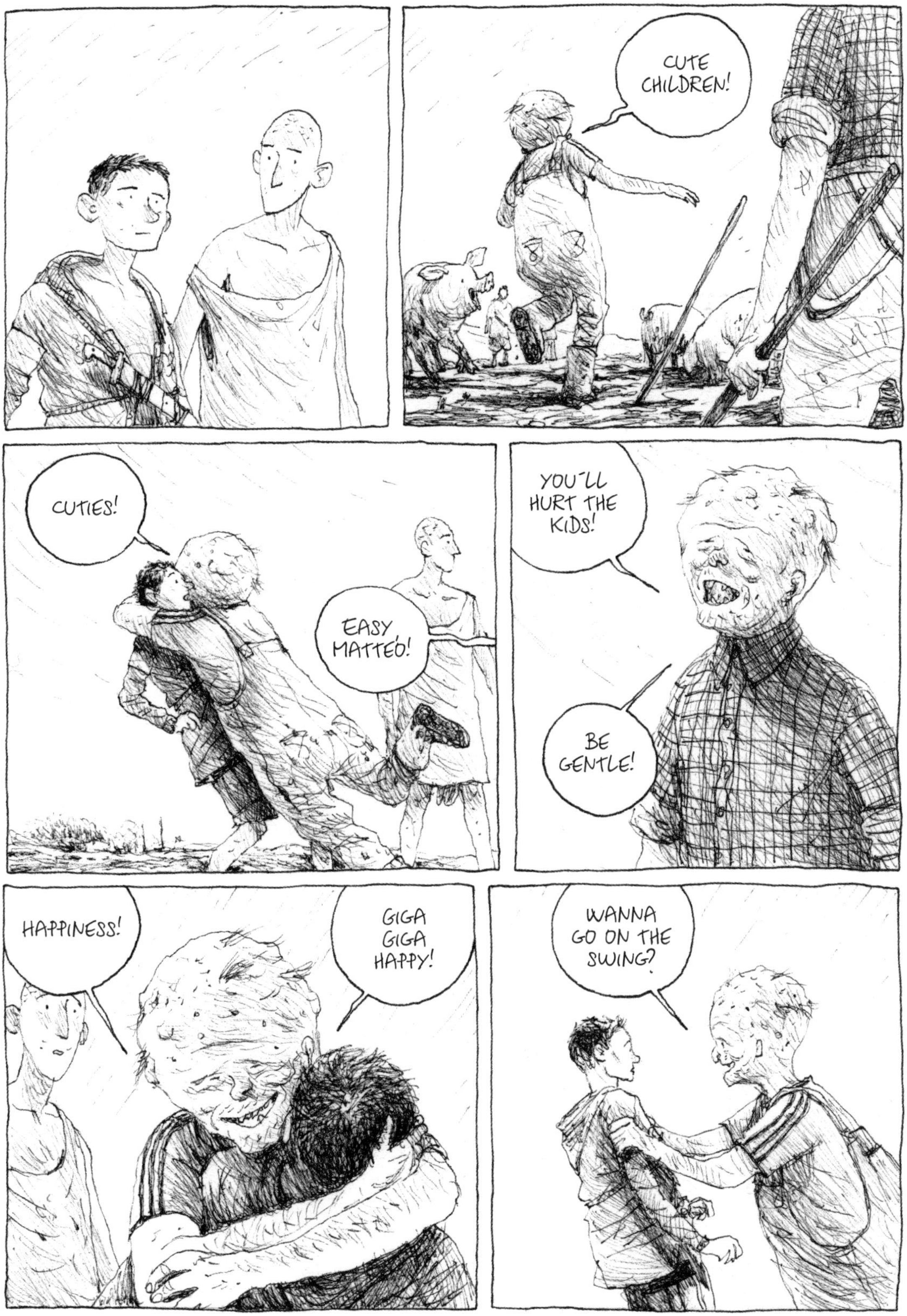
CUTE CHILDREN!
CUTIES!
EASY MATTEO!
YOU'LL HURT THE KIDS!
BE GENTLE!
HAPPINESS!
GIGA GIGA HAPPY!
WANNA GO ON THE SWING?

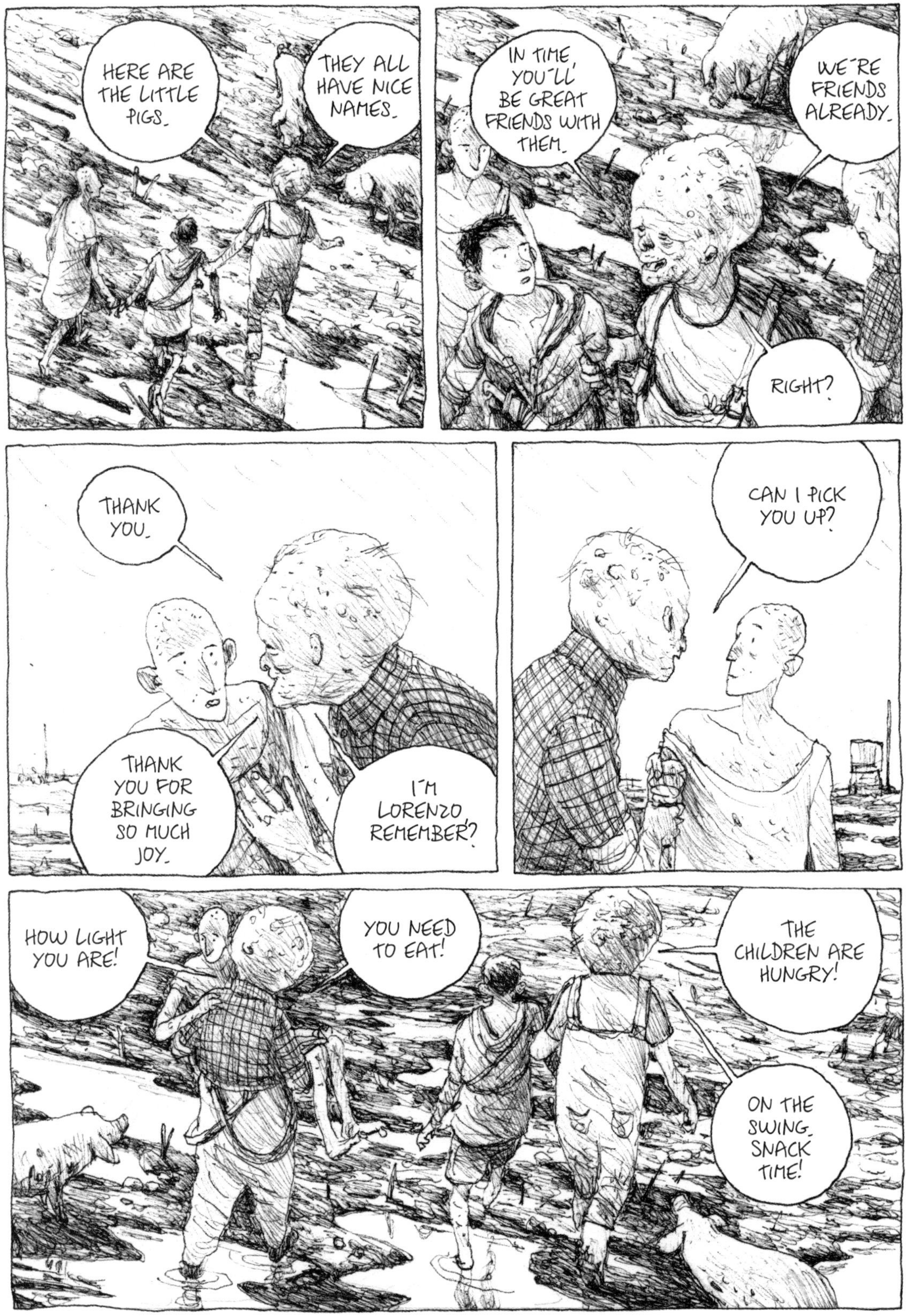
HERE ARE THE LITTLE PIGS…
THEY ALL HAVE NICE NAMES…
IN TIME, YOU'LL BE GREAT FRIENDS WITH THEM…
WE'RE FRIENDS ALREADY…
RIGHT?
THANK YOU…
THANK YOU FOR BRINGING SO MUCH JOY…
I'M LORENZO, REMEMBER?
CAN I PICK YOU UP?
HOW LIGHT YOU ARE!
YOU NEED TO EAT!
THE CHILDREN ARE HUNGRY!
ON THE SWING… SNACK TIME!

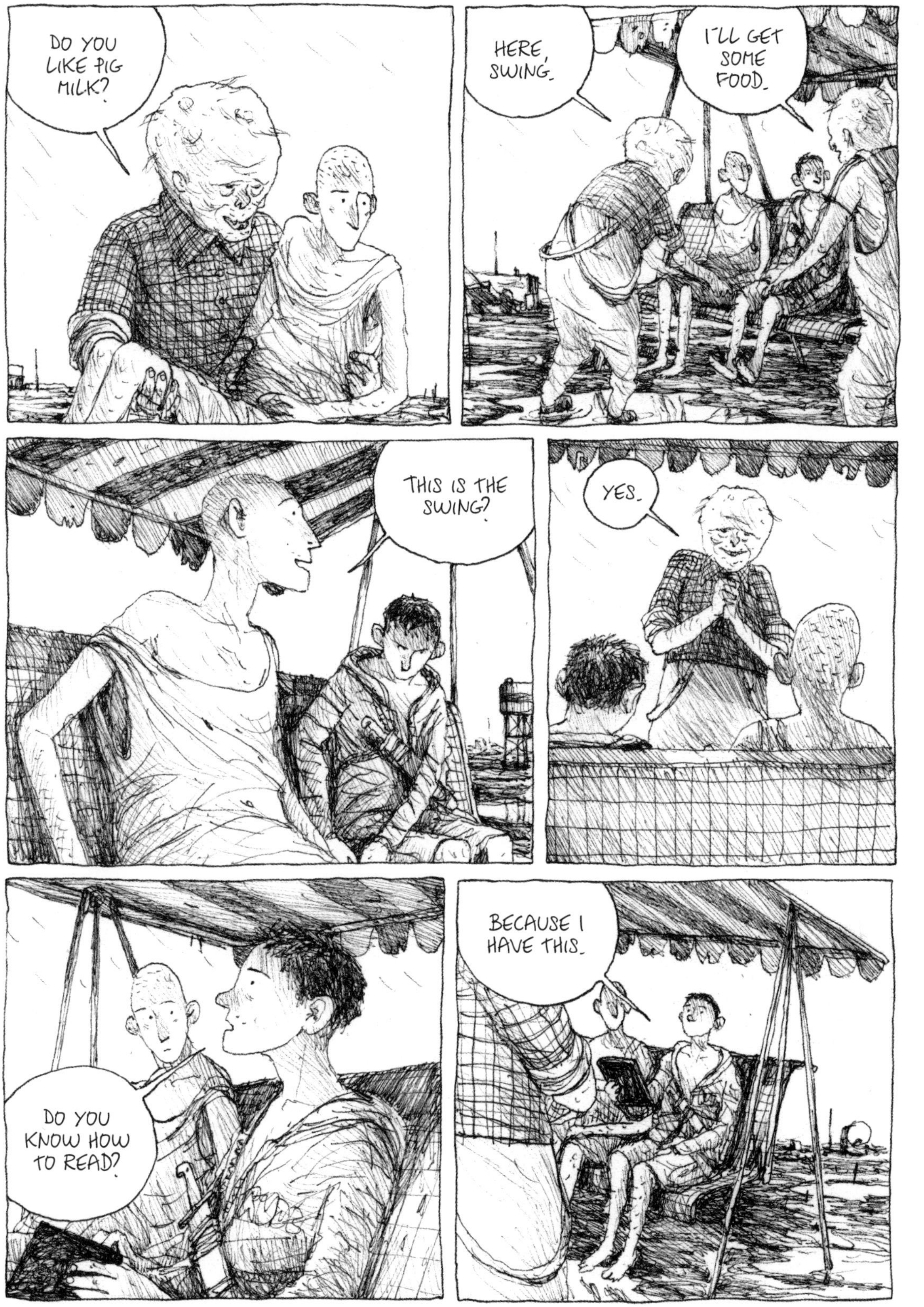
DO YOU LIKE PIG MILK?
HERE, SWING.
I'LL GET SOME FOOD.
THIS IS THE SWING?
YES.
DO YOU KNOW HOW TO READ?
BECAUSE I HAVE THIS.

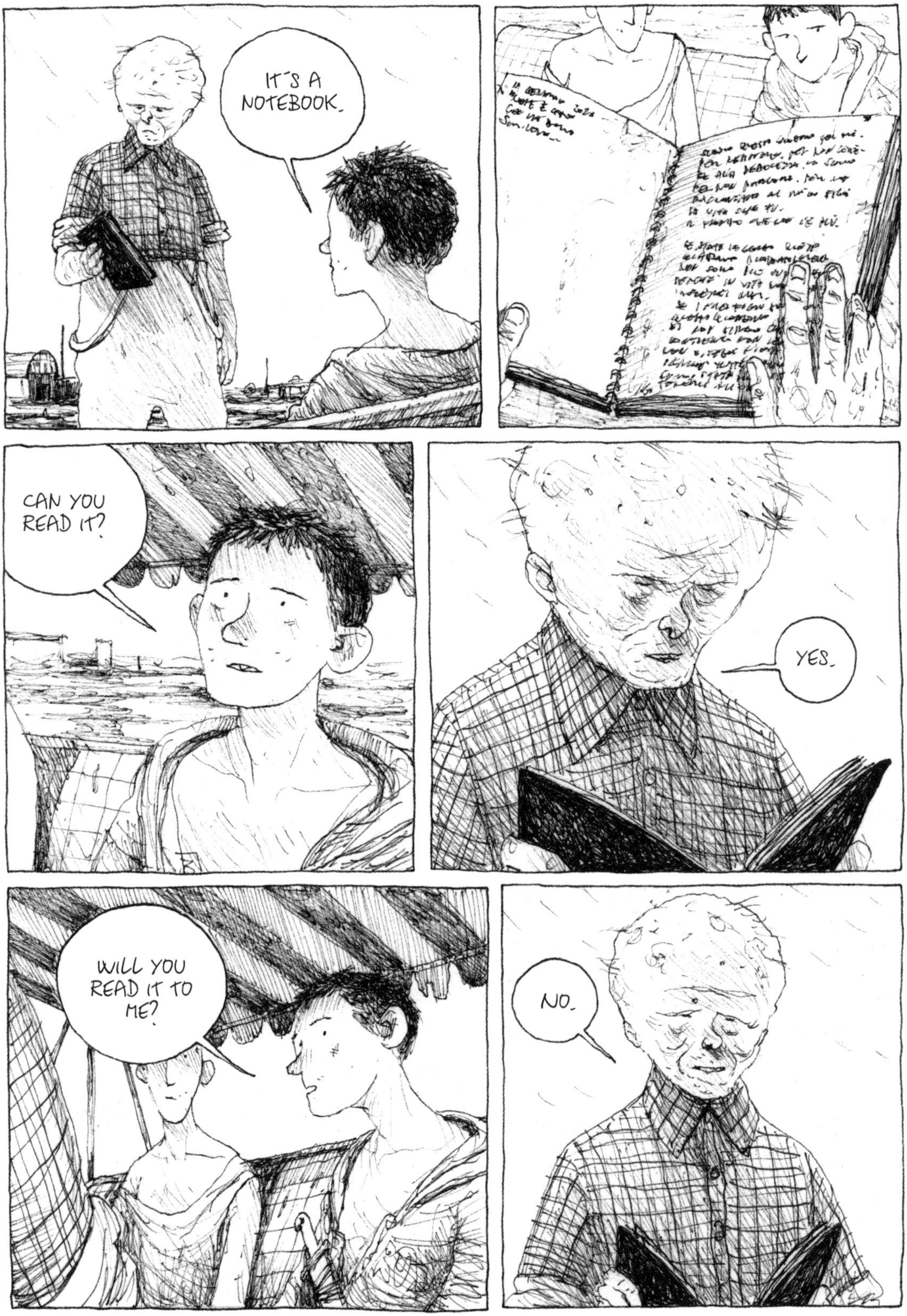
IT'S A NOTEBOOK.
CAN YOU READ IT?
YES.
WILL YOU READ IT TO ME?
NO.

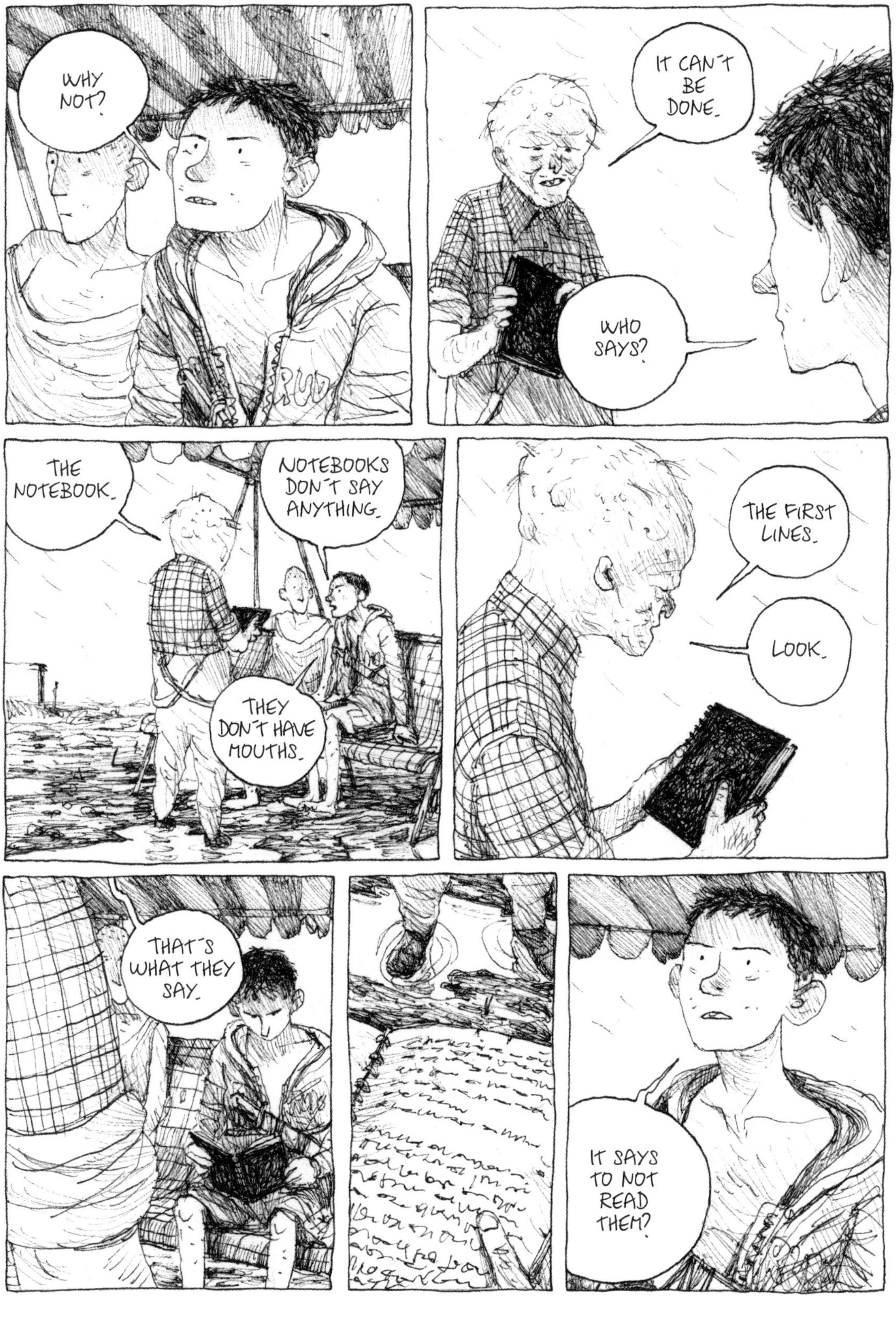
WHY NOT?
IT CAN'T BE DONE.
WHO SAYS?
THE NOTEBOOK.
NOTEBOOKS DON'T SAY ANYTHING.
THEY DON'T HAVE MOUTHS.
THE FIRST LINES.
LOOK.
THAT'S WHAT THEY SAY.
IT SAYS TO NOT READ THEM?

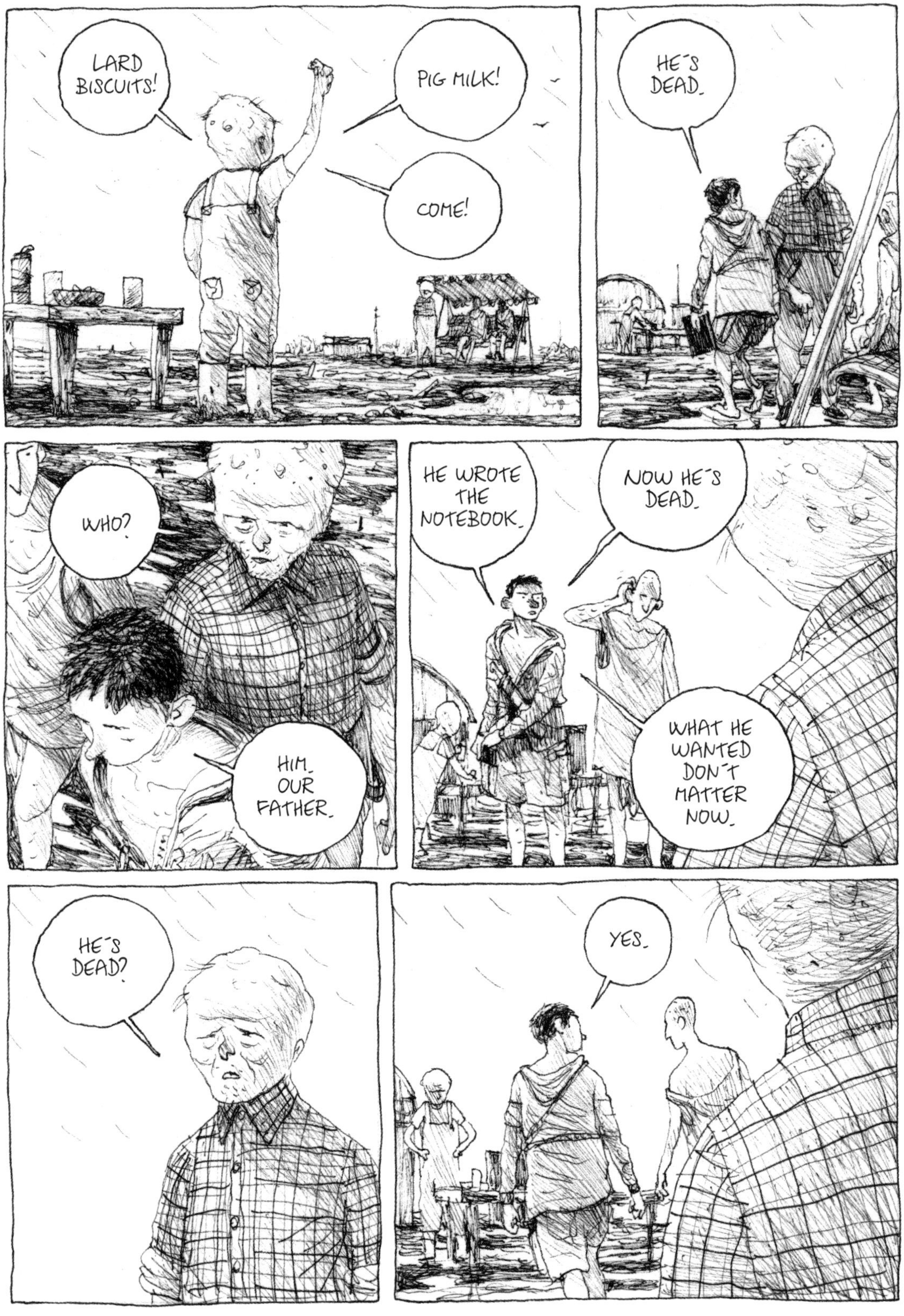
LARD BISCUITS!
PIG MILK!
COME!
HE'S DEAD.
WHO?
HIM. OUR FATHER.
HE WROTE THE NOTEBOOK.
NOW HE'S DEAD.
WHAT HE WANTED DON'T MATTER NOW.
HE'S DEAD?
YES.

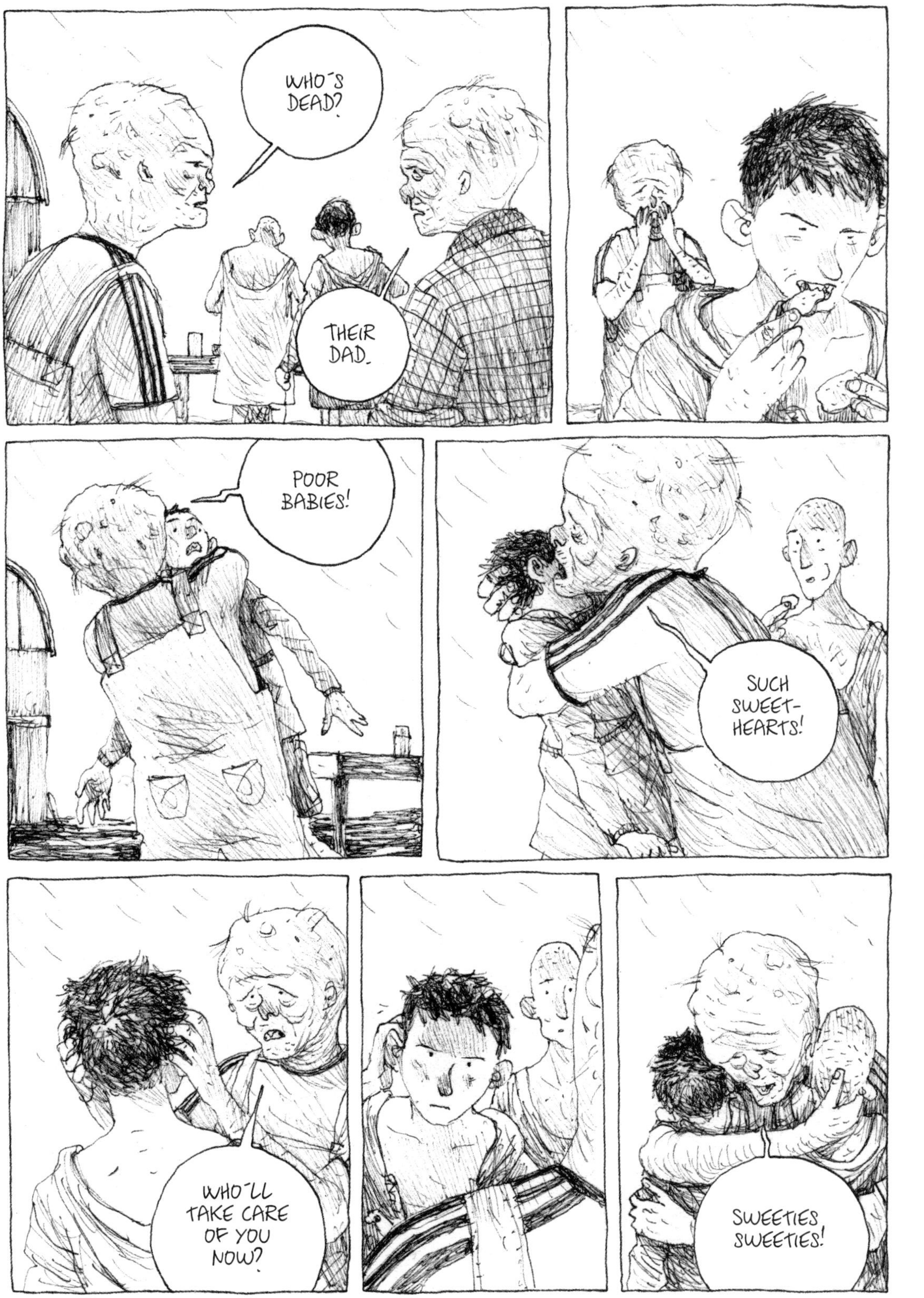
WHO'S DEAD?
THEIR DAD.
POOR BABIES!
SUCH SWEET-HEARTS!
WHO'LL TAKE CARE OF YOU NOW?
SWEETIES SWEETIES!

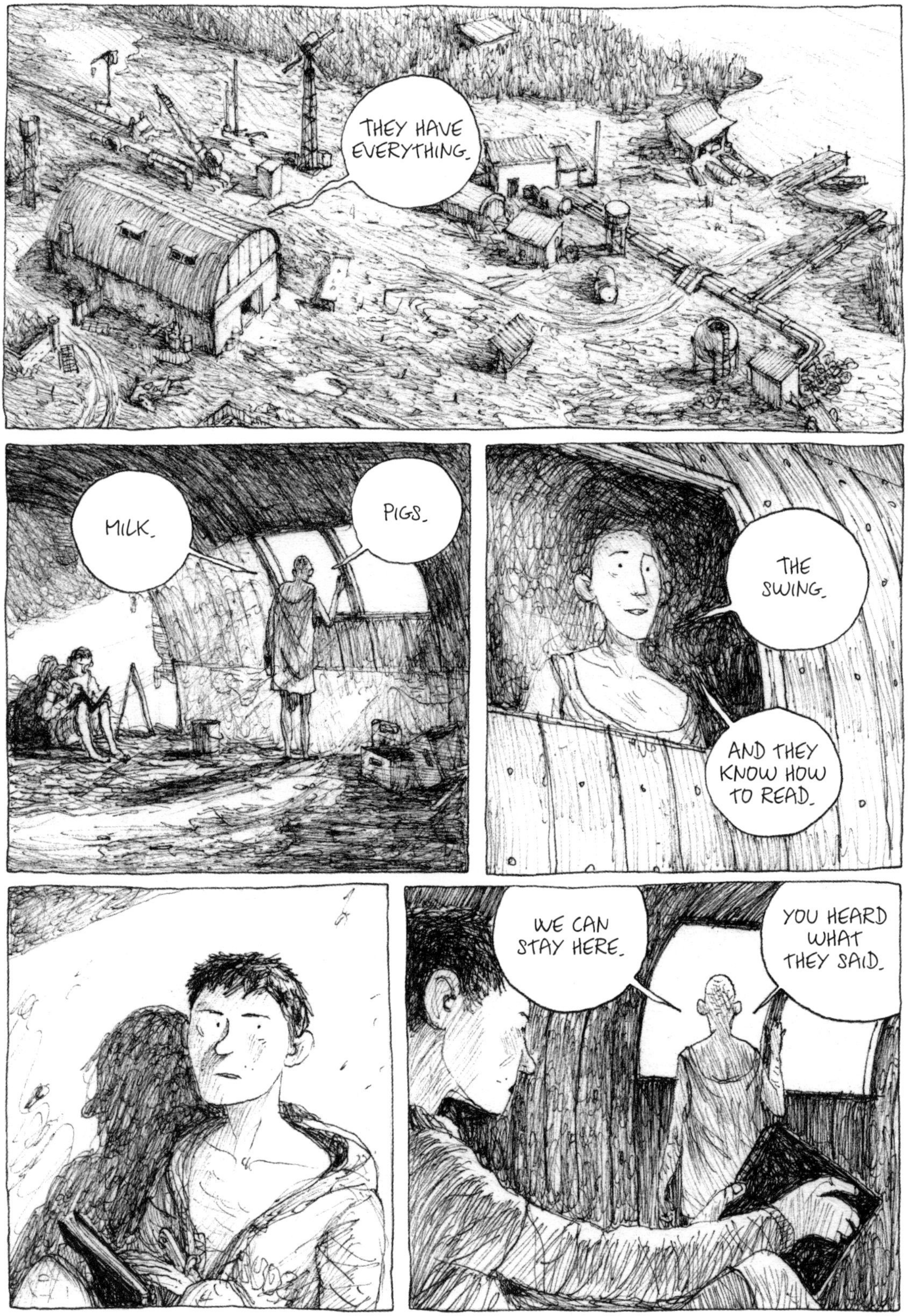
THEY HAVE EVERYTHING.
MILK.
PIGS.
THE SWING.
AND THEY KNOW HOW TO READ.
WE CAN STAY HERE.
YOU HEARD WHAT THEY SAID.

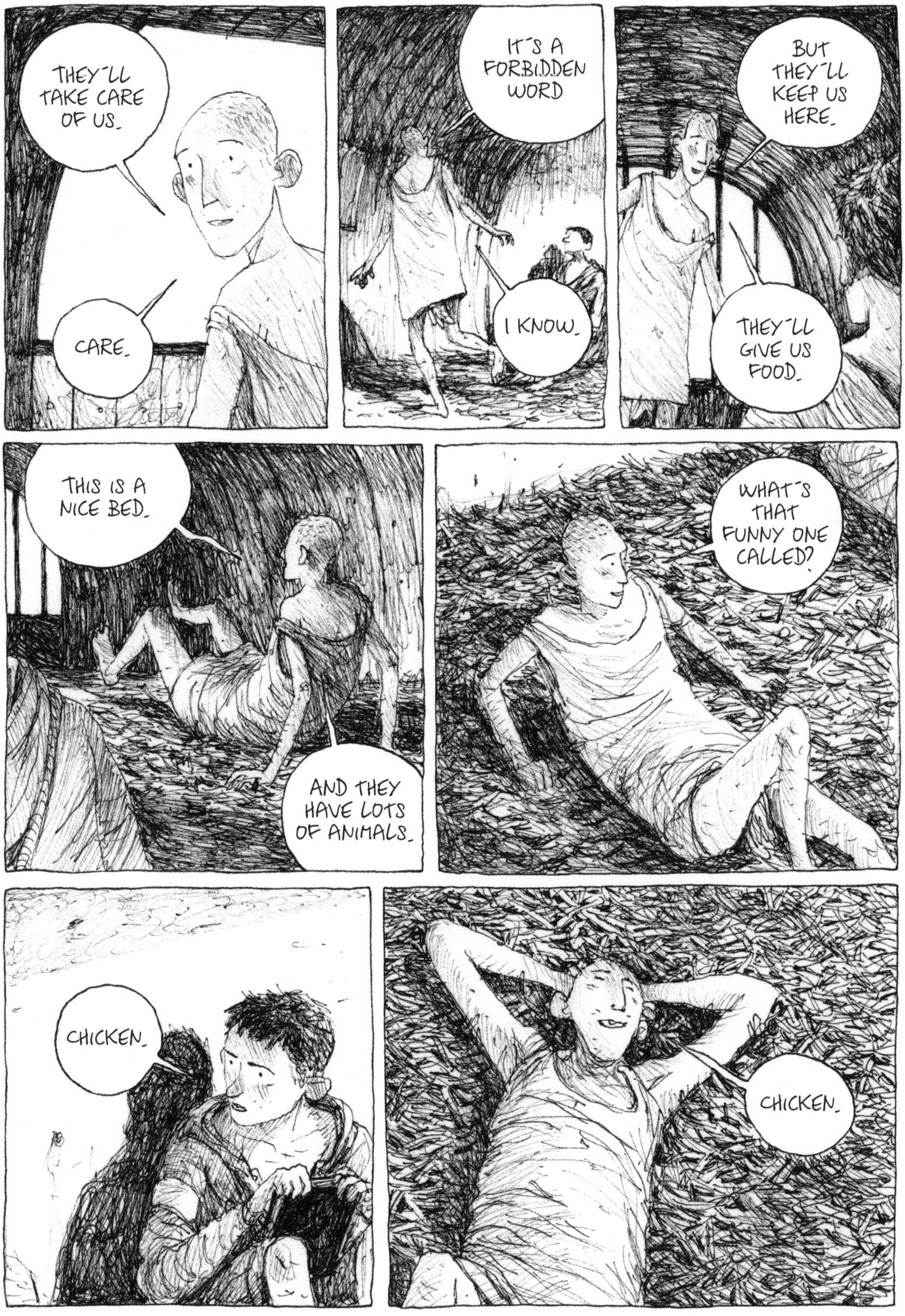
THEY'LL TAKE CARE OF US.
CARE.
IT'S A FORBIDDEN WORD
I KNOW.
BUT THEY'LL KEEP US HERE.
THEY'LL GIVE US FOOD.
THIS IS A NICE BED.
AND THEY HAVE LOTS OF ANIMALS.
WHAT'S THAT FUNNY ONE CALLED?
CHICKEN.
CHICKEN.

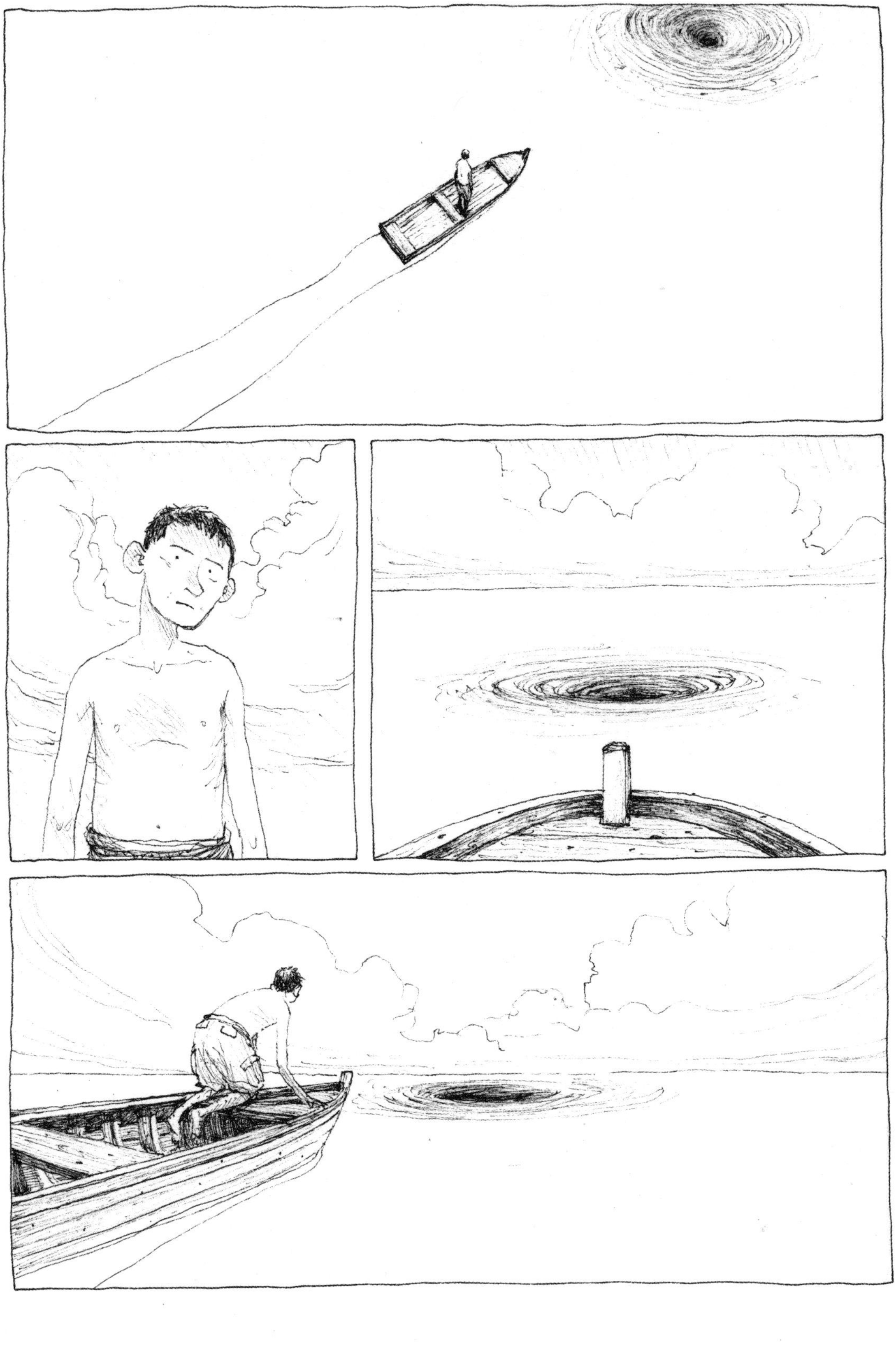

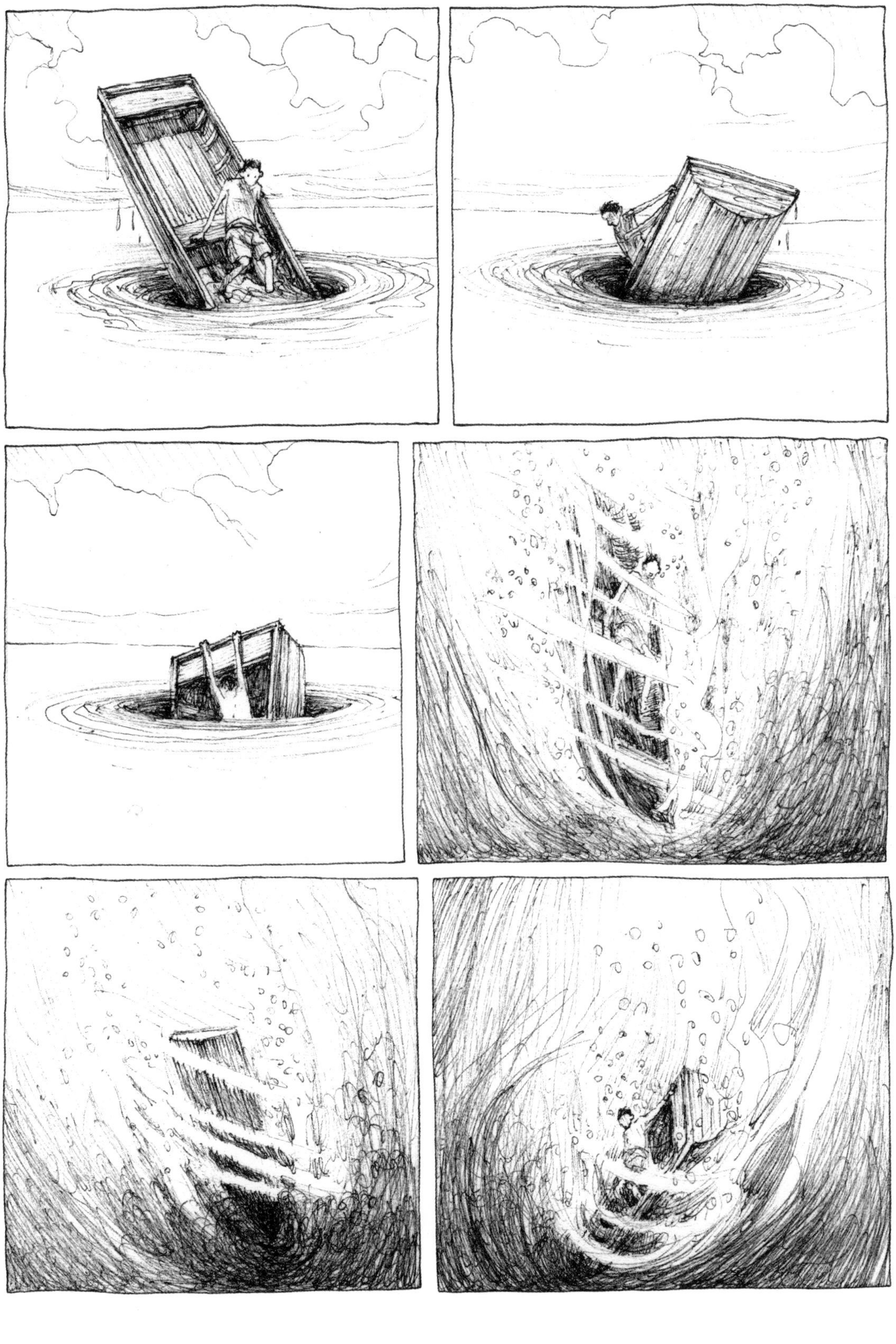

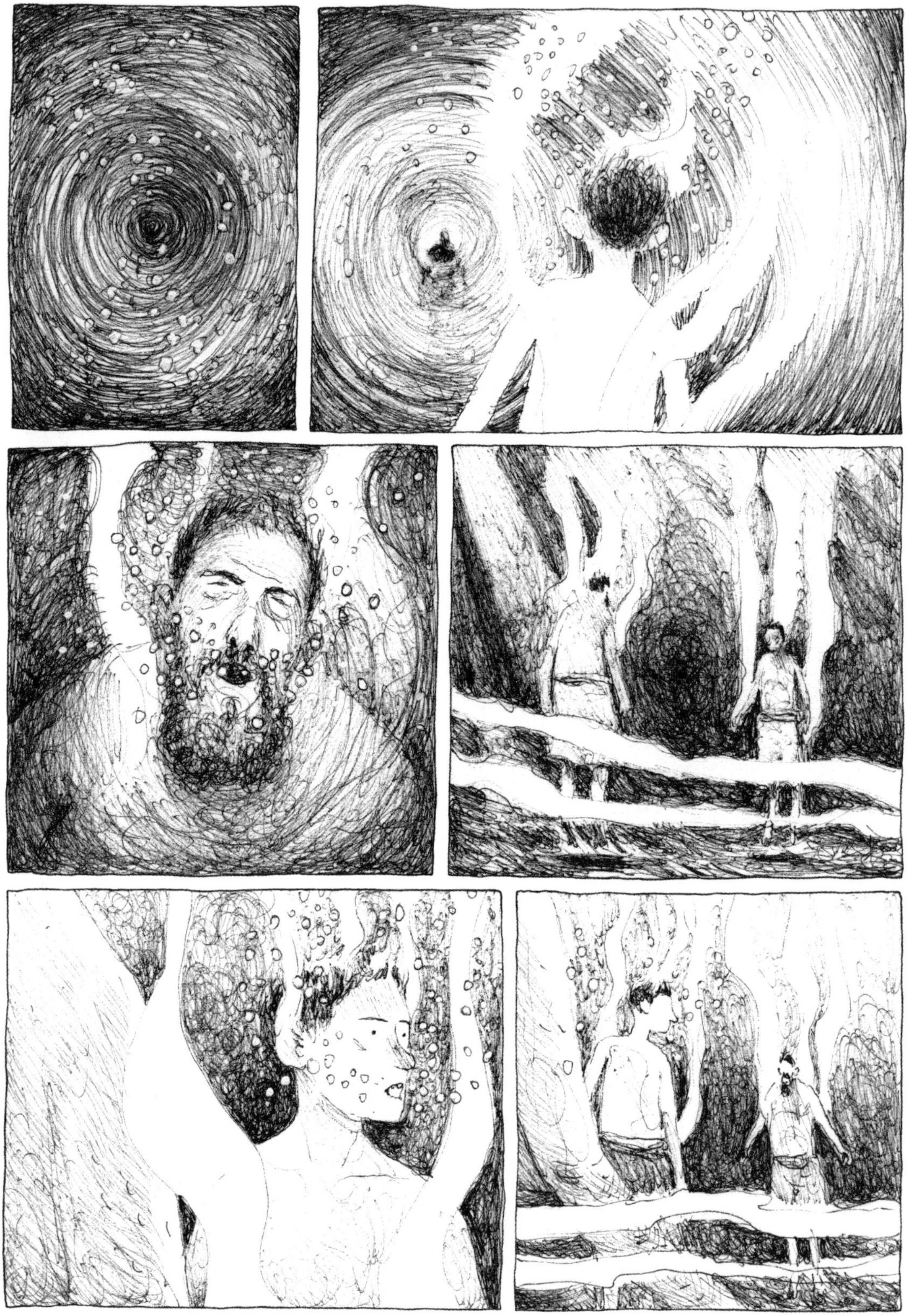

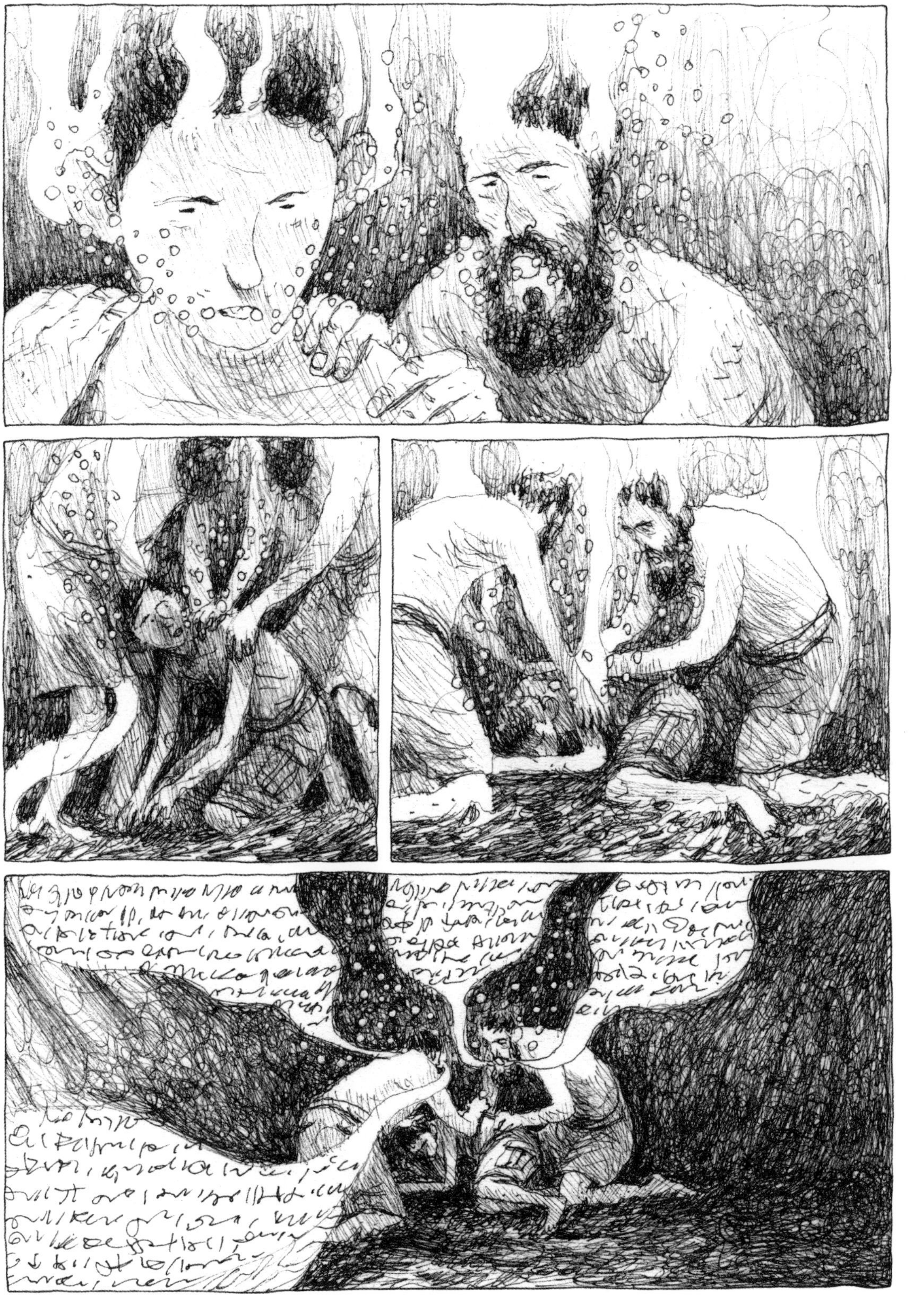

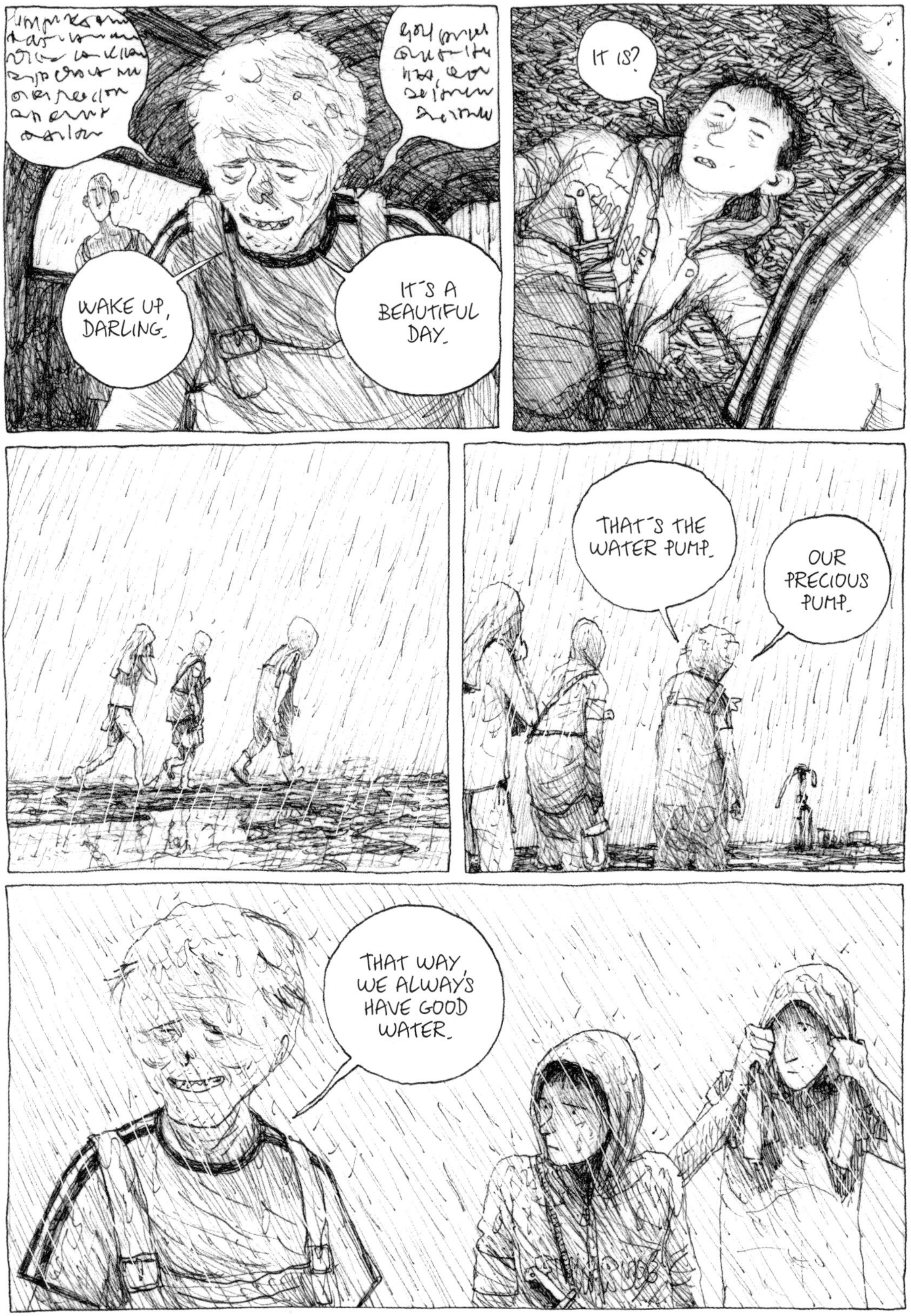
WAKE UP, DARLING!
IT'S A BEAUTIFUL DAY.
IT IS?
THAT'S THE WATER PUMP.
OUR PRECIOUS PUMP.
THAT WAY, WE ALWAYS HAVE GOOD WATER.

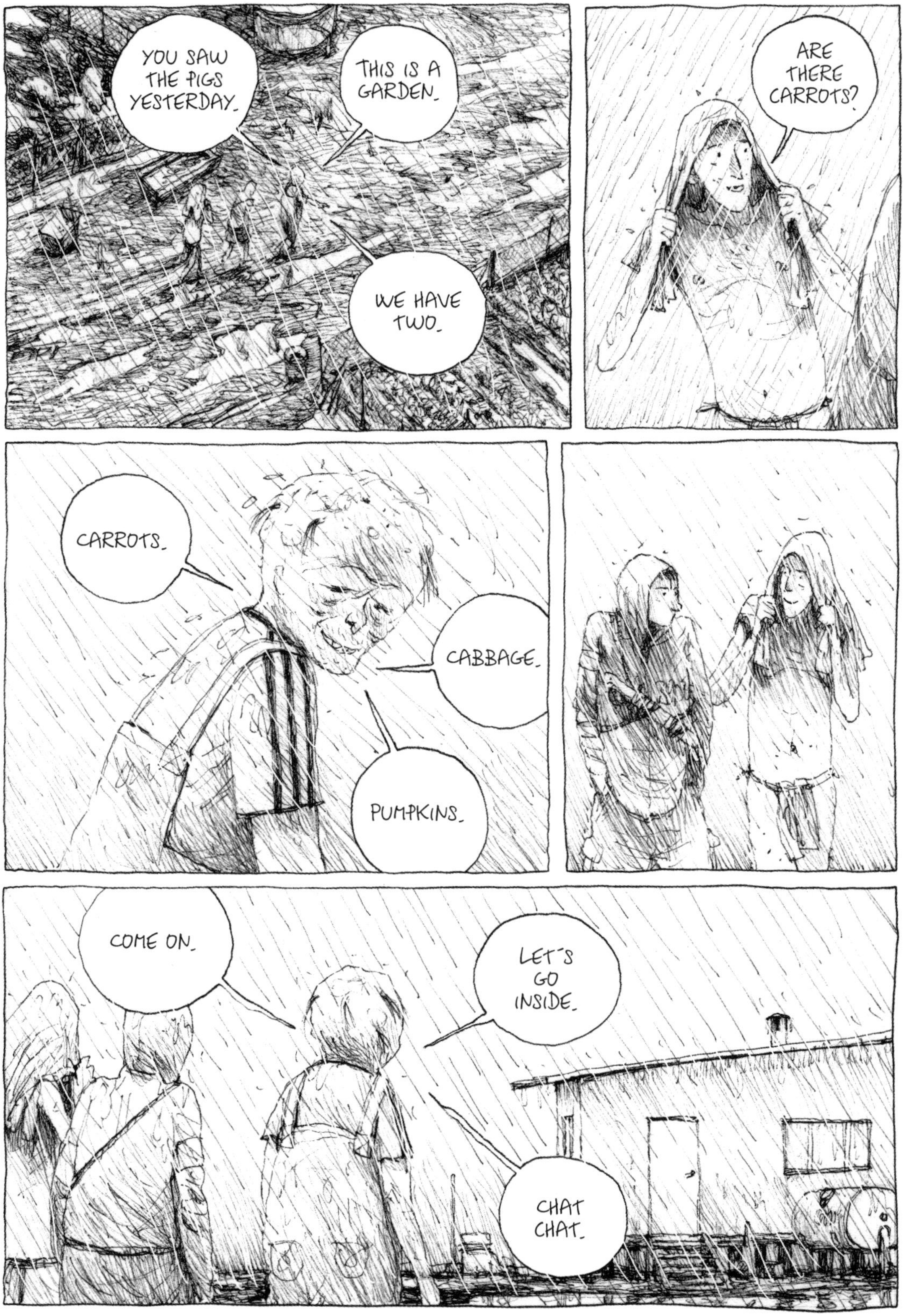

YOU SAW THE PIGS YESTERDAY.
THIS IS A GARDEN.
WE HAVE TWO.
ARE THERE CARROTS?
CARROTS.
CABBAGE.
PUMPKINS.
COME ON.
LET'S GO INSIDE.
CHAT CHAT.

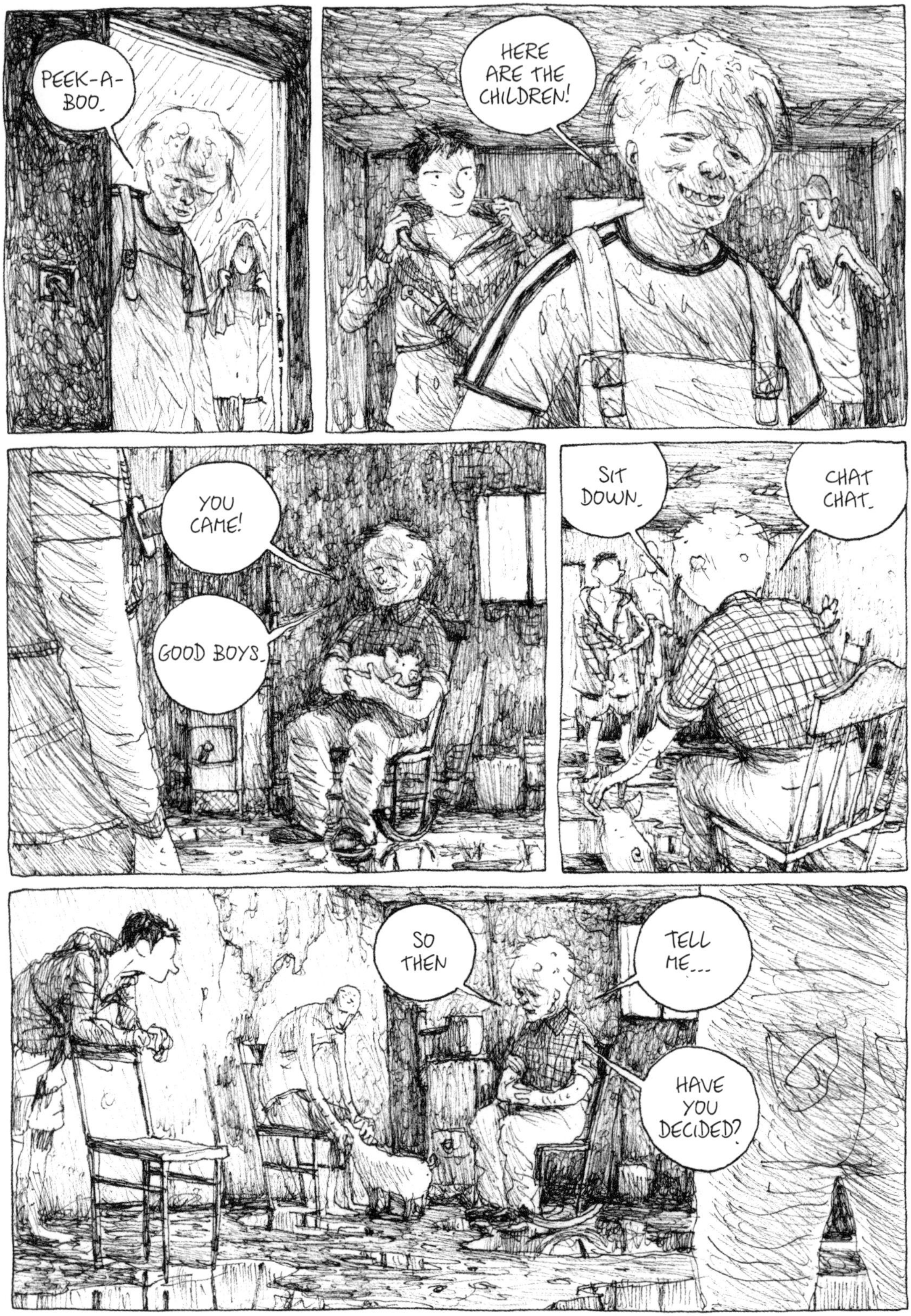
PEEK-A-BOO_
HERE ARE THE CHILDREN!
YOU CAME!
GOOD BOYS_
SIT DOWN_
CHAT CHAT_
SO THEN
TELL ME...
HAVE YOU DECIDED?

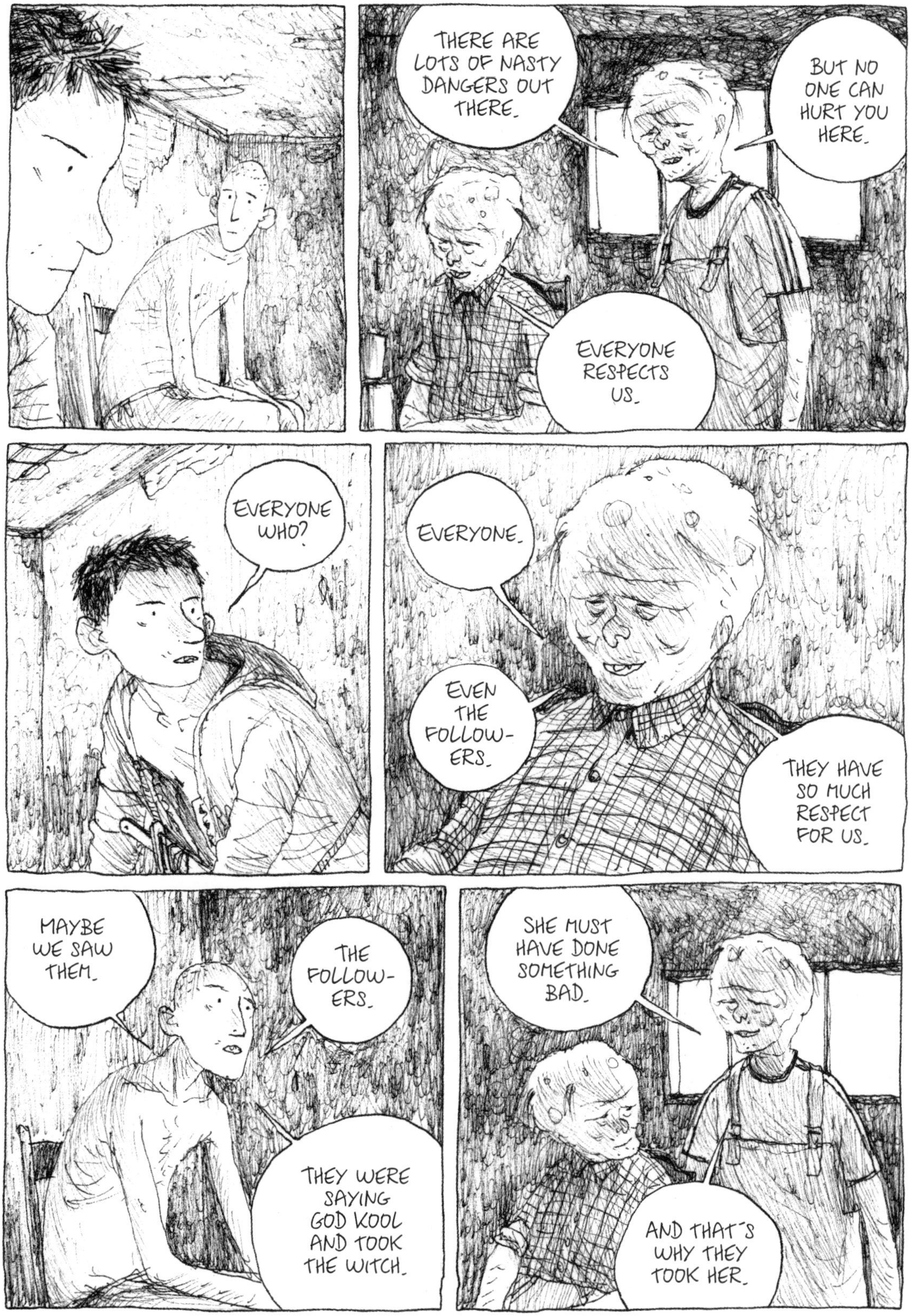

THERE ARE LOTS OF NASTY DANGERS OUT THERE.
BUT NO ONE CAN HURT YOU HERE.
EVERYONE RESPECTS US.
EVERYONE WHO?
EVERYONE.
EVEN THE FOLLOW-ERS.
THEY HAVE SO MUCH RESPECT FOR US.
MAYBE WE SAW THEM.
THE FOLLOW-ERS.
THEY WERE SAYING GOD KOOL AND TOOK THE WITCH.
SHE MUST HAVE DONE SOMETHING BAD.
AND THAT'S WHY THEY TOOK HER.

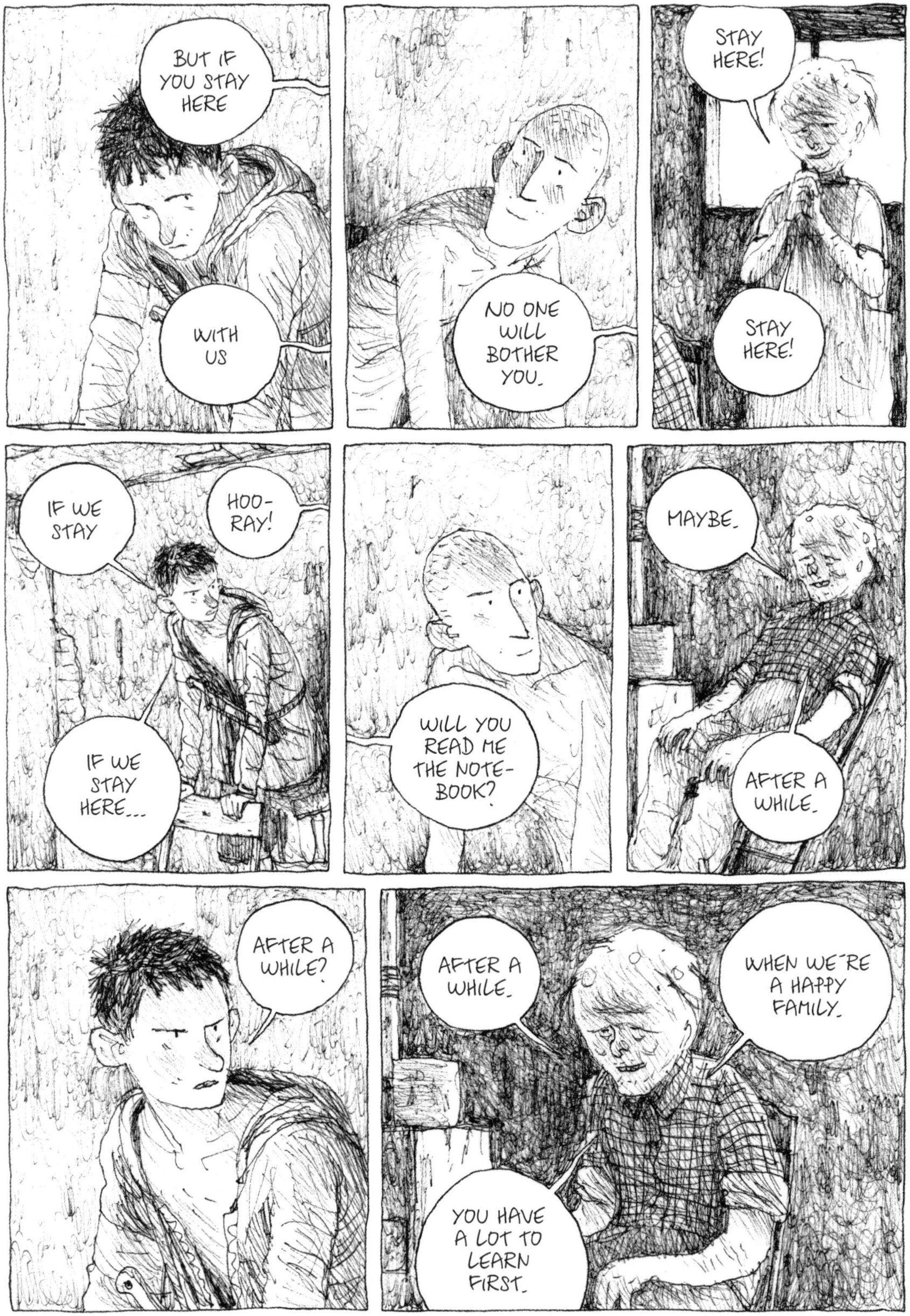
BUT IF YOU STAY HERE
WITH US
NO ONE WILL BOTHER YOU.
STAY HERE!
STAY HERE!
IF WE STAY
HOO-RAY!
IF WE STAY HERE...
WILL YOU READ ME THE NOTE-BOOK?
MAYBE.
AFTER A WHILE.
AFTER A WHILE?
AFTER A WHILE.
WHEN WE'RE A HAPPY FAMILY.
YOU HAVE A LOT TO LEARN FIRST.

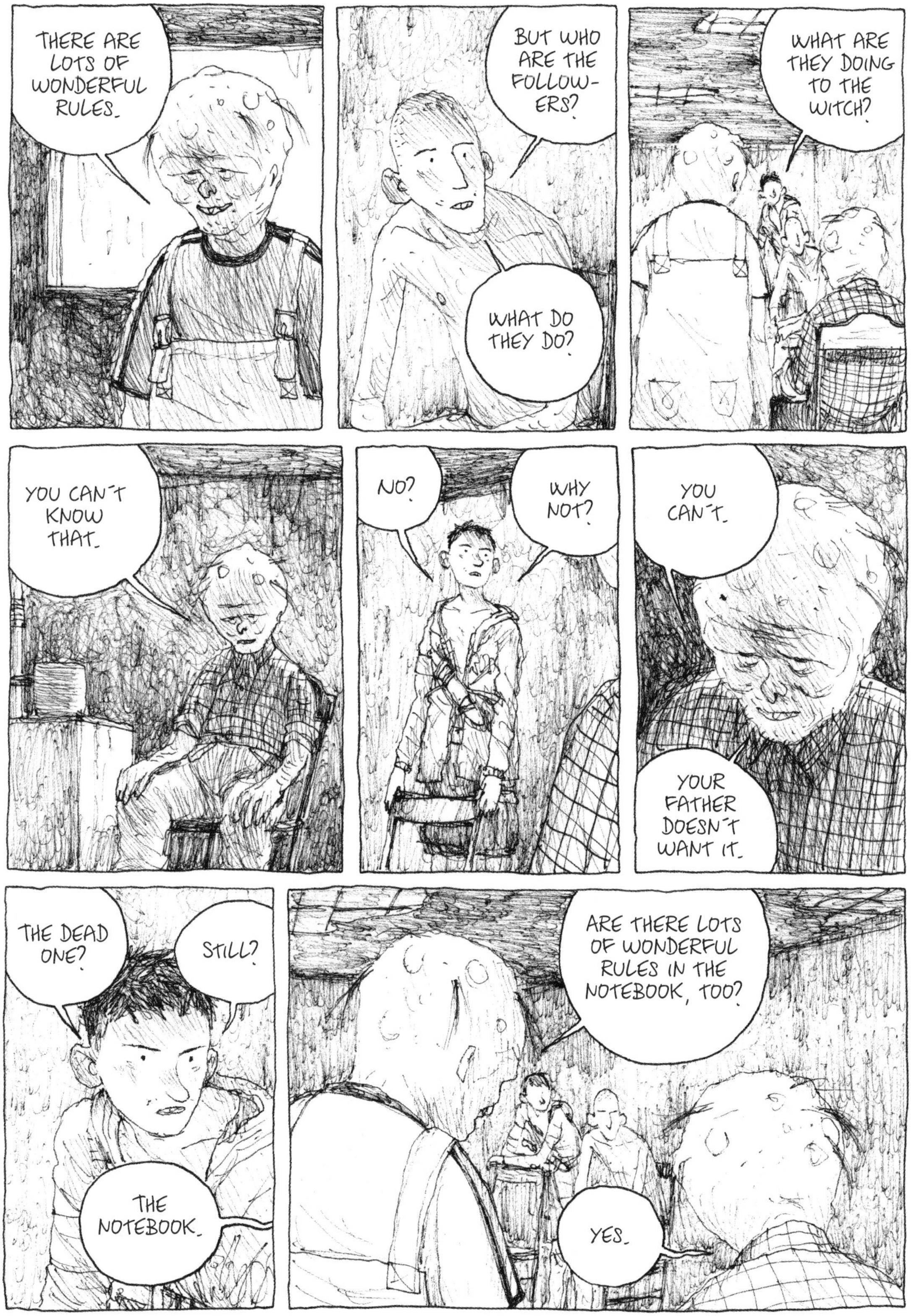
THERE ARE LOTS OF WONDERFUL RULES.
BUT WHO ARE THE FOLLOW-ERS?
WHAT DO THEY DO?
WHAT ARE THEY DOING TO THE WITCH?
YOU CAN'T KNOW THAT.
NO?
WHY NOT?
YOU CAN'T.
YOUR FATHER DOESN'T WANT IT.
THE DEAD ONE?
STILL?
THE NOTEBOOK.
ARE THERE LOTS OF WONDERFUL RULES IN THE NOTEBOOK, TOO?
YES.

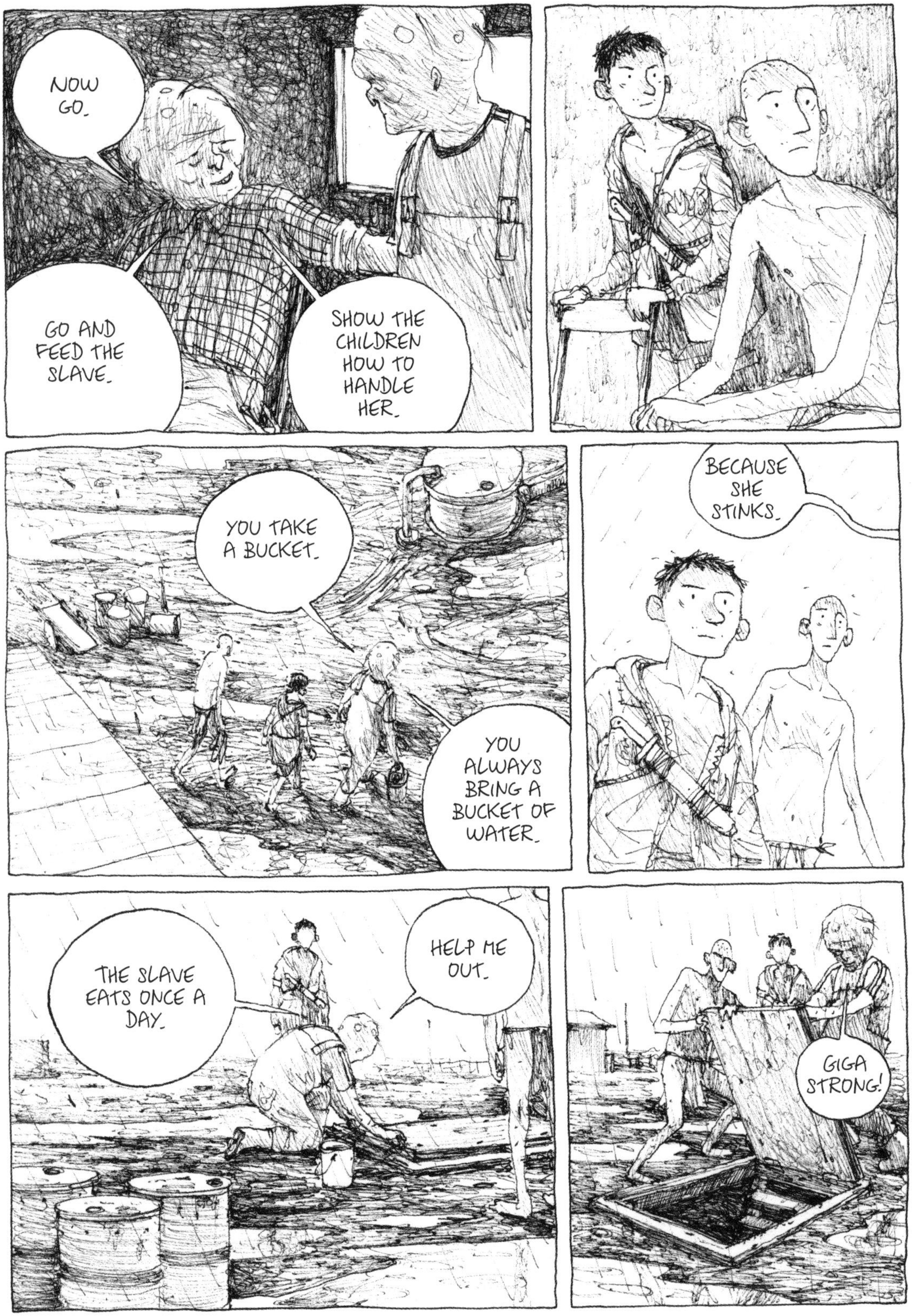
NOW GO.
GO AND FEED THE SLAVE.
SHOW THE CHILDREN HOW TO HANDLE HER.
YOU TAKE A BUCKET.
YOU ALWAYS BRING A BUCKET OF WATER.
BECAUSE SHE STINKS.
THE SLAVE EATS ONCE A DAY.
HELP ME OUT.
GIGA STRONG!

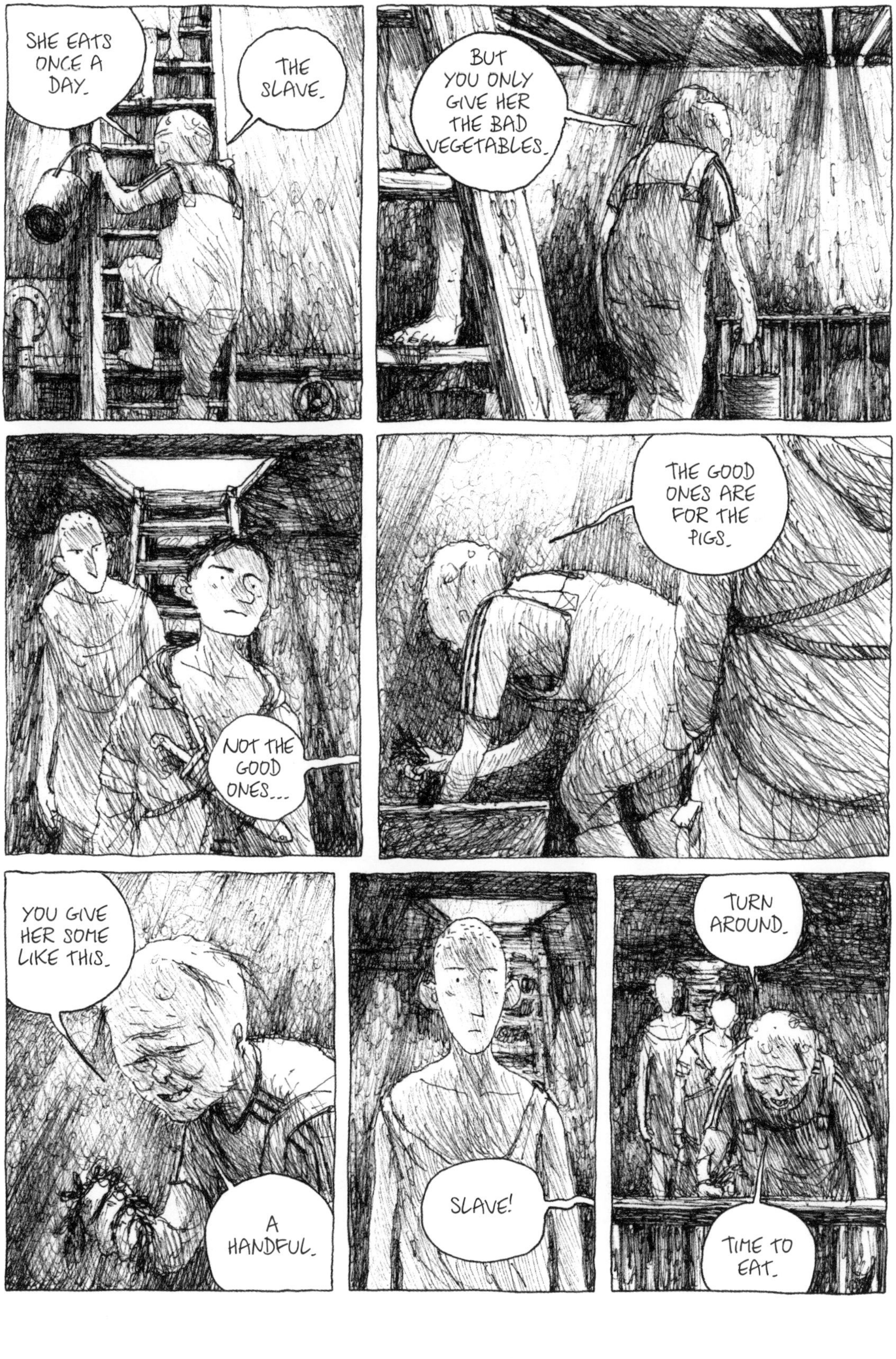
SHE EATS ONCE A DAY.
THE SLAVE.
BUT YOU ONLY GIVE HER THE BAD VEGETABLES.
NOT THE GOOD ONES...
THE GOOD ONES ARE FOR THE PIGS.
YOU GIVE HER SOME LIKE THIS.
A HANDFUL.
SLAVE!
TURN AROUND.
TIME TO EAT.

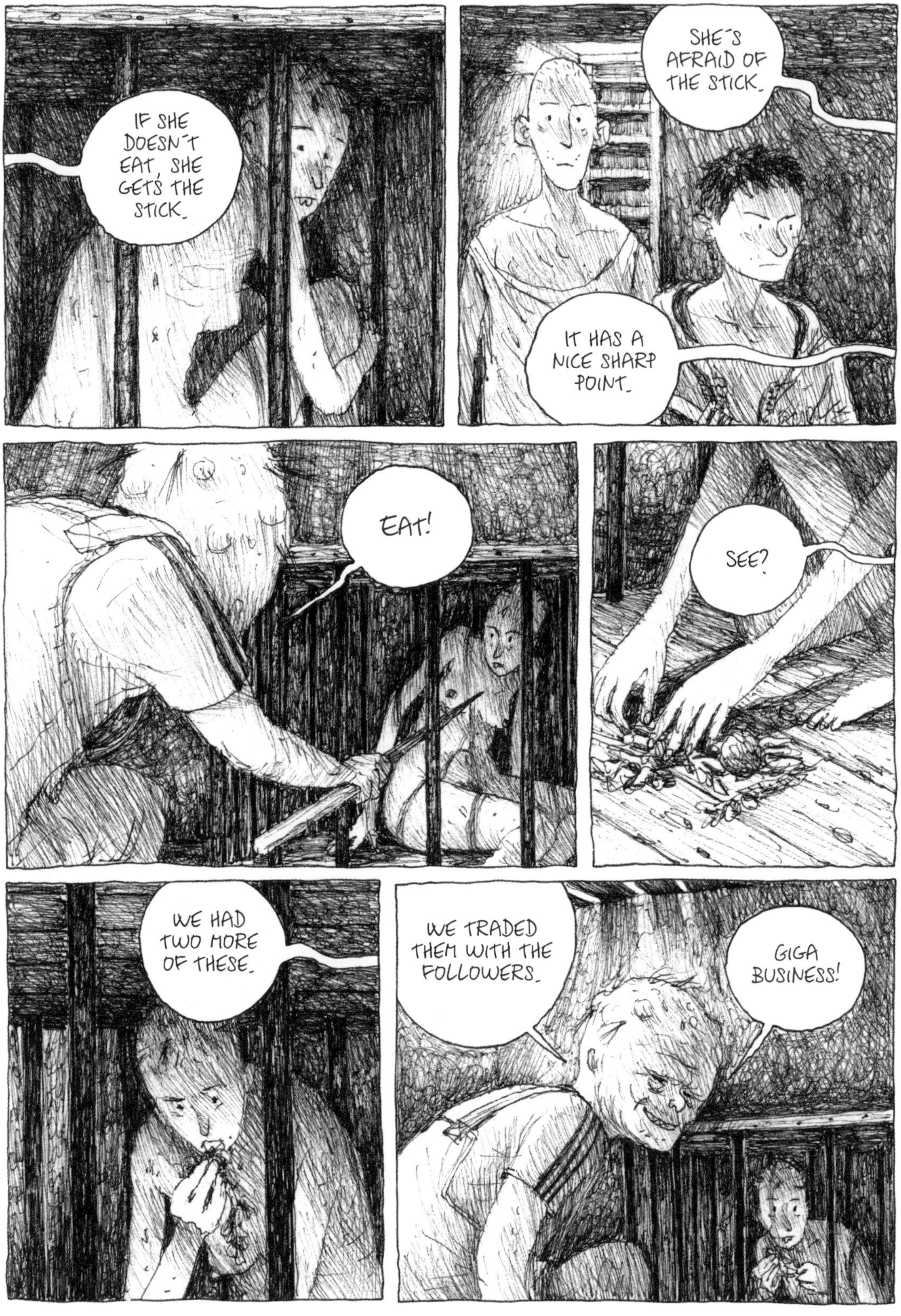
IF SHE DOESN'T EAT, SHE GETS THE STICK.
SHE'S AFRAID OF THE STICK.
IT HAS A NICE SHARP POINT.
EAT!
SEE?
WE HAD TWO MORE OF THESE.
WE TRADED THEM WITH THE FOLLOWERS.
GIGA BUSINESS!

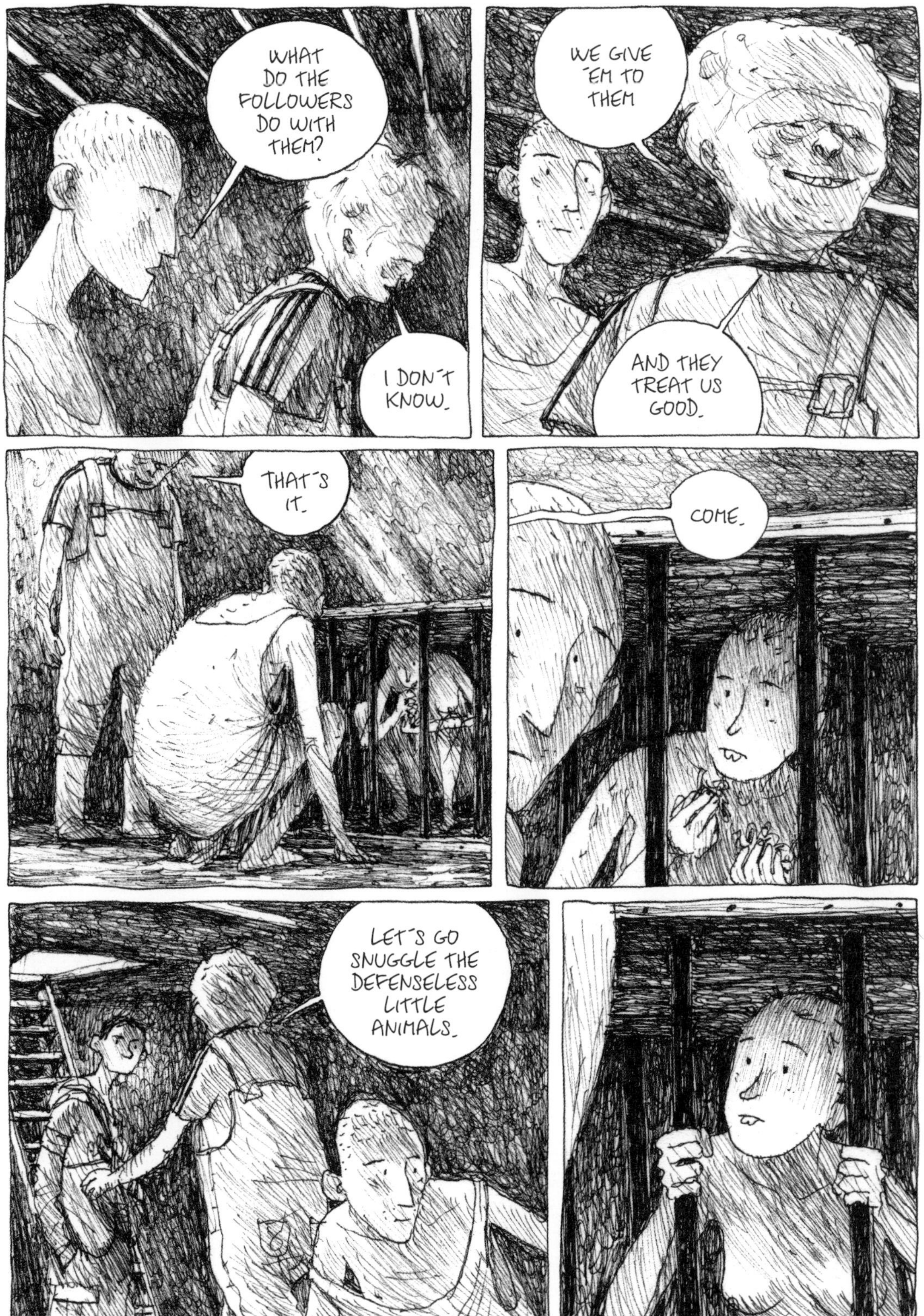
WHAT DO THE FOLLOWERS DO WITH THEM?
I DON'T KNOW.
WE GIVE 'EM TO THEM
AND THEY TREAT US GOOD.
THAT'S IT.
COME.
LET'S GO SNUGGLE THE DEFENSELESS LITTLE ANIMALS.

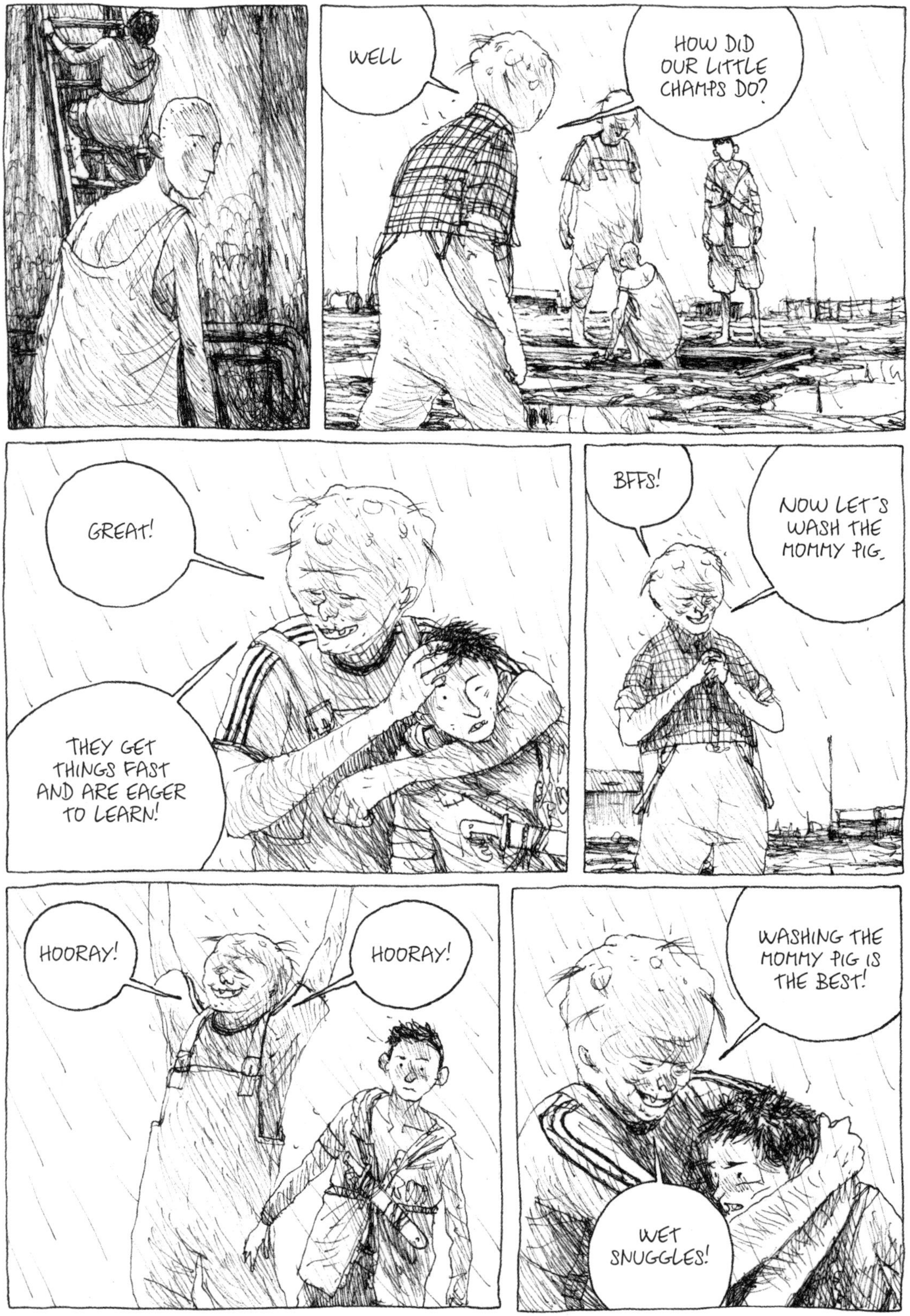
WELL
HOW DID OUR LITTLE CHAMPS DO?
GREAT!
THEY GET THINGS FAST AND ARE EAGER TO LEARN!
BFFS!
NOW LET'S WASH THE MOMMY PIG.
HOORAY!
HOORAY!
WASHING THE MOMMY PIG IS THE BEST!
WET SNUGGLES!

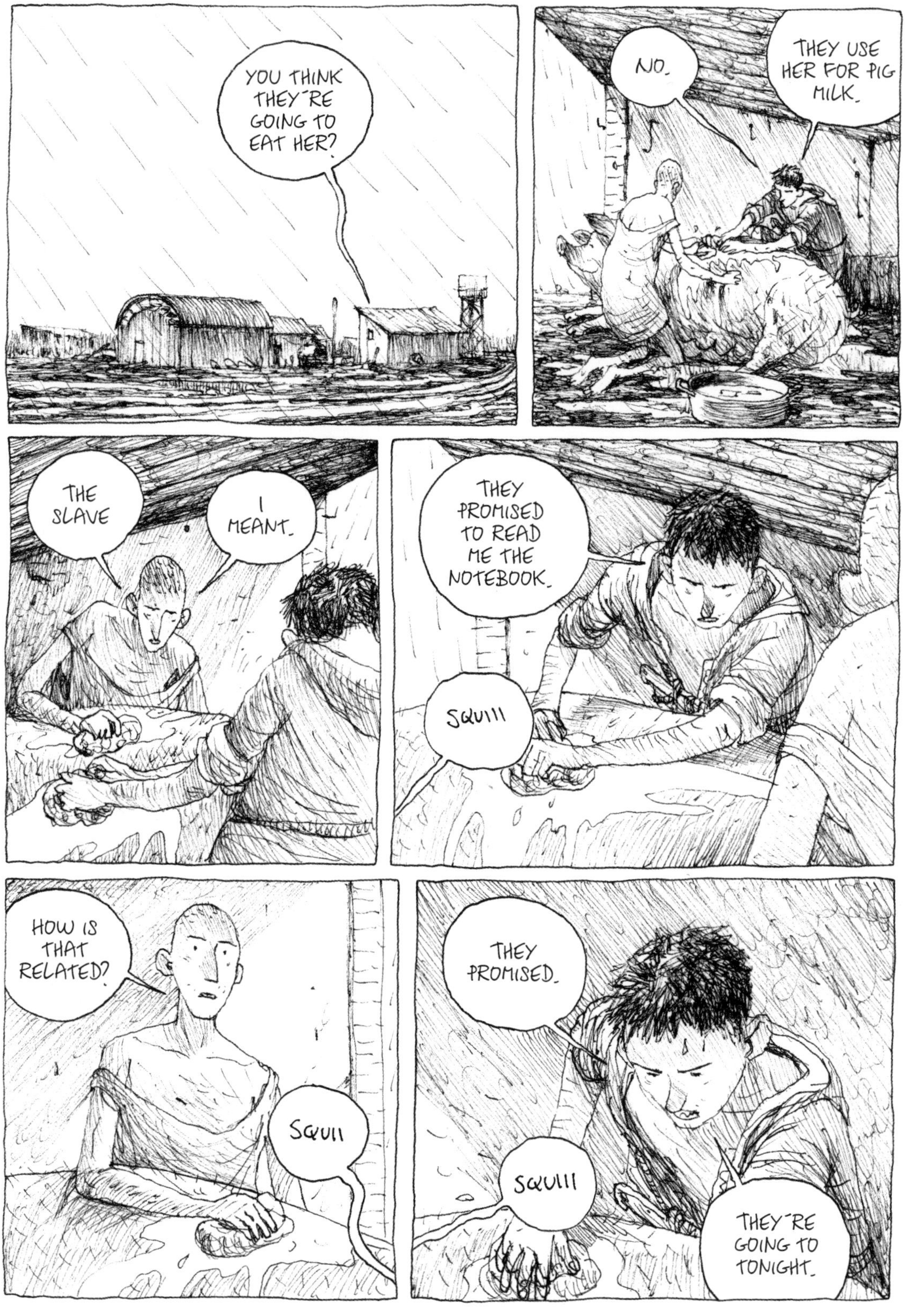
YOU THINK THEY'RE GOING TO EAT HER?
NO.
THEY USE HER FOR PIG MILK.
THE SLAVE
I MEANT.
THEY PROMISED TO READ ME THE NOTEBOOK.
SQUIII
HOW IS THAT RELATED?
SQUII
THEY PROMISED.
SQUIII
THEY'RE GOING TO TONIGHT.

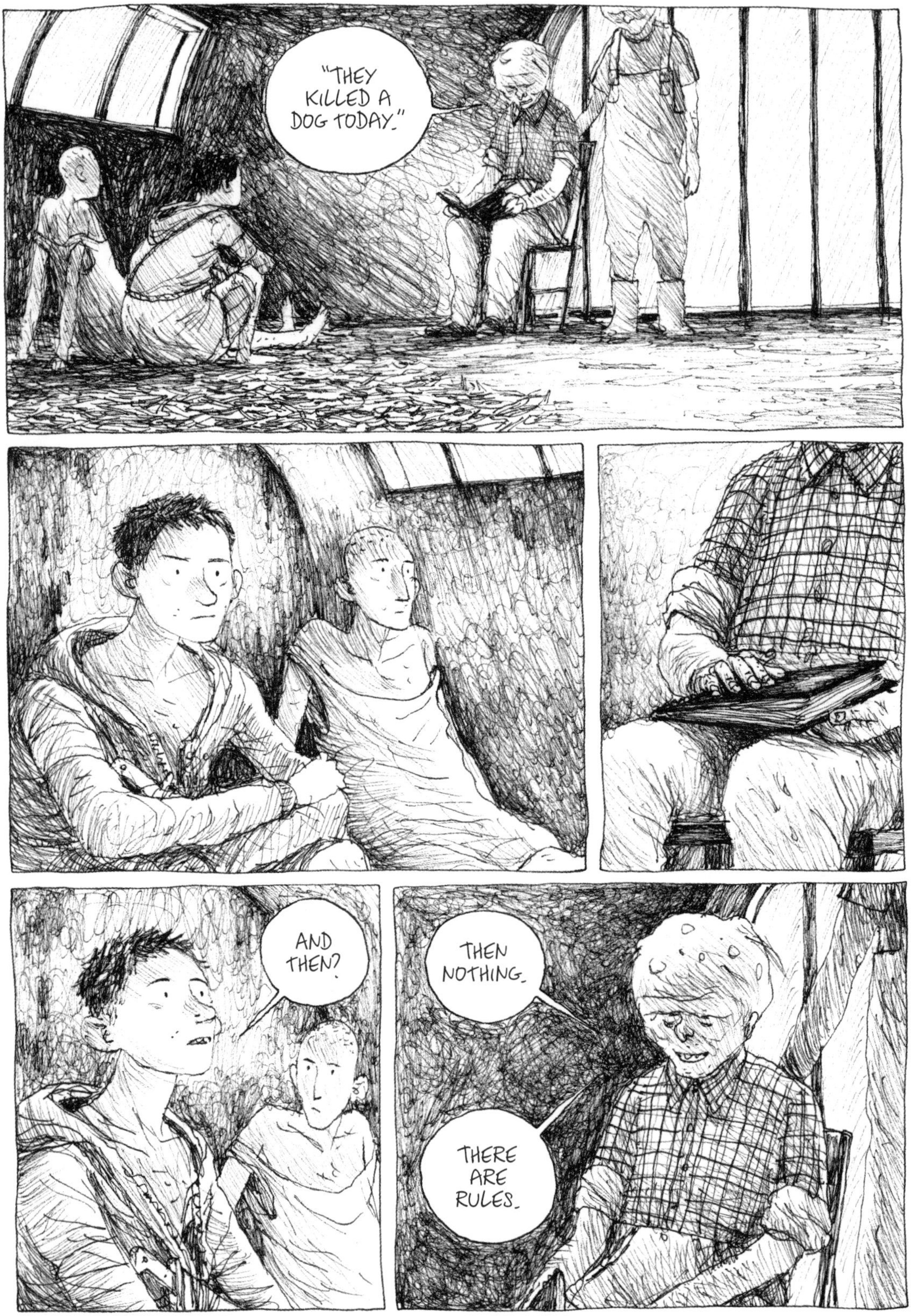
"THEY KILLED A DOG TODAY."
AND THEN?
THEN NOTHING.
THERE ARE RULES.

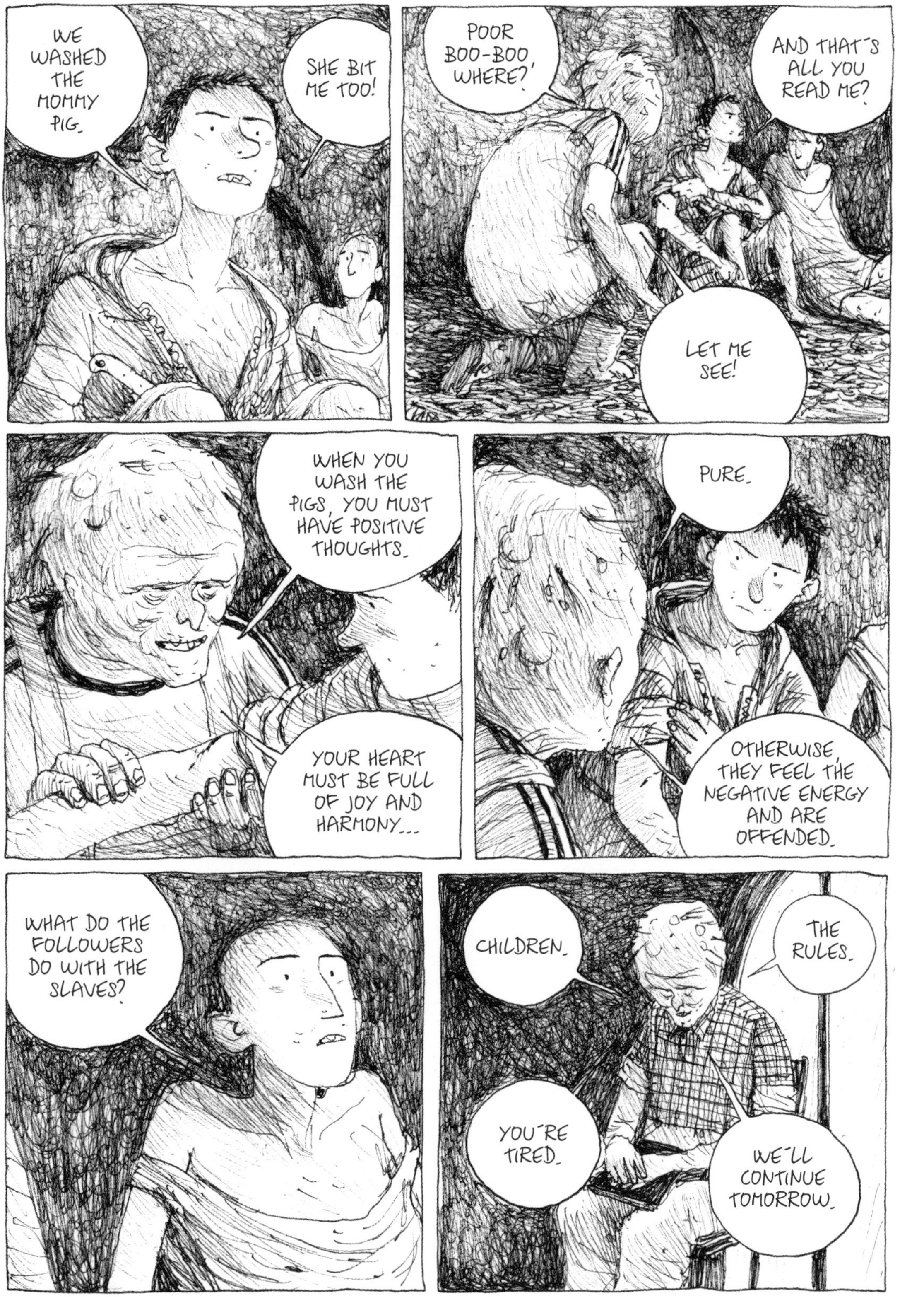
WE WASHED THE MOMMY PIG.
SHE BIT ME TOO!
POOR BOO-BOO, WHERE?
AND THAT'S ALL YOU READ ME?
LET ME SEE!
WHEN YOU WASH THE PIGS, YOU MUST HAVE POSITIVE THOUGHTS.
YOUR HEART MUST BE FULL OF JOY AND HARMONY...
PURE.
OTHERWISE, THEY FEEL THE NEGATIVE ENERGY AND ARE OFFENDED.
WHAT DO THE FOLLOWERS DO WITH THE SLAVES?
CHILDREN.
THE RULES.
YOU'RE TIRED.
WE'LL CONTINUE TOMORROW.

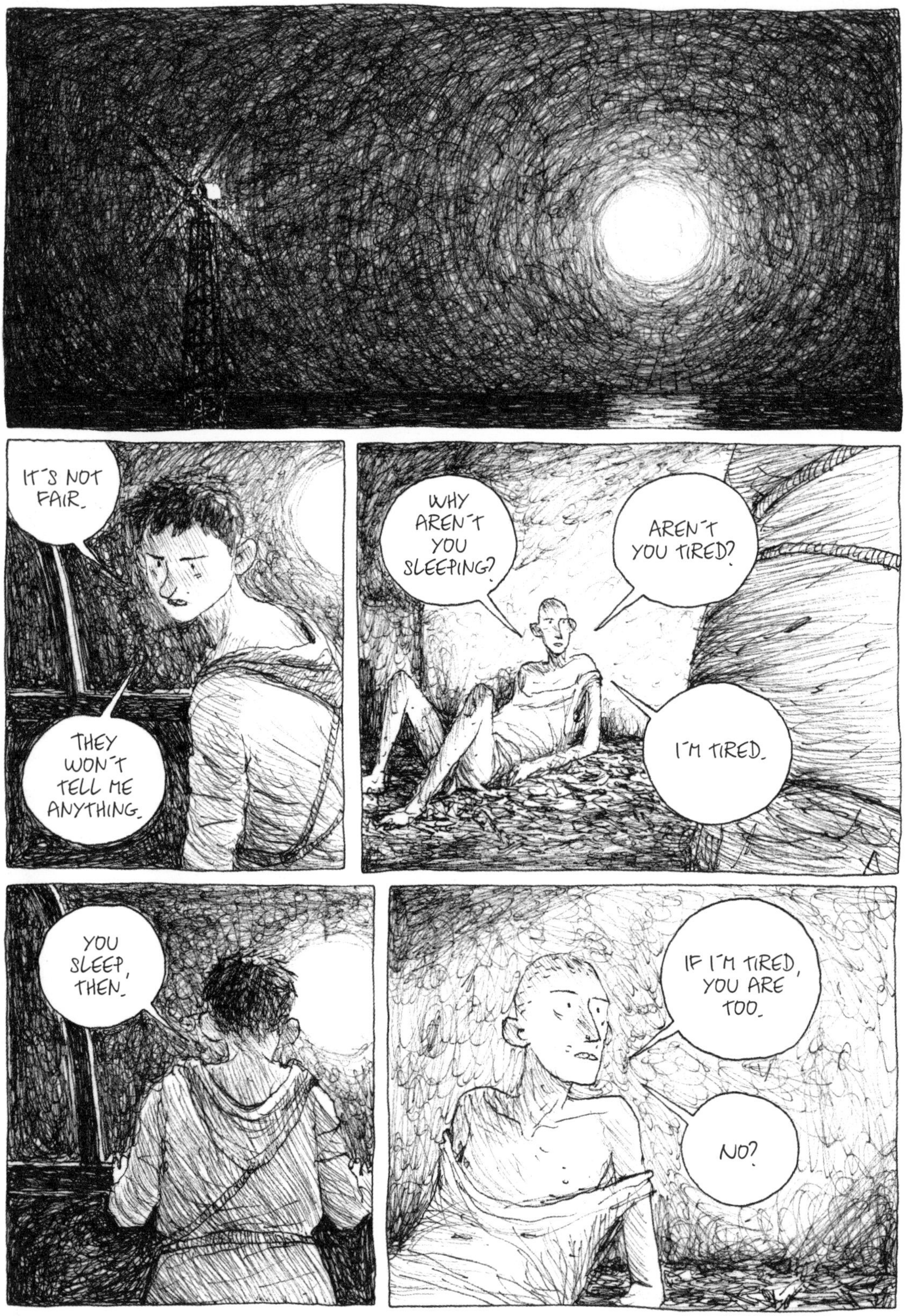
IT'S NOT FAIR.
THEY WON'T TELL ME ANYTHING.
WHY AREN'T YOU SLEEPING?
AREN'T YOU TIRED?
I'M TIRED.
YOU SLEEP, THEN.
IF I'M TIRED, YOU ARE TOO.
NO?

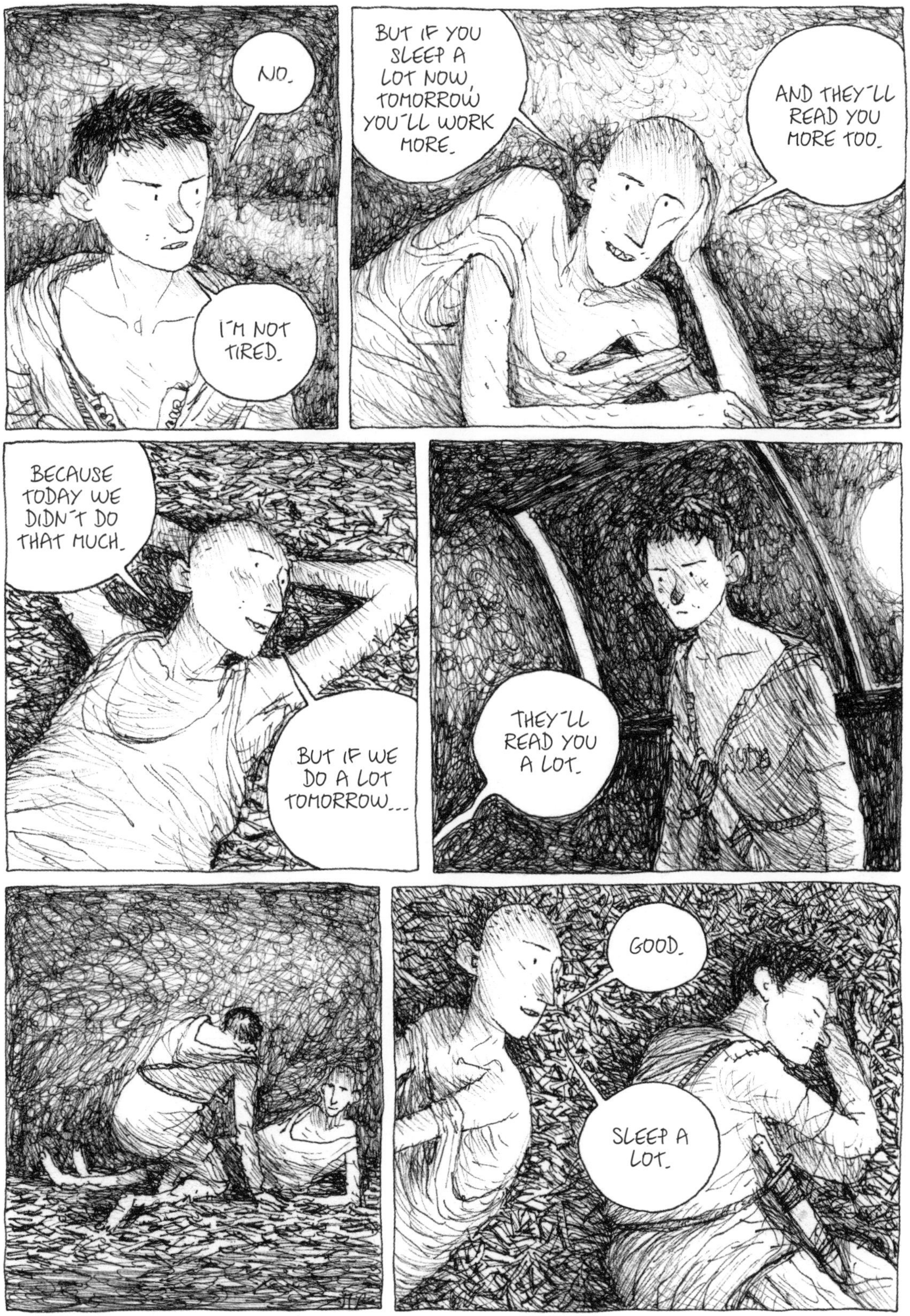
NO.
I'M NOT TIRED.
BUT IF YOU SLEEP A LOT NOW, TOMORROW YOU'LL WORK MORE.
AND THEY'LL READ YOU MORE TOO.
BECAUSE TODAY WE DIDN'T DO THAT MUCH.
BUT IF WE DO A LOT TOMORROW...
THEY'LL READ YOU A LOT.
GOOD.
SLEEP A LOT.

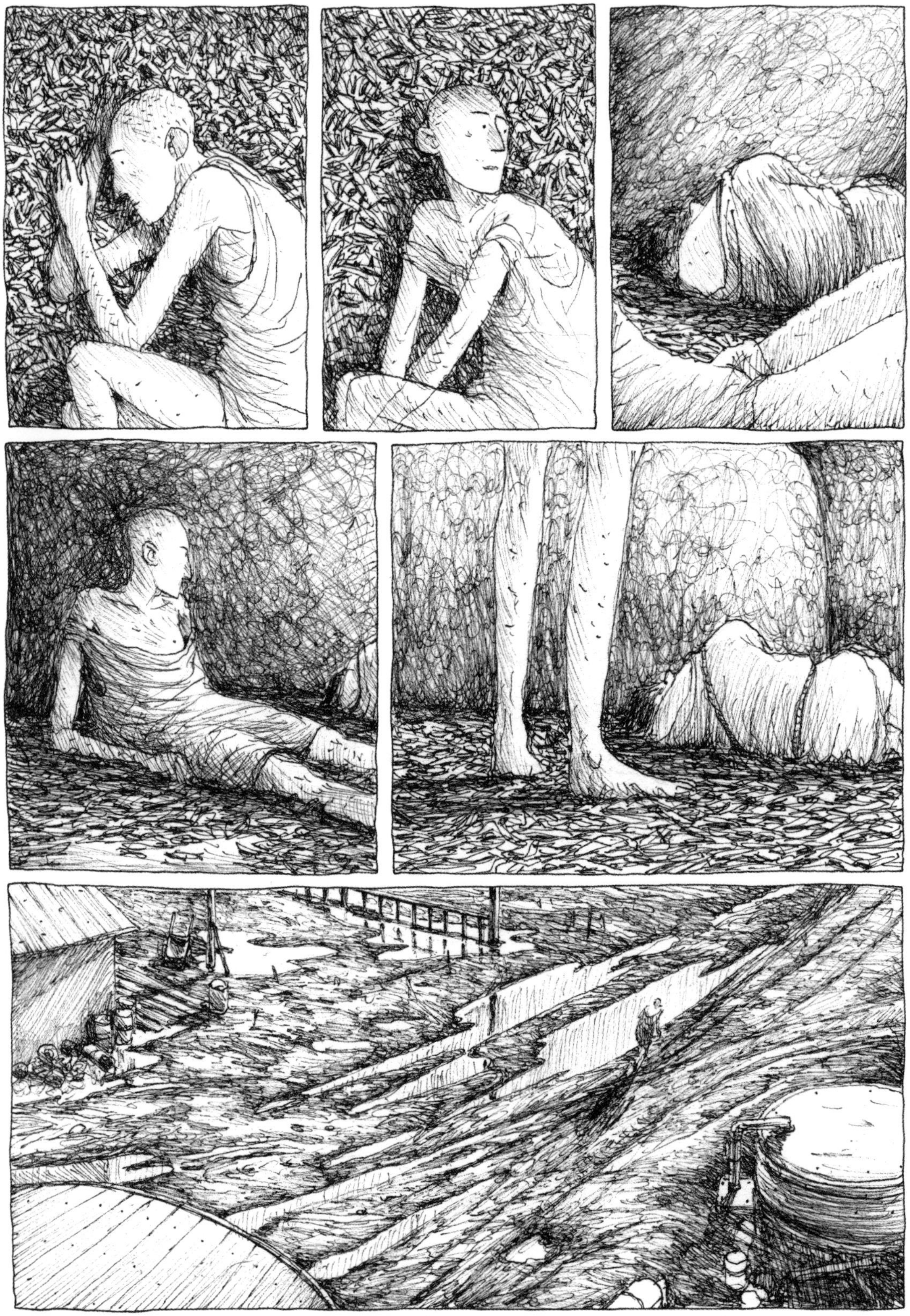

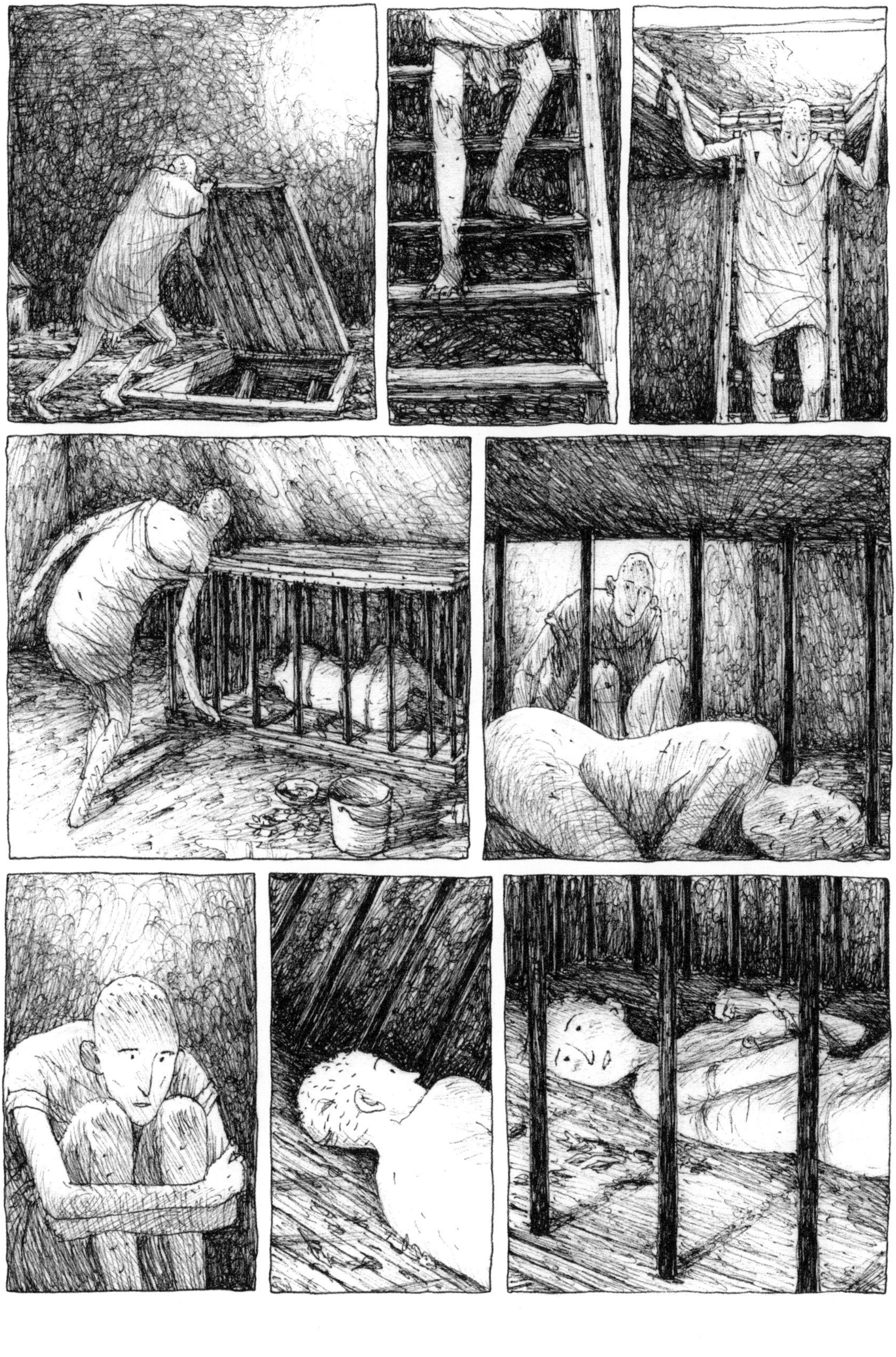

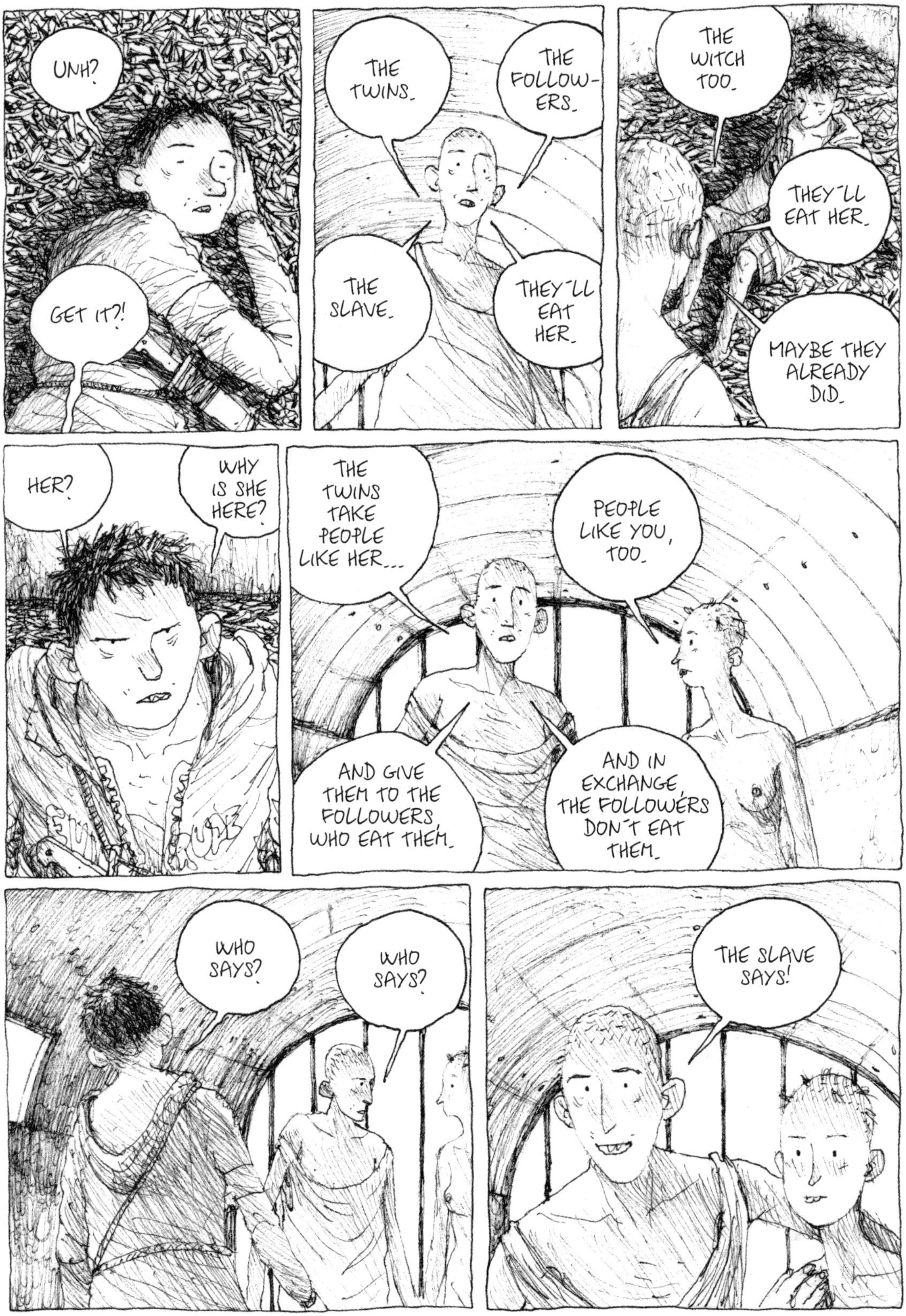
UNH?
GET IT?!
THE TWINS.
THE FOLLOWERS.
THE SLAVE.
THEY'LL EAT HER.
THE WITCH TOO.
THEY'LL EAT HER.
MAYBE THEY ALREADY DID.
HER?
WHY IS SHE HERE?
THE TWINS TAKE PEOPLE LIKE HER...
PEOPLE LIKE YOU, TOO.
AND GIVE THEM TO THE FOLLOWERS, WHO EAT THEM.
AND IN EXCHANGE, THE FOLLOWERS DON'T EAT THEM.
WHO SAYS?
WHO SAYS?
THE SLAVE SAYS!

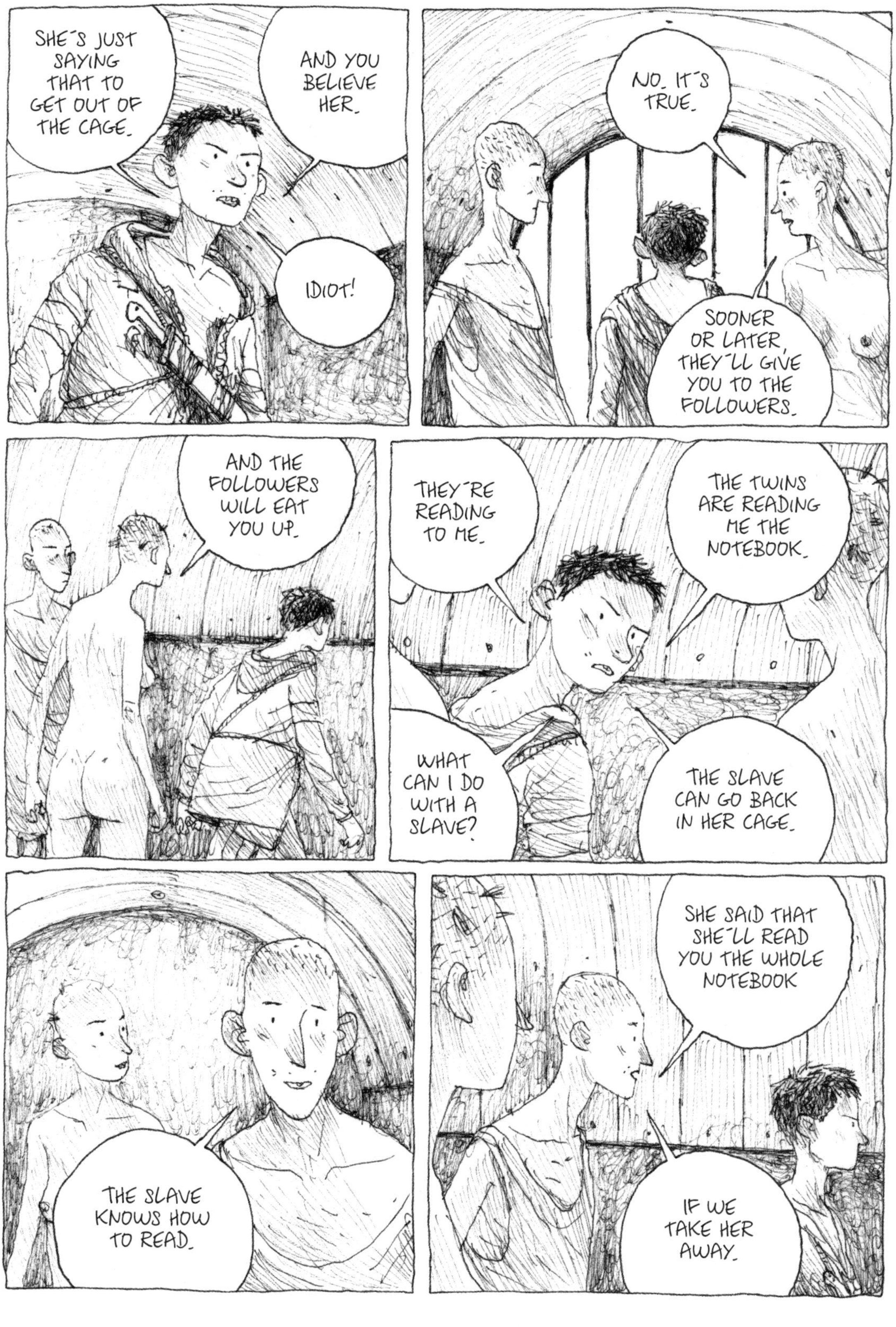
SHE'S JUST SAYING THAT TO GET OUT OF THE CAGE.
AND YOU BELIEVE HER.
IDIOT!
NO. IT'S TRUE.
SOONER OR LATER, THEY'LL GIVE YOU TO THE FOLLOWERS.
AND THE FOLLOWERS WILL EAT YOU UP.
THEY'RE READING TO ME.
THE TWINS ARE READING ME THE NOTEBOOK.
WHAT CAN I DO WITH A SLAVE?
THE SLAVE CAN GO BACK IN HER CAGE.
THE SLAVE KNOWS HOW TO READ.
SHE SAID THAT SHE'LL READ YOU THE WHOLE NOTEBOOK
IF WE TAKE HER AWAY.

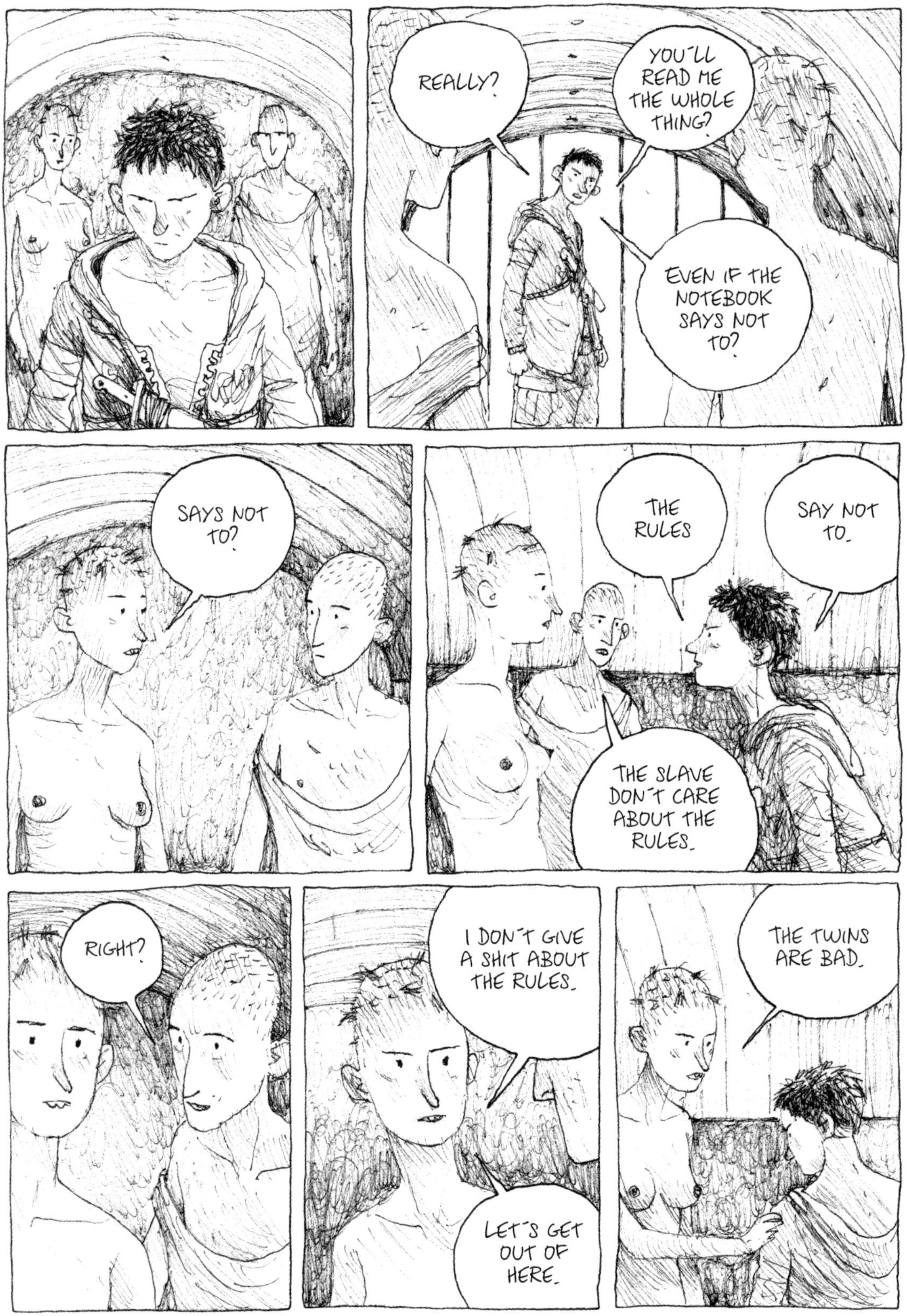
REALLY?
YOU'LL READ ME THE WHOLE THING?
EVEN IF THE NOTEBOOK SAYS NOT TO?
SAYS NOT TO?
THE RULES
SAY NOT TO.
THE SLAVE DON'T CARE ABOUT THE RULES.
RIGHT?
I DON'T GIVE A SHIT ABOUT THE RULES.
LET'S GET OUT OF HERE.
THE TWINS ARE BAD.

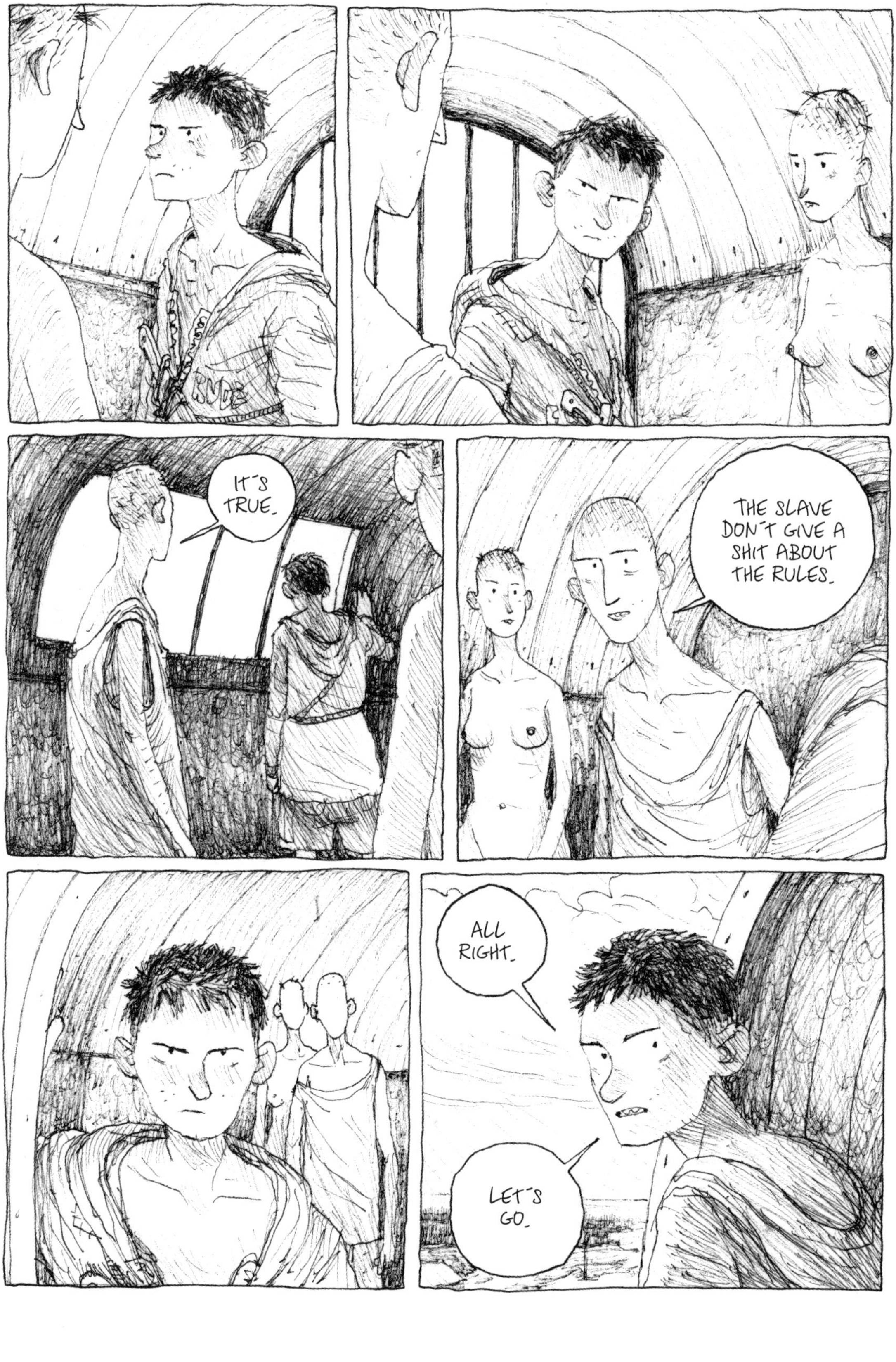
IT'S TRUE.
THE SLAVE DON'T GIVE A SHIT ABOUT THE RULES.
ALL RIGHT.
LET'S GO.

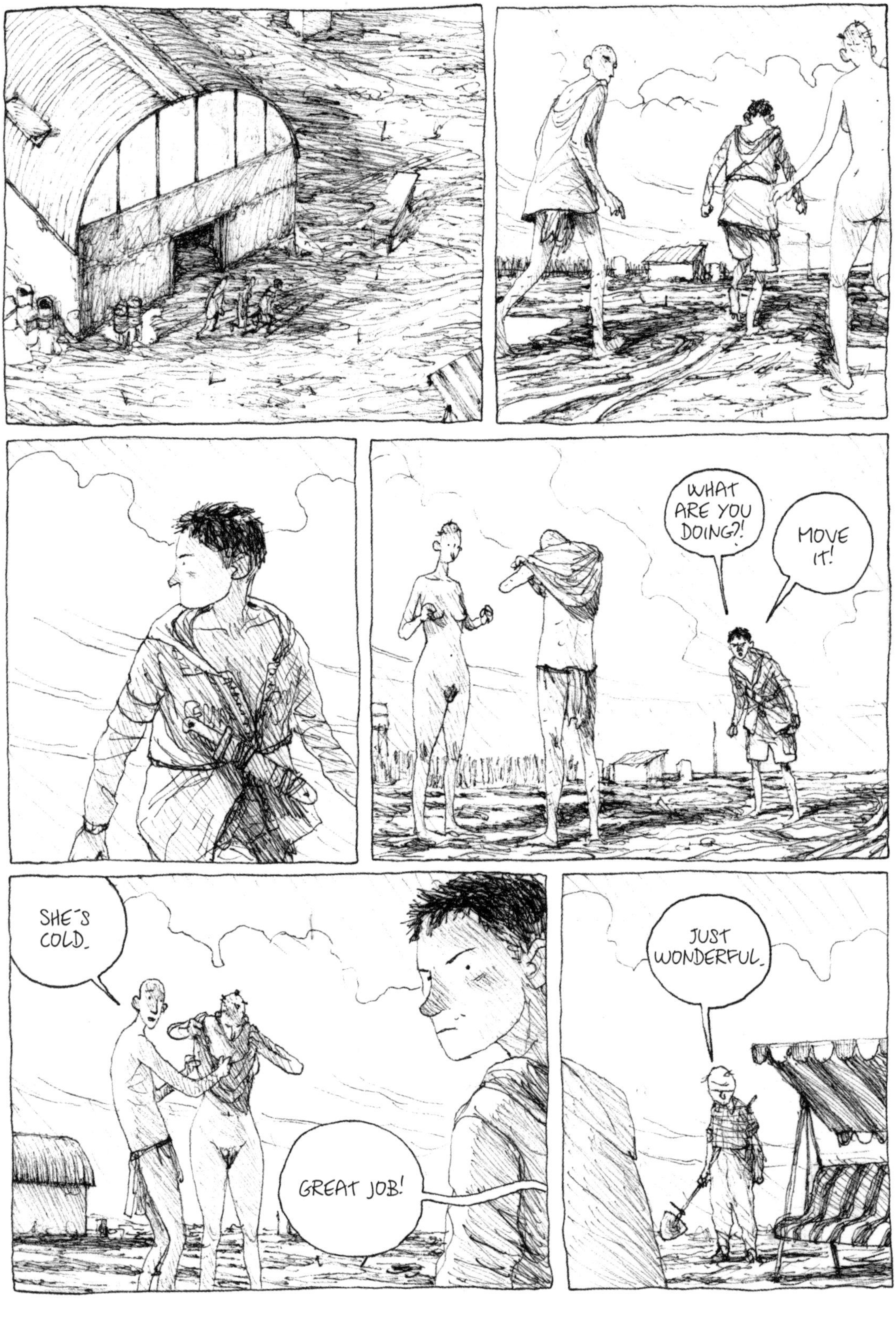
WHAT ARE YOU DOING?!
MOVE IT!
SHE'S COLD.
GREAT JOB!
JUST WONDERFUL.

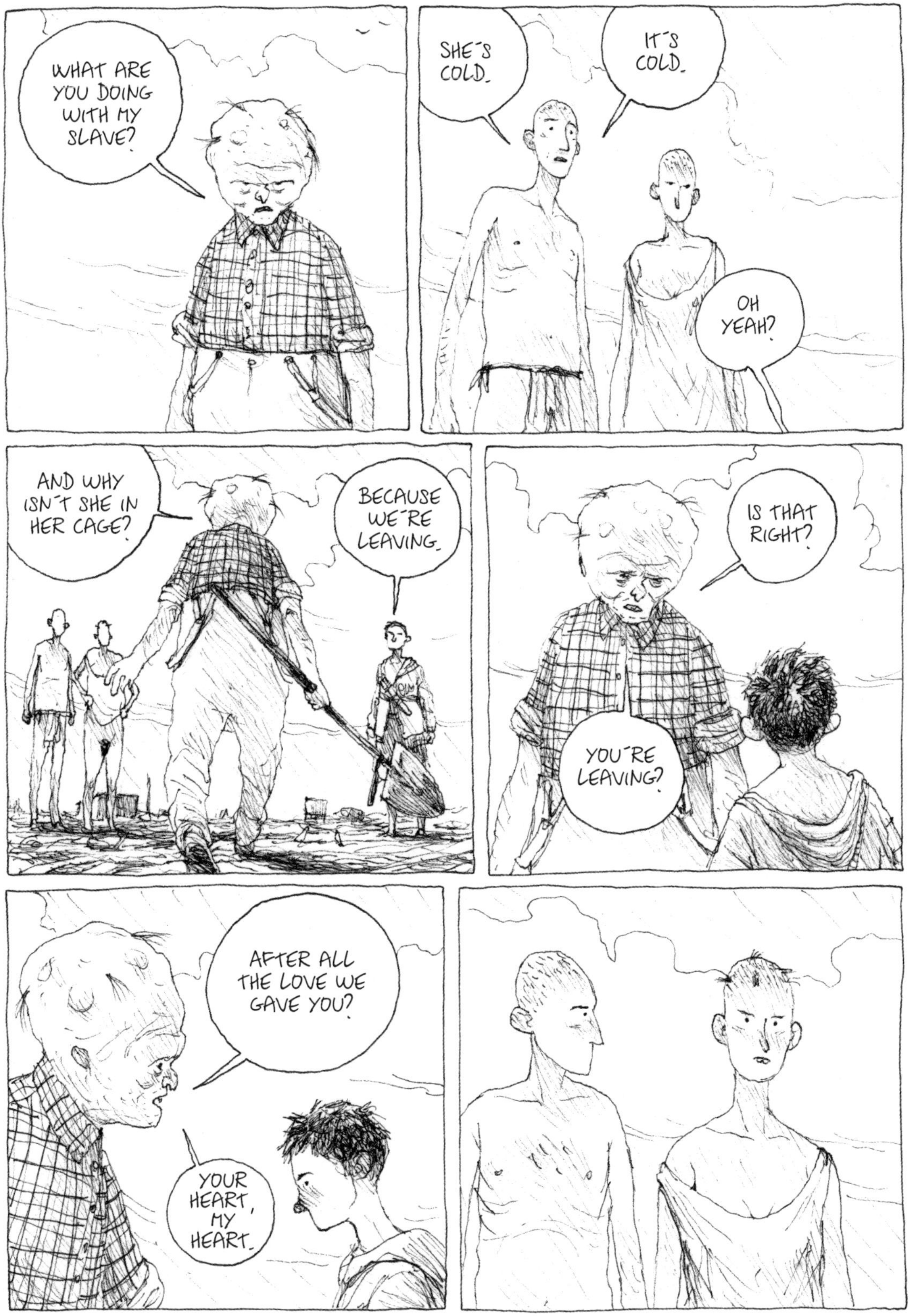
WHAT ARE YOU DOING WITH MY SLAVE?
SHE'S COLD.
IT'S COLD.
OH YEAH?
AND WHY ISN'T SHE IN HER CAGE?
BECAUSE WE'RE LEAVING.
IS THAT RIGHT?
YOU'RE LEAVING?
AFTER ALL THE LOVE WE GAVE YOU?
YOUR HEART, MY HEART.

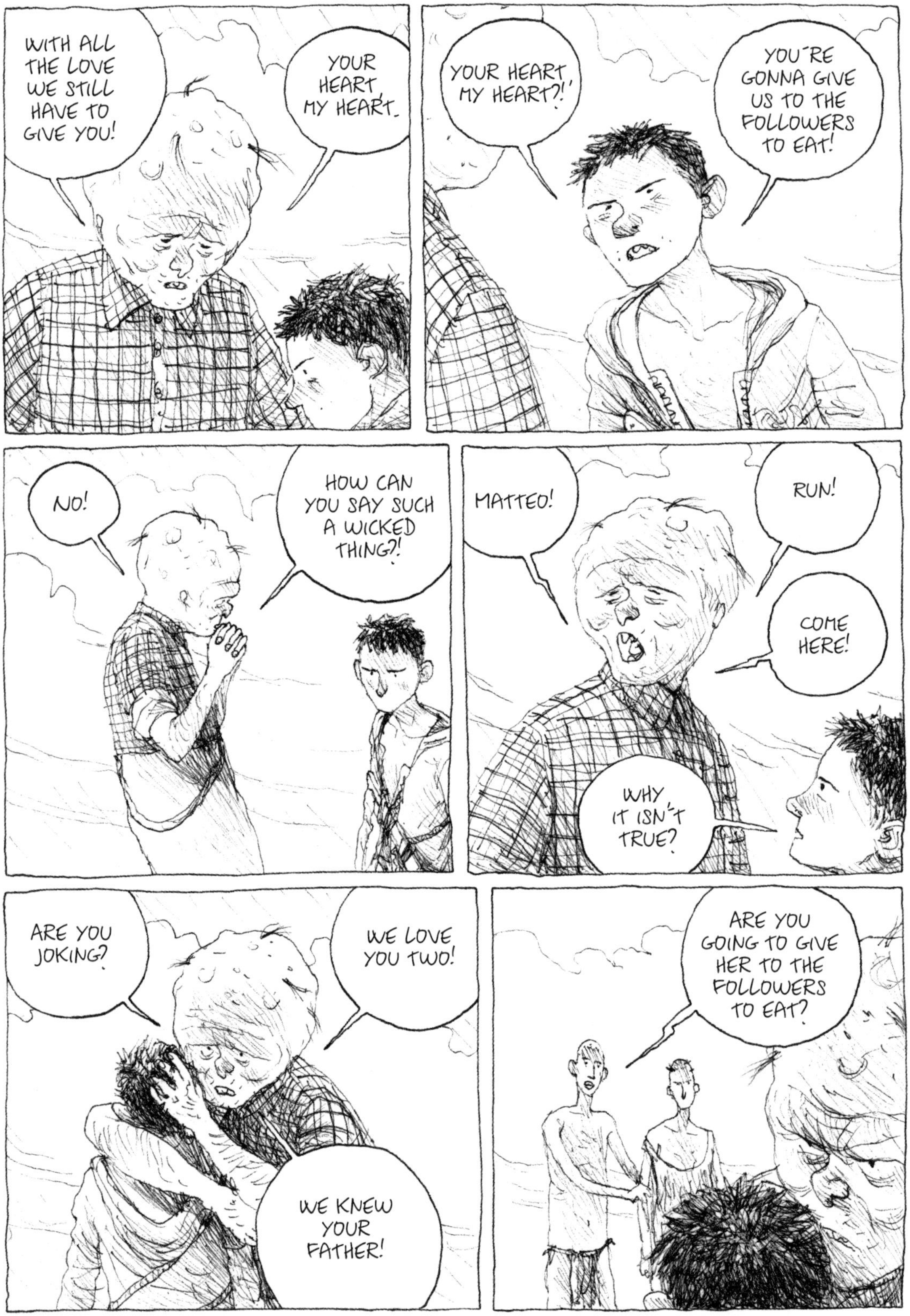
WITH ALL THE LOVE WE STILL HAVE TO GIVE YOU!
YOUR HEART, MY HEART...
YOUR HEART, MY HEART?!
YOU'RE GONNA GIVE US TO THE FOLLOWERS TO EAT!
NO!
HOW CAN YOU SAY SUCH A WICKED THING?!
MATTEO!
RUN!
COME HERE!
WHY IT ISN'T TRUE?
ARE YOU JOKING?
WE LOVE YOU TWO!
WE KNEW YOUR FATHER!
ARE YOU GOING TO GIVE HER TO THE FOLLOWERS TO EAT?

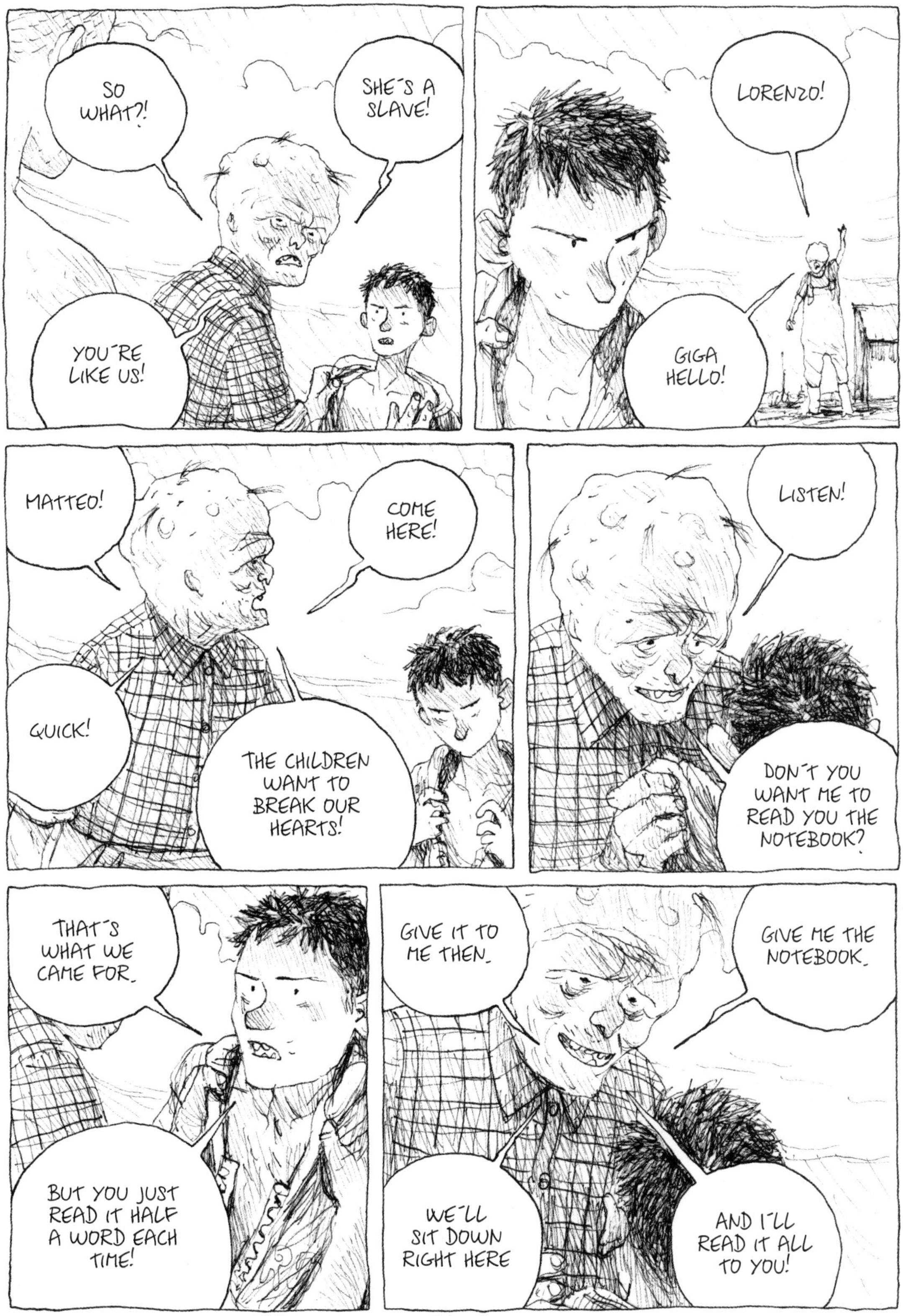
SO WHAT?!
SHE'S A SLAVE!
YOU'RE LIKE US!
LORENZO!
GIGA HELLO!
MATTEO!
COME HERE!
QUICK!
THE CHILDREN WANT TO BREAK OUR HEARTS!
LISTEN!
DON'T YOU WANT ME TO READ YOU THE NOTEBOOK?
THAT'S WHAT WE CAME FOR.
BUT YOU JUST READ IT HALF A WORD EACH TIME!
GIVE IT TO ME THEN.
GIVE ME THE NOTEBOOK.
WE'LL SIT DOWN RIGHT HERE
AND I'LL READ IT ALL TO YOU!

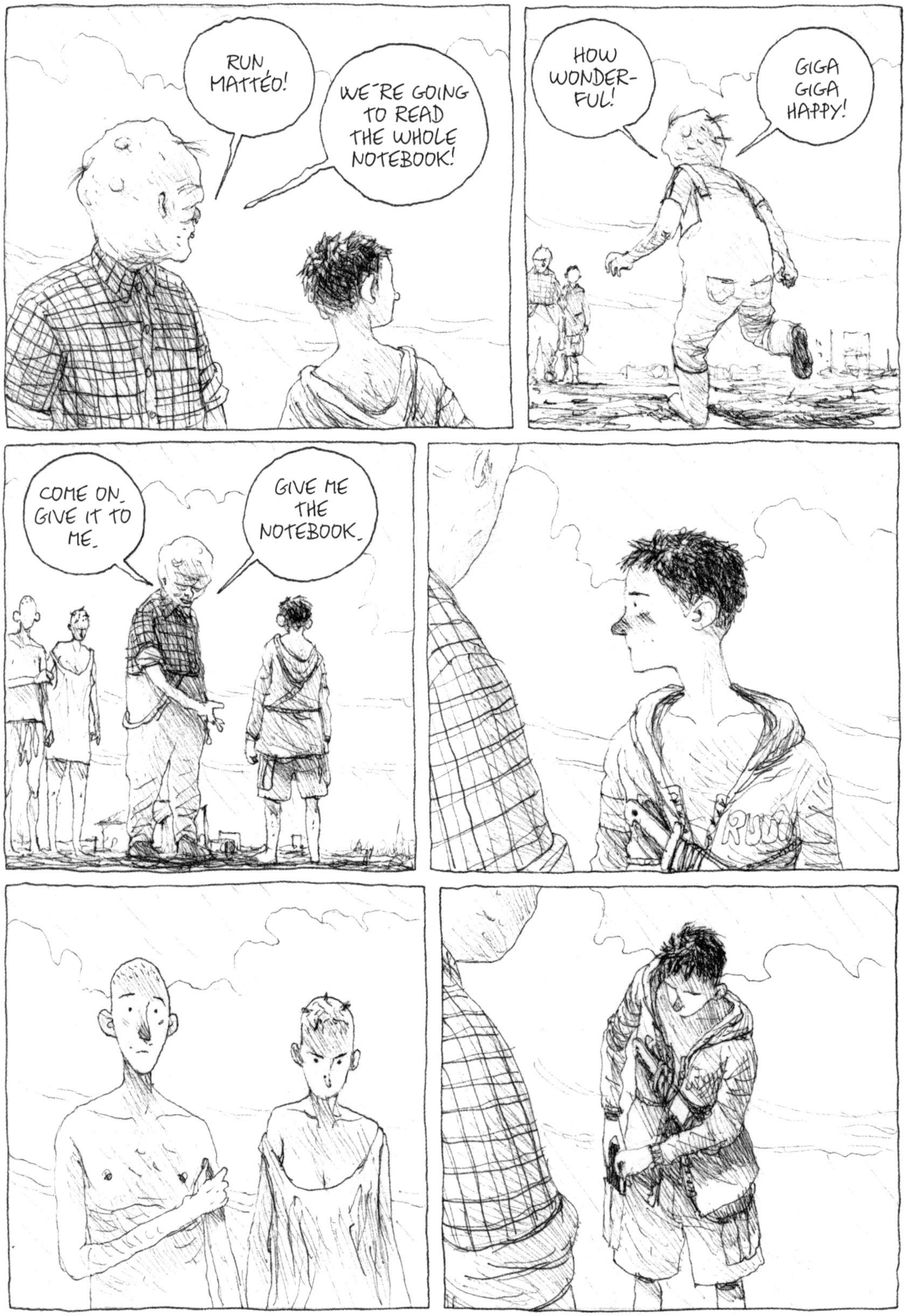
RUN MATTÉO!
WE'RE GOING TO READ THE WHOLE NOTEBOOK!
HOW WONDERFUL!
GIGA GIGA HAPPY!
COME ON_ GIVE IT TO ME_
GIVE ME THE NOTEBOOK_

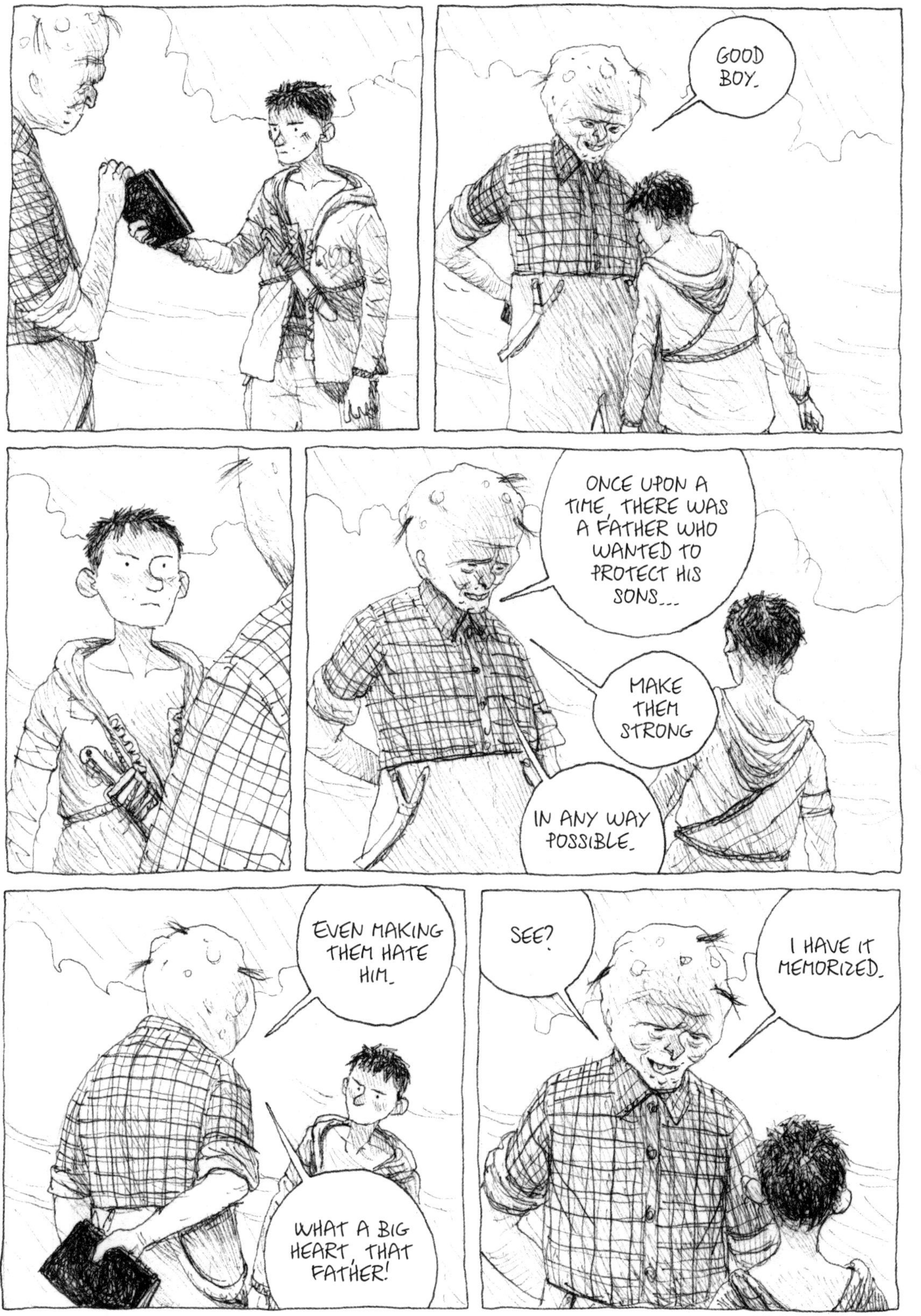
GOOD BOY.
ONCE UPON A TIME, THERE WAS A FATHER WHO WANTED TO PROTECT HIS SONS...
MAKE THEM STRONG
IN ANY WAY POSSIBLE.
EVEN MAKING THEM HATE HIM.
WHAT A BIG HEART, THAT FATHER!
SEE?
I HAVE IT MEMORIZED.

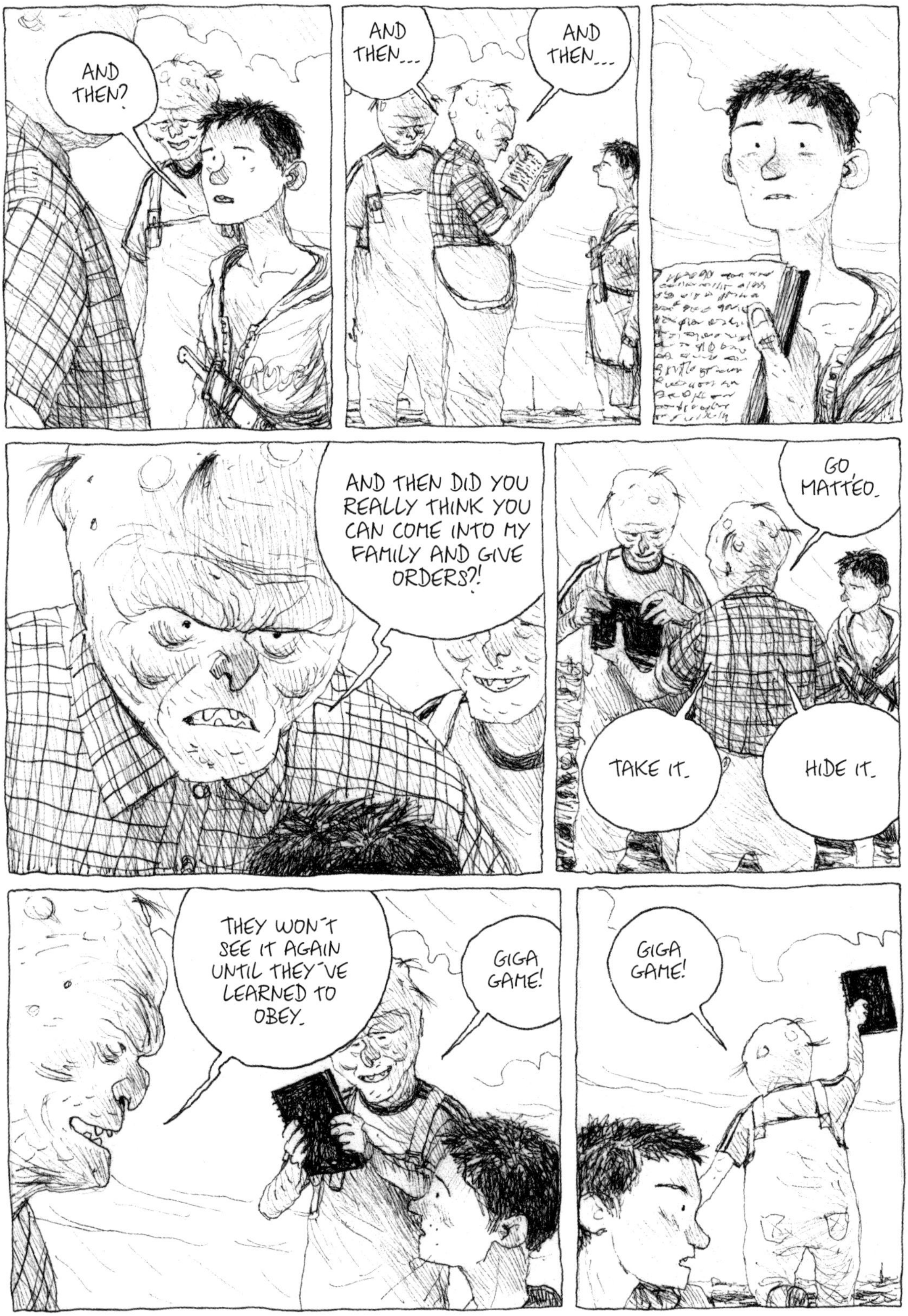
AND THEN?
AND THEN...
AND THEN...
AND THEN DID YOU REALLY THINK YOU CAN COME INTO MY FAMILY AND GIVE ORDERS?!
GO, MATTEO.
TAKE IT.
HIDE IT.
THEY WON'T SEE IT AGAIN UNTIL THEY'VE LEARNED TO OBEY.
GIGA GAME!
GIGA GAME!

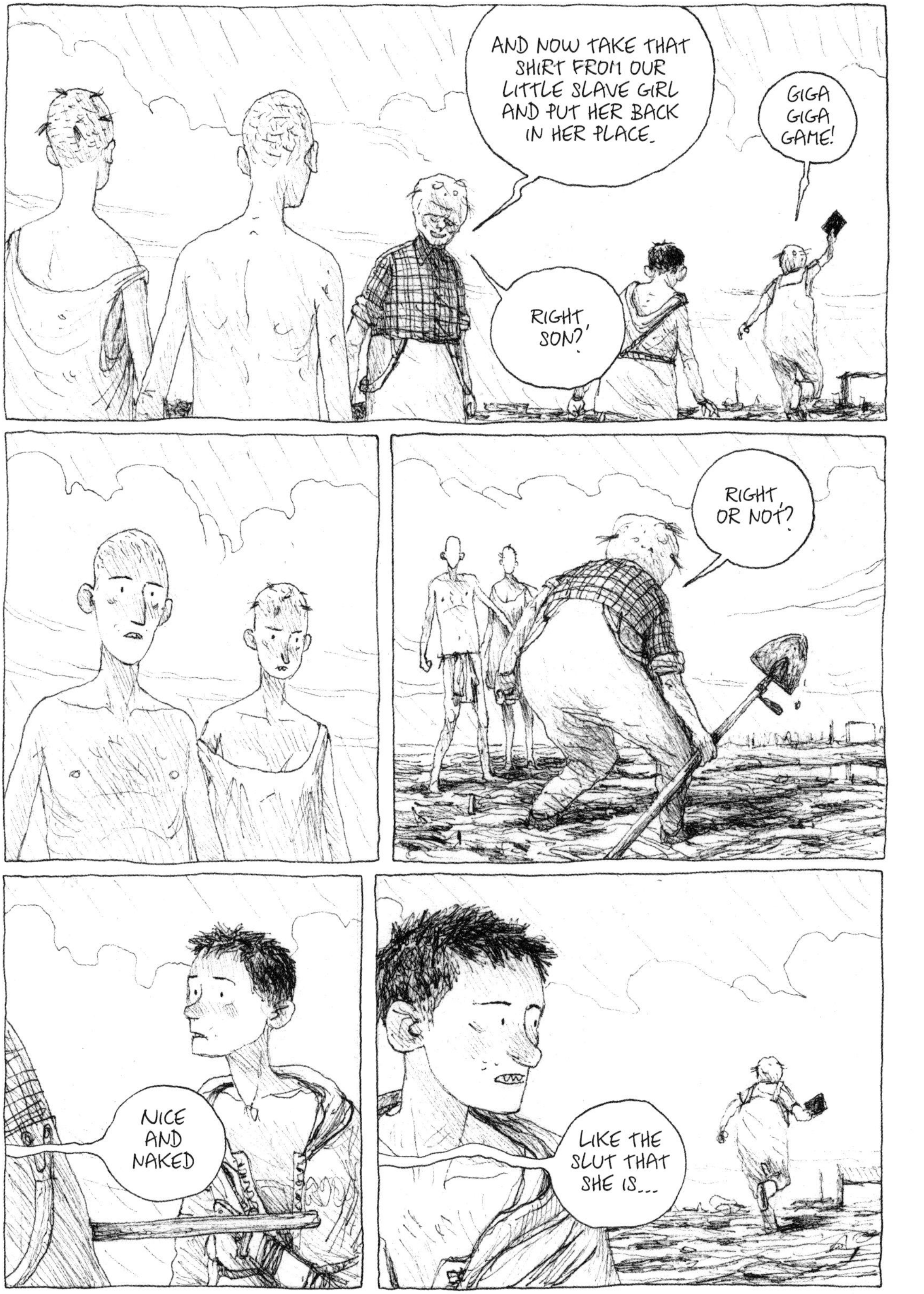
AND NOW TAKE THAT SHIRT FROM OUR LITTLE SLAVE GIRL AND PUT HER BACK IN HER PLACE.
GIGA GIGA GAME!
RIGHT, SON?
RIGHT, OR NOT?
NICE AND NAKED
LIKE THE SLUT THAT SHE IS...

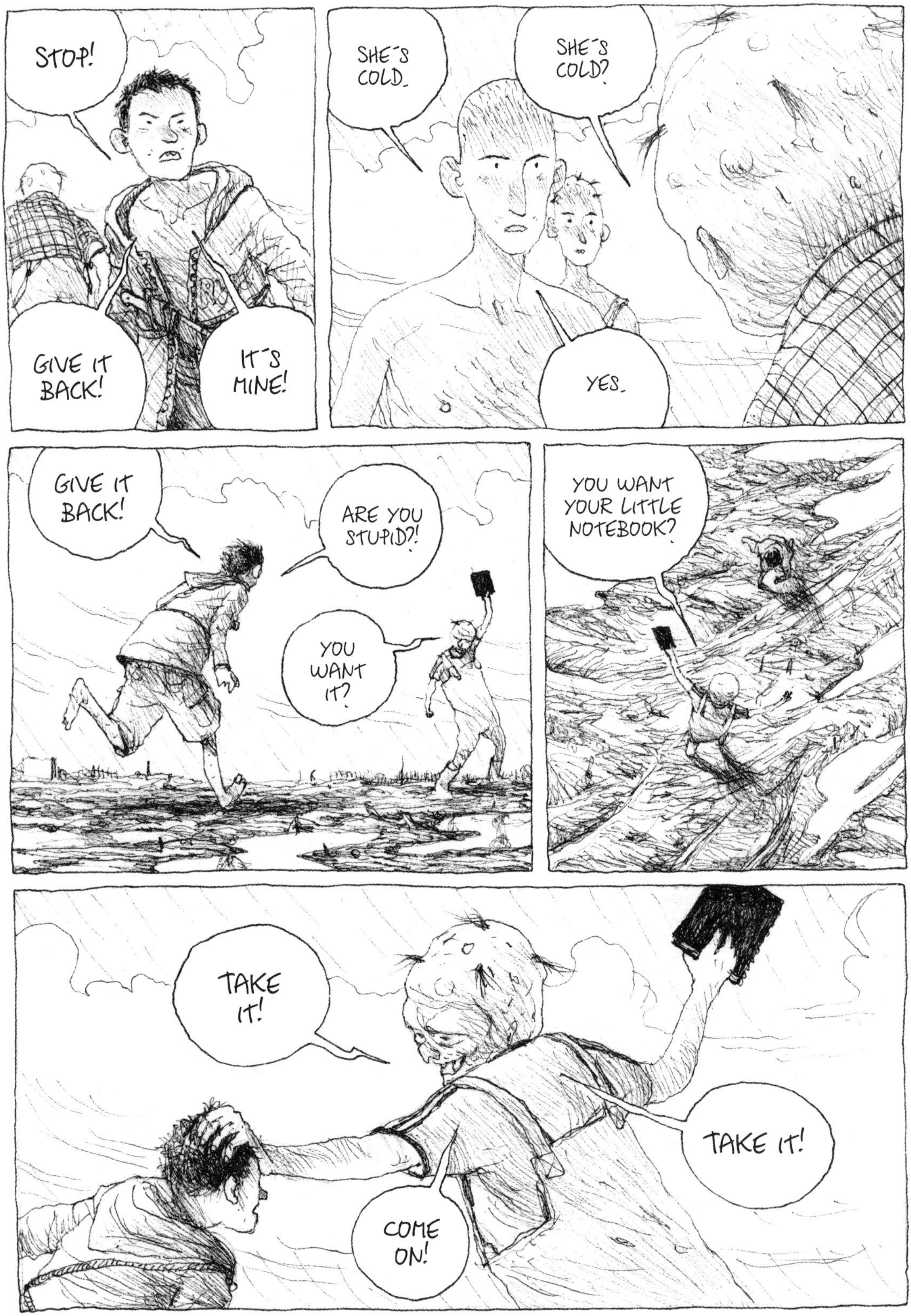
STOP!
GIVE IT BACK!
IT'S MINE!
SHE'S COLD.
SHE'S COLD?
YES.
GIVE IT BACK!
ARE YOU STUPID?!
YOU WANT IT?
YOU WANT YOUR LITTLE NOTEBOOK?
TAKE IT!
TAKE IT!
COME ON!

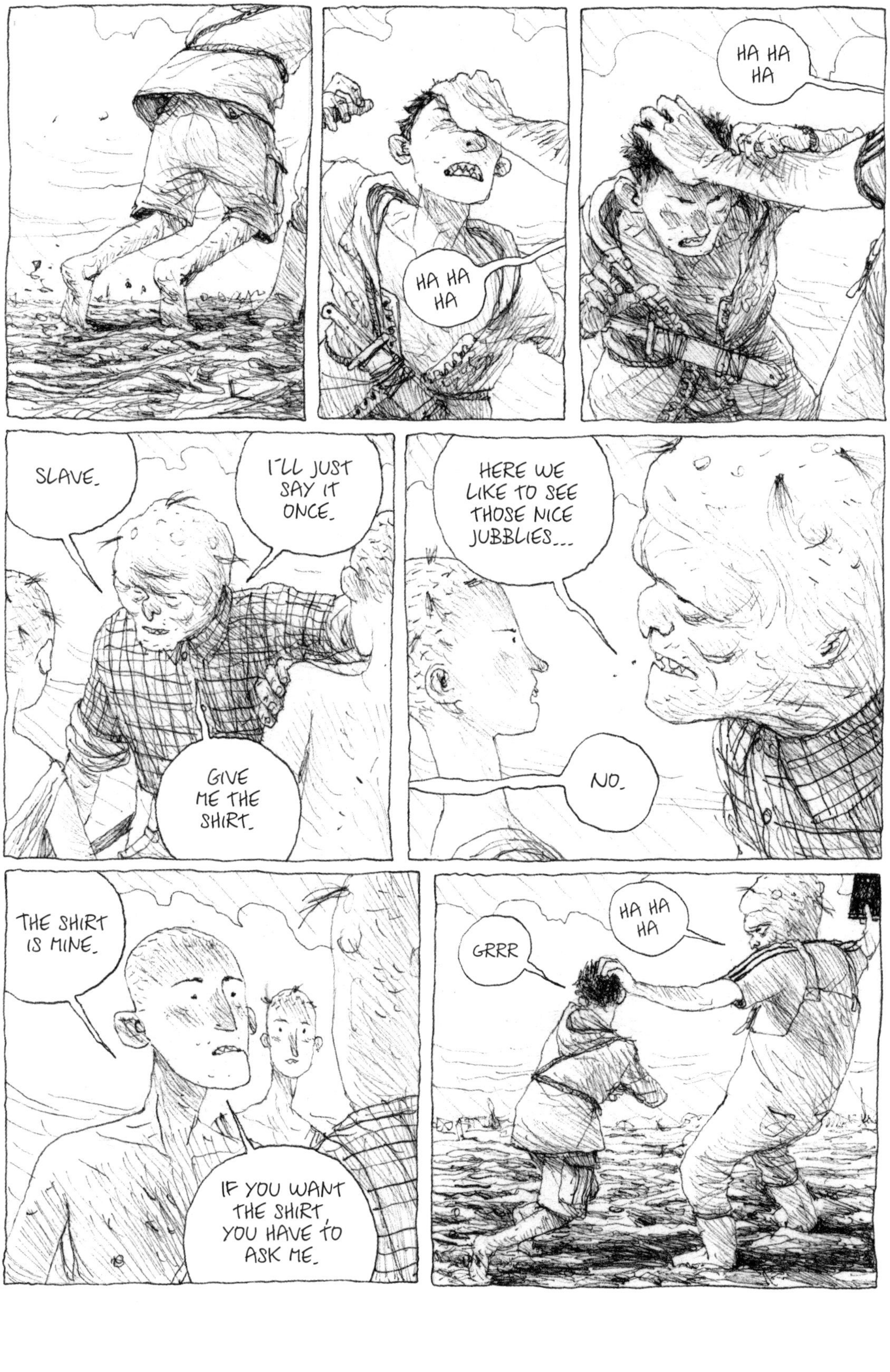
HA HA HA
HA HA HA
SLAVE.
I'LL JUST SAY IT ONCE.
GIVE ME THE SHIRT.
HERE WE LIKE TO SEE THOSE NICE JUBBLIES...
NO.
THE SHIRT IS MINE.
IF YOU WANT THE SHIRT, YOU HAVE TO ASK ME.
HA HA HA
GRRR

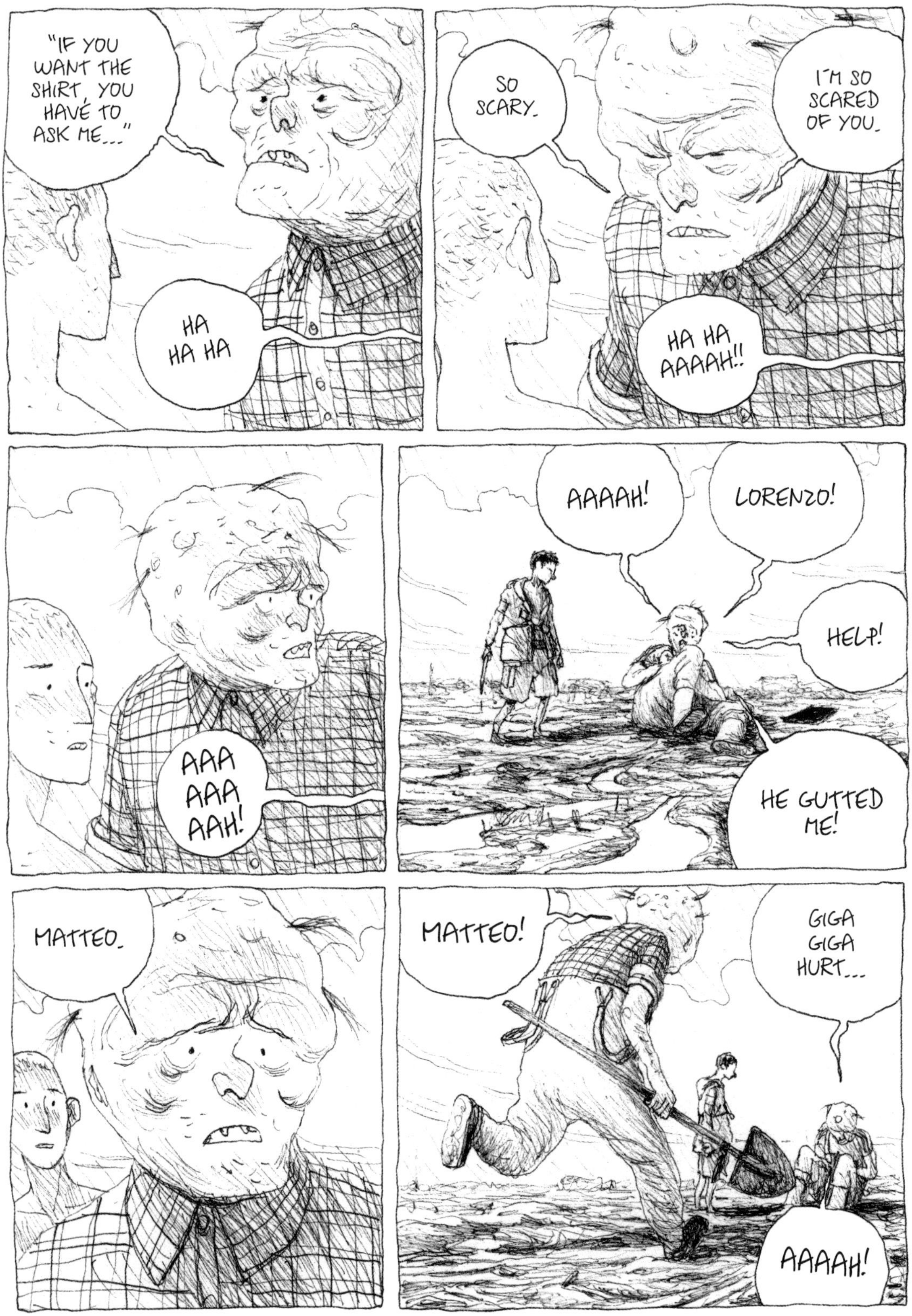
"IF YOU WANT THE SHIRT, YOU HAVE TO ASK ME..."
HA HA HA
SO SCARY.
I'M SO SCARED OF YOU.
HA HA AAAAH!!
AAA AAA AAH!
AAAAH!
LORENZO!
HELP!
HE GUTTED ME!
MATTEO.
MATTEO!
GIGA GIGA HURT...
AAAAH!

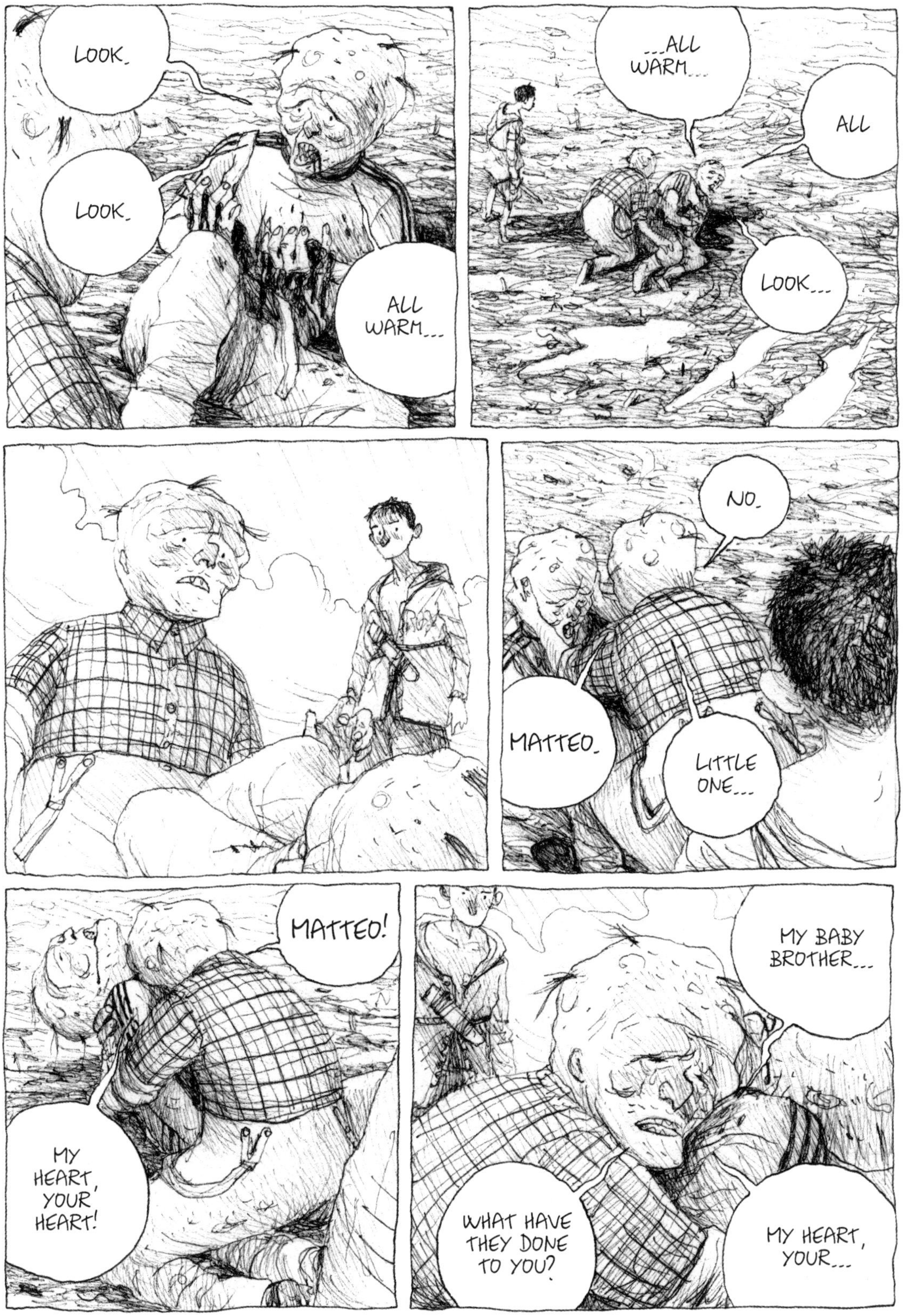
LOOK.
LOOK.
ALL WARM...
...ALL WARM...
ALL
LOOK...
NO.
MATTEO.
LITTLE ONE...
MATTEO!
MY HEART, YOUR HEART!
MY BABY BROTHER...
WHAT HAVE THEY DONE TO YOU?
MY HEART, YOUR...

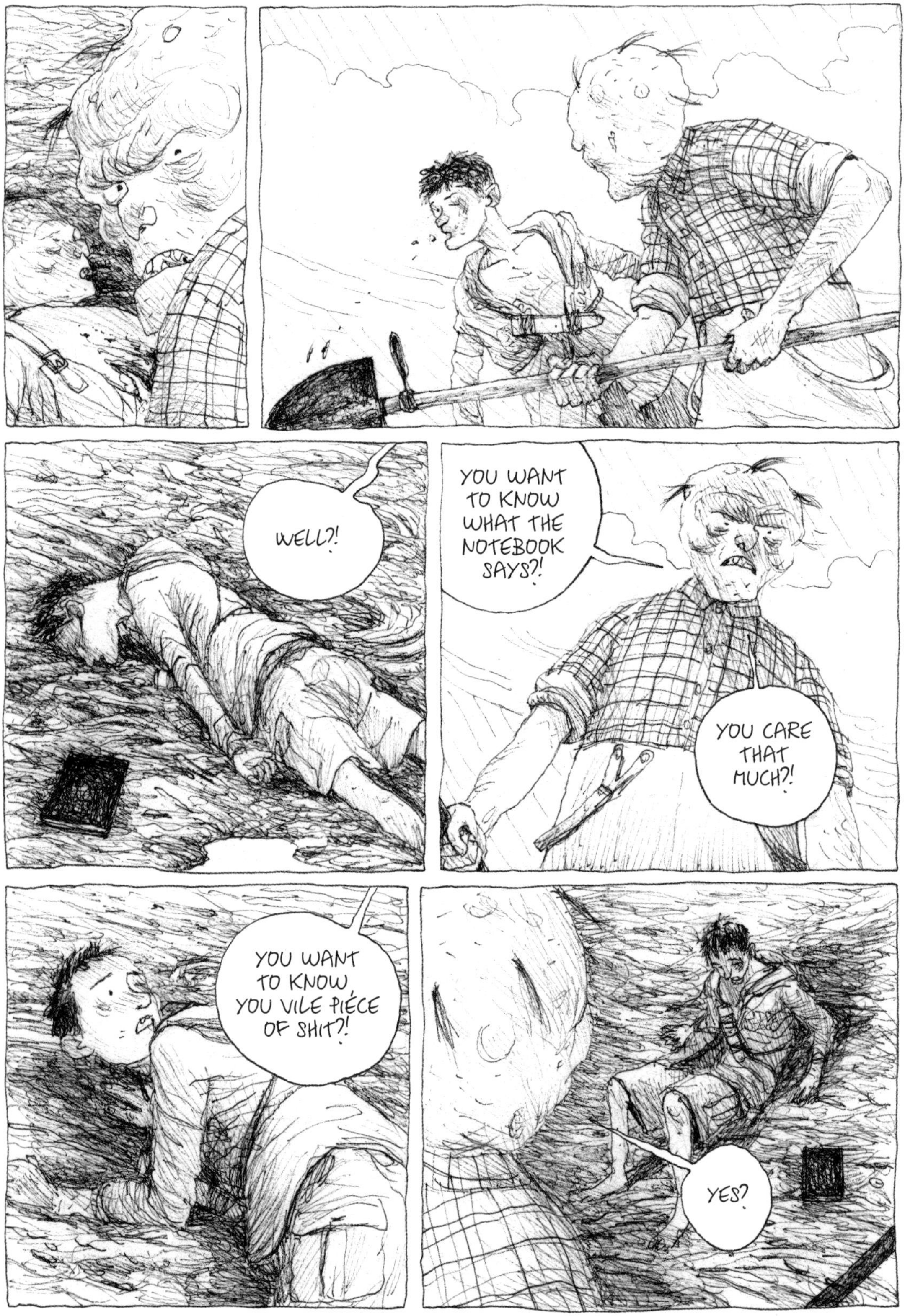
WELL?!
YOU WANT TO KNOW WHAT THE NOTEBOOK SAYS?!
YOU CARE THAT MUCH?!
YOU WANT TO KNOW, YOU VILE PIÉCE OF SHIT?!
YES?

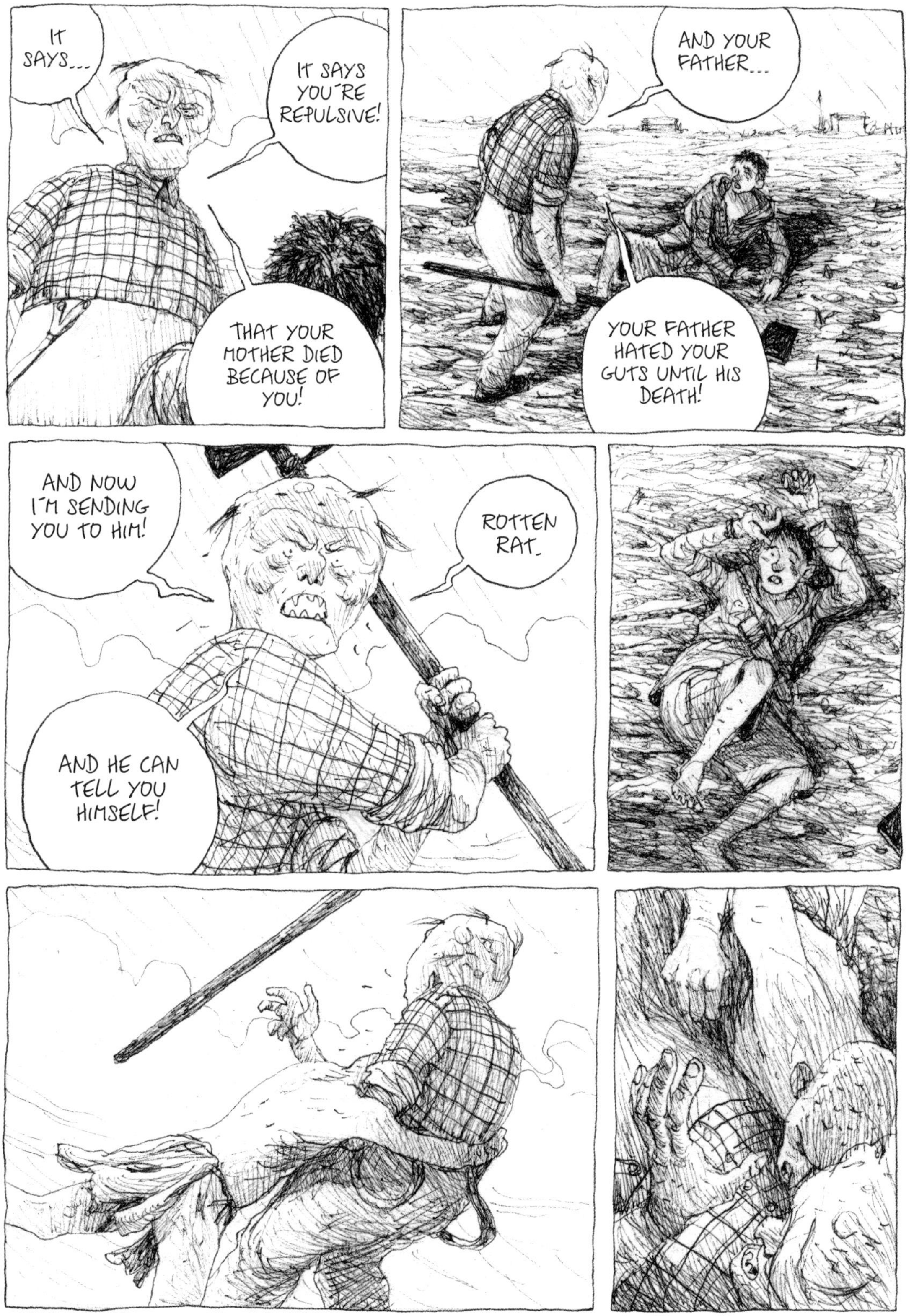
IT SAYS...
IT SAYS YOU'RE REPULSIVE!
THAT YOUR MOTHER DIED BECAUSE OF YOU!
AND YOUR FATHER...
YOUR FATHER HATED YOUR GUTS UNTIL HIS DEATH!
AND NOW I'M SENDING YOU TO HIM!
ROTTEN RAT.
AND HE CAN TELL YOU HIMSELF!

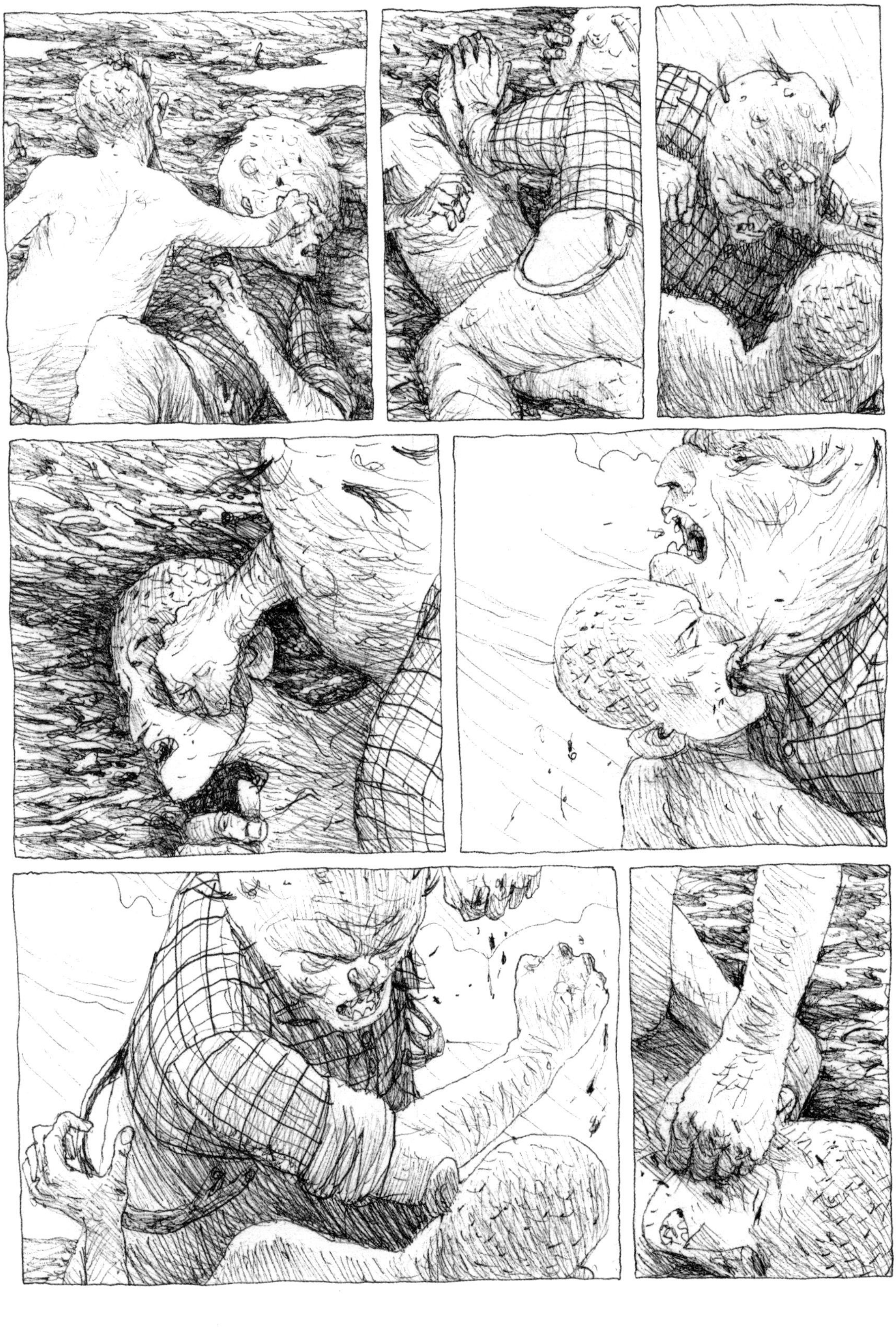

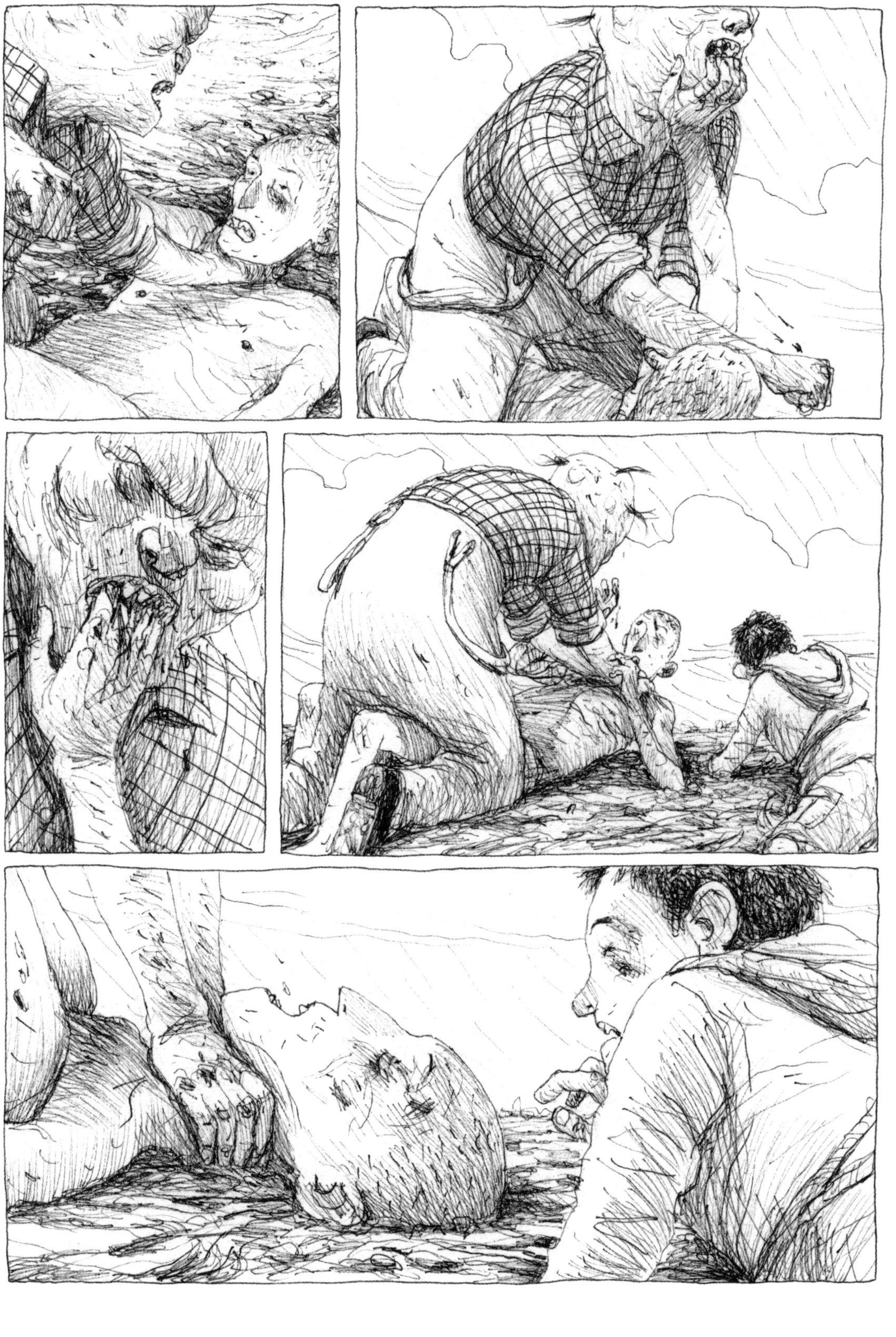

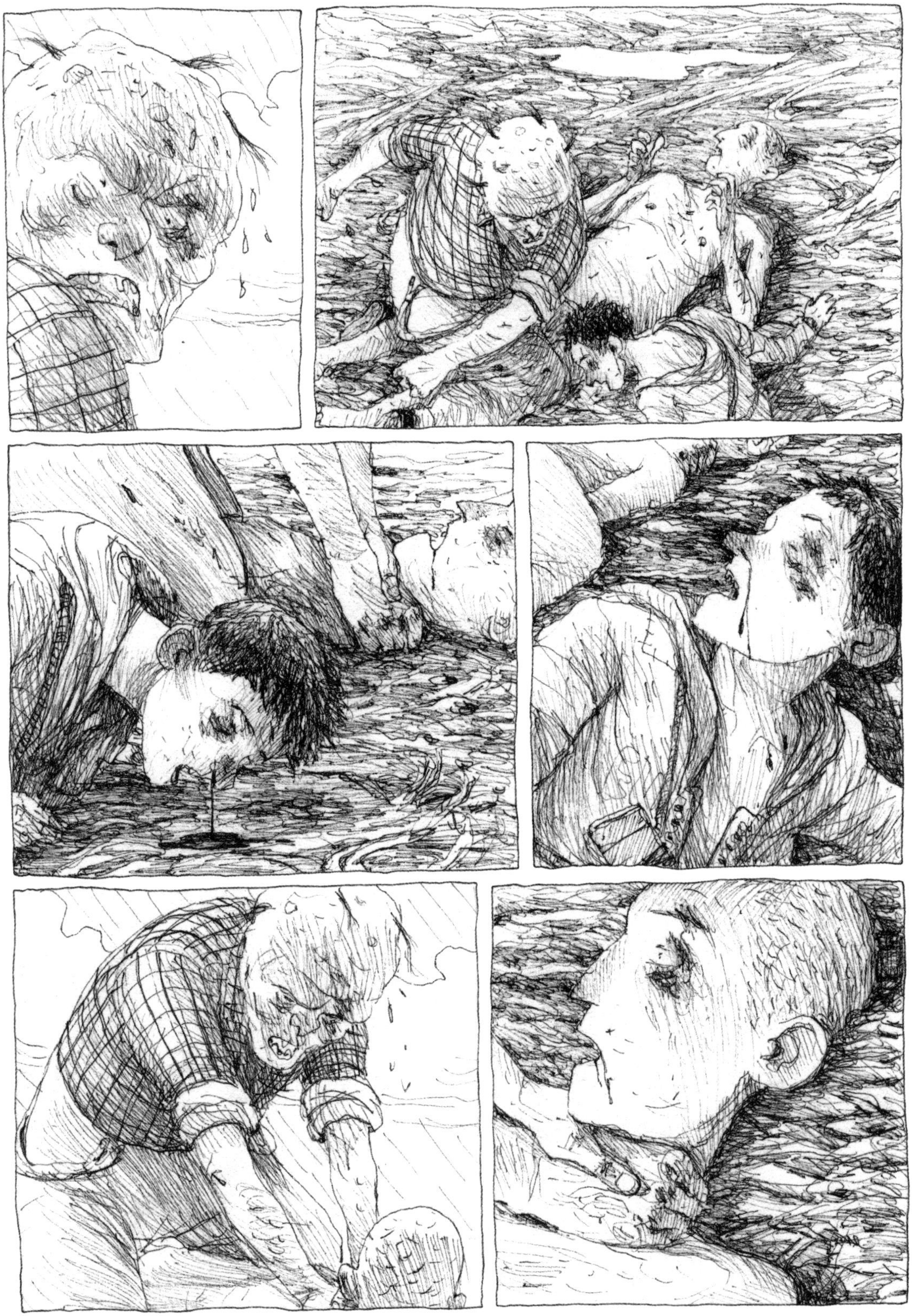

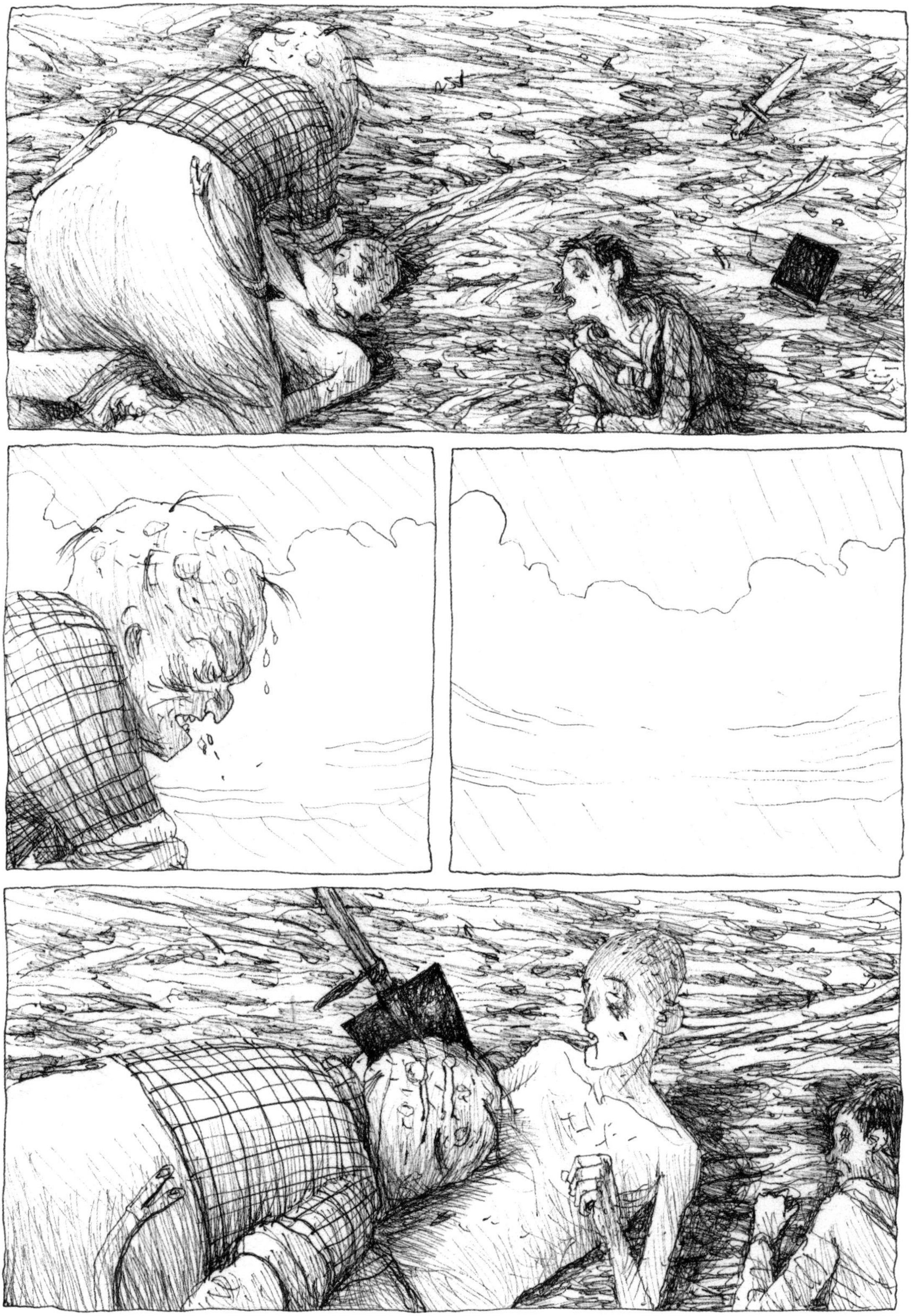

...
I TOLD YOU.
I TOLD YOU.
I TOLD YOU THE TWINS ARE BAD.

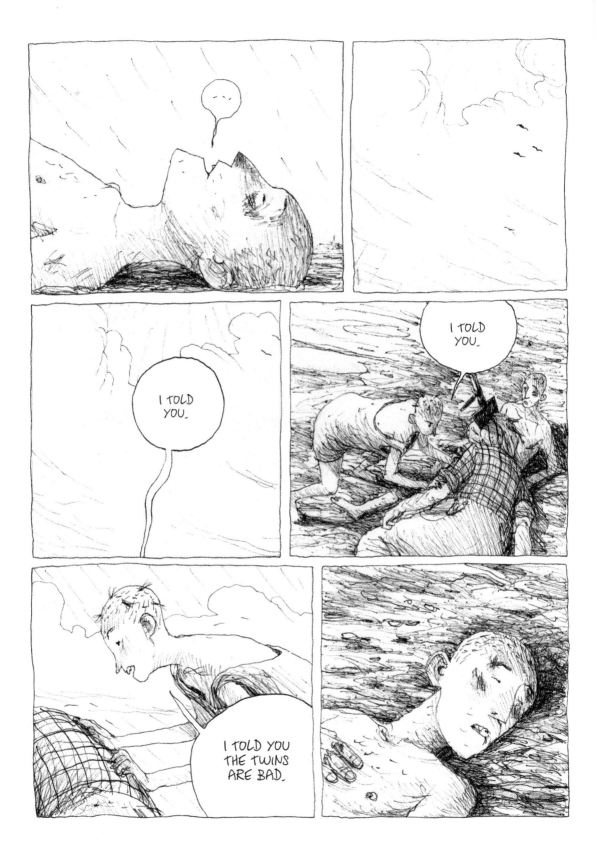

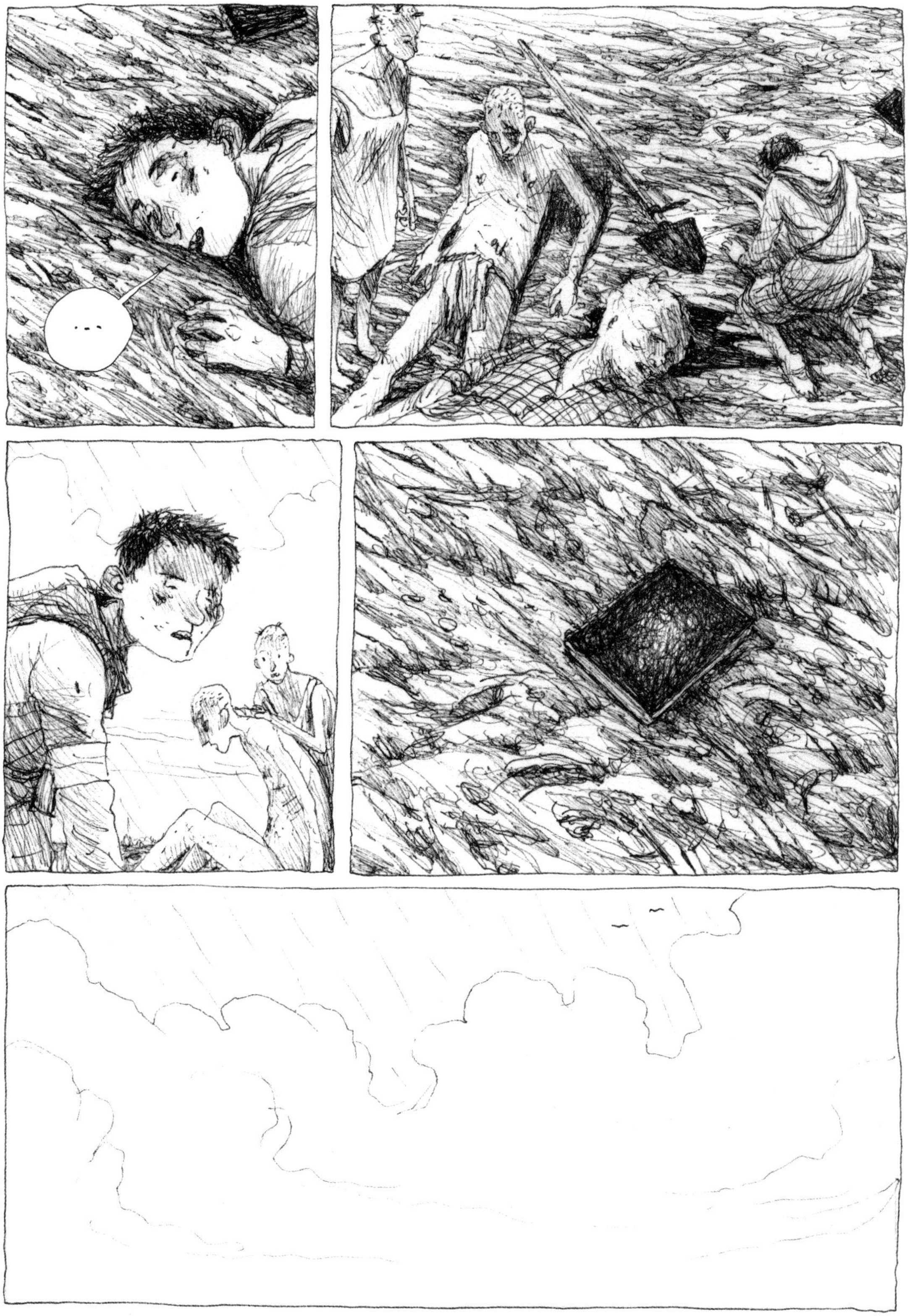
...

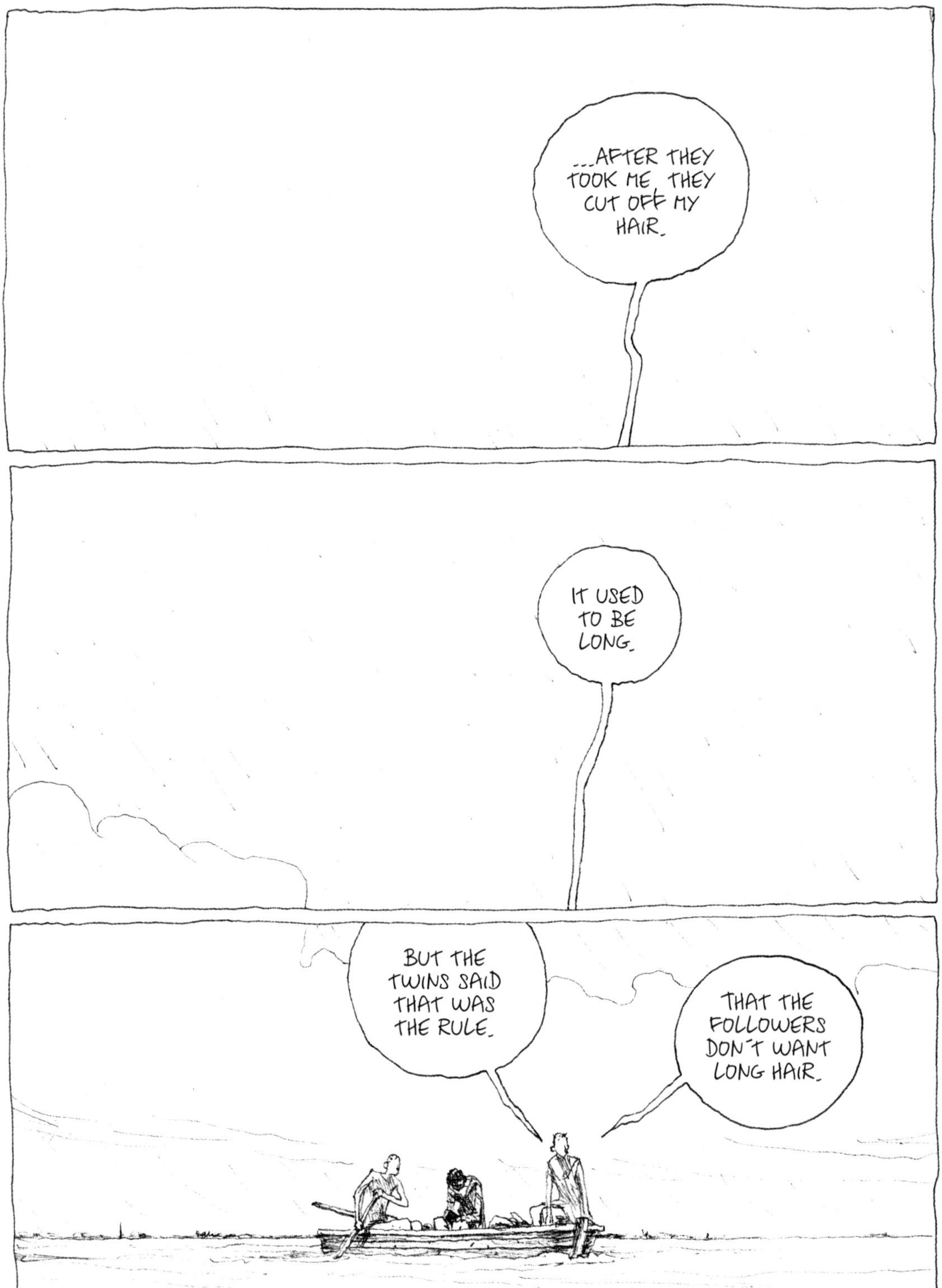
...AFTER THEY TOOK ME, THEY CUT OFF MY HAIR.
IT USED TO BE LONG.
BUT THE TWINS SAID THAT WAS THE RULE.
THAT THE FOLLOWERS DON'T WANT LONG HAIR.

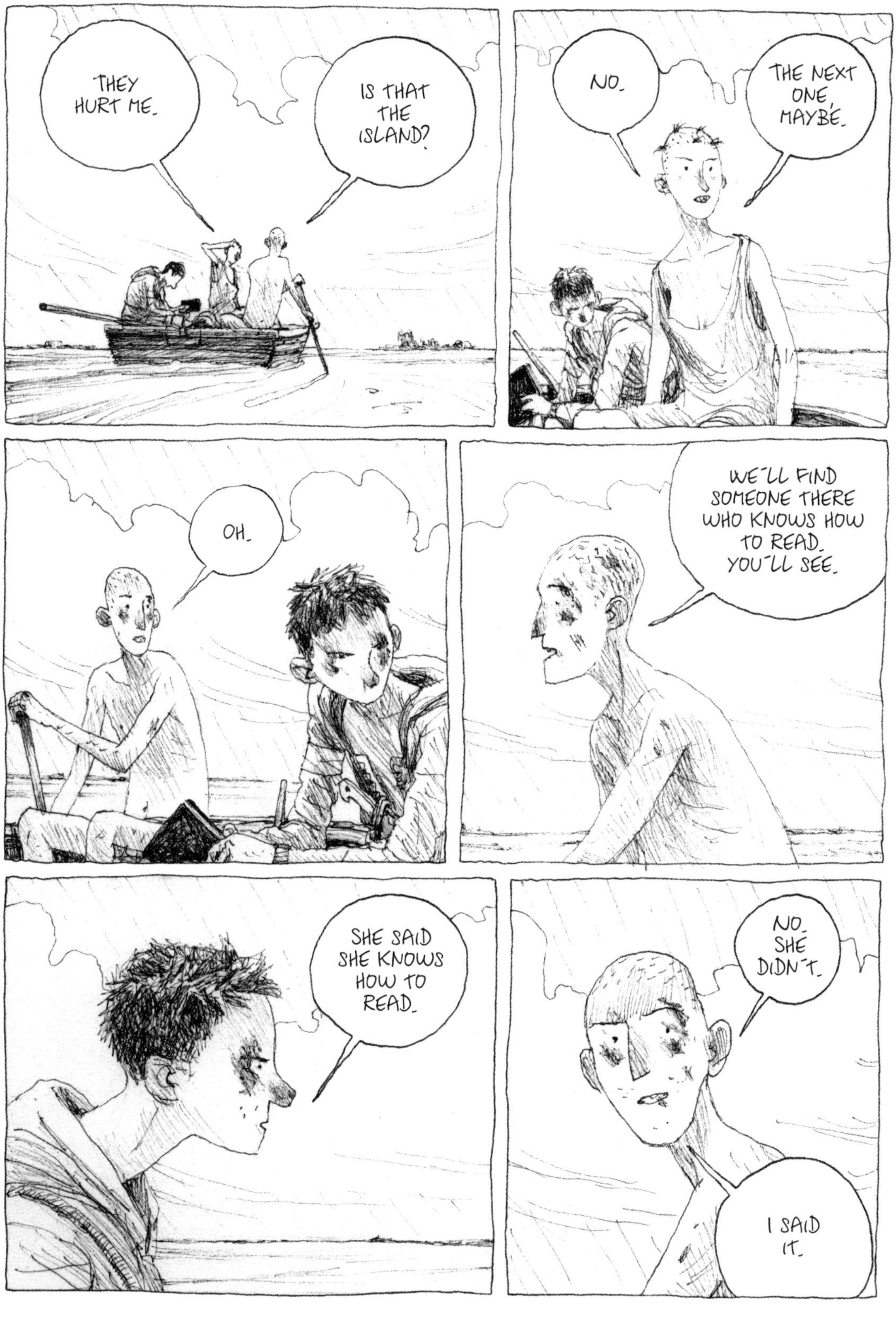
THEY HURT ME.
IS THAT THE ISLAND?
NO.
THE NEXT ONE, MAYBE.
OH.
WE'LL FIND SOMEONE THERE WHO KNOWS HOW TO READ. YOU'LL SEE.
SHE SAID SHE KNOWS HOW TO READ.
NO. SHE DIDN'T.
I SAID IT.

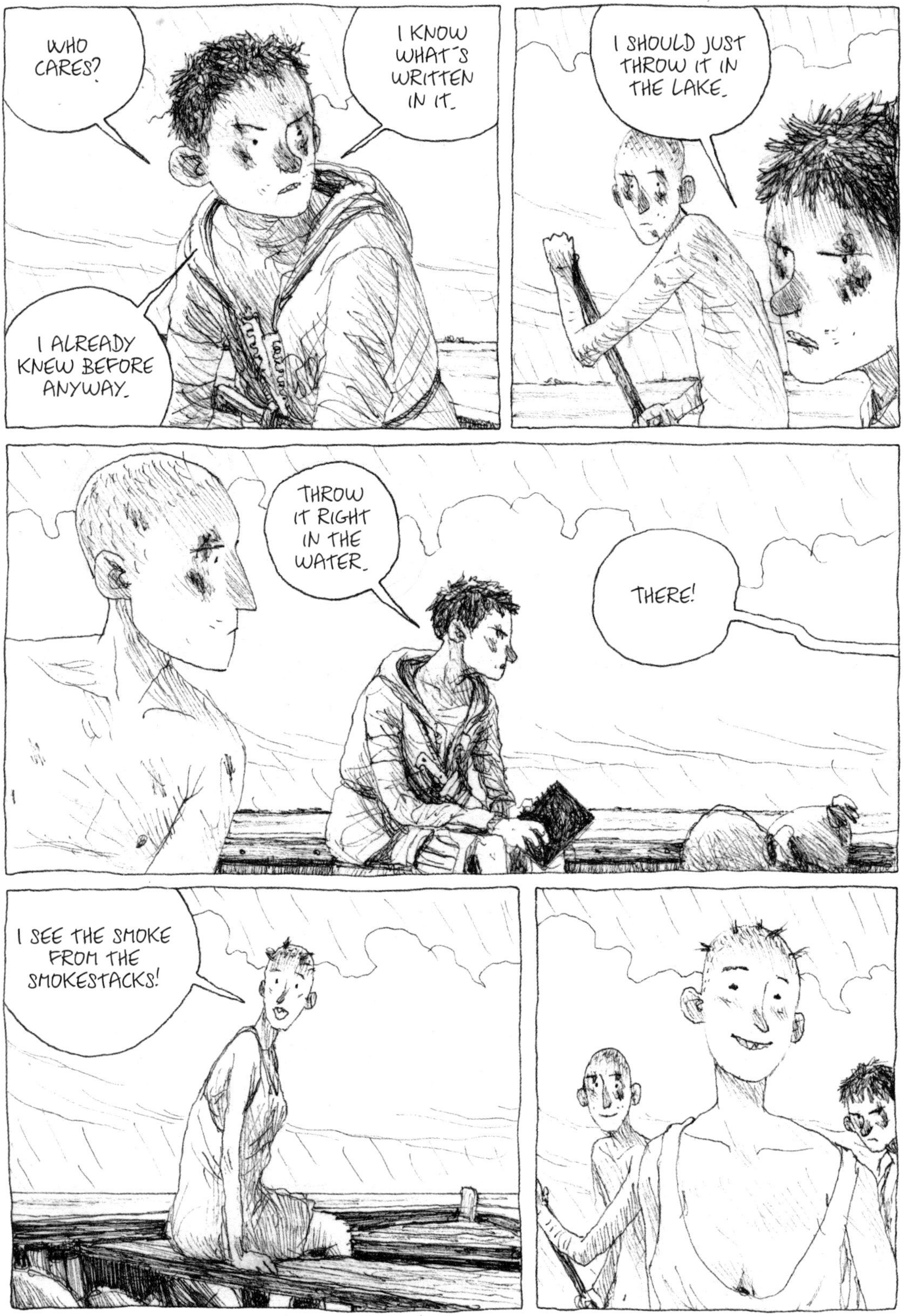
WHO CARES?
I KNOW WHAT´S WRITTEN IN IT.
I ALREADY KNEW BEFORE ANYWAY.
I SHOULD JUST THROW IT IN THE LAKE.
THROW IT RIGHT IN THE WATER.
THERE!
I SEE THE SMOKE FROM THE SMOKESTACKS!

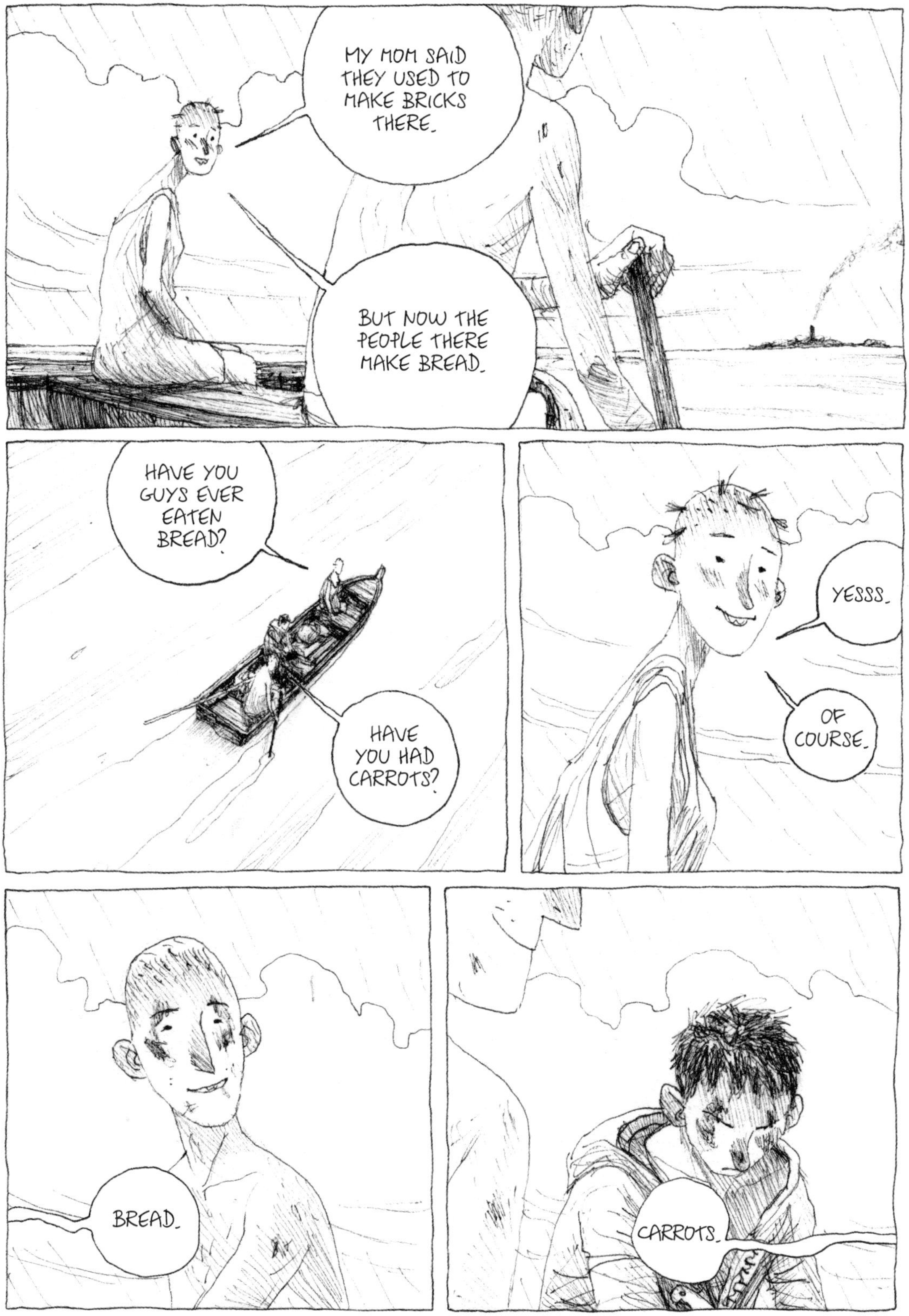
MY MOM SAID THEY USED TO MAKE BRICKS THERE.
BUT NOW THE PEOPLE THERE MAKE BREAD.
HAVE YOU GUYS EVER EATEN BREAD?
HAVE YOU HAD CARROTS?
YESSS.
OF COURSE.
BREAD.
CARROTS.

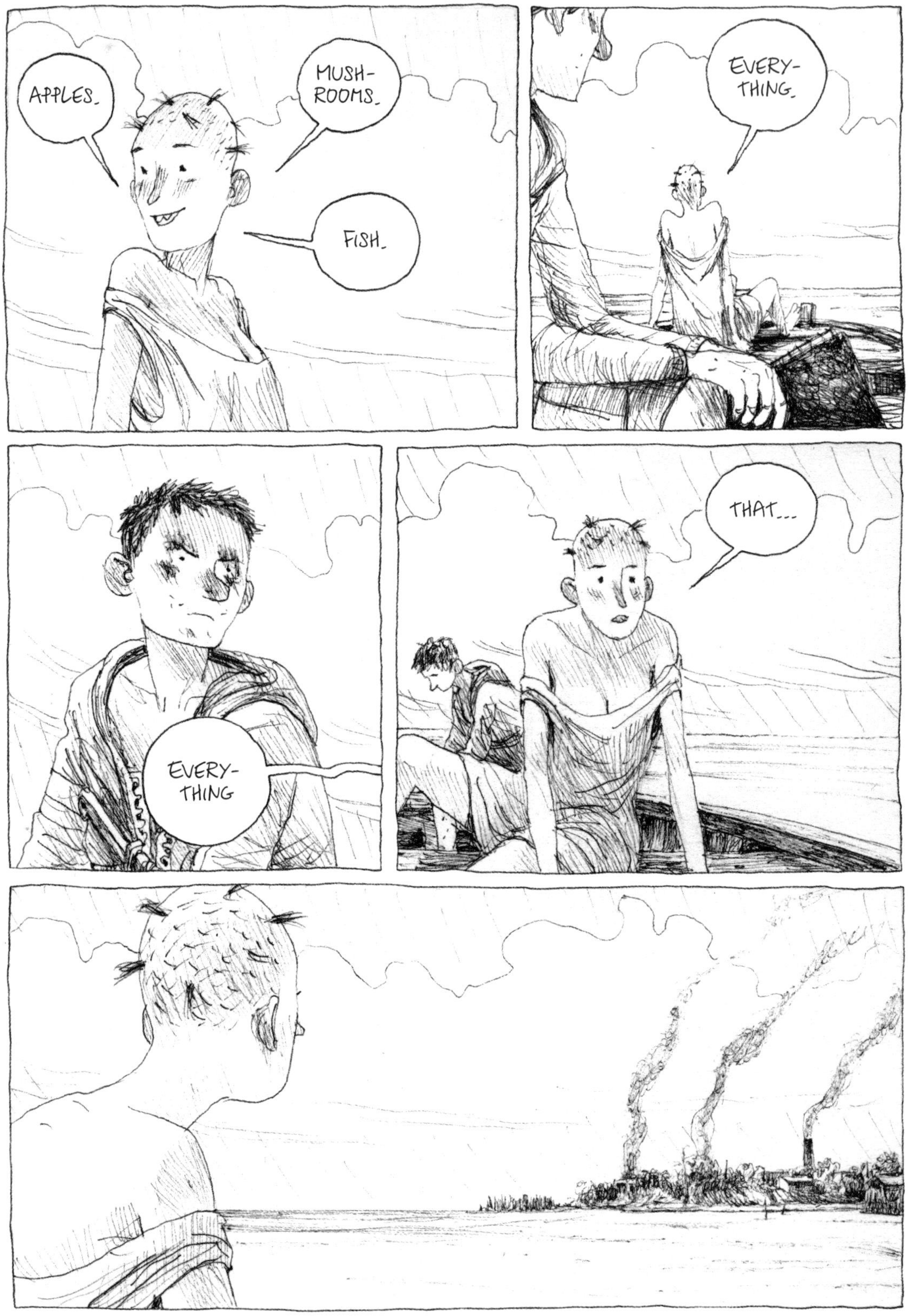
APPLES.
MUSH-ROOMS.
FISH.
EVERY-THING.
EVERY-THING
THAT...

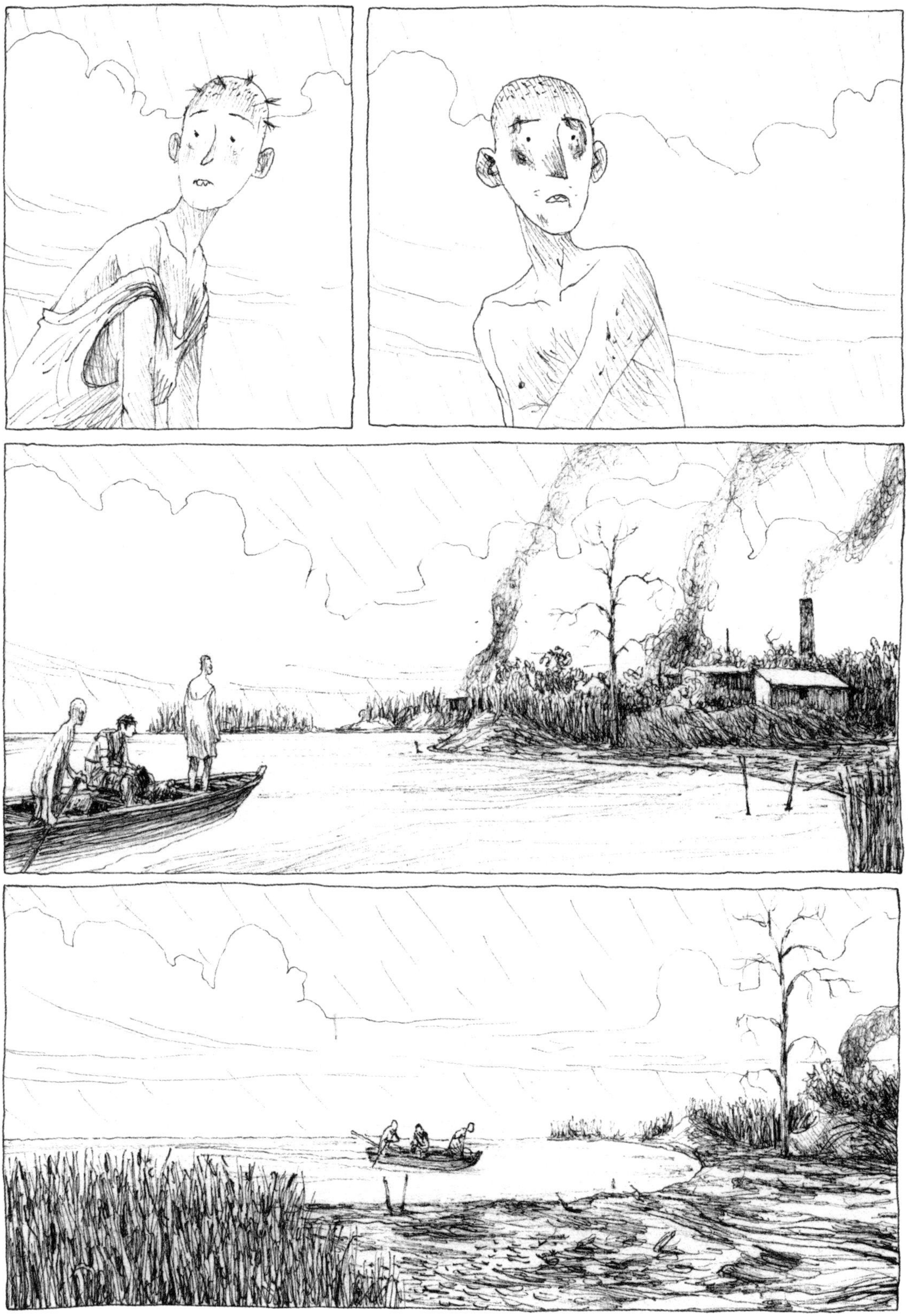

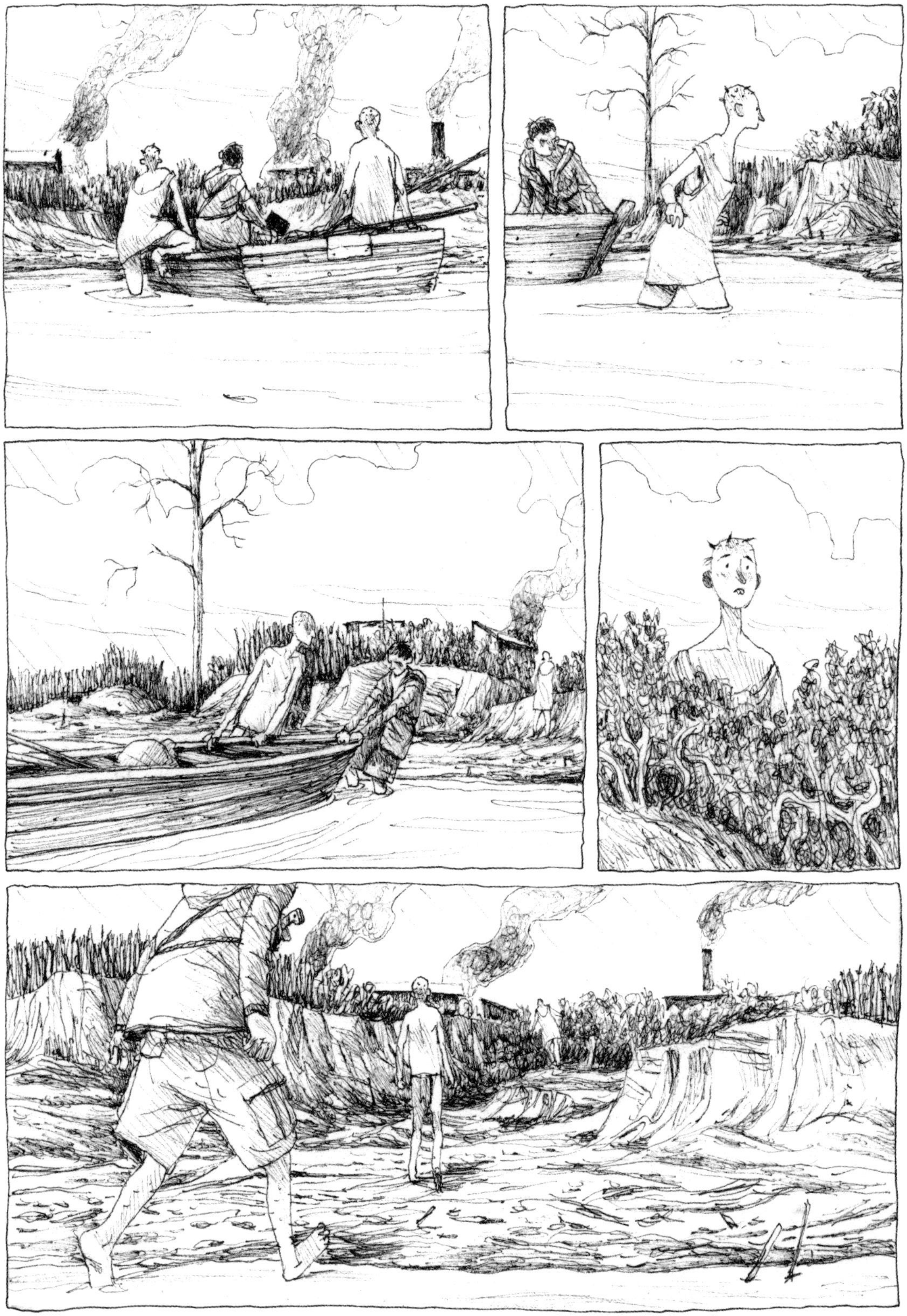

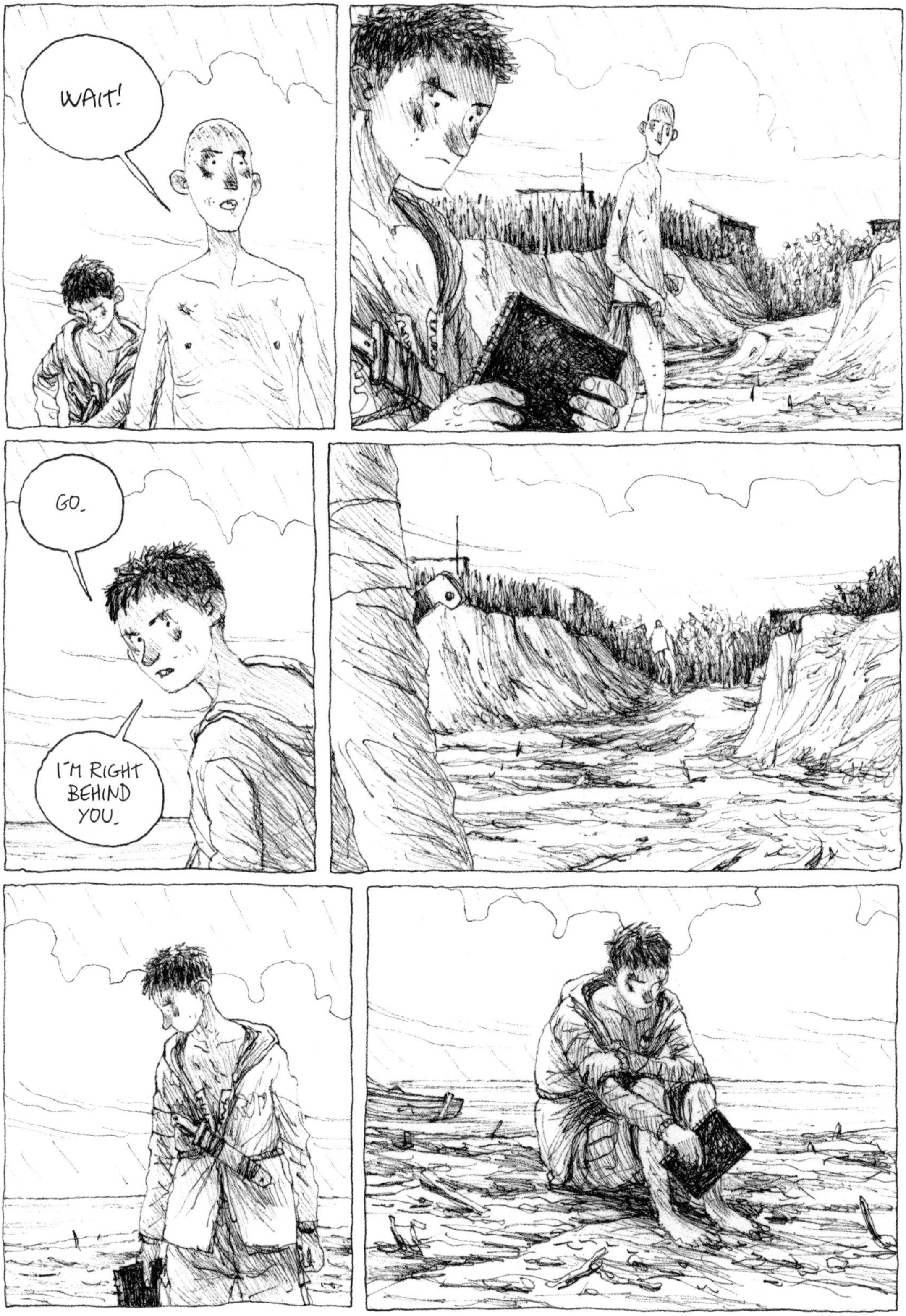
WAIT!
GO.
I'M RIGHT BEHIND YOU.

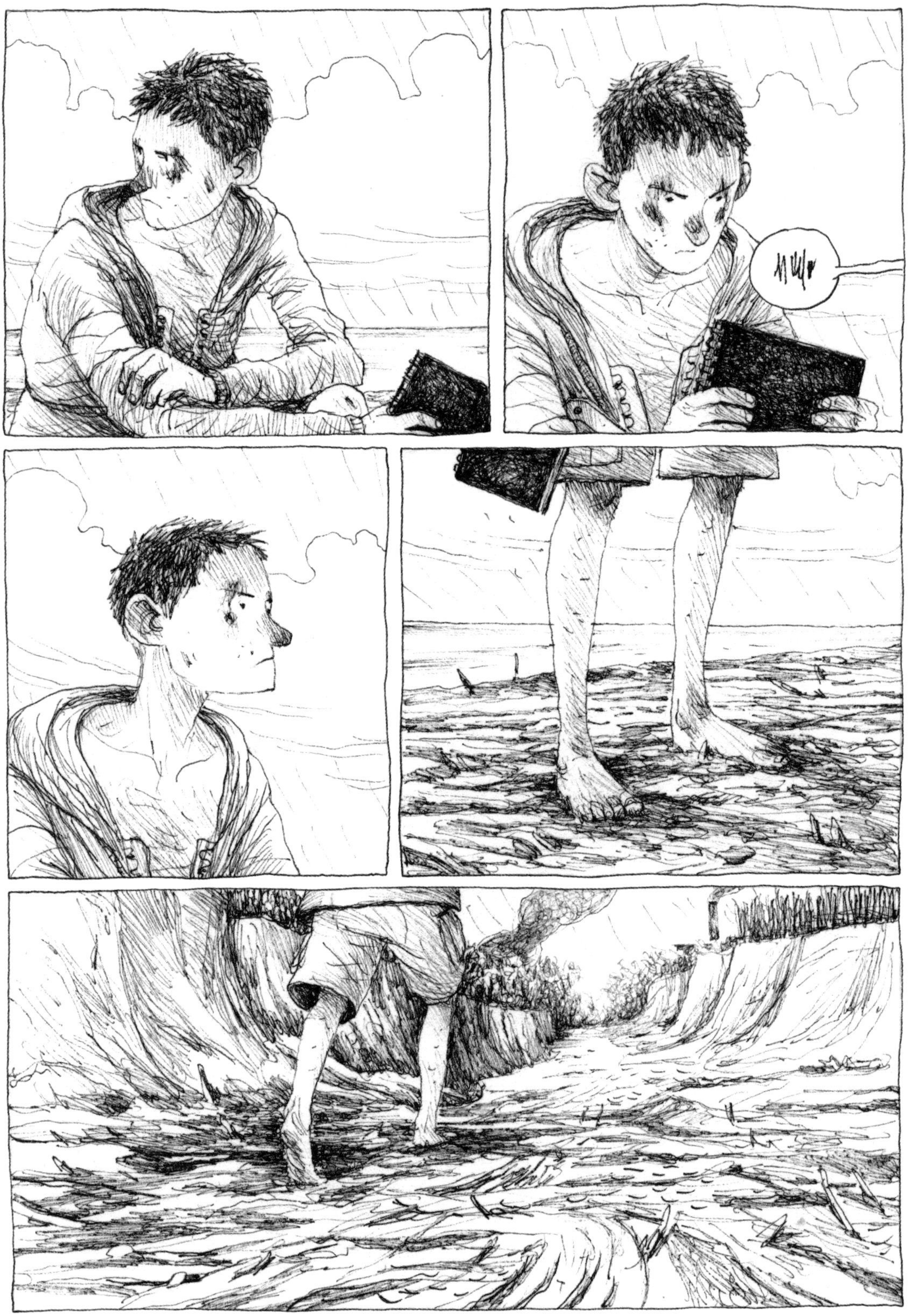

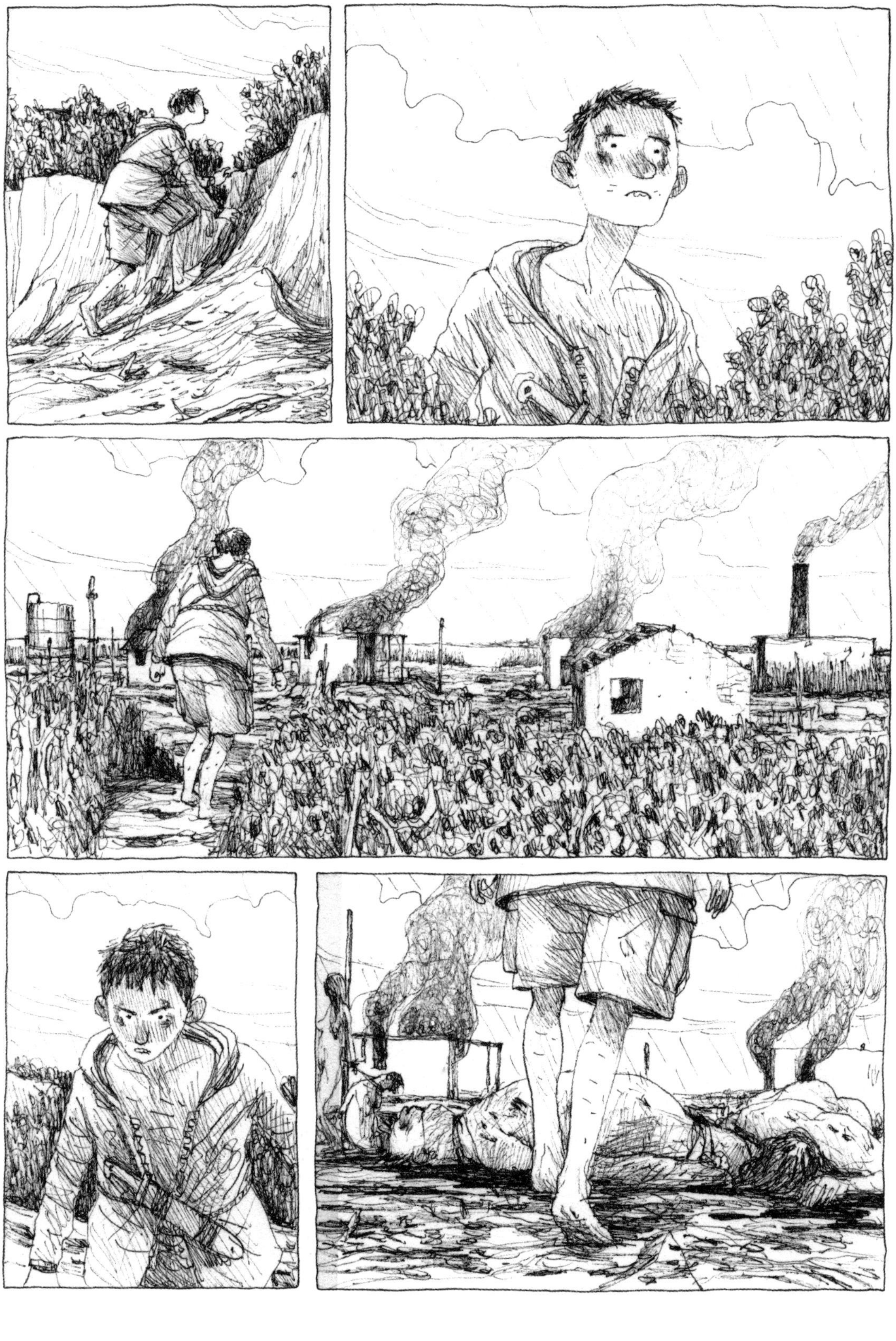

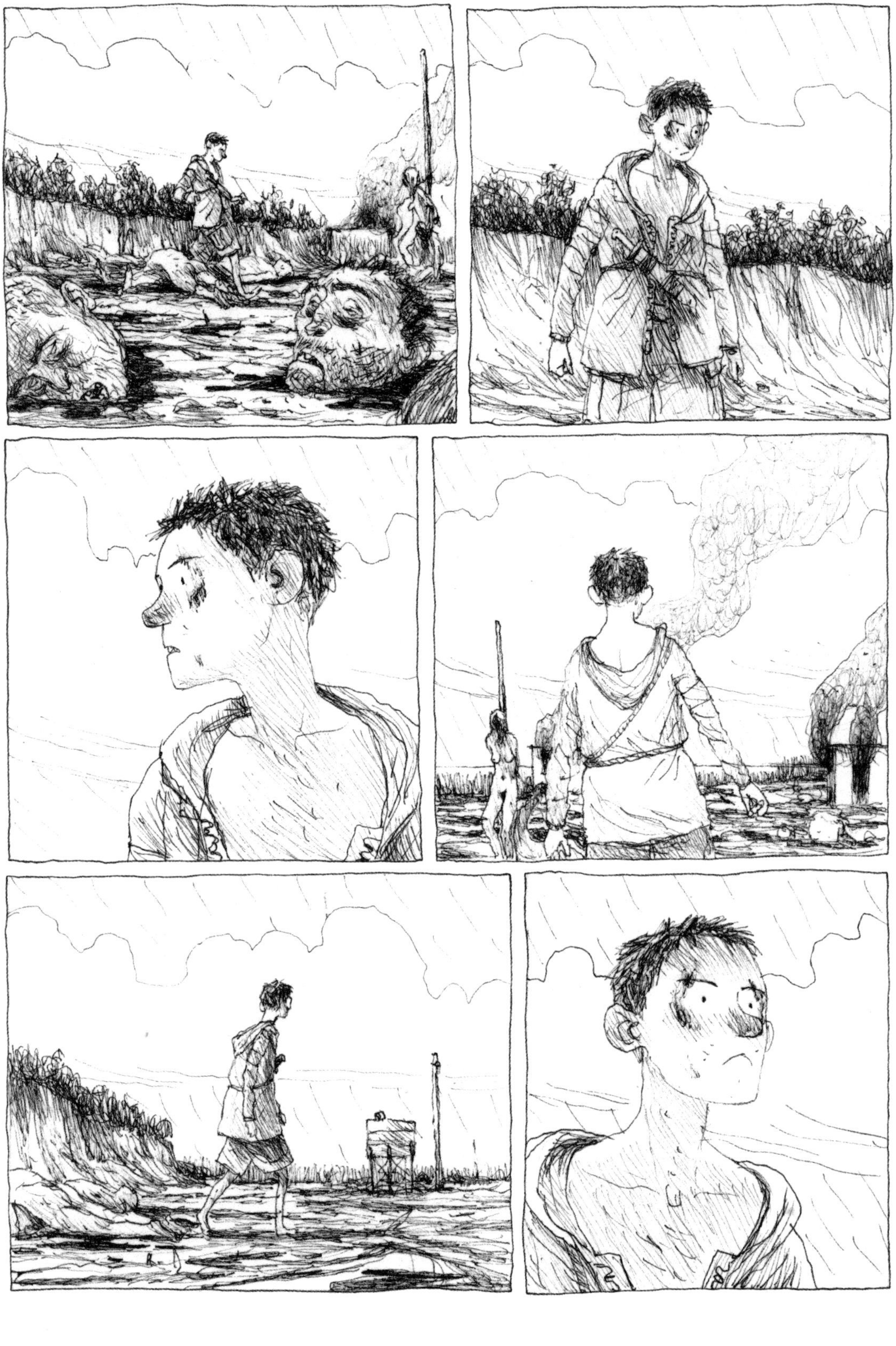

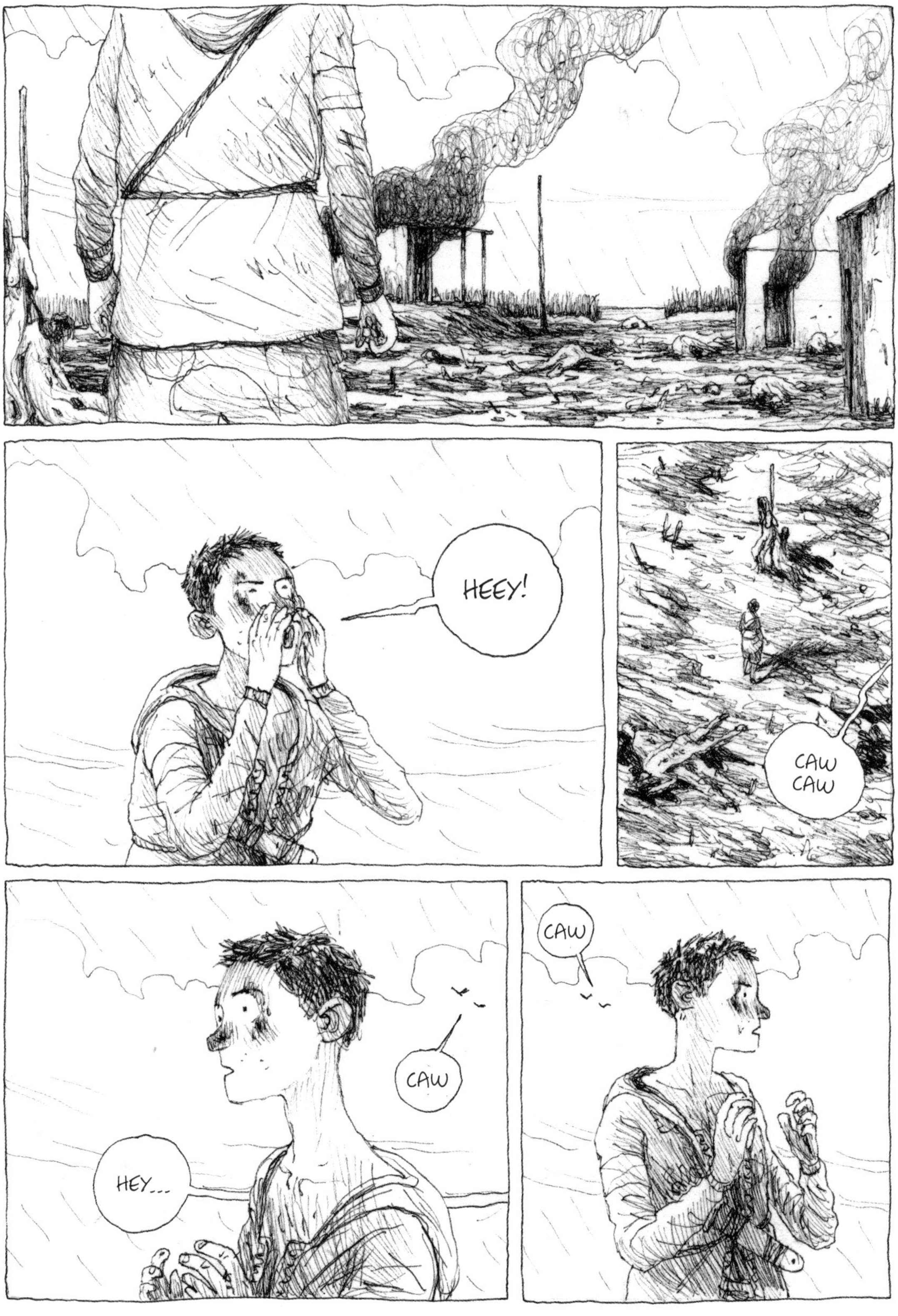
HEEY!
CAW CAW
CAW
HEY...
CAW

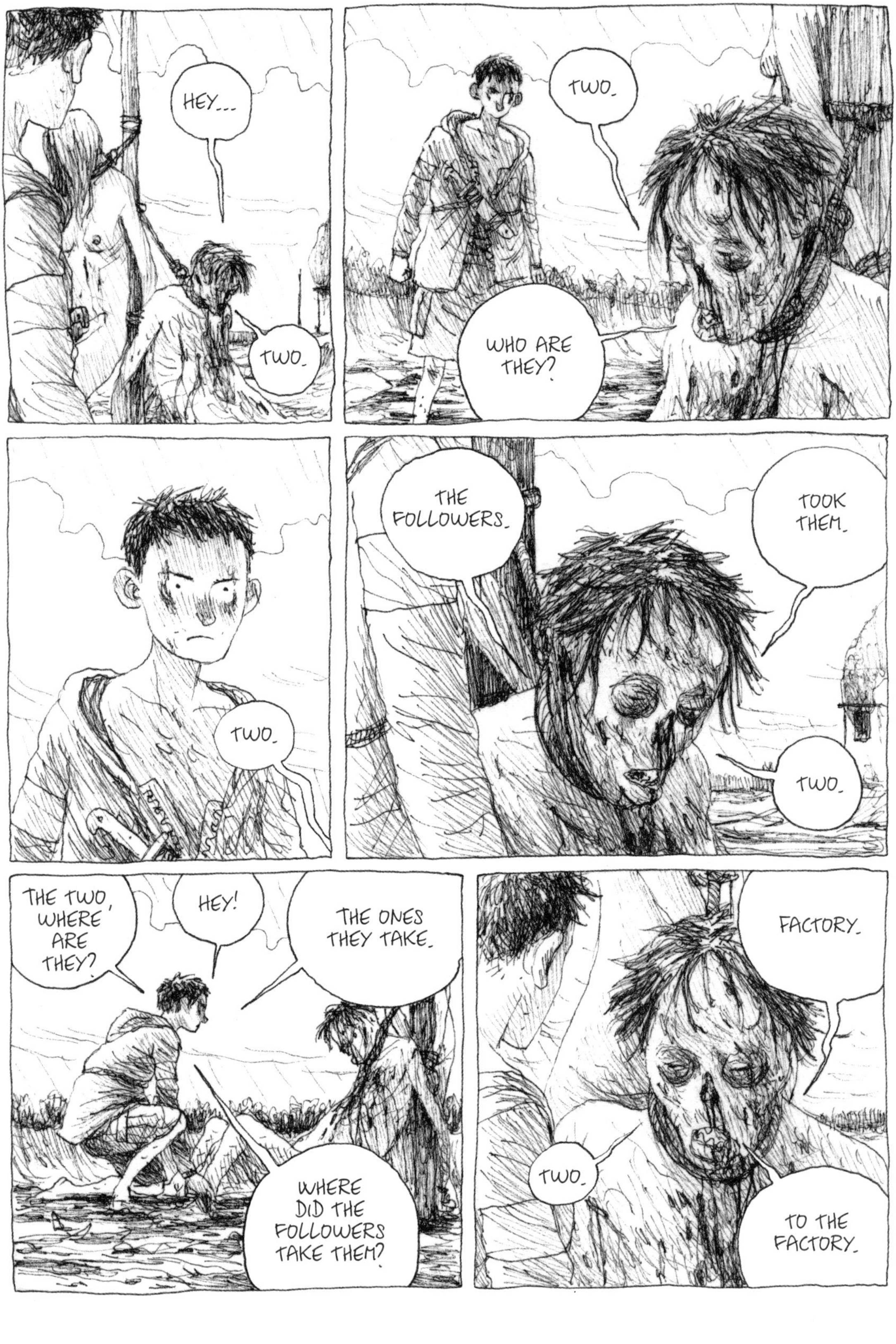
HEY...
TWO.
TWO.
WHO ARE THEY?
TWO.
THE FOLLOWERS.
TOOK THEM.
TWO.
THE TWO, WHERE ARE THEY?
HEY!
THE ONES THEY TAKE.
WHERE DID THE FOLLOWERS TAKE THEM?
FACTORY.
TWO.
TO THE FACTORY.

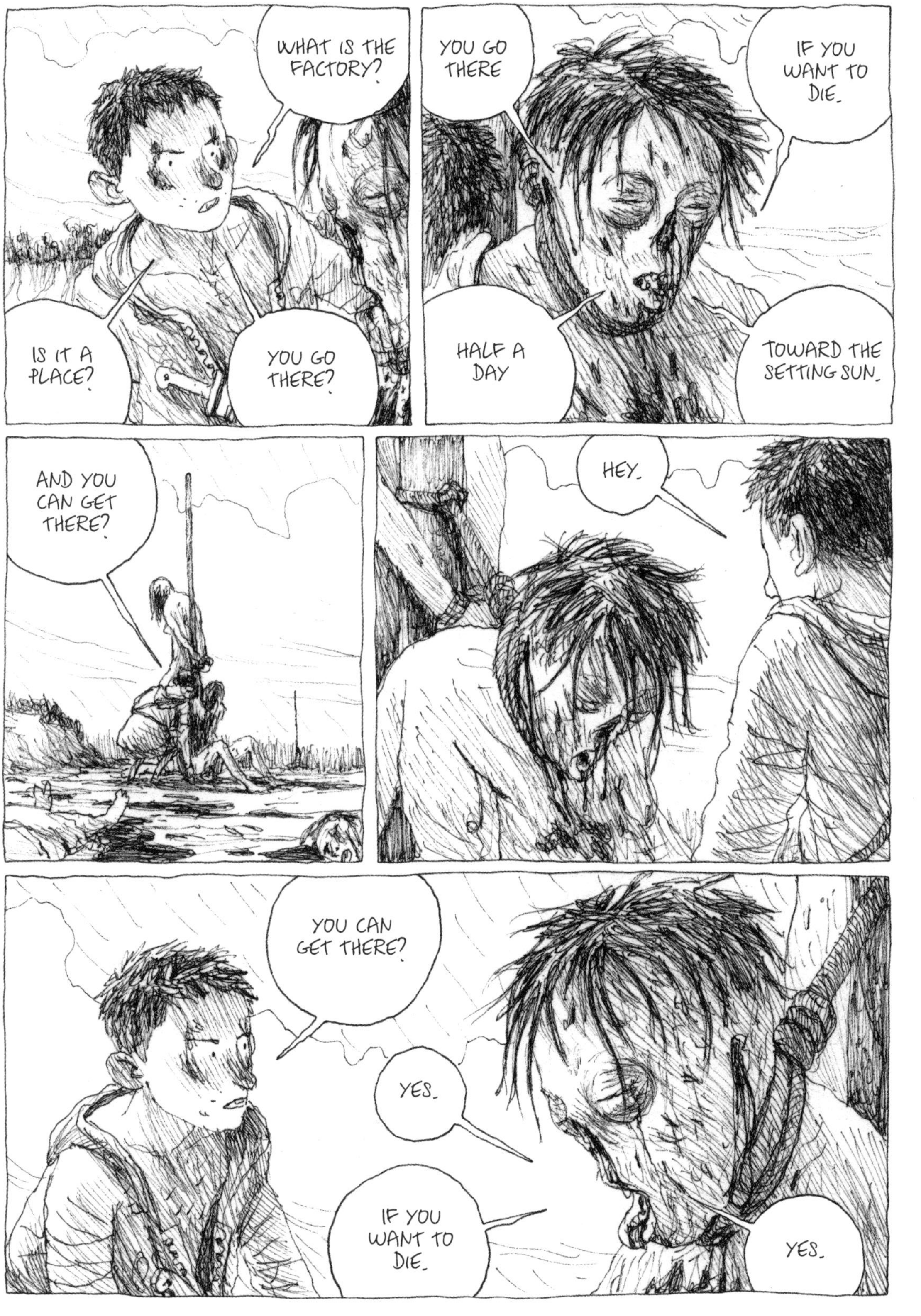
WHAT IS THE FACTORY?
IS IT A PLACE?
YOU GO THERE?
YOU GO THERE
IF YOU WANT TO DIE.
HALF A DAY
TOWARD THE SETTING SUN.
AND YOU CAN GET THERE?
HEY.
YOU CAN GET THERE?
YES.
IF YOU WANT TO DIE.
YES.

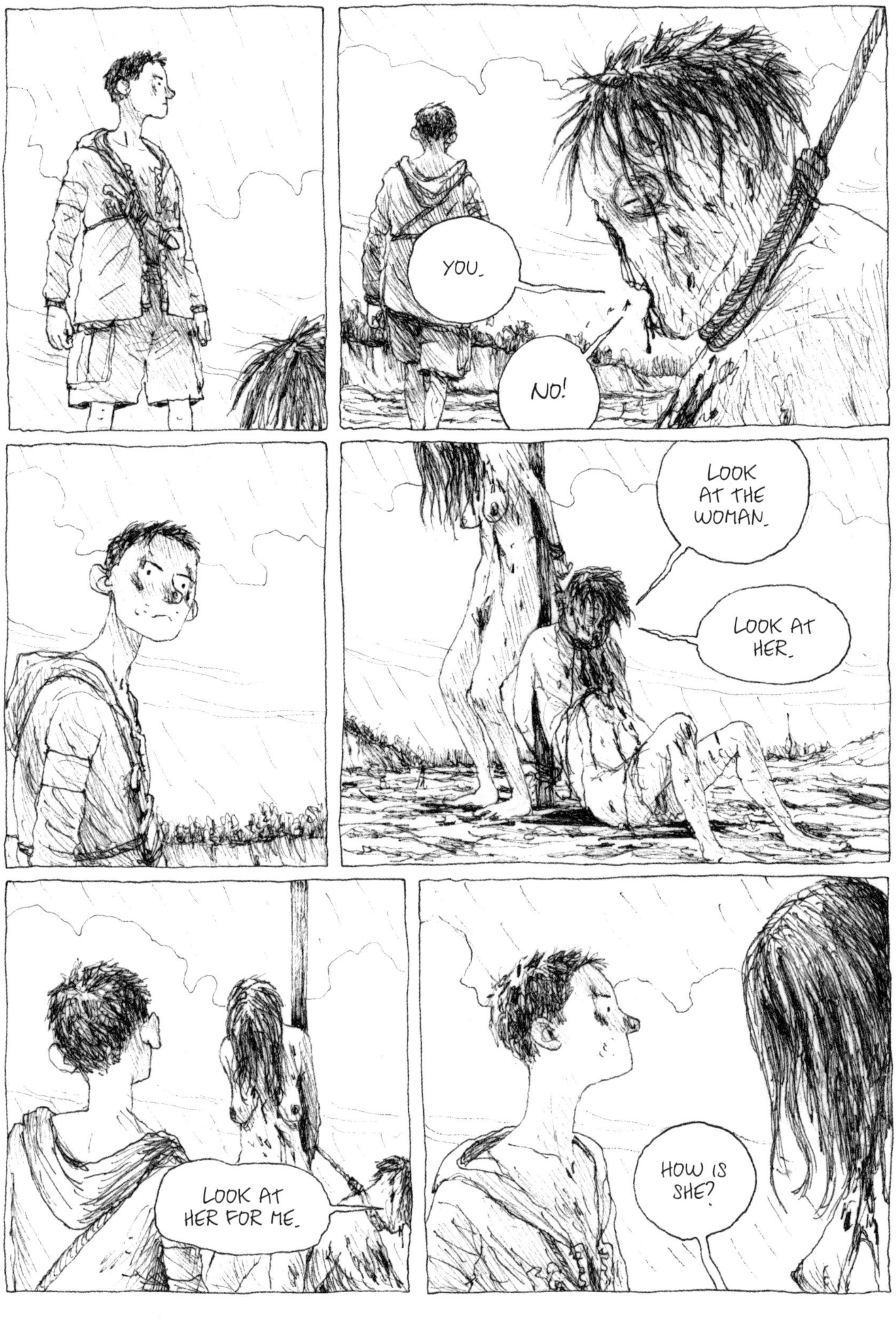
YOU_
NO!
LOOK AT THE WOMAN_
LOOK AT HER_
LOOK AT HER FOR ME_
HOW IS SHE?

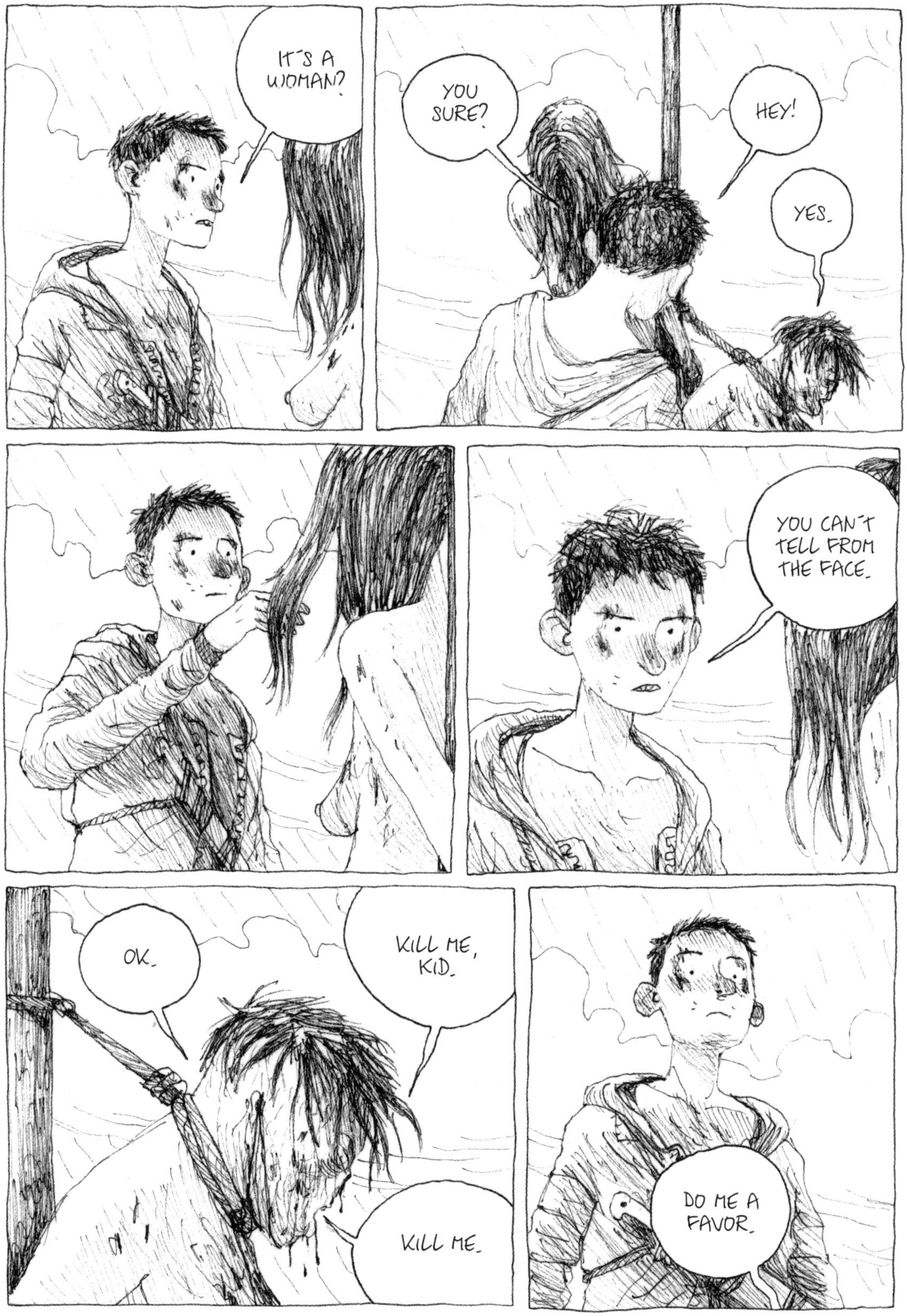
IT'S A WOMAN?
YOU SURE?
HEY!
YES.
YOU CAN'T TELL FROM THE FACE.
OK.
KILL ME, KID.
KILL ME.
DO ME A FAVOR.

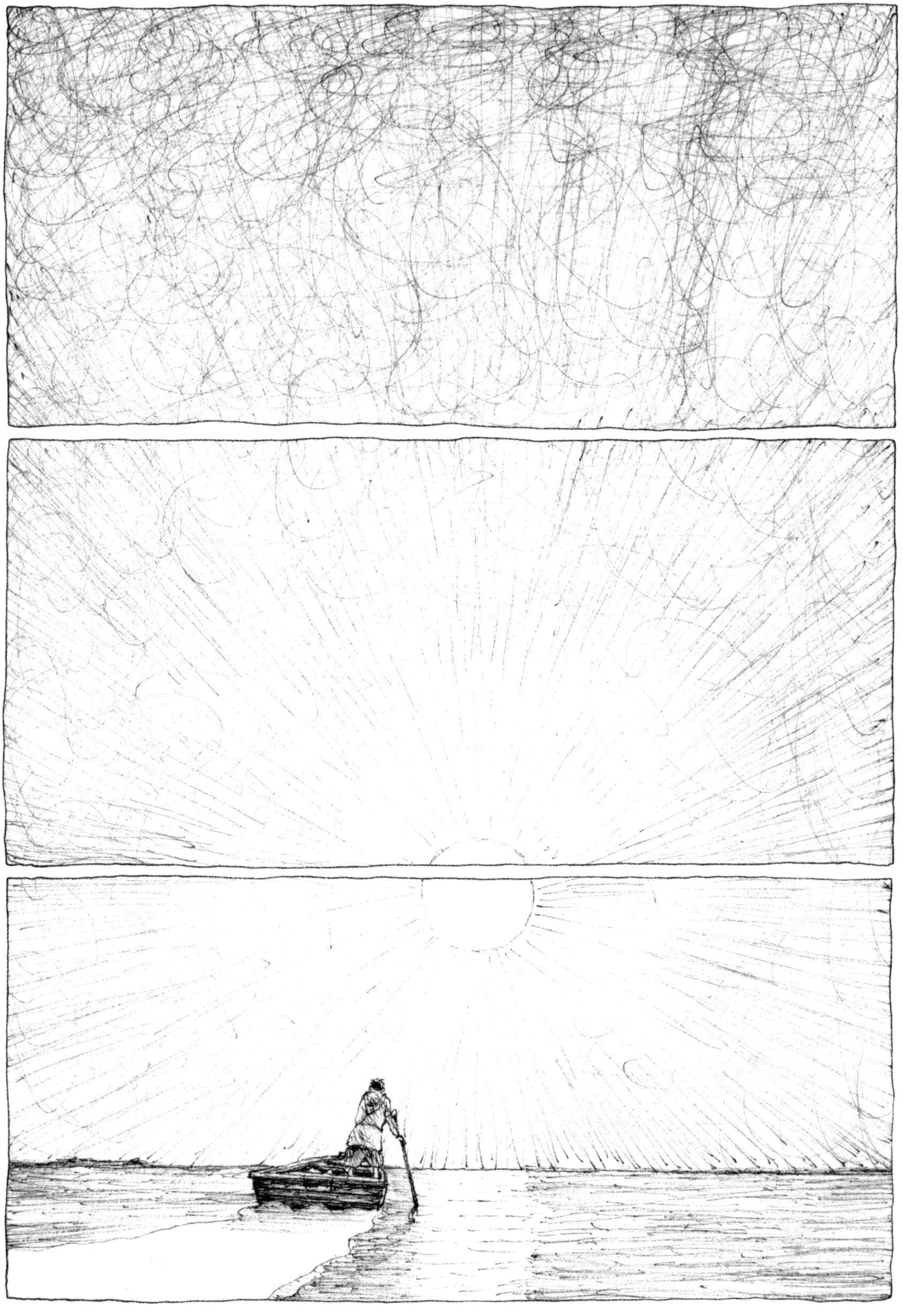

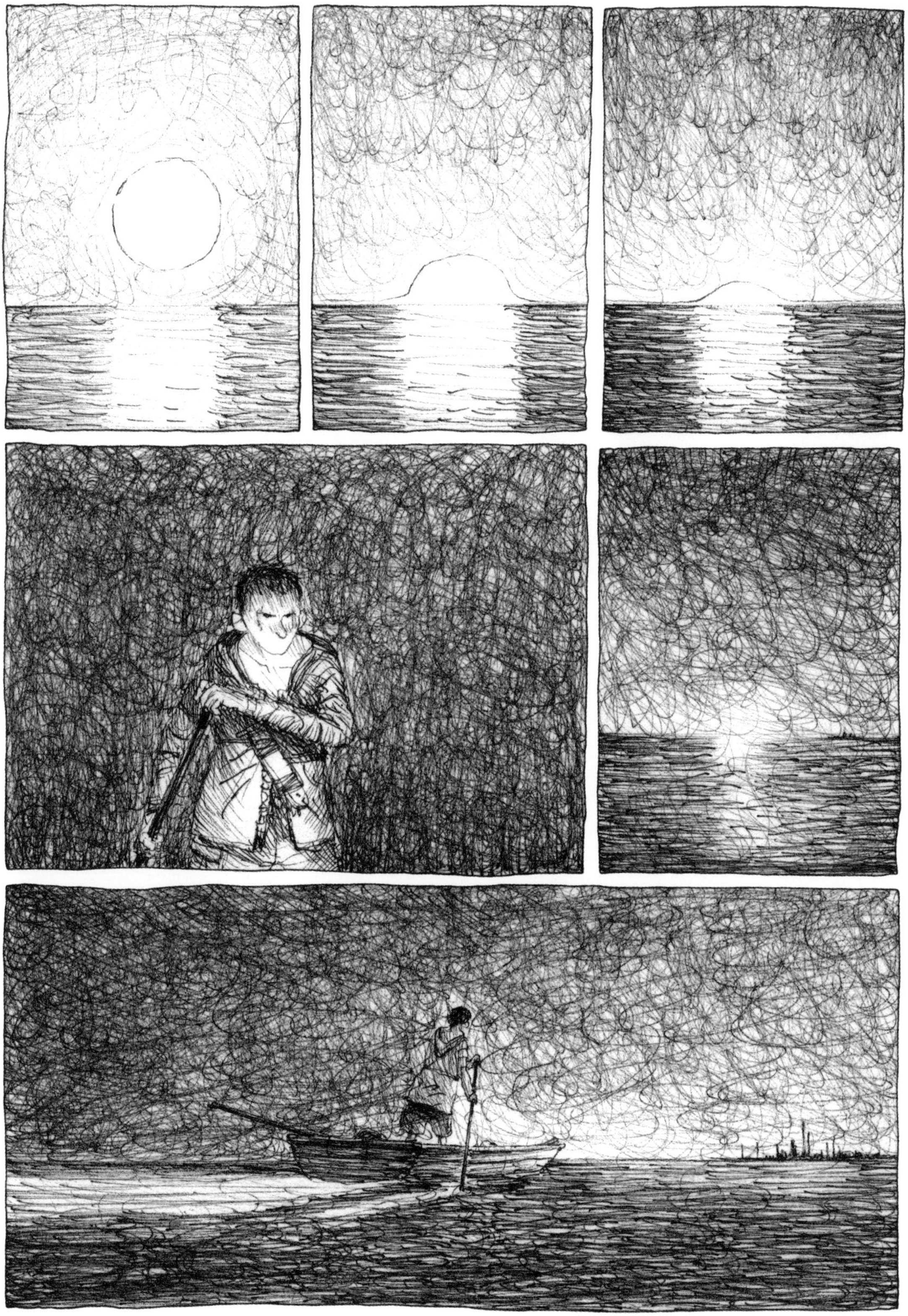

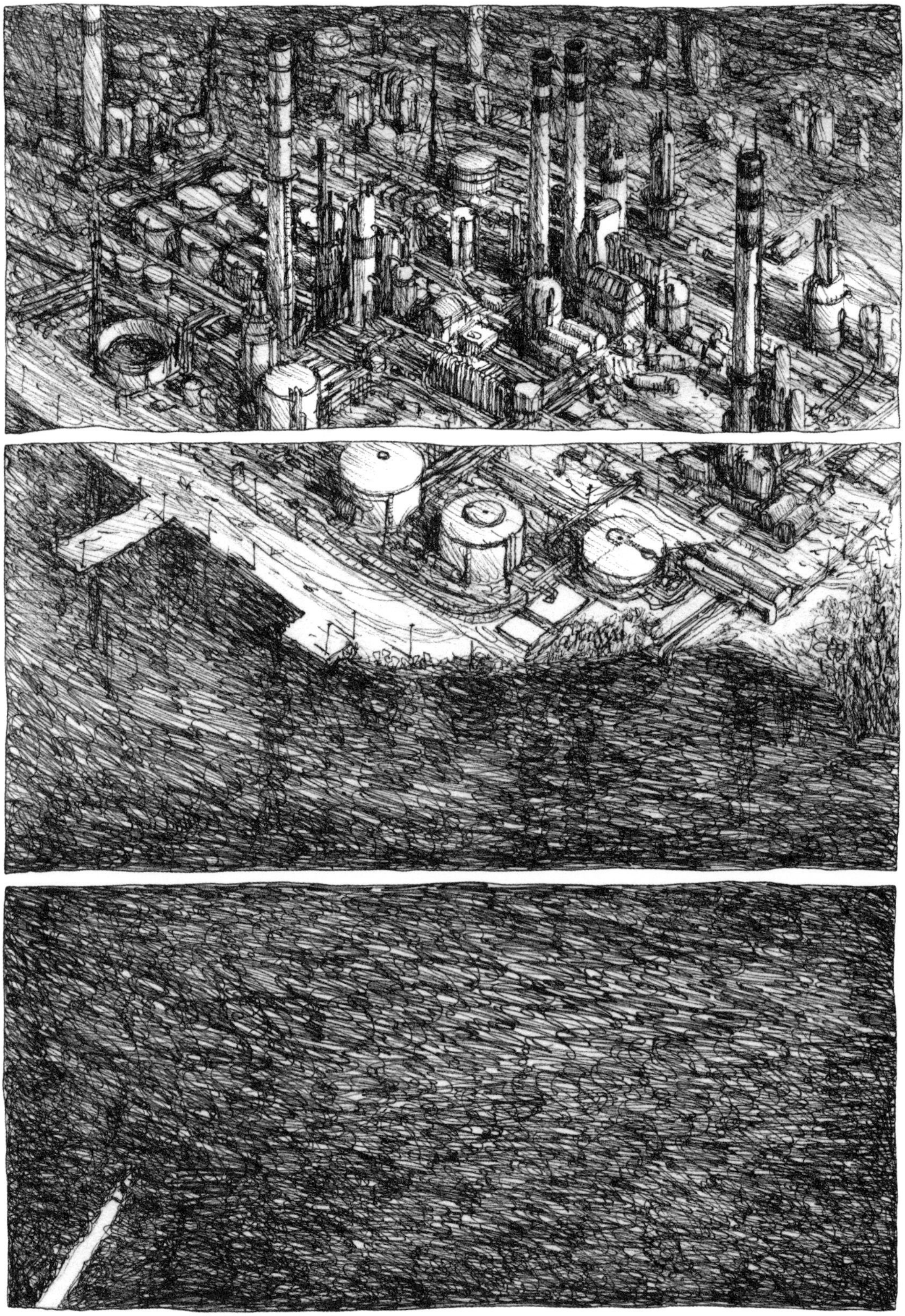

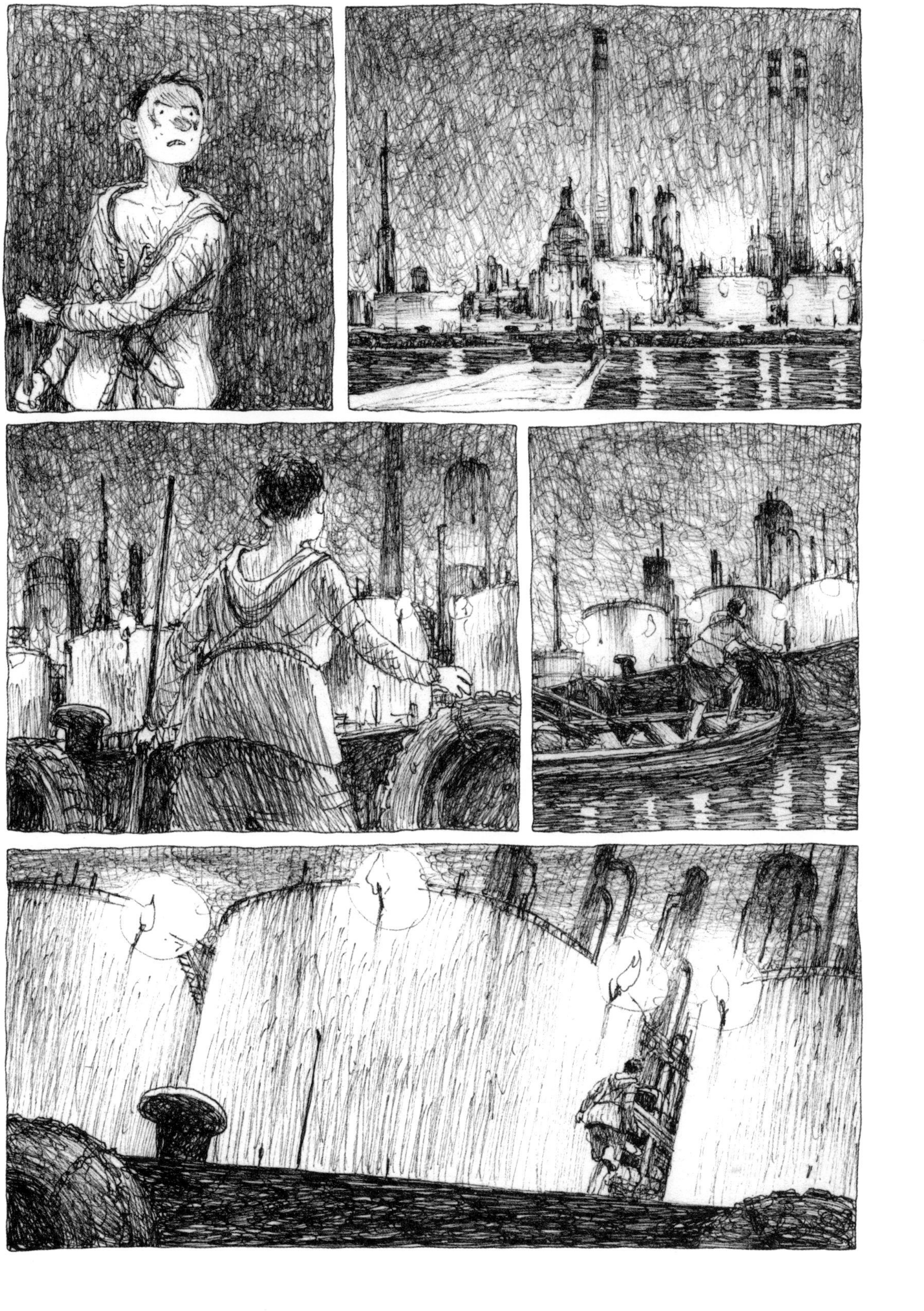

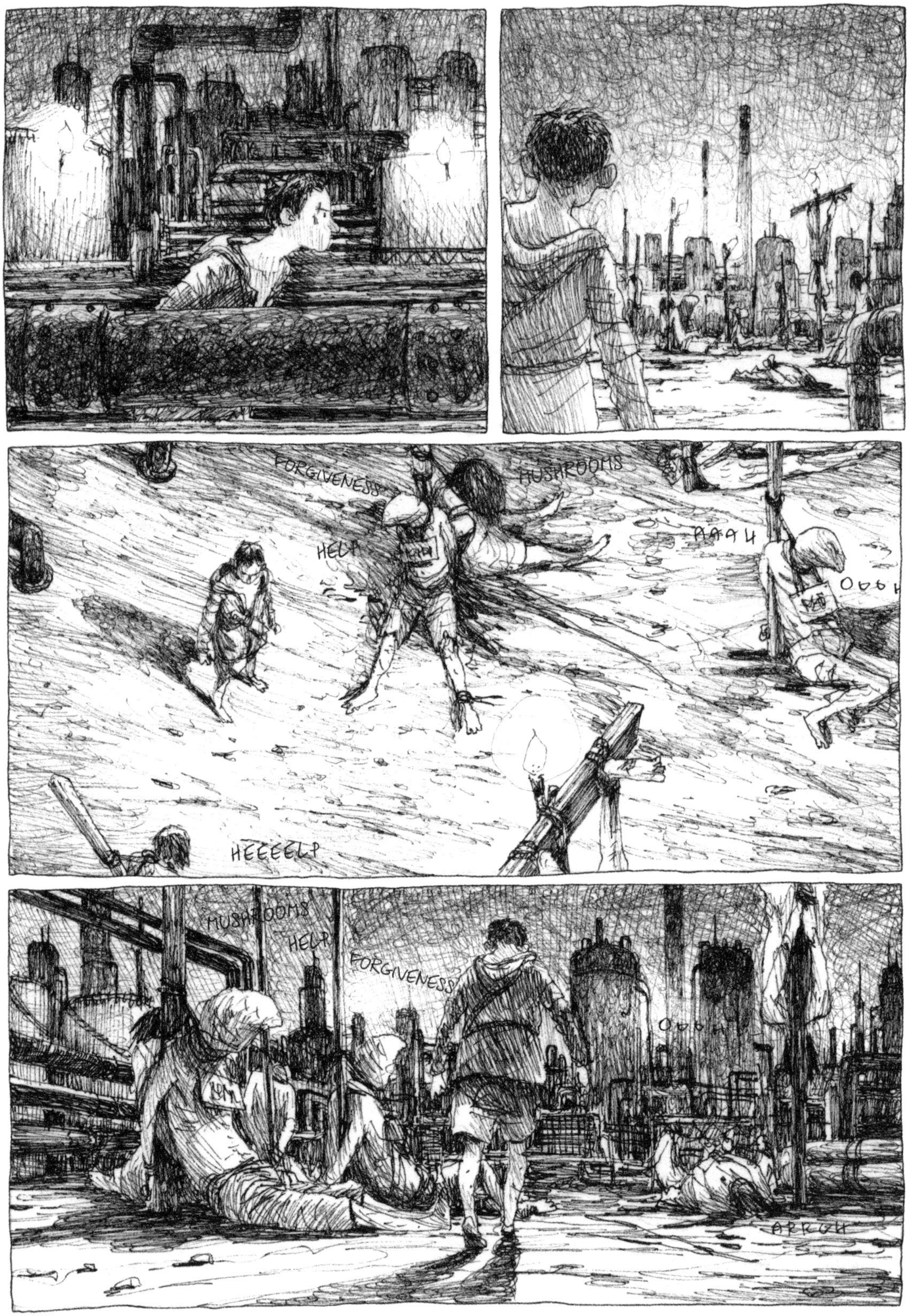
FORGIVENESS
MUSHROOMS
HELP
AAAH
OOOH
HEEEELP
MUSHROOMS
HELP
FORGIVENESS
OOOH
ARRGH

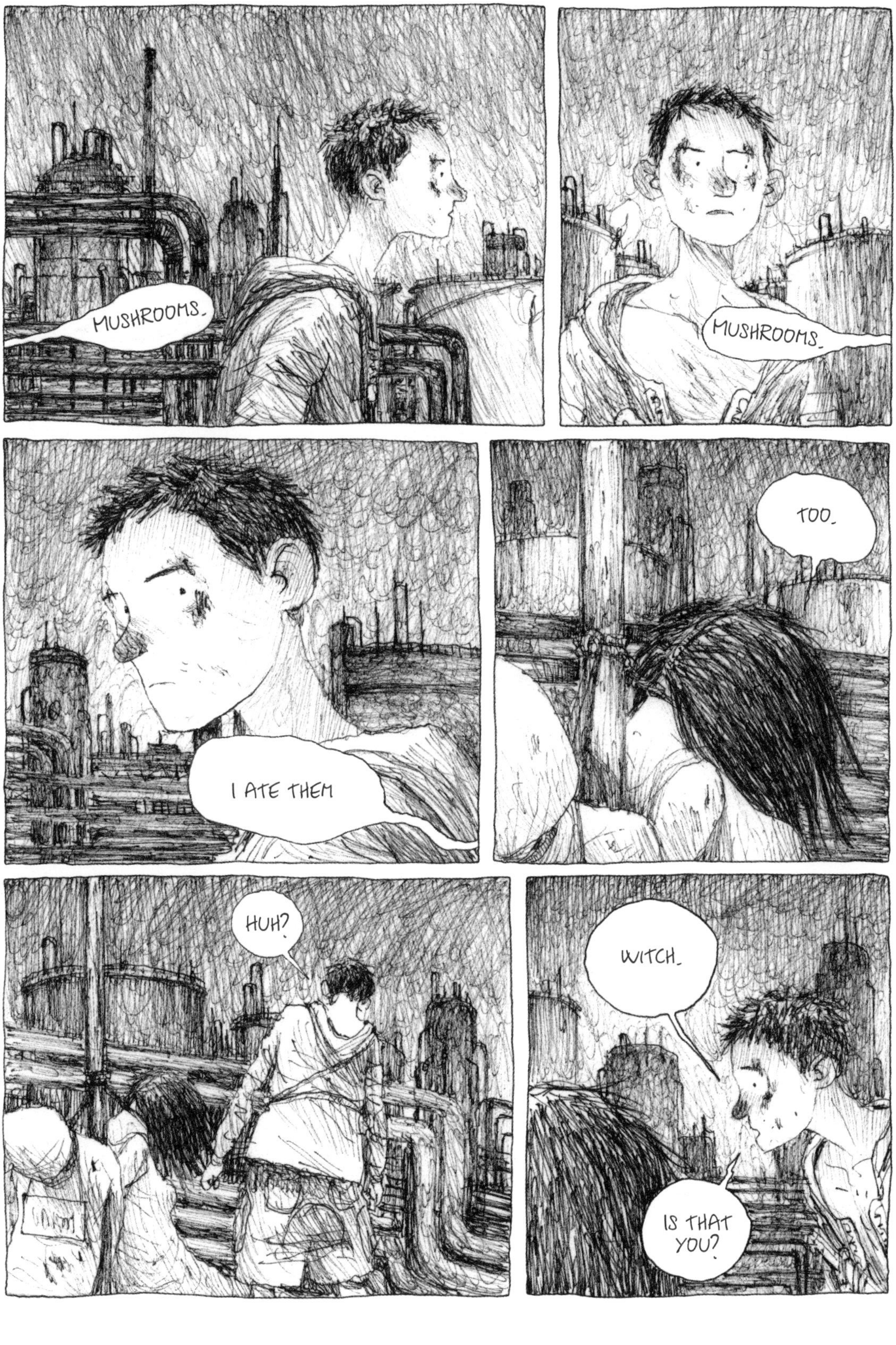
MUSHROOMS_
MUSHROOMS_
I ATE THEM
TOO_
HUH?
WITCH_
IS THAT YOU?

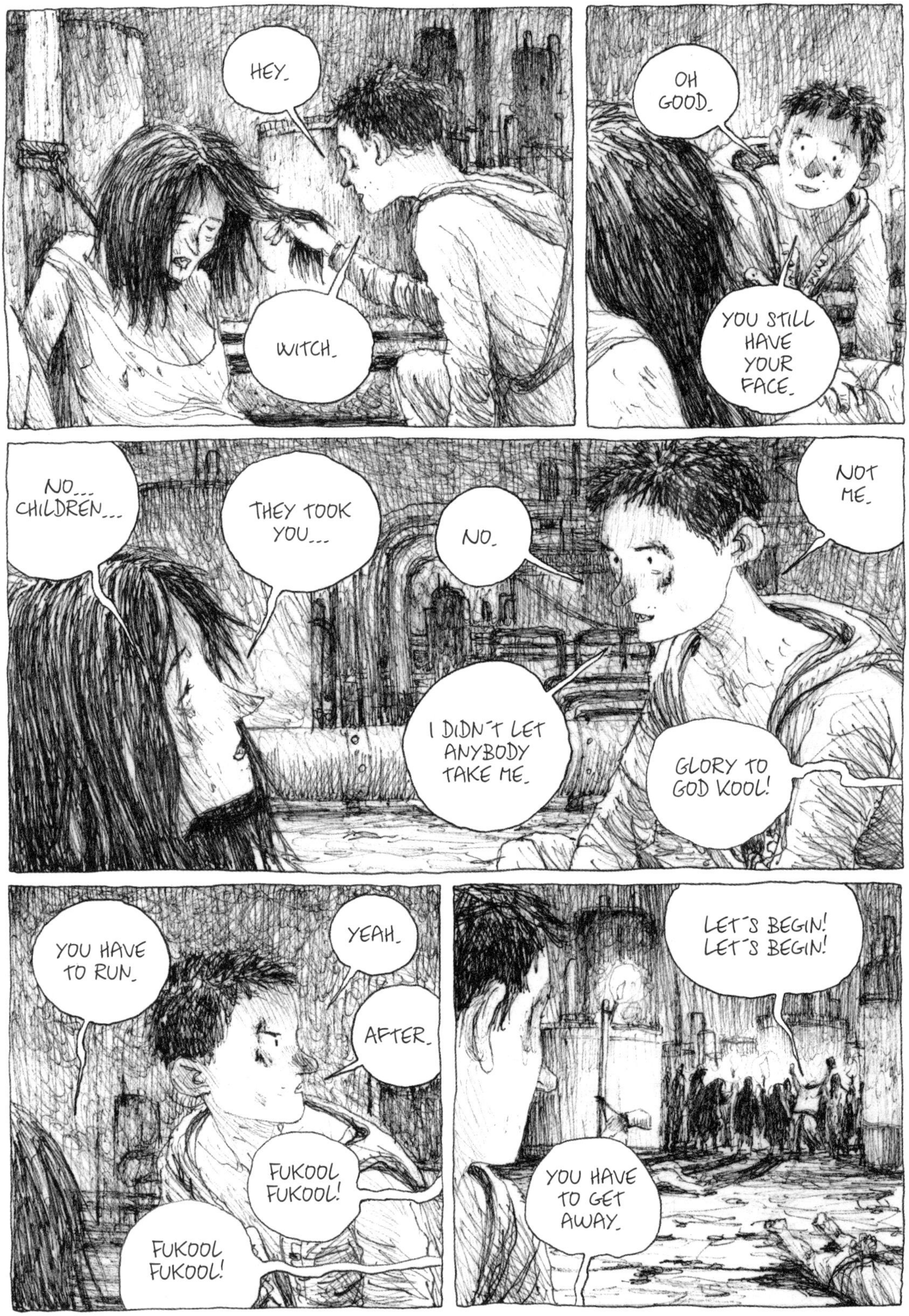
HEY.
WITCH.
OH GOOD.
YOU STILL HAVE YOUR FACE.
NO... CHILDREN...
THEY TOOK YOU...
NO.
NOT ME.
I DIDN'T LET ANYBODY TAKE ME.
GLORY TO GOD KOOL!
YOU HAVE TO RUN.
YEAH.
AFTER.
FUKOOL FUKOOL!
FUKOOL FUKOOL!
LET'S BEGIN! LET'S BEGIN!
YOU HAVE TO GET AWAY.

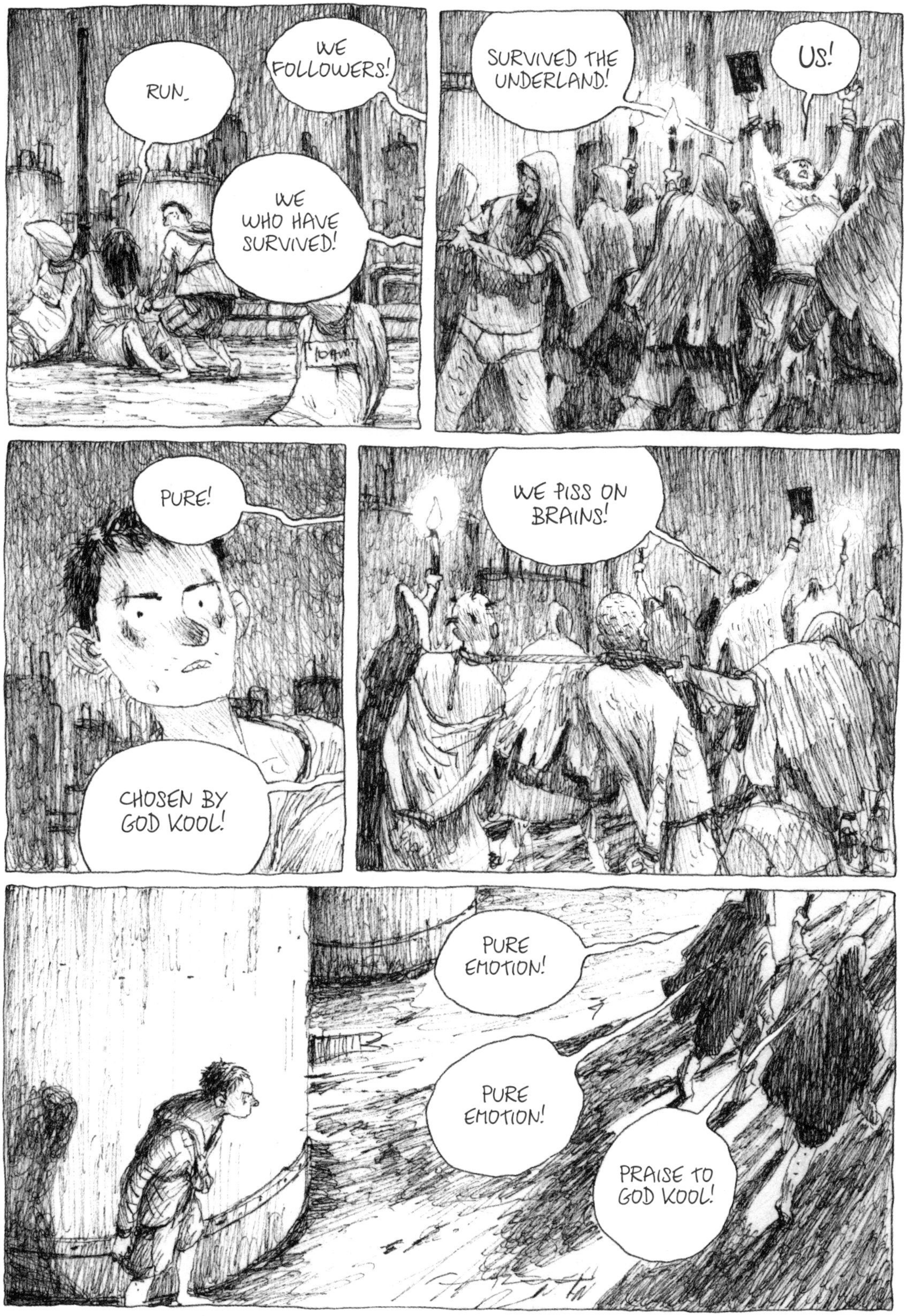
RUN_
WE FOLLOWERS!
WE WHO HAVE SURVIVED!
SURVIVED THE UNDERLAND!
US!
PURE!
CHOSEN BY GOD KOOL!
WE PISS ON BRAINS!
PURE EMOTION!
PURE EMOTION!
PRAISE TO GOD KOOL!

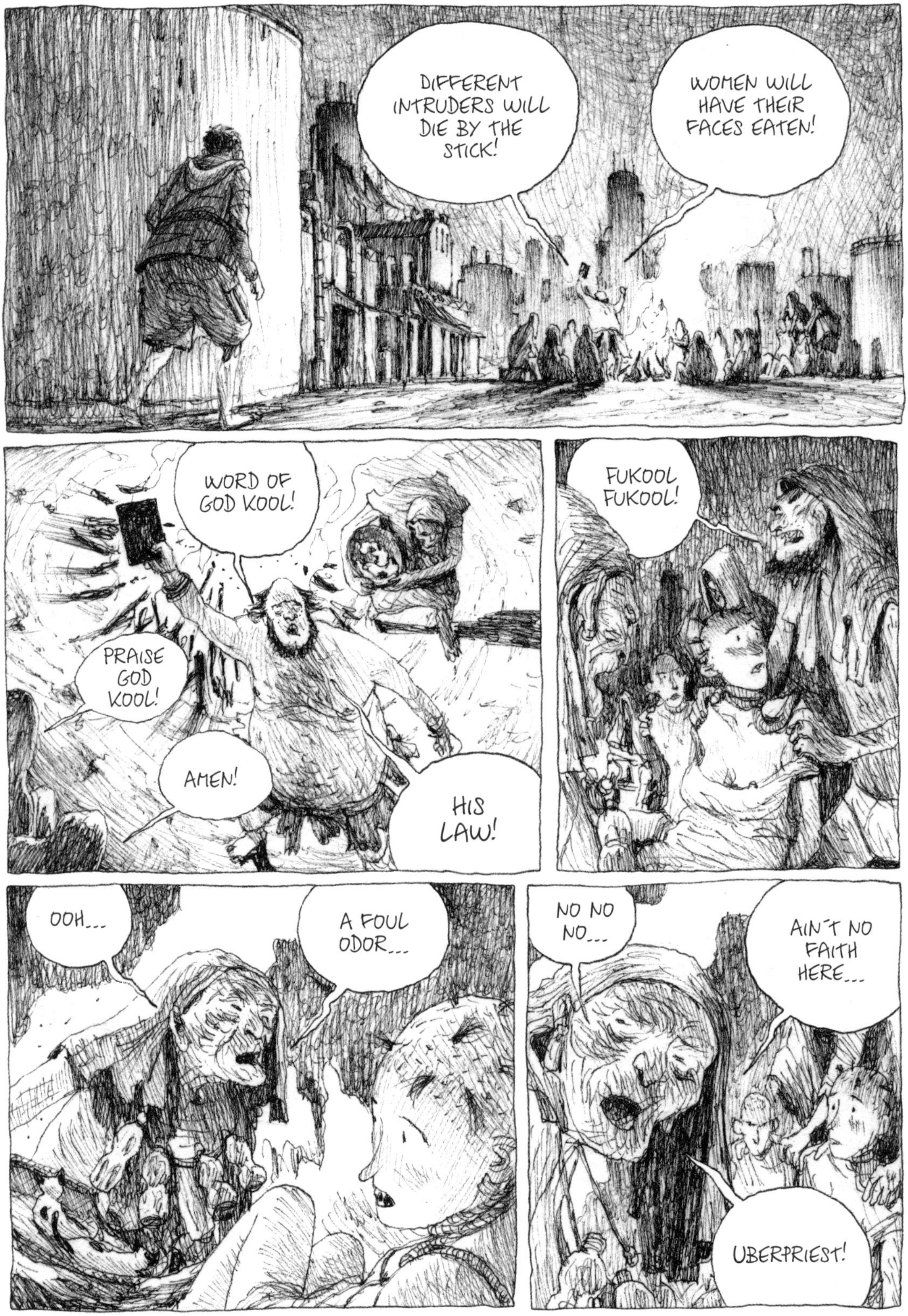
DIFFERENT INTRUDERS WILL DIE BY THE STICK!
WOMEN WILL HAVE THEIR FACES EATEN!
WORD OF GOD KOOL!
PRAISE GOD KOOL!
AMEN!
HIS LAW!
FUKOOL FUKOOL!
OOH...
A FOUL ODOR...
NO NO NO...
AIN'T NO FAITH HERE...
UBERPRIEST!

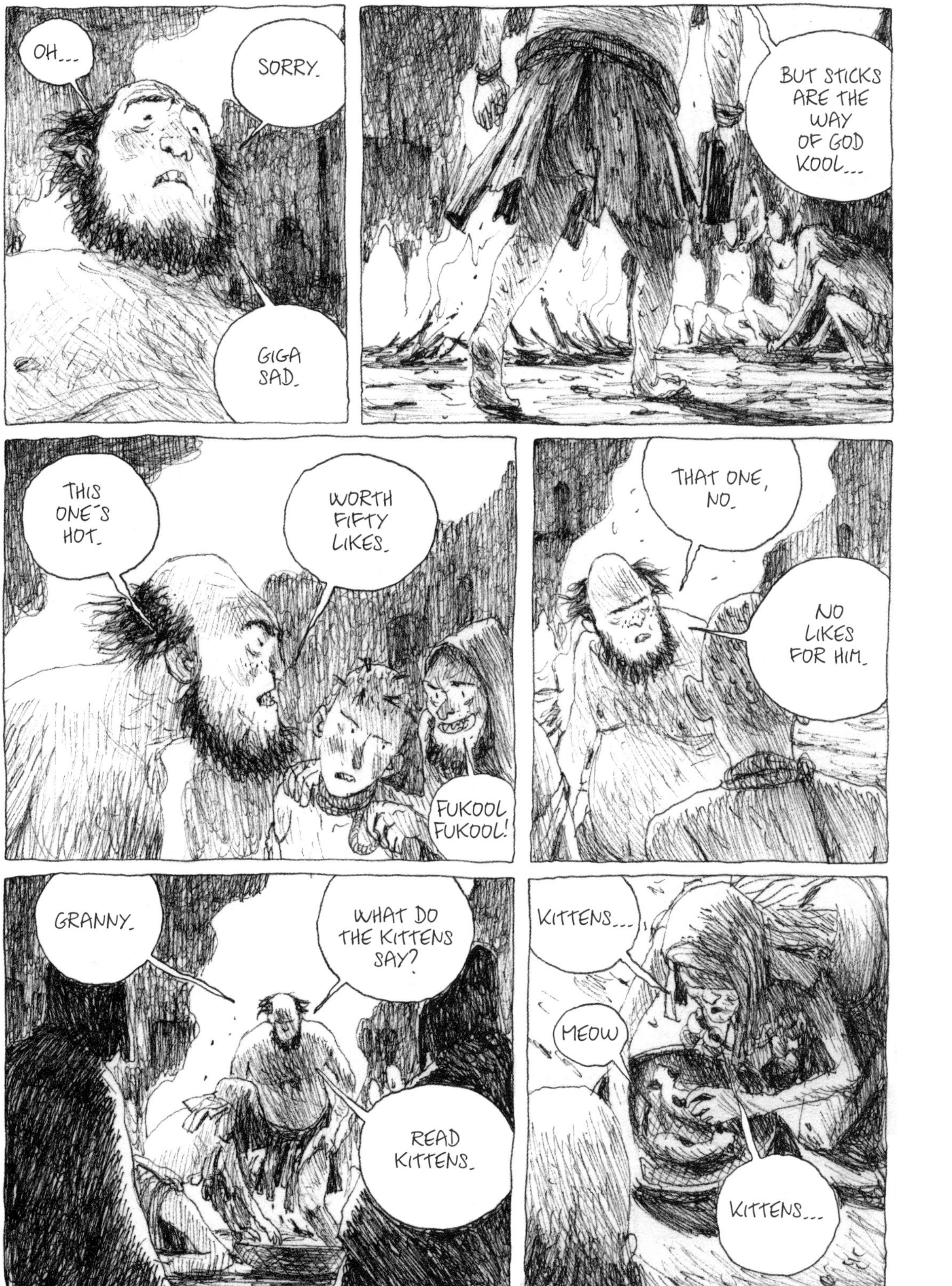
OH...
SORRY.
GIGA SAD.
BUT STICKS ARE THE WAY OF GOD KOOL...
THIS ONE'S HOT.
WORTH FIFTY LIKES.
FUKOOL FUKOOL!
THAT ONE, NO.
NO LIKES FOR HIM.
GRANNY.
WHAT DO THE KITTENS SAY?
READ KITTENS.
KITTENS...
MEOW
KITTENS...

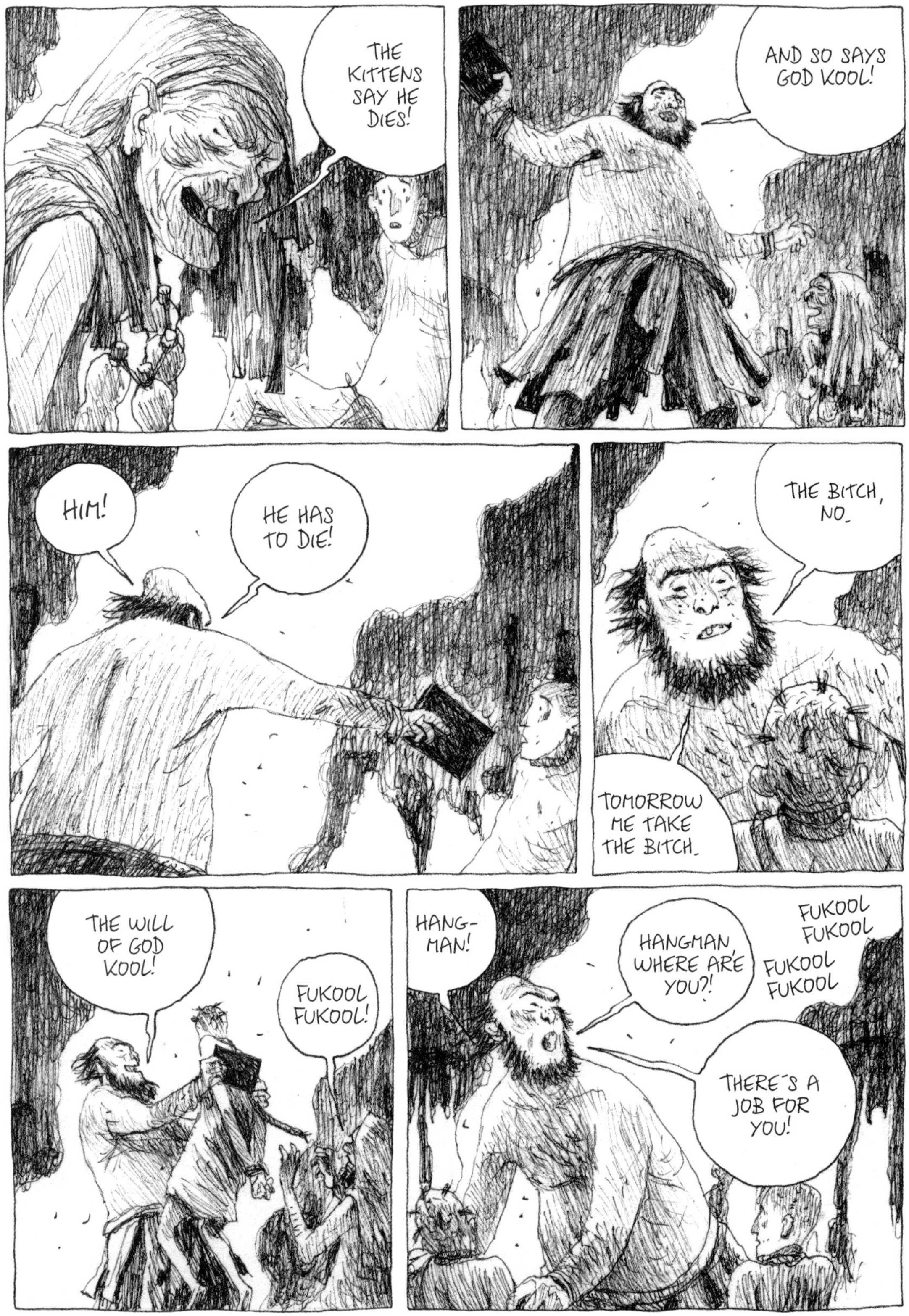
THE KITTENS SAY HE DIES!
AND SO SAYS GOD KOOL!
HIM!
HE HAS TO DIE!
THE BITCH, NO.
TOMORROW ME TAKE THE BITCH.
THE WILL OF GOD KOOL!
FUKOOL FUKOOL!
HANG-MAN!
HANGMAN WHERE ARE YOU?!
FUKOOL FUKOOL
FUKOOL FUKOOL
THERE'S A JOB FOR YOU!

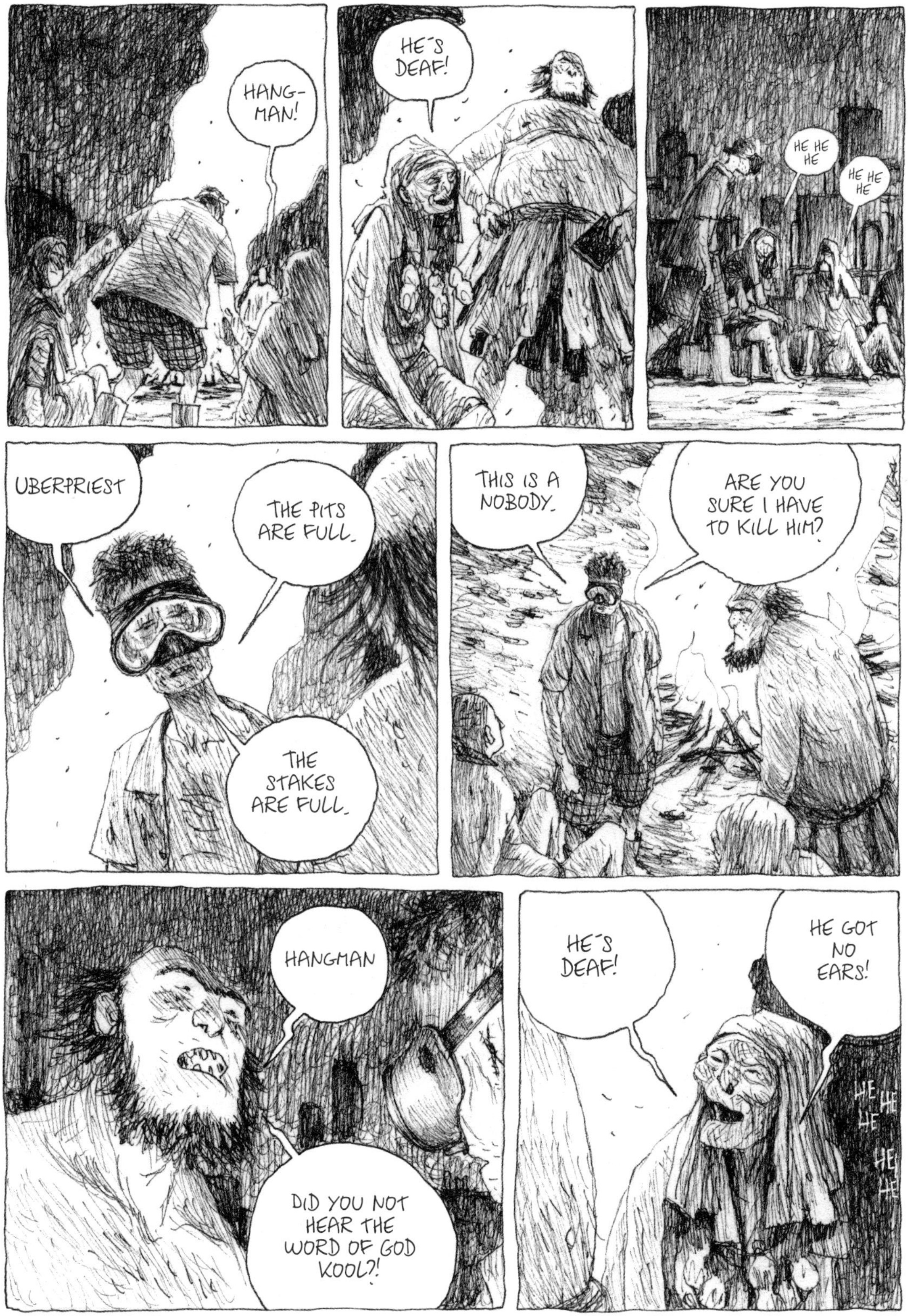
HANG-MAN!
HE'S DEAF!
HE HE HE
HE HE HE
UBERPRIEST
THE PITS ARE FULL.
THE STAKES ARE FULL.
THIS IS A NOBODY.
ARE YOU SURE I HAVE TO KILL HIM?
HANGMAN
DID YOU NOT HEAR THE WORD OF GOD KOOL?!
HE'S DEAF!
HE GOT NO EARS!
HE HE HE HE HE

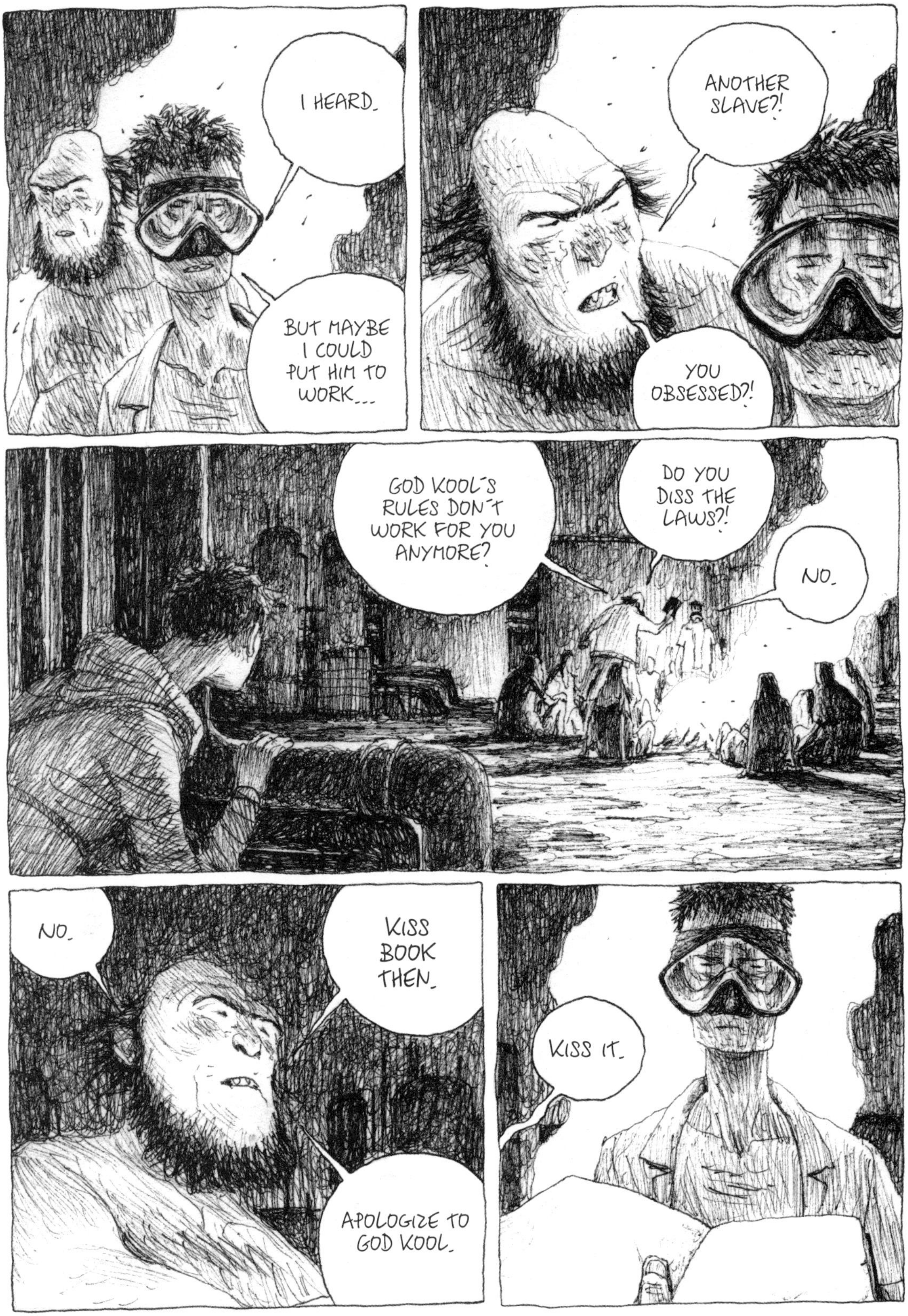
I HEARD.
BUT MAYBE I COULD PUT HIM TO WORK...
ANOTHER SLAVE?!
YOU OBSESSED?!
GOD KOOL'S RULES DON'T WORK FOR YOU ANYMORE?
DO YOU DISS THE LAWS?!
NO.
NO.
KISS BOOK THEN.
APOLOGIZE TO GOD KOOL.
KISS IT.

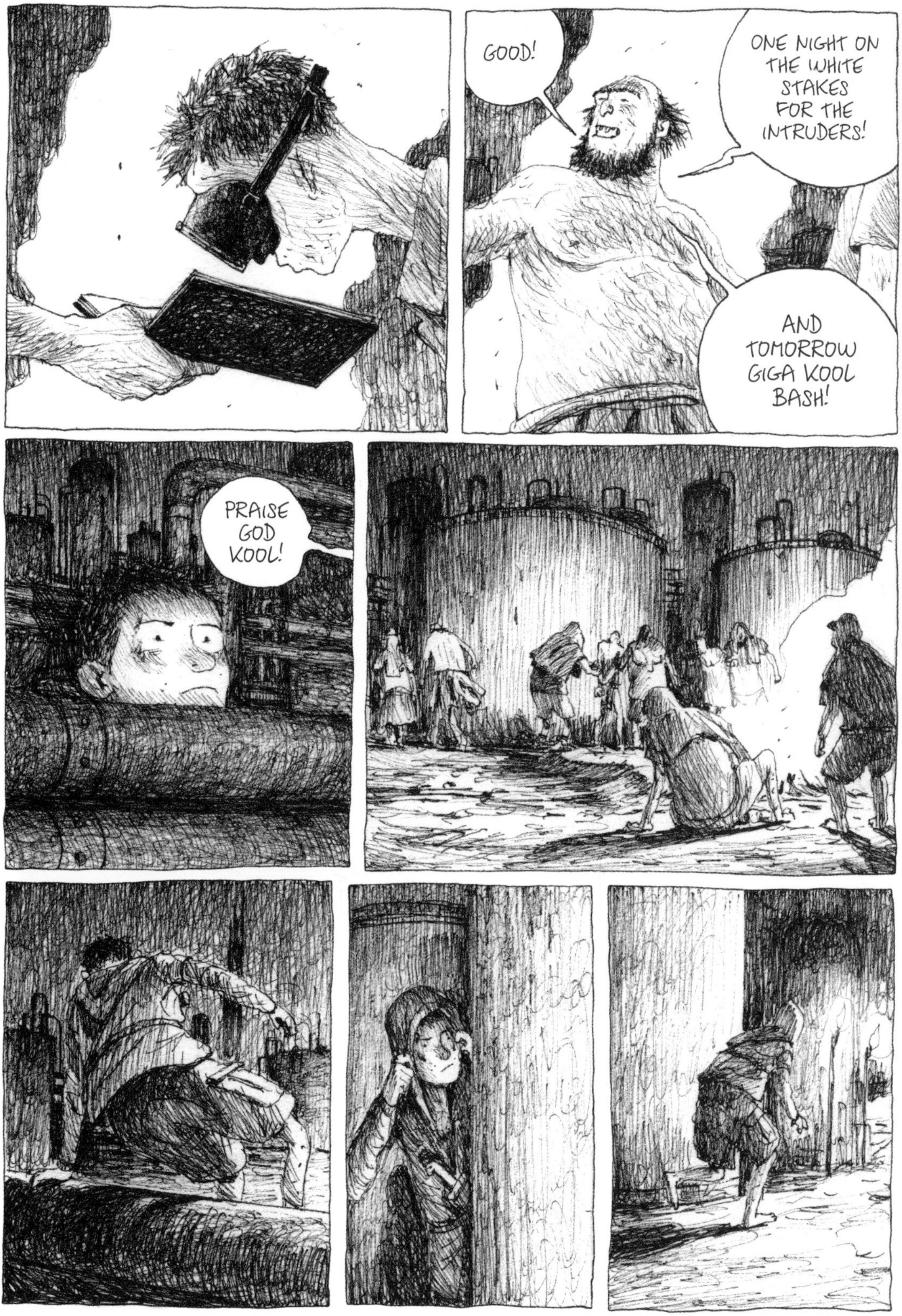
GOOD!
ONE NIGHT ON THE WHITE STAKES FOR THE INTRUDERS!
AND TOMORROW GIGA KOOL BASH!
PRAISE GOD KOOL!

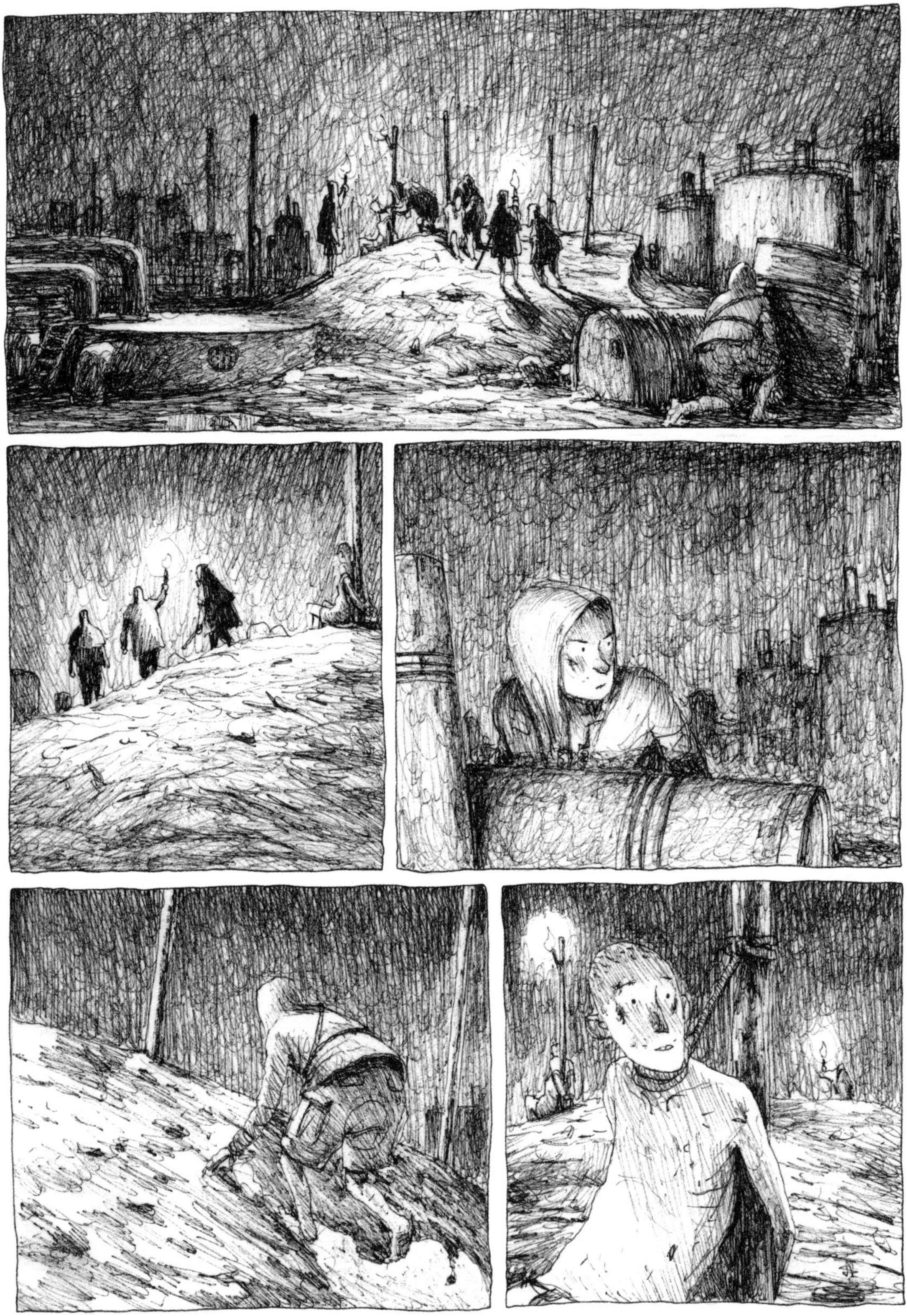

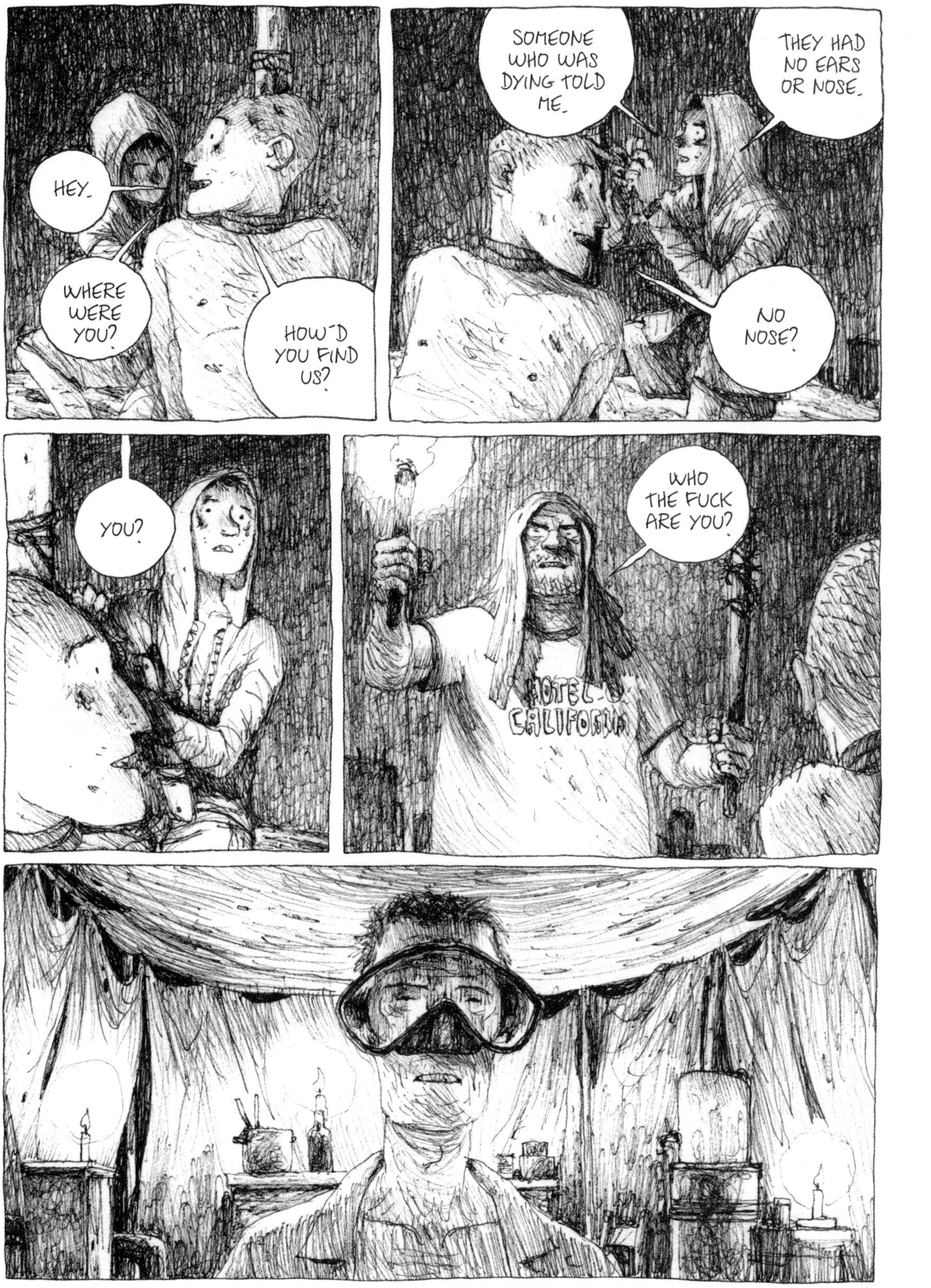
HEY.
WHERE WERE YOU?
HOW'D YOU FIND US?
SOMEONE WHO WAS DYING TOLD ME.
THEY HAD NO EARS OR NOSE.
NO NOSE?
YOU?
WHO THE FUCK ARE YOU?
HOTEL CALIFORNIA

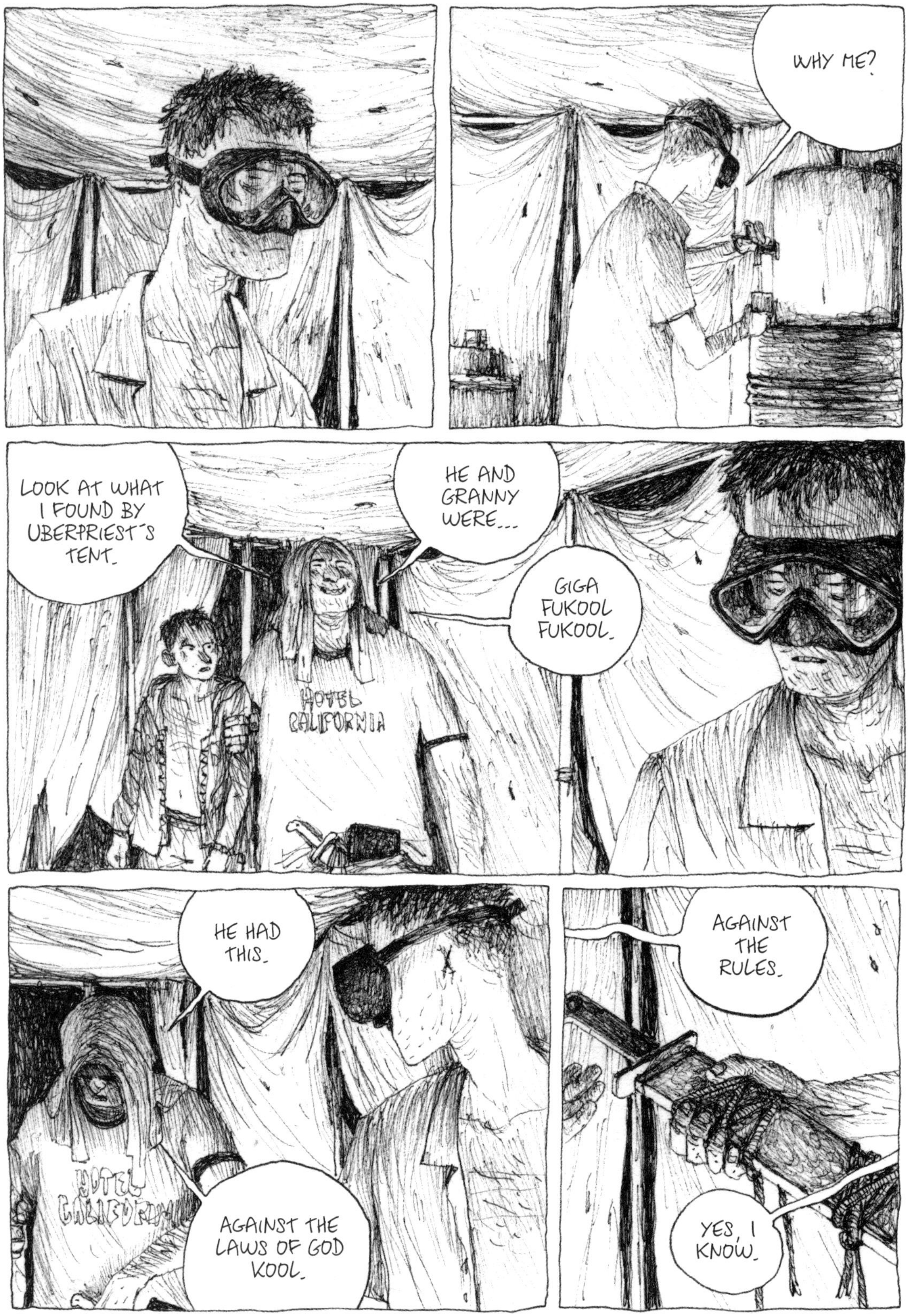
WHY ME?
LOOK AT WHAT I FOUND BY UBERPRIEST'S TENT.
HE AND GRANNY WERE...
GIGA FUKOOL FUKOOL.
HOTEL CALIFORNIA
HE HAD THIS.
AGAINST THE LAWS OF GOD KOOL.
AGAINST THE RULES.
YES, I KNOW.

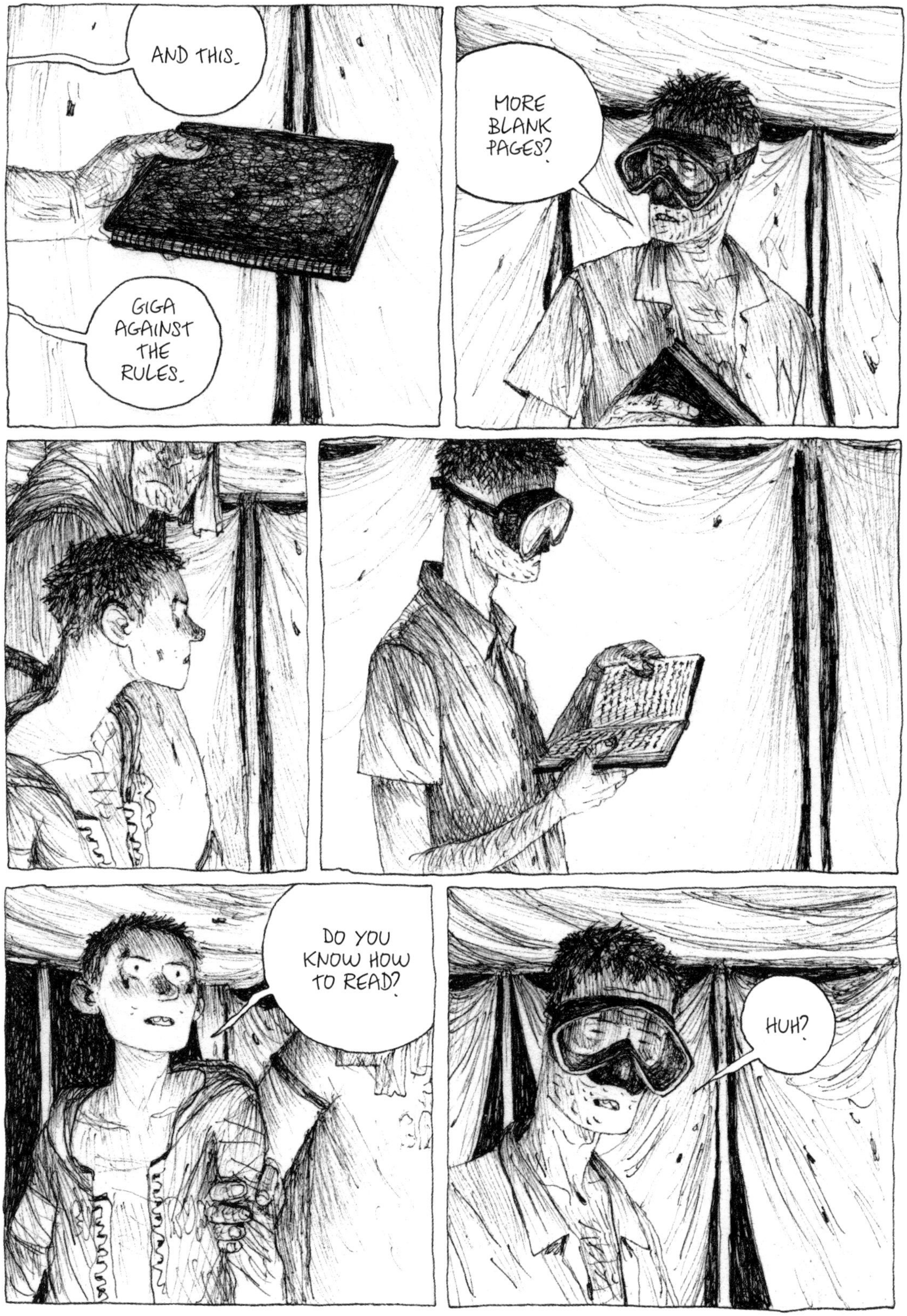
AND THIS_
GIGA AGAINST THE RULES_
MORE BLANK PAGES?
DO YOU KNOW HOW TO READ?
HUH?

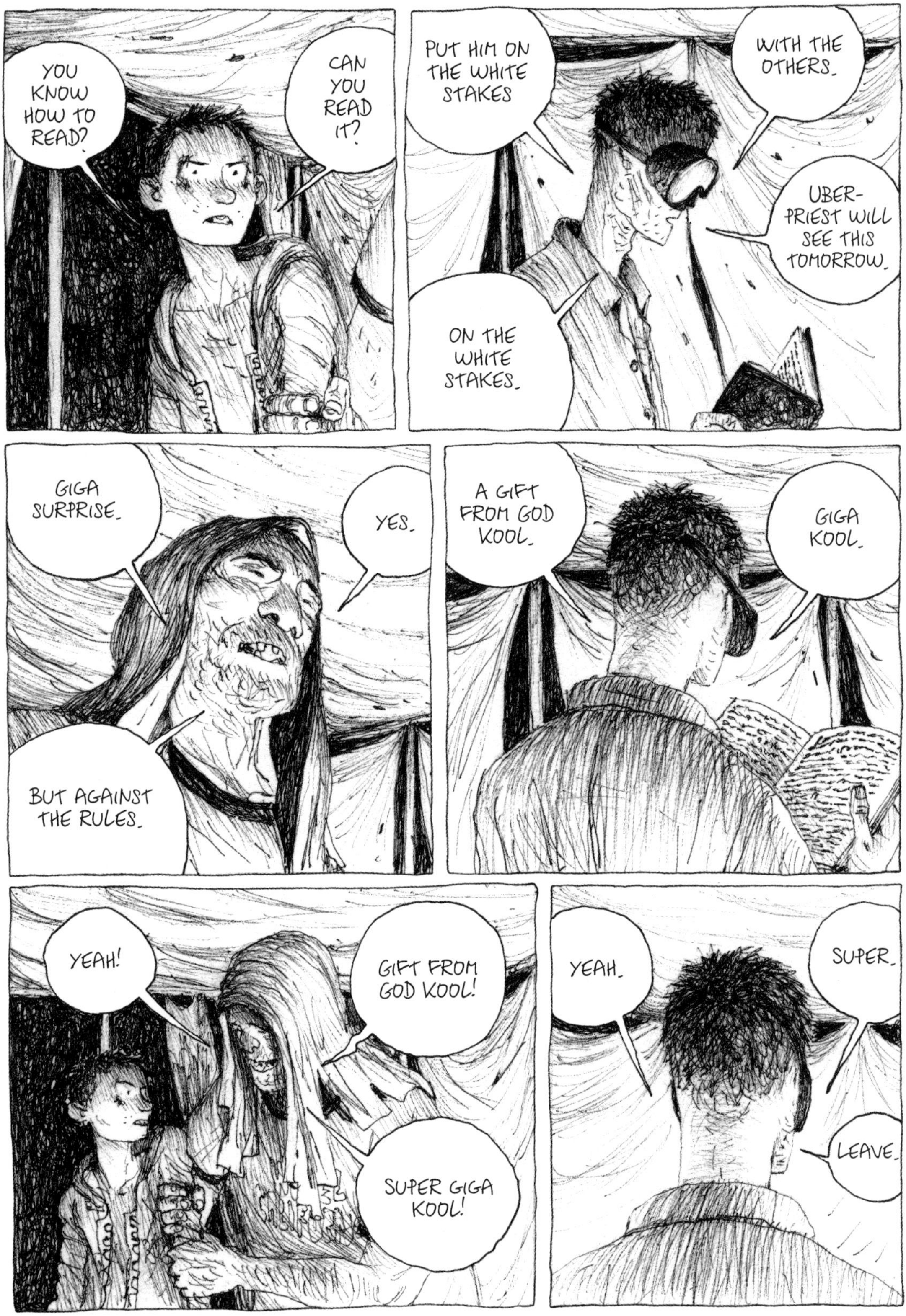
YOU KNOW HOW TO READ?
CAN YOU READ IT?
PUT HIM ON THE WHITE STAKES
WITH THE OTHERS.
UBER-PRIEST WILL SEE THIS TOMORROW.
ON THE WHITE STAKES.
GIGA SURPRISE.
YES.
BUT AGAINST THE RULES.
A GIFT FROM GOD KOOL.
GIGA KOOL.
YEAH!
GIFT FROM GOD KOOL!
SUPER GIGA KOOL!
YEAH.
SUPER.
LEAVE.

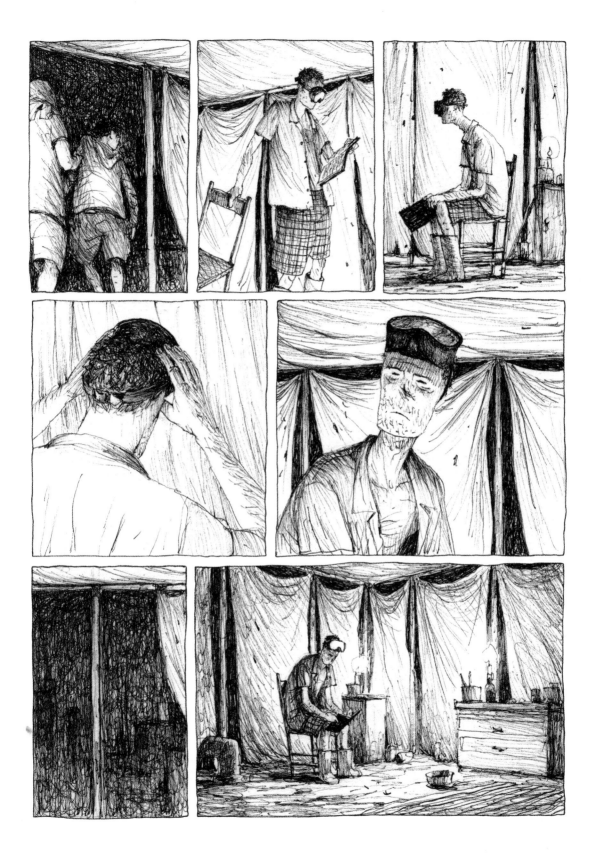

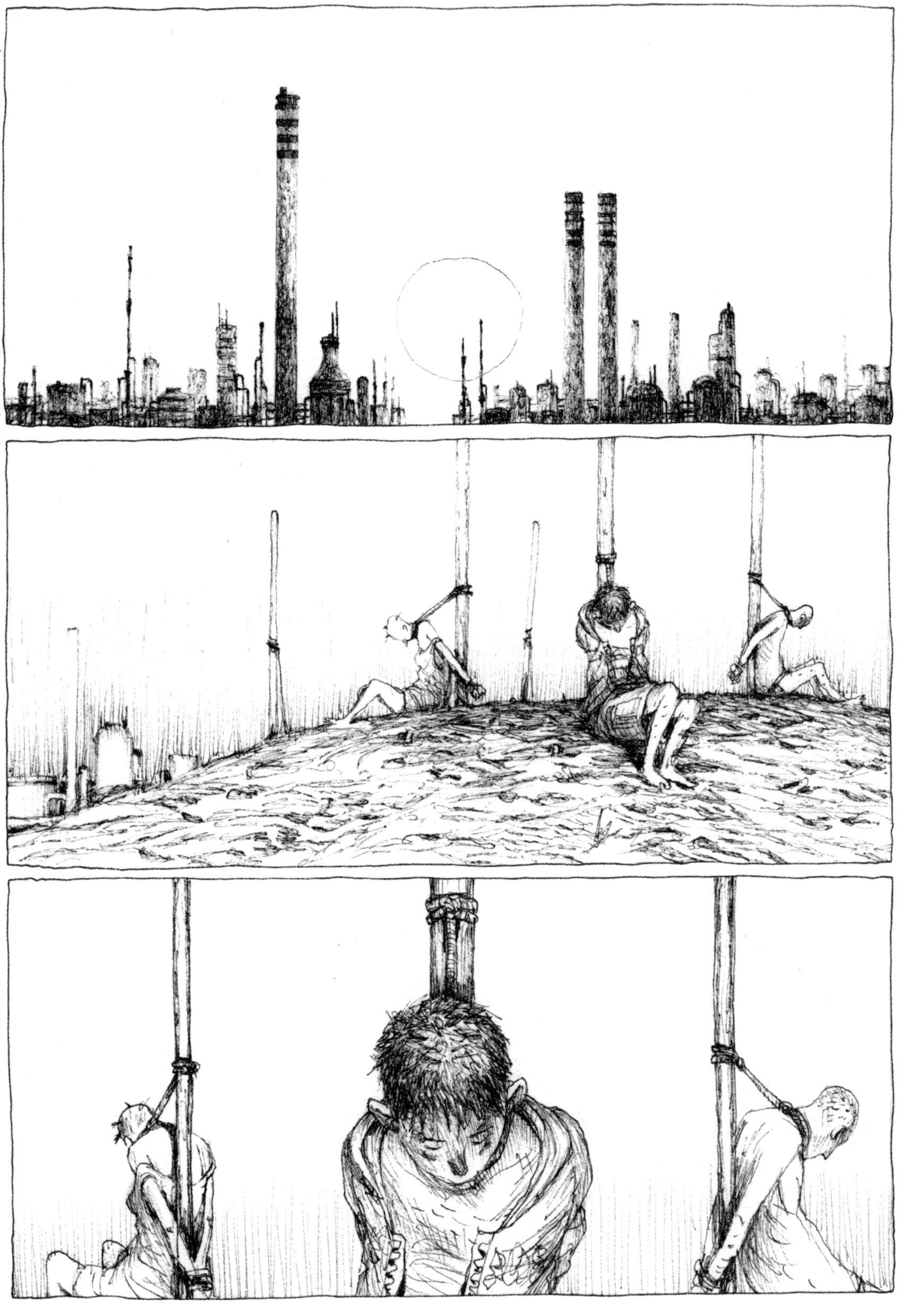

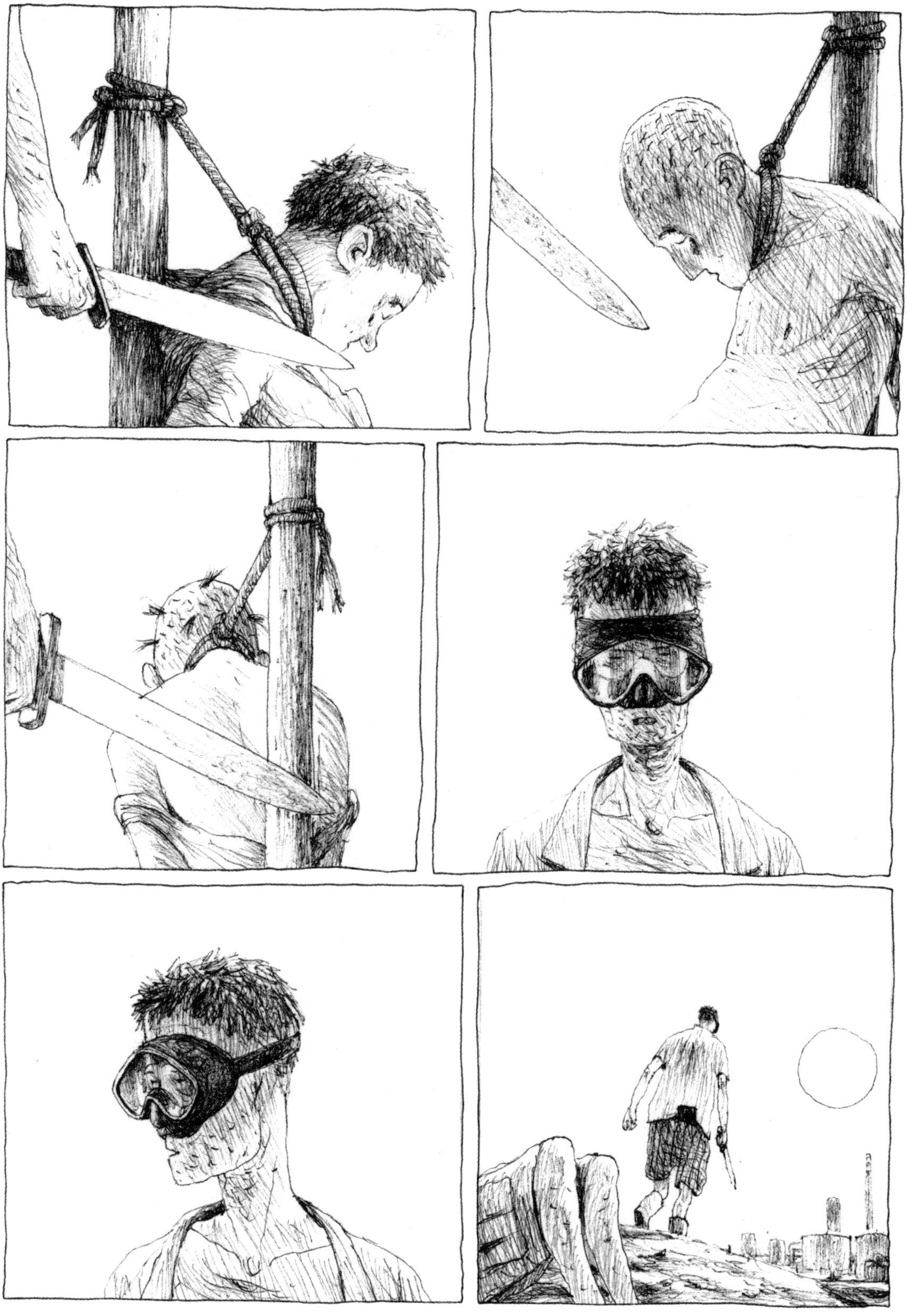

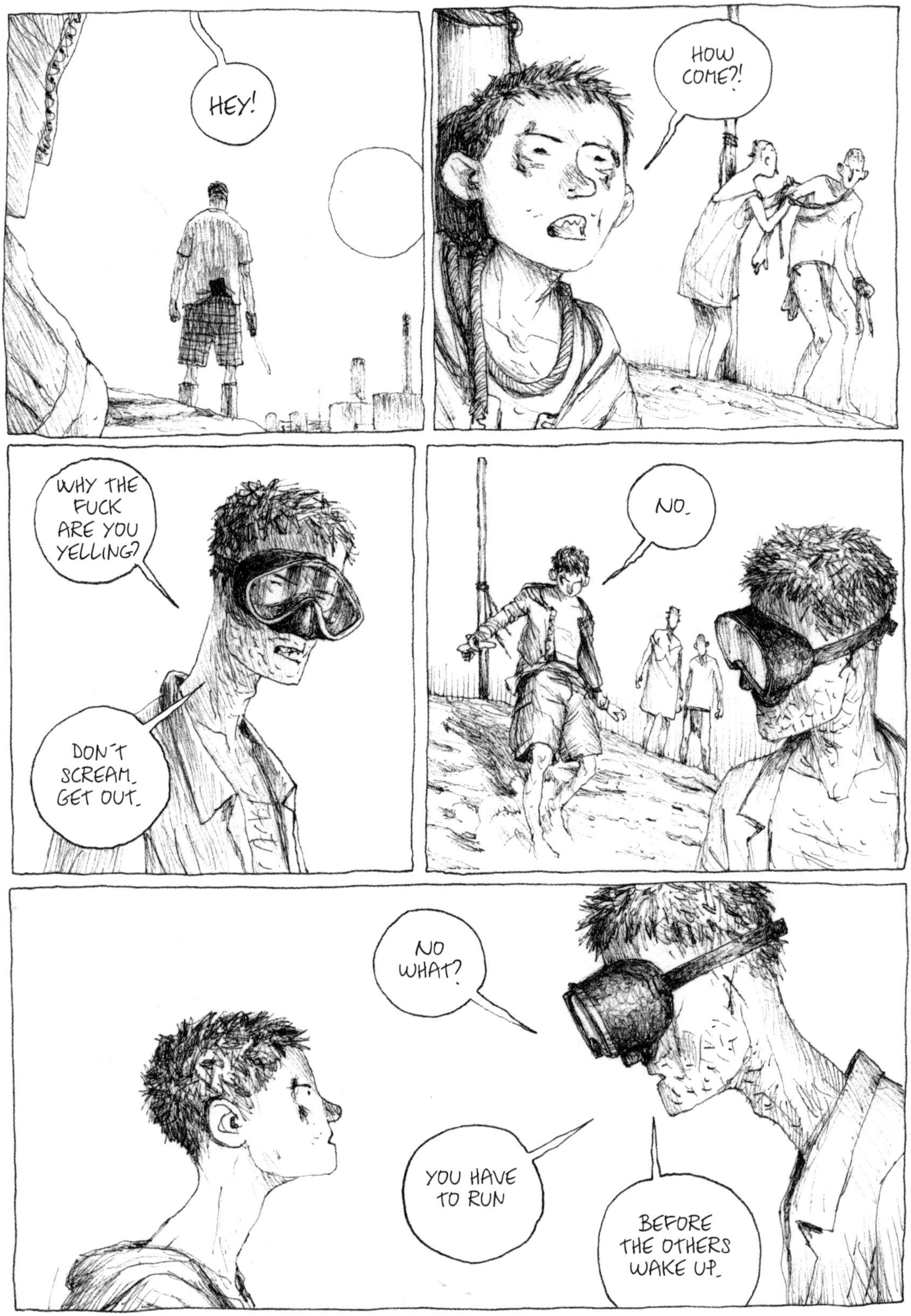
HEY!
HOW COME?!
WHY THE FUCK ARE YOU YELLING?
DON'T SCREAM. GET OUT.
NO.
NO WHAT?
YOU HAVE TO RUN
BEFORE THE OTHERS WAKE UP.

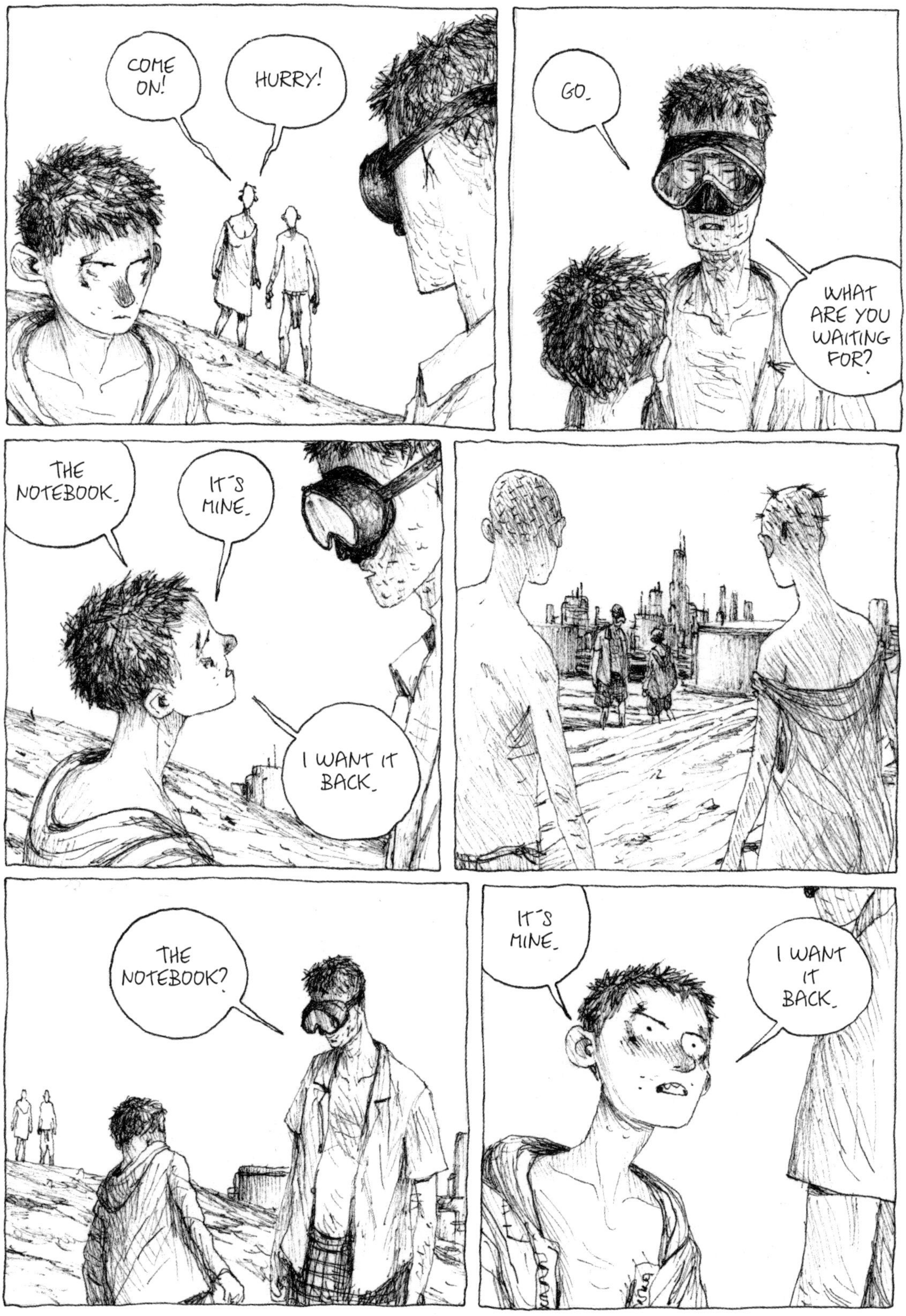
COME ON!
HURRY!
GO_
WHAT ARE YOU WAITING FOR?
THE NOTEBOOK_
IT'S MINE_
I WANT IT BACK_
THE NOTEBOOK?
IT'S MINE_
I WANT IT BACK_

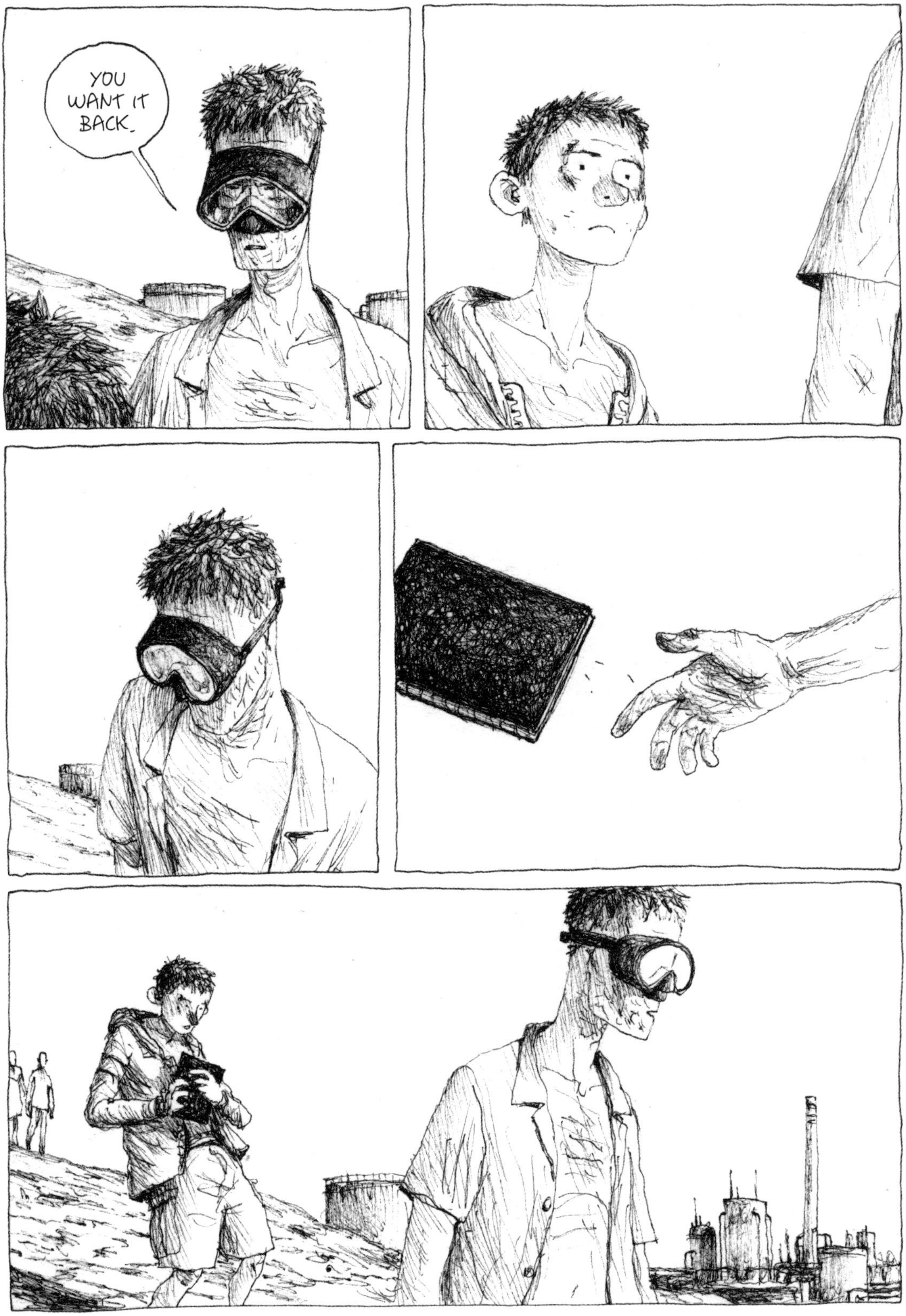
YOU WANT IT BACK_

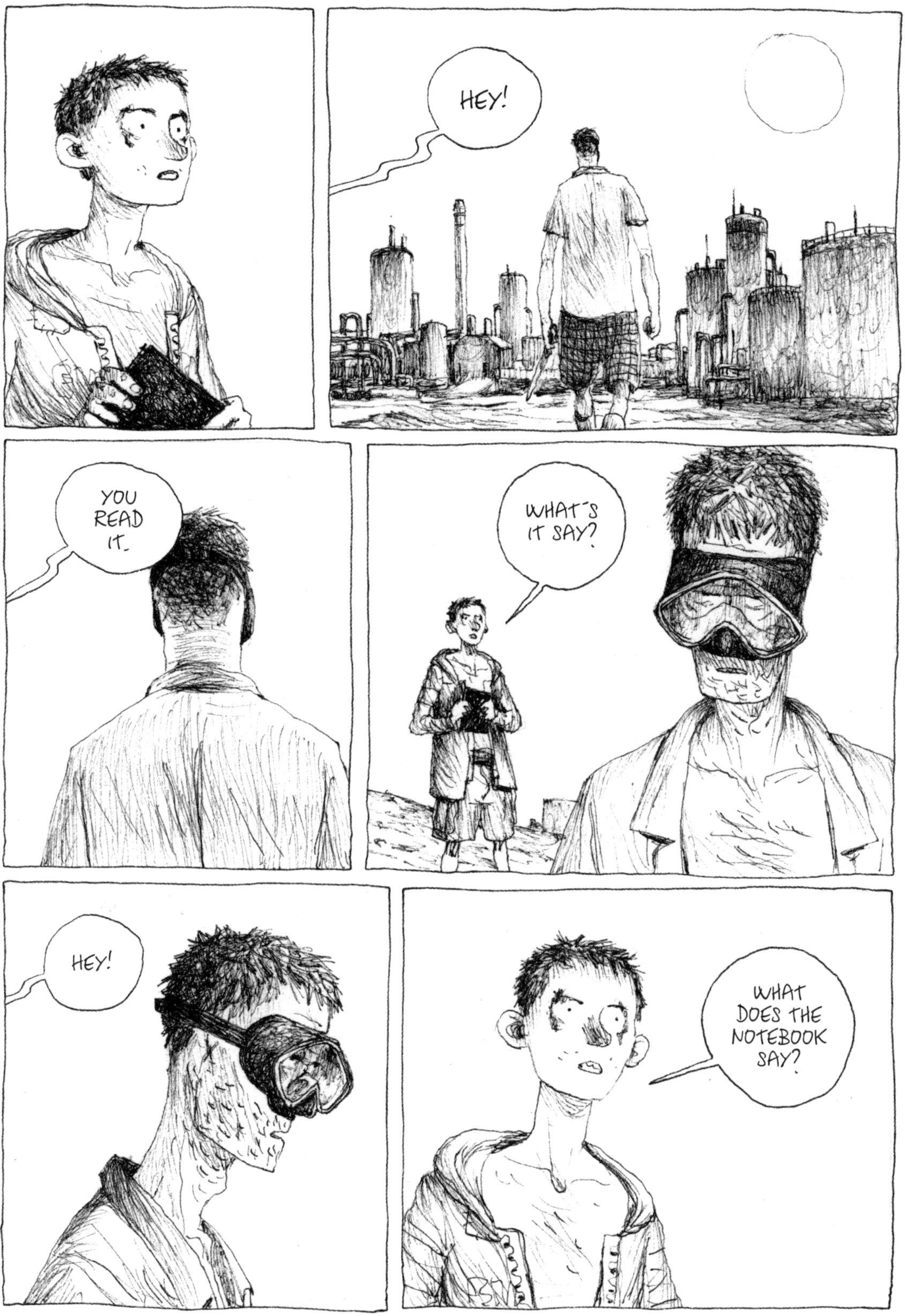
HEY!
YOU READ IT.
WHAT'S IT SAY?
HEY!
WHAT DOES THE NOTEBOOK SAY?

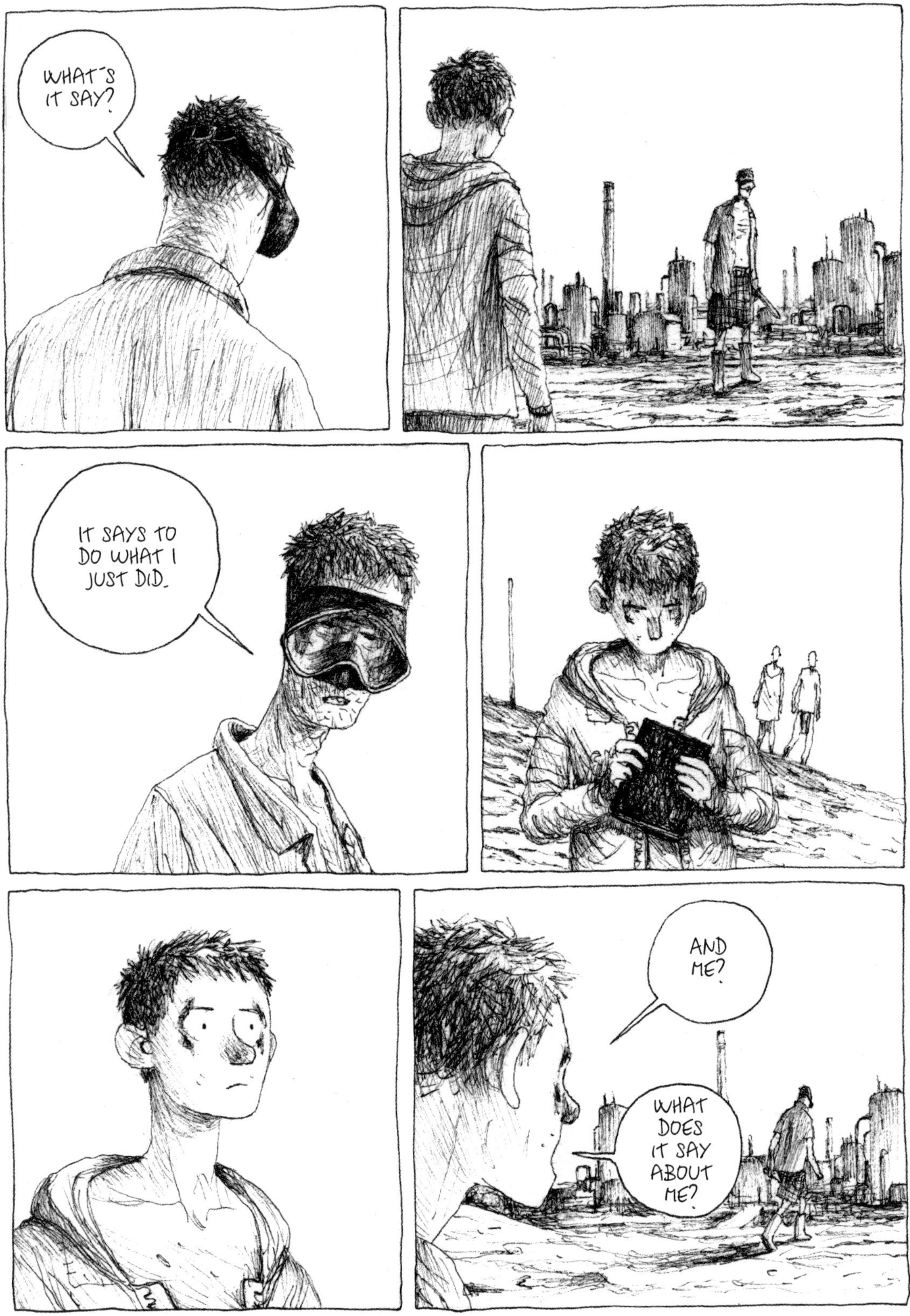
WHAT'S IT SAY?
IT SAYS TO DO WHAT I JUST DID.
AND ME?
WHAT DOES IT SAY ABOUT ME?

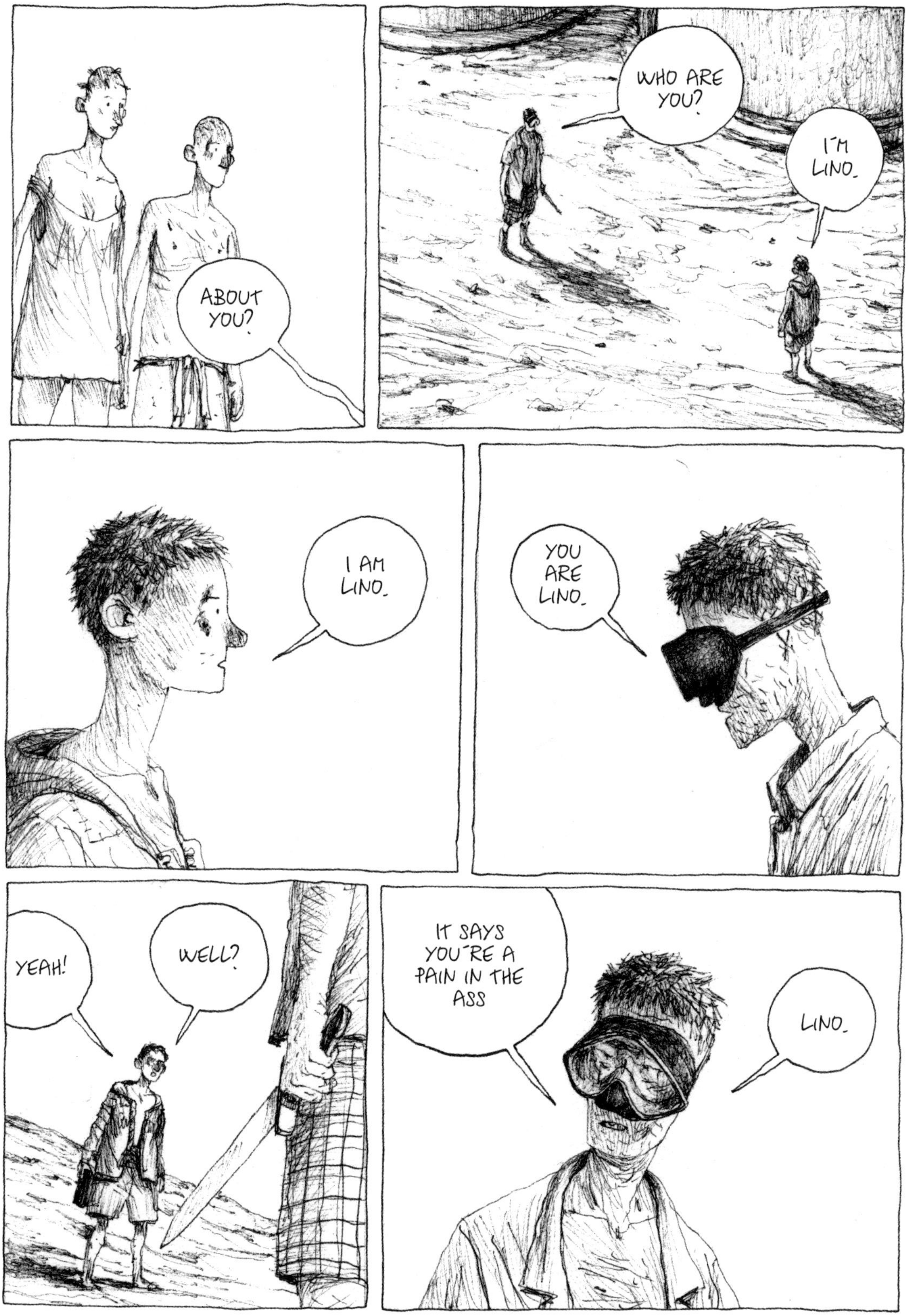
ABOUT YOU?
WHO ARE YOU?
I'M LINO.
I AM LINO.
YOU ARE LINO.
YEAH!
WELL?
IT SAYS YOU'RE A PAIN IN THE ASS
LINO.

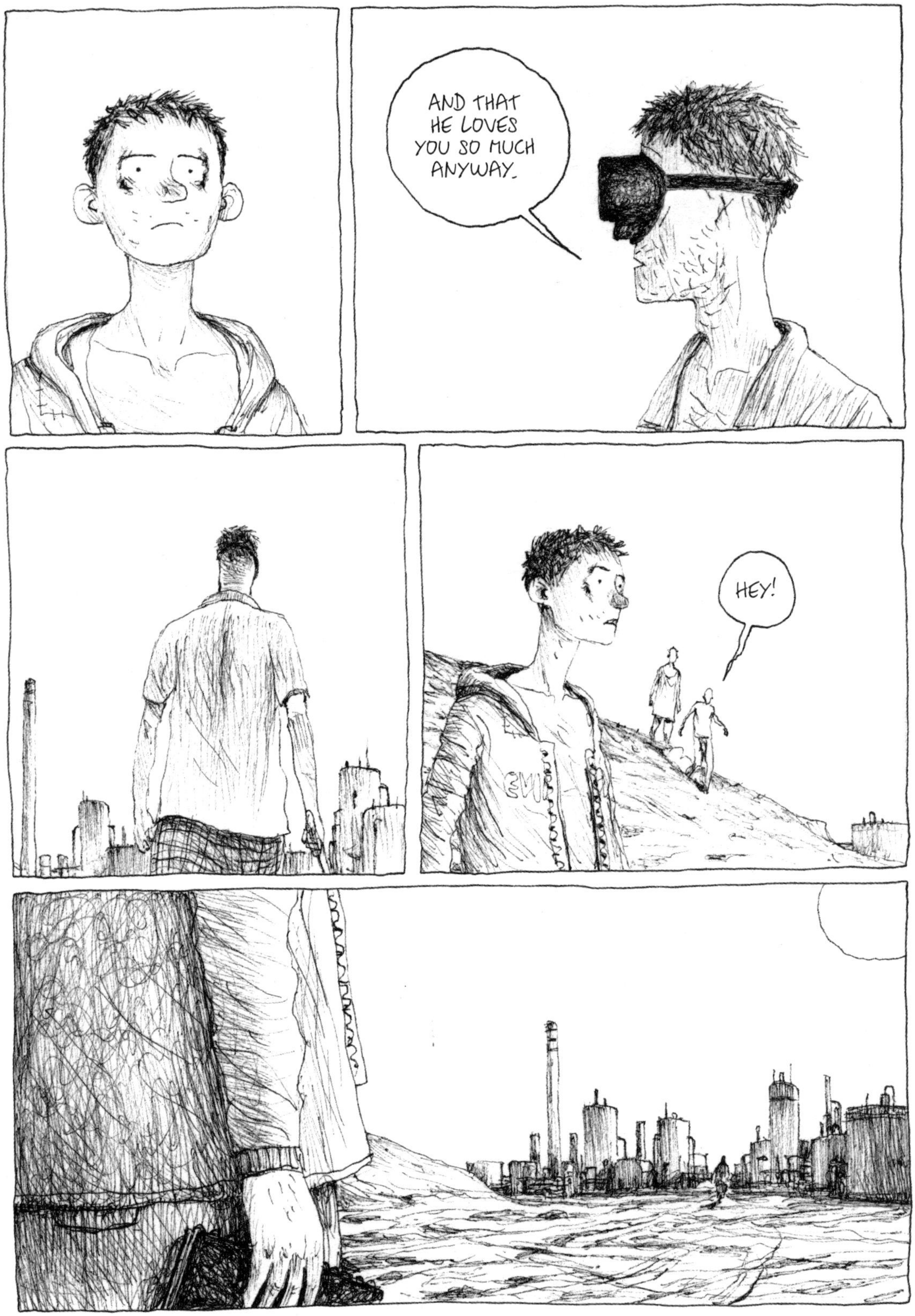
AND THAT HE LOVES YOU SO MUCH ANYWAY.
HEY!

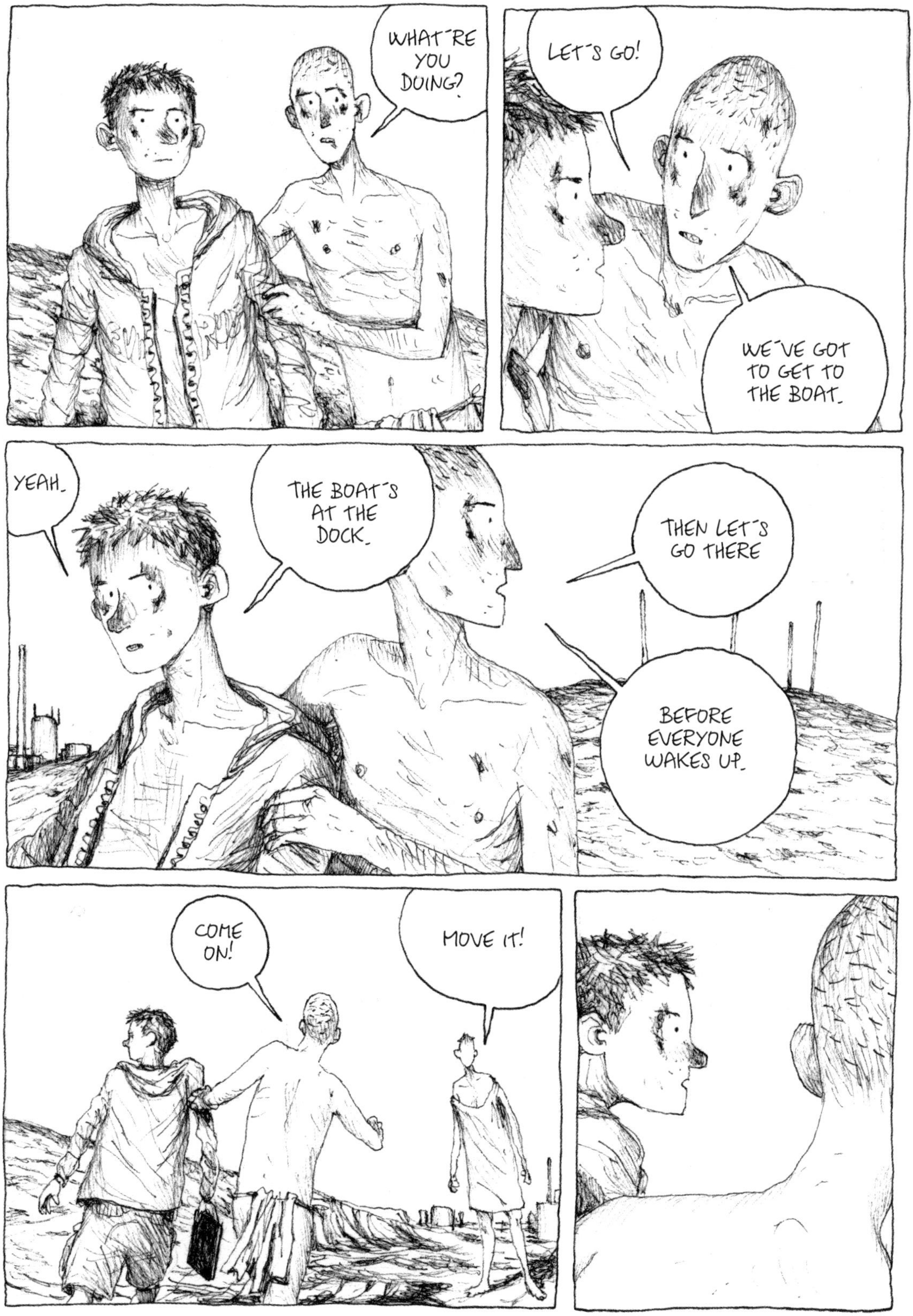
WHAT'RE YOU DOING?
LET'S GO!
WE'VE GOT TO GET TO THE BOAT.
YEAH.
THE BOAT'S AT THE DOCK.
THEN LET'S GO THERE
BEFORE EVERYONE WAKES UP.
COME ON!
MOVE IT!

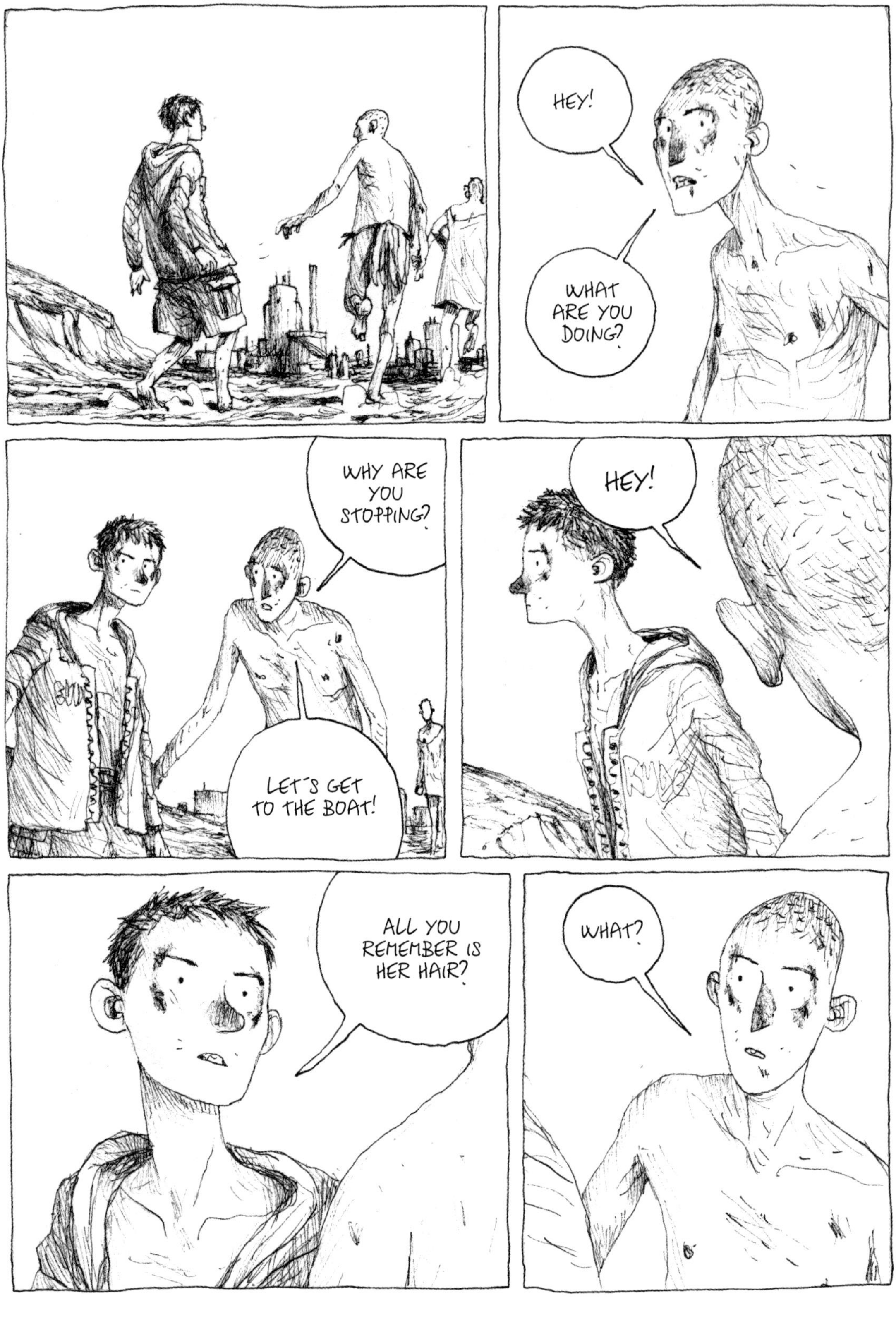
HEY!
WHAT ARE YOU DOING?
WHY ARE YOU STOPPING?
LET'S GET TO THE BOAT!
HEY!
ALL YOU REMEMBER IS HER HAIR?
WHAT?

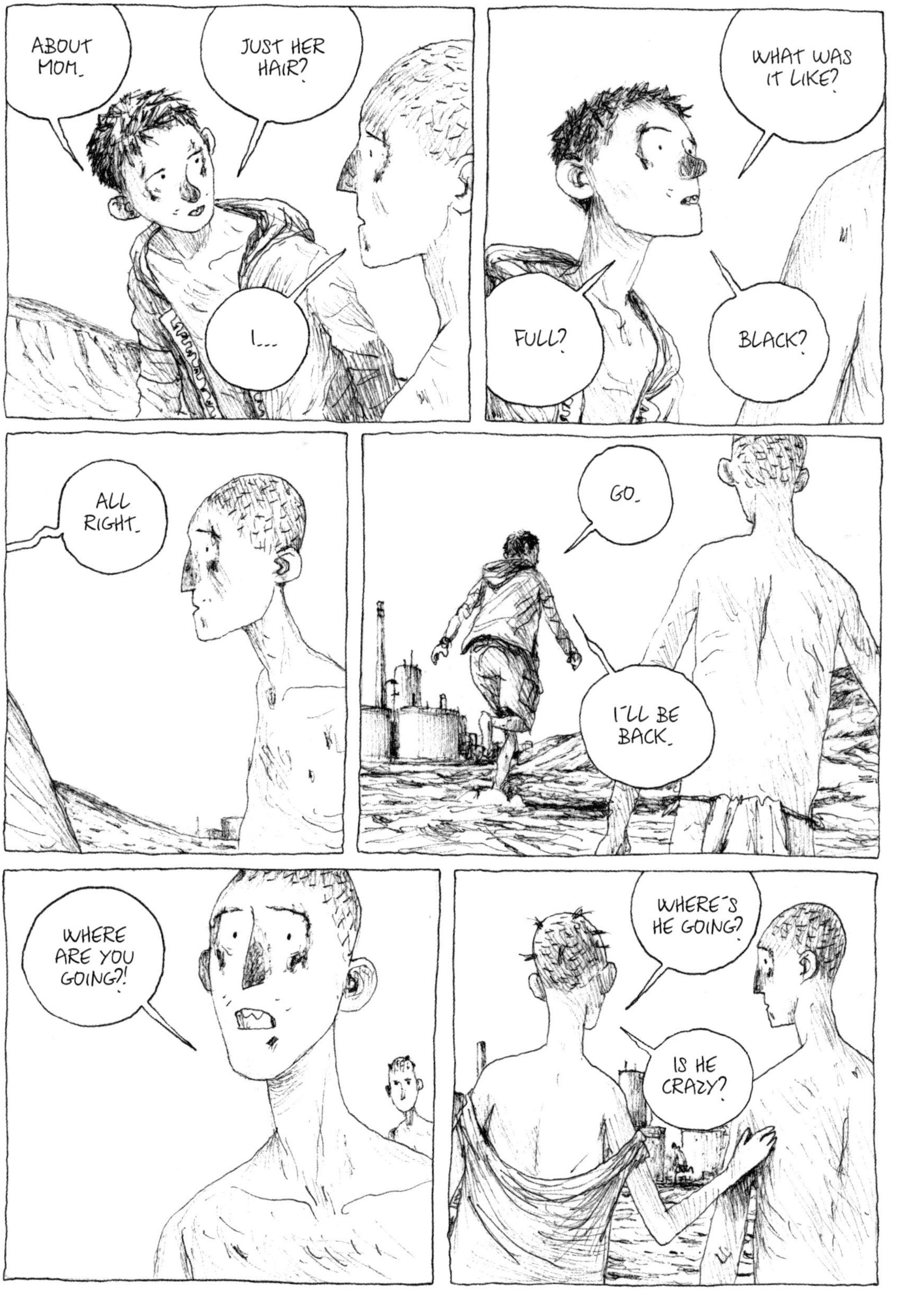
ABOUT MOM.
JUST HER HAIR?
I...
WHAT WAS IT LIKE?
FULL?
BLACK?
ALL RIGHT.
GO.
I'LL BE BACK.
WHERE ARE YOU GOING?!
WHERE'S HE GOING?
IS HE CRAZY?

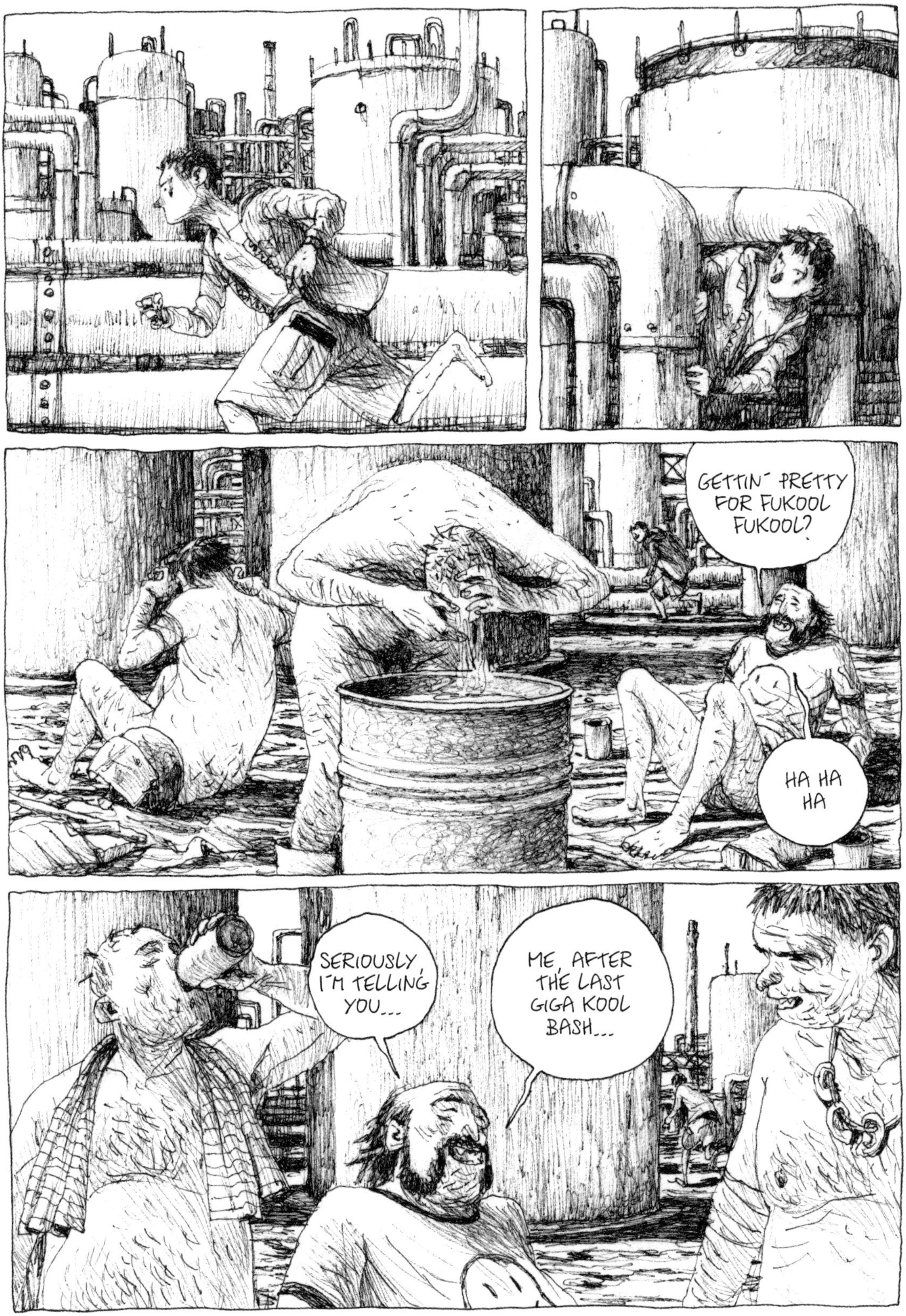
GETTIN' PRETTY FOR FUKOOL FUKOOL?
HA HA HA
SERIOUSLY, I'M TELLING YOU...
ME, AFTER THE LAST GIGA KOOL BASH...

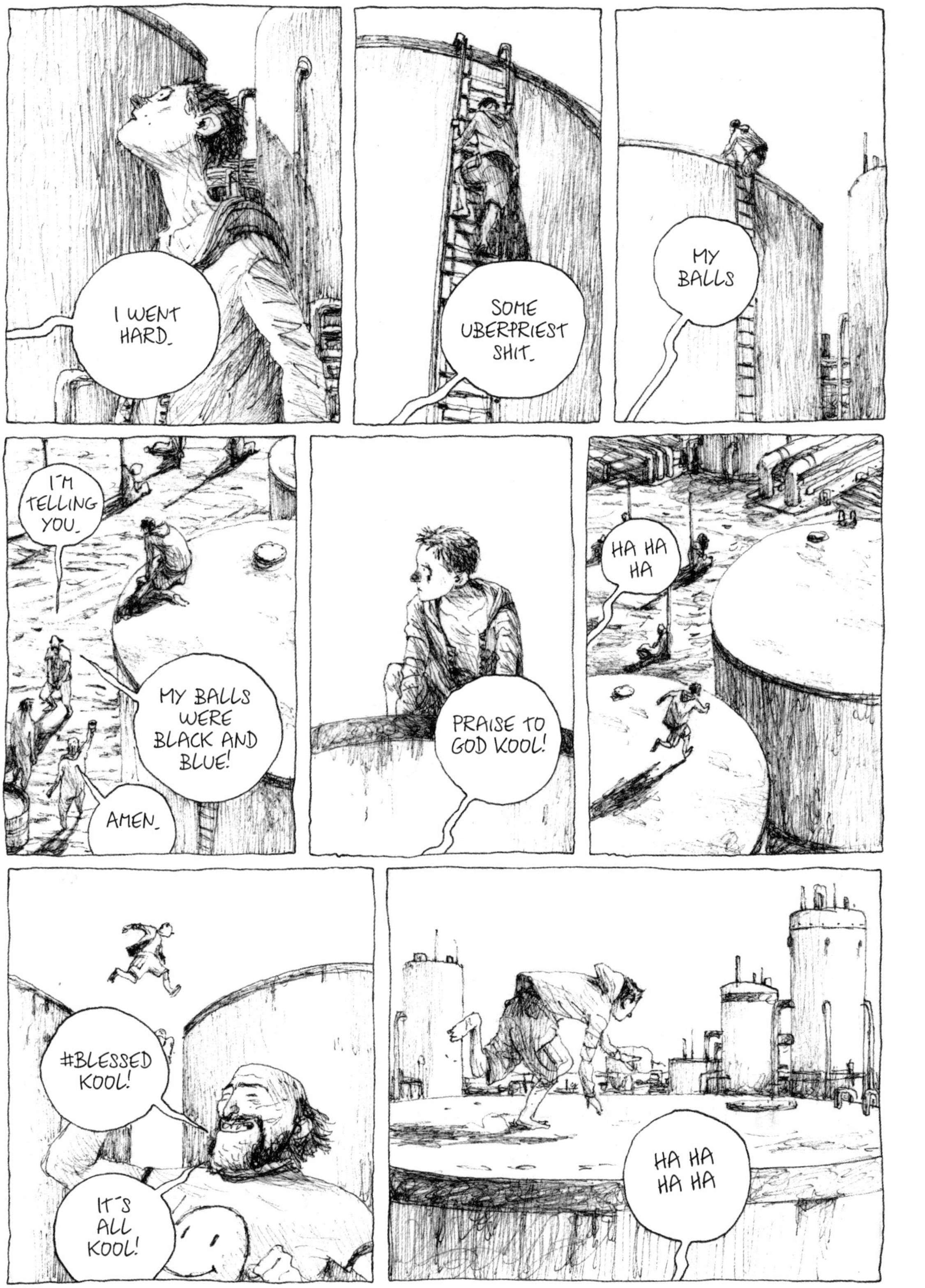
I WENT HARD_
SOME UBERPRIEST SHIT_
MY BALLS
I'M TELLING YOU_
MY BALLS WERE BLACK AND BLUE!
AMEN_
PRAISE TO GOD KOOL!
HA HA HA
#BLESSED KOOL!
IT'S ALL KOOL!
HA HA HA HA

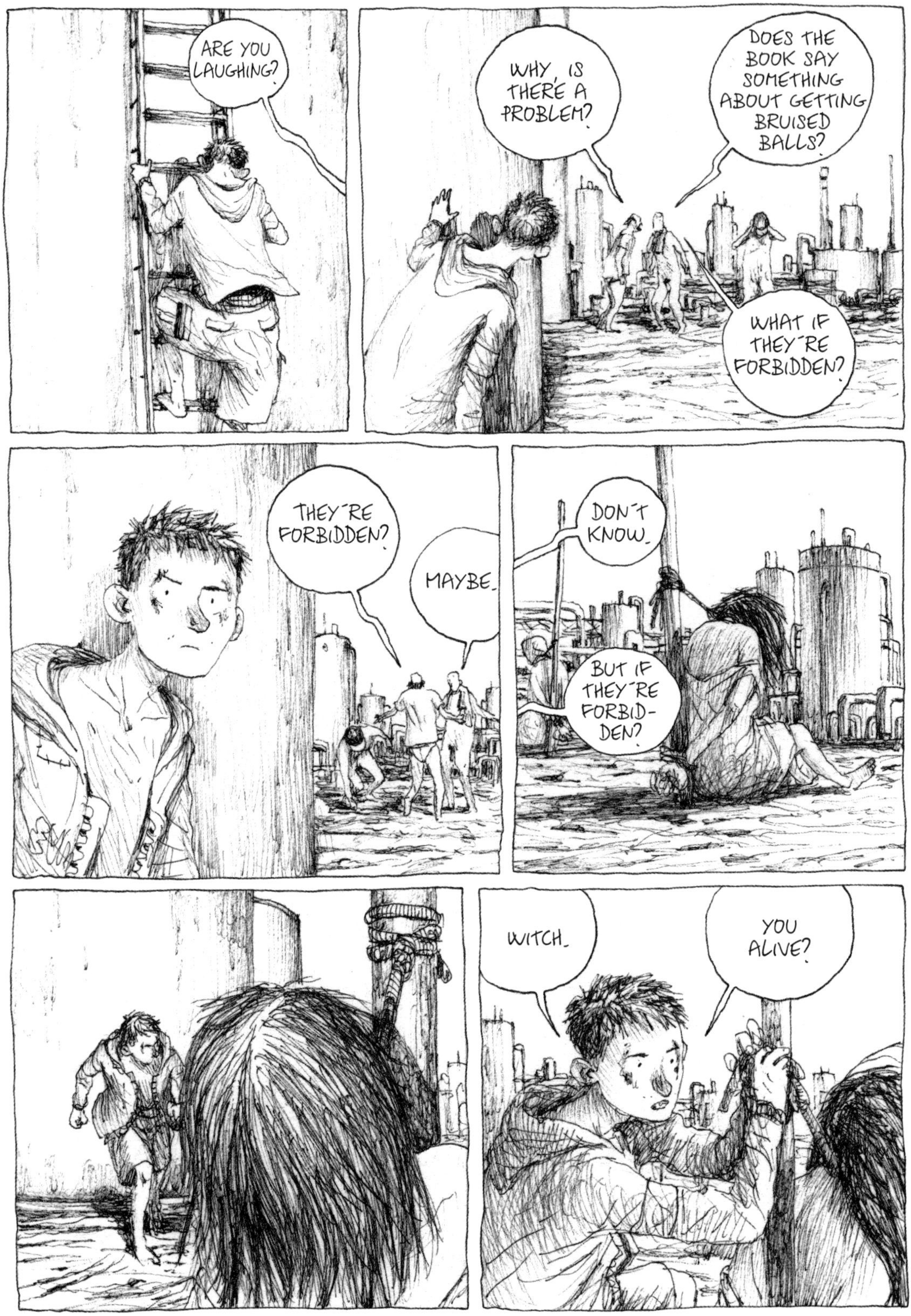
ARE YOU LAUGHING?
WHY, IS THERE A PROBLEM?
DOES THE BOOK SAY SOMETHING ABOUT GETTING BRUISED BALLS?
WHAT IF THEY'RE FORBIDDEN?
THEY'RE FORBIDDEN?
MAYBE_
DON'T KNOW_
BUT IF THEY'RE FORBID-DEN?
WITCH_
YOU ALIVE?

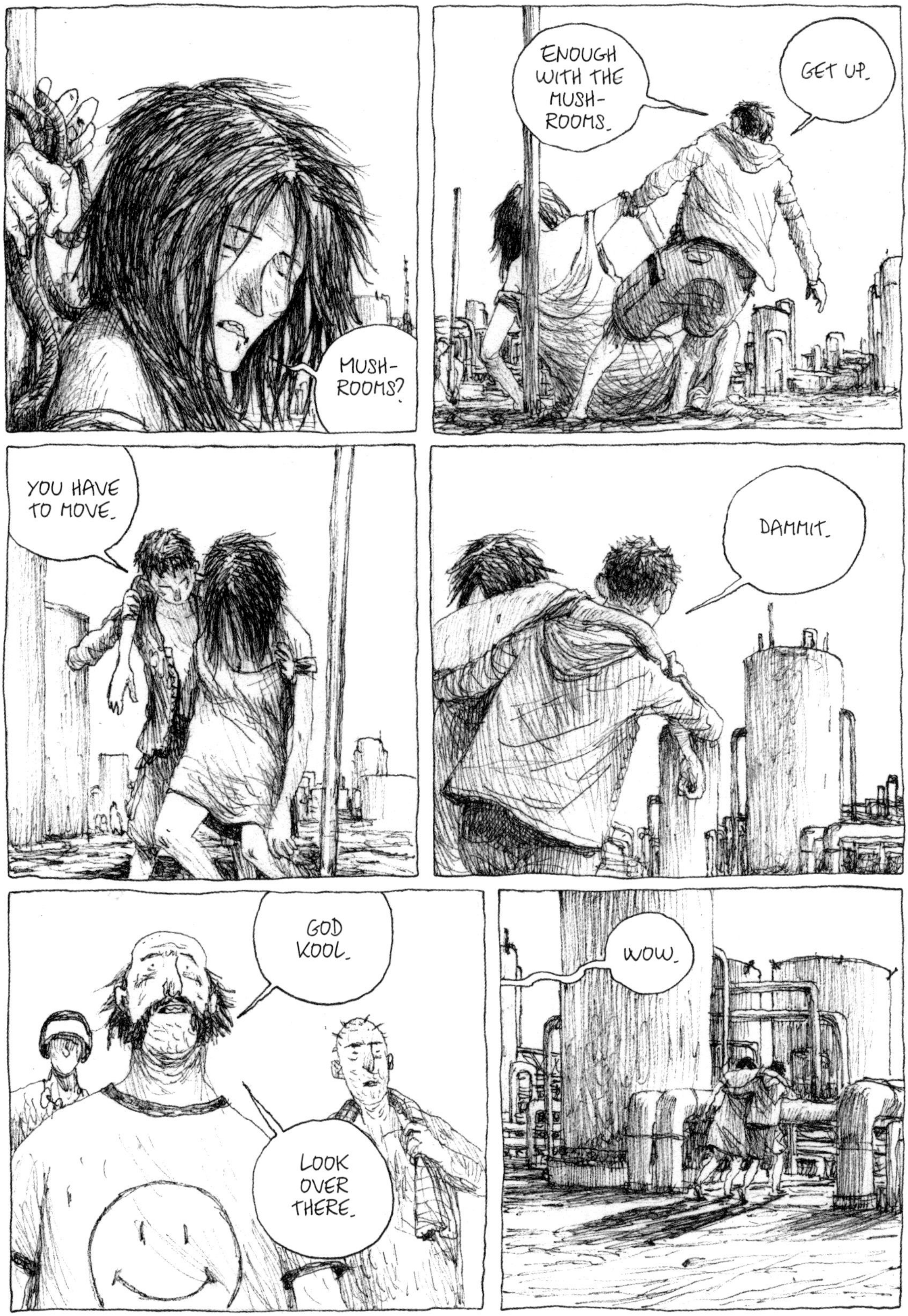
MUSH-ROOMS?
ENOUGH WITH THE MUSH-ROOMS.
GET UP.
YOU HAVE TO MOVE.
DAMMIT.
GOD KOOL.
LOOK OVER THERE.
WOW.

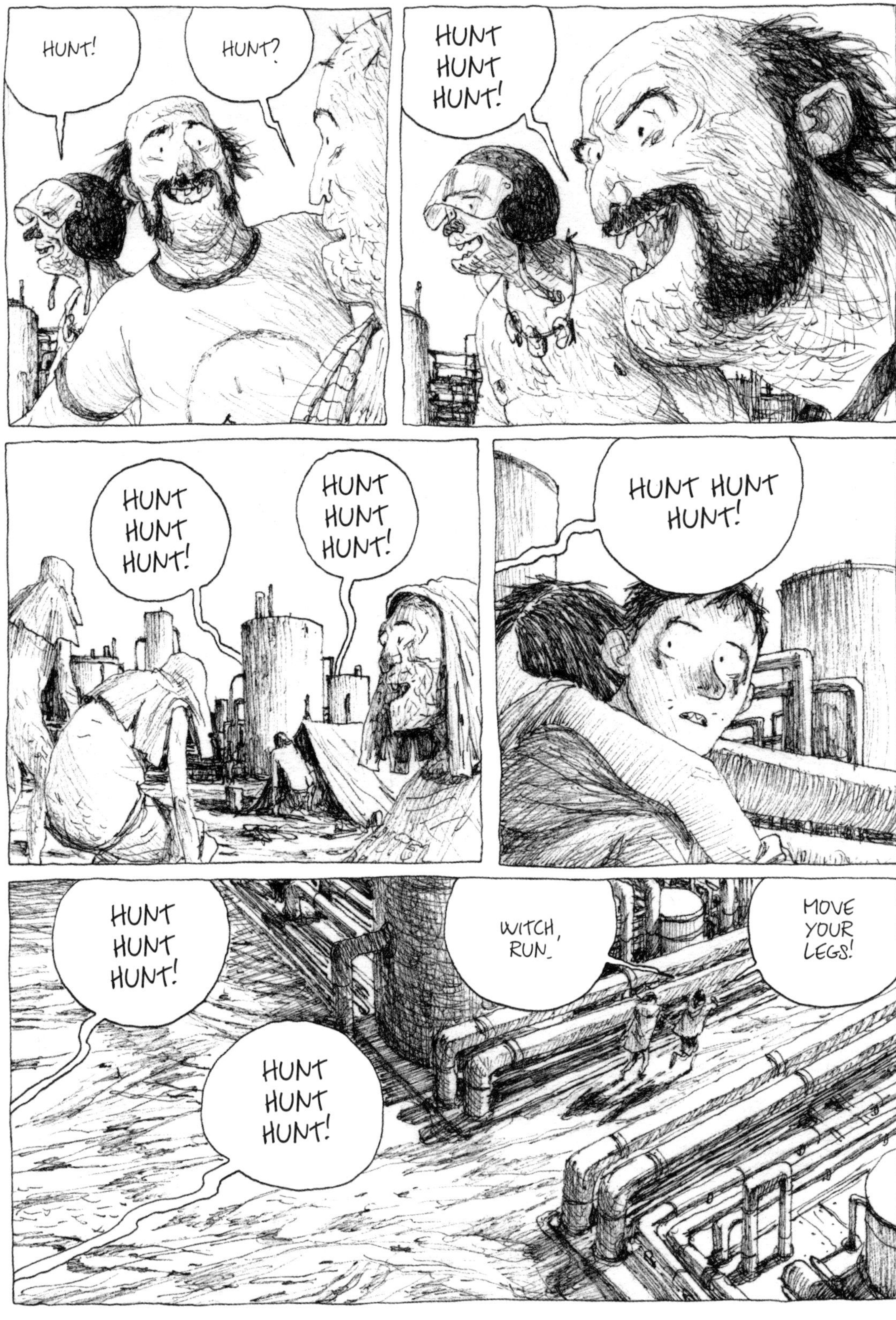
HUNT!
HUNT?
HUNT HUNT HUNT!
HUNT HUNT HUNT!
HUNT HUNT HUNT!
HUNT HUNT HUNT!
HUNT HUNT HUNT!
HUNT HUNT HUNT!
WITCH, RUN.
MOVE YOUR LEGS!

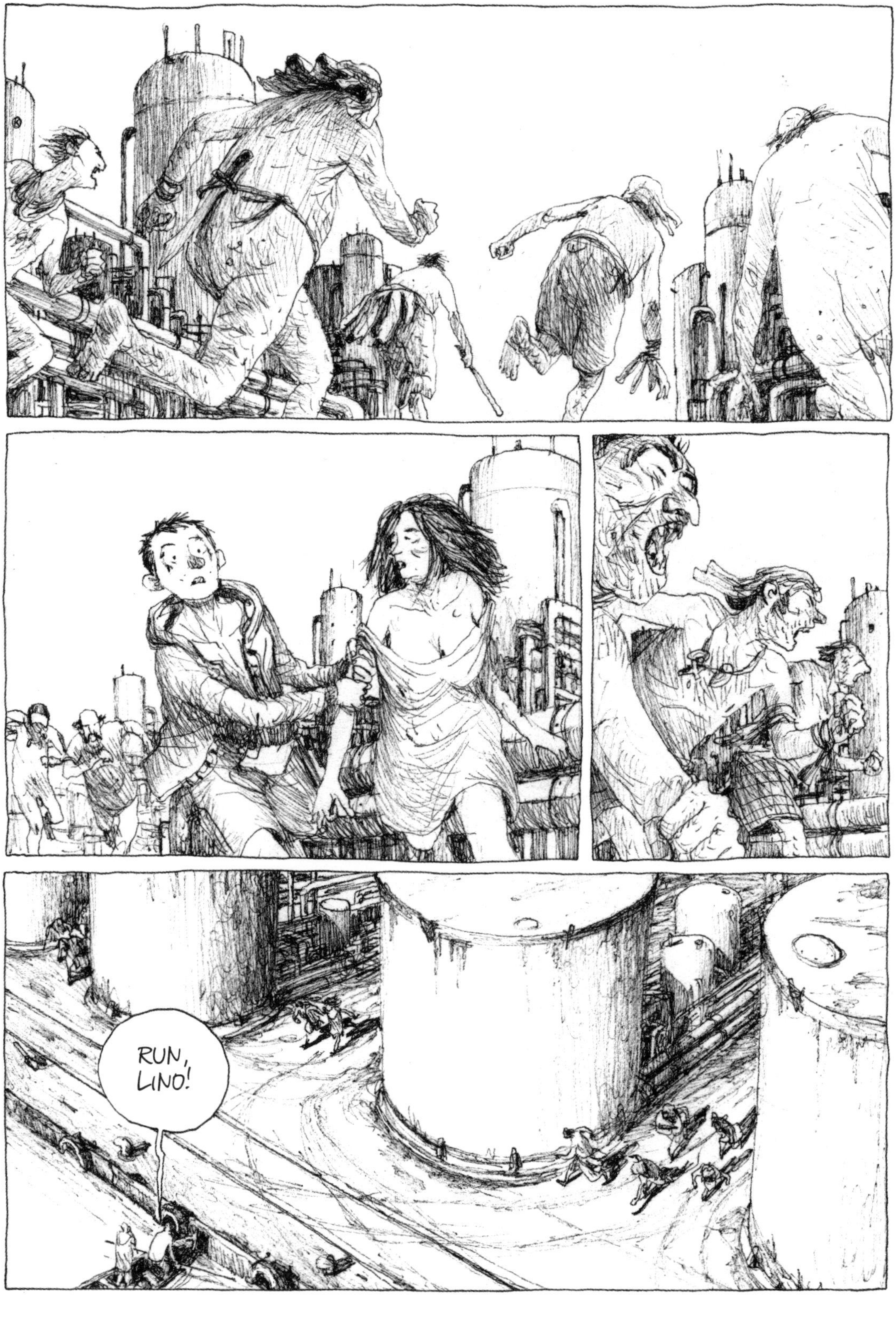
RUN,
LINO!

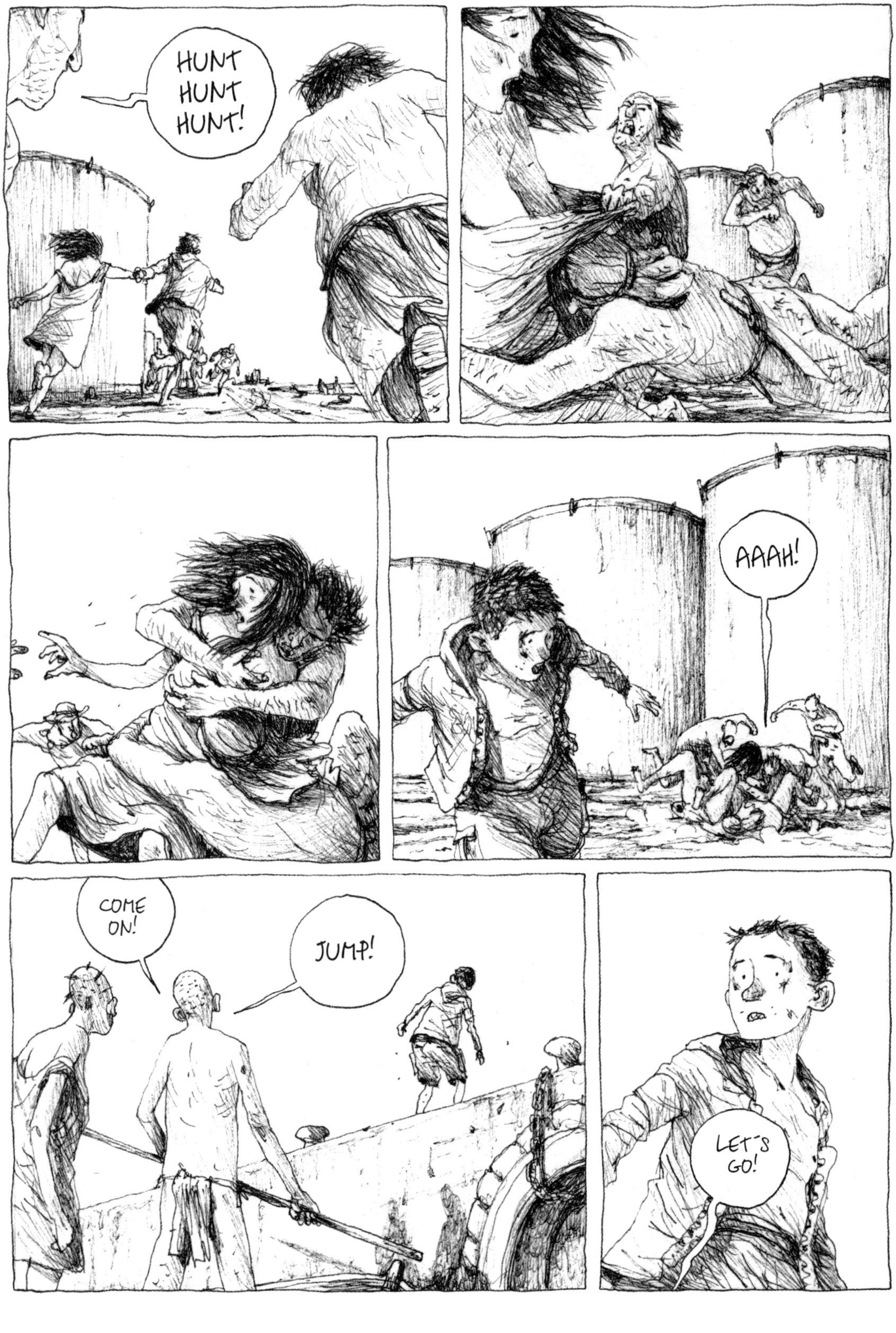
HUNT HUNT HUNT!
AAAH!
COME ON!
JUMP!
LET'S GO!

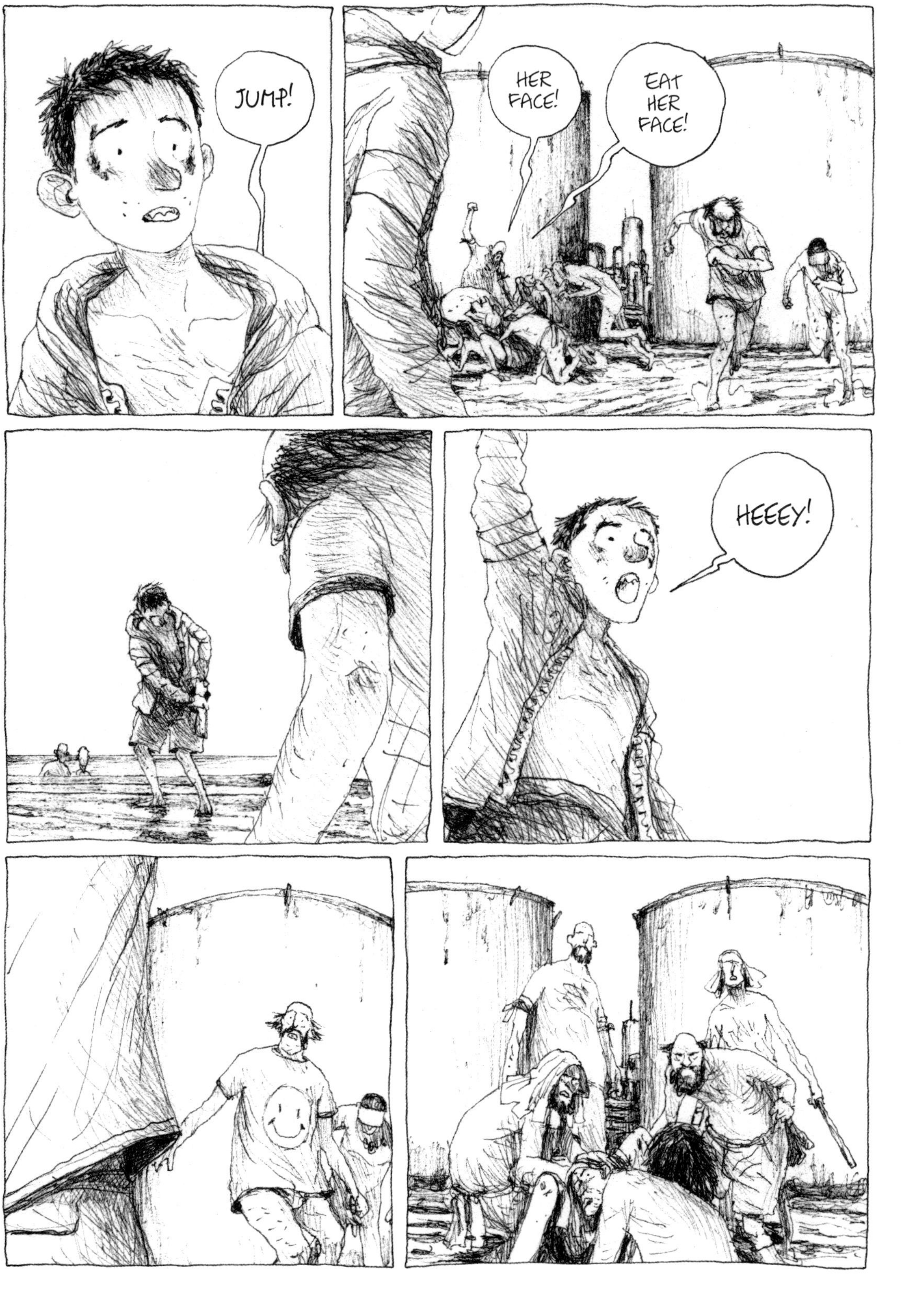
JUMP!
HER FACE!
EAT HER FACE!
HEEEY!

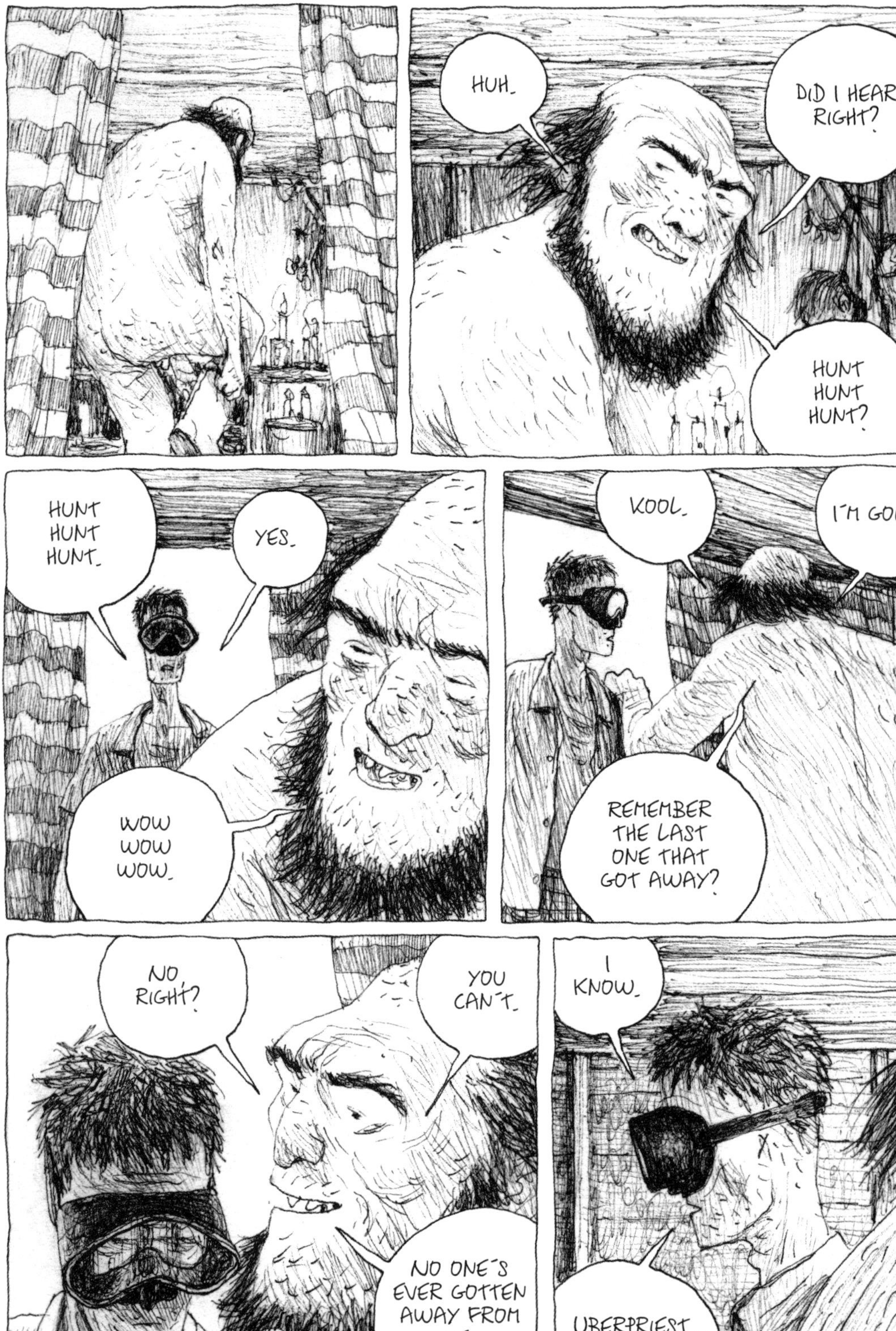
HUH.
DID I HEAR RIGHT?
HUNT HUNT HUNT?
HUNT HUNT HUNT.
YES.
WOW WOW WOW.
KOOL.
I'M GOING.
REMEMBER THE LAST ONE THAT GOT AWAY?
NO, RIGHT?
YOU CAN'T.
NO ONE'S EVER GOTTEN AWAY FROM ME.
I KNOW.
UBERPRIEST...

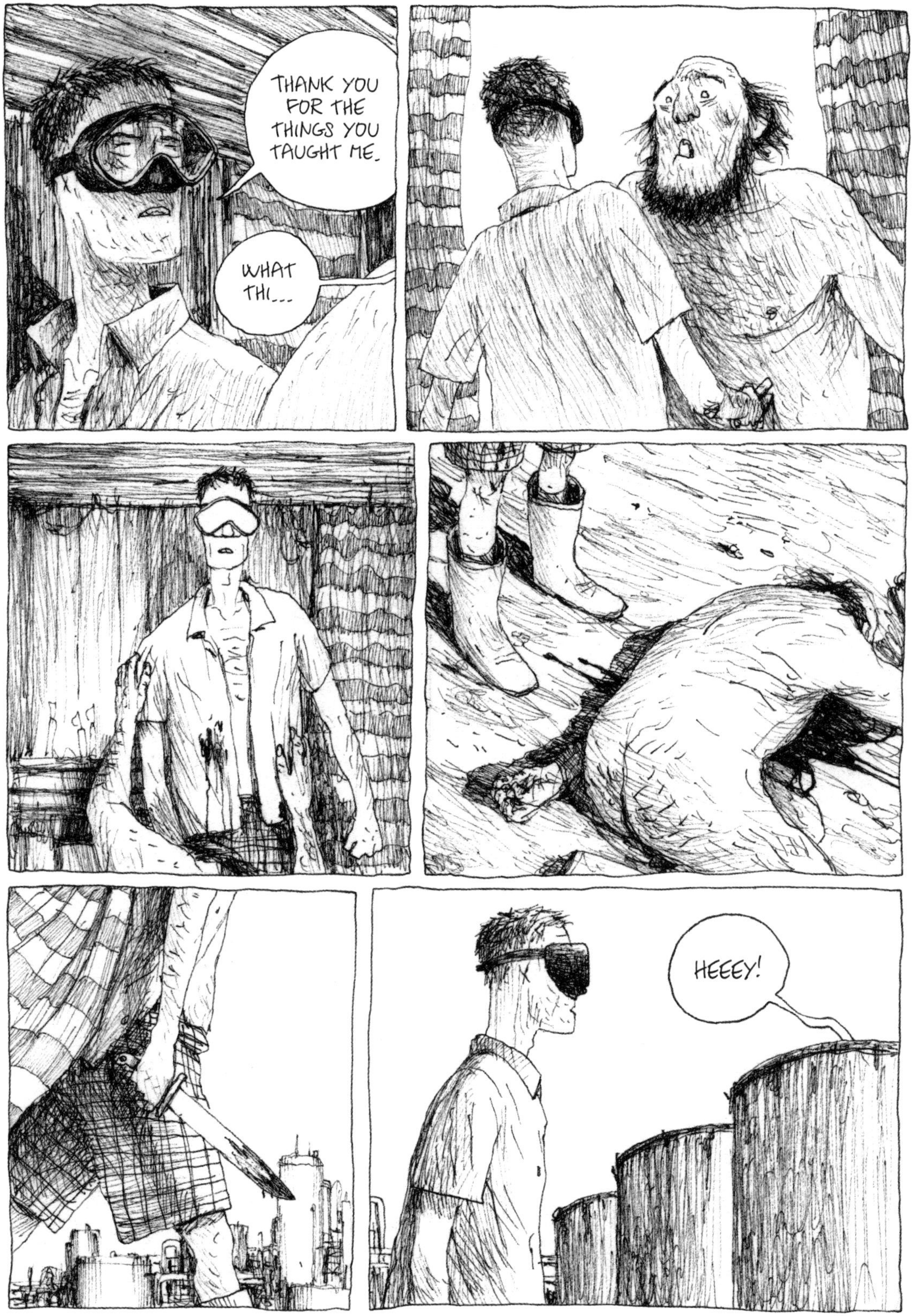
THANK YOU FOR THE THINGS YOU TAUGHT ME.
WHAT THI...
HEEEY!

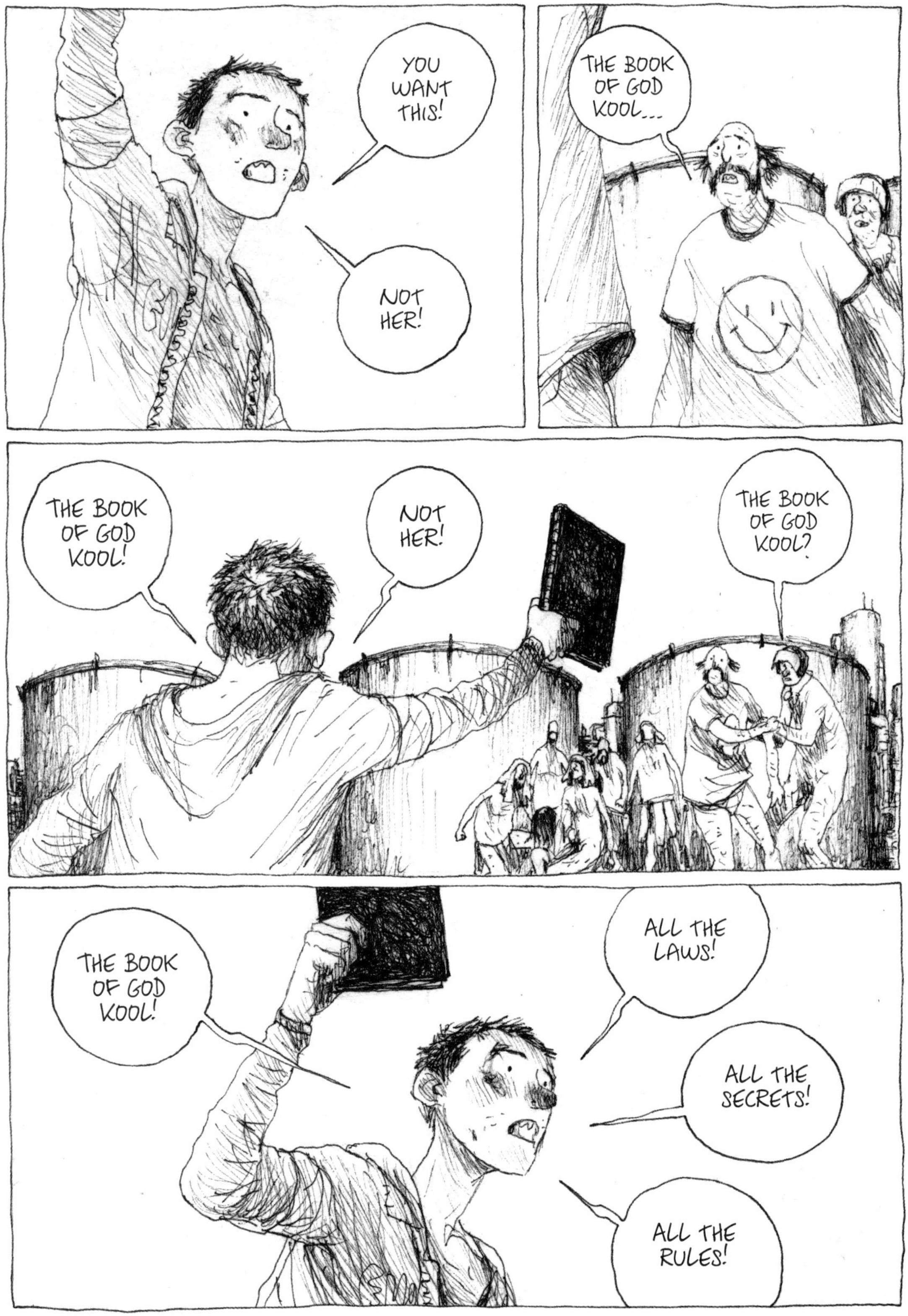
YOU WANT THIS!
NOT HER!
THE BOOK OF GOD KOOL...
THE BOOK OF GOD KOOL!
NOT HER!
THE BOOK OF GOD KOOL?
THE BOOK OF GOD KOOL!
ALL THE LAWS!
ALL THE SECRETS!
ALL THE RULES!

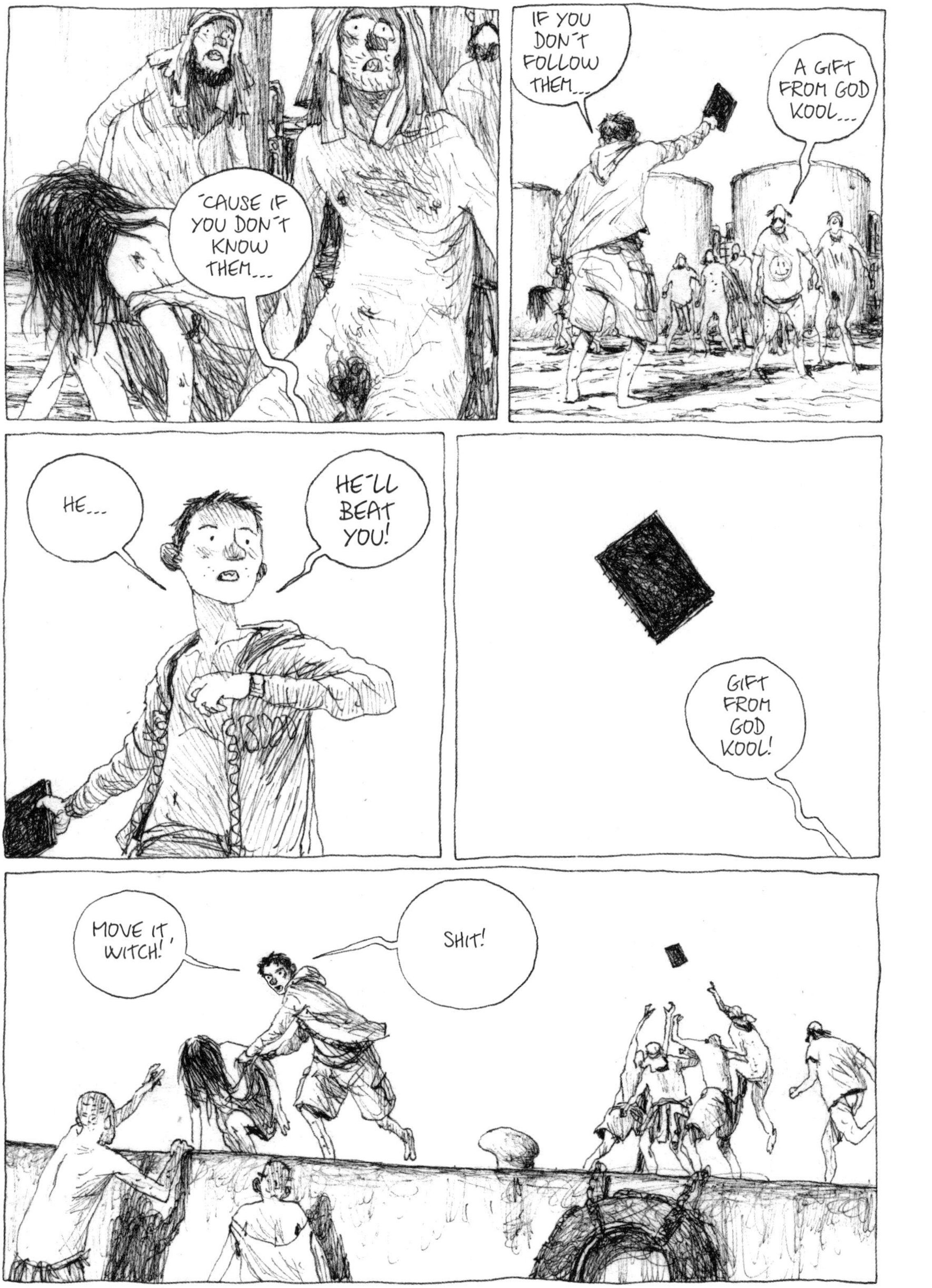

'CAUSE IF YOU DON'T KNOW THEM...
IF YOU DON'T FOLLOW THEM...
A GIFT FROM GOD KOOL...
HE...
HE'LL BEAT YOU!
GIFT FROM GOD KOOL!
MOVE IT, WITCH!
SHIT!

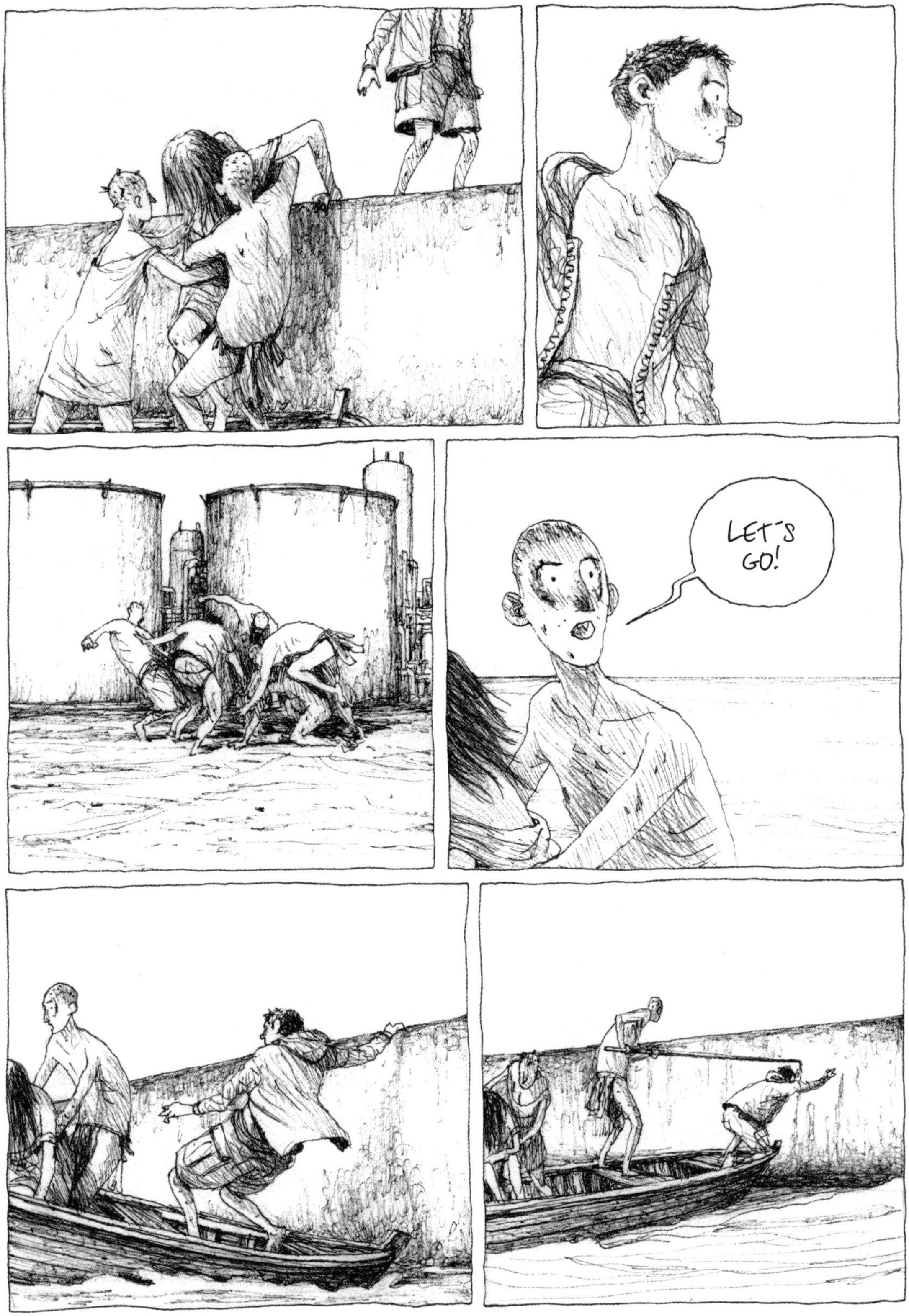
LET'S GO!

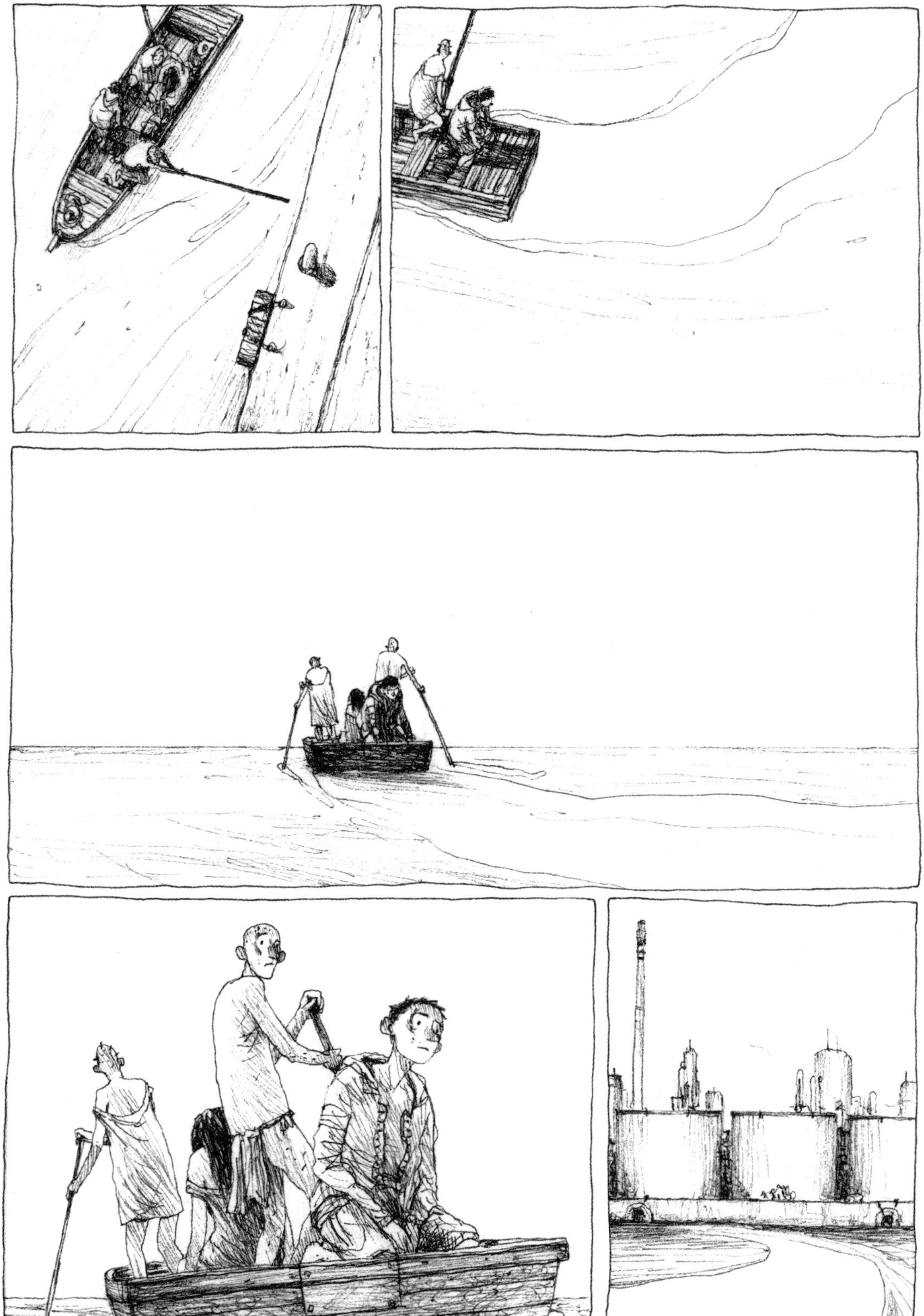

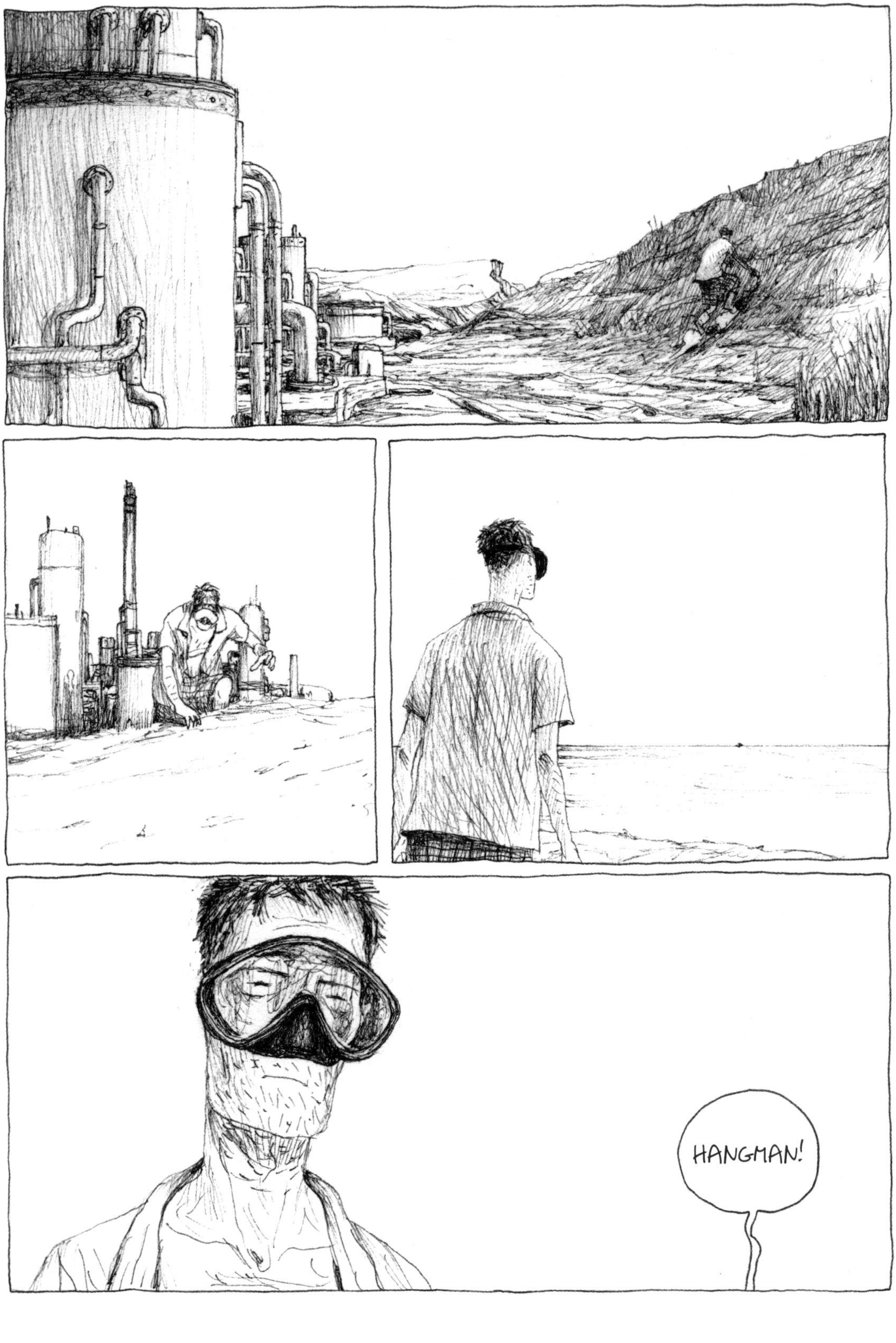
HANGMAN!

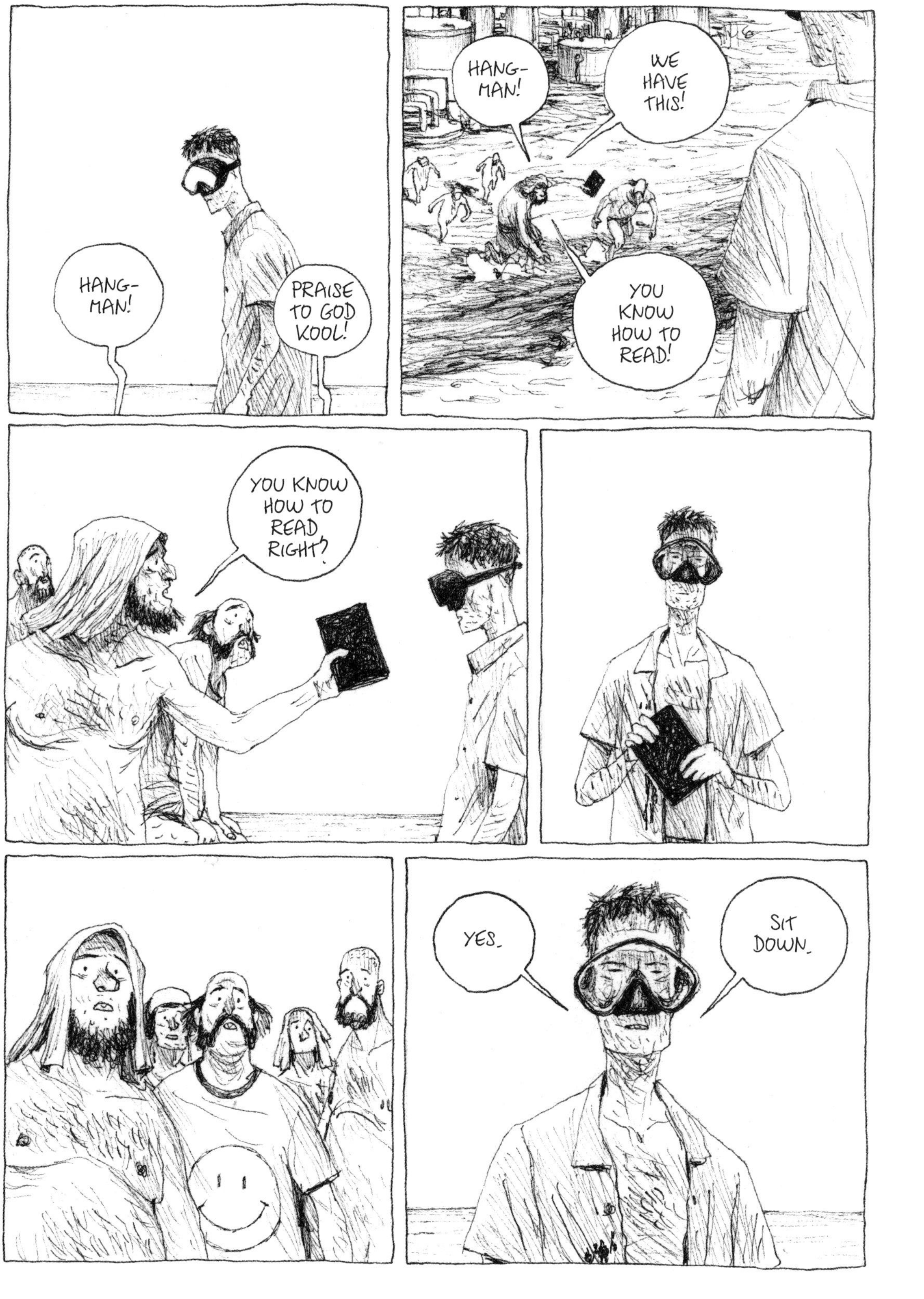
HANG-MAN!
PRAISE TO GOD KOOL!
HANG-MAN!
WE HAVE THIS!
YOU KNOW HOW TO READ!
YOU KNOW HOW TO READ RIGHT?
YES.
SIT DOWN.

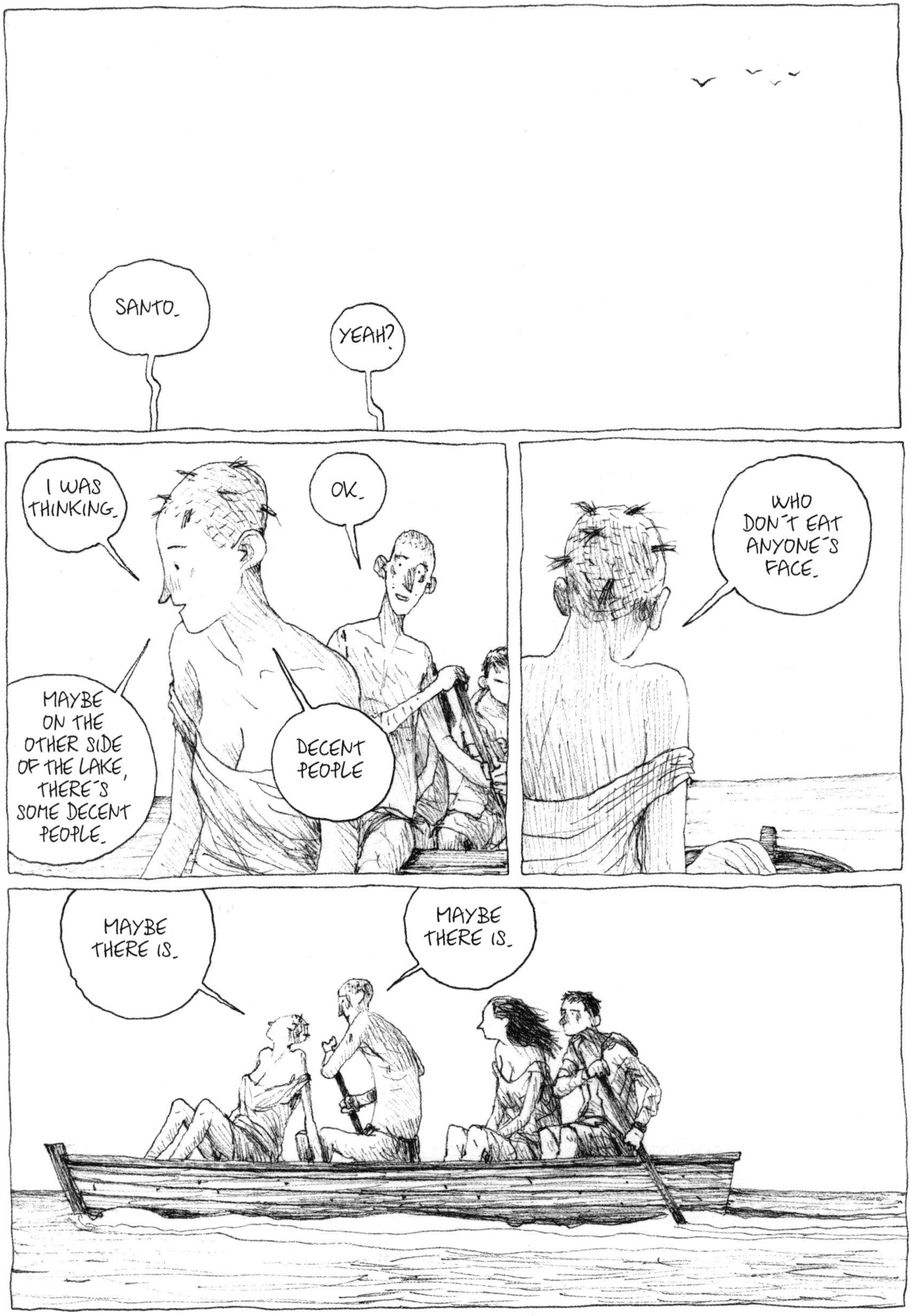
SANTO.
YEAH?
I WAS THINKING.
OK.
MAYBE ON THE OTHER SIDE OF THE LAKE, THERE'S SOME DECENT PEOPLE.
DECENT PEOPLE
WHO DON'T EAT ANYONE'S FACE.
MAYBE THERE IS.
MAYBE THERE IS.

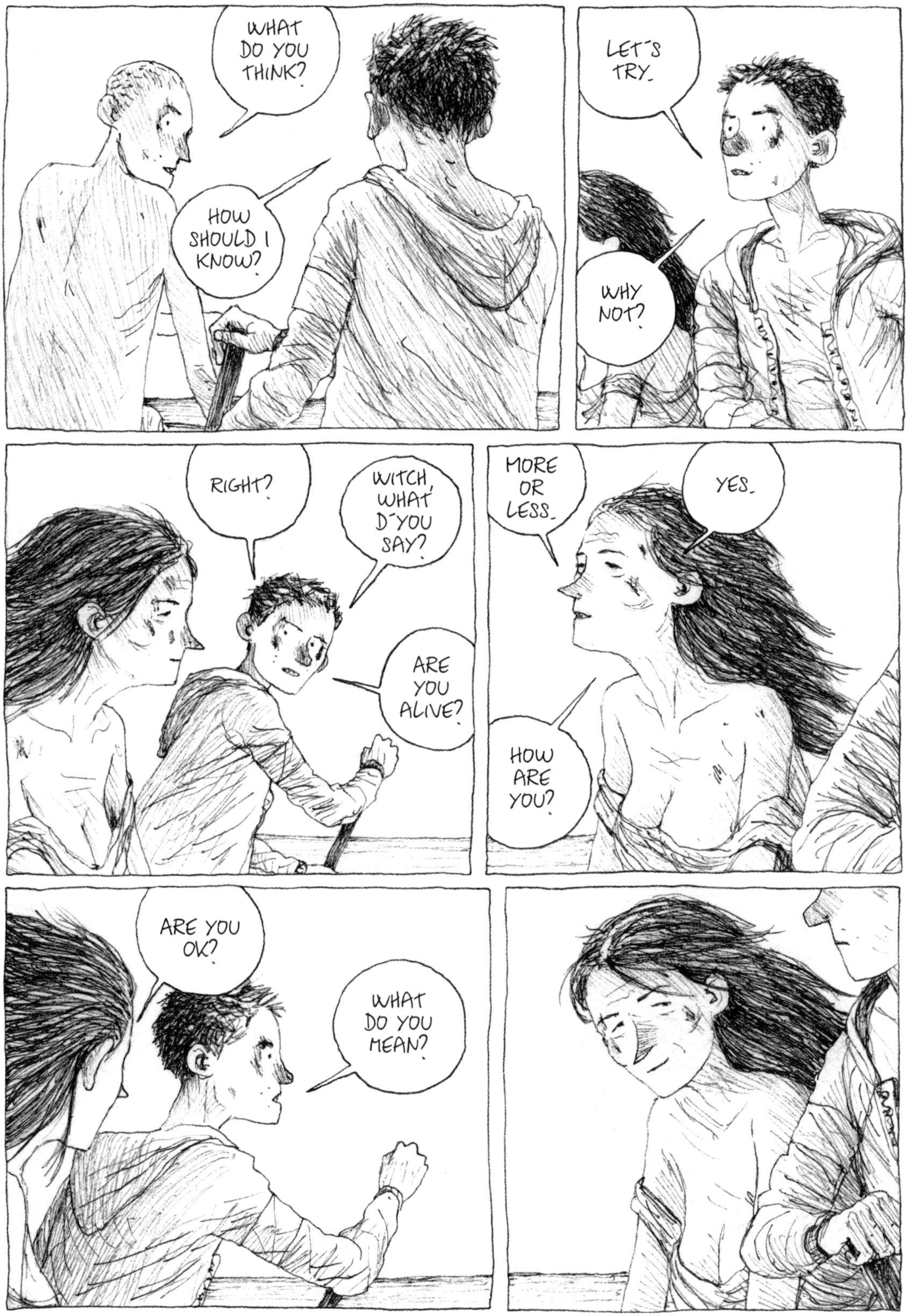
WHAT DO YOU THINK?
HOW SHOULD I KNOW?
LET'S TRY.
WHY NOT?
RIGHT?
WITCH, WHAT D'YOU SAY?
ARE YOU ALIVE?
MORE OR LESS.
YES.
HOW ARE YOU?
ARE YOU OK?
WHAT DO YOU MEAN?

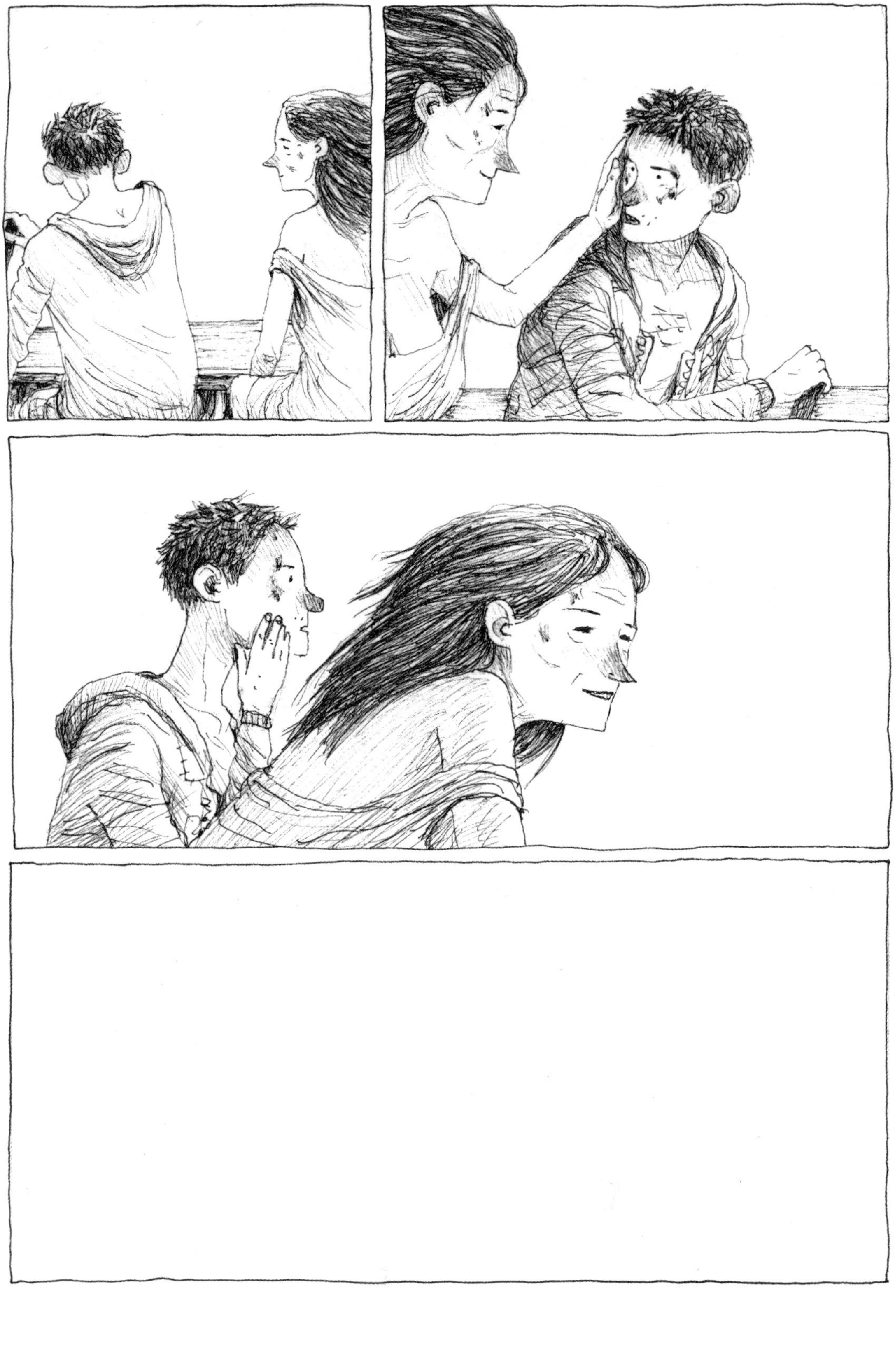

LAND OF THE SONS

GW 2016

FANTAGRAPHICS BOOKS

Translator: JAMIE RICHARDS
Editor: GARY GROTH
Design: GIPI and COVEY
Assistant Editor: RJ CASEY
Production: PAUL BARESH
Editorial Assistance: AVI KOOL
Associate Publisher: ERIC REYNOLDS
Publisher: GARY GROTH

FANTAGRAPHICS BOOKS, INC.
7563 Lake City Way NE
Seattle, WA 98115
www.fantagraphics.com

ISBN: 978-1-68396-077-5
Library of Congress Control Number: 2017950386
First Printing: April 2018
Printed in China